A Year Long Journey With You

Laura Garrett

NFB Publishing
Buffalo, New York

Copyright © 2021 Laura Garrett
Printed in the United States of America
A Year Long Journey With You/Garrett- 1st Edition

ISBN: 978-1-953610-28-7

1.Title. 2. Fantasy. 3. LGBTQ. 4. Romance.
5. Science Fiction/Fantasy.

NFB
<<<>>>
NFB Publishing/Amelia Press
119 Dorchester Road
Buffalo, New York 14213

For more information visit
Nfbpublishing.com

To my loving husband,
family members and friends
who have helped to push me to finish my book,
and my cats

A Year Long Journey With You

"WITH ANOTHER HOT *scorcher to end the month of June, people have flocked to the streets for the week- long festival provided by the Elite Global Organization in most major cities around the world. With prizes to be won, and a feast happening every night during the course of the festival, who wouldn't want to join in on the fun?"* The voice of a female news anchor read the teleprompter in a cheerful tone as to excite those who were tuning in. The words seemed to echo in the background of the empty kitchen as the news was being played on the small portable television resting on the marble countertop. The wooden cabinets that were once filled to the brim with food and various cans were now bare and empty. The screened windows rested open, allowing for the hot air from outside to enter the vacant home. The sounds of the cicadas resting on the nearby trees grew louder as the hours passed, a large orbital structure clung to the sky, visible for everyone to see. It was a large space station that had been built over the course of a few years by the Elite Global Organization to save humanity from the war that had been raging over the past couple of years.

The Elite Global Organization was formed as a way to help society save itself from killing off humanity for good. Funded mostly by celebrities and politicians in an attempt to bring a sense of hope in the time of war that caused men and women to die in senseless battle. With the war pulling most of the food resources away from the private sector, major cities found their streets full of angry people rioting in protest demanding that the politicians do something about the food shortage as the people's hunger fueled their rage against those in power. The shortage of food was made worse when countries all over the world started to deal with one natural disaster after another. This caused a limitation on the world's food supply, making it harder for those in the working class to provide enough food for their family to keep from going hungry.

With the threat of droughts making it hard for farmers to grow enough food, the Elite Global Organization came up with a plan to be able to use a large man made and operated space station that would be built to control the weather, allowing for the Elite to control the planet and what regions would receive aid. Or so that was the plan. Many people were excited for such advancements in technology that they didn't see the lies that were put in front of them.

The week-long festival was a means to make the people docile. It was as if the Elite Organization was trying to display that the finished space station would bring an end to all of the misfortune that cropped up over the years since the war had started. The same war that had brought an end to so many people's lives. How did the war start? Or better yet, why did it continue?

Some say that the war was due to one country trying to invade another for land, while other people say that it was because of some sort of political matter that escalated to the point of another war breaking out as allies seemed to turn against each other. There were some who even claimed that this was just a huge ploy in order for those with enough wealth and fame to build the space station without people becoming suspicious as to the nature of the large orbital structure clinging to the sky. But at this point, no one could agree on how the war started, though it had escalated to the point where innocent blood was being shed on each side.

"ALRIGHT, this should be the last of it grandpa." A young man spoke, placing down two boxes. One of the boxes was already opened, showing off that it was full of cans that had a light coating of dust that seemed to linger on top of its folded flaps, giving the impression that these cans came from the basement or some sort of storage in the house. The other box was still neatly wrapped tightly in its taped down condition that would have seemed like it was brand new, if it wasn't for the corners of the brown cardboard box sporting water spots along the base as if it had been exposed to some sort of water leakage.

The younger man wore a pair of faded jean overalls with a white t-shirt underneath, the edges of the undershirt was visible due to the heat, resulting in the man becoming a bit sweaty. His brunet hair was covered by a white bandanna to help reflect the sun to keep him cool, though it seemed to do very little in that regard.

Pulling out a pocket knife from a front pouch of his overalls, the man opened the bottom box up to inspect what was inside to make sure that it was edible food and not something that would just be a waste of space in the shelter. Inside was a top layer of cans with pull-able tabs, meaning that if something were to happen to him, at least his grandfather would be able to eat without much trouble.

"Ah, thank you my boy." An elderly man spoke, his feet slowly shuffling closer towards the younger male, a wrinkly smile lingering on the old man's lips. "Most of the preparation has been complete. By this time tomorrow, we'll have everything locked up before those bastards can even strike." The elderly man continued as he bent over, pulling out one of the cans from the box to inspect the label, only to grimace at the can being that of canned mackerel. It was better than something he couldn't completely digest.

"Are you sure about this grandpa?" The younger male spoke, pulling the bandanna off and scratching the left side of his temple under his sweaty locks. Normal pale skin had been burned red from his time in the field working to produce what little crop possible with the soil barely able to retain nutrients. "I mean, if the E.G.O was really going to kill off the rest of humanity, I don't see why they would throw a week-long festival for everyone. Especially with how limited food has been, it seems like a waste to not go." The young male replied with a small frown, wondering if perhaps people in the community may have been delusional, or at the very least paranoid at all of this. "It would just be a waste of money. I mean, we're nearing the end of this war, right? At least that's what the news reports say. We could finally have peace since this stupid war even started.. Killing off everyone now, it would just be pointless."

"World peace only happens when those Elite bastards have killed off everyone. When that happens, they will be able to build up a whole new society where they can control every aspect of a person's life! What part of that don't you understand?" The old man shouted, causing the younger male to shake his head a bit, becoming a bit tired from debating on the intention of the station since the prior year when the station was near its completion. The younger man sighed as he couldn't believe that an organization who did everything to help save humanity would do something that would kill off the rest of the world. Trying to debate the whole concept itself was rather pointless with his grandfather. The old man was just set in his ways after all.

"I just can't see them killing trillions of people just for a simple thing like wanting to re-build a whole new society for them to govern when we already have a society here on Earth. It would be like making a whole new batch of scrambled eggs simply because the eggs you had just made were too milky or something." The young man remarked, bending down to pick up the now opened box to continue inspecting its' contents.

"I mean, could they really live with that much blood on their hands? Is their morality so far gone that they would be willing to do a hard reboot without knowing if it would work?" The man asked, picking up the three opened boxes with a small grunt. "If they kill us off, how would they be able to know when it is safe to come back? The planet might not even be habitable in their lifetime! It would just be pointless grandpa." The conversation seemed to continue as the two men headed down into the underground shelter that was built out of an old fallout shelter that had been expanded over the last couple of years. Ever since the station started coming into view, most people started to build the shelters in case something were to go wrong with the station and it would come crashing down to Earth.

"All they care about is creating a perfect world where they can control how people live and die. To use fear as a means of control without having people revolt against them." The old man snapped back, following his grandson deeper into the shelter. It wasn't very big, but his cattle seemed to be enjoying the makeshift meadow that was put in place that allowed for them to graze in it. The shelter had a single tunnel that led towards the rest of the community. The large barn looked brand new where the old man would be able to store his cattle for the night as well as keep most of his supplies for when he would alternate the crops. It seemed that the discussion had been put to a stop by Alex, who seemingly refused to give his grandfather a comment about the topic as it was leading them nowhere.

"So, have you moved into your place in the shelter yet my boy? Janet will be due soon, right?" The old man asked, a smile creeping on his lips, proud of the fact that he would be able to see his great grandson. "Awfully proud of you boy. Though you should think about getting married to her." The old man remarked, giving Alex a light nudge with a small wink. The nudge wasn't hard given the man's weakening state, but it was enough to put a light smile on Alex's face as an amused chuckle left his lips.

"Yeah, I made sure to finish moving things into our shelter before coming here to help you gramps." Alex smiled, a bit relieved that he got them moved in as Janet was resting in the bed in their shelter. Their place wasn't all that big, but it was in close proximity to his grandfather's shelter so that Alex could take the tunnel up to see him. Janet had wanted to go to the festival, but the doctors advised her against it. Since the baby was due within a couple of weeks, she was ordered bed rest until the due date. With the hot temperatures, it wasn't wise to have her moving about.

"That's my boy Billy." The old man spoke, giving a pat on the young man's back, a chuckle leaving his lips before coughing. The old man wore some faded brown slacks with a white buttoned up shirt and suspenders. On his feet was some faded steel-toed boots where the steel was starting to show through the worn down leather. Hunching over a bit, the old man had a shiny bald spot under his large sun hat. Tusks of silver hair were tucked behind his ears as his hair was slicked back by some gel.

"My name is Alex, grandpa. We don't even know a billy. Or a William for that matter." Alex spoke, using his foot to open one of the barn doors as his hands were full with the three boxes. "Anyways, we're going to be having some chicken and rice with vegetables for dinner tonight. Would you like us to bring you some?" Alex asked, smiling at the older man before heading into the barn.

The interior of the shelter was rather open with the smell of hay lingering in the air. The sound of the resting chickens clucked while they opened their eyes from the sound of the two men entering, causing a sound of some feathers ruffling as the chickens tried to get comfortable enough to go back to sleep. Inside of the barn was a bit dark, but thankfully the old man was able to flip a switch to light up their way. Hay seemed to be scattered on the ground while the pens for the cattle laid empty. Each one had a small basin for the cattle to drink when they were inside of the barn instead of grazing out in the small meadow.

"As long as you make the chicken juicy like your grandma." The old man spoke, resulting in Alex growing a shocked look on his face, which in turn caused the old man to bust into laughter. "Juicy like how she made it." The old man corrected himself, before a small devious grin landed on his face. "Though your grandma was very-" The old man started to speak as if he was about to reminiscence about the fun times he had with his wife before getting cut off by Alex.

"I don't want to hear about your sex life grandpa!! Especially not with grandma!" Alex shouted, cursing his hands being full at the moment. "God rest her soul." Alex muttered under his breath. "I don't know how she put up with your dirty mind!" This seemed to cause the elderly man to laugh until he started coughing once more. "It's bad enough when dad talks about it, but to hear it from you and imagine it, it's just too much." The images caused Alex to cringe. "Seriously, what is wrong with my family?" Alex muttered under his breath, moving towards the shelves that seemed to be stuffed full of food that didn't seem like they would expire any time soon. Years of hoarding canned food seemed to be handy in their current state. With everything going crazy, many people had to resort to canning food in order to make it through the years.

"It just means you're grown up enough to hear the juicy stuff that happens in the bedroom." The elderly man spoke, ignoring the grimace gaze coming from his grandson, who seemed to start putting the cans on top of the shelf in sections that were barren. There had been plenty of cans that had been placed on the shelves a few months in advance, but if Alex could focus on this task, then perhaps he might be able to tune out the rest of his grandfather's story.

"I feel like I am going to give myself a lobotomy the next time I hear someone mention *that* word." Alex mumbled mostly to himself, his hand shaking a little bit as he placed the cans on the shelf. Thankfully Alex was tall enough that he didn't need the step ladder, unlike his grandfather. It used to belong to his grandmother, since she was a rather short lady, but now it was used to aid his grandfather.

Alex always made sure that the screws were still tightened, that way his grandfather wouldn't fall while getting something on the top shelf. After all, his grandmother had passed away shortly after she had fallen off of the step ladder and broke her hip. It was best to be safe rather than sorry.

"Relax Alex. You're a Flores. You can't give up so easily just because you don't like hearing about other people having sex. Sex is a natural part of life." The old man remarked, smiling as he placed a hand on Alex's shoulder. "After all, with the amount of porn that was on your computer as a teen, it seems that you really know your stuff in order to get yourself a bun in the oven." He finished, giving Alex a few hard pats on the shoulder, all the while Alex looked at him with disbelief that his own grandfather had said that sort of thing. Just how shameless was his family?!

"Grandpa!!! Stop already!! I don't want to hear another word about it!" Alex stammered, his face a bit flushed as he covered his ears. The old man continued to chuckle, only stopping to cough as he enjoyed the little banter that seemed to make his grandson squirm.

The last bit of the items in the house didn't take long to move into the shelter. Having to start their life underground wasn't going to be easy, but within a few weeks, they should be able to emerge from the shelter like nothing happened. At least, that's what the plan was. To simply show that people were believing a mass hysteria that would result in nothing happening, allowing for life to continue on as normal. But nothing ever goes as planned.

As the third of July rolled around, people were gathering a few last minute party supplies in their local store in preparation of the holiday. The weather was hot, reaching close to a little over a hundred degrees while people struggled to cool down. The fire hydrants were popped in the inner city to cool the hot asphalt, people were out and about to catch up with their neighbors who were getting ready for their mid-summer vacation, while people were already heading out of the city in order to head towards their destinations if they weren't going to take part in the festival happening close by to them.

During this time, there was a live broadcast of the last members of the Elite Global Organization boarding the rocket that would take them up towards the now finished space station. Most people seemed to ignore it, feeling like they had more important things to worry about than to see the last of the rich and powerful make their way up into space. Though, that should have been a warning to those wise enough to see what was going on. For that was the cue to head into the shelters before the disaster that changed the landscape would happen.

A loud static scrambled the signal of all televisions and broadcasting channels, only to have an image of the high ranking members of the Elite Global Organization appearing on the screen catching everyone's attention. "Greetings inhabitants of Earth." Came the voice of the man who stepped forward, wearing an odd mask over his eyes and part of his nose.

The mask that covered the man's upper facial features had long ridged goat horns as goat-like ears stuck out from either side, making them more apparent was the fact that the parts of the ears were covered in gold. The eyes were blacked out as it seemed that the cheeks of the mask were covered in black and white goat fur. A semi long black beard resting below the man's lips seemingly trickled down towards his chest had a small gem-like beard bead that sparkled in the light shining on him.

"With the festival reaching its' third day with an all out feast for everyone, the members of Elite Global Organization would like to take this time to thank you for all the hard work that everyone has done for these last couple of centuries." The man continued, causing those who were watching the broadcast to become confused as to what was going on. Cars seemed to stop in the road in some cities where the broadcast could be seen, causing people to peek their heads out of the window to listen to the broadcast as it was certainly unusual. Those on the street stopped in their tracks while gazing up towards the virtual billboards with a puzzled look on their face.

"With the recent war coming to a close, us here at the Elite Global Organization would like to extend a helping hand in making sure that this war will finally end once and for all. We all know how much the endless killing and bloodshed of good men and women on either side has been affecting either side. So, what better way to bring world peace to this wonderful planet than to make it all end at once?" The man continued, his voice echoing between buildings and on computers for those who were tuning into the broadcast at home.

"What's going on?" A male voice could be heard from the street while those around him couldn't provide answers. After all, how many people could really say that they knew what was happening at this point in time.

The man on the screen continued to speak with a devious grin steadily creeping onto his face. With a tilt of his head backwards, the man started to raise his shoulders. "Now you must be asking yourself, how could a single group end all of the war at once, right?" The man continued, only to flash a single red button on the screen that had the man's gloved fingers carefully wrapped around the button.

With the button being enlarged on the screen, people turned to one another with a mixture of confusion and worry lingering on their face, softly muttering in confusion to see if anyone knew what was going on. Those who were watching at home started to panic as they didn't need much convincing to head towards the safety of the shelter. Collecting the few things they needed before rushing into the shelters close to them, those who were on the streets started to yell for people to head towards the public shelters. Those who were inside darted towards the entrance, collecting those who were trying to make their way into the shelter and helped them. The screaming in the streets and the pandemic that ensued was pure chaos. In the panic there were some people in their shelters that were cowardly and closed off some of the entrances to save themselves rather than help out those who were banging and pleading to get inside of the shelter, fearing that it would be too late to get them into the shelters in time.

"With this." The man continued, his thumb resting beside the flashing button. "Now you shouldn't fight this, you filthy little vermins." The man spoke in a cold tone before letting out a sharp hiss as his thumb caressed the button. "We all know that the human race today is just lacking the proper discipline needed to create a perfect world." The man taunted, a creepy smile still lingering on his lips as his full body appeared on the screen with a silhouette of people behind him, the black and white tuxedo he was wearing coming into view as the camera panned out to the members who were already on board with a champagne glass in hand.

"So, to celebrate the birth of a new humanity, one full of the best and brightest to lead the charge to make humanity truly great, we give you pathetic rats a spectacular firework display that will leave you all breathless. A grand exit to you flea infested pests and a grand send off what remains of worthless beings who dared to call themselves humans. Let's hope that you all enjoy the fireworks. I know we will." The man's voice cracked a bit towards the end as he clicked the button, resulting in the broadcast ending on the man's maniacal laughter.

Those who were outside would hear the sounds of the sirens echoing through the skies would be many who ended up the casualties of the tragic event that would be left to decay on the streets, their shadows frozen in time, never to fade. A constant reminder hundred of years later of what the Elite did to those not worthy for their new age of humanity that would be ruled under their thumb. On the station overlooking the Earth, the figure from the broadcast pressed a secondary button that was able to hijack the satellites in orbit, resulting in the computers on Earth to shut down.

All the technology seemed to halt, resulting in mass confusion to those who were unaware of what happened. Before long the computers started to reboot by themselves, resulting in every screen starting to flash red with white letters and symbols that danced across the screens. As people tried to fix their screens or tried to get the image off, dark pixels fell into place among the red and white, forming a goat's head with a counter above its head ticking down. As the timer was counting down, one missile pad after the other around the world started to open to expose the war heads held inside of them. This caused mass panic within the silos as people frantically tried to get the timer to stop, or to try and bypass the lock down but to no avail.

A taunting tone seemingly rang from the goat's mouth, sounding like children singing a ghostly song as those inside of the missile silos lost control over their computers. The abort sequences refused to work, only to be greeted with random goat screams as they tried to stop the missiles from being launched. Helplessly, those inside of the control centers couldn't stop whatever virus this was, dooming the planet with no way of stopping it.

The death and destruction that was caused in those few short moments left the planet completely devastated. Those who were lucky enough to make it inside had to hear the begging pleads of those trapped outside banging on the doors, up until they eventually died from either the blast or from the radiation sickness. People huddled together for comfort. This was the end of times. The planet was going to be left as nothing more than a ruined planet underneath the United Space Station Millennium. The Elite watched with delight, their champagne glasses clanging against each other as they watched the mushroom clouds color the planet with bright red dots followed by a dark brown as the clouds lifted up into the air.

With the last nuked drop, the party could finally commence. The Elite and their chosen associates were free from the burden of the unwanted pests that were not up to their standard. They were finally able to form their own society and those in the lower sections would be grateful after witnessing the horror that happened on the ruined planet. These people would be trapped in a never ending hell aboard the space station for the rest of their lives, bound to forever serve the Elite as the gods they so desperately desired to be. Even though most would rather have been down on Earth to be with their friends and loved ones, they would simply accept their fate, unless they wish to be killed as easily as those on the ground.

Through the passage of time, the remaining humans would continue to live and die on their twisted version of Noah's Ark. Blissfully unaware they were being held captive by the very monsters that killed off everyone they loved. The Elite Global Organization had finally formed their ideal society, and they were not going to allow anyone to take it away from them. The only way they would give it up was over their cold dead hands.

CHAPTER ONE: *Dark Truth*

ABOVE THE DRIFTING planet that was once called Earth, there lies a large structural satellite that is known as the United Space Station Millennium. The large satellite appears in the sky like a secondary moon to the dead planet, though unlike the moon that was once the solo orbital structure close enough to be seen from the surface, the Millennium holds the last remaining humans that survived the destruction of the planet it now orbits. The large orbital satellite appears as an oval shape pod with layered rings around the main core to act like a protective barrier from space debris. The importance of those rings is significant, as it holds most of the agriculture to allow fresh vegetation and cattle as a steady food supply for the inhabitants of the station.

Each ring holds two classes of the remaining humans, while the large main core holds the highest class known as the Elite Class, home of the wealthy and descendants from the main original pioneers that boarded the station so many years ago. Upon these rings, Dean Torres finds himself among the lowest section of the classes, the Bronze class. That particular class holds those who are considered poor, thus not allowed the same privilege as those of either the Silver or Elite classes.

Inside one of the smaller pods lining the outer wall of the station's rings, there lies inside a studio style pod, a sleeping figure of a man resting on his bed. The glow from the ruined planet that was once Earth was barely visible in the circular window above the bed, its beauty seemed to shine brightly as if the Earth was a painting fixated on the pod's wall. The blanket that barely seemed to fit the man was a thin felt blanket, his toes seemed to stick out of the covers due to the short length, causing the man to shiver ever so slightly in the cold room. The blanket seemed to have small holes in various spots along the main body, making it appear like some type of decoration, though it just simply gave away the blanket's age.

A dull roar echoed through the station's haul and in the pods connected to it, acting as white noise to those living on the station. It wasn't long before there was a sound of a repetitive beeping noise that could be heard throughout the room, causing the man to reach out a hand to turn off the digital clock, a soft grunt escaped as the man raises from the bed allowing the blanket to slip down to his belly button, showing off the man's well fit body as he slept bare naked with only the blanket to cover his lower half. Reaching both of his hands up, the man known as Dean started to rub his eyes to wipe away the dried crust from his turquoise green eyes. His dark brunet hair was a little disheveled from tossing and turning in his slumber as the length was about medium, just barely grazing over the top edges of his ears as his bangs parted evenly as their edges brushed over his temples.

"I really don't want to work today..." Dean grumbled to himself as he had to force himself awake. Slicking his hair back before ruffling the back of his head, Dean got out of bed. It wasn't long before Dean's bare feet hit the floor, though he was a bit hesitant from how cold the metal floor was against his bare feet, before making his way lazily towards the small bathroom. It resembled a smaller closet than anything else. There was only enough room to allow a singular person to rotate 360 degrees in the bathroom, though without being able to extend one's arms without hitting anything inside. On the right side of the doorway rested a small sink with a mirror hanging overhead. The sink resembled a flat drinking fountain more than anything else, while the mirror that was above it appeared like a picture frame but with a reflective surface.

The shower rested on the left side of the door, it was small to the point where it looked like an old phone booth, with nothing more than a thin sheet of see-through plastic to act as a shower curtain. Directly in front of the door was the small toilet that looked as if it belonged to a holding cell, one that was found on Earth before its destruction. It barely functioned, but it was what Dean was given. Seeing as how Dean was 5'11" his legs would always brush against both the sink and the wall by the shower if he were to sit on the small toilet, giving him little to no movement. How anyone his size could function in a small space like this was beyond anything that Dean could comprehend.

Turning on the hot water, Dean had no issue in simply stepping inside of it. The hot water was relaxing enough, though the timer above the shower head was always a pest as it counted down the time that was allowed for a person to use the hot water for the shower. Any more, and it would be docked from his paycheck. Which granted wasn't very much to start out with, but considering that the Bronze class had less time for the shower than everyone else, it showed just how little the Silver and Elite classes cared about those in the Bronze class.

If it were up to Elite, the Bronze class would only have cold water or no water at all. Many would consider themselves lucky with the time that they had gotten, but it wasn't enough for Dean. Especially when he had the dirtiest job of being in the janitorial section of the Business class. Hauling all of the garbage from the different sections of his route always left Dean feeling like he was swimming in garbage, but it fueled the station to keep everything running without much issue, so he couldn't really complain.

As the steam began to rise, Dean focused on using what limited time he had to wash his body. Rubbing the bar of soap over his torso, the suds started to roll down his pale skin. Dean was fairly well built in his stature, despite the fact that he was once a pudgy boy in his youth thanks to the meals his parents made when he was in the Silver class, Dean was forced to slim down due to their restriction of food he received after he was put in the Bronze class. As tall as Dean was, he always had to bend his knees in order to fit under the shower head if he was to wash his hair, making him waste more time in doing so. But seeing as how he didn't have enough shampoo or conditioner to wash his hair properly, Dean was left to only wash his body.

Letting out a soft sigh, Dean rinsed the rest of the soap off of his body before turning the shower head off, watching as the droplets from the shower head fell down to the swirling drain always made Dean feeling disgruntled as the drips seemed to waste what precious shower time he had left. Casting a soft glare at the faulty shower head as if to curse the station for purposely giving the lower class the cheapest faucets possible, simply because the fat cats in the Elite class could make more off of them, Dean softly shook his head to get any lingering water droplets off of his scalp. There was no point in trying to do anything about it. If he did, there would be more problems that would seem to pop up to make him spend more credits than he really had.

"Keep quiet and obey... right?" Dean thought bitterly as he grabbed a white towel to start dry-

ing off his body as he pulled back the thin curtain to the side. Looking at the fogged up mirror in front of him, Dean slowly wiped the mirror to clear it off with the towel, allowing him to actually see his reflection in the mirror. With his medium hair slicked back, a single thick strand of hair rested a few centimeters from his forehead.

"Bags under my eyes again...pale complexion, but at least my cheeks aren't sunken in like most people here in the Bronze class." Dean muttered to himself as he examined his face, poking and prodded his features in the mirror. "Guess I should thank my folks for giving me a decent life when we were in the silver class...Or rather, when they were alive" Dean spoke softly, his eyes glancing down towards the sink as he hated the fact that his parents died and no one would take him in. Not even members of his own family would take in the orphaned boy. Despite that, it was because of those years growing up in the silver class that has taught Dean how to survive in the hellish class of the bronze world. Though in hindsight Dean should have paid more attention when his parents tried to teach him the importance of cooking and cleaning. Dean simply never took to it. At least not like how he did with reading or gardening.

Glancing towards the closed bathroom door, there rested the uniform assigned to him hanging on a hook. The top of the uniform was skin tight, the coloring of the mesh short sleeve top was that of a mixture light gray and white with a thin aqua blue seam separating the two colors. The arms and shoulders had the light gray texture while the white rested on his mid torso. Having to wear a harness that wrapped around Dean's chest, there was a small orb that rested in the middle of the chest, it glowed a light bronze color as it displayed his initials. This was a way to identify Dean as well as provide what his class was currently in.

The light gray gloves he would wear to protect his hands from the grime of picking up garbage was resting on the edge of the sink, dried from the night before as he washed them after work. The pants that he would wear were a bit more on the loose side, unlike how the top was, it allowed a bit more freedom to move about, though it was better than having it feel like some type of prison uniform. Only the Elite and selected members of the Silver class were allowed to wear whatever they wanted.

Matching the design of the mesh shirt, the gray coloring looked more like Dean was wearing chaps as the middle section of the groin sported the white coloring with the aqua blue seam separating the two. The design for the uniform often changed depending on the current fashion trends designed by the fashion section of the Elite class. Lately everyone seemed to wear chaps, making those who served under those who were higher than them more apparent. Even though the latest design was built like an odd western movie design sketch, Dean was grateful that the sides of the uniform pants came with various pockets that were helpful with carrying various tools for cleaning. It came in handy more times than Dean could count.

Slipping on the uniform, it didn't take much time as Dean was out of the humid bathroom, and back into the cold room of his pod. Walking past the small table with the single chair that was barely used tucked into the table, Dean headed to the small kitchen that had a small wall against the refrigerator as to make it seem like the kitchen was open rather than have it be its' own room. The kitchen itself was practically the same size as the bathroom, only difference was that the kitchen was against the wall rather than have it bunched together in a closed off section like the bathroom.

Dean opened the fridge to pull out a cold hard boil egg, a single slice of bread, and butter for his breakfast. It wasn't much of a meal if you asked Dean. After all, the living conditions were a joke, almost laughable really. Everything that a member of the bronze class did was drained from their paycheck. Even if one were to work hard enough to make a living, the Elite would find a way to overcharge them to make sure that the Bronze level stayed poor.

They promised that no one would ever have to worry about bills ever again. That there was a universal income that everyone would be able to live on. But the truth was, the Elite would just take the money from both classes while they didn't have to pay for anything. Seems like they made the universal income more for the Elite rather than for those in the either class. It was damned if you did, damned if you don't, type of mentality that everyone on the station was forced to deal with, and Dean was getting sick of it.

Water, food, even electricity was automatically taken out of one's pay if they had a job. Even when someone didn't have a job, they were still forced to pay for the living fees. Disabled? Still had to be subjected to living fees. Retired? Not for the Bronze class. One had to work until they died in order for a household to survive.

Even when a family member died, that particular family would receive less due to the number of people living in that household decreasing. What about their belongings? Would that go to the family? Unfortunately that wasn't the case. When a member of the Bronze class died, the Enforcement officers would come in to repossess everything that belonged to the deceased. The family wouldn't even be able to legally gather family heirlooms before the repossession would begin. It was basically the same for the Silver class as well, but not as harsh. At least those in the SIlver Class could choose what they wanted to keep before they would have the Enforcement officers come in and take whatever they wanted from the deceased residents.

Shoving the limp bread into the small toaster, Dean took out a fork and knife from the utensil drawer that was located in one of the two counter drawers. Glancing at the time, it seemed like the time was going faster than normal. It wouldn't surprise Dean much if the Elite had been increasing or decreasing the time in order to gain more profit off of the slave labor placed on the Bronze class. A small groan escaped his lips before Dean's attention went to peeling off the egg shell, all the while the bread was being toasted.

"If the Elite are really making it to where we are getting less sleep, that could be why I have bags under my eyes. Not that I could prove it, living in this hell hole is always so stressful. Makes me wish that I could have my youth back. Or at the very least, back before my parents died anyways...Back when I could still remember their voices." Dean thought to himself, watching as the egg shells landed in the small bin. Dean could feel the weight of the bags under his eyes, as if they weighed ten pounds each.

With the small buzz coming from the toaster, the sound of the toast popping up caught his attention as Dean went straight to work fixing his meal. With a small amount of butter on the toast, followed by cutting the egg in half, Dean popped the other half in his mouth. With his mouth full, it didn't take long before Dean started to smash the other half of the egg against still hot toast. With a bit of pepper and salt on the mushed up egg, Dean was ready to enjoy the other half of his breakfast. Sure it would have been nice if he got a chance to actually eat his food in the morning, rather than having to scarf it down with fear of choking on said breakfast, but that was only afforded to the higher classes.

Swallowing the last bit of the food, the alarm rang above the door through the small speakers to indicate the start of the day. Dusting his hands off of any crumbs, Dean left his small pod to head towards his work station. Just like every day, Dean would walk the crowded hallway with those of his ranking. It seemed that everyone was too busy with their latest gossip to pay too much attention to Dean. Though it wasn't like he cared too much for attention as it was, it always felt like it brought disaster when people seemed to notice him.

Even when he tried to teach others on how to grow their own food, like his parents and others in the Silver class did as their contribution to the station, it only backfired on him. The enforcement officers came in and removed, or rather destroyed the small gardens people were growing in their own homes while they were away at work or school. Because of that people started to blame Dean for their misfortune as the Elite punished those who tried to grow their own food by restricting their food budget.

The Elite didn't take a liking to those who would try to break away from their dependency. It was simply because those who grew their own food would take away the profits that the Elite received when it came to selling people their groceries. It caused Dean to grow a strong resentment towards everyone living on the station. A resentment that would follow him for the rest of his life.

"This whole space station could blow up and I just wouldn't care anymore." Dean thought bitterly to himself as he got onto the large elevator that was used for the Bronze class to be brought up to their assigned floors for cleaning duty. Even though the elevator was fairly big, it still seemed to feel like they were nothing more than a can of sardines, packed into a neat little metal box and shipped off to the nearest store. But there was at least one good thing that seemed to come out of being packed into an elevator with people pushing him towards the back. At least Dean was able to at least admire the view of the ruined planet through the oval window behind him, though he was allowed fleeting glances the further up they went, it was better than looking at the exhausted workers before Dean.

Gazing at the destroyed planet, Dean couldn't help but wonder if there were any humans left. How long ago was it since the planet was deemed too hazardous to live there? How long has it been since there was a person who stepped foot on the lonely looking planet and wasn't dead upon landing there? Not like there was a way for one of the remaining humans on board the Millennium that would be able to make it back if they went down there.

Even if there were people on the planet, it wasn't like they would be the same anymore. Not with all of the radiation left behind from when the nuclear missiles were launched, it would have wiped out any trace of humanity left. Not only that, but the lingering effects it would have on the environment alone surely would have mutated those who were once human into something else. Nothing would have been safe to either eat or drink for a normal human. But there was hope, hope that maybe there was a way for people to survive without any harsh side effects from the blast. But that wasn't physically possible, was it?

"To think, it's been a little over 500 years or so since the idiots in charge decided that they wanted to simply use this space station as their own little Noah's Ark. Allowing only for their personally selected human beings that were well off enough to be brought into space. I can only imagine the type of orgy they must have had to try and re-populate in order to make for a diverse race." Dean thought bitterly to himself. *"Too bad we*

can't simply go down to the planet. Too damaged they say. What a load of crap. But whatever. Not like there is anyone still living on that planet anyways." Dean was lost in thought, he almost didn't get off on his floor when it arrived. The dangers of daydreaming, but it was Dean's only escape from his personal hell.

Without saying a word, Dean got off of the floor that he was assigned to. It was the same floor he would always head to for over eight years. Walking over the same black and golden marble flooring, Dean kept his eyes against the floor out of habit since he started to work in the Business Elite's section as one of their janitors. The air was filled with a heavy scent of chlorine, thanks to the fountain that took up half of the lobby, it's elaborate design of faceless humans reaching towards a smaller replica of the Millennium always seemed haunting to Dean.

The way that the water seeped out of the top of the Millennium replica, though on a smaller scale, the glistening water washed over the faceless golden models below made it seem like those without any faces were crying because they were simply abandoned. Left behind to die by the Elites' greed, having to simply look out for themselves while the world was destroyed around them. It always made Dean sick to look at it. How anyone could find it beautiful or a piece of art baffled Dean.

"Red pointy shoes... Mrs. Donnaven. Black ankle strap shoes ... Ms. Joyce. Black penny loafers... Mr. Robertson. That means I have a couple of steps left before I spot the tile slate with a small crack that none of these assholes seemed to notice. Round the corner, and I'll be at my station to clean up after these assholes messes once again. Always the same thing day in and day out. Nothing ever changes around here." Just like most creatures, humans always stuck to their habits.

If they found something that they liked, humans would often stick to it. Rarely taking in a chance to change something about themselves. Only when they are tired of those habits would they be willing to change. For all Dean knew, he could have been wrong. Maybe it wasn't those individuals' feet that seemed to huddle by the drinking cooler. Maybe they belonged to someone else? But once Dean had gotten towards the corner that led to his door, he glanced towards the individuals he had passed to see if his hunch was right. Sure enough, the three individuals mentioned were going on about some trivial rumors, wasting company time for their idle chit chat and laughter.

Mrs. Donnaven was a bit of an older woman who often loved wearing brightly colored clothes to give her a bit of a younger appearance. This time she was wearing a shimmering red blouse and matching skirt that rested just above her knee as she wore tanned pantyhose to give her usually pale legs some color. Her face had small traces of wrinkles that were more noticeable around her eyes, that was if her face wasn't caked in what seemed like pounds of makeup to hide the wrinkles. It was a sad attempt in making her look younger. Her black hair was tied back into a tight bun, as if to try and hide the bits of graying hair that was trying to stick out in her locks.

The woman's fingers were decorated with different jewels that it almost seemed like they were little weights on her skeleton thin fingers. Sure the gems and gold seemed to sparkle in the light, but they were a bit off putting when it looked like she could barely lift her fingers because of how heavy the rings were. Against her wrinkling neck was a large pearl bead necklace, it was like she was showing off just how well off she had been thanks to getting married to someone in a higher class. Despite her riches, it seemed as though Mrs. Donnaven wished that she could be young again, but there was nothing to hide her real age. If she didn't try so hard, maybe she could have found some happiness in being able to grow old. Maybe pass her wisdom off on those much younger than herself? But like most in the Elite and upper Silver class, there was no happiness to be found.

Standing next to Mrs. Donnaven was Ms. Joyce, a single woman who was decent to look at if you were into dirty blondes that wore slightly revealing tight clothing to get the attention of an older rich Elite male, one that would be willing to drown her in wealth for a piece of action. Though she would never admit it, it was well known that she would flirt with men who came from a wealthy family regardless of what their relationship status was. Be it married, engaged, in a relationship, or even widowed, she would be there ready to take on the role of a beautiful piece of eye candy that any man would want to show off.

Ms. Joyce was the type of woman who would rather go for the older looking men rather than a younger one, simply for the fact that she would be more inclined to be included in a will and given some sort of inheritance for letting an old man 'stick it' to her. Roughly in her late twenties, Ms. Joyce could be found undoing the few buttons on her silky blouses to give a man a sneak peek of her decently sized breasts. There was no way that she would give someone like Dean a pass however. Then again, Dean wouldn't go for that type of woman anyways. Dean would rather have someone like him for who he was, not with how much he was worth.

Then there was Mr. Robertson, a rather robust man with a belly that jiggled like a fresh uncut jello mold, Mr. Robertson was a man who rather enjoyed the attention of an attractive woman trying to hit on him. As noted with how his eyes eagerly gazed down at Ms. Joyce's parted blouse. Even though the man was already married, it seemed like he was willing to give Ms. Joyce the thrill she was aiming for, considering that Mr. Robertson did come from the upper Silver class.

To think, Dean could have ended up like that man. With just a single glance at the man, it was evident that he was able to eat his fill to give him such a robust gut, the suspenders seemed to be ready to snap off and hit either one of the two ladies standing in front of him. Though it would have been funny to see, even more hilarious to think about. Dean continued towards his work station as he didn't want to be caught loitering around. No need to be beaten for simply standing around after all.

Turning the key into the locked door, Dean walked into the supply closet to collect his usual tools needed to clean up the messes that the 'real' working class often created. The mess ranged from leaving half eaten food on important documents or misplacing said documents in places that they shouldn't be, but it didn't matter to them. After all, they wouldn't be the ones who were punished if anything happened to those documents. The only people who would be punished if anything was thrown out that shouldn't have been was those on the lowest totem pole. Otherwise known as people like Dean, the Bronze class.

The first time Dean made a mistake, it almost cost him his hand, like he was some thief. At the time, Dean had mistakenly thrown out an important document that had coffee rings all over the piece of paper, making it impossible to read. When the office manager found out, he had beaten Dean badly. Dean's right eye was almost swollen shut and his nose wouldn't stop bleeding. There was a cut just under Dean's right eye from the sharp edge of the man's ring, even though it took a few years to heal, Dean could sometimes feel the phantom pain of the ring cutting into his skin from time to time. Dean's stomach was covered with bruises and his hand was almost crushed by the man, mostly due to the fact that the large man decided to step on it, as Dean 'dared' to touch the important document. Even to this day Dean could still feel the weight of the man and the imprint of the shoe lingering on his left hand.

Imagine being a sixteen year old boy making a small mistake, only to have some large man that was close to twice your age and size, stepping on your hand in an act to break it. The weight of his large body trying to break someone's fingers as if they were fragile tree sticks, causing your fingers to almost snap, only to have the muscles swell up to act like a shield to protect the delicate bones of your hand. The sneering cold gaze of someone who viewed an orphaned teenager as being nothing more than trash. How he seemed to ignore the cries of protest and begging for him to stop crushing the Dean's hand, only to grab the teen's hair and pull him up while still trapping his hand. The amount of pain and humiliation that Dean felt helped him learn an important lesson that day. He couldn't rely on anyone. Only himself. The more he tried to help others out, the more Dean got hurt in the process. This was true even later in his life when he tried to help his neighbors with growing their own food, only to be shunned by said people later on.

With the trash bag rolls filling the various pockets in his pants, Dean grasped the large cart that he would use to collect the trash before heading out into the hallway. Keeping his eyes level with the edge of the cart, he went from room to room collecting the trash from the two separate bins located in the corners of the office rooms. Even though most of the time it was pretty straight forward which bin had documents that needed to be shredded or which one was normal garbage, it wasn't uncommon for Dean to find food in the documents bin. It was almost as if they were doing that sort of thing on purpose. As if it was an act of defiance or something. Either way, Dean would have to make sure that there wasn't more trash in the documents bin, having to manually pull the food or other non-documents out of the bin before placing it back into the trash bin where it belonged. It was often a pain to fix, but it was better than letting the shredder get destroyed from food going through the machine.

"Great... a half eaten pastry that has sticky jelly that would jam up the shredder. Just what I needed." Dean mentally grumbled to himself as he took a tissue from his back pocket to wipe the slightly crusted jelly off of the paperwork. *"What a waste. This could have been split in half to feed two people. It's a shame that they waste good food like this... Assholes..."* It was hard to imagine why one would simply toss out food that was half eaten. It made Dean think about the amount of food he wasted as a child, even if it was for a moment, he felt ashamed that he could have ended up like the people he resented now.

Tying off the ends for each of the two different colored bags from the bins, Dean started to wonder why some people had problems telling the difference between what was trash and what was to be shredded. It wasn't that hard to figure out where the trash belonged, all they had to do was look at the coloring of the bag or the location of the bin to know the difference. Just looking at the lining, one could easily see that the white bags are for the documents while the black bags are for trash. Returning back to his cart with the bags in hand, Dean tossed the bags into the bin, only to head towards the next office to repeat the process. One right after the other until the cart was full, leaving Dean with no choice but to head towards the assortment hall to toss them out. It was a hallway used to keep the Bronze class out of sight from the "public" eye. No one wanted to see a person carrying a bunch of trash after all, not like Dean could really blame them.

In the hallway there were two large slots, each with a label that read 'Trash' and 'Shredder'. It didn't take an expert to realize how simple it was to put the bags into the correct slot, even a child could understand it. Tossing the black bags first as they were usually the heavier of the two, considering that it was full of food or other waste that could be used for burning as the stations main source of fuel that was available, Dean crushed down the bulks of the trash with his gloved hands in order to make it fit. It wasn't easy, but he was able to make the bag fit into the slot.

Tossing the last bit of the document bags into the slot, Dean lifted his right arm up to wipe off the sweat lingering under his slightly parted bangs with his forearm. The sound of a grumble left Dean's stomach, causing Dean to peel off one of his gloves. Lightly placing a hand on his stomach, Dean stroked his clothed stomach, giving it a soft caress, as if that would stave off his hunger. The thing was, Dean wasn't even all that hungry. Though the last time his stomach growled like that, it seemed to catch some unwanted attention from someone in the Silver class. They would often say such horrible things that often made someone feel ashamed for being stuck in his class.

All Dean wanted to do was to lay back on his bed with a good book while occasionally glancing towards the planet. To enjoy the sounds of the dull roaring of the station gave off being the only noise in the room. If the conditions were just right, Dean could even fall asleep with the book on his chest and dream about a better life than what he was subjected to.

There were times in which he even found himself dreaming about living on the planet, before everything went to hell that is. With the stories he read about what was found on the Earth before its destruction, Dean would imagine himself walking along the busy streets of some city somewhere, no matter where it was on the planet, only to gaze up at the vast sky with actual clouds that covered the sun. The only thing he had ever seen that was somewhat close to that was the artificial sky given to those in the Silver class.

Just being able to look at pictures of beaches made Dean want to travel to one and experience a warm gentle breeze. To hear the sounds of the seagulls cawing as they seemingly floated in the sky, all the while the sound of the waves crashing against the shore replacing the familiar sound of the dull roar of the station. To be able to feel the warm sand sticking between his bare toes, only to have the cold waves washed over his feet as he stood on the shore, admiring the view of the ships in the distant horizon as they sailed to unknown lands. Though it seems like he would never be able to experience anything quite like that, it was always nice to dream of such a thing. It was an unfulfilled wish, and Dean was alright with that.

THE hours seemed to pass by as Dean kept himself busy with his work. The time for everyone to head home for the day seemingly crept up on Dean before he even knew it. After locking his cart up, Dean headed towards the elevator, only to have to wait a bit before getting a spot towards the back. Floor after the floor the elevator stopped, allowing for more passengers to get on, causing the elevator to become more crowded as it made the slow descent down towards the different living quarters. If Dean had to compare this to anything, it would be equal to rush hour traffic, though it wasn't like Dean knew what that was. Sure he could have used the shuttle his parents had left him, but he wasn't the best at driving it, on top of the fact that fueling it was a complete nightmare.

As the elevator shifted before descending, Dean glanced towards the top of the elevator as he often did, trying to forget about the day he had by closing his eyes, shutting out those around him. Dealing with only a few breaks that was barely five minutes long, with no days off, it was just a pointless job that was given to Dean by the so called hiring committee. With no education available to him, those in the Bronze class were not afforded the luxury of education, Dean had to figure out a way to make money once the allowed amount of inheritance was given to him had dried up. Getting a job at the age of sixteen meant that he had to choose between being a maintenance personal or janitorial. One had the dangers of being out in space from time to time, while the safer of the other job meant that Dean got to stay inside.

Mentally counting down the number of stops till they would land on his floor, Dean hurried himself out of the elevator as fast as he could, wanting to free himself from the fishing net that was the inhabitants of the Bronze class. Upon entering the main corridor, Dean felt like there was something wrong. His feet felt a bit heavy, like he could barely lift them up past his knees. Shuffling his feet the best he could, it didn't take long before Dean couldn't even walk, causing someone behind him to bump against his back.

"Sorry." The man spoke quickly, walking around Dean in a hurry, though Dean couldn't blame the man for wanting to get away from everyone else, he wanted to get away from everyone the most, but his feet refused to budge. It was worrisome to say the least, not being able to move as a cold sweat trickled down his body, all the while people walking past him in a hurry to get home.

Before Dean could even say anything, the man was gone. *What's going on with my body? My legs... they feel as heavy as sandbags. I can't move them at all.* Dean thought to himself, his mind started to feel a bit fuzzy, all the while his vision blurred. The cold atmosphere in the station caused Dean to feel like he was freezing, the cold sweat trickling down his body didn't help matters either, all the while his feet refusing to move. Dean could feel his heart beating against his chest, the voices of those around him became inaudible. There was a low ringing in his ears, his breath picking up to small pants. What was happening to him? Dean wasn't getting sick was he?

Seconds felt like hours. The people seemed to glance back at Dean who stood frozen in place as they passed him. Their faces became blurred to the point where there weren't any facial expressions, yet Dean could feel them staring at him even for a second.. A sense of doom washed over him, leaving Dean feeling scared for the first time in years. The pounding of Dean's heart started to beat louder in his ears as those around Dean started to walk in slow motion. Even if they were not actually walking in slow motion, it felt like they were. It was as if time was slowing down around Dean, and he was simply stuck in place. Unable to escape while everything moved to a small crawl.

It was only when someone else bumped into Dean that it felt like he could move again. At first his steps were wobbly, as if he was a newborn calf. It didn't ease the fact that Dean's heart still pounded against his chest though. Finding a spot to rest by the wall and away from the flow of traffic of everyone walking to get home, Dean reached a hand up to his forehead to see if perhaps he had a fever. His skin felt ice cold from the sweat that was pouring out of his pores with a small flushed coloring to his already pale cheeks.

Being able to simply rest seemed to do the trick at least, despite the fact that people gave him puzzled looks as they walked by him, Dean was able to stabilize himself to walk once more. As Dean took small shallow breaths, he was able to get his footing down. Sure his steps may have been a bit unsure as Dean fought the urge to simply collapse in the middle of the hallway, but eventually Dean made it back to his little sanctuary that was his pod.

Closing the door behind him, Dean pressed his back against the cold metallic frame. It didn't take long before Dean took his gloves off as his hands were soaked, tossing the thin gloves off in an unknown direction as he didn't want to look at the stained gloves any longer than he already had to. However, after tossing them, the familiar dizzy sensation caught back up to Dean as a wave of nausea washed over his body. Tilting his head forward and slumping down against the ice cold metal door to the floor, Dean's hair fell forward as some sweat started dripping from his locks and onto the metal floor between Dean's legs. The ringing felt like it was getting louder this time. Reaching his left hand up to his face, Dean covered his eyes as the lights in the ceiling felt like they were blinding him. Did he get sick? No way, Dean couldn't afford to get sick!

Pulling his legs in closer to his core, Dean curled up into a small ball in an act to try and keep himself warm while recovering from either this illness or sense of dread that washed over him. The minutes passed slowly before Dean finally felt somewhat normal. Stretching out his legs, Dean softly sighed as he stared up at the small speakers above the door. "How am I supposed to keep going like this?" He murmured softly to himself.

An exhausted gaze brushed against his face, his eyes seemingly appearing dim, like all of the life was slowly draining them. "Day after day, it's the same. I get up in the morning after barely getting any sleep, I work myself to the bone only to have everything taken away from me. What kind of existence is that?" Dean's voice trembled as he spoke to himself, small tears forming in his eyes as a small sniffle escaped the exhausted man. "Is it wrong to actually want to live a life that doesn't work me to death? To be able to do as I please without the need for an invisible source of so called money?" His words echoed into the vast void of his room. "Why am I being punished like this?" Dean whimpered as he closed his eyes as his shoulders slumped a bit. "It's not fair…."

Burying his head into his hands, Dean stared down at the floor. "I just want to break free from these chains. To go on some type of adventure, even if it is just once in my lifetime." Perhaps Dean felt this way because his youth was being sapped from him. Having to go from being a child one day, to having to grow up into an adult at the age of twelve after the death of his parents, it wasn't easy. The mental exhaustion that Dean was feeling was the norm in the Millennium.

Taking a deep breath in to regain his composure, Dean was finally able to stand up. Making his way over towards the kitchen, it seemed that perhaps Dean needed something to drink to help calm his nerves. Seeing as his hands were shaking as much as his legs, Dean needed to find a way to calm himself down. Grabbing the small handle bar to open the refrigerator, Dean opened it up with a small grimace on his face. There wasn't much that would provide Dean with something that would help to calm him down, or make the man feel better. Too bad he could never afford alcohol as he felt like he could use some. Instead, Dean grabbed a bottle of water out of his small fridge in hopes that it would help him feel more refreshed.

Taking out a bottle of water, Dean twisted the cap off, though he did struggle with it at first as it felt like all the strength had been sapped from him. Bringing the smooth rim up to his lips to drink the cold refreshment, moistening his throat that felt like it was on fire, it felt as if Dean had swallowed a piece of sandpaper with how scratchy his throat was. After taking the sip, Dean wiped his lips as he stood against the counter to help support his body.

After everything that happened, Dean didn't exactly trust himself to move around so freely. With the bottle in hand, Dean walked back to his bed where he would be able to simply relax for the rest of the night with a good book, that is if his vision would permit it. Making his way towards his bed, which was only a few steps away, it didn't take long before Dean had practically fallen on top of the firm mattress out of exhaustion. "Finally... my favorite place in the whole station..." Dean mumbled with a hint of bliss as he landed on the bed and rested his face against his worn down blanket.

Moving to sit back up on the edge of the bed frame, Dean started to peel his uniform off of him. It was a bit harder to get off than it was to get back on, mostly due to the fact that his body was soaked in sweat, but once the uniform was off Dean tossed the wet uniform towards whichever direction he deemed right at the time. Pulling a drawer out by his left leg, Dean grabbed a pair of sweatpants to slip on as he felt like a cold turkey being pulled out a freezer to thaw. Slipping the sweat pants on, Dean collected the felt blanket in his arms as he got into the bed. If he was going to rest for the night, he at least wanted to be comfortable. Propping the pillows up behind him, Dean leaned back before spreading the blanket over top of him as if he was casting a fishing net. It was a bit of a ritual he did since he first moved into the pod. Though at that time the blanket was still big on him.

Once he was settled into the bed, Dean grabbed the book he had been reading for a while now from the side drawer on the frame of his bed. Flipping through the pages until he found the page that he had left off on. It was the old story of a young boy who dreamed of flying to another land in search of adventure. Emily used to read it to Dean often when he was a child. The worn down cover showed its age and the pages faded and Dean knew the story by heart, but he still liked to read it.

BEFORE he knew it, Dean had nodded off to sleep. The book rested on Dean's stomach as the makeshift bookmark was barely visible against the edges of the pages, the book rocked back and forth ever so gently against Dean's sleeping frame. He was too exhausted to read further than he would have liked. Everything seemed quiet on the ship in that moment, only to have their whole world turned upside down in an instant. Seemingly, out of nowhere, the pod just above Dean's exploded from the station, causing Dean's pod to shake violently, disturbing the slumber that Dean rarely ever got.

Bolting up from his slumber, the book Dean was reading was tossed towards the edge of his bed facing the wall. The same wall that was once lined with different books and a few photos that he was able to keep before his parents' home was repossessed by the Enforcement officers, now had all of its contents spewed over the hard metal floor. The sound of glass breaking was masked by the sirens going off above the door as the emergency lights started to turn on. The whole room was flooded with the color red, making it hard to see what was going on in Dean's dazed state.

After collecting his bearings, Dean crawled towards the circular window to see if he could see what was happening. It took only a second to see it, but what Dean saw before him was something he wouldn't be able to look away from. Among the debris that floated around the space in front of his window, a singular pod was spotted seemingly spinning wildly towards the planet out of control. For a second Dean was able to spot the image of a woman pinned against the window as the pod hurled towards the planet. The look of fear in her eyes was prominent as she knew that she was being flung towards her death, and there was nothing she could do about it.

Watching helplessly as the occupant and their pod were burned up into the atmosphere, leaving hardly anything left of the poor individual to be found, it was something you couldn't look away from. How could this have happened? There was no way that these little pods should have been broken off so easily. To think, her screams were left unheard as everything around the woman literally spiraled around her or was pulled into the vacuum of space, only to be burned alive as she was pulled by the Planet's gravitational force. That is, if she was even that lucky to survive the vacuum of space suffocating them. There was no way that anyone could survive something like that. Clenching his teeth, Dean wondered what would have happened if he found himself in that situation. What if his little pod had been the one sent out like that? Could that still happen?

Dean couldn't watch it anymore. Placing a hand on the small handle for the blinds, Dean closed them. The floor above him must be in a chaos as they didn't know what happened either. Mothers' would keep their children inside, people would become scared of every little bump or creak that they would feel from their pods now. But then again, who could really blame them? They were in a floating space station with nothing to keep them safe from either inside or outside of this death trap. This was their fate after all. All they could do was simply wait for their own death, regardless if it was natural or 'accidental'.

Pulling the blanket off of him, Dean glanced around at the mess that was caused from the pod dislodging itself from the station after the lights went back to normal. The photos of his parents had been knocked down causing glass to litter the floor, making it unsafe for Dean to walk around barefoot. Dean didn't exactly have a broom close by, so the only thing he could do without stepping on a bunch of glass was to use the little robot cleaner. It was expensive to use in large moderations, but with everything that had happened earlier, Dean didn't have the strength to clean.

Carefully placing his feet on the ground, Dean made his way over towards the panel by the refrigerator. With a press on the sweeper icon followed by the targeted size of the mess, a small panel opened up under the bed. A small silver oval robot hovered off of the floor, its' purple digital eyes blinked as if it had just woken up from a nap. It didn't take the small robot long before it started to go to work as its small claws extended from its main body. The little robot was quick to stack the books and picture frames with its' claws, piling them up in a neat stack before it started to sweep up the glass. Taking the glass over towards the bin, the little robot dumped the glass with a swift movement, only to head back into the slot it came from as the task was finished.

"It may be adorable, but it sure is expensive. I could have gotten a whole series worth of books with the price of a small clean up job by this guy." The first time that Dean learned about the robot, he over used it and had to eat food he found in the trash at work, the price of the little robot cleaning was equal to the price of Dean's food budget for a month.

Walking over towards the pile, Dean started with collecting the books first since it was easier to do the heavy part first before having to replace his parents photos. Placing the books in no particular order, as he was too tired to deal with organizing them, Dean bent down to collect the broken frames soon after. It was one of the few things that he could carry with him after the Enforcement officers kicked the newly orphaned Dean out of his parents' old home. Gazing at the photos, Dean couldn't help but remember the good times he had with them.

Emily Torres, Dean's mother, was a beautiful woman with piercing Aqua blue eyes. Her brunette hair was always shoulder length as it softly grazed her pale skin. Her smile always seemed warm, much like her personality. She was always a bit stubborn on her beliefs, but she had so much love to give to her son and the children that she taught. She was a school teacher for the Silver class in their district and often had a positive effect on the children that she taught.

In the photo she was holding a much younger version of Dean who appeared to be about four years old at the time in front of their old home. The house was a lovely two story brick house with different flora surrounding the porch. They often used the porch on weekends to enjoy the yearly beautiful weather of the Silver class. Not a single dark cloud in the makeshift sky or any clouds for that matter that were real and not projected onto the high ceiling. In his youth, Dean was often found on the porch reading books while sitting on one of the patio chairs with a side table that would hold a mixture of a small drink, a snack, and the next book he would read.

Turning the frame over to open the back as it was a safe way of getting the photograph out, Dean noticed that there was a piece of paper that was hidden underneath it. Bringing the photos over towards the table and chair, Dean sat down so that he could see what the hidden paper had on it. Blinking a bit in surprise, Dean unfolded the faded looking piece of paper to see what was written on it. He could clearly see some type of letter that was hand written in his mother's style, but it was barely legible with how the paper was folded and the ink looked a bit smeared as if it was quickly folded and hidden before the ink could dry. Carefully unfolding it, Dean read the note left to him by one of his parents:

Dean, there isn't much time to let you know what is about to happen, but you must know the truth. Every decade a child is sacrificed by the Elite who perform unholy acts on a child of their choosing to ensure that the station continues to run in their favor. Most of the children sent to the Elite class are forced to engage in the debauchery of the Elites. You must-

It seemed that the letter had been cut off, almost like Emily was in a rush to hide the letter before her untimely death. Dean couldn't believe what he had read. Sure he had heard rumors of some orphan children being put into questionable situations if they were 'selected' by the Elite, but to think that they would be subjected to debauchery? It churned Dean's stomach just thinking about what they would do to those kids, but there wasn't much that he could do to help them. Perhaps if Dean was in a higher status, he would be able to do something about it. Since he was in the Bronze class, he couldn't exactly do much about it.

A soft sigh escaped from his lips as he crumbled the letter. Tossing the paper ball towards the bin with a scowl on his face, Dean felt a heavy pressure forming on his shoulders with this new discovery. "I must what, mom? What were you trying to tell me?" Dean grumbled to himself bitterly. Perhaps it was best to simply disregard the note. But that made Dean curious about if his father's picture frame may have held secrets to it as well. Picking up the empty frame that held his mother's old photo that was now empty, Dean tossed it towards the bin as well, not caring if it made it into the bin or not.

"Not like I can do much when I am constantly suffering in this pit of hell you left me in." Dean spat bitterly, though he wasn't really angry with his mother. He had no power nor influence to help anyone, not even himself.

Spotting the other broken picture frame that held his father's Max's photo, Dean picked it up before he started to undo the backing to the frame. Pulling out the photo, Dean couldn't help but gaze at it. In the photo Max was holding Dean as a baby all wrapped up in the hospital blankets shortly after he was born. Frankly Dean looked more like his father than he would have liked. With brunet slicked back hair, and a bushy goatee around his lips, Max had piercing emerald eyes with a tanned complexion to him. Emily would often complain about how Dean didn't even look like her, but Max would always disagree. It was a silly thing to fight about, but thinking back on it, it was rather sweet.

Pulling off the back of the cracked frame, Dean noticed a piece of paper that had some of the ink appearing more visible with scribbles that Dean was faintly familiar with. Unfolding the paper, Dean realized that it was his father's writing on it. In the center of the paper was a body chart with different notes lined with findings on a body.

Glancing over the chart, Dean noticed that it was for a boy, around Dean's age at the time. The details on the chart were sickening to say the least. Bite marks on the boy's upper thighs, lacerations on the boys' wrists and ankles that seemed to indicate that the boy had been tied up, there were different spots of bruising that were made by either hickeys and strike marks from paddles hitting the young boy. But the worst yet was on the backside of the body. Deep whip marks that reached the boys' entire length of his spine. His rectum was torn, meaning that even if this boy survived, he would have irreversible damage to him. Ultimately what killed him was strangulation followed by the removal of his heart.

It must have been gut retching for his father to see a child around Dean's age at the time be killed and horribly defiled before and after death that he couldn't simply keep quiet about it. Though with a big secret of what the Elite had done to this poor child, there wasn't anyone that Max could have told that would even believe him. The only person whom Max could have trusted was Emily. She hated the Elite even more than ever after learning about the horrible deed, so it wasn't like she would go and sell him out when it would end up killing the both of them and perhaps Dean in the process.

Even with hard concrete evidence like this, it was hard to deny the truth as to what happened to his parents. One way or another, the Elite had found out that Max had worked on the body of the child who they had sacrificed. Though at the time they didn't know that Max had drawn up the notes on the body on the wrong chart on purpose. Perhaps a nosy neighbor had overheard the two talking about the discovery and reported it? After all, those who reported any wrong doing often got rewarded. Nothing like selling out your neighbor for an extra bonus to your household. Meaning that anyone in Dean's old neighborhood could have been a guilty party in his parent's death. It filled Dean with an anger like he never had before. But now wasn't the time to dwell on the past. He had to focus on what was right in front of him.

Laying the chart down on the table, Dean found himself in an interesting position. On one hand, he did have the power to show the station what kind of sick bastards were in control of everything on the station and could possibly get a following behind him to get his revenge, but on the other, he could very well end up like his parents. Dead with no trace of what really happened to him. Or at least if there were people who saw, they wouldn't say anything.

Taking a deep breath through his nose, Dean glanced at the date, it seemed that the date in which the boy died was on Hollow's Eve. It was a time in which everyone would take part in a festival for the harvest of the fall season. It resembled Halloween, a holiday that was celebrated with candy and costumes on Earth before it was nuked.

Leaning against the table with his right elbow propping his head up while leaning his cheek into the palm of his hand, Dean sat there and wondered how they could have tortured this boy and what he went through. Was it really for some type of ritual? It was around a decade ago that this happened, so perhaps they stopped doing this sort of thing?

The more that Dean dwelled on it, the more things started to click to the current events that were folding in front of him. Was that explosion the result of the steps necessary for them to find their next orphan? Shaking his head as that felt like a crazy conspiracy, Dean knew that he had to do this right. If he became too suspicious, what happened to his upper neighbor could very well happen to him. This was a dark truth that no one will believe or would even want to believe. Considering the letter that his mother left for him to find was hidden from the Enforcement's clean up crew, Dean was left with a double edge sword.

Placing the photos on the table, Dean tapped the chart with his right index and middle finger in thought. As a nobody on the ship, it wasn't like Dean could simply go around flashing the chart to people. He would seem like he was some kind of nut case. The Enforcement officers would be called in, and Dean would be executed, all the while the officers would lie and deem Dean 'safe' in their custody. Eventually over time, people would forget about him, and everything would be right in the world. There was no way that Dean would ever allow that to happen. He'd just have to bide his time is all. Question was, how long until they would find the evidence?

Getting up from the table, Dean collected the photos of his parents, before walking over towards the cabinets. Pulling one of the empty drawers open, Dean placed the photos in the drawer for safe keeping. He'll get new frames later, but for now he didn't want them to get dirty. Heading back to the table, Dean knew he had to do something with the chart. But where could he hide it?

Folding up the paper and chart, Dean walked over towards his bed. Lifting the edge up of the thin mattress, Dean shoved the folded piece of paper into the narrow opening of the bed frame. The worst that could happen if it fell into the bed was that Dean would have pulled the top of the drawer open in order to have the papers fall down for easy access, but not many knew about that little hidden feature, so it would be safe from prying eyes. "Most guys keep dirty magazines under their beds. But what do I hide? Dark secrets." Dean mused to himself as he put his mattress back down.

Sitting on top of his bed Dean laid back to gaze up at the ceiling. All of this information was a bit too much. His parents died because they discovered the truth about what happened to a boy around Dean's age as part of a dark ritual. Since it had been over five hundred years since the last of the humans went into space, that meant that the Elite have gotten away with the ruthless killing of children for over fifty years. That raised the question, were they doing this sort of thing before they came up to the station? Back on the Earth below? That thought alone was chilling.

Despite the heavy mind set of the rather dark topics that recently surfaced, Dean was able to fall asleep. It was probably due to his lack of energy from the illness that plagued him earlier that made Dean feel exhausted, allowing him to sleep despite waking up in a cold sweat from the following nightmare he had remembering what happened to his parents.

Sitting up, Dean brought his hands up to wipe the sweat off of his forehead. Groaning as he did so, Dean glanced out the window as he pulled the blinds back up to look out at the planet below him. There wasn't as much space debris as there once was from the last time he gazed out of the window, but the unsettling fact that he witnessed someone's death still haunted him. The last time he witnessed a death, it was the after effect of his parents.

Looking up at their cold dead bodies, even to this day it sent a chill down Dean's spine. "Thought I was over these nightmares." Dean grumbled to himself, rolling over to his side. His eyes felt like sand bags. Dean was a bit torn between wanting to sleep and staying awake, mostly due to the fact that he was scared of returning back to the nightmare.

With a soft sigh, Dean reached the blinds to pull it down. He couldn't deal with looking at the planet right now. As much as he loved gazing at the cloud covered planet, Dean just felt sick looking at it. His mind wavered slightly, drifting between sleeping and thinking about what happened. Unfortunately, in the end, sleep won and caused Dean to fall fast asleep. Unaware of the movements being taken place to turn his life upside down the very next day that he was to go back to work.

Chapter Two: *Crash*

A FEW DAYS PASSED since the accident, the station seemed to be abuzz with rumors or speculations regarding the cause of the pod becoming dislodged from the space station. The thing that really stuck out in the rumors was the fact that no one was in the corridor when the so called accident happened. The only casualty was that of a young mother who occupied the pod, while her only daughter seemingly disappeared an hour before the dislodging of the pod occurred.

Deep down Dean could sense that the Elite were moving onto their next target. The time line seemed to match up with the events that happened ten years ago. A child being chosen by the Elite, seemingly becoming an orphan around Hollow's Eve, there was no way that the chosen child would come out of this ritual alive. Much like that boy ten years ago, she'll be beaten and sexually assaulted before having her heart ripped out by the sick Elite members.

Frankly if the dislodging of the pod was indeed an accident, there would have been more deaths from the number of people that often walked around the corridor during that time. Rather it was coming back late from work or collecting groceries from the store in preparation to make dinner, there would have been at least ten or so people walking around at the time. If this was really an accident, like the Enforcement officers were claiming it was, their bodies would have been floating among the debris.

Coincidentally it seemed like the maintenance personnel had been able to respond to the distress in a timely manner. It was like they were on standby, ready at the scene, even before it happened. Normally it would have taken much longer for the hole to be patched up. Usually taken up to five or so hours, but this time they had seemingly patched up the hole in half the time.

The Enforcement Commander had first congratulated the maintenance staff who responded to the breech, only to later throw them under the bus. Remarking that the whole tragic event could have been avoided if the structure of the station had been up to code. Seemed like they were trying to shift the blame onto those in the Bronze class once again, making it seem like everything that went wrong was because of that class in particular.

"I still can't believe it. That poor family being hurled towards the planet like that. I heard the pod decentagrated when it fell into the atmosphere." The voice of an older woman reaching Dean's ears as they rode the elevator up towards the top floor. The woman looked to be roughly past sixty as her face was decorated with wrinkles. Her eyes were a dull blue and her silver hair curled this way and that on top of her head. She was wearing a gray babushka that wrapped around her head, the scarf having a floral design made with white and teal thread to keep up with the colors assigned to the Bronze class.

"Oh my. Were the mother and daughter aboard the pod when it crashed?" Another woman asked, only slightly younger than the elderly woman standing next to her, she seemed to be a few years younger in appearance. The woman had a bit of red still lingering in her locks, though they were slowly being taken over with bits of graying hair. Brown eyes glanced towards Dean, as if she could sense that he was eavesdropping on the two, causing Dean to glance away, not wanting to take part in their idle chit chat.

"I don't know. Some people said that they had seen the daughter with one of the Enforcement officers. But others say that, there was no way the mother could have gotten out of there in time. It was so sudden after all. I do wonder what happened though. Maybe they will do an examination on the outer walls? Don't want that to happen to anyone else." The woman remarked with the babushka as she too looked towards Dean, wondering what it was that her friend had been looking at. It was almost as if they were trying to cue Dean into talking about it with them, but he wasn't going to budge. After all, it wasn't his place to speak ill of the dead.

"What a time we're living in. It seems like every couple of years something like this happens, and it's always to the young ones. Sad, really." The elderly redhead remarked, shaking her head as she went back to looking straight ahead of her, giving up on the idea of trying to get a young man to talk about the gossip as well. There was always something about the elderly that seemed like they wanted to include as many people as they could to their little gossip. Then again, younger people tend to do the same, but are much more selective about it. Or at the very least try to be.

"Indeed. Guess we should count ourselves lucky to still be alive and kicking." The babushka woman remarked, a small chuckle leaving her before the elevator stopped. It had appeared that the elevator had stopped on the floor that the two elderly women were stationed at. Watching as the two ladies walked out of the elevator with their small shuffle, Dean was a bit relieved that he could get a break from the constant gossiping surrounding him.

Every day the gossip was getting worse, and each time it felt like eyes landed on him in an accusative gaze like he was the cause of it. It was either that, or he had known what had happened. Replaying it in his mind, Dean couldn't figure out what could have caused it, but from the rumbling it must have been some type of controlled detonation. Though if that was the case, they would have to make sure that it wouldn't cause too much damage to the space station, only to force that particular pod to dislodge from the station.

Thinking back on the person he had seen when the pod was heading towards the Earth, there was only one person visible being trashed about inside, but then again his window wasn't all that big. At least not big enough to get a decent look as to what happened. If there was another person, it wasn't like Dean would be able to see them. But if what those ladies had said was true, about the daughter being seen with one of the Enforcement officers just before the explosion, then was it that time again? For another child to be sacrificed? They only had a couple of weeks until Hollow's Eve would be upon them, it would make sense now that there was movement on the Elite's part for the next ritual.

"So if they make sure that it looked like an accident in which a child is orphaned, it would only make sense that they do the preparations a few weeks in advance in order to keep people from questioning what is going on." Dean thought to himself, walking his usual path by memory as his eyes kept to the ground. *"Everyone would think that it is just simply the station showing its age. But considering that there had been no issue until now, most would see this as just an unfortunate event to one family in particular."* As messed up as that sounded, it could very well be the case.

"The way that the Elite had set this up, they made sure that nobody would ever guess the true reasoning as to what is going on. They have done this so many times that they figured out the formula." With the Elite controlling everything, they were able to convince people that they saved humanity from its

own destruction, though really they ruined any chance for humanity to grow and get away from the Elite's grip.

"This is so frustrating! Why can't people see what is going on?! They're too busy looking at the Elite as if they are some type of hero when really we're being held captive! We're nothing but cattle to the hungry wolves." Dean thought bitterly as he clenched his fists. A dark scowl washed over Dean's face as his gaze was set upon anyone ahead of him. He wasn't going to allow more innocent people to die. He was no longer going to sit back and watch helplessly anymore. He would take his findings, and show them to everyone. Dean didn't care anymore if it would result in his death. People had to know the truth!

As Dean rounded the corner, his gaze was set ahead of him instead of his usual lowered gaze. He no longer looked like someone who was an obedient dog, but rather someone who had enough of taking orders from people who were 'above' him. With a scowl on his face, Dean's pace quickened as he made it to the busy office only to find that something was off.

The cubicles were empty. It was oddly quiet to the point that you would be able to hear a pin drop onto the marbled black and golden tiled floor. The sounds of the printing machines and telephones ringing were gone. This didn't feel right. The usual three weren't standing around the water cooler, much of the office workers were gone. It wasn't a weekend, otherwise this would have been the norm. Maybe the Elite decided that those in the Silver class got some time off to deal with the death of the woman hurled down towards the planet? That didn't make sense. They never did that before. Especially not for someone who was in the Bronze class.

Turning the corner towards his station, Dean was surprised to see two Enforcement officers standing near the door that held his equipment. Dean froze in place, the seething anger quickly disappearing from his face as it was replaced by fear. Now it seemed to make sense. The Enforcement officers didn't want to have any witnesses around when they were about to do their dirty deeds. Did this mean, Dean's little plan was being snuffed out before it even began?

"What the hell are they doing here?" Dean panicked as he could feel a cold sweat running down his temple. His first instinct was to run, but that would be assumed that he was guilty of something he clearly didn't do. Dean knew he had to face this head on. Who knows, maybe they were just there to question him? It didn't ease his nerves though, then again, bad things tend to happen with Dean when the Enforcement officers were around.

The two officers standing in front of the door had their backs turned to Dean. The design of the officers' uniform was similar to how Dean's was, though unlike the short sleeved version that Dean was given, the officers' uniform were long sleeved to give them extra protection. The gray was turned to black. The seam was golden and the white that rested on the lower torso was turned to blue. The belts that the officers wore had been decorated with the tools they needed for whatever emergencies they were dealing with.

Their belts did have a bit of a dip according to which side the officer was more dominant with, whether it was their left or right hand, making it easier for them to reach down for their smaller side arm if need be. Their armor was a sleek black coated chest plate that made sure to protect their vital organs. Along their collar were stars or circles to indicate their rankings.

Circles were assigned to regular officers while the stars were higher rankings for captain, lieutenant, and so on.

Two names were etched onto the officers backs to identify them, one reading Harrison and the other McCoy. Swallowing a bit of saliva to moisten his dry throat, Dean lowered his head as his gaze moved towards the floor as he walked towards the two men. Each step had Dean's heart racing, there was a faint ringing in his ears as the silence made Dean's heart sound like a loud drum being beaten. It was only when the two officers had taken notice of the footsteps that the two turned towards Dean.

"Dean Torres?" One of the two officers asked, though their faces were blocked out from the helmet that they wore, making it hard to really know what the officers looked like when they were wearing their helmets. Maybe it was used as a way to keep people confused to the point that they would mistake which officer that they were dealing with, which was unsettling if you think about it.

"Y-Yes?" Dean answered as he stopped walking, timidly looking up at the officers. He had to be corroborative, otherwise he may very well be charged with something that he didn't even do. The stories that he heard about the Enforcement officers never seemed to go well with those in the lower class, which meant that Dean had to keep his wits about him, unless he wanted to be part of those horror stories as well.

"I'm officer McCoy and this is my partner officer Harrison. We're here to ask a couple of questions regarding the incident of the pod detaching from the station a few days ago." The more muscular of the two spoke. It was almost as if Officer McCoy was trying to intimate Dean into behaving, though Dean wasn't doing anything but simply standing here. Though Dean's body language was a bit defensive for the officers liking, which may have been why McCoy had to speak up.

"How can I help you officers?" Dean's voice was calm, not wanting to show any of the aggression that he had previously. Even though Dean felt anger towards these two due to his own personal history with the Enforcement officers, he wasn't going to do or say anything stupid that could cause them to become aggressive towards Dean.

"If you'll follow us." The man continued with a small gesture of his hands that indicated that he wanted Dean to follow him, all the while the other officer seemed to keep his eyes on Dean. Even if Dean couldn't actually see the other officer glancing towards him, it was the unsettling feeling that Dean got while facing the officer. How could anyone feel safe seeing their reflection against those helmets?

"Certainly..." Dean spoke, glancing at his door before the two officers turned to escort Dean to a more private setting. Something seemed off about this whole situation. Even though Dean couldn't put his finger on it, it felt like the officers knew that Dean had some evidence on the Elite, and they were here to silence him into his submission. With how quickly things have moved to keep individuals quiet, it wouldn't surprise Dean if this was exactly what was happening right now.

Dean had heard some horror stories that dated back to when the last of the humans arrived on the space station. The Elite took the chance to round up those who were deemed a threat to expose their dark secrets, and were brutally executed in front of the large masses. The sound of gun fire and the bodies seemingly landing on the ground below with crunch from their necks breaking was used as a demonstration that those in the Elite class were able to kill anyone that they deemed unworthy to be in their ranks.

Rather that the story in itself was true was still up for debate, but as long as he could remember, Dean read a couple of notes that used to linger in his father's den that suggested that some deaths were suspicious. How you may ask? Well, there was a case in which a man was found in his bathtub with a red mark around his neck. Though the water was over flowing, and his wrists had been cut to indicate suicide, there was more to it with the evidence left on the body that seemed to make it more like a homicide than a suicide. But there was no way that the Enforcement Officers would rule it a homicide. Possibly because they had their part in it. Either way, Dean knew that these guys didn't exactly mess around.

Walking down the hall, Dean took notice that there were some people around, though they seemed to be peeking out of their little hiding holes. *"So they are here. Trying to be sneaky and take a peek, wondering what will happen next? Cowards."* Dean thought bitterly to himself, his eyebrows knitted together as he wanted to scoff, but that would draw the attention from the officers. Dean didn't need to add fuel to the fire. Besides the few people who actually seemed to be sticking around were simply hiding in their little office, leaving the hallway empty.

Dean had walked the same halls day in and day out, but he never really got a chance to look around. Along the walls were portraits of the Elite, the descendants, and those who were dubbed the pioneers who brought everyone into space. This was the first time that Dean got to see their faces, as most of the Elite liked to hide themselves in the inner sections of the core. They appeared like any normal human to Dean, but in their own minds, the Elite saw themselves as gods.

It didn't take long for the three to enter into a small conference room with a table and chairs on either side. Taking a seat, Dean tried to relax his body, but there was no way to relax around the group of murders that didn't even get punished if they killed someone. *"I didn't do anything wrong. So why are they questioning me?"* The thought that they might pin this on Dean wasn't exactly comforting.

Considering that they always looked for some type of scapegoat in these types of situations in order to calm the public. They probably would make up some lie about Dean being able to find his way outside, plant some sort of explosive, and be able to get back in when people weren't around. Dean stuck with the janitorial duties to avoid that type of thing. As much as he loved looking at the Earth he never wanted to go outside into space where he would die a horrific death.

One of the officers cleared his throat before taking his seat next to their partner, as if to indicate the start of the interrogation. "Around seven in the evening yesterday you were in your room, correct?" The police officer known as Harrison asked, reaching down to his belt to get out a notepad. Pulling a pen out for the spiraling side, the man waited for Dean to start talking before writing down the answer given to him.

"Yes. I just finished my twelve hour shift." Dean spoke, clearing his throat a bit as he was trying to stay cool, calm, and collective. Just like every single day for the past eight years, Dean always worked a twelve hour shift. Though Dean failed to mention that he wasn't exactly feeling the greatest at the time, but he didn't see how that would benefit this so-called investigation.

"I see." Remarked Harrison as he wrote something down on the notebook before he flipped a couple of pages in the notebook after that. "We have a report here that you had stopped a tad bit before reaching your room. Seemingly refusing to move despite someone bumping into you. It was only when someone else had bumped into you that you started moving again. Only to slink into a passage for an unknown time, before finally making it home past your normal time. Care to explain what happened there?" The man asked before flipping back to the previous page for his notes, the pen pressing against the paper while the movements of their helmets seemed to face directly at Dean.

Dean's reflection in the man's helmet showed the shocked look on Dean's face as he was unprepared for the question. "I-I wasn't feeling well." Dean started out in a bit of a shaky tone before clearing his throat before he continued. "I worked through my lunch. Perhaps I was simply low on sugar." Dean tried to make up some type of excuse, but it seemed like there was just a list of excuses that came to mind.

"I haven't been feeling well since that morning. After getting off of the elevator after the long shift, my body felt heavy. I might be getting sick due to the lack of warmth in my pod. With the nights getting colder, and my blanket looking like Swiss cheese.... mostly because I can't exactly afford to replace it since things seemingly keep taking funds out of my account..." Dean trailed off, his left leg started to bounce under the table as he could feel the anxiety creeping up on him. Dean's heart was pounding against his chest as he didn't think stopping in the hallway to compose himself was a bad thing. Did they really find that suspicious? How would they even know about something like that?

"I see..." The voice of Harrison remarked as his voice seemed to echo in the helmet, his doubt was showing in his voice. Even if Dean couldn't see the man's reaction under his helmet. It was clear that they were starting to think that somehow Dean was involved with this 'accident'. Even if Dean told them the truth, which he was despite his nervous demeanor, they would probably doubt anything that he said. "Moving to the time of the pod breaking free from the space station, do you recall anything out of the ordinary?" Harrison asked, tapping the paper almost impatiently.

Out of the ordinary? Watching someone being hurled towards the planet below was clearly something out of the ordinary! Finding out that the Elite were using children as sexual play things before killing them and ripping out their hearts was something that was out of the ordinary! Hearing that one of their officers was seen with the now orphaned girl was suspicious to say the least. To say that there was something out of the ordinary going on was an understatement.

"I had decided to lay down once I had gotten to my pod since I wasn't feeling the greatest." Dean started to recount the events of what happened after he reached his pod. "I was sleeping before I felt a rumble from above me. It knocked everything down from my shelf. Other than that, there wasn't anything else out of the ordinary." Dean spoke, his voice more flat tone as he looked between the two officers. It was the truth, but he wasn't going to head into the details of finding out the evidence that could put their superiors in danger of being exposed. He had to choose his words carefully.

It seemed that the two had shared a glance as their helmets turned towards each other. They were onto something, and it seemed like Dean had said something that could cause them to be suspicious of him. It was a bit unsettling, but Dean wasn't going to back down. Perhaps they were expecting Dean to say something that would sound like he was a crazy conspiracy person.

"I had a couple of books on the shelf that were knocked down in the explosion. Along with a photo of my parents that shattered once they fell. I used the cleaning robot to clean up the shards of glass that broke. You can look at my charge history if you don't believe me." Dean added on, watching the body language of the two in front of them. It seemed as if Dean had said something that had caused them to become slightly uncomfortable. They knew something, even if they weren't going to say it.

"Was there anything else? Did you notice if anything was out of place?" The man asked, trying to change the subject. The change in their body language went into a bit of a defensive and guarded position, seems like Dean might have said something that he shouldn't have. This caused Dean's eyebrow to rise a little, his interest perked as to what these two knew.

"I saw a woman being hurled down to the planet below. The way she screamed into the empty void while being thrown around like a rag doll, I can only imagine how horrible it sounded inside. But I guess in the vacuum of space, no one can really hear you scream. The strange thing was, she was the only one inside. If I recall correctly, the woman had a daughter right?" Dean asked, glancing at the two officers.

"Seems like her daughter was missing from that horrific picture if that's the case." Dean spoke, his cocky attitude shining through as his agitation only seemed to grow. "After all, the two of them would have pressed against the window as their pod rolled down into the gravitational force of the planet. Seems a bit suspicious when it should have been around the time that they would be getting ready to eat." A small smirk formed on Dean's face, like he had just solved the case of what happened like some type of mystery solving detective.

"Though I did hear that she was spotted with one of your kind. Kinda interesting if you think about it. A little girl goes missing before the untimely death of her mother. It's almost like this has happened before, but where?" Dean spoke in an accusative tone, his voice showed the disgust and bitterness he felt for the Enforcement officers in general. "So do you know where the little girl is? Because she wouldn't be a charred skeleton to be picked apart by whatever is left on the planet, right?" Dean asked, leaning into the table. Watching his own reflection on the tinted surface, Dean glared at the two men in front of him, acting as if he had them cornered. Not like they were going to admit anything.

It seemed at that point, the other officer who had been sitting idly by decided to start on his bad cop routine out of nowhere. They stood up, slamming his hands one the table before pointing towards Dean. "Did you hold a grudge against her? Did she really deserve to die?" McCoy shouted, acting as if Dean was the one who caused the pod to detach from the station. It was evident with the way that had acted in response to the unspoken allegation, that they were going to turn this whole mess onto Dean.

"What the?" Dean spoke, a bit baffled by the sudden turn from the muscle bound cop. "I didn't even know the woman!" Dean yelled, standing up and kicking the chair behind him backwards. "I see exactly what you're trying to do here. You're trying to blame me simply because I am in the Bronze class. I didn't know the woman, nor would I ever have a grudge against anyone on this damn station." That was a bit of a lie, but the Enforcement officers didn't need to know that.

"I didn't do it! You know I didn't do it!" Dean yelled, his voice seemingly echoing against the walls of the room. It was one thing to question Dean about what happened, it was another thing when they spouted nonsense that he was the one who caused an explosion to hurl the poor woman down towards the planet below. "I wouldn't have been able to get access to her pod and you know it!"

"Relax you two." Shouted Harrison as he stood up, glancing over towards his partner. "We're not here to arrest anyone. We've been asking the other neighbors if they have seen or heard anything unusual as well. We're not here to arrest or accuse you Mr. Torres." Officer Harrison remarked, trying to calm the two who were ready to tear out each other's throat. " Due to the pod being dejected from the station, we're just going to move you to another section. This is for your safety, whether you want to believe us or not depends on you." Harrison continued, pulling out a piece of paper that had a section with a room number on it.

"Your area has been deemed hazardous. There was a fracture above your pod." Harrison started to explain in a stern voice, like a parent scolding a child. "Though the damage was on the outer part of your pod, it is deemed best to have your stuff moved to another section. As a result, you will also be assigned to a new location starting today." By the way that Harrison had been talking, it seemed like he was confident that this was the best choice of action to take for someone like Dean. To be firm yet strict.

Listening to Harrison talk, it seemed like he was the most level headed of the two. Either that, or he was able to manipulate other people with his calm demeanor. Perhaps that was why they partnered him up with McCoy. One would seem to be a bit unhinged, while the other was more calm and collective. Making people trust him and follow Harrison's directions. This was triggering a lot of red flags in Dean's brain, making him trust Harrison even less now. But he had to be corroborative.

"Take your shuttle over to the new coordinates for your living situation. You'll find that most of your stuff has already been moved there. Upon entering the dock, you'll be briefed on your new assignment. It will still be the same position you have currently, only you'll be working in the west wing, rather than the east." Harrison explained, his voice calm and collective to bring down the tension in the room.

"Wait! My stuff was moved over there already? But I just left not too long ago. When did you even have time to move it?" Dean asked, his mind boggled at the fact that they already moved his stuff out. Sure he didn't exactly have a lot of stuff to begin with, but it didn't make sense as to why they were doing it while Dean was supposed to be at work.

Then it dawned on him. They must have found evidence that indicated that Dean knew the truth. During the accident, it uncovered the hidden documents in his room, and Dean foolishly threw the piece of paper that pointed out the dark truth that got his parents killed. If he could, Dean would have smashed his head against the table. The more he thought about it, Dean came to the realization that this could very well be the death of him. That sheer fact caused Dean's stomach to churn. He was going to die today, wasn't he?

"Regardless of how long ago you left your pod, the fact remains that your stuff has already been moved. I suggest that you do the same. You don't want your pay to get docked now, right?" Harrison spoke, more in a stern and commanding tone than anything else.

Closing his notebook, it was a sign that the two officers have done their job in setting a man up to die before any type of damage to the Elite could be done. Dean was left speechless. They had the gull to move Dean's things without his permission, and now they made snide remarks about his pay? Unbelievable! A small growl left Dean's clenched jaw as he balled his hands into two tight fists. His body felt hot and tense as the two officers got up.

As the two men started to make their way towards the door, Dean could tell that McCoy was smirking under the helmet as the man's head was tilted back in victory, as if he had won some kind of pissing contest with the help of his partner. With a slight sneer, McCoy walked with Harrison towards the door, rudely bumping into Dean to shove the poor janitor to the side. Dean could even hear McCoy chuckling after they left the room. It took everything in Dean's power not to want to pick a fight with the Officers.

Placing his hands on the table after unclenching his fists, Dean stared down at the wooden top, sweat slowly trickling down his temple as a heated knot rested in the middle of Dean's throat and chest. There was not enough saliva or water on the station that could cool down the burning sensation in Dean's throat. A wave of nausea rushed over Dean's body as his vision blurred with the realization that Dean was a dead man. A dead man who would be walking towards his death as soon as he left this room.

"They found mom's note ... the note she warned me about the danger of the Elite. A-And now.... I'll be killed." The panicked thoughts took over and the feeling of nausea grew stronger as Dean glanced towards the door. Dean's fingers twitched uncontrollably, causing him to clench his hands.

Raising a fist up, Dean punched the wooden table with all his might. "Damn it!!" Dean shouted, only to collapse to his knees as he grasped his hair. Pulling on the brunet locks, Dean felt like his whole world had come crashing down. A sharp sting heated Dean's eyes as he felt the tears swelling up. Despite the fact that men shouldn't cry, Dean couldn't help it as he never felt this helpless before. Not even when his parents died. Sure he did cry when reality hit, but Dean was still a kid. Now, as a grown man who was forced to walk to his own death, he had every reason to let his emotions take over.

It took a couple of minutes for Dean to compose himself. His eyes, much like his hand, stung with a dull throb. Slumping over as he exited out of the room, Dean made his way towards the elevator, his feet barely lifting off of the floor with each step he took.

"Let's see...how will they kill me?" Dean started to speculate as he made the long trek towards the elevator. *"It's not like they would be dumb enough to try to explode the new pod that I'll be heading to. That would raise too much suspicion."* It was a bitter thought, but it seemed like the thought process as to how Dean could die seemed to help deal with the morality of it. Even if it did seem messed up, it was better than jumping at every little bump he felt while walking around the station.

"Though I wouldn't put it past them to have someone hiding out inside the pod. Waiting until the night to come out and kill me... like they did to my parents." At the time Dean had been asleep when it

happened, so he was spared the gruesome details of their death, but he wasn't as lucky when it came to the aftermath of it.

"It's either that, or they messed with the shuttle. Not like they would risk losing an elevator just to crash with me inside of it. It would probably break my bones, though I would beg for death afterwards since I can't afford the medical cost right now." Dean would be lying if he said that he wasn't scared right now. His body felt like jelly. The blood seemed to drain from Dean's face, all the while the sound of a loud whistle blew in Dean's ear despite there not being one.

Pressing the button, Dean had time to think back to what happened on the night his parents died. How his parents were put into some type of a gruesome display, spread out as a warning to anyone who dared to oppose the Elite, though many people didn't realize it at the time.

IT was around ten years ago when his dream life turned into a never ending nightmare. The day had started out rather peaceful, just hours before the stench of decay would fill Dean's nose and the sight of his parents' dead body to be etched into his mind forever. As Dean sat at the kitchen table, the smell of roasted sunflower and pumpkin seeds lingered in the air. Emily was already dressed up in her witch outfit, it appeared more cheerful rather than scary with the coordination of color with the glistening design of all the 'spooky' decorations that was often found all over the section in people's homes.

Her dress was a mixture of orange and black with different pumpkin faces decorated with the hem of the puffed out dress. A small trail of spider webs in black pigment brushed up towards her slender waist. The edges of the top of the dress had the design of a skeleton's rib cage as the long sleeves of her dress had black cats circling the hem of the sleeves. Her earrings were little skeleton hands that were colored orange as little black bats dangled down off her earlobe. The fishnets she wore on her slender legs had small decorative gems that sparkled in the light as the black flat shoes she wore were far more comfortable to wear for long walks better than high heels ever could. The last time she wore heels, Emily couldn't move around for a week, mostly due to falling on a small tree branch, causing her to sprain an ankle.

"Ah, I love this time of the year." Emily spoke as she pulled the roasted seeds out of the oven to add to the collection of different treats that she made. There were small sandwich bags that had an assortment of treats she made to be passed out for the Hollow Eve's trick-or-treaters. Small pretzels, bits of raisin and chex mix lingered in one set. Some bags were filled with candy kisses and gummy worms, those seemed to rested on one side of the kitchen island counter, meant to be given out for the first wave of tricksters for the night. On the other side were different patches of cookies that she made for the older kids who wanted to have some type of treat. It acted more as a bribe to keep them from doing nasty 'tricks' to the house. The third batch, the one in which would have the roasted seeds and other healthy alternatives was used by those who had over protective parents.

"That's what you say about Festival Eve. You bake a lot of treats during that time while blasting that annoying music during all waking hours." A young pudgy Dean grumbled as he sat at the table, doing the last bit of his homework that was assigned before the start of the winter break. Dean never really understood the reason behind the teachers handing out homework over the long break, but from what Emily had remarked, it was to keep kids busy while their parents were still working.

"Aw. Don't be like that. You know I love celebrating all the seasons with my little Dean bean." Emily chimed happily, licking her finger tips from the collective salt that lingered from the treats she made. Making her way over to Dean, the smile never left her face. It always gave away what she was going to do next, and that was to smother her son to help cheer him up.

"I told you not to call me that!" A grumpy Dean yelped, the flush of embarrassment lingering on his face as he pouted. "The kids at school pick on me enough as it is. I don't need some nickname my mom calls me to add to the bullying." Thankfully Emily seemed to keep that little nickname away from the public and only in private. Dean was into the teenage years, and this was just one of the signs that her boy was becoming a man.

"Aw. You're still growing. You just haven't reached puberty just yet, my little Dean bean sprout." Emily spoke, wrapping her arms around Dean's shoulders. "Your father was a little pudgy too, before puberty hit him that is, and now look at how handsome he is." Emily added, nuzzling her cheek against Dean's pudgy cheeks."Just look at how handsome you are, we'll be batting off the girls in no time." Even though Dean squirmed to get away from the affection, Emily took great pride in making her son suffer a little bit.

"And yet we eat a lot of food. You honestly think me reaching that particular milestone will really change me so much that I would go from being porky to studly?" Dean asked, his voice showing his unimpressed attitude as he picked at a slice of bacon. The plate before him had two sunny side eggs as eyes and two slices of bacon were placed to represent a smile. A piece of toast that was cut in half looked like thick eyebrows over top of the eggs. It was cute for someone who was a kid, but Dean was becoming more of a teenager at the time, meaning he found it to be childish more than anything.

"Well, we'll start working out when the spring comes around. Or if you want, we can find ways of fitting in a work out routine after the festival. But if you don't want to wait, we can work out while you're on break. What do you think?" Emily asked, letting go of Dean though ruffling his thick hair. "We'll need to get you a haircut soon kiddo. Just look at this mop of hair." She teased as a soft mused chuckle left her lips, using both hands to ruffle his hair up a bit more as Dean shook his head to make her stop. Dean's hair seemed to puff out ever so slightly, making it appear that there was more volume to it than normal.

"Fine. Just please don't mess up my hair too much, 'kay? I worked hard to get it just right this morning." Dean spoke, a light smile finally landing on his face before his father walked in wearing his usual lab coat, black buttoned up shirt and black slacks. It seemed that Emily's attention went from embarrassing her son to greeting her husband who finally got up for the day.

"I see you were busy cooking up a storm. How long have you been up?" Max asked, walking over to Emily before giving her a kiss on the cheek. This was a bit of a usual morning routine for the both of them. Despite how long they have been married, it always seemed that the two were still in love like they were newlyweds. At times it could be nauseating, but it just showed that they still loved each other.

"Long enough. I think a power nap will help with the night ahead. Gotta do a lot of walking if I'm going to take Dean out for his last year trick-or-treating. He'll either want to stay home or go by himself after tonight. They grow up so fast, don't they?" She replied, smiling sweetly at Max though her exhaustion was showing.

Covering her mouth as she yawned, Max took it as his cue to take over the duties of the house while she went to rest. Much of the cooking had already been done, so there wasn't much for Max to do. Though the least he could do was wash the dishes before getting things ready for the night full of trick-or-treaters.

"Go get some rest. I'll take Dean with me to get some weapons for warfare in case any punks try to egg our house tonight. Can't let my castle fall while the beautiful queen is out escorting our young prince for one last raid." Max chuckled, lightly patting Emily on the back, reassuring her that she'll be fine to sleep for a couple of hours. As silly as it may have sounded, it was a way of setting her mind at ease. With their long talk the night prior, it seemed like both of them were on edge.

"My knight in shining armor." Emily remarked before leaving the two men alone, the sound of her shoes grew quiet in the distance as she went towards the living room where her favorite nap spot was on the couch. One could have sworn that Emily was like a loving house cat rather than a person. Maybe that was why Max loved her. Or least, that's the only reason that a young Dean could think of.

Picking up one of the half pieces of toast, Max scooped a piece of the bacon and one of the eggs onto the piece of toast. "So what do you plan on being for Hollow's Eve this year?" Max asked, carefully balancing the egg on top of the bacon and toast. "It'll be your last year of going out with your mom to get some candy and treats. You gotta look decent for your last outing. Don't want to bring shame to the Torres family, right?" It was a little bit of a teasing joke, as noted with the big grin that rested on Max's face as he shoved the food into his mouth.

"I'm going as a bum this year." Dean remarked, picking up the other piece of bacon and taking a bite out of it, not wanting his dad to eat more of his meal like when Dean was a child. He was a growing man after all.

"Oh, so you're going as yourself?" Max teased, chewing the food a little, only to swallow it in one gulp. It was something that Max often did with Dean to help break up any type of tension that his son may have been feeling, helping to put Dean in a lighter mood. It was never easy dealing with a hormonal son, though at least they didn't have a daughter. That might have been worse.

"Hey! I'm not a bum!" Dean grumbled in a cracked voice, his brows knitting together as he took offense to the comment, but he knew that it was simply in good nature. Though at this time in his life, Dean would take offense to much of the things that his parents would tease him about. But that didn't mean that they didn't love him. In the later years, Dean would miss these little pep talks that his father would give him.

"I'm kidding." Max finished picking up the small pitcher of orange juice and pouring himself a glass. "I'll help you with the makeup bit later on. After all, in my line of work, making dead people look fresh is part of the job. So making you look natural will be simple." Another little playful jab at Dean as his father was someone who loved to joke around and make people smile. After all, it wasn't like the dead could smile. Not unless he dolled them up to smile. Thinking about it would just be seen as creepy.

"I'm not a bum dad. I'm just going to dress up as one." Dean grumbled once more, finishing the last bit of the bacon before working on the eggs. Even though Dean would never say it, he did appreciate his father for helping him with relaxing and not dreading walking around with his mother when he could be bullied for it. Being called a momma's boy wasn't exactly flattering. Then again, it wasn't like Dean wasn't used to being bullied.

"Well, we're going to head for the store in a few minutes. So hurry up so we can stock up on eggs. While you're out protecting our queen, I'll hold down the fort and do everything in my power to keep the assault down. Hopefully our castle won't have a single egg on it." Setting down the empty glass, Max brought a napkin up to wipe his mouth. "And if we're successful, and have a bunch later on, we'll be having a bunch of egg dishes for the next month or so. It'll be a good source of protein for your growing muscles if you're going to start working out." That was one way of putting it.

"Oh, you heard that?" Dean asked, a small flustered look crossed Dean's expression. It wasn't like it should have been embarrassing, but considering that it was coming from his father, Dean felt a bit more ashamed of how his body wasn't perfect like the other kids. Even though his parents didn't seem to mind it, it always made Dean feel self conscious about his body image.

"There's nothing to worry about Dean. Even I had to do some exercises when I was your age to get rid of my baby fat." Max spoke, lightly patting Dean's back. "If you want our help, all you have to do is ask." Dean felt more reassured after that, but he didn't expect that he would never get a chance to work out with his parents. He would have to learn everything on his own after that night.

"Thanks dad... that really means a lot to me." Dean spoke, a soft smile lingering on his features. Relaxing his shoulders, Dean felt like a weight had been lifted off of him. The fact that he would be able to work out with the help of his parents, it meant that he wouldn't have to do it alone, though that didn't happen either.

Whether or not Dean had cared to admit it, he loved how dorky his parents could be. They always seemed to make him smile or laugh, despite his growing teenage angst. That's why when the night that his mother took him out trick-or-treating for the last time, only to come back and find his father gone was worrisome. Little did the two of them know the type of danger that would happen later on that night.

***

After walking around for an hour, both Dean and Emily started to make their way home for the evening. It had appeared that, with his limited movement, Dean grew tired of walking around collecting candy. Though there seemed to be another reason behind Dean's sudden need to head back home, he felt embarrassed that his mother was still walking around with him, even though she kept her distance. Either way, Dean was able to get a fair amount of candy in the time that they walked around, so it wasn't that big of a deal.

Walking down the line of white picket fences with different decorations lining them, they came back to their quaint brick home to an odd sight. Normally they would have seen Max standing on the front porch dressed as Dracula with a bowl in his hand for passing out the treats. But instead, their porch was completely empty. Void of both life and light.

The fact that Max was gone sent alarm bells through Emily's mind. She didn't want to worry Dean, who seemed to be puzzled by his father's disappearance. Emily grabbed Dean's hand before giving him a reassured smile. Though it was a fake one, Dean didn't know it at the time. "Come on, let's see if maybe dad is trying to scare us." Emily mused, giving her a son a small nod before walking up the path towards the door.

The door appeared to be slightly open, causing Emily to be a bit hesitant. If Max was indeed trying to scare them, he was doing one hell of a job. Quickly she swallowed the lump in her throat as she opened the door, expecting Max to jump out and yell 'Boo!' before laughing at the fact he had successfully scared the two. But sadly, that wasn't the case.

Walking inside, Emily felt that something was off. Though the chatter from outside of their home was loud, the inside was completely silent. It was like the house had witnessed something horrible, keeping silent of what happened, while trying to appear normal. It was a subtle shift, but one that Emily could sense. To Dean, it simply felt the same as he did when he came home before his parents arrived. Sure there was something different about it, but it wasn't as alarming for him as it was for his mother.

"Hey mom? Where did dad go? Wasn't he supposed to be outside passing out treats?" Dean asked. bringing up a hand to scratch an itch on his face, the makeup he was wearing made his face feel itchy, causing some of the makeup to get under Dean's nails.

Ironically he was wearing paint that looked like dirt. The overalls he was wearing had patches of different fabrics lining his body, even the pillow case matched the pattern of his costume, all thanks to Emily knowing how to stitch. "I wanted to show him my haul." As silly as it may sound, it was a tradition of going through and seeing exactly what Dean had gotten, as a way to make sure he didn't get anything dangerous. It was either that, or his parents wanted to see if they could snatch their favorite treats after Dean went to sleep.

"Oh, that's right. I asked him to go to the store to pick up something for me before they closed for the night." Emily lied, but with her kind smile. Dean didn't seem to catch onto the lie. "He'll be back soon. There are a lot of people walking around, so he wouldn't want to hit them." Another reasonable lie, enough to make Dean believe her anyways. Emily always hated lying to her son, but in this case, it was to keep him safe. "Now, head upstairs to wash the makeup off. I'll be in to tuck you into bed in a few minutes." It might have seemed a bit early for bed, but Emily needed to make sure that the downstairs was safe enough while locking up the place.

With a small shrug of his shoulders, Dean headed up the steps. As he reached the top, Dean headed straight to his room. The doors for the bathroom and his parents room were closed like normal, nothing seemed out of the ordinary. Dean's body swayed back and forth, seemingly tired and sore from walking around. Opening the door to his room, Dean made a small b-line for his bed, tossing the pillow case on top of it, before kneeling under his bed to get out a set of pajamas.

With a fresh pair in his hands, Dean headed back out the door and towards the bathroom. Glancing over the banister, he could hear his mother putting away the dishes as the light from the kitchen was the only light coming from downstairs. Opening the bathroom door, Dean sighed as he flipped the light on. Having to scrub the makeup off was always the worst.

Twisting the knobs of the faucet, Dean pulled the small wash cloth from the dangling ring on the wall. Using the bar of soap, Dean went to work getting the makeup off. It wasn't the first time he had to wash makeup off, but it wouldn't be the last. The rough texture of the washcloth always seemed to tickle Dean's face, it was like a cat's tongue, just not as rough as sandpaper. The heat from the wet washcloth always made Dean feel relaxed. Even if he could barely breathe, it always made him feel refreshed after the damp washcloth was removed from his face.

The scent from the soap filled Dean's nose, it smelled a bit like oranges, which made sense as it was an orange colored soap bar with lines of white mixed in. There was a time when Dean was little, he took a bite out of it since it looked and smelled like a treat. Naturally he got a little sick from it, but it was something that he could laugh at now.

Peeling off the costume, Dean tossed it into the little bathroom hamper. It didn't take long to put on a pair of sweatpants and a baggy shirt, allowing Dean to be out of the bathroom in no time. Walking back to his room, Dean sat down on his bed. Pulling the bag close to him, Dean dumped the treats in his lap, the pile practically covered his chubby legs. Shifting his hands through the wrappers, the sound of them crinkling was music to his ears. This was his favorite part of the night. Being able to dive in and enjoy the rich treats that would give him cavities.

Taking a wrapper, Dean untwisted the golden colored wrapper to reveal a perfectly round milk chocolate ball. Eagerly popping it into his mouth, Dean bit the chocolate ball before feeling the rush of caramel brush against his taste buds. A delighted moan escaped from Dean's mouth as he closed his eyes to enjoy the sweet texture of milk chocolate and caramel in his mouth. It was no wonder he was so pudgy, with treats like this, who needs friends?

The small creak of the door caught Dean's attention, causing the young male to glance over to see his mother smile with a small weary smile. "So, enjoying your treats?" She asked, walking over towards Dean before picking up a piece of candy.

Of course, with his mouth full, Dean couldn't help but simply nod as a hum of agreement left his lips. "Good." Sitting down on the other side of the bed, Emily untwisted the same treat that Dean was enjoying before popping it into her mouth as well. A small hum left her lips as she took delight in the candy as well. "Mrs. Anderson always makes these. I would kill to get her recipe." It was a bit of a joke, but it made Dean laugh a little bit with the treat in his mouth..

"Then I wouldn't be able to get in shape. I'd be bugging you to make these all the time." Dean remarked, tossing the wrapper into the small bin beside his bed. Glancing at the different treats, Dean was ready to pick out another piece of candy to enjoy, though he feared that his mother would slap his hand if he did so. The rule was one piece of candy on Hollow's eve. Afterwards, they would be used as reward for when Dean did his chores or even when he cleaned up or did a task without being asked to.

"True. Plus mommy would gain weight with you. Then your father would get angry at us and tell us to brush our teeth so that we don't get cavities." Emily mused, a soft chuckle leaving her lips. Glancing towards Dean, Emily couldn't help but smile before ruffling his hair a bit. She often did that as a way to make herself feel better. She couldn't allow Dean to know what might have happened to Max, but she wouldn't let anything happen to Dean. Not while she was alive that is. "Speaking of brushing..." Emily remarked, her voice trailing as if to signal to Dean what he was supposed to do next.

"Yeah yeah... I'll go brush my teeth." Dean groaned, scooping up the candy to put back into the bag. "Do you think...maybe I could have at least one more piece of candy?" Dean asked, looking up at Emily with hopeful puppy dog eyes. It was something that Dean learned that his mother couldn't really say no to. "Just this once?" With a small pout of his lips, Emily couldn't help but sigh ever so slightly, a sign that she had been defeated.

"Just this once. But don't tell your father." Emily mused as she could see the excitement in Dean's turquoise green eyes. The real issue at hand wasn't the fact that Dean had to worry about his father finding out. Knowing the Elite, Max was more than likely dead. A way to keep silent after the dead boy was carted to Max's morgue rather than that of the Elite's mortician.

Emily saw how jumpy Max was the other night. Muttering things like he was being followed, they were going to kill him, they were after him. It wasn't until Emily sat Max down to listen to him that everything was revealed. The night before Hollow's Eve, the child was sacrificed, his heart torn out to be devoured that night. The body was still a bit fresh when it was brought over to Max's morgue. Emily's heart sank when she heard that. How anyone could even do such a thing to a child, it was sickening.

"Thanks mom! You're the best!" Dean gasped excitedly, giving Emily a tight hug before taking another golden wrapper and eagerly popping it into his mouth. Hearing Dean say that made Emily feel better. Being able to make her son happy was the best feeling for a mother. To know that her son loved her, even as he aged, she couldn't ask for anything more. Though this would be the last time she gotta see her son this happy, in her final moments, she would at least know she was a wonderful mother.

"Alright, time to brush your teeth. I'll get your medicine ready. Don't want the Enforcement officers to come and take me away for being a bad mother, right?" Emily half heartedly joked, but it wouldn't be the first time that something like that happened. Even though they lived in the Silver class, they had just as much restriction as the Bronze class did, though they seemingly got away with more. That was, as long as they fell in line with what the Elite ordered them to do. If you were not in the Elite class, you were nothing more than an underling.

"You always say that, but I don't see why they would take you away." Dean remarked, closing the pillowcase full of candy before setting it aside on top of his dresser. "I hate taking that medicine. It always makes me so tired." Dean whined a bit, only to have Emily softly chuckle as she got off of the bed.

"I know sweetie. But what the Elite says goes, right? Don't need them getting angry at us." That was a huge understatement. Considering the events that would happen soon after, it would be best if Dean slept through the horrors Emily would be subjected to. Though, knowing the Enforcement officers, they would simply take Emily away in the night. Heading towards an unknown location, free from any witnesses, to finish her off.

Walking with Dean towards the bathroom, Emily took out the medicine from the locked cabinet. There were different bottles that housed all kinds of medication, some of which Emily didn't find them to be all that safe. The ones that housed toxic chemicals that had no benefits were always flushed down the toilet first thing she got them. There was no way she would subject Dean to horrible treatments if they didn't benefit him in any way.

Pulling out a small pill box, Emily placed the pills in Dean's hand before watching him swallow the pills with a glass of water. A weary smile lingered on her lips as she stood in the doorway, watching as Dean started to brush his teeth. At least he never had any cavities, unlike most kids his age.

Locking up the cabinet, Emily walked back with Dean to his room. Hopping into the bed, Dean pulled the covers over top of him. Walking towards the bed, Emily knelt down so that she was level with Dean. Giving him a soft kiss on his forehead, Emily brushed some of Dean's hair from his face. "Good night my little Dean bean." Emily spoke, a soft smile lingering on her lips. Even though Dean hated that nickname, she loved calling him that.

"I told you not to call me that mom." Dean softly grumbled, turning onto his side, facing away from Emily. "Night mom. I'll see you in the morning." Dean remarked, though a yawn escaped him towards the end.

Even though it wasn't long after Dean took the medicine it knocked him out rather quickly. Emily stood there, softly stroking Dean's hair as she wanted a bit more time with her son. Though she could never tell him what would happen to his parents, the least she could do was at least watch him sleep. Just like she did the first time she brought Dean home for the hospital. How she would stand at the crib side, exhausted but still admiring that sleepy face. She had to get ready for what awaited Emily that night, knowing that when everyone settled down for the night, death would soon be knocking at her door.

As the morning came, Dean woke up more groggy than ever. Peeling back the bed sheets, Dean glanced around to see that everything was still the way that it was when he had fallen asleep, except for one key difference. There was no noise coming from the kitchen. Usually his mother made an awful lot of noise when it came to cooking. She always loved to listen to music and sing to it, even if it was poorly. But now, it was eerily silent. Bracing himself, Dean opened the door to his closed bedroom, which he could have sworn he left it slightly open like he always did. His parents didn't believe in letting him completely shut the door, in case of something happening.

The creaking of the door sounded like a roar in the empty hallway. Dean glanced around timidly as he walked down the small hallway. The sound of the clock downstairs was the only ambient noise in the whole house. "Mom? Dad?" Dean called out, heading towards his parents bedroom, seeing if perhaps they were still sound asleep in their bedroom.

Dean's footsteps sounded as if he was stomping in the quiet house. The chiming of the downstairs grandfather clock struck seven, the chimes muffled thanks to distance separating Dean from the living room, though it did startle him from how quiet everything was. Stopping just shy of his parents bedroom, Dean noticed that it was slightly opened, meaning that perhaps his parents were in bed and just haven't woken up for the day. This would have been normal if it was around Festival day, but the day after Hollow's Eve, it shouldn't have been like this. "You guys up?" Dean asked timidly, pushing the door open with a loud creak.

As the door swung open, Dean saw that the room had been void of any type of life. His parents' bed was still freshly made as if no one had laid in it since yesterday. "C-Come on guys. This isn't funny." Dean stammered, his heart feeling as if it was sinking to the pits of his stomach.

Walking into the room, Dean glanced around and noticed that everything was in its original spot, which made Dean wonder what happened to his parents last night while he was sleeping? "You're supposed to try and scare me before Hollow's Eve... not after." Dean called out timidly, his voice shaking. When it was clear that his parents were not anywhere near their bedroom, and no sounds could be heard from the bathroom, Dean walked out of his parents room and headed down towards the lower foyer, hoping that perhaps he would be able to spot them somewhere downstairs.

Heading down the steps, Dean glanced around for any type of movement inside of the house. To his dismay, there weren't any signs of movement within the household. Swallowing the heated knot in his throat, Dean carefully walked towards the kitchen, the last place he had seen his mother the night prior. Inside the kitchen everything was the same. The pans rested neatly against the wall, the sink was clear of any dishes from the night prior. The only thing that seemed out of place was one of the large kitchen knives seemed to be missing.

It was one that was serrated, used for carving up the pumpkins earlier in the day. There was a small trail of blood that was barely noticeable, but it showed that someone must have gotten injured. Dean felt his mouth start to dry up as he looked for any other signs that might have explained what happened. But there wasn't any. Glancing towards the pantry, Dean noticed that it was open. Walking towards it, Dean cautiously opened the door to see nothing inside. Dean felt a bit of relief, but he still had no clue where his parents were.

Letting out the breath that he was holding, Dean was a bit puzzled as to where his parents were. Closing the pantry door, Dean's eyes went towards the living room. Usually his mother would be napping on the couch if he couldn't find her. She was usually either there, or in the garden. But considering that it was the winter months approaching, the station would get colder, so there was no reason for Emily to be out in the garden.

Walking into the living room, Dean glanced around to see that everything was tidy. The couch looked brand new, almost like no one sat in it. Considering that it was his mother's favorite spot, that seemed suspicious. Glancing down towards the rug that lingered underneath it, Dean was surprised to see a few droplets of blood that looked darker on the rose petal decorated rug. The more blood he saw, the more worried Dean became for the safety of his parents.

It was only when Dean had noticed some movement outside the windows that he noticed the large gathering of people around his home. Blinking in surprise, Dean found the strength to rush towards the front door. Finding it unlocked, which was unusual as his parents always locked the door at night, Dean was greeted with the sight of people standing just outside of their fence.

The look on their faces was a mixture of awe, sorrow, and disgust. Some people seemed to be pointing towards the roof while some people seemed to hold onto each other. With shaky steps, Dean walked out on the porch with a confused look on his face. There was an unpleasant smell in the air, unlike anything that he had ever smelt. It smelled a bit like rotted guts, the same smell that he often associated with his father's job.

"W-What's going on?" Dean asked, his voice cracking a little as he stepped out from the shade of the porch. But it seemed like no one heard him. Walking down the few steps, Dean noticed that there was some type of dark substance that seemed to pool out by the gutter. Once Dean was far out from the porch, he slowly turned around. Looking up towards the gutter, Dean couldn't see much. But as he started to walk backwards towards the fence, the sight he witnessed was unspeakable. There, resting on the black tiles of the slanted roof, were the deceased bodies of his parents.

His mother and father looked as if they were beaten and bloodied. Their mouths were gaped open as flies buzzed around their bodies. The flies crawled in and out of their gaping mouths, both of his parents' tongues had been cut out with a jagged knife. Their eyes were completely gone, seemingly ripped out from their sockets, allowing for more flies to enter into the deceased bodies of the two. Their guts rested just outside of their bodies, slowly dangling down towards the gutter. With the guts, a single word was sprawled out. *Traitors.*

The sight alone would be the cause of nightmares for many years to come. His parents weren't traitors. They would never do anything to risk the livelihoods of the people around them. Tears stung Dean's eyes as he slowly fell to the concrete path below him. The sound of sirens and the people chatting seemingly faded from Dean's hearing. He wanted to vomit, but nothing seemed to come out. Even though he couldn't break the concrete, Dean dug his nails into the slab below him. As he sobbed, Dean hung his head as a way to keep people from seeing him cry. Even though Dean tried his best to keep quiet, it wasn't long before he really started crying. Never in his life would Dean think that he would lose his parents like this. And yet, it happened so easily. This was the start of Dean's distaste in the Elite completely.

REACHING the bottom level that held the shuttles for the residents, Dean shuffled out of the elevator to the cold concrete garage. How long has it been since he was here last? It wasn't like he used the shuttle very often. If anything, he would rather not have to deal with the storage fee, but unfortunately there was no way to back out from it. Sure it was handy for when people had to go from one side of the station to the other, but how often did someone in the Bronze class have that luxury? It was one of the few things that his parents left for Dean, and there was no way to return it or even trade it in. So it simply sat in an occupied section of the shuttle port without moving.

"Let's see... 2086... where is 2086?" Dean mumbled as he walked over towards the map that outlined the layers for the garage. Pointing his right index finger at the map, Dean scrolled past the numbers before reaching the 2080's section. Finally he had found the location, it was still in the original place that the Enforcement officers placed it in. "Man, I hope that old piece of junk still works. Probably covered in dust." Dean was trying to make light of this whole situation, even though he was on his way to the death sentence.

Walking to the elevator separate from the one he came down in, Dean pressed the button for the floor that housed the shuttle. The ride was quiet, considering that he was the only one there as everyone else had been at work, thus making the silence even more deafening the longer he was there by himself. Every little noise would put him on edge. When the elevator stopped, Dean stepped out, half expecting someone to come up to him and shoot him or something. But glancing around, it appeared that wasn't the case. Dean didn't know if should be relieved or upset at this point. Counting the rows until Dean got to the eighth row, he started to head down the section while glancing around. "2...4... and 6." Dean muttered as he reached the shuttle that had a tarp drape over it.

The whole time that Dean had the shuttle, he rarely took it out for himself. Instead, he simply let it sit in the cold garage for years. Since there wasn't any way for parts to rust, it was ideal for people to be able to store different types of space shuttles in the garage. It was always monitored, so no one really had to worry about their property being messed with. But in this case, Dean didn't have much confidence that some Enforcement officers didn't make a quick stop to his shuttle and 'inspect' it to make sure it was still in good condition.

There wasn't much dust on the covering, considering how long it has been since the last time he touched the shuttle was a couple of years, it was suspicious. "So that's their game." Dean remarked to himself, his eyebrows knitting together in a small scowl. "Sending me to my death with the shuttle. Cowards." Dean grumbled, pulling the tarp off of the shuttle, Dean was always surprised at how brand new the shuttle looked.

The sleek design of the center pod displayed the two frontal seats. In the back was a third seat making it a perfect vehicle for the Torres family at the time. The wings were narrow, barely sticking out of the sides, they were arrow dynamic as they could extend or retract depending on the situation. The shuttle was a prototype for being able to go back to the Earth once it was deemed safe, but due to the fact in later years of the shuttle breaking up in the atmosphere, the shuttle was discontinued. Or at least, that's what the Elite had said.

Walking around the shuttle, Dean checked the corners and underside of the shuttle to make sure the shuttle wouldn't just magically explode once he was inside of it. Not like the Elite would do something too underhanded, but this was the Elite and their goons that Dean was dealing with. Crawling out from the underside of the shuttle, Dean placed his hands on the glass.

Taking a look inside the clear glass, Dean didn't see any tampering, at least that he could see any evidence of tampering on the inside of the shuttle through the large window. "So there was no tampering on the outside. But that doesn't mean that they didn't mess with the inside of it" Dean remarked to himself, as he moved towards the handle for the door. Pressing the code in, which happened to be Dean's birthday, the door popped open to allow Dean to get inside.

Resting his knees on the wing, Dean checked under the seats to make sure that there wasn't any type of 'surprise' waiting for him. Wanting to be thorough, Dean made sure to check every last corner of the shuttle before he felt like it was safe enough to actually travel in. Nestling himself in the driver's seat, Dean took a deep breath in. This was the first time he was actually going to drive it without another person inside teaching him.

Dean could feel his fingers shake from being nervous, his heart beat increasing as he put his feet on the pedals. Like the vehicles on earth, the shuttles operated the same as an automatic. Strapping himself in, as well as making sure that he was secured, Dean pressed the start up button for the shuttle to turn on. Like magic, the door closed the shuttle up tightly, making it completely air tight. The blast of air filled the shuttle up from the vents, making it possible for Dean to breathe, cooling off the sweat that clung to Dean's forehead. There was a lingering scent that Dean never thought he would be able smell again. It was the scent of his father.

The cologne he wore the time that they went to the store to buy eggs. It was oddly comforting, even if it was for a second.

The lights on the dash lit up the dark panel, illuminating Dean's face as the display for each of the sections of the shuttle showed up on the dashboard. "Well, this certainly isn't going to be easy. But, at least I'll be able to enjoy the view of the Earth... even if it would be for one last time." Dean mumbled to himself, as he placed his hands onto the steering wheel.

With a deep breath in, Dean put the shuttle into the right gear before pulling out of the spot. Taking it a bit slow, Dean got into position for the take off. With the section being walled off, and the sirens with lights indicating that someone was going to take off, Dean waited for the signal before slowly pressing down on the gas pedal to gain enough speed to break free into space. Before too long, Dean was out in space, flying among the stars and away from the station. For the first time, Dean felt like he was able to break free from the cage that bound him in place all of his life.

Ahead of him was the ruined planet known as Earth. It looked much bigger than he originally thought. Taking his foot off of the gas pedal, Dean sat back to take in the view of the planet. For something that was supposed to be ruined, it looked full of life. Though a fair amount of clouds covered the ground, Dean could still see bits of land through the opening in the clouds. He could see green lights dancing across the edges over the northern parts of the sky. Though half of the planet was covered in darkness, the other half that was covered in light shined brighter than any light Dean had ever seen. It was almost blinding honestly.

The further out that Dean had floated from the station, the more he came into view for two familiar officers to press a button that would change Dean's life forever. As soon as the shuttle received the signal, the dash board started to flash red, causing the shuttle to shake ever so slightly.

The gas pedal pushed forward, causing it to push towards the Earth's gravitational pull. "What the?" Dean muttered to himself, as he tried to press on the brakes. It was a no go. Dean was going to crash into the planet he had admired for so long. "So this is how you're going to make my life end? Crushed by this beautiful planet you scared?" Dean growled, a small smirk formed on Dean's face as he grasped the steering wheel tightly.

"I'll gladly throw myself into the pits of hell you created, but you better hope I don't survive. Or I'll come back and make your life a real living hell!" Dean spat at no one, the shuttle moving closer towards Earth, only to feel an invisible force capture the invading shuttle, pulling Dean into the Earth's grasp.

As Dean entered the atmosphere, he could see the front of his shuttle starting to burn up. The fire was intense, but that didn't mean that Dean was just going to willingly let himself die like this. He was going to do whatever it took to survive this crash. The grip on the wheel was tight, causing Dean's knuckles to turn white. The shuttle shook and bucked, the land was coming closer and closer. The view would have been breathtaking, if it wasn't for the fact that Dean was fighting to stay alive, he would have easily enjoyed the view more.

But from what Dean had seen as he glanced up, he was blown away by the sight before him. Large vast trees lingered all around with traces of old ruined skyscrapers decorated with different colored trees. Large craters dented the planet, but it seemed that life had reclaimed those craters by filling it with water. It was all so surreal to him, like he was stepping into a whole new world.

If Dean stared any longer, he would have missed the ground creeping closer to him. He was only a few seconds from crashing into what appeared to be a field with some types of crops being grown. A button with the words eject started to flash, Dean didn't waste much time before he slammed his fist into it, causing the slowly breaking glass to pop off before the seats were ejected high into the air. Breaking off into three pieces, a large parachute deployed above the seats. The empty seats drifted off into different directions, while Dean's seat started to drift away from the two.

Grasping onto the cords, Dean held onto the thin cords for dear life. The air was cold, causing Dean to shiver. What he wouldn't do for a blanket or something right about now. His feet dangled over the edge of the seat while the wind ruffled his hair this way and that. Drifting slowly towards the ground, Dean watched the shuttle crash into the field below. Small bits of ember seemed to drift from the exposed shuttle, the crackling of the fire reached closer to Dean's ear the closer he got to the ground.

As Dean was getting close enough to safely land, a large explosion from the fire reaching the fuel line sent Dean flying backwards into the trees. At least the heat warmed Dean up a little bit, too bad the parachute wrapping itself up in the tree branches took precedence. Being dangled from off of the ground wasn't ideal. But it was better than being dead. If Dean didn't press the eject button, he would have ended up like the woman a few days prior. Just another burned up husk on this dead planet.

"Oh man..." Dean spoke, a weary sigh escaped Dean's lips as he glanced down at the ground. There were a bunch of roots that seemed to line the ground under him. Glancing around, Dean noticed that there were no tree branches that Dean could use to safely climb down, not like how he used to climb the trees on the station when he was a little kid. Before he had gotten pudgy that was. If Dean was going to get out of these straps, he would end up falling hard on the ground below. Though he wasn't looking forward to it, it might be his only means of escape.

"No ship...no tools... no way I can really survive in this world." Dean muttered to himself, hanging his head in defeat. "How am I going to survive in this world alone?" Dean asked himself, glancing down to see a strange sight. It took him back a bit, but there was some type of mutated Deer looking up at him. Dean blinked a bit in surprise. How was there life on this planet if the reports indicate that there was no life here?

The antlers of the deer seemed to be that of a ten point. The skull was exposed, and it was standing upright. Was the deer wearing clothes? "Hey there, are you alright?" The voice of a man seemingly called out from the deer. What in the world was going on? "Don't worry, we'll get you down." The man called out, turning away from Dean, the man walked away a bit, waving towards a group of people who seemed to be busy putting out the fire caused by Dean's shuttle exploding.

Just what in the world was going on?! Dean was left speechless as he watched the whole thing unfold. A single man ran over towards the deer headed man, he was wearing the skull of a wolf. The two seemed to converse a bit, before the man with the deer head pointed towards

Dean who was stuck in the tree. With a nod, the man with the wolf skull raised up a bow pointing towards Dean. Within a blink of an eye, the first strap was cut loose, making Dean dangle on his side.

"W-Wait a minute!" Dean shouted, but the man was already shooting the second arrow, missing Dean, but grazing the other strap. "I'll get myself down." Dean stumbled as he took off of the belt straps. Falling onto the hard ground below, Dean landed on his back, taking the air out of him.

Wheezing as he struggled to breathe, Dean glanced up at the seat still dangling. The sound of leaves shuffling caused Dean to shift his attention to the man with the deer skull. With the man being so close, Dean could take in all of the others' features so clearly now.

With porcelain white skin like that of a doll, medium silver hair covered the right hole of the skull. The man pulled off the skull, giving more for Dean to look at. The man reached up to tuck his silver hair back behind his left ear, exposing the man's upper ear that showed the piercings along the edges of his ear lobe and on top of his ear. There was a bright sapphire squared earring that took up most of the man's lower ear lobe. The piercing on the side of his ear appeared to dangle like a rope as it caressed over the man's covered shoulder. Around the man's neck was a large choker with some sort of engraved stone over it that Dean couldn't read or understand what the ruins meant. From the angle, Dean was able to see, the man was wearing some type of dark robe, but not much detail really stuck out.

"Seems like he hit the ground pretty hard. We should get this Coward over towards the hospital." The silver haired male spoke, getting a simple nod from the other with the wolf skull. Before the man could take a step forward, Dean started to slowly roll over onto his stomach, trying to get up himself rather than have someone grab or carry him.

"W-Wait...w-what did you just call me?" Dean asked, wheezing as he struggled to get on his hands and knees. This seemed to make the two men stop in their tracks. Giving each other a quick glance, the silver haired man knelt down in front of Dean. The sunlight seemed to peek through the clouds, almost blinding Dean with how bright it was.

"I called you a coward. That's what your kind is. The last of the so-called humans in space. Cowards who left the rest of humanity to die when you dropped the nukes on us. Anyone who comes from space is referred to as cowards." The man spoke coldly, no warmth in his silver eyes. It seemed that Dean wasn't the only one who seemed to resent the Elite. He'll need to get these people to understand that he was on their side. He hated the Elite more than anyone, even more so considering that they literally sent him to his death.

"But I-" Dean started to defend himself, though before he could continue, the eighty pound seat fell onto Dean's back, causing the male to scream in pain. The sheer weight on his back caused Dean to pass out, his head hitting the hard roots below.

This seemed to startle the two other men as they were quick to push the seat off of Dean. Collecting him into one of the men's arms, they rushed in an unknown direction, seemingly bringing Dean towards some type of medical center to treat his injuries. The smell of burning smoke in the distance, the warm sun seemingly beating down, and the sound of leaves rustling as the wind picked up. Any audio that came from people surrounding Dean was inaudible. Dean was fading fast, his body unable to take the pain as he was shutting down.

CHAPTER THREE: *The Sins And The Past*

As the distant sound of crickets reached Dean's ears, the man slowly began to stir from his sleep. The room he was in seemed to be dim, only a small light that didn't seem to hurt his eyes provided enough light to look around. Besides the small said light, the only other type of light that provided additional light came in the form of lunar light from the opened window as the moon was visible outside. It seemed to be in the shape of a crescent moon. Though he had never really seen the moon, it was oddly beautiful. Tilting his head back to look around, Dean had found that the bed was already in a sort of sitting up position. It allowed Dean to glance around the room without hurting himself. It seemed that Dean was in some sort of medical room, at least it resembled one of the medical rooms on the station but almost barren.

Unlike the medical bay that had rather expensive devices in it, making it seem like they were more for decoration than anything else, this room looked almost empty. Sure there was a bed and what looked like a railing for curtains without any curtains attached to it at the moment, but other than that there wasn't much. Besides perhaps a single chair that rested close to the wall and a little night stand that appeared to be wooden in nature. As he looked around, Dean took notice of a single white board that sat in front of him as it hung on the wall, the words John Doe was written in curved letters.

"John Doe?" Dean mumbled to himself before bracing himself to sit up a little bit as he pushed up with his arms. The pain was more in his back than anything else, though his arm was still tender from the fall. "Oh right. That's when they can't identify someone. Been a long time since I saw that name written on anything." Dean mused to himself, remembering times in which he would read some medical books that his father had in his den. Dean was a bit of an odd ball when he was growing up, though most children tend to act that way. Trying hard to be like the man that they idolized, which was typically a father or father-like figure. Due to the nature of looking over the different types of documents that lead towards a person's death, Dean often felt like he was some sort of detective. Besides taking after Max's looks, Dean had a natural curiosity for the more morbid side of death. If it wasn't for the smell, Dean may have very well fallen in his father's footsteps to be a mortician.

"Well, it wasn't like we found any type of real identification on you, so we had to call you something." A voice seemed to call out from the bit of darkness that covered the room. It was a bit familiar, but Dean couldn't put his finger on where he heard the voice. The voice was fairly light, almost like it had a bit of a younger tone to it. Though Dean's voice was a little deep, the voice belonging to the unknown being was lighter. It almost had a bit of an air to it, light and soft, though clearly masculine. It was different, but in a good way. Even though Dean wouldn't admit it, it was soothing.

"Who's there?" Dean growled a bit as he knit his eyebrows together. He was in no real condition to fight, so he had to be on guard. Dean wouldn't be able to know for sure why these people were keeping him alive. After all, there wasn't supposed to be anyone on this planet. It was deemed a wasteland since the nukes had gone off. If word got back to the station, this could very well cause chaos as many would want to come back. Perhaps that was the reason the Elite had lied to everyone about the planet being deemed too hazardous to return. Trying to think about this was making Dean's head ache a bit, though that could also be due to the fact that his head was injured in the fall.

"Relax. I'm not here to hurt you." The voice called out, the sound of beads jingled as the mysterious person walked along the wooden floor boards towards Dean. "I've just come to see how your condition was." The man paused, taking note of Dean's injuries and seeing if he could understand him. "It's not every day we get a coward surviving the trip down from that wretched station. Most of the time they burn up as soon as they enter the atmosphere." The man spoke, an amused chuckle leaving his lips. "Must have been one hell of a ride for you though. I couldn't imagine staying calm during the whole ordeal." The figure spoke, coming into view for Dean. Even though there wasn't much light, Dean could still make out some of the features that matched the man Dean saw before passing out. The man stood roughly 5'9", only two inches shorter than Dean, and he looked roughly around the same age as Dean if not younger, at least that is what he figured anyway.

"Don't lump me in with those assholes." Dean softly growled, his body ached as he moved a bit on the bed to get in a more comfortable sitting position. "I may have come from the station, but I am in no way a coward." The way that this guy had given Dean a cold glare when he first arrived, it was much like the way that Dean often glared at the higher ranking class.

"So I'm guessing that you must have gone through hell as well down here? I thought that everything and everyone was destroyed when the bombs dropped." It was a silly question to ask, but it was a way to start up some type of conversation. "Glad to see that there are actual survivors. I'm surprised that I can even understand you. I figured that if there were any remaining humans, they would have made up some type of universal language or something." It may not have been comforting to hear that remark coming from a being who lived on the Millennium, but Dean was relieved to know that people did survive.

Watching the other take a seat in a metal chair that frankly didn't look very comfortable to sit in long term, Dean felt a bit uneasy considering that he had seen this man wearing the skeleton head of what was once a deer. No matter how Dean looked at this guy, all he could picture was just a porcine doll all decorated up and sitting on a shelf with how pale he was. Did this guy never get out into the sun? With that pale complexion, it would seem like this guy was a vampire or something. Even Dean didn't look as pale as this guy, and Dean was never exposed to the true sun, only the artificial light that was built into the Silver class to aid with the growth of the crops.

"Well, we all know the ancient languages from around the world. It wasn't hard to figure out that you would have spoken the same language as us." The man remarked, knowing that it was just easier for people to learn the different languages from the nations that survived the destruction of the world. It seemed that the man noticed how Dean was gazing at him, seeing how he shifted a bit in the seat that he was sitting on, glancing to the side.

"You know, it's actually a miracle that you were able to make it out of the crash in one piece." The man spoke up once more, clearing his throat a bit. "The fire from your ship did burn up a bit of our crops, but it wasn't anything too serious."

"From my-?" Dean started to speak before he remembered what happened. That's right.

He crashed his ship into a field. While this man was trying to help Dean get out of the tree, the fire from Dean's shuttle started to burn the crops. That was, however, until a group of other survivors rushed to put out the fire before it could spread.

"I'm sorry about that. I didn't exactly have much of a choice where I landed." It wasn't exactly a lie. If Dean had crashed into the water, he could have drowned or sunk with the shuttle. If he landed in the trees, he could have likely started a much bigger fire that would have caused more damage than what already happened.

There was a small bit of silence in the room after that. Glancing down towards the blanket, Dean formed a small frown thinking about the woman that had crashed a few days earlier. Since her pod had disappeared in the darkness of the planet, Dean wasn't exactly sure where she could have landed. "Guess I really should count myself lucky then, huh?" Dean muttered, moving to lean back with a small hiss from the pain he felt in his spine. It felt like he had a boulder had landed on his back. "I could have burned up just like that woman did..." Dean trailed off, not wanting to think about it. But seeing as how it caught the man's attention, Dean shook his head a bit.

"Eh, forget about it. Not like it would matter anyways." There was the awkwardness once again, and Dean didn't seem to like it. He needed to change the subject, even if it wasn't something he was very good at. "So how long have there been people on the surface?" Dean was a bit curious about the humans living on the surface. Seeing as how a lot of them looked as normal as a person on the station, minus the coloring of hair of course, this was his chance to learn more about what happened on the day the bombs were dropped.

"We haven't been on the surface for all that long actually." The male spoke, seeing as how this guy didn't seem like the typical Elitist that one would almost expect on the station that hovered over them. "Thankfully our ancestors were smart enough to catch wind of what the cowards were planning and built or modified existing shelters that were underground. Granted it wasn't ideal, considering that most of the shelters at the time were still under construction as they were going to be brand new and state of the art. But it was better than the alternative." The man continued, Dean taking note of the grim tone in the man's voice. So many people died that day, it was just a reminder of how human kind wasn't meant to be ruled over a few who garnished power by any means necessary.

"Better to have people live in a shelter while they waited for the fallout to settle. Though it takes at least four hundred years for radiation to settle down towards safe levels for humans to be around." Dean remarked, moving a hand up to ruffle his hair a bit. "But it goes to show how humans are able to overcome and adapt to their changing surroundings." Dean mused to himself a bit, a light chuckle leaving his lips. "Human self preservation." It was only natural that humans would want to survive in a hectic world. That change was part of evolution after all. Making for better descendants and all that scientific jargon that Dean didn't pay too much attention to in class when he attended.

It was only when Dean had pressed his back into the bed that a small hissed escaped Dean's lips. There was an ache unlike any Dean felt against his back side. "Damn, did a rock fall on my back of something?" Dean cussed, his back felt as if it was throbbing. The smallest movement caused his back to spasm in pain. The only pain worse than this was when Dean broke his arm from falling from a tree when he was little. Moving to arch his back and pinch his shoulder blades together, Dean could feel a small pop like a bone being put back into place, relieving some of the pressure on his back in the process, though it still hurt the more he seemed to sit up right. It was only when the pillow that rested behind Dean's head had slipped, falling behind Dean's back, that the other had a bit of relief.

"Close." The man spoke, crossing his arms in front of his chest. "It was actually the seat that landed on your back after the strap holding it in place broke off, causing it to fall right on top of you." Thinking back on it, it did make sense as Dean remembered how heavy it was landing on him. It literally took the wind out of him. "You should have stayed in the seat. But it seemed like you were impatient and decided to fall down on your own. You probably wouldn't be in as much pain if you had stayed seated." The man lightly nagged, causing Dean to feel the same guilt he often felt when his mother would scold him.

"Yeah... I guess you're right." Dean spoke, a soft sigh escaping him. He never thought that he would be getting a lecture from someone who wasn't his mother. She often would remark how careless Dean was as a child. Often trying to get things done quickly rather than take his time. "Thank you though." Dean spoke, watching the look of surprise appear on the man's face.

"Huh? For what? I didn't exactly do anything." The man remarked, his silver eyes seeming to catch Dean's attention. Those eyes held a lot of emotions behind them, though the man tried to act formal in front of a total stranger, his eyes expressed both amusement and surprise from a simple thank you. Dean was used to seeing so many empty and lifeless eyes, it was a refreshing change of pace to be able to see such expressions displayed like that. Not to mention, this guy's eyes were silver like the moon shining above. It was almost hard to look away from them as they seemed to shimmer.

With a quick shake of his head, Dean was quick to explain. "You told someone to shoot me down before getting the heavy seat off my back. After that, you brought me to some kind of medical facility. Not many people would have done that. Especially for someone that they might have deemed a threat." At least not anyone on the Millennium. Everyone would have left him, forcing Dean to get himself down. No one would ever lift a finger for him, not even someone in his own class. "By the way, my name is Dean, Dean Torres." Dean added. "I figured it would be better than simply calling me something other than my real name."

"Dean Torres huh?" The man spoke, tilting his head ever so slightly to the right. "Interesting name." He remarked, a soft smile landing on the man's lips. "You can call me Kane Flores. I'm one of the tribal leaders." Kane introduced himself, but the last part did confuse Dean since he had never heard of someone being a tribal leader.

There had been so many people who would flaunt their social status as Silver or Elite class, so hearing that someone was a tribal leader was something that Dean would have never expected. Regardless, Dean at least had a name to call the other, even if the first name was a bit too biblical for his liking. Like the old story about the brother's betraying each other. Hopefully this guy wouldn't betray Dean.

"A tribal leader?" Dean asked, his confusion becoming more evident as he was trying to wrap his mind around it. The first thing that Dean thought of when he heard the phrase 'tribal leader' was usually an older gentleman with wrinkles decorating his features to show his age, sort of like the old gossiping ladies that often rode on the elevator with Dean. A man full of wisdom and could guide the young towards the right path, someone who could easily say something so wise and simple at the same time. Not someone just like the guy in front of him who looked like a young adult.

"Being a tribal leader means that I take care of those who wish to be in my clan. You see, it was a way for everyone to be united as a whole." Kane remarked, figuring that he might as well explain to the outsider how things functioned. "Even though I'm nineteen, I'm in charge of the Gluttony clan. There, we tend to focus mostly on agriculture. We grow crops, tend to cattle, and focus on distributing food to the other islands." To Dean, it reminded him a lot about growing up in the Silver class.

"There are times in which we act like nomads." Kane seemed to continue his explanation. "Those who were either born into or wanted to be part of the Gluttony clan, they tend to move about between the other islands to help raise animals or tend to the field. We even go as far as to help the other clans use all the parts of the animal so nothing goes to waste. But that's not all that we do. Just like with any type of trade or skill, we allow people to pursue their passion without restriction. It's what helped to progress us in furthering our attempts to reclaim what was left of humanity after the bombs dropped."

"Wait..." Dean spoke, trying to let all that information sink in before he continued his thought. "You're a leader at nineteen?" Dean asked, a bit surprised since the other was so young to be running a whole nation or clan. "You look older than that. I thought you were closer to my age or something." Dean spoke, his confusion seeming to grow, though it seemed to entertain Kane as the other let out a small chuckle. "What?" Dean asked, his perplexion showing even more as he didn't know what was funny.

"I just didn't figure that you would have been so focused on the age part." Kane remarked, a light amused smile lingering on his face. "Not the fact that my clan is full of nomads, or that we use all the parts of the animals we kill, but my age." Kane added, the light dimples on either side of his lips seeming to grow as it seemed like Dean was at least entertaining to him.

"Sorry, it's just, when I was nineteen I was barely able to cook rice without burning it." Dean spoke, remembering that day like it was yesterday. There was always that lingering smell of burnt rice that lingered in his old pod. "But I'm impressed. You're able to do more at such a young age here than most people on the Millennium." Dean added, leaning forward a bit as he did want to know more about this place now. If he could use some of his skills here, maybe he would be able to fit in after all. "So what else do you use the animal parts for?" Dean asked, taking note of the spark that seemed to light up in Kane's eyes.

"Well, we tend to use the animal parts for medicine, food, or clothing." Kane remarked, though it seemed like Kane was getting a bit self conscious since he wanted to impress Dean with his wisdom. "Before we had the tribes set up, food was hard to come by." Kane explained, figuring that he might as well let the man know a bit of how hard it was after leaving the shelter.

"The radiation had mutated the plants on the surface to such a degree that we didn't know if it was possible to eat them. The animals also mutated to the point where even harmless creatures became dangerous." Even though Dean didn't seem like he would be able to understand, he at least was trying to imagine what it would have been like for those exiting out of the shelter to be met with such changes, Dean wouldn't even know how to handle something like that.

"It was only when our food supply was getting low that we had left the shelter." Kane continued, a light sigh leaving his lips as he planted both feet on the floor. "We did a bunch of tests to make sure that the plants and some animals were safe to eat before we moved back to the surface to retake it." Though it wasn't like Kane was part of the group that first emerged, but the way that Kane talked about it, you could almost say that he was.

"But, because of that, we have gotten better than when we stuck to the shelters. We were able to build up stable farms, till the land and alternate crops, and even start to really expand since first leaving the shelters." Kane smiled more towards the end, obviously happy at the effort that was put in to help rebuild humanity as a whole.

"It's amazing that you were able to accomplish that much just on your own." Dean remarked, a soft smile spreading on his own face. "Knowing the Elite, they would have simply drafted those in the Bronze class to act as sacrifices in the attempt to collect data." Knowing how the Elite tended to act, it wouldn't surprise him. Seeing as how they viewed everyone on the Millennium like pieces to a chess board, those in the Bronze class were obviously their pawns.

"So you must have killed a deer then?" Dean asked, trying to get to know a bit more about the other. It was actually nice to have a decent conversation with someone. Sure there were people on the station, but they just didn't appeal to Dean. Talking to someone like Kane, it felt a bit more natural. Sure it could get to be a bit awkward, but most conversations with someone new usually was.

"Yup. I killed my first deer, well... if you want to call it a deer, when I was thirteen." Kane seemed to chime happily, obviously excited about it to this day. "I was able to take it down with a couple of arrows. Though the fall down the steep cliff helped to kill it off. Otherwise I would have tracked it down before finishing it off." Kane spoke, relaxing his shoulders at this point, as if the weight of formality had been lifted from his shoulders. "I was able to make a warm blanket out of its' hide, enjoyed a nice stew that night with the deer's' meat, and decorated the skull later that night." Kane finished, seemingly proud of his achievement.

"Decorated? But it doesn't seem like it had any type of decoration to it." Dean spoke, noticing that there wasn't much that appeared on the skull when Dean had seen it the first time. The top was completely white, say for maybe a few little feathers dangling from tips. But otherwise, there was no way that it could have appeared decorated like the other seemed to indicate.

"That's because we used a type of phosphorescent paint for it. It tends to make the paint on the skull glow in the dark." Kane added, seemingly getting up from his chair before sliding it closer towards Dean. Because it can wash off easily, we used resin as a cast. It's like a plastic shell for the skull, making it act like a helmet for battle." Kane finished, sitting back down in the seat, though he was much closer to Dean than before.

Dean wasn't used to someone wanting to actually sit next to him, considering that most people found him to be odd, so it was a little startling that Kane actually wanted to be closer to him. "Seems like you had a better childhood than I did." Dean lightly joked, though now he wished that he had been born on the planet where he could have at least made at least one decent friend like Kane.

"Sure it was fine when my parents were still alive, but getting placed in the Bronze class, my life was a living hell. When I was a bit older than you when I almost got my hand crushed by some asshole because I was simply trying to do my job." Dean remarked, reflexively clenching his hand that had been stepped on, as if reliving that pain again.

"What did you do in the space station?" Kane asked, taking note of the tone in Dean's voice that seemed to indicate that his job was dangerous. It was further from the truth. Dean felt a bit ashamed to admit he was a janitor, the most safest job one could have in the Bronze class. He could have easily lied to Kane and say that he had some type of important job, but what was the point of lying to someone who seemed like they wanted to get to know him for who he was as a person, and not just his ranking?

Dean never had someone look up to him in a way that seemed genuine the way that Kane was looking up at him right now. There was some warmth in Kane's exposed silver eye. This guy really had a childlike heart despite saying that he was a tribal leader. What happened in their life to make it seem like they had to grow up faster than should have? Was life expediency low considering that they seemed to lack the same tools that the Millennium had?

"I was a janitor..." Dean softly admitted, the shame seemingly washing over him as he glanced away from Kane. "Everyone on the Bronze level was either a janitor or worked maintenance. I actually had it pretty safe compared to those in the maintenance. Those guys would actually go out into space, while all I did was simply clean." Dean explained, though it wasn't as exciting as being a leader of a tribe, it was something that he knew how to do well enough. If Dean was free to do what he wanted like his father was able to, perhaps Dean would have liked to be a doctor or perhaps someone who dealt with forensics. If his parents were still alive, that would not have been much of a problem, but sadly that wasn't the case for those who were put into the Bronze class.

"Really? Someone your age is a janitor?" Kane asked a bit surprised as he brought his crossed arms up to rest his upper half against the bed. Kane seemed to study Dean as he wasn't sure exactly what a janitor was, but it must have been something important. It was almost like Kane was hanging off of every word that Dean would say, making it a bit intimidating to try and impress this guy, despite the whole age question. There was a sense of wonder in Kane's eyes, making Dean feel like he was letting the other down for having something as trivial as a janitor job.

"Someone my age?" Dean asked, raising an eyebrow as he was curious as to know how old this guy thought that Dean was. Did people on Earth not live that long or something? Exactly how old did Dean look to this guy? He wasn't that old looking, though stress and poor dieting might have caused Dean to look older than he really was. Dean didn't have wrinkles and his hair wasn't turning gray, so he clearly wasn't that old looking. Part of Dean was worried about the answer that Kane would give him regarding his age.

"You know, someone in their thirties." Kane remarked a big eager grin on his face, only to get a light smack on the back of his head by Dean who was not having any of that thirty year old crap when he was in his twenties.

Grabbing the back of his head and jolting up from the pain, Kane had groaned while rubbing the part that Dean had smacked him. "Ow! What was that for?!" Kane grumbled, closing his exposed left eye. It seemed like Dean had hit him a little too hard, but in a way the other did deserve it.

"I'm only twenty four!" Dean shouted, his annoyance evident as he grasped his wrist with the other hand. His hand seemed to be stinging a bit from the smack as his body was too sore to do much damage to the other, or the guys' head was as tough as steel or something.

"Seriously? You're only in your twenties?" Kane asked, a bit surprised at the fact that Dean was old as the other leaders. "I could have sworn that you were at least older than Amelia." Kane gently whined, the pain from the smack started to ease up as he could look at Dean now. "Guess it's true what they say then. Space really does age you faster." Even though that was meant to be more of a mumble to himself, Dean could still hear what Kane had said.

"There's no way I look older than someone my age, right?" Dean muttered to himself, fearing that people would get the wrong idea about his age. Nothing like a younger person telling you that you look almost ten or so years older than your actual age to make you feel self conscious. Talk about kids these days. But then again, taking a look at Kane, it was clear that he was still very much someone who was still young with a bit of innocence left in them. This tribal leader still had much to learn about the real world.

"I wouldn't worry about it too much. Honestly you look the same age as Felicia, Amelia, and my good friend Miles. They are the other leaders of the tribal clans. Keaton and Ashley are more around my age, though Ashley is the youngest leader out of all of us." Kane explained, crossing his legs once more as the robe he was wearing shifted with a fluid movement that made it seem like the robe was a solid piece, though Kane didn't lean on the bed in fear that Dean might strike him again if he said something that Dean didn't agree with. Kane seemed to resemble a puppy being lightly smacked on the nose for doing something wrong.

"You said that there were six leaders right? Why don't you explain to me who they are? That way I would be able to better understand how your society works down here." Dean asked, getting a bit confused since he had no idea who those people were and what they would represent when it came to the different types of sins there were. It would have been just as confusing if Dean had picked out some random people on the station and said that they were so and so.

"Of course. I'll explain who everyone is and what they represent for the clans." Kane spoke before clearing his throat. "I'm sure that you'll end up meeting them anyways, so at least if you do end up meeting them, you'll be able to guess who belongs to which clan." Kane continued as if he was going to give a lecture. Even though Dean would have no idea when or where he would be meeting these people, it was nice to have a bit of an inside scoop about what may come in his future.

Ashley Greenlee, the youngest of the leaders at the age of eighteen is the leader of the Envy clan. Often sporting knee high dresses with long sleeves, Ashley's hair is just as long as it nestled towards her thin waist. Wearing her hair up in a ponytail most of the time, her golden locks often sported a small cow lick on the top of her head. Though most of her hair was straight, the ends often curled this way and that in no particular order. Her eyes were a piercing green but cold and judgmental. Standing at a height of 5'2" she was more stubborn than a mule and knew where to hit a man who would try to pick on her due to her height.

Unlike Kane, she had a bit of a rosy color to her features. Through her artistic work, she has been able to redesign different towns to make sure that the buildings work with nature rather than try and destroy the buildings if they were still functional. Even though she can often be a sadist with her actions or comments, she does tend to still act childish while throwing small temper tantrums when she becomes angry or flustered.

Kane Flores is the youngest of the male leaders at the tender age of nineteen. Being the leader of the gluttony clan meant that he often ate a lot of food, while at the same time being good at hunting. Standing at 5'9" Kane was often seen wearing robes since working in the fields often meant that he was exposed to bugs and mud. It was easier to simply roll the hem up and tie it off to keep it from getting dirty.

Kane is more in touch with the surroundings than most, often being rumored to understand the planet better than anyone, which has allowed the crops of any land to be bountiful. Kane doesn't let his youthful appearance keep him from being serious at times, but there are moments when his child-like nature can pop up. Though he looks like a fragile doll, he is a lot tougher than he appears. There are some personal secrets that Kane doesn't talk about, but only when he gets comfortable around certain people is when he lets his true self shine.

After Kane, the next oldest at the age of twenty two would be Keaton Fox, the clan leader of Lust. Standing the tallest of the leaders at 5'10", he is on par with Miles who is the same height as him. Despite his position, Keaton isn't some type of sex addict nor is he really a playboy. Often looking like more of a thug with his piercing golden eyes, Keaton's deep voice could quiet a room if he shouted, but he tends to keep his voice at a normal volume. His short medium length dark brunet hair wasn't exactly tamable as the locks often go this way and that.

Always wearing a mask to keep other people's scents away from him, Keaton sported his pierced ears that trailed the edges of his ears. Often a man of reason, he helps with teaching others about sex education and how to give safe births by using cattle, it has helped expected mothers and fathers with handling child birth at home if they were not able to safely make it to a nearby hospital. Other than that, Keaton is able to train those who want to hunt using archery.

Miles Mayworth is a twenty three year old medical herbalist in charge of the sloth clan, and he also happens to be best friends with Kane, though Miles acts more like a brother than a friend to Kane for personal reasons. The man was an inch taller than Kane, standing at 5'10", the two of them basically looked like brothers.

Miles sported a thinner yet darker version of Kane's hair, but it seemed that his gray locks seemed to suit him. With the help of Kane, the two men were able to come up with some powerful medicine to help fill in the gaps that traditional medicine didn't seem to cover. Every time that Kane would make trips to visit Miles, the two would indulge in some herbal medicine and food. Unlike Kane's silver eyes, Miles has piercing steel gray eyes that looked as if he could see right into your soul. Another opposite of Kane was the fact that Miles had more color to his skin, giving him a peach color.

Felicia Manwell was the same age as Dean, twenty four. Felicia stands at 5'8, making her fairly tall for a woman on the planet. Felicia is the leader of the Pride clan. With her desire to have everything in a state of perfection, she uses her skills to design different ways to engineer transportation and finding different ways to harness the use of crystals for their energy source. Even though her platinum blonde hair isn't as long as Ashley's, her loose curly locks did rest against her back. As she often wore corset style dresses, Felicia's skin had a bit of tan to it due it always working outside on her designs.

Lastly was the oldest of the leaders. Amelia Park was the Head Leader of the other clans as she is the leader of Greed. Despite the fact that she comes from that particular clan, she doesn't let the greed control her. In fact, with Amelia's help, they were able to establish a type of currency using poker chips from the old casinos that cannot be replicated. There are alternative sources of currency with the use of gems and jewelry as well. Typically every place around the earth uses the barter system rather than have set prices for everything. Standing at 5'7" Amelia's dark brunette hair barely brushes past her shoulders.

Unlike the other two female leaders, Amelia's hair doesn't have any curls to it as it was perfectly straight. Her piercing silver eyes on the other hand, they were just like Miles, able to look straight through someone. As one would expect of the Head Leader, Amelia often showed her displeasement if one were to try to lie straight to her face, her wrath was merciless. Often looking as if she was some type of rock star or pirate with the amount of studs that decorated her body, often wearing tight and slightly revealing clothing, Amelia had a definite tan to her body.

Three guys and three girls for the leaders, seems like it would only make sense, though it seemed that there were only six leaders while there are seven deadly sins. "So how come there isn't a seventh tribal clan? You have all of the sins except for Wrath." Dean commented, wondering if perhaps there was something going on with that. What would be the point in having all but one of the seven deadly sins as their leaders?

"Well, we used to have a Wrath clan, but things... sort of got messy with that." Kane remarked, moving to rest his upper half on the mattress once more. "You see, the leader at the time was trying to cause a bunch of conflicts between the leaders. It was getting so bad that eventually our first war broke out. We lost a fair amount of people during that time since the Wrath clan pushed everyone over the edge with empty promises, but when news of all the leaders dying was announced, it just abruptly stopped." Kane explained, remembering how bad it was, though he was only fourteen when it had started, it was still fresh in his mind.

"Distrust was an all time high at the time. It was like someone from the space station came down to try and ruin what little we did have when we first came out of the shelter. But it was one of our own. An unstable man who had big ideas, but seemed to become more twisted the more he was away from his shelter." Studying Kane's face, it seemed like this war caused a lot of heartache. The sadness was evident on Kane's face, it seemed that Dean could read this kid like an open book.

"How long ago was it?" Dean asked, his tone was a bit more serious as he looked concerned, though it wasn't like he could have really changed anything. The fact that Kane remarked about the distrust was something that Dean knew all too well. To think that people on Earth knew how it felt even after they were abandoned, it said a lot about what they went through. Hell, Dean was down on the planet because of the distrust that the Elite felt with those of the lower class. Though the evidence he had on the Elite didn't exactly help matters either

"It was only a few years ago that it stopped. We're still trying to recover because of it." Kane started his explanation, the frown that he wore was evident that Dean was not going to like what he would be hearing. "Amelia's father was the one who finally put an end to it." There was a bit of a pause, almost like Kane was trying to make sure that got the facts correct. "Her father ended up killing all of the leaders himself before he had Amelia kill him. At least, that's what she had said." To think that someone would easily kill another person, Dean could never understand that type of mentality.

"After that, the oldest children of the previous leaders got together and agreed that we would work together to bring peace to the other clan members." So it seemed that the leaders had siblings? Well, humanity did have to repopulate after all. "Using an even number, we could all keep each other in check." Or least, that's what it seemed. It was certainly better than what the Elite had done in the past.

"Amelia took it upon herself to carry the burdens of being the Head Leader for us, since a lot of us were fairly young at the time. If anything went wrong, she would take the blame. Perhaps it is her way of trying to atone ...To stop the endless greed of wanting power and fame." Which would have been reasonable. "I know the others might not say it, but we all think that she probably killed her father while saying that he instructed her to do the horrible deed, trying to save us from more death and heartache." The amount of guilt that Amelia must have felt during that time, Dean could understand to a certain degree. It was one thing to lose your parents by the hands of another person, it was another thing to have to kill them yourselves.

Hearing all of that, it seemed like Dean's hunch was correct about not liking what he was going to hear. It was bad enough having to see his own parents being torn apart and disemboweled as to keep the secrets safe even beyond death, but to have to personally kill your own father with his own weapon took the type of guts that Dean knew that he didn't have. Whoever this Amelia was, she certainly had been through a lot, just like his own mother.

"I may not know much about how things went down here, considering that I literally just showed up, but from what you had said, you were able to recover from this war." Dean spoke, trying to find out the best way to finish what he needed to say. "Then perhaps killing her only flesh and blood was the best way to go about it, to put an end to this war. Doing it in a way that saved more innocent people from dying." Dean let out a sigh as he knew how messed it sounded when he wasn't even there to see what had happened.

"You see, in the Millennium, I discovered a secret that my parents had kept hidden, it didn't go into too much detail about what the Elite did, but it was enough to have the Enforcement officers try to kill me. They tried to use the shuttle to crash towards the planet in an attempt to kill me. Lucky for me, I was able to eject from my crashing shuttle, allowing for you to find and save me." Dean continued to explain how he got there. Since Kane had been so open about what happened to allow young kids to be in a position of power that they were not ready for, it was only reasonable that Dean at least someone else knew about what happened.

"The pod that crashed into the planet recently, killing the occupant inside, she was above me when her pod-" Dean started to before bringing up his hands to make a quoting motion.

"Accidentally..." The exaggeration on his voice was prominent to get his point across. "Exploded from the station. During the time in which her pod was detached from the station, it had knocked down a couple of things from the shelf close to my bed. Mostly books and the photos of my parents who were murdered on Hollow's eve had fallen down and-" Dean started to explain, though could see the confusion on Kane's face. Oh right, it seemed like maybe Kane couldn't keep up with the conversation because of the holiday, since those on Earth wouldn't know what the holiday even entailed.

"Hollow's eve?" Kane asked, his brows knitting together as the confusion was evident on his face. Seems like Dean was able to figure it out even before Kane asked the question. Not like Kane would really understand it, considering that the holiday was really made up to either boost morale or to carry on a tradition, though it could have been used for both. Despite the fact that it was used for more satanic worshiping from the Elite, but Dean had no physical proof that would back up his claims. At least not anymore.

"Oh, it's a type of holiday that we have where we pass out some homemade treats to give thanks for a good harvest. It used to be called Halloween on Earth before everything went to hell and the Elite decided to head up into space." If the old ways were still being taught, that would be the best example for the obscure holiday that the Elite came up with as a means to hide their dark secret ritual.

"Anyways, I found a letter and a body chart that my parents kept hidden in their photos. That had the evidence that the Elite were using orphaned children from the Bronze class, my class, to perform some kind of dark ritual. I don't know exactly what they did, but I think they sexually and physically abuse a child every ten years as part of that ritual. As a result, a child's heart is removed, resulting in the death of said child." It was a lot to unfold, and it still churned Dean's stomach just thinking about it. How anyone could participate in that thing was something that Dean couldn't wrap his mind around.

"It wouldn't surprise me." Kane remarked, moving to rest his head in his own hand. Needless to say Dean was taken back by that comment. Surely it should have been a bit surprising. Did Kane know something that Dean didn't? Dean's eyes seemed to widen at the fact that this wasn't exactly mind blowing for the tribal leader to hear.

"What do you mean?" Dean asked, a bit confused considering that this type of news should have gotten someone like Kane up in arms about it. Hopefully this wasn't common practice on the planet. If it was, Dean would have to figure out what he was going to do, even if he had to go about it all on his own. He couldn't even imagine going through that again. Discovering the extent of how the Elite abused a poor child, it would make Dean livid if the tribal leaders were doing the same thing.

"They were doing that sort of thing before they went into space. It always seemed to be in a forest too. Those in the higher positions tend to use dark arts to continue holding onto a power that really isn't there." Kane seemed so nonchalant about it that it practically boggled Dean's mind. "You honestly thought that they would stop their dark practices just because they went into space?" They were doing it even before they went into space? How the hell was Dean supposed to react to that?

Laying his head back against the mattress, Dean had to pretty much sit back and start to reflect about what he was being told. "I don't know... I guess when they control every aspect of your life...when you actually open your eyes to the fact that other people have known about this just sort of thing makes you wonder what else is out there to ruin your outlook on life." The defeat in Dean's voice was apparent, but it seemed to at least get a chuckle out of Kane as the man sat back up in his chair.

"Well it's not like there is much that we could have done about it. As long as they are up there, that's all that matters." Kane remarked, glad to be away from the horrors he heard about the Elite. "We finally have a chance to be ourselves without the influence of those who come from money to control everything." Kane spoke, a bit of reasoning in his voice.

Dean was not able to exactly see it, but he could tell that there were less restrictions here than on the Millennium. It was easier to breathe down on the planet rather than be cooped up on the space station. It was like the noose that had been slowly tightening around Dean's neck was finally broken. He was finally free from the Elite. Though many people would still have to suffer, hopefully Dean would be able to find a way to free them from the Elite's chains.

"Speaking of money..." Dean spoke, feeling the unease of a subject considering that everything he did to survive circled around the aspect of money. "I don't know how I would even go about paying for this room or any type of medicine." It must have cost a lot of money in order to stay in what seemed like a private room. A private room would cost roughly a thousand credits per day. So who knows how much they would want to charge Dean for a room like this. How would he even be able to pay it off?

"We aren't charging you." Kane remarked, surprising Dean as he looked at the leader with widened eyes. "You needed medical help after all." Kane spoke, flicking his wrist as he waved his hand as if to disperse the doubt that might have come from the remark. "You see, we work more like a colony of ants. We look out for each other." It seemed too good to be true for Dean to really accept the reality of such comments. Working like ants without being expected to work themselves to death? Talk about living in a dream.

"Won't people take advantage of that?" Dean asked, his gaze being a bit more suspicious as he tried to figure out what the catch was. After all there was no such thing as a free lunch, and in this regard, there was no such thing as free medical care. Sure it had been talked about on the station, but it never came to be. The Elite said such things like they had limited resources and could not replicate the medicine used on Earth. Naturally that was all a bunch of lies, but people tended to believe those lies coming from their so-called gods.

"Why would they?" Kane asked, a bit curious as to how a person who came from the orbiting space station thought about how things were supposed to work when there wasn't a large group of people trying to bleed them dry. Not like Kane would have known about how greedy the Elite had become, but he did have his suspicions when it came to the way Dean was reacting.

"Well..." Dean started out, trying the best way to explain this. "In a hospital, you get a nice bed... some clean sheets... And medicine that helps you get better. Don't you have a limited resource on the planet?" Dean asked, not exactly sure what he was expecting as he never went to the medical bay after the death of his parents. "I'm sure medicine isn't all that easy to come by nowadays." Not like they had the technology to continue their research with everything being destroyed.

"And yet you think that the planet that is much larger than your space station couldn't provide the necessary materials to be able to cover that?" Kane asked, a bit of a smirk forming on his face as he couldn't believe the gall that Dean was trying to push onto him. "What good would it do if we couldn't provide medicine for those who are sick? If there are too many who are sick and injured, who would help to take care of the crops? Sure you can have people rotate to help cover the ground needed to keep something like a hospital working, but eventually it is just going to cause more stress and more people to become either injured or sick." Kane explained in a way that anyone could make sense out of it. "So instead of focusing on trivial things as making a profit that would cause more harm than good, we focus more on making someone better." Even though it seemed like a sound argument, it just wasn't wrapping around Dean's mind. Possibly because of the years he was brainwashed that you had to have money in order to get proper treatment.

"Don't you need money for things like food, water, and shelter?" Dean figured that perhaps he could figure out something to drive the point that money was necessary in order to have a civilized society. After all, to live on the Millennium, money is pretty much what determined if you were able to eat or not. To live in a society where money didn't have to be used to cover basic human necessities, it seemed like a dream. Sure you didn't need to have credits to live in the Bronze dorm like pods, but it was still taken out of one's pay in order to keep some type illusion that money was a sign of sophistication.

"We don't waste food here, every part of the animal or vegetation is used so there isn't anything wasted. The bones are used to help make tools that we use for common day items. For example, you can use a hollowed out bone to turn it into a handle for a weapon or tool." Kane remarked, figuring that he would be able to explain what his tribe did. "There are plenty of empty homes in good condition that made it easy for people to have a roof over their head." Kane added. Considering that much of the world had to live underground, the land above was ready to be used for the survivors to expand their growth once more.

"The water is still a bit iffy, which is why we used some of the water we used for our hydroponic system during the winter season." It was too complex to really explain it so easily without having Dean actually see it. "As for shelter, everyone has a home. It would be wrong to watch people suffer from the harsh weather conditions we have. From heavy rains that tend to flood the lower areas, to harsh winters that could freeze anyone who remains outside for too long, it would be more trouble to have people dying on us if they can't find shelter." It seemed like the people on the planet had it much better off than those on the station. Though it seemed like mother nature wouldn't exactly agree to that type of statement from what Kane had described to Dean.

"There are apartments for those who live either alone or together. Then we have homes for people who want to start families." That sounded a bit like what the station had, but everyone was cramped into a small little pod to try and make ends' meet. "Having to depend on money for something that is a basic human need, it's cruel. Everyone deserves to have their own little space where they can live a happy life." Kane remarked, moving a hand to brush some of the hair from his right side. To have their own space and to live a happy life, huh? It was starting to sound as if Dean had crawled his way out of hell and into heaven.

"So you guys don't waste food here? And people can actually move up in the world regardless of class?" Dean asked, his disbelief showing along his features. Dean would almost suggest that he should be pinched considering that he couldn't believe what he was hearing. Hell, maybe Dean did die and this was paradise. There was no social class that would engage in a class war. Everyone was deemed equal, and he didn't have to worry about not having enough money to eat.

"Class? We don't have classes here. Everyone is equal. Despite having tribal leaders to help to make sure that things run smoothly, we don't make more than anyone else. Everyone is a working class. Rather we help to teach the future generations by using our skills to be passed down, or working in the field. We all do something to make this world a much better place." Kane remarked, his smile never fading as it seemed like he was able to convince Dean that he would be better off working with them rather than against them, though he didn't know much about Dean but it seemed like he had a rough time on the space station.

"But didn't you say earlier that you use casino chips and gems as currency? How could you have currency if you don't charge people for things like food, water, shelter, or medical?" Dean asked, a bit of doubt washing over him as he didn't know how that would exactly work if the basics of human needs were not being charged. After all, people had charged for their goods and services for years.

"We use those as a way to promote growth. We need to pay people for their labor, to make them feel accomplished more or less. If people don't get paid, it would just end up feeling like slave work. You can still have a nice place to live and have food on the table, but it's always nice to have a bit of extra on hand to feel like you're doing well. But as we see it, you don't need money to be human." Kane wasn't the best at explaining how their money system worked as he wasn't the one who came up with the concept.

"Seriously…. how it is that a bunch of kids came up with this concept when the Elite are not able to think of such ways to make society as a whole function without a shit ton of restrictions and fees?" Dean grumbled, mostly to himself. It didn't seem to matter at the moment anyways. Not like Dean would be able to get back there. He never meant for the comment to be an insult, rather to show how amazed Dean was that people younger than himself were able to make this work out.

"Well to be fair, this isn't something new." Kane remarked with a small tilt of his head. "It took a lot of trial and error before we were able to get a decent grasp on everything. There are still some things that don't exactly work, but we were able to improve on it to get this far. Before everything was so chaotic that most people didn't know what to do once they were in the shelters." Kane spoke as he leaned back in his chair, it was clear that the chair was getting more uncomfortable as time passed.

"In the shelters?" Dean asked, though it would make sense if there were small communities that were able to take shelter in something that was built to last as the world above was completely destroyed. Maybe Dean could get a chance to see some of these shelters that Kane talked about since the shelters did save humanity as a whole.

"Yeah, that was the only way that people were able to survive for so long after the bombs dropped. To think people were able to live in those shelters for about five hundred years."

Kane spoke in almost a daydream tone as he shifted once more in his seat to get comfortable enough to explain the process to Dean. "Frankly you had more radiation surrounding you in space than what we had to deal with on Earth. At least we had the atmosphere to keep the radiation from space free from the surface. I'm surprised you don't have any weird mutations for being out in space." Kane remarked, but it was just a little bit of playful banter.

"Unless you count on the fact that I seem to be a lot weaker here than on the space station. I don't think that would be considered a mutation. Though if it was, I sure have some bad luck." Dean spoke, a small chuckle leaving his lips as he leaned back in the bed. The fabric of the hospital gown felt loose on him. It was quite different from the tight clothing he had been used to. Though the fabric didn't feel like it would be able to keep him warm. Thankfully Dean had the blankets for that.

"To be honest I'm surprised you only had to deal with a bit of sore muscles. I would have thought that you broke something when you fell on top of the roots." Kane remarked, a bit impressed since most people would have easily broken a bone. "So perhaps you have some good luck on your side. After all, you did survive the crash on top of not breaking any bones when you fell."

"I certainly don't feel lucky." Dean remarked, a soft sigh escaping his lips. "I've dealt with nothing but bad luck when I was a kid on the Millennium. If I start getting some good luck now, it would only seem like a fluke." Dean lightly grumbled, moving to brush some of his hair back. The heat coming from the mattress felt amazing against his spine. Dean wasn't exactly sure if it was due to his own body heat or if the mattress used some type of device that allowed for heat to be trapped, but it made the pain in his back ease up a bit.

"Well, I would consider yourself lucky. After all, if you were like the astronauts that would come back from missions in space, your life wouldn't exactly be the same. They had to deal with changes regarding their bone density, vision, and even taste once they came back to Earth." Kane remarked, his tone was a bit of a matter-of-factually more than anything. "It's amazing how much the world has changed since the bombs dropped. Our whole diet had to change since the old flora and fauna had mutated during the time of our ancestors being trapped in the shelters." It seemed like there was still much that Dean needed to learn about this world. Everything that he was taught before seemed so out-dated now.

"Yeah, guess if you put it that way, I'm finally getting some good luck on my side then." Dean couldn't help but smile a bit at the end. He had been through so much hell before he came to this planet. "I was actually wondering, when I am able to heal up, maybe we could go around and I could meet some of the other leaders and get to know how things work around the tribes." They needed to get back at the Elite that caused trouble to the human race due to their own selfless goals, and if Dean could convince the leaders to come up with a way to destroy the station, the better life would be for them. After all, if he could get down to the planet in one piece, there would be no stopping the Elite from coming down if they wanted to.

"You want to see the others?" Kane asked, blinking a bit in surprise was it took Kane off guard that Dean would suggest something like that so early on. "Well, I guess I could bring you with me when I meet with them for the crop rotation for the winter months..." Kane trailed off, a bit of doubt resting on his face. Something was telling Kane that this was probably a bad idea. "What do you want to talk to them about?" It didn't hurt to get inside of Dean's mind to see what his thought process was.

"Well, you're going to find out one way or another." Dean started to speak, taking a small deep breath as he closed his eyes. "But I was thinking, maybe it's time for the Elite to pay for what they did to humanity as a whole?" Dean remarked, letting the idea seemingly sink into Kane's mind. Surely the other wouldn't mind the idea of getting some revenge on those who destroyed the world and made everyone's life a living nightmare.

"If we could somehow blow up the Millennium, I think society would be able to grow even faster. Wouldn't you agree?" Dean asked, a bit out of character for someone who barely survived the first death attempt from the Elite. But Dean had been holding in his grudge ever since the death of his parents.

Sure he could tell that their deaths were not natural, and that when he went to the Enforcement officers about opening the case back up, they simply dismissed him. Dean figured that if they believed that he was dead, they wouldn't be searching for him. This would give him the leg up on a surprise attack that could end everyone's suffering.

"Are you crazy?!" Kane shouted, quickly standing up as he couldn't believe what he was hearing from someone like Dean. "Why would we want to draw attention to ourselves? We've lived on the planet long enough that the cowards have forgotten all about us." Kane remarked, his voice showing his utter disbelief.

"Do you honestly think that I would just go along with your plan simply because I took pity on you?" It was clear that Kane was not in the mood to risk his own people for personal revenge for someone else. Dean was clearly livid at the thought that he had been sent to his death, so maybe this was just a crazy scheme that Dean came up in order to deal with the shock of surviving the crash landing. But judging by Dean's silence, Kane knew what was going to happen.

Taking a deep breath, Kane sat back down in the chair as his hands moved down to grasp onto the arm rest of the seat. With his back straight, Kane narrowed his eyes towards Dean before crossing his arms over his chest. The way that Kane presented himself now was much more like a leader trying to figure out if he should exactly trust Dean now.

The stoic gaze and piercing silver eyes seemed to be distant and cold. "You have to give me a damn good reason that I would even consider helping you get revenge on the cowards above. After all, what you are asking is something that would be suicide for you, myself, and everyone on the planet." It seemed reasonable since what Dean was suggesting could very well be the complete destruction of the planet once more if they were not careful.

"Because if we don't stop them, they'll just keep making people suffer, and eventually they will come down here once they learn that people are still alive." Not a real valid reasoning, but at least it was starting somewhere. The look on Kane's face showed that he wasn't going to simply allow that though. "Every day I have witnessed so many people in the Bronze level suffering at the hands of the Elite. The way they practically starve us while wasting food that could have easily fed a whole family or even a whole section...it's disgusting the amount of food that goes wasted while they charge those in the lower class until they are bleed dry of their money." Even though Dean was trying to appeal to the gluttony side of the leader, but to no avail.

"They don't allow us to get any type of medical treatment, as we cannot afford it. They make it so we waste water by giving us faulty faucets to use, which only racks up the amount we owe them. The Enforcement officers can come in and destroy everything that you own, only to expect you to pick up the pieces. You don't get a single say in what happens. Not only that, but they tried to destroy the planet for their own Utopia." Dean explained, trying his best to think of what could change Kane's mind to help him get revenge.

Watching Kane's eyes study Dean made him feel a little uneasy. What he had said wasn't a lie, but perhaps there was something more that Kane wanted Dean to say. "What's the real reason Dean?" Kane asked, wanting to cut through the crap that Dean was spilling. "Don't try to appeal to the fact that I don't like wasting food or that money isn't a big issue for us. I want to know the real reason why you want to get revenge on these people." Kane added, wanting to know the real drive behind Dean's actions.

The comment had caught Dean off guard. The real reason? Glancing down at the blanket that was against his lower half, Dean had to be real with himself for once. What was driving him to have so much hatred towards the Elite? Where did it really start? Closing his eyes, Dean tensed his body as he knew that it would have been brought up eventually.

"It's because I want revenge for what they did to my parents." Dean finally said it. After all this time, he finally came to grasp with the reason why he wanted to see the Elite destroyed. Why his life had been a hell. If it wasn't for the death of his parents, he probably would never have thought that the Bronze class deserved better. That they should simply know their place. But being forced into the situation, he knew how wrong it was to think that way.

"What did they do to your parents?" Kane asked, his voice showing his concern, it seemed like Dean had gotten through to Kane with that one at least. Sure Dean talked about how the Elite killed his parents, but being able to know what happened could very well give Kane an inside to Dean's train of thought. Maybe this was Dean's chance to gain an ally?

"They killed them." Opening his eyes, Dean could feel the hot stinging sensation in his eyes. "They killed them out of the home so that they could easily resell it after they washed the blood and guts off of the roof." Dean added, taking a deep breath through his nose as his throat felt like it was trying to close on him.

"They labeled them as traitors because my father discovered that they raped and killed a child around my age at the time, a little ten year old boy. They didn't want my father to let those in the Silver class know what kind of sick bastards they were." Dean explained, taking a deep breath before he would continue.

"The only one that my father could trust with this information was my mother, as she didn't like the Elite for the rumors that were being spread about them. Little did they know, it was all true." Another deep breath was needed for the next part. After all, losing his father was bad enough, but losing his mother on top of it was a real low blow for Dean. "So, since he told my mother about his discovery, she was killed as well." Though Dean didn't know how they were able to do it without raising suspicion, he wasn't exactly sure how it all went down. He only saw what happened afterwards and how it seemed to spread around the community.

The silence in the room was deafening. There was a small flicker from the light, but over all the room looked as if it was frozen in time. Dean didn't seem like he could really relax with the emotions he had been holding in for so long starting to rise to the surface. Not that anyone could really blame him. He had no one to really talk about this to. It was only now that he finally got someone to listen to him to his side of the story. Someone who wouldn't say that his parents got what they deserved, unlike those on the Millennium. They would rather believe that the 'traitors' had gotten what they deserved rather than face the truth that two innocent people died.

It was only when Dean let out the breath he had been holding that he seemed to relax. "They didn't even give me a day to pack up my stuff before they kicked me out." Having to relive the day that his parents die was never an easy one. "I was given an hour max to pack my stuff in a duffle bag before I would be removed from the property. I didn't have any relatives that could take me in. So I was forced to move into a small dorm-like pod where I would have to learn a majority of adult tasks on my own. I had to learn how to cook, and learn how much it cost to be able to keep myself from starving with how much they took out of pay for the food..." That seemed to bring to light the issue for why money seemed so important to Dean, at least to Kane that is.

"Being a janitor was physically exhausting. Not to mention how cruel the Elite were when I made a small mistake." Dean continued, bringing his knees close to him as he looked at the injured hand from that day. "A guy almost crushed my hand because I was throwing away an important document that had a bunch of coffee stains on it. It was hard to read, so I thought that it was meant to be thrown out. He didn't have to nearly crush my hand in the process." Dean explained, not so much in detail, but he gave a very condensed version of what happened on that day.

"Each day I prayed that it would just end so I wouldn't have to suffer anymore. To be simply taken out of my misery so I could be with my parents again. Sure they may have been annoying and overly clingy... but they were still my parents. And they didn't deserve to die the way they did. Like they were cattle brought out from the butcher to be displayed like choice meat." Dean's voice wavered as his body started to relax to the point where it was visible as Dean's shoulders slumped downwards ever so slightly.

Kane remained silent as Dean seemed to continue. "I even tried to help those around me save on money by teaching them how to grow their own food, but that ended up a disaster as well." Dean remarked, bringing his right hand up to run his slightly sweaty palm through his hair before he started to continue the tale of his woes. "The Enforcement officers came in and destroyed the plants that the people were growing for their food so they wouldn't have to pay so much just for basic food they were already getting. To have some actual fresh fruits and vegetables to replace the slightly deformed or rotted food that they were getting" Dean added, shrugging his shoulders as he was still trying to figure out what he did wrong exactly to deserve the hate he received by those around him.

"After that, it seemed like everyone shunned me, like they blamed me personally for the officers coming in and destroying their hard work." Dean paused, taking another deep breath in while Kane remained silent, observing Dean who had enough of holding it all in. "Eventually it seemed like no one really wanted me around, so I kept quiet. Only talking to myself mentally as a way to keep from completely shutting down from the loneliness that seemed to follow me like a curse." The loneliness seemed to make it hard to live day to day for Dean.

This was probably why he seemed to talk to Kane so easily. The other was actually willing to listen to what he had to say.

"It was a lonely existence that I lived with every single day of my life after my parents died. For ten years, I had been in silence, though not by choice. Because of the Enforcement officers ruining everyone's personal garden, and in turn they started to resent me, I in turn started to resent the people in the Millennium. It didn't matter what class they were from, rather they were from my own class or if they were part of the Elite class, I just didn't care what happened to all of us so long as the whole station died out. I just wanted it to all end." Dean finished, feeling like a weight had been lifted off of his shoulders.

"I would rather watch the Millennium get blown up with everyone on board than watch more people suffer at the hands of the Elite." At this point, Dean's hands were shaking a little, his body finally free from the resentment that held for ten years. Though the resentment and anger wasn't completely gone.

Not even glancing over at Kane, Dean could hear the other get up from the seat with a small creak from the metal chair as the chair was pushed back in the process. It didn't take long for the fabric of Kane's clothing coming to view as he sat on the bed with Dean. "Do you feel a bit better after talking about it?" Kane asked, his voice calming Dean a bit more, almost like when his mother would comfort Dean after throwing a temper tantrum. Though Dean felt like he would feel a lot better watching the Millennium explode like a firework, this was better than nothing.

"...Yeah... " Dean spoke through a hoarse voice, nodding his head a little in the process. Feeling like it was so much easier to breathe with all of that off of his chest. His body felt a bit heavy, considering the negative emotions he held for so many years, it was liberating to have it out in the open. Clearing his throat, Dean slowly started to turn his gaze up at Kane. It was as if the moon knew that Dean was gazing at Kane as it started to shine even brighter in that very moment, the light making Kane almost glow like a heavenly angel.

"Even though I may not personally like the thought of killing humans, I do understand where you are coming from." Kane spoke, brushing his bangs back to show his face. There was a scar over his right eyebrow, missing his eyelid but seemed to head towards his right ear. "It wouldn't be the first time that I had to kill someone." Kane's shoulders seemed to dip slightly as it appeared that he was recalling a bad memory at that moment.

"Revenge....it's a bitter pill to swallow and it sits in your throat. Slowly decaying at the base of your throat. It would feel like nothing that you swallow would be able to force it down." Kane remarked, seemingly finding the right depiction of how it felt to hold onto the idea of revenge. Taking a small breath, Kane continued with his remark after hearing Dean's story. "But if this would give you a bit of closure, then perhaps I'll make arrangements for us to go and visit the others." Kane spoke, leaning back a bit as he placed a hand on the edge of the bed to keep him from falling back all the way.

"R-Really?" Dean asked, a bit surprised that Kane was actually willing to give him a chance. The look of surprise seemed to be amusing to Kane as it seemed to make the leader chuckle a little. Even if Kane was able to understand where Dean was coming from, then perhaps he would be able to get the other leaders to work with Dean to bring down the Elite once and for all.

"Don't look so surprised. But it's not like I can help you try and convince them. I have my own personal matters with them." Kane wanted to at least make that point clear before he would continue his little speech. "But if you want to gain their trust, you'll have to be honest with them. Some might be easier than others." Knowing at least some of the other leaders wanting some type of vengeance against the Elite, not all of them were ready to jump on board so easily.

"Keep in mind that I haven't really said that I was on board with your plan. But if you can convince the others to join you, then you'll have my support, regardless of if I agree with it or not." Kane remarked, knowing how the others tend to react around strangers, it'll be difficult for Dean, though it would be a lot easier if Kane was able to at least travel with him.

"Just you wait, I'll make sure that you won't regret helping me." Dean spoke, a big smile on his face. It seemed like they would have to go on a bit of an adventure together, not like Dean wouldn't mind someone like Kane traveling around with him. It seemed like Kane knew a lot about the world and was eager to teach Dean a thing or two. Someone who was willing to be the logical part of the two while Dean was a bit of an unknown factor to all of the tribal leaders when it came time to move forward.

"I'll be looking forward to it. Though I do have to warn you about one of the leaders. The one who is my best friend, Miles." Kane spoke, his smile slowly fading as he knew just how Miles was when it came to the safety of the remaining survivors on the planet. "You see, he may be lazy, but he has a sharp eye. It'll be pretty hard to get his full support." Kane paused, his smile slowly coming back as he continued. "But if you can impress most of the leaders, it shouldn't be all that hard to get his approval." Kane remarked, slowly getting up from the bed with a small groan.

"We'll be heading out within a few weeks. This should give my tribe time to get the seasonal saplings ready for transport and the volunteers ready for their transfer to the other tribes." Perhaps it was a good thing that Dean arrived when he did, considering that it was around the time that the seasons were changing and the leaders were getting ready for the change, it meant easier access to the leaders.

"Are you sure it would be alright to leave your tribe though? Wouldn't they need you for harvesting?" Dean asked, wanting to at least make sure that it would be alright for their leader to be off on some type of adventure. Though by the sounds of it, it seemed like this was something that Kane had been used to. Traveling around all the time probably wasn't as easy as it sounded.

"They'll be alright. I do this at the start and end of every season. For me, it's just another part of the job. It's a good way for me to keep in contact with the other tribe leaders." Kane remarked, a small shrug of his shoulders. "I get to see how they are doing with their harvest, what products they can make with their yield, and if there are any major concerns that we could help with." Even though Dean had no idea what concerns could arise, it seemed that Kane was used to this.

"Plus it would be fun seeing your face when you get to go around to the different tribes. See how different we all are and see how humanity has come back from the ashes like the phoenix it is." Kane remarked, moving back to sit on the chair. "I can even show you some old maps and photos to show you just how much the planet has changed." The excitement seemed to return back to Kane.

Dean couldn't help but grow a small smirk as it seemed like he would at least be able to take in the sights. To be able to see the surface for the first time, after seeing the surface from brief glimpses out his pod's window, it seemed like it would be quite the experience. The main goal that Dean would have to focus on now would be able to heal his injuries. Even if he had to take it easy, being able to see this world for what it really was had always been a dream of Dean's. After all, he could only see so much from the windows aboard the U.S.S. Millennium. "Sounds like it would be an amazing time." Dean remarked, a soft smile crossing his face as he looked at Kane.

"Since it is getting to be a bit late, I'll have them bring you something to eat. I'm sure you're starving by now. Traveling through the atmosphere must have been like an old amusement park ride. Though I've never been to one, I could only imagine how bumpy it was." Kane spoke, heading towards the darkness where only a small bit of light peaked through the slits. "I'm not sure what you'll like, so I'll have them give you something simple. If it's not to your liking, let the nurses know so we can make something for you that you might like." Not wanting to make Dean sick or anything, but he did need something to eat.

"Hold on... before you go. I do have a question." Dean called out, looking at Kane's back the best he could with the limited lighting. Even though Kane had said that they used all of the animal parts for various reasons, Dean's curiosity had gotten the best of him.

"What's wrong?" Kane asked, tilting his head towards Dean to listen to his question. The small beads seemed to jingle a bit when Kane had stopped moving, his face showing up clearly even when in the darkness of the room.

"You were the one who found me under the tree, right? Why were you wearing that skull?" It may have seemed like an odd question, but it was still something that Dean wanted to know. It wasn't something that he had really expected. Just what was the story behind it? Other than it was simply something used for decoration.

"Like I said, I had killed the deer when I came of age to go hunting. It was a beautiful beast. My father was so proud of me at the time." Kane spoke, turning towards Dean. "I told you we use all parts of the animal, right? Well, usually we use the skulls for special occasions, or in some cases, if there is an attack. The skull is thick, so it can be used as a type of armor." Kane remarked, turning his left foot towards the door.

"When we saw you coming out from the sky, we figured that the cowards were finally coming down to attack us. Seeing as how the ship was different, we could only figure that it was time to fight for our land." Kane continued, a slightly smug look landing on his face as he turned towards the door.

"So we grabbed our gear ready for battle for our planet. Little did I know, I would find someone interesting, though too weak to move." Kane remarked, a soft mused hum leaving his lips at the end. "Since you couldn't move, we didn't deem you a threat. And given what you had told me, I don't think you would try to hurt us." The last part was a bit surprising. It certainly wasn't what Dean expected the other to say.

"How did you know that I wouldn't hurt you?" Dean asked, a bit confused as to what Kane had meant with that comment. Raising an eyebrow as Dean wondered what the answer would be. Not like Dean was in any real shape to fight anyone at the moment.

"Well, if you meant to harm me, you would have done so when I got on the bed. Instead, you sat there looking like an injured sparrow more than anything else. Your wing is broken, your pride hurt. If you were really wanting to kill me, you wouldn't have looked so dejected after telling me your story." Kane spoke bluntly. Though there was still a lingering smile on the man's face as Dean looked up at Kane with a puzzled look on his face. Kane turned to leave, leaving Dean puzzled as to that remark.

Dean had no idea how he should have taken that. On one hand, it seemed like not doing anything but talking about his own personal past had gotten Kane to trust him, but on the other hand he felt a bit insulted to be compared to a swallow. He didn't know what it was, but from the description, Dean figured that it must be some type of bird.

"A bird huh? Even though I know what they sound like, I have never been able to see one up close." Dean thought to himself as he leaned back all the way on the bed as his body felt a bit heavy. Listening to the door open, Dean's eyes squinted from the light coming from the hallway. Being left alone after the door was closed behind Kane, Dean gazed out at the moon light. It wasn't as harsh to his eyesight as other lights, so that was at least a bit of a relief. He also seemed to become a bit adjusted to the small flickering light attached to the wall. Gazing over at it, Dean was surprised at what he had seen.

There, seemingly producing enough electricity was a small white crystal that was smoothed out to look like a crystal cut into a baguette. Not like the bread, but a rectangular square that allowed the electric to pass through with a small wire crossing through the middle. So they were able to use crystal as their means of a way to light up their world? It was impressive to say the least, though Dean would have no construct on how they were able to do such a thing. After all, the mainframe on most electrical devices would have been fried when the bombs dropped. To think, they were able to come this far, it was certainly impressive. This was just the beginning pages of Dean's adventure. Rather he was able to be successful or not, he did have a plan to make sure that the Elite paid. They spilled enough blood on their own, now it was time for Dean to get his hands bloody. Even if that meant he would later come to resent himself, it was better than allowing the Elite to continue their cruel ways on the innocent people they victimized.

CHAPTER FOUR: *First Meeting*

IT HAD ONLY been a couple of weeks before Dean had been up and moving around to the point where he didn't need any assistance while he was staying at the nearby hospital, if you could really call it that. According to the doctors, it had appeared that the lack of actual sunlight for most of his life had caused Dean's eyes to become sensitive to the direct sunlight, but with enough exposure, his eyes would be able to adjust.

Besides his eyes being sensitive to the light, there was only one real issue that caused Dean some discomfort while he was resting in the hospital bed since his crash landing on the planet. Due to some bruised muscles along Dean's neck and back, the stiffness from the muscles swelling had made it hard for Dean to move around. Thankfully that was remedied with some type of herbal medicine that was given to him through an amber looking oil that he had to inhale. It seemingly did wonders for the pain, allowing for Dean to get up and walk around without much strain.

The time that Dean had to wait to be given the all clear to leave felt like it was taking forever. Sitting alone in the room, Dean started to collect his thoughts. Thinking about how the Elite must have celebrated watching his shuttle be pulled towards the planet, and watching as it started to burn up in the atmosphere, it filled him with anger. Sure he could simply ignore the large orbiting station as he lived his life on the planet, but what good would that do for the rest of the planet? To want to gaze up at the night sky, and see that large station as an eyesore, it would ruin any kind of mood that anyone might have while gazing up to the vast sky. Besides, if the Elite learned that there were survivors, it wouldn't be long before they would try to come back and reclaim what was theirs.

Since he already got permission from Kane to travel with him, it would only be a matter of time before he would be able to get the leaders on his side. Knowing that Kane wasn't exactly the type to be up for killing people in straight cold blood, Dean would have to wear the others down over time to see that what Dean was trying to do was for the best of humanity. To give a bit of pay back to the Elite for what they had done to the people on Earth when they launched the nukes, killing off those that they didn't feel would be beneficial to their ideal humanity.

Just thinking about everything that the Elite did caused Dean's blood to boil. Clenching his fists, Dean's brows furrowed together as he clenched his teeth. The only sound to bring that seemed to bring him out of his train of thought was the sound of someone knocking on his door. Before Dean could really say anything, the door opened. There was Kane standing with some sort of bag by right side and the doctor on his left.

"Sorry to keep you waiting." The doctor remarked, walking in with Kane, a chart that was Dean's seemed to linger in the man's hand. The doctor was a bit of an older male, his black hair slicked back as he wore some type of gray uniform that had a little red cross on the breast pocket on the man's left side. The doctor wore a surgical mask that could hide any type of facial hair that the man had. Though by looking towards his neck, it was clear that he hasn't shaved in a few days. His round glasses almost took over half of the man's face, which made Dean wonder how bad his eyesight was.

"Come in, doctor." Dean spoke, though his voice sounded a bit defeated. Not like there was much that Dean could do but sit and wait for the doctor to do his business and be on his way. Watching as Kane walked towards the spare chair in the room, Dean couldn't help but eye the bag that Kane had brought with him. Out of all the times in which Kane had come to visit him, this was the first time that he brought something. It certainly did peak Dean's interest, but he would wait until the doctor had left before questioning the tribal leader about it.

"It's good to see that you are up and moving around." The doctor remarked, his voice seemed to show his age, though there was still a bit of youth to it. "It shows that you are making an incredible recovery." The doctor lightly chuckled towards the end, his smile creasing the wrinkles that decorated the man's eyes. "Now, since you're going to be traveling with our dear leader here, I just want to make sure that you don't push yourself too much. Your body is used to artificial gravity, is it not?" The doctor asked, raising his slightly bushy eyebrow, waiting for Dean to respond.

"Uh, yes." Dean answered, giving a small nod of his head in the process. "I've slowly started to get used to the gravity, but it'll just take some time." Dean added, giving some feedback towards the doctor. Not like it has been all that easy adjusting. He did have a hard time adjusting to rolling in the bed, his body not used being on something as solid as the planet. It had made him rather sick the first few nights that he was in the hospital, but slowly he has gotten used to it.

"I'm sure you'll be able to adapt to your new environment." The doctor spoke in a cheery tone. The way that this doctor was friendly was something that Dean wasn't exactly used to, so it was a bit off putting. He was used to doctors who felt like they knew everything and that they were a god because other people's lives were in their hands. Then again, Dean was just starting his puberty the last time he had seen a doctor, and even during that time the doctors were complete assholes to him. No bedside manners. Unlike this doctor.

"Now then," The doctor spoke up once more, though this time he was looking in Kane's direction. "I trust that you won't push him too hard on the journey, yeah?" The doctor asked, seemingly smiling through his mask as he had a bit of a twinkle to his dark brown eyes.

"Don't worry doctor. I'll make sure that if Dean needs to slow down, I won't push him too hard." Kane reassured the doctor with a kind smile. Dean was a bit surprised by how genuine the smile was. It seemed like Kane was looking forward to this long journey to meet up with the other tribal leaders and discuss the demise of the Elite as a whole. Or perhaps, he was just putting on an act for the old man so as to not worry him? Either way, Dean didn't know what he was going to expect while the two of them traveled together.

"Right right." The doctor remarked with a small chuckle, turning back towards Dean now. "Just remember to take it easy. We do have different measures of treating your pain in the other tribes, but you still need to take it easy. As long as you can keep that in mind, you're free to leave when you're ready." It felt like the doctor was almost lecturing him like his mother used to when he was sick. Maybe it was just old age that caused some people to act like that, but it seemed like the doctor was just trying to be helpful.

"I will doctor, thank you." Dean thanked the man, figuring that it would help to get him out of the room faster. One good thing about being able to put on a fake convincing smile through his years of being pushed around by those who thought that they were better than him, was that it was able to fool pretty much anyone who didn't know Dean. With that, the doctor had left the room to attend to the next patient, leaving Dean and Kane alone.

With a sigh escaping his lips, Dean leaned back on the bed once more and closed his eyes. He was just a bit overwhelmed all of a sudden. Plus it wasn't like Dean was ready to deal with visitors just yet. Not while he was focused on how he would go about killing off those in the station without there being a possibility that they would come and try to hurt the survivors on the planet.

As the silence filled the room, Dean could feel his curiosity growing as his eyes landed on the bag that seemingly clung to the side of the chair. It seemed that Kane caught Dean's gaze as he reached down to pick it up. Dean carefully watched the movement of the bag before it was placed onto Kane's lap.

"Since you're getting out today, I figured I would surprise you with some new clothes." Kane remarked, a friendly smile lingering on Kane's face as he pulled out some odd looking clothes that Dean had never seen before. "I took the liberty of getting some other outfits prepared ahead of time as well. I did bring you a backpack of your own, it's just sitting at the front desk with mine. We'll just have to pick it up on the way out." Kane continued to explain before placing the bag down.

"That's fine and all," Dean remarked, casting his eyes away as he knew that he was caught watching the bag a little too closely. "But do you even know my measurements?" Dean asked, knowing that he didn't exactly have anything that would give Kane any indication what his measurements were. Sure wearing a thin gown was one thing, but wearing actual clothes that would fit him was another thing entirely.

"Well, when you got here, they took some standard measurements." Kane remarked, standing up with the clothes after taking them out of the bag and pressed to his chest. Walking towards Dean, Kane smiled as he set the clothes onto the edge of the bed.

Dean looked at it, a bit confused as he saw more layers with these clothes than he would have seen with a sandwich. Dean had a skeptical look on his face as he looked between the stack of folded clothes and Kane who seemed excited for Dean to try them on. Eventually Dean relented as he couldn't say no to Kane's eager smile and the imaginary tail that would have been wiggling back and forth behind the tribal leader.

"We'll see how it goes. But if I don't fit in it, you can't blame me." Dean grumbled, leaning forward to take the clothes off of the blanket. Looking the layers over, Dean saw the different types of clothing fabrics that were chosen for him. Some pieces were made up of either leather or some type of thin fabric. With a sigh through his nose, Dean peeled the sheets off of his body.

With his feet planted on the ground, he knew that he would have to get dressed. "Alright, let me see if I can piece this together without any help." Dean remarked, not wanting to have the embarrassment of watching Kane's face contort with amusement at the spaceman struggling to get dressed. With a curtain attached to the railing to give him some privacy to get dressed, Dean started to change into the gift that Kane had given him.

At first it didn't seem like it would have been all that hard to get into, but the more that Dean looked at it, the more he was getting confused by the style. He had never seen the type of design that Kane had picked out, especially since it seemed like no one else was wearing it. Not the nurses, and certainly not Kane. In all honesty, Dean figured that it was a robe type outfit similar to what Kane often wore, but this outfit had too many different layers that it was a bit confusing to Dean.

"Need any help in there?" Kane asked, parting the curtain back ever so slightly, only to peek in to see that Dean was in nothing more than underwear, lucky for Dean, Kane had brought him some before today. There was still a bit of bruising on Dean's back where the seat had fallen on his back, but it was slowly disappearing now, though it would be a bit tender to the touch if pressure was applied to it. Kane's eyes did wander down a bit, surprised that Dean was in such good shape for someone who lived up on the space station. Dean's back was broad and lean with small dimples towards the lower waist. His shoulder blades peaked out subtly, but not enough to be completely visibly.

"No no... I'm sure I can manage. After all, it's not like I don't know how to dress myself." Dean spoke, figuring that Kane wouldn't push the issue further and leave the poor man alone to dress himself. Though maybe it was just Dean's pride that made him not want to ask for the help in the first place. Getting a grasp on the pieces of clothing that were laying on top of the messy hospital bed, Dean grabbed the pants first since they seemed easier to pull on himself. It was the top section of clothing that was a bit more confusing for him.

The slacks that Dean picked up were black in color, they looked like they would be a bit snug, especially around the thighs and buttocks area. The first leg went on easy, however the second leg not so much, mostly due to the pain in the back, it made it harder to get dressed. It took a bit of balancing for Dean to slip his other leg in, but once he had gotten them inside the pants, he pulled them up to rest just above his knee caps. Dean had to take his movements slowly to keep from straining his back.

Bending over to slip them pants further up his body, Dean was able to lift them up over his thighs and up around his waist. Once it was secured, there was only one thing that Dean had to do, and that was to reach into the opened pants to adjust himself to make sure that everything was in its place to keep from having to reposition his crotch all the time.

"Alright... now I need your help." Dean called out, only to watch as Kane quickly pulled the curtain back with ease. It was a bit embarrassing to be seen with his pants undone and no shirt on, but what other choice did he have? He didn't know how to put the layers for the top on. The fabrics were different than what Dean had been used to. After all, he came from a place that wore single layers though they were in space. Seeing that there were at least three pieces of clothing just for his shirt, Dean wanted to understand what he was supposed to do with them, as to avoid using Kane's help all the time. He wasn't some child who didn't know how to change his clothes. It was just an interesting set piece that Kane gifted him.

"I knew you'd need my help." Kane remarked as he pulled back the curtain. With a smug grin on his face, Kane walked over to see some of the clothing on top of the bed. "First you will need to put on the thin white top before you put on the vest. It will give you a bit more a sleek look when we're on the airship." Kane remarked as he picked up the red and black leather vest that had some type of binding strings in the back.

As Dean started to slip the shirt on and buttoned the shirt up, Kane waited patiently for

Dean to finish before handing him the vest. "Funny how the vest reminds me of the leaves changing in the autumn. Sadly you were in the hospital when they changed. Now most of the leaves around my tribe have already started to drop towards the ground." Kane remarked, watching Dean struggling with trying to put the vest on.

Walking towards Dean, Kane started to close up the buttons in the front. "Speaking of my clan..." Kane remarked as he finished the last button. "I hope that you'll at least be able to see it more after everything is said and done." Kane continued, his finger gently brushing over the metal button. "Turn around for this next part." Kane ordered, catching Dean a little off guard, but he did what he was instructed.

"When the fall starts to change to winter, it's quite something else. The lush trees that once gave the buildings life, now look empty and barren. Just like when the bombs had dropped, and no life remained on the surface for hundreds of years " Kane continued in almost a daydream tone, despite the cryptic image that was associated with it.

"I've seen trees change colors. So I don't think it would be a big deal. But I never saw them bare." Dean spoke, though a few small grunts escaped towards the end as Kane started to tighten the string in the back. "Which reminds me..." Dean trailed off before glancing over towards Kane. "What do you guys do during the winter time? Does it snow?" It was a simple question. If Kane was in charge of the harvesting of crops, what was there to do during the winter time when it was hard to grow crops.

"Well, my tribe still tends to the cattle. But otherwise, they relax during the winter months. Most of the time that's when people do a lot of catching up. The snow is oddly relaxing when you've had a long day." Kane remarked with a faint smile on his face as he remembered watching the snowfall from his small cottage.

"Nothing like watching the large flakes of snow swimming in the cold crisp air while you sit by a window, a fire warming you while resting beside a fireplace." Kane remarked, watching as Dean zipped and buttoned the pants on to complete the look.

"As for myself, I tend to head towards Miles' tribe to help them out. I have a couple of volunteers who come with me for some extra pay. You'd be surprised with how many single people come with me in hopes of finding a partner." Kane mused, a soft chuckle leaving his lips. Stepping back from Dean, Kane studied the other to see that the other male liked the outfit picked out for him. "There, how's that?" Kane asked as Dean started to look over the outfit himself. The other did look good, Kane couldn't help but be a bit proud of himself as he was able to pick out a decent outfit.

Placing a hand on his own chest to feel the fabric of the vest, Dean was surprised at how well it seemed to fit him. "Seems good to me." Dean remarked, the satisfaction in his voice. "Mind helping me with those weird gloves?" Dean asked as he picked up the long gloves that Kane provided him. They were unlike anything that Dean had ever seen before. It was almost like something one would see an Enforcement officer wearing rather than what Dean would wear himself. Dean was used to the smaller gloves that only went to his wrist, but at least these ones covered his fingers.

"These are weird to you?" Kane asked, raising an eyebrow before he started to undo the buttons on the side of the gloves. "It's funny, your previous outfit looked weird to me." Kane coyly remarked as he worked on the gloves for Dean. "But, it did look good on you. Guess those cowards still have some fashion sense up there." Not that Kane knew what it was like to live up on the space station.

"I'm used to small gloves that don't travel past your wrists." Dean commented as he could feel the fabric sliding over his arm. "These on the other hand look like they are going to swallow your forearm, like a snake or something." Dean commented, earning a small chuckle from Kane. It wasn't like Dean was lying though. But seeing Kane fuss with it, it wasn't as bad as Dean originally thought.

"You're too much." Kane remarked with a soft chuckle towards the end. "Sometimes it's funny to think you're older than me and still have the mindset of a child at times." Kane commented, finishing the one glove before grabbing the other glove to repeat the same procedure on Dean's other hand.

"Well, we were never allowed much in the way of accessories. That was usually reserved for the Elite and higher Silver classes." Dean sighed a little. "Regardless, I'm surprised that you bring other people with you. I would figure that they have their own people working in their tribes." When you think about it, who wouldn't want to be able to travel around and see the sights? To be able to find love in places that they never expected it? It was something that Dean often thought about, when he wanted to get away from it all on the Millennium.

"They do." Kane started off as he crossed his arms against his chest. "It's a way to keep our tribes from hating each other and it makes for a more diverse population. In fact, there are a couple of members from my tribe mixed in with the others and vice versa." Kane continued to speak as he put the old clothes into the bag he brought with him.

"Some act as teachers, others act as harvesters or butchers. It's a way to help each other out. Working to unite our tribes rather than spy on one another. Something that the cowards never understood by what you've told me. " Kane explained, though there was a bit of a sad look to him.

"What about their personal belongings? Their pets? That is if they have any." Dean started to ask in curiosity. "I'm sure their families would be worried." Dean finished as he sat down on the bed to slip on some boots that were mid calf in length with a small zipper in the back to keep the boots in place. They were a solid dark brown with some straps on the outer edges of the boot's length that matched his gloves.

"It gets shipped to their new housing. Well. . . not their pets. They travel aboard the ship. But the animals are restricted to their owners' corridor until we arrive at our destination." The last thing that anyone wanted was poor animals to suffer. "We don't allow any cattle on board due to the fact that it would be too much stress on the animals, as well as the fact that there is limited room for cargo." Kane explained, watching as Dean tried and struggled with some of the other accessories that were laying on the bed.

"Interesting." Dean remarked, trying to figure where he was supposed to place a pouch looking accessory, finding that there was no way to keep it attached to his pants. "How the hell are you supposed to keep this damn thing on?!" Dean grumbled in frustration, watching the pouch fall to the ground for the fifth or so time. If it was this frustrating to get a little pouch on, there was no way that Dean would have made it in the Enforcement course. Not with how many accessories that they had to wear.

As Kane grabbed the red belt off of the bed, he brought up the belt to be eye level with Dean. "You attach it to your belt, letting the loops go under the pouch before passing it through the other loop to lock it in. You want to keep it more towards the front to keep someone from snatching it." There was an amused smirk on Kane's face as the male took a bit of pleasure watching the space man struggle to put on so many layers. After the explanation, Dean was able to figure it out for himself as he watched Kane demonstrate how to put on a belt.

"You take pleasure in watching me suffer, don't you?" Dean grumbled before taking the belt from Kane, a bit of irritation washed over Dean's facial features the more he saw the smug look on Kane's face. One could practically see how annoyed Dean was with having to put on a bunch of clothing, not to mention how warm it was getting with so many layers on.

"Perhaps a little." Kane remarked back, an amused smile on his face. With how tight the outfit was, Kane did admire the way that it looked on the spaceman. You could almost say that Dean could pass as one of the members of the clan rather than actually coming from the station. Kane wondered if perhaps Dean could settle down in his clan, perhaps share some of his experience with Kane, and they could continue to be good friends once everything had settled.

"You're the devil." Dean grumbled a little, though in a teasing manner. "Even though this is torture, I guess it's better than going around wearing the old janitor uniform." It wasn't like Dean cared much for that outfit anyways. He would rather focus on being able to move on from his past. Nothing was waiting for him up there anyways. No family or friends, just an empty pod that would go to waste. By this time, Dean figured that most of his stuff had been burned. The last of the photographs of his parents were gone, erasing any evidence that Dean Torres ever existed on the Millennium.

With everything on except for the jacket, Kane leaned up to take in Dean's face as he noticed something different about the male. "Ah, I see that someone not only got all cleaned from the stubble he was growing, but he also got a bit of a haircut." Kane spoke as he took notice in the slightly embarrassed look that came over Dean at that remark.

"Yeah? So what?" Dean spoke a bit defensively as a flustered look crossed his face. "I asked one of the nurses to take care of it." Dean continued as he glanced off to the side. "Besides, I was starting to look a bit like my old man with my facial hair growing out. I didn't want to feel like I was looking at his ghost when I looked in the mirror." Dean finished as he couldn't look Kane in the eyes. To actually have a chance to talk to his old man wouldn't have been a bad thing, but Dean didn't want to see the disappointment in his own eyes being reflected into a similar image of his father.

"No need to get defensive. I was just commenting on how good you look cleaned up. To be honest, you did look decent with a little bit of facial hair, but the clean look really is more of your style." Kane spoke, taking a step back before crossing his arms over his chest. There was an unsettling silence that grew between them before Kane spoke up once more.

"I'm sure you'll have an easy time getting a partner." Kane spoke, nodding his head a little bit, speaking his thoughts out loud, catching Dean off guard by the comment.. "Not everyday someone gets to have a little bit of romance with a space man." It was as if Kane was trying to pass it off as some sort of joke as he saw the discomfort in Dean's posture.

"Doubtful." Dean quickly dismissed the comment as he shrugged it off as an innocent joke. "Not like there is much for me to provide for someone. Especially being an outsider." Dean didn't see there being much of anyone who would find an 'Elite' member to be attractive. Not with the resentment the survivors had.

"But speaking of partners," Dean paused, glancing over towards Kane. "Do you have one?" Dean would be more than surprised if Kane didn't have a partner. With his soft almost doll like appearance, who wouldn't be attracted to someone like him? The two of them were a bit on the opposite end of appearance. Where Kane looked a bit more like a feminine yet masculine man, Dean was more well built with a slightly muscular frame with some decent features.

Gazing at Kane, Dean noticed that the other seemed to smile at him with a bit of mischief lingering in Kane's eyes as he thought about it. A minute or so passes in silence before Kane brings his finger up to his lips. The exposed silver eye closes half way before he spoke: "That's a secret." A hum left Kane's lips as he turned around to head towards the bathroom. "I can't tell you that just yet." A soft chuckle escaping Kane's lips once more. "Anyways, I'll be getting dressed. It'll be only a few minutes. Unlike you, I know how to dress in layers." Another little tease as Kane closed the door to the bathroom where a small bag was tucked away by the door.

"Wait, what? A secret?" Dean asked, a bit surprised that Kane wasn't direct towards him. Kane had usually been so straight forward with Dean, granted they have only known each other for a few weeks that Dean was in the hospital, but for a majority of that time that Dean was there Kane would come in to visit with him.

It was nice to have someone to whom Dean could form some type of friendship with. Even when Dean was in the Silver class, he didn't have any friends. Often bullied due to his weight more than anything, and maybe his weird obsession with reading different types of medical books that his father had around, Dean never really had a friend. Kane was the first real friend that Dean has had in his life. Even if Kane didn't feel that way, Dean considered him a friend at least.

"You'll have to figure that part out on your own Dean." Kane called out from the bathroom. The light in the bathroom flickered on as the sound of the bag rustled reached Dean's ears. Seemed like Kane wouldn't need help, unlike Dean. Which made sense, considering that Kane was used to wearing the different styles on the planet, unlike Dean who was used to one particular style all his life.

Visibly shaking his head, Dean picked up the only piece of clothing left for him to put on. It was a fairly large red leather trench coat with hooks to help close up the middle zipper that rested on his chest. The hood of the coat was large enough to block out the sun's harmful rays, which would come in handy for someone not used to being exposed to natural sunlight all of their lives. The hem of the coat reached Dean's mid-thigh as the coat hugged his body.

Sitting down on the messy bed, Dean could feel himself already becoming a bit too warm. Pulling the hood off of his head, Dean slicked back his hair ever so slightly as he tried to free any trapped sweat from his scalp as they were trapped in his thick locks. It was rather funny how Dean could recall a memory he had of a time where Dean and his father were sitting around bored while they waited for his mother to get ready for their dinner reservation. Though unlike that time, Dean was simply by himself. He didn't have his old man there to make idle chit chat. Instead, he could simply hear the chatter coming from the hallway. It wasn't coherent, so it wasn't like there was much for Dean to pay attention to.

It took around what seemed like ten or so minutes before Kane walked out in a completely different outfit than what Dean was used to seeing on him. The large earrings that once dangled from Kane's ears were now replaced with small silver and black hoops that lined his earlobe. The large necklace that partially hid Kane's Adam's apple now held a crystal gem attached to some silver links. The others' skinny frame was more evident without the robe.

Wearing a mono-sleeve leather gauntlet that wrapped up his arm and slightly over his right shoulder and around his neck, a small black and white robe-like shirt seemed to be draped over Kane's chest like a tunic that had one sleeve that draped loosely over Kane's left arm. A sash wrapped around Kane's torso that acted like a belt to close the gap where the white top and black tunic met over his stomach. On the right side of the sash was a pouch that looked more full than Dean's.

Dean's eyes glanced down Kane's body to take more of others' appearance. At first it seemed that Kane was wearing some type of shorts that only went to his mid thighs. With the coming winter months coming in, one would think that Kane would have the common sense to wear pants instead of shorts. But looking down, Kane was wearing tall boots that broke the gap that Kane would have just wearing the shorts. There was a small dagger attached to Kane's left boot, just a bit above the knee. Were they going to deal with fighting some monsters or something?

Blinking a bit in surprise, Dean watched as Kane brought up his left hand to brush back some of his hair to show off his right eye. Sure the scar that barely missed his eye was something Dean had to get used to, but it looked like it was a couple of years old and was slowly fading. But in a strange way, it did look good on him. With the left arm a bit more exposed, Dean noticed that Kane was wearing a long sleeved glove similar to his own. Though unlike Dean's, the gloves appeared to be finger-less.

"Aren't you going to be cold like that? You'll freeze out there wearing that." Dean asked, wondering how Kane wasn't going to freeze in the winter like that? Did it not get all that cold on the planet? Knowing that the after effects of the nukes being dropped was a nuclear winter, the temperatures didn't exactly agree with something like booty shorts.

"Nah. I got on some warm thermal long johns pants underneath. I'll be fine." Kane simply brushed off the remark like it was nothing. "Besides, my cloak is basically a giant blanket." Kane remarked, pulling out a large black cloak that seemed to cover Kane from his shoulders down to his knees.

There were a few hidden clasps that were on the inside of the cloak that Kane could close it from inside of his cloak. There was a small hoodie as well that protected Kane from any of the hash elements, like if the sun if it got too bright for himself. The inner part of the cloak appeared to be white. So it seemed that the cloak was a special type of reversible garment? It would be interesting to see exactly how it worked, considering that Dean had never seen anything like it. Slipping the cloak on, it appeared that Kane was ready to head out.

"How did you get pants on under those boots?" Dean asked, walking towards Kane, seeing the eagerness in Kane's eyes as the other was already slipping his right boot off as if to show him. Despite the cloak being closed, it seemed that Kane was still able to move around as he pulled off the long boot with ease.

"Check it out, they hook under my ankle with a strap and it stays in place." Kane remarked excitedly, though Dean noticed how Kane was barely keeping his balance on one foot, making him appear like a flamingo. It was amazing that Kane wasn't practically falling over, though if he did, it would have been hilarious.

"You know, you look pretty funny with your wobbling stance. Though I am curious as to why you decided to wear that instead of your robe. At least they would keep you somewhat warm." Dean spoke, watching as Kane tried to put the shoe back on. With a couple of jabs with the tip of his shoe, it seemed like Kane was able to get it back on.

"Well, usually I wear them when I go commando. I doubt the other leaders would appreciate me showing up wearing nothing but my robe." Kane spoke bluntly as he grabbed the bag with his other change of clothes inside of it

"The summers get really hot here." Kane started to explain as they walked towards the door to exit out of the room. "Forcing people to wear underwear is kind of cruel if they don't want to. Not to mention it feels more free. If you get too hot, you can just spread and cool down." Again with the bluntness coming from Kane. Mentally shaking his head, Dean didn't want to exactly picture Kane spreading his legs to cool off while wearing the robe.

"So you're saying that all the time that you came here, you were completely naked under your robe?" Dean asked, an unimpressed gaze being pointed towards Kane. Now if Dean saw Kane wearing the robe, he would have to figure out if he was wearing underwear or not.

"No way, that would have been rude. I always came to visit more towards the evening when it was getting cooler outside." Kane smiled towards Dean. Now Dean didn't know if the other was being serious or if he was joking to make Dean feel less uncomfortable about knowing that Kane sometimes goes commando. Then again Dean couldn't get angry at Kane for being naked under his robes, most of the time Dean liked to lay in his bed in the nude, so he had no room to talk.

"Well at least you have some tact." Dean spoke with an exasperated sigh. The rest of the walk was silent. Passing by patients who were up and moving around, Dean considered himself lucky that he was able to get out today. Some of the people in the hallway looked rather sickly or had serious injuries. The worst was seeing kids in the hospital who resembled the kids in the Bronze class. Seeing their cheeks sunken and their skin sickly pale, it always made Dean's heart sink seeing them like that.

It wasn't long before Dean arrived at the main entrance with Kane. The two had to stop at the nurses station in order to get their backpacks. Putting his own on, Dean groaned as he felt some nerves pinching as he slipped the backpack on. Turning to face the doors, the sun had already been starting to set. The coloring of the sky was that of an orange and purple mixture, almost making it seem like the sky was on fire. The orange glow on the floor that passed through the door made it apparent that they were heading out at dusk.

Walking under the small covering above the door, the pair stopped to take a look at the sky. Even though the place seemed like it was covered with the tree branches, there was still a bit of light that reached down to the surface. The branches almost made it seem like dark claws were reaching along the ground towards them, ready to grab the pair and drag the pair off into the awaiting darkness.

Staring up towards the setting sun, Dean brought up his right hand to shield his eyes from the sun. Looking up at the sky, Dean was practically in awe of what he had seen. Small dark figures flew above him in a V shape, the noises coming from sounded like deep honks. The more that Dean looked up at the sky, the more that Dean noticed that it had different pigments of colors that Dean had never seen before. It was breathtaking as he never saw something so colorful yet dark at the same time.

Pink, orange, blue, red, purple, and bits of white decorated the sky, it almost looked like an art piece. Bits of stars seeped through the clouds where the sky was the darkest. The air around them was cold with a bit of a crisp to it. Seeing his breath come out like a white cloud was a bit startling for Dean at first, never experiencing something like that before, but he wouldn't comment on it, seeing as how the same thing happened to Kane.

"Before everything went to hell, I was told that most of the world never had to deal with the darkness that creeped out at night." Kane spoke, taking steps towards the stone and vine covered courtyard. Most of the leaves had started to wither as the nutrients were being pulled back into soil as the end of winter was creeping closer. "When the sun would go down, everyone would be inside to enjoy their meal as family, only to get ready for sleep soon after." Kane continued to further comment as Dean hurried to be by Kane's side as he walked past the crumbled sign, the letters long faded and barely made it readable.

"But now, the darkness isn't all that scary." Kane continued as he pulled the gate open for them. "We mostly use the crystals to light up the roads and some of the streets, though it doesn't take away the darkness." As Kane remarked about the crystals, Dean noticed small flickering lights in the distance that resembled the same crystal fixture in the hospital started to turn on and give them light. "It provides enough light for people to be able to walk around at night without getting completely lost. See?" Kane remarked as a soft white glow from the light made it easier to look around at the surrounding buildings.

The smell of rust was evident on the gate as he passed it, but Dean didn't seem bothered by it. "It may never be the same as it once was, where you would be able to see the lights even from space, but it still offers us some light, like little fairies guiding us home." A soft smile lingered on Kane's face as the pair started to walk down the pathway between the buildings in an old looking neighborhood. "We'll have a ways to walk to get to the bay. But if you ever get lost, just look for the giant tree and you'll know where you're at." Kane remarked before turning to look behind them, causing Dean to turn around to look at it as well.

Dean was surprised to see where he had been staying the last couple of weeks. On top of a crumbling hospital building, there was a gigantic tree sprouting on top of the hospital. Though the sun was starting to set, Dean could see the tree perfectly. The building itself reached several stories high, and the tree on top seemed to reach even higher into the darkening sky. The width of the tree seemed like it was a whole city block. Though the branches were bare as it prepared for the winter months ahead. The tip of the branches looked like they were scraping the sky as the wind brushed against the heavy branches, causing the sound of the branches to creak against the howling wind. Was this a result of radiation and time away from humans that allowed it to grow this big?

The surrounding trees seemed pale in comparison. The lights scattered around the lining of the tree showed just how well humans were living with nature. The lights ranged in color, largely due to the different types of crystal used for particular lights, making the tree practically sparkle like a Christmas tree as it appeared that some buildings were sticking out of the sides of the tree. If this were a real life fantasy world, it would make those of the Gluttony Clan to be like some sort of wood elf.

"We have these trees to thank for protecting us from being discovered by the cowards up in space. Even though the crystal lights help to give us enough light without exposing us, it's really thanks to the trees for making it possible for us to breathe the air as well as keeping any light shielded from the spring to fall. During the winter the snow storms tend to keep the light from being seen as it is always cloudy here." Kane spoke about the lights and tree as he closed the gate behind them, only to see Dean avert his attention from the tree that encased the hospital and other similar buildings to gazing down at Kane.

"Seems like you guys have done a lot to protect yourselves from being seen. But how does a couple of trees help protect you?" Dean asked. It seemed pretty evident since not even Dean could tell that there were humans on the surface. For how much he spent gazing at the planet, he never knew about people living on it. Not like the Elite could have sent troops down to investigate if there was a possible sign for life. They would have lied and said that there wasn't any life on the planet, just to keep their cattle secured and docile. After all, who wouldn't want to return to their true homeland?

"Well, you were really surprised to see a normal person living here. Which means that you didn't know about our existence, which could give us a bit on an edge." Kane remarked as they walked down the road with the least amount of foot traffic. "If you didn't know about us, then perhaps we can take out those cowards with a surprise attack." It seemed like it might work, but the question was, how could they orchestrate an attack?

"Though, it may end up killing everyone on that space station. Are you willing to have their blood on your hands, Dean?" Kane asked, his voice serious as he stopped in his tracks. "We might not be able to save people who you knew. Family, friends, or even co-workers that you may have gotten along with" It wasn't like there was anyone waiting for Dean on the station, so asking the question was a waste of time in Dean's eyes. "Is it worth killing innocent people who didn't do anything to you for revenge?" Kane asked, giving Dean some time to think about it.

Would Dean really get any type to get some type of satisfaction by killing innocent people just to be able to get revenge on the Elite? It wasn't like there was much for Dean back on the station as it was. There was no real way to save those people. They were beyond saving in Dean's eyes. After all, they didn't put much effort into trying to save themselves from being bleed dry by the Elite all of their lives. But that wasn't the answer that Kane was looking for.

"I want to try to save them. But if they are part of the casualties, I won't be heartbroken over it." Dean spoke bluntly as he looked Kane in the eyes. "After all, they shunned me for the rest of my life after I tried to help them and it backfired. I was only a kid when it happened too. So sorry to break it to you, but it won't break my heart if they end up dying as well." Dean finished as he averted his gaze from Kane, clenching his fists to hold back the anger swelling inside of Dean.

After all, why should he shed even a single tear for those who ignored his cries for help? They didn't grieve for him, so why should he? The fact that Dean had become cold hearted to those who were in his class was worrisome to Kane. He didn't want to see Dean go towards that path. Not when he knew how destructive it could be.

As much as Kane wanted to save everyone, it seemed like Dean's mind was already made up. "Have it your way then." Kane spoke, a hint of bitterness lingered on his lips as he headed down the dark road that led out of the city. Hearing the tone in Kane's voice, it caused Dean to pause as he wondered if maybe he was letting his emotions get the better of him.

It would take an hour or so on foot to get to their next location, seeing as how no one would be around as the sun went down, Dean and Kane would be the only two walking around. The road that they walked was lined with dried curled leaves from the trees surrounding the area. Some of the leaves settled down into the potholes of the road, giving them protection from slipping into the old worn parts of the road.

The leaves seemed to differ in size and shape, some much larger than others, while the smaller ones were barely noticeable. The sound of the leaves crunching against their feet was a new sound that Dean found to be pleasant. The trees on the station never seemed to drop, rather they kept their shape with only changing color in the fall. If the leaves had fallen, there would have been plenty of children who would have been eager to play in them.

As they traveled down the country looking road, Dean couldn't help but notice that there was a lingering smell of rotted hay drifting in the wind. He knew the smell from the time his school took a small trip to a farmhouse. The cows on the station seemed to resemble the ones that were on Earth before the devastation happened, only they were much smaller. Possibly due to being in space that changed the cows physical attributes.

There wasn't much light on the road, which was a bit worrisome, but Dean could see the night sky peeking out of the clouds. Glancing up, Dean saw a sight unlike anything he had seen before. Though it was still distant, he saw the very station that he was practically exiled from. The lights gave it away. It looked otherworldly when seen from the surface of the planet. Dean felt like a rock was pushing against the base of his stomach the more that he gazed up at it. How could anyone stand looking up at that sort of thing?

Stopping in his tracks, Dean placed a hand on top of his stomach. Kane stopped to look back at Dean when he didn't hear Dean's footsteps behind him. "Something wrong?" Kane asked, though Dean didn't say anything. Trailing the line of sight, Kane's eyes went towards the brief view of the Millennium. Now it made sense. "Hey, don't worry about it. Thanks to the clouds, you rarely have to see that ugly eyesore in the sky." Kane commented, trying to cheer Dean up a bit. With the passing clouds moving to cover up the station, Dean seemed to come back to his senses. "See? Gone. Just like that."

A small relieved sigh escaped from Dean, glad that he didn't have to see that station for very long. The way that the red lights lined up, it looked like a giant eye peeking down at the planet, trying to catch people out of their homes or something, it always seemed to be unsettling. Dean had to push the unsettling feeling to the back in his mind, not wanting to focus on it. He needed to bring down the station. He needed to make sure that they paid dearly for what the Elite did to everyone around them. For far too long they have been at the top of the class. Now, it was time for a change, and Dean was happy enough to take that position. "Thanks....I don't know what got into me." Dean spoke, his voice a bit weary.

"Don't worry about it. After a while, you just sort of forget that it is there." Kane spoke, a small shrug of his shoulders. "We've got a lot of ground to cover. The longer we stand around, the more Felicia will complain about us taking too long." Kane finished, a small annoyed sigh leaving his lips. It seemed that Kane didn't like dealing with this Felicia leader.

The rest of the walk was relatively silent. Though when they had gotten closer to the ocean, Dean could hear the waves. The smell of salt seemed to linger in the air as well, a smell he knew thanks to the salt his mother often added to their food. Reaching the edge of a cliff, Dean gazed out at the vast ocean ahead of them. The clouds appeared darker with bits of lightning in the distance. It seemed that a storm was approaching. Taking an overview of the harbor in front of them, Dean noticed a pathway that was on the steep side, but would bring them towards their destination.

As Kane turned to Dean, there was a slight annoyed look lingering on Kane's face. "Since we're going to head overseas, we're going to need to get a ride from Felicia." Kane practically shouted over the sound of the roaring waves and howling wind. "She controls most of the traveling across the sea, so we'll be visiting her at the inn." Even though it was a bit hard to hear Kane, at least Dean got the premise of what Kane was saying.

With a simple nod, the two made their way down the cliff. Watching where Dean stepped, there seemed to be a few lanterns that lined the way towards the inn. Glancing down, Dean took notice that the wood used as the steps resembled that of driftwood as the path was lined with a mixture of large rocks and sand to help keep even footing.

The bay appeared to have a more rustic appearance to it, unlike how the area that Dean had landed, the difference was quite apparent. Kane's tribal area was covered with trees that lined most of the area. Some of the trees grew in the building and made it hard to really settle down in those buildings. Those who were lucky enough to find homes that were in one piece seemed to live scattered throughout the once lived-in city. There were a few blocks that had a fair amount of people living together, but it wasn't a common sight.

Looking at the bay ahead of him, Dean could see for miles. Wrecked ships drifted in the distant darkening ocean. There even seemed to be bits of large buildings that collapsed into the ocean which made Dean wonder how any ship could even come close enough into the bay without becoming another sinking boat in the ship graveyard. The waves seemed to crash against the rustic buildings, spraying water up into the air. If there was anyone sailing in the choppy waters now, they would surely get into a wreckage. So how were they going to get across the ocean?

The houses that decorated the area ranged from a white gravel structure to wooden cabins that resembled a shack more than anything else. The streets weren't decorated with crystal light posts like in the city. Instead they used lamp posts with small flickering candles behind glass panels that allowed for the heat to rise through small slits at the top. Keeping both the candle from melting faster and to keep the elements out from blowing out the candle. As the two of them walked, it felt like the bay had been long since abandoned. There was no indication that there was life around them as they headed towards a single area that seemed to be glowing with lights. It was like a beacon of light as the night crept up behind them.

Following a single path that was used more than the alleyways between the homes, Dean took notice of how clean it was compared to the side paths that laid next to them. A small shiver ran through Dean's body as he felt the temperature getting colder the closer they were to the shore. Was it really possible for the area around the water to make it colder than it already was?

Glancing towards the sea, the water looked pitch black at night, making it look like moving tar. Dean couldn't help but shutter at the thought of what creatures could live in the sea now, if there was any that is. Who could have guessed that the beautiful blue sea that Dean once gazed at from space, could turn into a void that lacked any type of light inside? Visibly shaking his head, Dean focused back at the path ahead of them, seeing the large two story inn ahead of them.

For a building in the area, it looked pretty brand new. The white coating of paint helped the light from the candle lamp posts make it glisten in the darkness. The wooden plaque above read *The Dizzy Cups* in large black letters against the white background. It certainly was a unique name. The sounds of life seemed to catch Dean's ears, giving the male much relief that there were more people here than he had originally thought.

Once they reached the steps at the base of the inn, Dean followed behind Kane up the wooden steps towards the front patio that had some people sitting at tables outside, already drinking out of some type of mugs that appeared to have wooden handles that nestled around glass. The people talking around them sounded incoherent to Dean for it to make sense of what they were talking about, but it wasn't like he would be able to listen for very long as the two men went inside.

Once they were inside, Dean could feel the warm air from the collection of people and heat from the candles that decorated the wooden interior of the bar. Gazing around, Dean couldn't believe the level of detail that went inside of the large inn. Even though everything was made of wood and stone, it meshed well together. The top of the bar was wooden in nature, though it had some type of shine to it that almost made it look like glass. Despite the fact that Dean couldn't exactly touch it, he could tell that the surface had been sanded down to give it a flat and smooth texture.

Under the counter facing them, the base of the bar looked as if it was made out of differently shaped rocks to give it a unique appearance. But what was most impressive had to be the design on the walls. The four pillars on the main floor looked like trees with the way the ceiling was designed to look like branches spreading outwards and upwards to the second floor. The tangled branches gave a bit of privacy for the doors that lead to the inn's bedrooms. Dean was almost half expecting to find the branches covered in leaves in the warmer seasons, but that was doubtful.

Tracing the edges of the woodwork with his eyes, Dean glanced towards the middle of the ceiling. Dean was taken back by the chandelier that hung in the middle. The pyramid of antlers from deer that had been killed, mixed with glass beads and pearls, was a beautiful display of what Kane meant about using all of the animal. The beads and glass were perfectly evened out to make it shimmer with the reflecting lights from the crystal lights hidden within the core. It was simply breathtaking and something that Dean had never imagined possible.

Glancing at the tables, Dean noticed that they were all differently shaped. It was almost like the tables were made from the trunks of the tree that were cut down to make them. Of course Dean couldn't get close enough to see, but if one were to look close enough, they would be able to see the rings under the glassy top. The people around them seemed to glance over towards the two, making Dean look away as he didn't want to make any type of trouble that could make for a bad first impression in case the leader of the Pride clan had seen them. If what Dean recalled was correct, the person that they were looking for was a woman named Felicia.

Glancing around a bit more, Dean took in more of the design of the place. There was a staircase close by the bar, which meant that upstairs was where people would be able to stay the night, for a certain price that is. Along the edges of the stairs seemed to be little small lamp posts to help guide the way in case it was late at night and everyone was trying to sleep. It seemed like they were well connected to the stairs, as they barely moved when someone came down the steps.

Glancing at the woman from her feet, it appeared that she was wearing boots similar to Kane's, except the top rested just below her knees. At least, that's what the impression was when her left leg was exposed from the slit in her ragged skirt that went down towards her ankle on the right side.

"It's about time that you showed up." The woman remarked, gaining a glance from both Kane and Dean. As she reached the base of the steps, Dean noticed the top that she was wearing. A corset hugged her frame tightly as the top she was wearing barely covered her chest. With the middle split in half, her lush and supple chest seemed like it was barely staying inside the tan colored cloth. There were some accessories that draped around her arms, two bracelets that clung to cover her biceps and triceps with a small loose piece of clothing seemed to connect to the pair of bracelets she wore on either wrist.

She looked decently tanned and well in shape, her platinum blonde locks pulled back into a messy bun at the time. Silver eyes gazed towards Dean and Kane, leaving Dean wondering if this was really the leader of the Pride clan. "So is this the man from space?" She asked, looking Dean up and down, making Dean feel a bit self conscious about himself at that moment. This woman had the same type of energy that Dean felt from those of the Elite class. The constant judging that made Dean feel like he was never good enough in their eyes, and it made him angry. Instead of speaking, Dean clenched his jaw, waiting for Kane to say something, but he didn't.

"Yes ma'am. My name is Dean Torres, it's a pleasure to meet you." Dean remarked, offering out his hand, wanting to be civil with this woman. After all, just like Kane had said, first impressions were everything. It seemed to at least impress her as she raised one of her thin eyebrows, taking Dean's hand and giving it a good firm handshake.

"At least he has manners." The woman spoke, glancing towards Kane before shifting her gaze back towards Dean. "My name is Felicia Manwell. I'm the leader of the Pride clan. I'm sure Kane has told you that much, yes?" She asked, keeping her head held high as if she was preening like a peacock.

"Yes he has." Dean spoke, placing a hand on top of Kane's shoulders, causing the smaller male to almost jump from the slightest contact. It raised a bit of concern that Kane reacted in the way, but he'll bring it up a little later. "In fact, if it wasn't for Kane, I probably would have been dead." Even if Dean didn't know the history between the two leaders, he wanted to at least put a good word in for Kane.

After all, it wasn't a lie. Kane really did save Dean's life. "I couldn't be more thankful to have Kane in my life. He's the first real friend I've had. Which isn't saying much honestly, but I do appreciate everything that he has done for me." Dean added, glancing down at Kane, who seemed to be looking up at him with a bit of a surprised look on his face. Was what he said considered weird or something?

"Friend, huh?" Felicia asked, a bit of an amused smirk formed on her face as she brought a hand to rest against her cheek. "Well, how about we get settled in the back and get some food. It'll be on the house of course." It seemed like a good offer, but Dean wanted to make sure that it was at least fine with Kane. After all, they were here to talk about destroying Dean's old home, potentially killing millions of innocent people. "It won't be too much, just some chicken and local vegetables."

"That sounds delicious. I can't wait." Dean spoke, offering her a smile before giving Kane's shoulder another pat. Looking down, it seemed like Kane wasn't his usual self. There was no smiling, there was no positive energy coming from the other at all. It almost seemed like Kane didn't enjoy coming here. Was there some bad blood between the two of them or something? Either way, Dean figured that they would be able to talk about it when it came time to rest for the night. After all, they were getting a free meal and room out of it.

As they were being escorted towards the back by Felicia, Dean took notice of the design of the door that led towards the private section. The door was made up of some type of dark wood with an elegant design while the door handles were clear. As they headed inside of the room, Dean was surprised to see that the interior was similar to a captain's quarter on a ship. The walls were lined with different book shelves with rather ancient looking books, some of which looked as if they had been read through a decent amount of times, while others looked like they were waiting to be read by the layer of dust settled on the covers.

A fireplace rested between two windows that faced towards the bay. A small chandelier rested above a round table as the trimming of the chandelier was similar to the one in the main hall, except it didn't have glass beads and pearls hanging off of it as it was a single ring of ant-lers rather than a pyramid. Besides the door they had entered from, there was one other door that was connected to the kitchen. "I'll inform the kitchen staff of the meal to make. I'll also make sure to bring some type of food for Kane to enjoy while we get down to our business." Felicia spoke, only to head past the door, closing it behind her to leave the two men alone.

There was a little bit of an awkward silence in the room as Kane walked over towards one of the two couches to sit down. Kane's body language showed that something was wrong, even if he didn't say anything.

Dean softly frowned as he walked over to sit next to Kane. "Is something the matter?" Dean asked, his concern for his friend compelled Dean to at least try to make the other not feel like he had to stay quiet around the other tribal leader. It seemed the question had worked as Kane finally looked towards him.

"Yeah..." Kane spoke his voice trailing off towards the end. "It's just...I have a complicated relationship with Felicia." Kane spoke, knowing that it would be a little while before she would even come back. "We're sort of rivals." That wasn't exactly what Dean had expected to hear, but it was nice to know that Kane wasn't mad at him personally.

"What do you mean rivals?" Dean asked, raising an eyebrow as he couldn't really image what the two of them could be rivals about. After all, Kane had said that all of the leaders tend to work together in order to make their tribes function as a whole. Did their tribes see each other as potential threats?

"We like the same person." Kane started off as he looked dejected. Dean was surprised since earlier Kane said that his love life was more or less a secret. "Sadly she was able to win their affection. Despite how close we were, I just wasn't enough..." Kane admitted, a soft sigh escaping his lips as a frown formed on his face. Kane looked like a dejected puppy who was sulking in the corner. "They are even talking about getting married." Kane added, bringing his hands close to him before clasping them between his legs. "I mean, I'm happy for them, but I just wish it wasn't so complicated." Kane finished, lowering his head in defeat as he closed his eyes.

"Wait, married?" Dean asked a bit surprised as he didn't know that there was such a thing as getting married on Earth. "You guys allow same sex marriage?" Dean continued to ask, surprised that Felicia would be the type who would settle for a woman. "What's her name?" Dean asked, wondering if perhaps there was a way in which he could at least make Kane happy.

"It doesn't matter anyways." Kane mumbled, almost like he didn't hear the questions that Dean asked. "Not like I really stood that much of a chance." Kane continued to mumble to himself dejected. "She's everything I'm not. It was no wonder that I didn't get picked." Now it just seemed like Kane was self loathing himself.

"Listen," Dean spoke up as he moved to sit down on the couch beside Kane. "Just because you may have lost the battle of love to another chick, it doesn't mean that you're not as good." Dean commented as he tried to cheer Kane up the best that he knew how to. "If anything, it seems like they are missing out." Dean spoke, reaching out to lightly rub Kane's back.

"You're a good guy, Kane. Anyone would be lucky enough to be with you." Dean smiled towards the other male, watching as Kane glanced at Dean before moving to sit back up straight. "You're a really nice guy. You go out of your way to make people feel welcomed." Dean remarked with a smile on his face. "At least, that's what you did for me. It shows the type of person you are." Dean added, trying to find the right words to be able to comfort his friend, who desperately needed it. "You're not someone who could easily be replaced."

"Sadly being nice hasn't worked out for me." Kane continued in a dejected tone of voice as he averted his gaze from Dean. "In fact, it has gotten my heart ripped in half more times than I care to admit." Kane trailed off, a defeated sigh leaving his lips. Sulking over once more, Kane's eyes went to the little table in the middle of the two couches. "It's hard in this life trying to be nice to the wolves in sheep's clothing." Kane added, closing his eyes as he tried to hold himself together. Leaning his head back behind the headrest of the couch, Kane looked just like Dean did after every shift on the Millennium.

"Well, you always got me. I won't abandon you." Dean piped up, moving to sit sideways on the couch. "You've been good to me so far. Unlike a lot of people, it's actually a nice change of pace when you come from a place where people are self centered and bitter." Dean remarked, earning a side glance from Kane, the look in his eyes wondering if Dean was being serious or not.

"It may be a bit foolish to believe in the good of people, but just by the few encounters I've had, you're far better than she could ever be." Dean added. Kane's brows knitted together as he thought about what Dean was saying. It was almost like the leader was weighing the words coming from Dean. "You didn't have an attitude with me, which is a good thing considering that I am used to people always looking down on me. Sort of like that chick. It was sorta off putting and I don't see why anyone would want to be with someone who thinks they are better than others." Dean continued with a smile on his face, his eyes lighting up at the positive things that Dean thought of when it came to Kane.

"The only time you ever looked down on me was when I was on the ground. You made sure that I was safe after crash landing on the planet. You had someone carry me to the hospital. Hell you even came and visited me every single day while I was there." Dean started to list off a few reasons as to why Kane was a special friend to Dean. "I wouldn't even be here if it wasn't for you." Dean added, giving Kane's back a good couple of pats before standing up.

"So who cares if some chick won your crush's heart, you are a thousand times better than she could ever be. You'll find the right person in no time. And I'll be by your side through it all. You can count on me." Dean finished, not sure if it made sense or not, but it was worth trying to cheer up Kane.

Kane looked at Dean with a puzzled look at first, but soon smirked as he could see how hard Dean was working to try and cheer him up. It was a sweet jester nonetheless, causing Kane to grab a hold of Dean's hand before being pulled into a hug as they faced each other.

"Well, I guess as long as I have you by my side, I'll be alright." Kane remarked, only to be pulled into a tighter hug by Dean. With a flustered face, Kane's face peaked over Dean's shoulder. Dean's arms were loose on top of Kane's shoulders. Kane's body felt a bit tense from being hugged by Dean all of a sudden. "W-What are you doing?" Kane asked in a stammering tone, Kane's shock showing in his face with tinted cheeks.

"It's a bear hug." Dean started to explain with a grin on his face. "My dad used to give me one when I was sad and needing comfort. A hug between men as he would call it." Dean commented, giving Kane's body a small squeeze as a groan escaped his throat. Giving Kane a couple of pats on the back with his top hand, Dean could feel Kane seemingly beginning to give Dean a hug back as he clenched onto Dean's sleeves. That was, however, until they heard the creaking of a door slowly opening. Felicia cleared her throat as if to signal that she was there with three plates of food on a tray.

"My, seems like I'm interrupting something. Should I come back later?" Felicia asked in a bit of a teasing voice, causing the two men to pull back from each other with faces as red as tomatoes. The way they reacted caused a small chuckle to escape from Felicia's lips. "Relax, I'm only teasing. It's not every day that you walk in on two men hanging all over each other." Another little jab at the two as she walked over to the table to set the tray down.

"It was just an innocent hug between two men. It's called a bear hug, right Dean?" Kane tried to defend the misunderstanding. Though the fluster still seemed to linger. It must have been quite the showing to simply come in and see two guys in an embrace, hardly any space between them. Then getting completely red in the face out of embarrassment. How could one see that and not think something was going on between them?

"Yeah! It's totally normal for two men to hug." Dean remarked in self defense as he felt his cheeks heat up from the tease. "I mean, at least that's what my dad always told me." Dean muttered the last part under his breath. He could feel the awkward tension in the room as he moved to sit down. His father wouldn't lie about that, right?

After they had their meal, it was time to sit down and actually focus on the task ahead of them. The three had glasses of whiskey with a large chunk of ice in front of them. "Now that we've gotten food in our stomachs, let's talk about exactly why you're here Dean." Felicia spoke, taking a small sip of the whiskey first, clearing her throat a little before speaking directly towards Dean. "Kane told me a bit about your situation... but I want to hear the whole thing from you." Felicia remarked, she crossed her arms as to her chest with the glass still in her hand as she crossed one leg over the other.

"I see..." Dean spoke, his voice trailing a bit. He couldn't exactly repeat the whole story the way he told Kane. "Simply put, I want to get vengeance on those who made all of our lives a living hell." Dean started out, seemingly to catch Felicia's attention with that remark. "I figured that most of you have only recently gotten out from whatever shelter humanity had when the Elite had decided to go full nuclear warfare on the world, right?" Dean asked, but didn't give either one of the leaders time to respond before he started to talk again.

"Well, after that happened, the Elite used those on board to start their own version of No-ah's ark. Those at the top would live in the lap of luxury while those underneath were nothing more than servants to them. They made everyone's life a living hell after that." Dean spoke in a bitter tone as he glared at the glass in front of him. "Those who weren't good enough to be in the silver or Elite class were put to work like slaves. We were treated worse than street rats." Dean grumbled as he clenched his fists.

"You try to get ahead in life, and they just find something else to make your life miserable." Dean continued as he glanced up at Felicia, who seemed to weigh what Dean was telling her. "Children went hungry. People couldn't even mourn a death in their family in peace without the Enforcement officers coming in to rip away what little you had." Dean continued as he sat up straight. "Children were uneducated...forced to work as soon as they were able to walk around without stumbling over All for the sake of profit." The list could have gone on forever about what they would do to children, but considering that they had just eaten, it was best not to go into that type of detail.

"Despite everything that people went through on Earth before they nuked everything, it only seemed to continue on the Millennium." Dean continued to talk, despite the fact that his knuckles were white from clenching his fists tightly. "They just had more room and power to control the aspects of their workers' lives..." Dean trailed off as he released his clenched fists. "They killed people in cold blood by ordering others to do their dirty deeds. And worse yet..." Dean paused as he tried to collect his bearings for the next part. "They killed my parents and labeled them as traitors because they learned those bastards darkest secret." There was a small strain in Dean's voice as he talked about, still feeling the sting no matter how many years had passed.

"My parents aren't traitors." Dean spat as he grabbed a hold of his knees. "They were innocent! And those monsters killed my parents because my father learned that they raped and killed a little boy around my age at the time for their sick ritual." Dean shouted in anger, taking note of the expressions on the other leaders' faces. Kane heard the story already, as evident by how the male glanced away from Dean. Felicia on the other hand, her eyes widened when she heard it.

"When the pod above mind exploded, it knocked down some photos.." Dean trailed off in a shaky voice. "In those photos... my mother hid the evidence of what the Elite did to the child. Apparently, through observation in the cameras above our doors, they learned about the pieces of papers and decided that I was too much of a risk to keep aboard." Not that it was comforting to know that the Elite watched everything that people did in their pods, but after a while one just gets used to it.

"The Enforcement officers were probably planning on using me as a scapegoat for what happened to the woman above me." Dean continued, relaxing his shoulders a bit. "They decided to tamper the shuttle my parents left for me, using the excuse that my pod was in danger from the explosion. Because of that, I was sent on a one-way trip here so that I would die alone...and isolated..." Dean trailed off, his eyes glancing back down to the watered down whiskey glass that had small pearls of water dripping down its side.

"I can't just sit by and let the Elite harm any more people." Dean spoke up in the quiet room after a few minutes had passed. "They continue to kill those who get in their way. I can't let what happened to me and my parents happen to someone else." Dean continued before bowing his head to both Kane and Felicia. "So please!" Dean shouted in a begging tone. "Please help me get revenge on them!"

Kane glanced towards Felicia who sat back against the couch. The drink she had was almost gone, her face showed that she was studying Dean's body language to see if he was speaking the truth. With a soft bounce of her left leg, Felicia lowered the glass to set it on the table between her and Dean. The silence in the room was almost deafening if it wasn't for the fire roaring close by.

"That's quite the story..." Felicia trailed off as the clank from the glass sliding against the table reached Dean's ears. Dean glanced up to meet Felicia's gaze, seeing his reflection in her eyes. "If it wasn't for the fact that Kane told me pretty much the same thing, as well as knowing how the Elite tend to act, I probably wouldn't have believed you." Felicia's voice was rather cold before she cleared her throat once more.

"But I'm telling t-" Dean spoke up before Felicia brought up a hand to stop Dean in his tracks. A soft growl escaped Dean's throat as he was still worked up over his story.

"I know." Felicia scolded Dean in a stern voice before her eyes shifted over towards Kane.

"This isn't the first time that I heard horror stories of the Elite." Felicia continued as she moved a hand to tuck some loose hair behind her ear. "But seeing as you still hold onto those feelings of hatred, it's understandable that you want revenge."

Dean didn't like this feeling of being scolded. He tried his best to stay calm, but if Felicia wasn't going to be on board with trying to bring down the Elite, how was he going to convince the others? Reaching to grab the whiskey glass, Dean gazed down at the golden drink before bringing it up to his lips. Perhaps some booze would help to keep Dean's nerves calm. Otherwise he may very well lash out against the Pride leader.

"Wouldn't you want revenge if someone killed your family?" Dean asked, his voice echoing in the crystal glass before the watered down whiskey splashed on his tongue. The flavor was bitter, burning his taste buds in the process, making Dean almost want to spit it out right away. With a hard swallow, Dean could feel it burning his throat as the liquid made its way further inside of Dean's body.

"My father's death was already avenged." Felicia remarked in a cold tone, her displeasure resting on her face. "Sadly it wasn't by me, but he got justice in the end." Felicia continued as she moved to rest her arms against her legs. "It's not like we're not sympathetic to you Dean…" Felicia started to speak in a softer tone of voice as she frowned.

"I would do anything to bring my dad back. He was my whole world." Felicia continued before crossing her arms loosely over her stomach. "But getting swept away by revenge, it's not healthy. It costs more lives in the end after all…" Felicia trailed off as she glanced towards Kane. "But that doesn't mean I won't help you." This remark surprised Dean the most as he was expecting Felicia to tell him no.

"So," Dean paused, trying to make sure that he had heard right. "You're willing to help me?" Dean's voice wavered in disbelief. It felt like a weight had been lifted off of Dean's chest when saw the small nod to reaffirm that Felicia was on board with the plan.

"Of course it won't be easy…" Felicia spoke up, bringing a finger up to lightly tap her chin in thought. "With the station being out of the Earth's gravitational pull, and no real way to collect any information on it, it's hard to figure out what sort of weakness it would have." Felicia muttered mostly to herself

"Most of the information was lost when the electrical grid went out." Kane spoke up, causing both Dean and Felicia to look towards the quiet leader. "So even if there was some sort of blue print, it would have been lost on the day that the bombs were dropped." Kane continued, which only seemed to spark something inside of Felicia.

"The Electrical grid… of course." Felicia remarked with a small grin on her face. "We can try and use the resources we have here and make something that can deal damage from the ground." Felicia spoke as she got up from her seat. Walking over towards one of the book cases, Felicia's index finger brushed past the worn down books before finally landing on something. Pulling the book out, Felicia started to skim through the pages. "I have an interesting question for you two." Felicia paused as she turned towards the two men.

"What can travel into space at high speed that could actually reach the station without them knowing?" Felica asked, a grin landing on her face while Dean and Kane glanced at each other in confusion. When both of them seemed to fail, Felicia sighed as she flashed them the page that she was on.

"The fastest thing in the universe is light." Felicia spoke up as she scurried over to the two with the book in hand. "Light is able to reach speeds that most modern man made devices couldn't reach. As hard as people tried in the past, they couldn't make anything faster than light!" The excitement in her tone was giddy, almost child-like. "We always have sunlight breaking through our atmosphere. So it would only make sense that we use something like that to weaponize it against the Cowards." To think that something that helps give them some type of source of energy could now be used as a weapon.

Both Kane and Dean exchanged a glance between them before figuring that Felicia was onto something. "But light doesn't have much in the way of destructive power." Dean spoke, before thinking about what Felicia had said earlier. "Unless we can use some type of force that could disrupt the signals on the ship. Everything there uses the space station's main core computer to keep things running. So we'll need to make some type of weapon that can use light as a source of destruction..." Dean sighed towards the end, figuring that it almost seemed impossible.

"Actually we do." Felicia remarked as she flipped the pages in the book before landing on an old photo in the book. "It was something that was discovered way back in the early 1920's." Felicia continued, the giddiness growing. "There was someone who was able to use electromagnetic radiation to make a heat ray cannon. Even though they called it a death ray, it was still powerful enough to produce a light that was visible even in a photograph." All three of them looked over the photo in curiosity, wondering if it was possible to make something like this with the resources that they currently have.

"If I can use the designs from the original, I'll be able to experiment with it and create something even deadlier. We'll have to test it out on the ground a couple of times to figure out exactly how fast it would move to be able to hit an object in space, but we'll be able to do it." Felicia remarked, figuring that it would take a bunch of trial and error before getting the exact science down.

Both Kane and Dean looked over at the old black and white photo. "It looks like it is coming out of a cannon." Dean remarked, tilting his head to take a better look at it. "If we can really use this as a way to get back at the Elite, it won't take long to see that space station being taken down once and for all." Dean remarked in a chipper tone, feeling better than ever about this whole thing.

"Of course!" Felicia chimed as she picked the book up from the table. "Now if I can use lightning to give it more power, we could easily direct it to where we need it. Then, when it is in position, we can blow those cowards out of the sky!" Felicia remarked with a big grin on her face, making it apparent that she was more than eager to hope on board of this now that she had something to work with.

"Lightning? I've heard of it, but I have yet to actually see it." Dean commented, though if he had to guess, it must have been something powerful if it could generate enough electricity to feed into the cannon. Dean had no idea that the purple spurts in the clouds that he would rarely see was the lightning that Felicia had been talking about.

"We tend to have severe rain in the early spring and fall. So we'll have to wait on collecting the key element to be able to see if it can work on a large scale." Kane remarked, figuring that if they were going to go through with this, they would need to do a fair amount of testing before they could know if it would work.

"For now, I can make smaller scales and build them up until spring. If need be, when we have the larger scale of it, we can wait until the next fall season to accomplish our main goal." Felicia commented as she was brimming with excitement for this to happen. It seemed reasonable, and if they were going to do this, they needed to make sure that everything was in alignment for them to succeed.

"Right. I'll work with Ashley with the design." Felicia nodded, before glancing towards Dean. "Well, that is, if she actually agrees to help you." Seemed like this was going to be a collaboration with the other leaders after all. "But seeing as how she doesn't like the cowards either, it won't be that hard to get her on board." It seemed that more of the leaders would be willing to listen to him by Felicia's point of view. Which was a relief since Kane had mentioned that it would be hard for Dean to get their approval for going against the Elite?

"Ashley, she's the tribal leader of which sin again?" Dean asked, trying to remember all of the people. It was going to get confusing when he didn't know them all that well. But thankfully, he had Kane by his side to help him remember. After all, there were two other girls and two other guys to meet with.

"Envy." Kane spoke up, leaning against the armrest of the couch they were sitting on. "She's the youngest of the leaders. But don't let her size fool you." Kane added, a small smirk on his face as he could only imagine the type of things she would say to someone like Dean. "She may look cute and innocent, but she has a sharp tongue." Not that Dean was a fan of people with a sharp tongue, but it seemed like Ashley was the type who had things either go her way or no way at all.

"Not to mention she is almost as big of a pervert as Keaton. Those two are practically siblings when they go into their erotic talk. Like two virgin perverts who don't know the first thing about sex but often talk about it." Kane softly chuckled at the end, recounting something that happened in the past with the leaders. Seems like Dean would have his hands full when it comes to meeting the other tribal leaders.

"Oh that's right, he'll need to go through our right of passage, right?" Felicia asked, leaning back on the couch a little bit after taking her seat back on the couch. "Since you're going to head toward the other clans anyways, he might as well take the chance to kill an animal and become one of us. Might work in his favor, don't you think?" Felicia asked, raising a brow. This caused Dean to become curious as to what she meant by the right passage remark.

"You have a point…" Kane muttered mostly to himself before looking at Dean. "I'll see what I can do to help him out." Kane agreed, not like it made anything clearer for Dean. "Anyways, we probably should be getting some sleep then. Got the long trek ahead of us." Getting up from his seat, Kane wasted no time in heading out the door that they had previously entered.

"Kane's a bit of a loss cause, but he's a good guy." Felicia remarked, pulling out a key from the lining of her corset. "Here. This is the room in which the two of you will be sleeping in." She spoke as Dean took a hold of the key. It was still warm from her body heat.

"We'll be meeting up at my ship in the morning." Felicia remarked as she watched Dean gaze at the key. Dean had been a bit curious as to what kind of ship they would be going on, considering the amount of ruin in the sea just from the bay alone, it was highly unlikely it would be some kind of regular boat. But who knows, maybe they were able to make something that could get around the debris without causing damage to the ships.

"Right. Thank you very much for giving me this opportunity." Dean thanked the woman with a little nod of his head. "If the interior of the ship is anything like the inn, I'll be more than impressed." Dean spoke, a small smile on his face. After being surrounded by marble and gold all of his life, it wasn't hard to impress Dean with interior designs.

Leaving the room, it didn't take long for the smell of beer to hit Dean's nose. After being shut off from the rest of the inn, Dean almost forgot that most of the people who were there were drinking to help wind down after a long day. It didn't take long for Dean to be able to spot Kane standing at the base of the stairs where they had first ran into Felicia.

As the crowd continued to cheer in the background, having the time of their lives, Dean joined Kane's side before showing that he had the key for the room they would be staying in. Without another word, the two had headed upstairs. The wooden floors creaked a little bit with each step, the smell of the wood seemingly lingering in the air once they had gotten to higher ground. The door was the last one in the corridor, giving the two complete privacy for the night. As the door closed behind them, Dean locked the door to keep from having any lost guests making their way into the room.

The ceiling of the room was a bit slanted, though it did have a door that led out to a balcony. On each side of the door rested curtains were pulled back, showing off the scenery of the bay close by. Thankfully the door was closed, otherwise the sound of the waves and the drunk cheering from the patroons outside would have kept Dean up. There were two beds, only having a wide night stand between the two to give them some distance.

Watching as Kane went towards the door, the male started to undo the curtains to slide them over the door. It wasn't for the fact that they had anything to hide, but more so to keep the morning light out that would bring in more light when the sun would hit the water's surface. Heading over to one of the beds, Dean practically crawled on top of it.

"So, that went well." Dean spoke, glancing over towards Kane who was pulling his boots off after taking the other bed and sitting down. "I didn't think she would actually want to help us for a hot second." Dean added with a nervous chuckle at the end, trying to make conversation.

"Well, she is prideful." Kane remarked as he wiggled his toes, the sides of his feet a bit red from all the walking they did. "If she can make something that could take down those who tried to kill off humanity, she'll be on top of the world." Kane spoke, starting to peel off some of the layers of clothes that he had.

"Besides, she pretty much owes me one." Kane added, taking the tunic and gauntlet off, leaving him in the shorts with the long johns. Taking the bag that had his robes inside, Kane pulled them out before slipping it on over the current clothes he was wearing. Tying it off, Kane reached under to take off the clothing underneath. Once he was settled, Kane put the clothes into the bag before kicking it under the bed.

"How does she owe you one?" Dean asked, going to work on his own clothes now. Unlike

Kane, Dean had a lot of layers to undo. Starting off with the accessories, they were a lot easier to get off than putting them on. Dean could already feel the cold air starting to cool off his body after he was trapped in those layers while walking around.

"I don't want to get into it right now." Kane spoke bluntly, walking over towards the small wooden closet in the corner of the room. "Here's a spare robe for you to use. It's not much, but you'll have a bigger selection of clothes once we get on ship." Kane added, figuring that a change of subject was in order.

"Oh?" Dean asked as he glanced at it. It was rather plain looking. "Well as long as I don't have to always wear so many layers of clothing, the better." Dean remarked, pulling the vest and shirt off before taking the robe into his hand. Placing the robe over his shoulders, Dean didn't have much difficult tying it before doing the same thing that Kane did and taking the rest of his clothes off.

"You'll want those layers for the winter months. It gets really cold." Kane reminded him, collecting the clothes and sticking them on the floor close to Dean's bed. "Now, let's get to sleep. We have to travel to Felicia's territory in the morning. We'll be spending a day there before we have to travel to Ashley's place before the winter starts to hit." Kane spoke as he went to his bed to pull the sheets back.

"Yeah...Guess you're right. Best to get some sleep before we travel." Dean remarked, a small yawn slipping past his lips as he crawled into the bed as well. "Though I will be interested in seeing how the rest of the world looks from the ship. Seems like it will be an interesting way to travel." Though Dean didn't exactly know what he was in store in.

Turning off the light, Dean got comfortable in the bed that he wasn't used to. It wasn't as comfortable as the hospital bed, but it was at least something. Closing his eyes, Dean could faintly hear the waves crashing outside.

It might take at least a year for Dean to be able to get his revenge, but at least he wouldn't be alone on this planet. He would enjoy taking in the sights before reaping the benefits of watching the Millennium fall into pieces from the sky. The day of his revenge would happen later than he wanted, but it would still happen. Dean would see to it that it would happen, even if he had to do it himself. But with Kane by his side, anything was possible.

CHAPTER FIVE: *Setting Sail*

THE MORNING SEEMED to come sooner than Dean thought. There was a small splashing noise that Dean was unfamiliar with caused the male to wake up from his slumber. Opening his eyes, the curtains to the balcony were parted ever so slightly. Glancing to the other bed, Dean noticed that Kane was nowhere to be seen. The bed in which the other had been resting in was already neatly made. The small creaking from the bed that Dean was sleeping in filled the room only to be followed by a groan that Dean's lips. There was a cold breeze that seemed to slip from the crack of the door, causing Dean to shiver as his legs were exposed. The robe was disheveled from Dean tossing and turning in his sleep. Adjusting the robe before getting up, Dean walked towards the slightly ajar door, pulling the door open a bit more before spotting Kane already dressed up in the outfit from yesterday as he seemed ready to go.

"Oh, morning." Kane remarked, glancing back at Dean as the sound of the low tide rumbled in the background. The early morning seemed to be peaceful compared to the loud roar of waves from the night prior. The wooden floor underneath Kane's boots was darkened, evident that the storm had come while they were asleep. The clouds seemed to be a distant gray with peeks of orange seeping through the clouds that covered the sea. The sight before him was truly stunning.

"Morning." Dean greeted, walking over towards the wooden railing that Kane had been leaning against. "You know, this is the first time being able to see the ocean so close." Dean spoke, moving to lean against the railing as well. His own hair was a bit messed up as the back of the head had different cow licks standing up. "I used to see bits of the blue and think how clear it must be on the surface. But I guess I was wrong." It almost seemed like Dean was a bit disappointed by what he was seeing. The cold air didn't exactly help as Dean was barely wearing anything that could keep him warm.

"It may not appear that way right now, but underneath the choppy waves, it's like a whole other world." Kane spoke, a soft smile linger on his face as he glanced out at the sea ahead of him. "Before the destruction of the world, I heard stories of people being able to see all kinds of ships against the horizon. But now," Kane spoke, bringing up a hand to rest against his own cheek. "Now it's just covered with debris." Kane paused as he glanced out over the ocean.

"Bits of old homes are nothing more than driftwood now." Kane continued, spotting the metal frame from an old corporate building that had fallen into the ocean. "Old metal frames that used to belong to large structures now act like a barrier reef for school fish to swim through." Kane pointed out towards the nearest one. "Old rusted cars line the bottom of the ocean, completely stripped of any coloring that it once had." Kane let out a small chuckle before draping his arms over the railing while gazing out to the ocean.

"It's sort of haunting to think about how much nature was able to take over while we hid in the bunkers. Forced to ration out food and other supplies. Not being able to advance as quickly as we used to before the bombs were dropped." The smile had seemingly faded from Kane's lips as he thought about the past. Dean could only imagine the horror people witnessed the first time they came out of the shelter. How drastic their world must have been. There wasn't anyone alive from the time that the bombs first dropped, so maybe it wasn't as bad as one might have thought.

"You know, this place is like a whole new world for me as well. I really do feel like a fish out of water." Dean remarked, earning a bit of a glance from Kane. "But it's fine. At least I was able to meet you." Dean added, as a soft smile grew on his face. Glancing towards Kane, Dean was able to take note of the subtle smile that Kane tried to hide from Dean's line of vision. "But now that you mention it, if there are a lot of obstacles in the ocean, how are we supposed to head out? Do you have a clear route or something?" Dean asked, he was a bit confused as he could see the bits of buildings lining the coast, making it almost hazardous to travel in the ocean in its current state.

A mused hum seemed to leave Kane's lips as he pushed back from the railing. "Well, I can't exactly ruin the surprise for you," Kane commented as he turned towards Dean. "But you'll see how we'll be getting across in no time." Kane teased, reaching a hand over to lightly pat Dean on the back before turning on his heels. "Hurry up and get dressed, otherwise you'll catch a cold out here." Turning to face Kane, Dean watched as the other went inside, leaving the door open so that Dean would be able to come inside. The flapping of the curtain gave small peeks of the interior of the room. Seeing how well the room was put together, Dean almost wondered how long it took to make the inn.

As much as Dean wanted to head inside, he was still compelled to gaze out at the slowly churning waters. There were soft caws from the seagulls that flew overhead, but they were flying far away from where Dean was. There was a single one that flew down into view, giving Dean a chance to actually see one of these birds in the flesh. He had often heard that the seagulls were small, often with white slicked feathers and long beaks, but what Dean was seeing seemed almost nightmare fueling.

The feathers were more rigid in nature, almost like rocks from a distance, making it stand out towards the tips of the back of its skull. Its' eyes were a bright yellow with the sclera bloodied, making the golden eyes stand out more. The seagull's beak was thick yet wide, watching as the seagull parted its mouth, Dean could see the line of sharp edges of its saw-like tongue. Its' body was a bit more round in nature, the feet having sharper claws as if to grab its prey easier from underwater. This was unlike anything Dean had ever seen from books he read. Was it even possible for something so small to grow big?

Sure Dean knew of creatures that once were massive had slowly scaled down, but it seemed like the small seagulls from before the bombs dropping got bigger thanks to the radiation. Seemingly changing the birds genetic coding. It almost seemed like the seagull had gone back to resembling more like a dinosaur than a small pesky beach bird. The seagulls' caw was deep, causing Dean to step back as the bird looked at him, watching its wings flapping as it took off, Dean figured it would be best to head back inside for now.

Closing the door behind him, Dean noticed that Kane was busy making the bed that Dean had been slept in. The clothes that he wore were laid out on the bed as Kane turned to look towards Dean. "If you want to take a shower before we head out, you might want to do so now. The water on the ship isn't exactly the hottest like it is on the main lands." Kane remarked, placing his hands on his hips, the pouch against his waist jingling a bit as the chips rubbed against each other.

"How much would it cost to take a shower? I don't have any money, remember?" Dean asked, walking over to the clothes to collect them in order of arrangement that he would have to put them on. Glancing at Kane, Dean took notice of the puzzled look on Kane's face, making it feel like Dean had said something odd. "What?" Dean asked, taken back as he might have said something weird.

"Did those cowards force you to pay to take a shower or something?" Kane asked, his eyebrows knitted together in both disgust and awe that they would even do something like that. Kane would never really understand the hell that Dean went through, but at least he could explain what happened when the occasion would rise.

"Yeah, unfortunately." Dean spoke, letting out a sigh. "We only got a set amount of time for any type of hot water. Then it would cut off the heat, making it slowly trickle down to being freezing cold." Dean started to explain as he held the clothes to his chest. "Not only that, but they would charge us for going over the amount of time allowed." An exasperated sigh escaped Dean's lips as he hated being charged for every nickel and dime. "On top of that, even if we got out early, they would make it so that the water would continue to drip. Forcing us to pay for the full amount no matter what we did." It was an ongoing nightmare, one that Dean was glad to be away from.

It seemed that Kane didn't know what to really say to something like that. He had never expected life to be so controlled to the point where someone couldn't even be allowed the decency of having a hot shower. With the food limitation, the cost of everything making it hard for people to even make a live-able wage, it seemed like there was so much Dean missed out on simply because he had the misfortune of being born on the space station.

"That's horrible." Kane remarked as his brows knitted together. "I don't see why a person should have to pay so much money just so that they would be able to have a hot shower or even a bath." Kane started to speak as he sat down on the bed he had previously slept on the night prior. "I mean, I could see there being such a thing in the ancient times when such technology to be able to make hot water readily available didn't really exist, or that only the rich could afford it at the time, but you lived in what would be deemed a luxury space station only for the wealthy." Kane finished, trying to wrap his mind around it.

"Is that what they had called it before it was launched or something? A luxury space station?" Dean asked, not really even knowing about the history of the space station. After all, why should you learn about something that was just going to be considered your coffin even while trapped inside of a mother's womb? It was just a large metal flying death trap for all Dean knew. Sure he may have been born on the station, but he would be damned if he died on it as well. Even if it came crashing down, he would much rather watch it burn as the last bit of ashes fell onto the soil, allowing the planet to take over the skeletal remains like it often did to anything that had been long sensed abandoned.

"They had built the thing in secret while up in space. People on Earth only knew about it when it became visible in the sky. You can only hide something that big for so long before people would start to notice." Kane remarked, getting up from the bed before making his way over towards Dean.

Lightly placing a hand on Dean's back, Kane couldn't help but smile a bit. "Now, hurry up and take a hot shower. Once you're done, we'll make our way to the ship." Kane remarked, pushing Dean towards the bathroom. "I can't wait to see the look of surprise on your face when you see it." Kane remarked with a big grin on his face. Dean glanced over his shoulder to see the excitement that Kane was displaying, taking note that Kane was more energetic this morning.

With the door closed behind him, Dean glanced around the bathroom. At least it was bigger than what he had expected. There was a countertop that was made from stone with a large indent that was the sink. The faucet had gears on either side of it with the only difference on each gear being the colors that indicated the temperatures being either hot or cold. There was a mirror that was oval in shape with a frame that had the same type of markings that one could see in the main lobby area of the inn.

The walls had a bit of a wooden panel that gave the room a bit of color to it. The wood was dark with a bit of red tints to it, making it a bit more homely. Glancing at the toilet, it looked much bigger than what Dean was accustomed to. It seemed to be made of ceramic with a wooden lid with a craving of some woodland creatures of the past. The cabinet under the sink matched the toilet lid, but it was more elaborate with all kinds of animals on, all seemingly under a mountain, almost looking like a photograph but in wooden form.

The flooring under Dean matched the paneling, but there was a place mat right by the shower. Glancing at the shower, Dean was surprised to see something that resembled a tub, much like the one his parents had him take baths in when he was little. Though unlike having it being a cube, the tub was more elegantly designed. The width of the tub could have easily fit two or three people inside of it. The handles for the faucet were seemingly wooden in design, but had little letters on them to indicate the water temperature.

On the ceiling, maybe a bit more in the middle over the tub, there was an oddly shaped square device with a bunch of holes on it. Dean had never seen anything like it before, making him wonder what the function of it could even be used for. Setting the clothes onto the countertop, Dean noticed that there was something sticking out of the side of the tub by the wall. Pulling on it, it seemed that it was some type of makeshift curtain that was used to keep the floor from getting completely soaked from a shower. Pulling only a bit out, Dean took a mental note to use it when he got inside of the shower.

As Dean stepped into the shower after he hung the robe on the hook that rested on the door, he pulled the wooden guard to the other wall before working the handles to get the perfect temperature. To think, he'll be able to actually enjoy a full hot shower without any worries about time restriction. Sad to say that it made Dean excited, but when you go without something long enough, it gives you an incredible feeling unlike anything you ever felt before. Feeling the water with his hand, it didn't take long for Dean to lift the tab that would cause the shower from overhead to start pouring down on top of Dean like a sudden heavy rain. At first the water was cold, causing Dean to step back from cold water. When he had seen the steam starting to rise, he slipped into the water with ease. Closing his eyes, Dean felt the hot water wash away all of his worries.

As Dean busied himself in the shower, Kane opened the door to allow Felicia inside. Unlike the outfit she was wearing yesterday, Felicia was wearing tight fitting black pants, a ruffled blouse with a tight corset around her slender frame. The boots she wore had a small thick heel as the boot came up just below her knee. She wore a light green sash that had colorful gems decorating the hem as the gloves she wore were made of leather that slid up to her elbow. Wearing her hair up into a messy bun, Felicia had her favorite silver necklace with a silver titanium ring. It looked too large to fit on her delicate fingers, so perhaps it belonged to a man?

"So he's in the shower?" Felicia asked as Kane closed the door behind her. She seemed to stop in front of the bathroom door, taking notice that there was steam coming from the cracks of the door as it seemed to answer her question before Kane did.

"Yeah…" Kane trailed off as he glanced at the door. "Seems like he had it pretty rough on that station." Kane remarked, walking past Felicia. There was a small frown on Kane's face as he walked towards the bed that Dean had been sleeping in prior. Sitting on the edge, Kane glanced up at Felicia who had stepped away from the door leading to the bathroom.

"Apparently they would charge people in his section just to use a certain amount of water." Kane started to explain as Felicia made her way to sit across from Kane. "They even had a time limit on the showers. How greedy can people up there get?" Kane asked, only to hear a small chuckle from Felicia as she made herself comfortable. "It was bad enough when they used to make the water here so toxic that people couldn't drink it." Kane spoke, closing his eyes and shaking his head at the end.

"The same type of people who can only see the monetary value of something, that's who." Felicia lightly scuffed, tucking a stray piece of hair behind her ear. "I can see why he would want to take revenge though. If I was cast out after my parents were killed, I would try to confront my killers too." Felicia remarked before a scowl landed on her face. "Though I would want to see their whole bloodline erased right then and there by my own hands before I could ever forgive them." It was probably due to Felicia's pride of knowing what it is like to want vengeance on people who did her wrong that caused her to easily side with Dean and wanting to take down the Elite for everything that they did.

"I just don't think it is right for us to kill people who are innocent of any wrongdoing simply because they live on the station." Kane spoke, a soft sigh escaping his lips as he bent forward to cup his cheeks in his hands. "We would be no better than those cowards who launched the nukes on the rest of society while they fled into space." Would it really solve anything if they did kill those people? All of those lives would be lost, and for what? To just get revenge? What was even the point of it all? Maybe some would call Kane a fool for not wanting to get revenge, but he had seen what happens when all a person can see is simply getting revenge.

"They didn't think about that when they tried to wipe out humanity." Felicia remarked, as she crossed her arms over her chest. "Why not give them a little taste of their own medicine?" An eye for an eye always makes the whole world blind in Kane's eyes. It didn't seem to make Kane change his mind unfortunately. If she tried to continue her efforts into winning Kane over, she would just simply be beating a dead horse. Instead, a small smirk formed on her lips as Felicia got up to move next to Kane. Sitting down next to the male, Felicia softly chuckled before lightly nudging Kane's shoulder. "So it seems like you've moved on." She lightly teased, causing the poor teen to blush a bit.

"Wha… what do you mean?" Kane asked, trying to play innocent. Though he knew exactly what was going to come next. Since he had known Felicia most of their lives, he could easily read her like a book. As the same could be said about Felicia. She knew exactly what was going on in Kane's mind at that moment.

"You know what I mean." Felicia teased as she wrapped an arm around Kane's shoulders. "You two have become awfully close, especially with that hug." A mischievous grin landing on Felicia's face as she gave Kane that knowing smile. "How he held you tightly in his arms. I bet it made you feel all warm inside." She continued to tease, slightly shaking Kane back and forth. "So does this mean that you no longer have feelings for-" Felicia started to ask before Kane cut her off.

"Shut it!" Kane snapped, shrugging Felicia's arm off of his shoulder. The expression on Kane's face showed off his irritation. "I'll always.. " Kane spoke, only to shut his mouth and close his eyes. It was just a sensitive subject for Kane to really even think about, much less talk about it. "It doesn't even matter.... " Kane's voice trailed off as he softly hung his head. "Besides, there's no way that Dean would even swing that way. I haven't noticed him taking a liking to anyone anyways." Kane finished, glancing away from Felicia.

"I wouldn't really say that." Felicia spoke up, a soft smile on her face. "After all, he didn't really even bat an eye towards me. His attention was all towards you." She remarked, leaning back on the bed a bit while using her arms to prop herself up. "Even while wearing my little get up yesterday, I didn't feel like he was checking me out. Or at least he wasn't giving me a creepy vibe as he looked at me from my toes to my head." Felicia mused, while listening in case the shower turned off. "But I noticed that he tends to keep his eyes on you. And you seem to be keeping your eyes on him too."

"Stop trying to put me in a relationship just because I'm single." Kane was quick to anger, almost like he had heard this song and dance a million times before. "You're just as bad as Keaton and Ashley with that. Always trying to figure out who is top or bottom, who would look good with each other. Life doesn't work like that." Kane snapped a bit, getting up from the bed, wanting to put some distance between the two of them.

"I just want a friendship with Dean. Can't two guys just be friends without making it weird? Just like with a guy and girl being friends, it doesn't mean that they are magically attracted to each other. Same with two girls. We don't need everything to be about sex." Kane spat, turning to look at Felicia who had a surprised look on her face. It wasn't like Kane said something weird. Just because two people simply glanced at each other every now and then, didn't mean that they were automatically attracted to one another.

"We're human Kane. Of course we'll want to have sex and explore another person's body. We crave intimacy." Felicia spoke, getting up from the bed. "To be able to connect to another person, especially if someone makes us feel amazing, it's our dream to be able to find someone we can fall asleep with without worrying that they are off trying to have sex with other people." Felicia softly argued as she watched Kane pacing around the room a bit.

"We want someone who can make us feel like everything is alright in this world. To go without it, it's like you're trying to deny a part of you that makes you human." Kane could see where Felicia was going with this, but there was always that fear of rejection. To be rejected by someone with whom you form a bond with, it was the worst pain that anyone could go through.

"I don't want to deal with rejection... not again..." Kane muttered soft to himself. "To be fooled into thinking that there is someone on this god forsaken Earth that would be able to understand how I feel. To be able to understand when I am feeling down..... or that I am trying to hide my emotions in fear that I won't be accepted...." Kane spoke as his voice wavered ever so slightly, feeling the weight of his problems making his resolve crumble. "I like just being myself around Dean, without the pressure of wanting to make things awkward when there is no indication that Dean feels that way towards me." Kane added, though he felt as if his throat was burning, he paid no attention to it.

"Kane.... you need to stop being a glutton to yourself." Felicia spoke, her voice softening as she could sympathize with the other leader. "You put yourself through such emotional hell. Stop being so hard on yourself. If Dean can see you for the wonderful person you are without making you feel like you have to force yourself into acting this or that way, then I'm sure you'll feel more free." Felicia spoke up as she tried her best to stop Kane from overthinking the situation.

"The chains of regret and self-loathing will slowly disappear before you know it." Felicia added, her heart was in the right place, but it was more complicated than that. "Our society is much better than the society of the past. No one judges each other based on sexual preference anymore. We've given up on following a religion that is centralized around that sort of hatred. That way of the past is gone. We're much freer than ever before." A gentle smile appeared on Felicia's face as she approached Kane.

"That doesn't mean that there aren't people out there who would look at me with such disgust simply because I'm different. I....just...." Kane started to speak, his eyes glancing down towards the floor as his shoulders visibly shifted. "I don't want to see that look of disgust on Dean's face if he found out the truth." Kane whimpered, clenching his hands as he knew the look well when it came to coming out towards people Kane thought he could be honest with. "Even if it means that he has to think that you're with another woman, I'll keep that lie going." Kane finished, closing his eyes, though the look on Felicia's face was that of shock.

"A-A woman? Is that how you're going to treat-" Felicia started to speak before the sound of the bathroom door started to open. It seemed like Dean had been done for a bit as he walked out wearing his clothes he had on yesterday. His hair was still a bit damp, but otherwise it looked to be mostly dry.

"Hey Kane, do you mind helping me with-" Dean spoke, carrying the pair of gloves in his hand, only to stop when he had noticed that Felicia had joined them in the room. "Oh, good morning Felicia. Did you have a restful night's sleep?" Dean asked Felicia. Dean couldn't exactly tell what was going on between the two leaders, but it seemed like they were having a serious discussion that Dean rudely interrupted.

"Oh, good morning." Felicia replied back, though she did have a bit of a nervous smile on her face. Hopefully Dean didn't over hear everything that they had been talking about. "I slept alright. After my second glass of wine, I was able to pass right out." She mused, placing a hand on her hip as she gave Dean a soft smile.

"We'll be heading out soon. Just make your way past the cave to the ship. I think you'll be pleasantly surprised with what we were able to make over the years with the scrap we had from the previous world." Felicia remarked before giving a brief glance to Kane, making sure that the other leader was alright before she would take her leave. Needless to say, getting out of the shelter meant that they had to quickly adapt to their new surroundings. Finding certain supplies wasn't exactly easy.

"I look forward to it." Dean spoke, watching as Felicia walked towards the door in a hurry. As she was leaving, Dean turned his attention to Kane, seeing as how the other seemed to be upset, it was up to Dean to try and cheer the other up. Despite appearing like he didn't know what the two leaders were talking about, Dean was able to hear everything.

While in the bathroom, it was pretty clear what was being said. Even though neither of the two leaders spoke about who exactly Kane had feelings for, it was evident that it was someone of the same sex. It had to be one of the other two male leaders from what both Felicia and Kane said. Dean wouldn't press his luck with trying to get more answers from Kane. Considering that Kane wasn't in the right state to talk about it, Dean knew he would have to be tactful when it came to the sensitive issue.

With the door closing behind Felicia, it was just the two of them. "So?" Dean started to speak as he got Kane's attention. "How did I do without any help?" Dean asked as he flashed a smile towards Kane, all the while Dean moved his hands up and down in front of him. "I'm just not really that flexible enough to be able to get the gloves on by myself. So I'll still need your help with it. If you would be so kind." Dean remarked, holding out the gloves towards Kane, who seemingly took them with a faint smile on his face.

"You did pretty well with this being your second time getting dressed." Kane spoke, grabbing the two gloves from Dean's hand to help the male out with putting them on. As Kane went to work sliding the gloves on, the silence in the room was deafening. Just outside of the closed door, life was starting to flood into the inn. Crew members were getting some early breakfast, causing the inn to fill with delicious smells that would greet the two once they got outside.

Once the last bit of the laces was tied, Kane took a step back to put some distance between them. "Well, let's head out. I don't want to keep Felicia waiting." It was a piss poor excuse coming from Kane, but Dean figured that the other had his reasons. There was plenty of time for them to talk later on as it was, no need to make things even more awkward.

EMERGING from the inn, the morning sun was starting to peek over the ruins that littered the sea. The clouds slowly drifted against the sky as the distant caws of the seagulls barely reached their ears. The tide seemed to be low as the waves barely reached the shore. The wind was still, being barely noticeable as the two men walked along a worn down path that led towards a large and darkened cavern. It almost resembled a cave one would have seen in a type of fantasy movie that had a dragon waiting inside of it with a mountain of gold, daring anyone brave or foolish to enter inside. The entrance of the cave even looked like a dragon's mouth with the stalagmite and stalactite looking like the fangs. The only thing missing was a cloud of hot breath being visible against the cold air, giving off an eerie sensation that one could be eaten whole if they weren't careful.

"Are you sure that this is a cave? Looks more like the mouth of a dragon." Dean commented, standing just outside of the entrance as Kane made his way inside. Glancing up, Dean could see some light entering from two round holes towards the top of the cave as if they were hollowed out eyes of a dragon's skull.

"You have a pretty big imagination. Almost like a kid." Kane teased, walking further ahead since he wanted to get aboard the ship so he could relax a bit. "I think I know what kind of book I should give you to read while we're on the trip. I'll just have to make sure that it is available in the little library section of the ship." Kane's voice echoed, the further he would walk, the further Dean would be left behind.

"That's rich coming from a guy younger than me." Dean called out, taking a step inside of the cave so that he wouldn't be left behind. Since there was really only one path, it didn't take long for Dean to catch up to Kane. As the two walked along the stone and sandy path, Dean couldn't help but look around.

As the morning sun reached the crystals that lined the walls of the cave, Dean was actually taken back a bit by the sheer size of them. The walls seemed to be covered with differently shaped rods of crystals. Some looked as if it was made out of glass from how transparent they were. There was evidence of where people have come to take the crystals off of the walls with the bits of empty spots that were spread throughout the cave. The sound of the waves and the soft breeze made it seem like the crystals were singing a haunting song as a few of the loose crystals gently clanged against each other. It felt like Dean was in a whole other world the further they went into this cave.

"Wow, this place is big." Dean spoke in awe as he glanced around, his voice echoing in the cave. "Is this where you get most of the crystals to use as your power?" Dean asked, seeing as how this could be the source for the crystals he had seen used for the different lights. Though thinking about it, if that was the case, they must not use very much of the crystals if there was still plenty around in this cave alone.

"We have a much bigger cave in which we use to mine them. Even though we could simply make our own, we use different types of crystals for various energy sources. The ones here have a lot of salt, which wouldn't really make for a good conductor. So we leave these ones alone." Kane remarked, making his way past small mounds of sand that seemed to have piled up from the wind blowing through the cave. Thanks to the storm the night before, there was at least a bit of a path from people walking towards the location of the ships. There were a couple of footprints in the sand already that seemed to go in both directions, leading them to the right place.

It wasn't until they reached the exit of the cave that Dean got to see what this so-called ship was. It wasn't anything like he was really expecting, but something that he thought was only possible in something out of a fantasy. Hovering in the sky was a large blimp. It moved slowly in the sky as it departed from the land, heading towards some unknown land. It almost looked like a low hanging cloud as it gained altitude. Soaring as high as the mutated birds that flew beside it, it seemed to fly so effortlessly towards its destination.

The length of the blimp looked to be equal to that of a large stadium, able to carry many people across the vast ocean like Kane had mentioned to him earlier. The underside of the blimp looked to have been made out of wood, giving it some type of ship appearance, per-haps it was used in case something went wrong, allowing those on board to be able to detach in the ocean to keep the cargo and people safe. It seemed like the past mistakes that lead to tragedy helped to shape the blimp into what it was today. Besides that, it seemed that this was a literal flying ship that Dean was seeing, and frankly it was more impressive than living on a space station.

"Wow....." Dean spoke in awe, his eyes unable to look away from the blimp flying into the horizon. "I can't believe that you guys were able to get something like this up into the sky." Dean added, finally turning his gaze towards Kane who looked to be unimpressed. Perhaps it was because this was the first time that Dean was seeing it that he thought that it was amazing, but probably seeing it all the time took the magic out of the flying ship.

"Before we had these airships, we only had one save route across the sea." Kane started to explain as he continued forward on the path before them. "One that was void of life since the water was too acidic for aquatic life to thrive through there, but it was our best route that we had." Kane spoke, moving a hand on the back of his neck to crack it.

"We had to use a fusion of glass and quartz in order to keep the ship from dissolving in the sea. Not to mention that the haul was made up of plastic as well to keep it light enough to keep from sinking. Anyone who was thrown overboard died shortly after, usually in a horrible way. There was no saving people back then." Kane continued to explain, as the wind started to pick up.

"When the storms would hit, everyone went inside. We just couldn't risk other people dying just by steering the ship. It was really hard for us back then." It was a grim reminder that their lives were one slip away from ending before it even began. "But now, we're doing much better with the blimps attached to the ships. So it's not so bad." Kane finished, shrugging his shoulders a little towards the end.

"How did the water get that acidic?" Dean asked, not even sure how something like that could have even been possible. But to think that they were able to make something to adapt to their ever changing environment was amazing. No one would have thought something like that in the Millennium. Or at least, they seemed to lack the knowledge considering that the Elite didn't want to change the station. Why mess with 'perfection', or at least that's how they saw it. Though there could always be room for improvement, the Elite just thought any type of meddling with the station to be hazardous for everyone on the station.

"Don't know." Kane remarked with a small shrug of his shoulders. "Not like we can safely dive in and check it out. But from what I'm guessing, there was probably some type of acid spring that opened up when the bombs dropped." Kane spoke, heading towards a path that seemed to go around the cliff.

"We don't need to use that path any more now since we have flying ships to take us to our locations. It's made traveling so much easier." Kane tucked his arms behind his back as he reached the set of steps that lead up a hill. "We were able to modify the old ships into a sort of luxury liner. It makes the long trips worth the slow pace. Gives something for people to look forward to each season." Kane mused, a soft chuckle leaving his lips as they walked up the steps towards a dirt path that was lined with white chains that were once made of iron that suffered from erosion of the sand and salt from the sea. Some bits of broken iron links were embedded into the path, but the two men didn't pay much attention to it.

"How did you even know that there were people alive when you came out of the shelter?" Dean asked, following Kane's steps on the worn down path. "I bet it was probably a surprise when the first people met others like them." Dean mused mostly to himself, though glanced up at when Kane seemed to stop just shy of the last step on the second set of steps.

"From what I was told, everyone was pretty much connected in the shelters." That comment from Kane made Dean wonder if it was anything like the station where everything was interconnected. "It was like a big underground city that had a small network of roads through tunnels that were always monitored." Kane explained as he turned to face Dean.

"We had a network of communication that used couriers to deliver messages between shelters. They are like the old fashion mailmen one could find before the nukes were dropped." Kane informed Dean about some of their old systems that were no longer in service. "Nowadays we use something similar, but with our airships." Kane didn't see the harm in at least educating Dean what he knew about how the old interstructor worked based on the teachings Kane's father taught him.

"So why were there so many shelters already available? I mean, it's not like you guys would have known what was going to happen, right?" Dean asked, a bit curious as to how there were so many survivors with little notice given. From what Dean remembered, it was a surprise attack when the last member of the selected few had gotten out of the Earth's atmosphere that the Elite launched the nukes to destroy humanity once and for all.

"It was actually thanks to people being a bit paranoid that resulted in the massive construction of shelters." Kane remarked as he crossed his arms over his chest. "There was this mass hysteria that the world leaders and celebrities were going to destroy the world. I mean, technically they did....but during that time people didn't think that was actually going to happen." Kane explained the best he could. "Since there was a rise in the shelters being built, communities came together to make little underground cities. And then... the bombs dropped." Kane chuckled nervously. "Ironic, huh?"

"I guess you could say that, huh?" Dean remarked, his own nervous chuckle leaving his lips. Who would have thought that mass hysteria actually saved people's lives for once. That their own paranoia would end us being the saving grace that humanity needed in order to be able to survive the worse case scenario?

"People were getting fed up with their government telling them that things would be alright while they were busy building a space station to house the rich and elite." The very space station that Dean had been living on for all of his life. "So, those who weren't blind to the falsehood of the so-called news, took action to protect themselves and those that they love." Kane continued to explain, knowing that his own ancestors were one of the few who didn't believe the news and took to their shelter before the end of the world.

"Using government funds for their farm, farmers worked on making sure that they could save their livestock as well as make sure that they had plenty of crops to last them until it was safe for people to come back to the surface. Believe it or not, I came from those same farmers." Kane remarked, almost boasting with pride that he was a result of those farmers who didn't believe the lies being fed to them. All the while Dean imagined the smell that must have filled the underground shelters.

"Sorry for rambling and giving you a bit of a history lesson." Kane apologized, figuring that Dean must have been bored by the lecture Kane was offering him. Not like Dean outright asked for the lesson, but it was appreciated.

"Don't apologize." Dean remarked as he waved a hand in front of him. "I want to know more about the shelters." Dean continued with a smile on his face as he kept his attention on Kane. "After all, I'm sure you have a lot to talk about. So I don't mind it at all." Not like they were going to be short on time or anything. They had to make a stop over in the Pride clan after all.

"I'm glad to hear it." Kane chimed up as he stepped away from the broken fence. "How about this, I'll tell you more about the history of the shelters when we're on the ship. If we keep standing around, the line to board the ship will get a lot longer than it already is." Kane suggested, though the last remark left Dean feeling a bit puzzled.

It wasn't until that Kane walked up the last step with Dean following behind him that Dean realized what the other meant. Glancing around, Dean was greeted to the sight of a bunch of people gathering in one spot. It was unreal with how many people were already gathered there so early in the morning. So many of the people there looked young, some were even around Dean's age.

"Wow, I can't believe how many people are here." Dean spoke, following behind Kane who walked towards another entrance that had a few guards blocking the entrance. In the middle of the group was Felicia, seeming to make sure that there was nothing wrong with the ship before they would take off. It seemed like they were coordinating the crew to make sure that the take off would go off without a hitch.

Glancing around as they walked, it seemed that the presence of an unknown man known as Dean had caught the attention of a small crowd of women. Even though Dean couldn't hear what was being said, it seemed that their attention was towards the brunet male. Dean was no stranger to getting odd looks as it seemed to be a bit of a trend. Rather he was on the station or on this planet, he seemed to always turn heads. Strange how in two completely different settings, there was still so much similarity that it wasn't even funny. Guess things never change no matter one's location.

"Well, this is the last ship to head towards the main land." Kane remarked, glancing towards the crowd of people who seemed to be looking towards the two men. "Look at that. Seems like you've gotten some admirers. It's not every day that you get to see a real life spaceman." Kane teased as he lightly poked Dean's side. "And with word spreading fast, seems like you'll have your hands full while we're on the ship." Kane mused a bit, a small smile on his face. It was still a bit unnerving that people would stare at him while covering their mouths with their hands to prevent someone from reading their lips. Dean simply wished that they had the common decency to at least try to talk to him, rather than talk about him.

"Oh? So this place is just an island?" Dean asked, surprised that the place he had landed was considered an island. He was sure that it was at least a continent from what he could see when entering the atmosphere. "With how large it seemed, it seemed like this was a continent." Catching up to Kane, Dean wanted to make sure that he would be able to hear Kane's explanation as the noise from the engines of the ship made it hard to hear.

"Well there is water surrounding all sides of it. So really it's an island. With the melting of the ice caps, much of the world has been sunk under water. What was once a continent is now an island." Kane explained, shouting a bit so that Dean would be able to hear him. "We'll chat more inside. Let's get in while our hearing is still intact." There was no need to blow out both their ears and throat after all. The roar of the engine was much louder than one would expect. It was a miracle that Dean was able to catch anything that Kane said while they were close by to it.

As they ascended up the set of steps to enter into the air ship, Dean felt a bit of nostalgia wash over him. The sound of the dull engines roaring through the cabin was similar to the roar of the space station that lulled Dean to sleep every single night for the last ten years. That small pod was the only piece of heaven on that hell hole. It made Dean feel a bit more at home, if that made any sense. Being trapped in a floating ship that was packed like a can of sardines might make other people a tad bit nervous, but it was second nature to Dean. After all, when that was the type of environment you were raised in, it didn't make you feel cramped.

Taking a look around the interior, Dean was surprised at the different design that was chosen for the air ship. Unlike the inn where they had stayed, the interior design seemed to have a mixture of dark cherry oak with more floral designs etched into the wood. The windows that lined the doors were stained with elegant designs that almost resembled paintings. Each one was completely different from the other. There was one that was like a meadow with different flowers with animals that Dean had never seen before. Another one stained window seemed to have a body of water like a lake with a mountain in the distance. The forest surrounding the lake was so well detailed that one could almost envision themselves standing on the banks of the lake and admiring the view.

"Dean." Kane called out, stopping at a door with a stained glass painting of deer in the middle of the frame. "This will be our room." Opening the door, Kane already headed inside as Dean caught up to him. Pressing the door open, it didn't take long for Dean to close the door all the way. Watching Kane take a seat on one of the two chairs in the room, Dean took this chance to glance around as he walked to the other chair to sit down.

Against the wall to Dean's right was a pair of bunk beds that had a single ladder at the foot of the beds. Underneath the ladder rested a black out curtain for the bottom bunk to allow for some privacy. In the middle of the frame separating the two mattresses was a wood piece of art work of a field surrounded by trees with a few deer grazing in the long grass. In a way, it sort of reminded Dean of the field in which he had landed in when Dean first arrived.

The trimming of the interior of the bunk beds was wooden, the corners of the bunk bed had small crystal lighting to give some type of light for when it gets dark. A switch for the lights rested just outside of the bunk by the headboard, allowing for each person to be able to turn the lights off and on for their own beds. Underneath the lower bunk rested a few drawers for personal use, which made sense as they were going to be on board of the air ship for roughly a week as they traveled towards this mainland.

"You'll want to strap in. Sometimes the take off and landing are a bit rough. Especially for new flyers." Kane explained, slipping straps from behind the seat. Dean couldn't help but blink a bit in surprise since he had never seen something like that before. If Dean wasn't traveling with Kane, he would have never known about the straps, unless someone actually told him about it before taking off. "It gets pretty bumpy at take off." Kane added, reaching over to pull something out of the drawer in the table that separated the two chairs.

Taking that advice in mind, Dean didn't say anything as he got into the seat. Just watching Dean fumble with the straps caused Kane to snicker a little bit, resulting in Dean becoming a bit flustered. "I've never had to deal with straps that were on the back of a seat before. How am I supposed to know how this works?" Dean grumbled to his defense as Kane laughed at him. "It would be like me expecting you to know how to buckle up in one of the space shuttles that we have. It's not as easy as it looks." Even though it was a decent comparison, it only seemed to make Kane brim with how embarrassed something so small could make Dean get defensive.

"I didn't think you would get so defensive." Kane teased, leaning back against the chair a bit. The chair didn't exactly have much to offer other than the royal blue coloring seemed to make it stand out in the room. There were some gold leaf designs that decorated the cushions, a bit of an odd choice, but at least it was comfortable to sit in. Considering that the two would be seated for a while, there were worse choices that they could be seating in.

"And you didn't have to grow that smug smirk on your face, and yet here we are." Dean remarked, crossing his arms over his chest, pouting in a way that seemed to keep a soft smile on Kane's face. "How bad is the take off anyways?" Dean asked, a bit curious now as to what happens when the ship actually lifts up from the ground. Considering how heavy the ship appeared to be, it caused Dean to ponder how it would lift up from the ground.

"Just bad enough to make you throw up if you get easily motion sick." Kane remarked as he instinctively placed a hand on his stomach. "Considering that today the wind is light, it might not be so bad." Kane remarked, opening up a small empty bag. If it was going to be bad taking off when the wind is light, Dean would hate to see how it would be like if the wind was really strong. Most likely there would be no way that the ship would be able to fly if that were the case.

"Sounds like how it felt when my shuttle came crashing down." Dean remarked, his eyes going towards the little white bag. "Like I was riding some kind of animal that was trying to buck me off." Dean commented, though he didn't want to go through that again. It was bad enough the first time. "What's that in your hand?" Dean finally asked, raising an eyebrow as he never seen anything like the small bag that Kane held open in his hands.

"Oh this?" Kane asked as he held up the small bag to Dean. "It's a throw up bag." Kane started to explain. "Normally I don't get sick. But considering how bumpy it can be, it's best to simply use the bag in case….something does happen." Kane continued, a bit of a nervous smile on his face. So it seemed that Kane had a bit of motion sickness. With how often the male had to travel around, Dean was surprised that Kane could get sick so easily. "You don't want to try and scramble towards a bathroom. You'll only make a bigger mess." Seems like Kane was speaking from experience.

"I can only imagine." Dean remarked, leaning back in the chair. It seemed that the talk was making Kane a bit self conscious. There was no shame in throwing up if one had motion sickness. Though Dean never experienced it, he was at least conscious enough to not bring it up.

ONCE it seemed like everyone was settled in, and everything had been checked for their take off, the ship was ready to take off. The ship started to shake slowly at first, before the shaking started to increase as the engines got closer to taking off until the ship started to lift up from the ground. The feeling of the ship taking off felt much like the elevator that Dean used to take to his work station. Sure it felt like it pulled on your stomach when it lifted up, but once you were used to it, it was something that wouldn't affect him for the rest of Dean's life. However, it seemed to cause Kane's face to get a little green. Thankfully Kane didn't seem to throw up, but he did seem to go limp in the chair.

"I hate taking off . . " Kane groaned, placing a hand on his stomach. "It never gets any easier." A small whimper from the other male made Dean chuckle a little bit. "It's not funny spaceman. Just because you might be used to it, doesn't mean us normal people are." Kane grumbled a bit, resting his head back a bit. Small whimpers could still be heard from Kane as the ship rocked back and forth ever so slightly.

"Can I get you something to help you recover?" Dean asked, feeling more fit to be able to do some errands for Kane while the other recovered. At least Dean could be somewhat useful. Plus it would give him a chance to be able to look around the ship while Kane was recovering.

"I guess I could go for a lemon lime drink. Maybe some rice crackers as well." Kane remarked through his groans, his eyes glancing up towards the white ceiling. "But we'll have to wait a bit before we can move around." Kane started to explain as he glanced towards Dean. "We have to level out the ship so that we don't hit a lot of turbulence. Don't need to have people slamming into each other like they are trying to do the horizontal dance." Kane remarked, placing a hand over his eyes, as if the lights above were too bright for him.

"Odd way of saying it, but I'll take your word." Dean spoke up, finding it a bit entertaining that Kane was suffering this much. For someone who seemed to like seeing Dean struggle, the same could be said for Dean. It wasn't like he took pleasure in seeing Kane suffer, but did find it a little amusing. "So where would I need to go to get you a drink and snack?" Dean asked, not knowing his way around the ship.

"You'll want to head towards the dining cart." Kane remarked as he kept his head tilted back. "You can put in an order for the room. We're on the Crystal floor, room 1109." Kane spoke, moving to undo the belt at this time. "After you put the order in, feel free to roam around the ship. I'll be in bed for most of the day." Kane continued to talk, slowly making his way towards the ladder. Dean watched carefully, making sure that Kane didn't need any assistance.

Seeing as how Kane made it up into the bed so easily, Dean unbuckled himself before hearing a chime over in the room. In one of the corners of the room, there was a small speaker that was used to make announcements. It reminded Dean of the alarm and speaker that was above the door in his little pod.

"Good morning ladies and gentlemen. You're free to move around the rooms now. Please keep in mind that there will be pockets of air that we will encounter during our trip, so keep your surroundings in mind as you travel around." An unfamiliar voice started to speak. "Breakfast will be starting soon, so if you wish to grab a bite, please make your way towards the dining cart located on the Ruby floor." Dean continued to listen, trying to take note of the different floors in this airship. Hopefully he could at least find a map to help Dean navigate the ship. "Lunch will be ready around one, and dinner will be available past four. If you need anything, feel free to contact any of the personnel working on the ship. Have a wonderful day." With that, the voice stopped and a small clicking sound could be heard to signal that the broadcast was over.

"Seems like things never change. Though the last time I heard an announcement like that, it was when I still went to school." Dean thought to himself, moving to get up from his seat with a little stretch. "Alright, I'll head down to the dining room." Dean spoke up as he made his way towards the door. "Is there anything else you want me to get while I'm away?" Dean asked, walking over to the bunk beds to see that Kane was already curled up in the blankets.

"No. I should have everything I need from the last time I went to the mainland." Kane spoke, nuzzling against the pillow that felt cold against his face. "Go and make some new friends. Maybe have something to eat." Kane spoke through the pillow, making it almost hard for Dean to hear him. "I can't exactly eat right now with how upset my stomach is. But I know you'll like the food." Kane remarked as he pulled his face away from the pillow to look at Dean, a small lingering smile featured on his face. Though it looked like Kane was ready to pass out, Dean at least wanted to make sure that Kane was at least comfortable.

"I'll make sure to have them bring you up something for your stomach." Dean spoke, lightly patting Kane on the back. It was something that Dean's mother often did, a bit of reassurance that he would be able to pull through. Though Dean didn't know if it would help Kane, it was at least worth a try, right?

Slipping out of the room, Dean glanced around the small hallway. Seemed like no one was really around, meaning that he would be able to be by himself. Glancing around Dean noticed that there was a chart with a small layout of the ship. It seemed that the ship was made up of four sections. The Crystal floor had a few rooms for crew members, as well as a small library and seating area for people to look out and enjoy the view.

The Amber floor housed the rest of the rooms for the passengers, with a bathroom seemed to linger in between four rooms at a time, with the rooms with pirate bathrooms being towards the stairway that lead towards the Crystal stars.

The Ruby floor seemed to hold most of the entertaining and dining sections of the ship. While the Emerald floors were where the cargo bay was located. So Dean would need to go down two flights of stairs in order to get to the dining room, at least that was good to know.

Taking a few steps back, Dean looked around his environment. There was a room right next to the one that Dean had just come out of, at the end of the hall, more towards the entrance that they had come in through had a door with the stained glass figure of an elk. Much like the deer, the elk had long antlers that branched out.

The design behind the elk was more mountain based than the one of the deer. Narrow trees lining the base in small clumps while the elk seemingly stared at you. Under the elk were the initials A.G. Blinking in surprise, Dean looked at the door he had previously come from. Sure enough, the initials K.F was etched into golden plates. "So, are these rooms mostly used for the leaders and their companions?" Dean asked, moving down to take in the other doors. Were they all the same on the inside or were they different?

Carefully making his way down, the next door next to Kane's room, had a bull in the stain glass. It seemed like the bull was in a prairie field. The grass seemed to graze against the bull's knees as the high hills of the prairie decorated the background. Underneath was the initials K.F. Dean couldn't help himself, reaching down, he took a hold of the door handle to see if perhaps the room was open.

Unsurprisingly, it was locked. "Huh. Well at least it seems that they have the common sense to lock their rooms when they aren't flying." Dean murmured to himself. A soft sigh escaping his lips as he glanced towards the next room. The next one had a bear on it, seemingly in a river bed with a fish in its mouth. The initials read A.P. Dean couldn't help but think about how ironic it would have been if the bear was in a pond rather than in a stream.

Moving down to the last two, Dean noticed that there was one with a wolf, seemingly howling at the moon surrounded by thick trees. There was a little unsettling feeling he had gotten from the wolf. Thinking back when Dean first landed, he had seen someone with a wolf skull on their head. Was that person that shot him down the same person that was staying in the room? With a small shake of his head, Dean felt like there was no way that was possible. Underneath the wolf stained glass portrait was the initials M.M. Glancing down, Dean couldn't help but wonder, would the deer prefer the company of the bull or of the wolf?

While in thought, the sound of a door slowly creaking open interrupted Dean's train of thought. Glancing towards the door with the stained glass tiger, Felicia came into view. "Well, if it isn't the wonderful spaceman." Felicia teased as she closed the door, walking over towards Dean who had been lost in through. "Surprised you're up and walking." Felicia remarked before moving to put her hands behind her. "But then again, I guess you're used to being pretty weightless considering where you came from." She continued before glancing towards the door that currently had Kane resting inside of it. "Poor Kane must be trying to sleep it off?"

"I was heading to get Kane something for his stomach in the dining room actually." It wasn't exactly a lie, as Dean was just simply looking at the stained glass lining the door. "I was just admiring the stained glass on the door." Dean commented as he looked towards the door closest to him. "They seemed really detailed. What do they stand for?" Since Dean couldn't exactly ask Kane, he might as well ask someone else who is a tribal leader.

"Oh these?" Felicia remarked, walking over towards the door she had just come out of. The stained glass on her door appeared to be a tiger, slowly slinking out of the tall grass with menacing eyes. Just like the rest, it had the initials F.M lingering on the bottom. "These are the animals that were our first kill when we came of age." Felicia remarked, a big grin on her face. It would be no surprise if Dean didn't exactly believe that she was able to take down a tiger on her own.

"Wait.... you took down a tiger?" Dean asked, the shock on his face only seeming to amuse Felicia. "How did you even kill something like that?" If anyone were to take down a tiger, Dean would have imagined it being a man who was strong enough to fight back against the tiger's powerful fangs and dangerous claws. Not some pretty girl who might have been able to take down something like turkey more than a tiger.

"I'm surprised you even know what a tiger is." Felicia mused as she crossed her arms under her chest. "Then again, it wouldn't surprise me if those rich assholes kept them around just to hunt them." Felicia commented in a bitter tone. Reaching a hand up to take out a key from a pocket within her shirt, Felicia moved close to the door and locked it since it wasn't going to be used. With the door being locked, Felicia tucked the key back into her blouse, keeping it safely on her at all times. It was a general rule that the leaders keep their doors locked when they aren't in there. It was mostly to keep nosy people like Dean from entering into their rooms and going through the leaders' belongings.

"Isn't that the pot calling the kettle black?" Dean remarked, glancing away as he didn't see the use of having to kill a dangerous animal for sport. It seemed pointless. Maybe if it were a life and death type situation, he could see the merit behind it. Dean could see Kane being the type of person who wouldn't kill something simply for sport. But then again, what do you expect from a tribal leader who used every part of their kill for everyday uses.

"I wouldn't exactly say that." Felicia spoke, moving a bit closer to Dean before patting the other on the shoulder. "I killed it because it was killing our cattle. I respect nature just as much as Kane. But I couldn't simply stand back and let the beast continue to kill our cattle." At least it seemed like she had some sense then, making Dean feel like a jerk for simply assuming that she killed for the sport of it. "The tiger was alone. It wasn't part of a pact. It looked as if it was starving, so I couldn't exactly blame it for killing our cattle for its food supply." She continued, retracting her hand. "We even put up a fence to protect the cattle, while keeping the tigers at bay." Felicia continued to explain as she tucked some hair behind her ear. "We even offer the wild animals parts of our fresh kill. We give them something to make their lives easier as well as our own. It's a bit of give and take. We take from nature and we give it back. That's how we've been able to survive for so long."

Give and take? The concept was a bit foreign to Dean, considering that all the Elite ever did was take without giving. Perhaps that was why they were not going to survive for very long. At least, not if Dean had anything to do with it. "Still, it's pretty impressive that you were able to take out a tiger." Dean remarked, figuring that he should at least show some interest in her story. Who knows, maybe she would even give him some information on Kane that the other wasn't willing to share just yet.

"Yeah…." Felicia trailed off, moving her right leg behind her a little. "Anyways, I'm heading down to get some breakfast. Want to join me?" Felicia asked, surprising Dean. Perhaps she was wanting to use Dean for some information of her own. Talk about a little give and take. Not like Dean could really refuse her. They would both be heading in the same direction anyways. So maybe having a bit of company wouldn't hurt.

"I don't see why not." Dean remarked, a small shrug of his shoulders. It wasn't like Felicia was bad company or anything. Besides, there were some things that Dean needed to get answers about. Answers that Kane wasn't willing to give, but maybe Felicia would.

Walking down the steps, Dean took note of the surface of the stairs. Different fragments of crystals lined the base of the tread, seemingly being covered by a thick protective case that could withstand people walking over it. A dim light seemed to shine through, making the different colored crystals shimmer. The railing hand a cherry wood banister, the iron bars that lined it had an elegant floral design as the bars were bent this way and that.

The amount of detail that went into the staircase itself was significant at the level of detail that went into making the ship's interior decorating show how much the designer wanted to make the flying ship into something that people would enjoy traveling in. As they reached the base of the steps, Dean glanced back to see the design on the riser. In a way, it sort of looked like an inkblot test with the way the white engraving design nestled on the base of the cherry wood.

As they reached the Ruby section, Dean was surprised at how large it was. It was almost like they were on some sort of luxury ship that used to sail the vast ocean of the Atlantic. Though it didn't have a large ceiling, due to the ship being four floors high, there were rows of seats that would be able to hold at least two people per table. There were some seats that were seated next to the windows, giving a view of the sea below.

Dean could only imagine how it must have looked. He had only seen the ocean up from space. Granted it wasn't much from the distance he was while in the station, but he still would love to actually look over the ocean as they flew directly over top of it. Perhaps not right away, since he did want to talk to Felicia. If they sat down next to a window, Dean would get lost at looking at the ocean, possibly making his food cold.

The tables had a thin white cloth on top of the square table. There was plenty of room for people to shift in their seat if needed. Glancing towards the ceiling, Dean spotted small flickering lights from the crystals dangling overhead. If it was dark, Dean would have sworn that he was gazing into the vast universe. Parting his lips a little, Dean was surprised at how well put together the lights had been. The sun from outside took away the beauty of the ceiling, at least for now, but Dean could only imagine how beautiful it must be at night when the sun went down. He'll certainly have to come back later for dinner to enjoy the lights. But with the help of the sun peaking through, Dean could see the thick black line connecting the lights. Making it seem like they were fairy lights. Regardless, when it was dark, the cords would become invisible, making for romantic lighting.

"Well, shall we pick out a seat?" Felicia asked, giving Dean a small nudge in order to snap him out from staring at the ceiling. It seemed that as Dean gazed up at the lights, it had caught other people's attention. Some people were wondering what it was that Dean had been gawking at, only to snicker since most were used to the lights. Considering that Dean was literally an outsider, he couldn't get over the fact that they were able to use crystals as a sort of light source.

"Yeah.... but I do have to head towards the bar to send Kane the items he requested." Dean remarked, spotting the large bar. There was a singular man standing behind the bar that was, much like everything else, made out of the dark cherry wood. The glasses hanging upside down sparkled in the overhead lights, showing that they were well taken care of and thoroughly cleaned. The seats didn't have much of a backing to them, but it seemed that they did pivot to a point. The man was an older gentleman wearing a buttoned up shirt with two bands around his biceps. He didn't look frail, but rather well put together.

"Alright. I'll find us a seat. Just remember to put it under Kane's tab." Felicia called out, watching Dean leave as she waited for someone to seat her. It wasn't very crowded yet, mostly because people were still unpacking their belongings or they ate elsewhere before boarding. Though Dean didn't know where they would be able to eat, possibly making their own food before getting on the ship? If it costs money to eat, Dean could see why some people would skip meals. After all, that's what he did when there wasn't enough money to get enough food for himself. Or perhaps they were getting much needed sleep? That's probably what Dean would end up doing if he didn't take a shower beforehand. Either way, as long as it wasn't loud, Dean didn't mind being around others.

"Hello. I need to have some room service delivered." Dean greeted the man with a curt nod. Even though he didn't exactly like talking to most people, at least Dean had the common sense to be straightforward and to the point.

"What room number?" The man asked, pulling out a pad of paper and a small pen that was tucked behind his ear. Seems like there were plenty of people who would get some room service. Judging by the amount of lingering bits of paper that seemed to stick to the spiral of the notepad this was only the start of the breakfast rush.

"It's for room 1109 on the Crystal floor. It should be under Kane Flores. He just needs a lemon lime drink for his motion sickness. Oh, and some rice crackers too." Dean wanted to make sure that the other something to eat. Even if it wouldn't be too much, something was better than nothing.

It seemed that the man was smirking a bit at the order. Was there something funny that Dean wasn't aware of? "Ah, Kane's usual." The replied, jotting something down on the piece of paper that Dean couldn't see. "We'll get it right up to him." The man finished, giving Dean a small curt nod before heading towards the door that led towards the kitchen. Seems like the members on the ship at least knew of Kane's motion sickness, so that was good at least. Now all Dean had to do was find Felicia and get some food in his stomach.

Turning around to scan the room, it didn't take long for Dean to locate Felicia. She seemed to be seating more towards the middle of the room, meaning that Dean wouldn't be distracted by the vast ocean they were sailing over. Taking the seat across from Felicia, Dean picked up the menu to have a look over what they offered. There certainly was a decent amount that he could order, but he didn't know what was good or what wasn't up to his liking. After all, Dean only had hospital food since he arrived on the planet.

Eventually Dean landed on something along the lines of an omelet for his dish. Felicia ordered something with an odd name to it that Dean wasn't even going to try and repeat as it sounded more like a tongue twister than anything else. Once their orders were placed, Felicia neatly folded the napkin in her lap. Dean copied her since he wasn't aware of there were any type of table etiquette. Catching sight of it, it seemed the way that Dean mimicked her caused Felicia to smirk.

"So Dean." Felicia started to speak, catching Dean's attention. "Would you like to know a bit of dark history?" Felicia asked, watching the look on Dean's face going from a bit confused to having his interest peaked. Felicia leaned in closer to the table, her elbows resting just on the edge of the table as her hands interlocked, her chin rested against her slender fingers as the smirk never faded from her lips. "I'm about to tell you the story of a brutal man named Nero. The very man, who started the sin wars, and how our precious Amelia put a stop to it."

It was a bit of a surprise how one person would be able to change the world that the others had grown in. How it seemed like humanity as a whole was able to advance so much just by one person's ideas. Even towards the end it seemed that the one behind the ideas that helped to advance society forward would easily turn everything on its head. The story of Nero wouldn't be an easy one to listen to towards the end, considering all the bloodshed that happened on the man's part before the current leaders took their new positions. It was easy to see why Kane opposed more bloodshed. Despite the history of one man's start to change the world to be a better and more productive place, it was still a lot to take in. Dean simply did his best to follow the story. Even if it was hard to hear.

CHAPTER SIX: *Nero*

FIFTEEN YEARS AGO a crew of expeditioners crossed the mountainous landscape towards one of the known shelters that had seemingly gone silent over the years. Whether these shelters had cut themselves off, or some type of misfortune caused the shelters to go quiet, the expedition team had to at least figure out what was going on with those shelters in order to have society come together as a whole. The notion of people coming together wasn't a new one, but being spread out without any means of contact was a new challenge that the remaining humans had to overcome.

After reaching a fair amount of shelters, the expeditioners found themselves coming up on a run down city with large pillars with elegant designs along the base of the ivory covered pillars. The air was warm as the flowers started to peel open to greet the new day. Though the sun was still behind the mountains, the crew settled down by some ruined buildings that housed the shelter. The place they settled at appeared to be an old market, which possibly saved many people who were out shopping on that devastating day. The shelter was located towards the back in a warehouse that could provide temporary shelter, allowing for people to file down into the shelter, as well as bringing down last bits of food to help stretch out the bit of food that was already down there.

The first three members of the team had started inwards, leaving a small crew behind in case anything happened. As the three members started down the basement steps of an old warehouse, two men and one woman, walked down the worn down steps. Each wore a gas mask to protect them from any type of fumes that may have lingered in the dark depths of the unknown warehouse. The steps were broken into uneven steps, making it tricky to reach the lower sections by foot if they were not prepared.

The first male who was leading the team seemed to have a permanent scowl on his face under his mask. His eyes were barely visible, in the darkness, but they were a cold earthy brown with scattered pigments of green. His skin appeared to be slightly reddened from the sun. The sides of his head had been shaved off, leaving a rugged punk mixed with military style for his hair. A tribal tattoo was etched on his neck, barely noticeable against his camouflage top. The sleeves were rolled up, exposing the dark black gloves he wore, the color seemingly matching the rubber overalls that was once used for fishing in a river, now used for protection when wading through murky water..

"I don't think we're going to find anything down here." The punkish man spoke, holding up an old hand flashlight that came from a previous shelter they had explored, using it to sweep some light against the basement walls, the water resting just above his knees. "You sure it's supposed to be in this one?" He asked glancing back towards a woman holding a map. Even though it looked brand new, the map was at least a couple hundred years old.

"Well it's either in here, or in one of the other buildings around here." The woman re-marked as she looked at the map, the light shining through to the other side. "But this is the city we were supposed to head to. Hopefully we'll find something here." The woman of the group spoke through the gas mask. Her short appearance was apparent between the two men. Her dark red hair was tied up in a short ponytail. The shirt she wore was a dark navy blue sleeveless top, a pair of worn down dog tags jingled against her top. Steel gray eyes scanned the surroundings, making sure that they weren't getting into anything too dangerous.

The water seemed to rise up to her mid thighs against the rubber overalls while the water rested just around the men's knees. With a small flashlight in her hand pointed to the thin map, a thin strap wrapped around her wrist to secure the small flashlight to her, the light was just bright enough to see where it was pointing to. "We're just lucky that this wasn't completely covered in water." She added, taking another step before tripping over something in the water. Landing face first in the water, the woman flailed around as she was mostly submerged in the water, leaving nothing dry. It would have been comical if it wasn't for the fact that there could have been some dangerous hazards in the water.

"Lizzie!" The other man shouted, rushing over to help the poor woman open up. The man was a bit more burly than the other male. With a slightly messy mop on top of his head. His dirty blond locks seemingly coming down towards his eyebrows that rested under the gas mask. Wearing a dark red short sleeve shirt, he helped the woman up by grabbing her arm. "Are you alright?" The man asked in a worried tone. Lizzy looked up at him, completely drenched, seemingly glad for his help as she struggled to stand up on her two feet.

"Y-Yeah. I'm fine." Lizzie reassured him as she clung onto the man who rushed over to help her. "Thanks Mark." She added, taking a step back from the man who helped her up. " I guess I should head up and get changed in some new clothes." Lizzy commented, feeling the water seep through her clothing. "I'll have to burn these now," Lizzy paused as she glanced down her soaked top. "Considering that we don't know what could be in this water, best not to leave it to chance." The very thought of what could even be clinging to her body was a little unsettling. "Not to mention I'll have to make sure that the map gets dried." She finished, holding up the damp map, the words on it slowly starting to become illegible. It was a shame that they didn't have a spare. But accidents were bound to happen.

"Good idea. We'll stay down here and look around." Mark spoke, watching to make sure that she was at least able to make it towards the stairs in one piece. A small sigh left Mark's lips though the mask before he turned to look at the other male. "Seriously? You couldn't lift a single finger to help her?" Mark scolded the man, crossing his arms over his chest, the rubber suit he was wearing mostly dry. "Come on Chris, the least you could do is talk to me. We're on the same team for crying out loud." Mark continued to nag Chris, resulting in the punk looking male to glare towards Mark in annoyance.

"The least you could do is communicate to us. You know, like what a team is supposed to do when they are on dangerous missions like this." Mark was the type of guy who tried to get along with everyone, wanting to see everyone coming together as a society once again. Most thought that Mark was a bit childish, or at the very least naive to believe that people could come together as a whole. At least, that's what Chris thought of him.

Chris tried to play it off, not wanting to really deal with the unnecessary drama, though almost having one of your colleagues drown wasn't exactly unnecessary drama. Chris just didn't like dealing with people altogether. He was here on a mission after all, one that he had taken of his own free will, though now he was regretting it. There had been a bit of drama as of late with the expeditioners. The typical need for some type of companionship while on a long journey, a budding romance if you will. Chris was more of a solitary creature, not wanting to get caught up in the typical human emotions that people would often find themselves in, especially if it meant that they could die along the journey. Chris figured that it would be easier to just not get attached.

"Fine…" Mark sighed in defeat. "Be the lone wolf of the group." Mark grumbled as he moved to take a step, only to stop when it seemed like there was something in the water. Pointing his own flashlight into the green looking water, Mark's eyes widened at his finding. There, in the dirty water, was a valve that was used for the purpose of making the shelter air tight. That is, if they had properly closed it once everyone was in the shelter. "Hey Chris! I think I found it!" Mark exclaimed, getting Chris' attention. If his mask wasn't hiding it, Mark would have been smiling from ear to ear.

The sound of the water splashing echoed in the basement, waves in the water distorting the image of the underwater valve as Chris approached the area where Mark had his light pointing. As Chris joined him, it seemed that the two had indeed found what they were looking for.

"Good work Mark. Seems like you're good for something after all." Chris spoke, kneeling down to take a better look at what he was seeing. Using his own light, Chris traced the edge of the entrance, old bits of rumble and algae nestled on the writing. Reaching a hand down, Chris was able to remove some of the blockage from the letters, seeing the words **Fallout Shelter** spelled out Italian.

"Well, it was Lizzie who found it." Mark spoke up, causing Chris to glare towards him in annoyance at the love-sick puppy Mark was for Lizzy. "You should really thank her when we get back up to the surface." Mark finished as he stood up. Chris couldn't understand why anyone would subject themselves to acting like a fool for someone who doesn't feel the same way. Perhaps it was just a primitive thing to want to show the person you have feelings towards just how eager you were to prove to them that they would have a better life with you. Lizzie wasn't exactly the type of girl who was easy to get along with. Considering that Chris was her half brother, Chris just couldn't see the appeal that Lizzie had to offer.

"Well, we should head back up and let everyone know we found it. The sooner we can get the water level down, the sooner we can rescue the people trapped in there." Mark remarked in his usual cherry tone. However, Chris had this feeling that the people weren't exactly trapped and helpless as Mark would envision.

"That is, if it isn't a watery grave." Chris grumbled, moving to stand up, the dirty water running off of the rubber suit. The reality was most of the shelters that had gone silent meant that people were dead. There was some that appeared to have been the overly religious type, going as far as to commit suicide as a whole rather than wanting to try and live out the rest of their lives underground. The smell alone in those places wasn't exactly the best. But they were able to find some interesting leftover items, at least ones that weren't covered in black mold that is.

There would be a couple of shelters that actually had a few people left, seemingly excited to be able to see other people still alive. Then there were people who seemed shocked that there were others still alive. Sure they were happy, but most of them seem uninterested to rejoin society as a whole. Typically they would just restart their own little colony once they got on the surface. Not like Chris had cared, he was just doing his job of getting some type of connection to that particular shelter.

"Why do you always have to be a downer about everything?" Mark was quick to snap, annoyed at how Chris could never find anything good about what they did. "Would it kill you to be a bit more optimistic about what we'll find in the shelter?" Mark grumbled, watching Chris walk past him.

No matter how often Mark tried to be friendly towards Chris, the other seemed to always bring the mood down. It could get annoying after a while, but Mark knew he had to get along with Chris if he wanted a chance to get with Lizzie. Sure Lizze was just as stubborn as Chris, but she would never look at everything as half full or empty. But then again, that could simply because Mark was in love with her and often tried to see nothing but the best in a woman like her.

"Because," Chris started to speak as he got to the edge of the steps. "Unlike you, I'm a realist." Chris snapped as he glanced over his shoulders to the other male. The lingering foot marks from Lizzie helped them find their way back. Though it wasn't like they had very far to go.

"I don't have my head up in the clouds, pretending that everything is alright when it's not." Chris spoke up to break the silence in the room. "For all we know, those people drowned and any type of research that we could use would be gone with it." It wouldn't be the first time that something like that happened. If they wanted to make the best of this world, they needed to have every type of culture come together to make rebuilding the world a reality.

"It's not likely that they are dead." Mark retorted back, trying his best to hold back any anger he was feeling at the moment. "They could be alive for all we know" A soft grunt came from Chris in annoyance, not wanting to hear Mark's positive outlook.

"Considering how much water was covering the base of the entrance, it appeared air tight." Mark remarked, again trying to see the best of things. "You'll see, once we use the back up generator to help pump the water out, we'll be greeted with open arms." The cheery tone in Mark's voice was muffled a bit thanks to the gas mask. "Who knows, maybe we'll even be able to get to enjoy some delicious food while we're there." Mark finished, a big grin on his face as he rubbed his stomach, almost like he was preparing himself mentally for a feast for rescuing the people trapped in the shelter.

"I don't think it will be that easy." Chris spoke, reaching the top of the steps before stopping in his tracks. "Something tells me that we won't like what we'll see. That...." Chris trailed off, almost lost in thought. "What we'll see down there, is nothing unlike anything we've seen so far." The tone of Chris' voice was full of dread. A cold sweat trickled down Chris' temple as he gazed back into the darkness. There was just something unsettling about the air down there. Granted that they couldn't smell anything through the gas masks, but there was something in the air itself that screamed danger.

"You're just overthinking things man. Lighten up." Mark spoke, passing Chris on the way up the steps, giving Chris a light pat on the back as Mark reached the top steps. Stepping into the sun, Mark raised his hands over his head before groaning as his muscles popped. Chris walked up behind him, wincing as the sun peaked up from the mountain's peak. It seemed that both Mark and Chris were the complete opposite of one another. Mark was like a bright sunflower, always getting his energy from the sun and standing up high. Chris was more like a moon flower, closed up tightly until the shine of the moon slowly opens him up. Perhaps it was due to their differences that they seemed to get along better than what most people had expected.

"Whatever. Let's just get this done already." Chris grumbled, walking towards the tent that the others had finished putting up. Chris' feet barely lifted off of the ground, kicking up much of the dirt as walked. The sun felt like it would burn him to a crisp, considering how red his skin was, it wasn't too far from the truth.

Entering into the tent, Chris took one of the white fold up chairs to sit down in the shade. Peeling the rubber overalls off, Chris tossed it off to the side, not wanting to wear it as it felt like it restricted his movement. It would need to be washed off later on, at least once they had collected some water from a nearby stream that is.

Bringing up his hands, Chris removed the mask from his face as he blinked a few times to adjust his eyesight. "Finally.." Chris groaned before taking a deep breath of fresh air. "Felt like I was going to suffocate." Chris grumbled to himself. Reaching into the front pocket of his camouflage shirt to pull out a pair of glasses that folded in the middle before slipping them on, it didn't take long before Chris could see better. The scowl that once lingered on his face softened.

Slumping down in the seat, Chris fumbled with the pockets of his jeans before pulling out a small case that was lined with some cigarettes. Putting one in his mouth, Chris pulled out a lighter from his other pocket, giving the lighter a few clicks before a flame shot out from the top. Closing his eyes halfway, eagerly taking the first drag of the cigarette as he let the nicotine consume him.

"You really should quit that habit." Mark spoke more clearly without wearing the mask. Entering into the tent as well, Mark started to snap off the buttons to the rubber overalls. The stench from the two soiled overalls would have been unbearable if it wasn't for the smell of the cigarette that Chris was currently enjoying. Thankfully the opening of the tent was opened, allowing for the breeze to pick up and carry away the unpleasant scents of the overalls and cigarette away from them.

"After all, we can't have you being breathless while we're trying to out run something. Besides, it'll make you age faster." The comment only seemed to make Chris scowl as the tip of his cigarette grew red from the deep inhale, almost out of spite for Mark's comment.

Chris could never understand someone like Mark who only seemed to nag at him like a nagging wife. During times in which Chris would get fed up with Mark's nagging, Chris would often remark about the muscular man being his unmarried nagged wife. It always seemed to slightly fluster Mark, so it was always worth it in the end.

"Like I really give a shit." Chris grumbled with the cigarette in his mouth. Leaning his right elbow over the back of the chair, Chris dug his heels into the ground. His eyes focused more at the opening of the tent more than anything.

It seemed like Chris was lost in thought as Mark went to work getting the overalls off of himself. The wind picking up seemed to rattle the tent a bit, kicking up the dust on the road.

The creaking of the worn down warehouse was a bit worrisome, but if it collapses, it wouldn't be totally devastating. The metal sheets had been worn down over time, making them much lighter than they used to be. The worst that could happen was that the collapsed building would set them back from being able to get access to the shelter to drain the water.

The jeans that Chris wore had some holes in the knees, showing off the sunburned skin that he was suffering from. Thanks to the amount of climbing they did, the climbs had ripped the jeans quite a bit over the span of their journey. When the crew had first started on the journey, Chris' jeans didn't have any holes, but with the test of time and the sharpness of the rocks they climbed over, the holes eventually formed through the material. Mark had offered to have Lizzie fix them, though just like a typical sibling, there was no way she would fix them for Chris. So instead of getting them patched up, Chris simply decided to rock the look. It really gave him the appearance of a bad boy, or at least, that's what Chris told himself.

"I'll go and tell the others what we found." Mark chimed in his usually cheery tone, causing Chris to look at him from the side. Mark was wearing a pair of tan cargo pants that were still intact, despite having climbed over the same sharp rocks that Chris climbed, Mark had Lizzie to thank for patching them up. "Right then, I'll be off." Mark gave Chris a short wave, figuring that the other needed to have a bit of space. Considering that Chris was a bit of a loner, he enjoyed his alone time.

Being left alone, Chris removed the cigarette from his mouth. It wasn't anything like what they had back before the nukes dropped. The paper used was rather thin, allowing for the tobacco leaves that were ground down into a fine powder to be visible. The end was connected into a small metal pipe, allowing for ones' lips to be safe as the cigarette would be used up. Cleaning the inside of the pipe after each smoke break was a pain, but it helped to stretch it out a bit. With the cigarette done, Chris pulled out a small miniature scrapper that was used to dig out the end of the cigarette. Scraping out the remains and tossing it on the sandy ground below, Chris stomped the still burning end to put the cigarette out completely. It wasn't like there were any harmful chemicals that could be left behind, so it wasn't like there was anything that could hurt the animals that might pick it up.

Once Chris was done, he walked out of the tent that he had to share with Mark. Considering that there was usually a traveling crew of six or more, two people of the same gender had to sleep in the same tent, mostly as a means to keep each other safe, but considering that Chris had to share his tent with the very man going after his sister, it felt a bit awkward at times. The sun was rising higher in the sky, the other members of the crew were starting to gather in the tent that the leader of their little expedition had set up. It seemed like they were going to go over the plan of getting to the shelter, of course after they would drain the water out to make it more accessible.

Heading inside, Chris joined up with Lizzie and Mark, standing between the two as it appeared that Lizzie wasn't exactly liking the idea of Mark being too close to her. It was apparent that Lizzie knew that Mark was trying to make advances on her, but she just didn't know how to reject him without hurting his feelings. Of course Chris told her to tell Mark the truth. That Mark just wasn't exactly what she was looking for when it came to finding someone she would want to spend the rest of her life with. But Lizzie was too nice to let Mark down gently.

"Alright, since everyone is here, we'll start planning our next moves." Davis remarked, the leader of the group. He was an older man, his dark brunet hair was mostly medium if not more on the short size as the tips barely brushed against the tips of his ears. Wearing a scowl with a scar that gashed his lips, his muscular form seemed to be littered with misshapen scars along his arms and parts of his chest that rested under his black muscle shirt. Wearing camouflage cargo pants, Davis' boots were tied tightly as the excessive string was wrapped and tucked into his boots. It was clear that Davis came from one of the shelters who made sure to train their civilians to be like soldiers. After all, if no one knew how to fight like a soldier, how were they supposed to survive for long in unknown territory?

"We already know that we'll be taking shifts to make sure that the pumps don't get overwhelmed. But the next mission will be getting the shelters opened." Davis spoke up as he pointed to the damp map. "If we find out that it is nothing more than a watery grave, we'll abandon the site and move to the next shelter." Davis spoke, glancing over the other five that surrounded him. On the table before them was the damp map that was starting to dry as the temperatures were starting to rise, as well as a map that was a layout of the shelter that had been similar to the structure for the others, making it easier to figure out what they would find once they got in there.

Though there had been a couple of shelters that were a bit different in their lay out, most of the standard ones would have a research and infirmary section, a monitor station, living quarters, schools, and a generator room to keep power going through the whole shelter. Some shelters even had other types of entertainment areas to keep people from getting bored, as a way to keep morality from dying. The type of entertainment often came as a form of a theater, saloon, or pub. There was always a center where people would be able to sell their goods and to teach others how to do their trade to keep the knowledge of said skill to continue on through generations.

"Are you sure we should just simply abandon the shelter so easily?" Lizzie spoke up, her concern carried in her voice. "It's not like there are many of the other shelters who would willingly join us. And we simply gave up too easily. If there are people there, I suggest we try our best to get them to join society again." It wasn't like there was any way that they could simply force the other shelters to join up with a new cause.

Considering that everyone had to fend for themselves on the few bits of scrap that they could collect, it wasn't hard to see why people would want to just live out the rest of their days in the safety of their shelter. After all, it was what they knew. People were not inclined to change if the only other option meant that they would be heading into the unknown.

"Listen Lizzie, you can't just lead a horse to water and make it drink." Davis spoke, crossing his arms over his chest. The two of them have done this dance a couple of times where neither of them could exactly agree on what course of action they should go with. Davis would rather let the people decide if they wanted to join, while Lizzie wanted to at least give an attempt to have the people join them.

Davis knew what Lizzie did may have seemed admirable, dedicated even, but it was foolish. What was left of society didn't have much in the way of materials that could be passed around. They were barely scratching by with what they had. More people being forced to join them just meant that there were more mouths to feed. Mouths that they might not even be able to feed.

"Don't give me that bull shit Davis!" Lizzie shouted, slamming her hands down on the table. Sure it made her hands tingle, but right now she wasn't not backing down. Glaring at Davis, Lizzie stared the man down. "We need more people to help with our crops. We don't know how much longer the hydroponics will be able to last if they are running all the time. Or do you remember how bad it got for your shelter?" That was an issue that Lizzie always loved to bring up, as if it was her triumph card that could get Davis to do whatever she wanted.

"You just love bringing that up." Davis muttered under his scruffy voice. "If you want to try and convince these people so badly, then do it yourself Lizzie. I'm not going to be the one to blame when all of this gets out of hand like a wildfire." Davis relented, figuring it was better to just let Lizzie do what she wanted this time, just so that he could see the look of defeat on her face. It wasn't like Davis hated her or anything, but more like he was getting tired of clashing heads with her. Sometimes you need to know when to pick your battles.

"Fine. I'll make you eat those words Davis." Lizzie remarked with a smug grin on her face. Crossing her own arms over her chest to mimic Davis, it seemed like the rest of the group wasn't exactly backing Lizzie. Some either sighed or groaned as they just wanted to get this mission done with.

Mark always seemed to find her stubborn side admirable, while Chris just found it annoying. This was always a constant thing that happened during the meetings as of late. Lizzie would put her two cents in, Davis would disagree, and they would just go back and forth before one of them finally backed down. It was almost like some type of foreplay with them, though Davis was not interested in Lizzie. Not by a long shot.

"Now if we can get back to the topic at hand." Davis spoke up, giving Lizzie a small glare before he pointed at the lay out once more. "If we're successful with being able to find other people still alive in the shelter, Lizzie will act as our recruiter, since she seems more than eager to prove herself." Normally on these types of missions there would be an acting leader who would try to convince those who were in the shelter without any communication for some years, if they would like to rejoin society. Oftentimes it never worked out. But the few times that it did, it helped to bridge the gap in the workforce. Not only that, but it brought in some unique skills that might have been lost to time.

"If we can get access to some of their records, we might be able to see what kind of crops can grow in the reign, see how much of the nuclear radiation still lingers in the soil, and how the wild life has been affected by the nuclear fallout." Davis continued, using his finger to map out the areas that the team would need to pay the closest attention to. "If they aren't willing to work with us, we could probably at least bribe them with some other goods we were able to bring with us." Davis continued as he glanced up to the others, making sure that they were paying attention.

"Some seeds could be used for other types of vegetation that they may not have, or perhaps we could work out a deal to send them some cattle that they might need, or at least would like." Davis started to list a couple of ideas that Lizzy would be able to use when it came down to negation. "We'll have to study them closely to figure out the best bargain chip to use when the time comes to recruit them." Since there wasn't much use for money between shelters, they at least had some type of barter system in place.

"In the event that everything fails," Davis paused, hating the idea that things may not go according to plan. "We'll wait three days before moving on to our next target." Davis spoke, glancing at Lizzie once more. "You got that Lizzie? We will only stay for three days." It seemed that Lizzie would have to pretty much agree to those terms. Any longer and she would risk making the others angry at her. Sure Lizzie had Mark, a man willing to stay close to her and was eager to meet any of her needs, plus having Chris along made sure that she had at least two people behind her. But Chris wasn't as loyal as Mark. Despite them being half siblings, that didn't guarantee loyalty.

"Yeah yeah." Lizzie grumbled a bit under her breath. The rest of the meeting simply went over the usual business. The etiquette that went behind how the group is supposed to act as a means of introducing the shelter inhabitants to rejoin the rest of the human race, going over what they could barter with, and what they were looking for in regards to information to the events after the communication had been dropped. The normal spiel that everyone in the group had heard a hundred times before.

Parting from the tent, Lizzie headed towards the generator that was in the process of being moved before they were called to the meeting. The generator was able to be broken up into three separate sections, allowing for easy mobility, as well as making it discrete enough to make it seem like it was just part of the cargo with the different tubes that lined the inside of the generator sections. Long circular tubes filled with water lined the inner workings of the generator. Inside of the tubes, mixed in with the water, was an odd concoction of coal and various oil that helped to create the fuel needed. Once the generator was placed out in the sun, the heat made it possible to create steam to power up the generator. Though it was only for a few hours that it would work, it was at least something they could use. With other types of fuel being in short supply, steam generators were all they had going at the moment.

Oliver and Rachel had brushed past Lizzie as they were going towards the generator to set up the pieces. Oliver was a rather scrawny looking guy, often wearing thick black rimmed glasses, his face was clean of most facial hair as he didn't like how scratchy beard hair felt. Wearing a white t-shirt that barely rested above his elbows, Oliver's light brunet hair was pulled back into a small ponytail. It's not like he didn't cut his hair often, but being out of these expeditions meant that he didn't have time to go and get it cut. His slender frame made it seem like he would be able to be blown into the wind if he wasn't careful enough. Though it might seem like Oliver would have a timid nature, he wasn't a push over. Sure he may not be able to fight, but that didn't mean he wouldn't be ready to back up his friends.

"Hey guys, ready to go into the warehouse and drain that water?" Lizzie asked, approaching the two. Rachel cast a glance towards Lizzie before letting out a small sigh. It seemed like Lizzie might have made things complicated during the meeting with her little outburst of wanting to put an effort in trying to make people join society once again. This only seemed to add a bit of a riff between the two women, not like Rachel liked Lizzie to begin with, but it wasn't helping.

"I can't believe you would be willing to make people come out of the safety of their shelter to join the surface." Rachel scoffed, kneeling down to inspect the generator, not wanting sand or dirt getting into the parts to make the generator act up while they were using it to pump out the water. Rachel was a lot like Chris, easily sunburned and often acting more like a realist to bring people back to their senses.

Rachel's usually pale skin was slowly tanning over, though there were still parts of her skin that was red like a lobster. Rachel's long black hair that usually went past her shoulders was currently tied up in a messy bun, sticking out of the white hat she was wearing to block the sun out of her eyes. With a camouflage jacket protecting sunburnt arms, Rachel wore a black muscle shirt with camouflage cargo pants.

"I don't see why we shouldn't at least try to bring them to the surface. It's better than being cooped up in one place for long." Lizzie started to defend herself against Rachel's bluntness. "Being outside in the fresh air, it's much better than breathing in the same air that has been in circulation for the last five hundred years or so." Lizzie spoke, causing Rachel and Oliver to glance at each other, the doubt showing on their faces.

"Look around you Liz. This isn't exactly the best place to live." Rachel spat, scooping out some dirt that seemingly nestled in the corners of the generator. "This place is covered in dust, it's hot as a dick after having some intense fucking, and the sun will burn you faster than pork on a hot skillet." The hot sun only seemed to add in Rachel's argument as the sunlight made it almost impossible to see right now. "Frankly, I would much rather be some place nice and cool, free of radiation, and not have to deal with extroverted bitches like you that feel the need to grow our little community when we have so little to give." It seemed like the heat always brought the worse out of people. The scowl on Rachel's face when she looked up at Lizzie didn't help matters either.

"I have to agree with Rachel on this one." Oliver spoke up, looking up at Lizzie, the shocked look on her face seemed to say it all. "We still operate out of our shelters as it is. The ruins around the world aren't exactly up to code." Oliver started to list reasons as to why this plan wouldn't work out in their favor. "We still have a lot of testing to do. Plus we need to find a way to communicate with each other long distance." Oliver continued, slowly standing up so that he could at least not have to look up into the sun while talking to Lizzie. "The best thing that we can do is at least plant the idea that there are people who would be willing to bring them back into society when they are ready, Lizzie." Oliver continued as he put a hand on Lizzie's shoulder. "The more you push, the more the other people are going to push back. We can't get anywhere with two groups of people trying to push their beliefs or ideas on each other."

Hearing that, it made Lizzie realize that perhaps she had been a bit selfish in her ideas of wanting to make the world a better place. The more she fought with Davis, the more she was hindering the mission. With a soft sigh, Lizzie slumped her shoulders as she brushed Oliver's hand off of her.. "When you put it like that, I guess you're right Oliver." Lizzie admitted, casting her gaze away from the two, though Rachel was busy making sure that there was no dirt left before grabbing the pieces and putting them together.

"I guess Davis just wants to at least make people know that there are people out in the world now, trying to at least rebuild society." It was comforting to know that they were at least getting the word out to the survivors. "Those who would want to join us, or at least entertain the idea of joining the good cause of coming together as the survivors of humanity, they would be able to make their way to us." Lizzie continued, placing her hands on her hips. "Thanks Oliver. You've been a big help." Lizzie thanked him, giving Oliver a soft smile before patting him on the shoulder.

"Don't mention it." Oliver spoke, shrugging his shoulders a bit. Watching Lizzie turn and walk away, Oliver made sure that she was a good distance away before sighing. "You know, I really don't care either way if these people want to come with us or not. I just want to get out of this damn desert." Oliver remarked in a blunt tone towards Rachel. "The longer she makes us stay, the more I want to make her suffer." Oliver spat, leaning against the brick building with the roof hanging off of it. The building looked as if it was an old store front for some candy shop. The letters on the sign had been long since faded. The only thing seemingly holding up the building was a well built structure, though it was still a bit questionable with how long it would remain standing.

"Right?!" Rachel agreed, a cynical laughter leaving her lips. "Why does she even care? Not like we'll really have a chance to see these so-called changes in our lifetime." Rachel groaned as she crossed her arms under her chest. "We have so much work to do that it's not even funny." Rachel continued to whine while dusting her hands off of any sand still clinging to her. "Honestly I think we should knock everything down and just rebuild with the good pieces of scrap we get from the rumbles." Leaning against the same building as Oliver, though she was careful to not put her whole weight on it, in fear that one wrong move could cause the building to collapse.

"Well it's not like Rome was made in a day." Oliver spoke up, glancing up at Rachel. "We will need more helping hands if we want to rebuild the world." Even if they couldn't have every single survivor join them, it was better than having no one around to help rebuild society. "There's plenty of land out there just begging to be claimed." Oliver remarked as he picked up a rock to toss it off to the side.

"Yeah, but at least we get to take this chance and see what land we can at least use." Rachel remarked, looking at the empty city in complete ruin before her. "As our numbers grow, hopefully we'll be able to make beautiful cities like before." Rachel spoke in a daydream tone as the wind started to pick up. "No more sad and pathetic wastelands. No metal structures lingering like skeletons of an old world long forgotten…" Rachel continued before Oliver chucked another rock to the side.

"I can't wait to see if we can revive the old tech." It was something that Oliver was good at. Studying old technology to see if perhaps they could replicate the forgotten tech or find ways to improve on it. Who knows, maybe we'll be able to find something to bring down that damn station." Oliver remarked as he glanced up at the sky as the clouds moved to cover the sun. "Maybe one day we'll be able to watch that damn station crumble in the sky as the last humans on the station die. " It was a dream that most of the remaining people on Earth had. To be able to witness the downfall of the cowards who went up into space, leaving them behind to suffer underground for so many years.

"I would pay good money to see that." Rachel mused, mostly to herself as she glanced up. Despite the cloud coverage, the station was still visible even during the day. Though the exterior was made out of metal, the way that the sun lit it up made it appeal like an eyeball.

The red lights that decorated the outside formed circles like a lens to a camera. It was like the rich were watching and waiting for the right time to come back to the planet they ruined, taking it back for themselves, and taking everything away from those left behind once again. If it came down to that, the humans that remained would have to fight for what little they had.

"To watch those bastards burn in a horrifying accident …the pieces of their beloved space station falling to Earth in beautiful colors across the sky, it would be more beautiful than a meteor shower." Rachel started to speak in a daydream like tone. "I would give up everything just to witness that beautiful moment." Rachel paused as she leaned back against the building. "Even if it destroys parts of the surface, it would be worth every bit of destruction to see their own demise." Rachel's voice husked as if she was imagining it right now. The way her eyes were half lidded, and the grin crossing her face, it was clear that Rachel would have taken great pleasure in witnessing something that would never happen in her lifetime.

"Damn, you would really give up everything just to see them burn like that?" Oliver asked, raising an eyebrow. He knew how much people resented the rich for what they had done, Oliver couldn't really blame them. But to see other people share the same reaction as Rachel was a bit disturbing. It seemed like the vengeance the survivors felt was sown deep into the passing generations.

One could only imagine how the survivors felt after they were tucked away safe from the death and destruction caused by the nukes landing in major cities. Huddling together as they knew it wasn't safe to head up to the surface. How the families were torn away from each other, their beloved pets killed as there was no way to save them, it was heartbreaking if you thought about it.

"Well, if you find a way to make them pay, at least invite me to show. I'm all in for a fantastic meteor shower." Oliver spoke, a small smirk landing on his face, figuring that if that would happen, he would at least like to see it. Hearing that, Rachel couldn't help but lighten up afterwards.

"We'll both have front row seats. We'll even make sure to drink some type of booze with us." Rachel remarked, lightly punching Oliver's shoulder in a friendly way, the smile never leaving her face. One would almost think that she was more into Oliver than Chris. "Now let's get this generator working. I don't want the little princess getting prissy that she can't be the savior the world needs." Rachel mocked, pushing off of the building that was falling apart, before the two headed towards the warehouse to join the others.

Oliver carried the heavy generator in his arms, it was a bit lengthy on top and heavy, but this was the burden of being able to have some type of portable power. Thankfully they wouldn't have to bring the generator down the steps, though the hose would have to travel down the steps. Setting up the generator, Oliver switched the button on, allowing for the sunlight to be stored, which in turn would give them the power needed to drain the basement.

As the hours went by, the water level in the basement slowly decreased to a manageable level. It wasn't possible for them to completely clear out the water, but it lowered the water to the rest around ankle level, meaning that they didn't have to worry about tripping and falling over the objects that remained hidden in the dark waters.

The decaying smell of the water had started to dissipate, allowing for the crew to breathe much easier. Gazing at the exposed ground, or at least more exposed that it once had been in some time, certain things had become noticeable. Old faded bottles with molded pigments splashed around in the liquid container, small critter skulls that still had bits of hair or tissue bobbed free from under the rusted shelves, and pieces of paper of old labels nestled into some of the corners of the room. The whole place seemed to reek of death and decay.

The algae seemed to cling to the walls, showing off bits of white walls as the colored coated walls faded. It almost seemed to be surreal with how much the water seemed to fade the old posters on the walls that once promoted sales for that particular week before the nukes landed. The group walked towards the entrance of the shelter door as it became more accessible. Stepping up the few bricked steps, the ones that Lizzie had tripped over, Davis knelt down in front of the floor entrance.

Studying it over, it appeared that not even a single crack had been spotted, meaning that there was at least some hope that there could be people around. With a glance towards the team, Davis gave them a small smirk with a thumbs up, seeming to relieve everyone, meaning that there was a chance that they would be able to rescue everyone. Slipping out a piece of paper, Davis started to work on the door's tricky opening sequence. This part often took the longest, meaning that the rest of the crew would have to act as guards to keep Davis safe while he cracked the code.

In order to protect the survivors from the cowards who went off into space, each door had a different code depending on their location, country, and shelter number assigned to that particular door. It was a way to make sure that only other survivors knew the code, in case there was some type of emergency and they needed to get to the other closed off shelters in the area.

Simply having a route underground didn't mean that it was always accessible. Damage from earthquakes had collapsed many of the tunnels in the early parts of the fallout. The survivors had to make sure to use other means of getting to each other. There was only so much a society could do when all forms of communication had been wiped out from the face of the Earth.

Once the door was opened, the alarms inside started to go off. Any survivors who were alive would rush towards the entrance, ready to either welcome those who were able to get into the shelter, or ready to kill them. The crew had started their descent down the steps one by one, leaving Rachel and Oliver at the top as back up. The first one down was Davis, followed by Chris, Lizzie, and finally then Mark. "Remember, we're not here as a hostile force. If they see us with any type of weapon, they might think we're here to hurt them." Davis spoke, waiting by the second entrance for his team to fall in line.

The four waited with held breaths, waiting to hear either the sound of the doors opening, or at least a voice over the speaker to talk to them. When the seconds started to pass to minutes, the crew looked at each other with a rather puzzled look. Were there no survivors?

"Don't tell me we came all this way for-" Lizzie started to speak before there was a loud buzzing noise that came from the speakers. Covering their ears, the crew yelled as the sound seemed to only get louder as it echoed against the wet walls.

"What do you want?" A male voice came through the speakers, though it was a bit hard to hear through the bits of static. As the crew seemed to recover from the loud buzz that felt like it was shattering their ear drums, they glanced at each other, making sure that this was exactly what they had wanted. Whether or not these people would be willing to join them was up to the residents. But for now, they needed to take the first step to invite these people to join them.

Taking a couple of steps closer to the door, Lizzie looked at the camera. Shaking the nerves from her fingers, she clenched her fists. "Uh, hello. My name is Lizzie and I'm here to represent a group of survivors like yourself." Lizzie started to speak, her heart racing against her chest.

"We came to see if your shelter had survived over these last five hundred years. We weren't sure if anyone actually survived.... " Lizzie trailed off before glancing at Davis. "After all, with the water we just cleared, we were almost certain that this shelter was done for." Lizzie spoke as she displayed a smile on her face. Lizzie was trying to be energetic, hoping that perhaps the person on the other end would see that she was not a hostile force, but rather a friend.

The silence on the speaker seemed to be deafening to the crew. Chris sighed as he shook his head. Mark looked concerned for Lizzie as this was the first time she was stepping up and acting like a real representative for the remaining human society. He wondered if she was really prepared for this. Davis cast his gaze down, bringing a hand up to cover his face, the disappointment was evident though he didn't say anything. Perhaps Davis should have been the one to talk to them first. If Lizzie could see the men, she probably would have felt either foolish or defeated. They didn't seem to have any faith in her.

"Uh. . . hello?" Lizzie called out, perhaps they couldn't hear her? "If you're talking, we can't hear you." Lizzie spoke up, figuring that there should be at least some feedback, in case the people inside didn't know that they weren't being heard. "Can you-" Lizzie started to speak before another buzz deafened them once more, causing them to cover their ears from the noise.

"If you wish to speak with our leader, you'll need to bring the other two down from the top of the stairs." The voice spoke up once more, causing everyone's eyes to widen. How did they even know that there were other people there with them? "The man and the woman. He won't speak to you unless everyone is down here." The voice spoke once more, a bit more irritated that these people seemed to be bold enough to have a small party left behind. The silence felt in that corridor was deafening. Panic seemed to set in, but nobody had the nerve to show it. They needed to be strong after all.

"How did they...." Mark muttered, glancing around as he scanned the trajectory of the single camera that it pointed towards. It wasn't like they would be able to see Rachel and Oliver from this one camera. Did that mean that they had other means of being able to see them? Some type of hidden camera in the area that was once flooded?

It was a bit unsettling to know that they had some intel about their group when this seemed to be the first time that the door was opened since the bombs dropped. The crew wasn't there for very long, so it didn't make sense that they would know how many people were there. Much less that they knew that the two people left behind were both a man and a woman.

"Fine.... " Davis grunted through his teeth, turning away from the camera. "I'll go and get them." Davis spoke, heading towards the stairs. "Mark.... Chris.... if they try anything, get Lizzie out of here. I don't want anything to happen to you guys." Davis muttered under his breath, close enough to the two. He didn't want the people on the other end being able to hear them talk. After all, if they knew about the two left behind, what other things did they know about? It was an unsettling feeling all around. The sound of the camera zooming in and out on them didn't exactly help matters either. The unsettling feeling that people were watching him, it sent chills down Davis' spine.

As Davis headed up the steps, the three remaining members of the crew huddled in close together as a means of talking with the camera picking up on what they were saying. The sound of the camera zooming in was audible in the empty stairway, seemingly trying to see what they were talking about, giving them an indication that the operator on the other side couldn't hear them in their current position.

"I don't like this already guys. What if they try to hurt us?" Lizzie whispered, glancing towards Chris. It was apparent that this whole situation had unnerved Lizzie. She crossed her arms over her chest, almost like she was trying to slip into an invisible shell like a turtle to protect herself.

"If it comes down to it, we'll make a run for it. We'll grab whatever supplies we can, and just run out of the city." Chris spoke, figuring that if they had to either fight or flight, the best course of action would be to run away. It may have been cowardly, but at least it meant that they had a chance to survive. After all, the foolish die young while the wise live on. Or at least, that's what Chris' philosophy was.

"Shouldn't we at least try and fight them off? Maybe if we do enough damage to their numbers, we could scare them into retreating?" Mark suggested, his right hand moving down towards one of the pockets. Even though Davis had said not to brandish a weapon, right now it seemed to be their only choice. If it seemed like they had weapons on them, perhaps the leader would think twice about trying to capture them, then perhaps seeing a modern weapon would scare them into actually working with the crew rather than against them. Though with only the six people in the crew, it wasn't like they had much of a chance regardless.

Before Mark could even pull his hand out of the pocket, no doubt wanting to sport the weapon he brought, Chris grabbed Mark's face to pull the man closer with a scowl on his face, taking both Lizzie and Mark by surprise. As their foreheads were pressed up against each other's, Mark was forced to look into Chris' eyes. "Don't you even dare try to flash that pathetic switchblade you idiot." Chris growled through some clenched teeth. "If they see it, they'll frisk us all. Then we'll be in some real trouble." Chris finished, slowly pushing Mark back. "You need to think before you act. Otherwise, you'll jeopardize the mission." Chris scolded Mark, taking a step back and resting against the wall.

"Oh.....yeah." Mark mumbled, feeling a bit foolish for almost giving away that a few of them did have some weapons on them. Though a switch blade wasn't exactly a weapon that screamed intimidation.

"Do you really think they would try and frisk us though?" Mark asked, unable to look at Chris directly. Even though the two didn't do anything, the thought that it appeared that they were closer than they really were was a bit unsettling. Though it seemed that Lizzie didn't mind, granted it was to save all of them, but seeing her usually cool headed sibling flustered made it all worth it.

"Who knows at this point." Chris mumbled under his breath. "Once the others get back down here, we'll know by then." Chris grumbled, glancing towards the stairs. It was as if on cue that Davis returned with Oliver and Rachel. "Geeze, what took you so long?" Chris continued with his grumbling, his posture showed his displeasure in everything that was going on. At least those three weren't there to see Chris make himself look like an idiot in front of the rest. The warmth from Mark's forehead still seems to linger against Chris' forehead.

"We took a little bit of time scouting the perimeter to see if we could find any cameras." Davis replied, as he reached the last step to join the others. "It appeared that they had a hidden camera set up on one of the shelves." Davis continued as he glanced between the three. "It was hidden behind some rusted cans. Blended in perfectly." Even if the flashlights had grazed over the cans, due to the lack of light in the room, it would have been kept hidden, making it hard to spot the camera as it was hiding in the shadows.

"It seems that some of the pipes had been sabotaged a long time ago. The waterline stopped at a certain point through the brick walls. Allowing the water to stay at a certain level to keep from damaging the camera." Davis explained, placing his hands on his hips, giving a small glance towards the camera as it zoomed in on him specifically. "Think of the wall like a sink. The ground behind the wall would absorb any water that spilled over. Brick and concrete are pretty hard to break down by the elements. Pretty ingenious if you ask me." If it wasn't for the fact that they were dealing with unknown factors, Davis would have been impressed.

"I'm glad you like my design." A different male voice seemed to chime in, this time sounding more like a younger male on the speaker. This caused the crew to glance up at the camera that was pointed towards them. "What better way to keep our shelter safe and keep undesirables away, than to make it hard for them to get in." The voice continued through the speaker. Most of the crew were surprised that there wasn't the usual loud buzzing that came from the speaker the first couple of times the speaker came on.

"So you're the one in charge I take it?" Davis' voice boomed in an authoritative tone, not liking the idea that this so-called leader sounded like a child whose balls just finished dropping. If this kid was the leader, then that meant that there weren't any 'adults' around with whom Davis could talk to.

Even though there could be some children who were very mature for their age, somehow Davis got the impression that he would be walking into a child's sick dream. All that research collected over the past four hundred years gone to waste, logic would give way to immature desires to which the children could never comprehend the consequences of their actions. They would be lucky if the walls weren't covered in fecal matter sigh misspell profanity decorating the walls.

"More or less." Came the voice of the male, almost in a taunting manner as the camera seemed to stop zooming in. "You see, the older folks we have in here....." The voice trailed off as a small hum in thought could be heard on the microphone. "Well... They aren't in the right frame of mind." The voice continued after a few seconds. It wasn't long afterwards that the door started to open, the smell alone was enough to make most of the crew cover their noise.

The smell was incomprehensible, like nothing that they could have even imagined. "Though, granted with how hostile you appear, you wouldn't even believe me if I told you half of the stuff the elders did to us before I took over." The voice spoke in a bragging tone. "So you'll just have to come in and see for yourself." The voice finished, a sound of the speaker clicking off, leaving the crew somewhat confused as they seemed to be a bit hesitant about whether or not they should head in. Everything was telling them to get out of there. To just simply run while they had the chance. But the mission came first.

The entrance to the shelter was dark, a slight musk came from the entrance though it wasn't as bad as when the door had first opened up. Rachel and Lizzie glanced towards Davis, their concern was apparent, but they had to go in and see for themselves what had happened. With Davis taking lead, each one of the six crew members walked past the threshold. It was fairly dark inside, with only a bright red glow from the emergency lights casting the only type of light that made it possible to see in the darkened area. Water seemed to be reflecting the light source, indicating that there must have been some type of flooding. So perhaps the water had managed to get in. The splashing sounds of their feet echoed in the dark hallway. Carefully taking out their flashlights, the crew started to look around.

Repent.... Blood Must Be Paid.... Crawl Like Beasts On Their Stomachs As They Enter Hell. Those were only a few letters that the crew was able to read on the blood smeared walls as they reached a room that was supposed to be a gathering room. The shock was apparent as the crew tried to stomach what they were seeing. Redden skeletons were pinned up on the ceiling, bits of muscle still seemed to linger on some as the rest were barren.

"O-Oh my g-" Lizzie gasped, quickly covering her mouth as she tried not to vomit. The overwhelming smell didn't exactly help matters either. "How could they have-" Lizzie couldn't even finish the sentence as she looked towards the floor. There were bits of the floor that seemed to be slick with blood. Old blood seemed to mix with new as they seemingly merged together before being washed away by the water that was kicked up.

"Sickening, isn't it?" Came the voice of from the speaker, the words seemingly echoing before he came into view. There before the crew stood a young man who appeared to be close to a little over five and half feet tall. His face was well defined and stoic for someone of his age.

White hair seemed to be a jumbled mess with a red scarf wrapped around the front of his head. It almost resembled something that a female gypsy would wear. The red scarf band had some golden coins decorating the middle section of the scarf, liming two separate lines with them. Tanned skin with bits of dirt and blood seemed to be cake to the bits of exposed skin on him. Golden eyes stared them down through some thick eyelashes. A scowl rested neatly on the young man's face, though he did have a bit of a Cheshire smile.

"What have you done to-" Davis growled, taking a step forward towards the young male, only to have sharp spears pointed towards him. Glancing to the side, it appeared that they were surrounded by some of the children of the shelter. Each ready with a weapon in hand, showing their demonstration that they were ready and able to kill as they pointed the sharp ends towards each other the crews' neck.

"Relax old man." The young male spoke, raising a finger, causing the children to push the spears closer to the group, seemingly herding them closer to one other. "Like I said, you

A Year Long Journey With You 143

wouldn't believe me if I told you half of the stuff that the adults did here before I took over." The young male continued. Crossing his arms over his chest, the young male started to walk over the crew. The golden earring dangling from his ears, bouncing ever so slightly as he walked towards them.

Taking a better look at this so-called leader, Davis took note that the young male was wearing clothing that appeared to have been torn up, like he had just gotten done fighting. The once white buttoned up shirt seemed to have the first three buttons already ripped off. The fabric was nearly see through with only bits of blood and dirt giving it color.

A red cape draped over the male's right shoulder, the edges torn along the hems of his sleeves. The black slacks were ripped in various sections as if he had someone slashing them with a dagger. Lastly a red sash seemed to be tied around his waist, acting like a makeshift belt. Thin boots seemed to be the only protection that this guy had from the dirty water lingering on the ground.

"By the looks of it, it seems like you were in a fight." Davis remarked, raising an eyebrow as he glanced towards the side to make sure that his crew wouldn't do anything stupid. "If what you're saying is true, then why is it that you look like you have fresh blood on you? You can't tell me that it's old. There's still a bit of shine to it. Old blood doesn't have that." Davis scowled towards the younger male, waiting for a reply. This only seemed to peak the boy's interest, causing him to grin towards Davis before speaking.

"Good observation." The young man remarked, bringing up the cape over his right arm to wipe away some of the blood on his face. "We actually just had a fight, to which I came out as the victor." The young male spoke in a bit of a bragging tone, cocking his head to the side. "But that point seems to be mute as of right now." The male spoke, moving to place his hands on his hips.

"After all, these *kind* people have decided to come and rescue us, right? Giving us hope that there are still kind people out there who are willing to take in a bunch of people who still have some sort of cognitive left that could be used to benefit the lingering remnants of mankind, right?" The tone of voice coming from this male seemed to be seething with sarcasm mixed in with some irritation.

"Or at least, that's probably what you would like us to think." The boy spat before glancing at the other children. "Trying to greet us with smiles on your faces before realizing that you were being spied on." The male spoke, leaning in close to Davis with a cocky grin on his face. "Yet those warm smiles quickly melted into cold blank stares before turning into hatred and paranoia right?" The boy asked as Davis growled under his breath. "Having the fear creep along your backside when you knew you were caught. Do you still want to rescue us?" It seemed that this little comment got under Davis' skin, though the crew seemed to cringe as they knew how short of a temper Davis had.

"Enough of this!" Davis shouted, taking a step towards the young male in charge, only to hear an audible gasp coming from Lizzie as the sharp end of the spear pierced into her neck ever so slightly. The sight of blood trickling down her neck was a clear message. With a small grunt, Davis relaxed his shoulders. "What's your name kid?" Davis asked, his irritation showing in his voice. If he wanted to keep his crew safe, Davis was going to have to play this little kids' game.

"My name?" The boy asked, almost in a sing-song tone with a cocky grin still lingering on his face. "Well... I guess it wouldn't hurt to tell you my name. Considering that I don't think you would last very long in the arena." The boy continued before bringing his hand up to inspect his nails, acting like these people didn't even have the importance of being looked at. "My name is Nero Cornix. But you can just call me Nero." The male spoke, giving them an irritated glance.

"Nero huh?" Davis spoke almost scoffing at the male's name, shrugging his shoulders a little bit as he didn't even know if he was dealing with someone special or not. "Well I guess we should-" Davis started to speak, only to have Nero raise his hand up to cut the older male off. This caused a confused expression to cross Davis' face. Did this brat really have the gull to cut him off?

"No names." Nero spoke, glancing towards the other children who were pointing their spears towards the adults. "At least, not yet." The taunting sing-song tone coming from Nero sent a chill down most of the crew's neck. "Take them to the arena." Nero spoke, turning his back towards the lot. "They'll have to battle it out with each other first." The confusion on the crew's face caused a quick chuckle to leave Nero's lips. "If they provide us with a good show, then perhaps we'll see if they can convince us to join them. That is, if they will even want us to join them once we're done with them." Davis didn't have any confidence that these kids were going to let them go freely. He needed to come up with a plan, but Davis' anger was blinding him.

"Why you!" Davis growled, before feeling the tip of the spear digging into his neck. An exasperated sigh leaving his lips. The annoyance of this kid was evident. Why did trying to reason with kids have to feel like he was pulling teeth? These kids were seemingly out of their mind.

Killing each other, or at least beating each other, purely for entertainment? Is this really what life has come down to? To be mere playthings for children? Either way, Davis knew that he had to at least convince these kids that violence was never the answer. That they could find other ways of contributing to society than what they were being subjected to. By the end of this, Davis would make sure that he retired from any more expeditions like this, and most likely the rest of the crew would agree.

CHAPTER SEVEN: *The Start Of Wrath*

U PON HEADING FURTHER down into the shelter, the sound of water splashing could be heard echoing in the hall, Davis and the rest glanced around the best they could with the visible lighting that was present. In order to save the limited battery life of their flashlights, the crew made sure to turn them off when they were being escorted to this arena that Nero talked about. The carved walls had elaborate designs on them that, at one time, could have been found in churches all over the world. The walls looked foreboding in the red emergency lights, as if religion fell the day the bombs had dropped. There were a few candles that lit up parts of the walls, illuminating them to show that they were white in color, but they were spaced out so far that they might as well save on the candle wax and run the power to the emergency lights.

The tiled floors underneath them looked as if it belonged to some old castle with the lay-out that could be somewhat seen in the dirty water. Bits of damped rug clung to the bottom of the water, giving a little bit of traction under the group's feet. Dirt had seemed to nestle down into the cracks, making it apparent just how dirty the water was. Glancing behind him, Davis wondered if they would all be able to get out of here.

The smell in this shelter was so bad that it reminded Davis of the time they had to walk through a shelter that was a pig enclosure. Just in that one shelter alone it made Davis vow to never eat pork again. But *this* was something out of an old horror film. The sound of the wind brushing through the empty halls almost made it sound like the shelter was alive and breathing. It sent chills down some of the crews' spine, but they had to keep going.

Walking past a sign, Davis tried his best to read it in the dark, but to no luck. It seemed that perhaps many people had gotten lost on in the shelter, resulting in the signs being set up in their place. Considering that the shelters were meant to be big enough to help humanity survive through the hell storm of the surface after the bombs were dropped, this would come in handy later if they needed to get around.

It was only when they came to a stop above a large stone stairway that the crew noticed what these children were planning. In front of them was a large stadium structure that was made to resemble the very Colosseum that Rome was known for. There were wide windows that were covered in stained glass, each having some sort of different artwork on them. There was one with two people racing each other on chariots, another one representing two people fighting with the crowd cheering them on in the background. In all honesty, they seemed to resemble more like a child's drawing made into a stained glass design, but the fact that they were able to do such a thing was impressive.

Surrounding the Colosseum replica seemed to have a bunch of houses made out of stone and dirt. This would have never been approved in the original building process, which meant that this must have come after the other shelters had lost communication with this particular shelter. Glancing around a bit more, at least while they could, it appeared that there were peo-ple of all different ages walking around. There were some young adults, typically mothers with their young children, walking around like it was just another normal day.

It seemed that there was some running water, allowing for fresh water to be collected by the townsfolk. There were some people down by the water, collecting it in buckets while some of the children seemed to play around. The crew would have to determine if there were harmful levels of radiation in the water at a later point, but that is if they can make it out without there being blood shed.

Davis and the crew tried to take in as much as they could, only to have the sharp end of the spears pointing against their backs. Glancing back, Davis scowled at the children wielding the spears, but it seemed that they weren't giving them much time to be able to look around. It might have been initially to prevent them from reporting things like the population of the shelter, what type of weapon advancement they had, and more. This Nero kid certainly knew how to train the young ones to be valuable soldiers. At least, that's what Davis' opinion was.

Walking down the steps, the crew were being led down towards the main street, which was in the direction of the arena. The area close by to the large structure appeared to be a marketplace. The buildings were filed neatly in a row, showing off a more modern society before the nukes were dropped resembled some sort of living quarters that the residents used. There was a little restaurant with some type of foreign smell that the crew had never experienced before. It wasn't bad or anything, certainly a welcomed change from the other scents surrounding them.

The further the crew walked and glanced around without being poked, the more the crew observed. It was like they walked back in time to ancient Roman times with the way the buildings were constructed. The one thing that seemed to stand out the most was the fruit stand. It was a good indicator that their hydroponic was still working. At least the residents were still able to get fresh water.

Standing in front of the Colosseum, the structure was very large in deed, and in much better shape than the one on the surface. With no one around to take care of the structure, the passage of time had taken its toll on the marvel of human engineering. Upon entering, the crew were broken up into male and female, meaning that they would be separated, making it hard to come up with some type of plan to get out of here.

"Stay strong you two." Davis commented, only to get a simple nod from Lizzie before the two women were escorted away. Then it was the men's turn to be escorted towards a section. Keeping their heads held up high, the men entered into an area that had a few benches where they would be able to sit down between matches. There were some variants of armor and clothing that they would have to change into.

Each of the four men sat down on the benches. Two guards were positioned around the door, meaning that they couldn't simply sneak out. This was getting to be a bit worrisome. Clearly this isn't the first time that they had people in here, ready to fight and die. It just seemed all too barbaric to even comprehend all of this. Did these kids enjoy slaughtering each other? Would they pit each other against their friends? With the tension rising in the room, Davis could only imagine what was going on with Rachel and Lizzie. It wasn't like they were the best of friends. If they had to fight against each other, who would come out on top?

As the men were forced to think about their situation, Rachel and Lizzie sat silently in their similar looking room. Lizzie's eyes were cast down to the ground, a soft frown lingering on her face. How could this have happened? Glancing towards Rachel, it appeared that she was more irritated being stuck in the same room as Lizzie. It was always like this, Lizzie tried to make friends with Rachel, but she would rather jump off a cliff than be friends with the likes of Lizzie. Or at least, that's the indication that Lizzie got from their interactions.

Whenever Rachel would see Lizzie in the tent, as long as it wasn't lights out, she would stay away from the tent. At first it didn't phase Lizzie, figuring that perhaps Rachel was just busy doing other things, but the more they traveled together, the more it started to weigh on Lizzie's mind. It really started to mess with her self esteem, to the point that Lizzie started to clam up around people who weren't Chris. There were times in which Lizzie was tempted to ask Chris for advice, but the situation never came up.

"So what do you think they'll have us do?" Lizzie finally asked, figuring that perhaps this was a chance for the two of them to at least talk things out. But with that classic click from Rachel's tongue, it was clear that things were not about to end well. At least, not for Lizzie.

"Like I care." Rachel muttered, a scowl lingering on her face. "As long as we can get out of here sooner, the better." Rachel scuffed, crossing one leg over the other as she sat down, keeping her distance away from Lizzie. Crossing her arms over her chest, Rachel leaned forward, as if to curl up into a ball. Rachel couldn't allow Lizzie to see her scared, having to look tough despite how she felt on the inside. Lizzie could see that Rachel was trying hard to act tough as the concern on Lizzie's face said it all. It would seem that this could very well be the end of the line for them.

Glancing around, Lizzie was trying to take in what she could in order to figure out how they could get out of here. Slowly standing up, Lizzie walked towards the stained glass window that had some white lilies as its display. Turning to glance at the door, the guards seemed to act almost like statues. Narrowing her eyes, Lizzie reached a hand up to the cut on her neck that she had received early. Thankfully it had stopped bleeding, but the fact that her neck was even cut, showed that these kids meant business. They were a force that was loyal to one leader, and that meant that any type of reasoning would be out of the question. This Nero brat really got these kids brainwashed.

Even if they did break out, meet up with Davis and the others, it wasn't like they could just run away. They probably would have their guards on the crew before they could even make it out. With a soft sigh, Lizzie walked back to the bench to sit down. She had never felt this defeated before. They only way that they could get out of this alive, it was to try to reason with that Nero brat. He seemed cunning, like he had the upper hand on the situation. Surely they could find a way to reason with the kid. Biting her lower lip, Lizzie pondered if it was even possible. Not like the kid would listen to reason. If given the chance, surely they could find some sort of middle ground.

THE time for the crew to get dressed in some type of fighting outfit came quicker than expected. Without the sun to give them some type of time base as to how long they seemingly sat in silence and deprived of food, made it harder to figure out how long they were actually there. It could have only seemed like an hour, yet they were probably in that room for much longer.

Before the crew knew it, they were forced to walk out into a large battle field that had everyone in the shelter spectating them. The center of the arena looked as if it was some type of battle ground. Not that they had lingering dead bodies, but rather there were parts that still had some fresh blood staining the dirt floor. Slash marks from swords or spears were apparent. The lights surrounding the arena were made of a bunch of torches, the heat from them seemed to keep the people from at least freezing. The place was three stories high and mostly jammed with people watching them, already chanting something that was inaudible.

The men wore identical outfits for their gender, though it was black in color, it did make it seem like they were a soldier unit as a whole. Odd looking sandals that seemingly wrapped up towards their calf, exposing their toes and the laces seemed to criss cross up the front. The laces were tight and slightly uncomfortable around their legs as the material was digging into their flesh, causing the men to shift in discomfort.

A sash wrapped around one of their knees, almost acting like a knee brace, was red in color as if to hide any type of blood that may spill down their legs. The edge of some type of battle kilt with melt balls etched into the hem made it feel awkward to wear, considering that they were wearing gladiator battle armor, it wasn't all that surprising that they would feel uncomfortable. Some of the men looked a little flustered, while the others looked indifferent to it.

Around their waist, they were wearing some type of leather belt that they had never seen before. On one side, there was a knife tucked in, mostly used for up close combat, while on the other, it seemed that they would have a holster used for their weapon of choice for battle. The chest piece they wore seemed to have been made of a thick leather material, bound tightly around their torso to protect the vital organs.

Pieces of metal and leather armor sat upon their shoulders, while their arms offered little protection. There was a metal plate tied around their arm, reaching the length of their elbow down to their wrist. This must be used to close daggers coming in close, which would come in handy. It appeared that they were ready for the battle that was about to commence despite appearing to be unprepared.

As for Rachel and Lizzie, they would be wearing a different sort of outfit. Unlike the men, the women were provided with metal boots that covered their calves. The metal seemed to be painted in a golden texture that accented their legs nicely. A thick white skirt moved to cover most of their legs, had long slits up the sides, offering movement in case they needed to get away. A decorative waist garment acted as a guard against exposing their genitals as the skirt was a bit see-through in nature. The garment had golden coins etched into the red and white fabric. The fabric was held together by a golden color belt with the same coins spread neatly along the belt.

A breast plate made up of gold seemed to fit perfectly against their body. A single white slash crossed over their left breast while a jagged golden plate hung over their right shoulder, their arms seemed to be covered more than the guys. With the sleeve ending just shy of the elbow, the women wore gauntlets made up of gold with some red fur like trimmings. They were dressed to stand out while the color choice of the men was basic in color.

Feeling the eyes of the men staring at them, Lizzie and Rachel glanced away, a bit of color flushing towards their cheeks out of embarrassment. "Wow, you look-" Oliver started, only to blink in surprise when Rachel held up her index finger with a scowl mixing in with her embarrassed gaze. It was clear that she was just as embarrassed as Lizzie at their appearance.

"Not, another word." Rachel growled under her breath, obviously uncomfortable in the outfit that had been selected for her. How was anyone supposed to fight in something that could easily get caught under someone's foot? It was like the hem was begging to be torn open. "It's already embarrassing enough to have you stare at it, let alone the freaks in the stands." Rachel continued to grumble before her eyes darted towards Chris. Oliver could already see the thoughts going on in her mind, so he didn't want to feel that gut wrenching feeling of jealousy to spoil the mood.

As the crew gathered, hoping to take this as a chance to strategize an attack to get out of this shelter and leave it behind them once and for all, the crowd behind them seemed to cheer loudly. Glancing around in a bit of confusion, the group's eyes started to trail towards a balcony that looked over the arena. Standing there, with a smirk on his face, was the brat known as Nero. Just seeing that smug look made Davis want to punch him repeatedly until Nero's face was nothing more than a puffy bloody mess of the boy's face with a couple of teeth knocked out of his mouth. Which was probably how the rest of his crew felt at the moment, but just didn't voice it.

"Sorry to call everyone here on such short notice." Nero spoke, his voice echoing from the speakers that surrounded the rings of the arena. "But I wanted to welcome a crew from the surface dwellers who came to our rescue after so many years of isolation." Nero continued, the statement seemed to turn the crowd that was once cheering and happy into a bunch of booing fans that would have been more than happy to see the group get slaughtered.

"You know, it's a bit funny how no one seemed to answer our pleas for help when we could barely grow enough food to survive for the whole growth season for our crops." Nero spoke up as he paced back and forth with the microphone in hand. "Did they reach out to us during that time, everyone?" Nero spoke as he looked down at the group with seething anger in his eyes.

"NO!" The crowd quickly shouted in unison, their voices echoing in the area as they all glared at the group of people standing in the middle of the area. Some of the adults were already starting to throw bits of rotten vegetables towards the group. However their aim was lacking as most of the vegetables didn't make it close to the group.

"Or how the time when the adults had drank radiated wine from the grapes growing in the underground water way when our hydroponic sprinklers failed to work for months on end." Nero started to list off another event that happened while the communication lines were down. "We all know what happened then right?" Nero asked but didn't give the crowd much time to answer.

"It resulted in those who tasted the wine to either turn mad and kill each other unprovoked....or they were slowly dying in front of us while begging them to put an end to their suffering." Nero continued. Lizzie winced in pain as she couldn't imagine that sort of pain. To beg a child to kill you instead of being killed by someone who was out of their mind? "Did these people help us out then too?" Nero paused as he waited for the crowd to answer in unison.

"NO!!" The crowd shouted, some of the adults even laughing about the matter. It was clear that there was no way that the crew wasn't going to get out of here. The more that Nero talked and got people on his side, the less likely they will convince these people to join up with them. At this point, Davis was willing to just suggest leaving and never coming back. But he had orders that he was given. So he had to at least try something.

"Hold on." Davis yelled, walking closer to the balcony, wanting some answers for what Nero was claiming happened after the communication was cut. "If that all happened, where is your evidence?" Davis spoke, placing his hands on his hips. If this sort of thing did happen, then there would have been some type of record on file. Even if these kids didn't know how to either read or write, surely there would have been evidence in the form of videos or audio that would back them up.

This seemed to only delight Nero, seeing as this was a bit of a challenge to him. To put some adult who thinks he knows how their world worked, when he had no clear concept of what was going on, on blast for what happened. As if it was all their fault for what happened to the shelter. Not the fact that a shelter that wasn't kept up to code would eventually fail, but rather the outside world was at fault for their mishaps.

"Well, if you can win the arena, I'll be more than happy to show you the evidence you seek." Nero remarked, a coy grin forming on his face as he glanced down at the dressed up outsiders. "Now then!" Nero spoke into the microphone. "Shall we introduce the other gladiators that will be fighting these trespassers?" Nero asked into the microphone as the audience started to cheer.

"Instead of this whole grand show," Davis shouted loud enough for Nero to hear him. "How about I take you on. One on one." Davis suggested, studying Nero's facial expressions to see if maybe Davis could bait Nero into agreeing to the fight. If this worked, then Davis would be able to hopefully spare his crew from fighting.

"Winner gets to decide the fate of everyone in the shelter?" Davis suggested, figuring that if Nero was as good as he boasted, surely the kid wouldn't have a problem battling it out with someone like the likes of Davis. This was the only real solution that Davis was able to count on. Using Nero's ego to get the better of him.

"Davis, what are you doing?" Oliver asked, giving the leader of the crew a nudge on his arm. "Do you really think it's a good idea to even battle this kid?" Oliver continued to ask out of concern. "He seems a bit on the unstable type if you ask me. Plus he might try to cheat in order to make sure that nothing happens to his so-called people." Oliver continued, voicing his opinion. It wasn't like Davis was the type who was ready to go and fight someone, but in this case, Oliver could see that this might be their ticket out.

"Listen, if we want to get out of here, the least we can do is entertain this brat with one battle rather than have all of us wear ourselves thin." Davis remarked, turning to face his crew. "Battling a bunch of kids, it's something that you guys don't really need on your conscious." Davis didn't want to have his crew feeling the continuous guilt of having to beat up a bunch of kids. Especially kids who were being ordered by some crazy power hungry child who didn't know right from wrong. "Besides, this kid has been asking to get his ass handed to him." Davis grumbled, a part of him seemed to look forward to battling this kid one on one.

"So what do you say?" Davis shouted loud enough to have Nero hear him over the crowd's chanting. It seemed like Nero had plenty of time to decide if the pros outweighed the cons. Not like there was much that these kids could lose while staying here in a run down shelter.

Sure they may have to change their way of life a bit, but they were at least young enough to be able to adapt and overcome any challenges that come their way.

"Very well, I don't see the harm in us fighting." Nero spoke, his voice showing his confidence. "If I win, then your crew would have to stay as our prisoners." Nero spoke, a sly grin forming on his face. "Meaning, that in order to be able to get their freedom, they'll have to battle and win at least forty times before they will be set free." Nero started with his prize first. "That is, if they can even survive that long against the other warriors I have." Not like they would really be able to get a chance to win that many times in a row. But at least it would make for some interesting battles in the future.

The collective shocked expression was apparent as Davis didn't know if he would be willing to risk his whole teams' freedom just so that they would be able to get out of this hell hole. *"Guess I'll have to make sure that I win now."* Davis thought to himself, knowing that there was a lot riding on this now more than ever.

"Fine." Davis agreed, not giving the others a chance to disagree with them being a prize. "But if I win, I want access to all of the records that you have and our freedom." It wasn't like these kids were going to simply come along quietly, so it was just easier to ask for important data and their freedom. One they were out of this place the better. Besides, if Davis could make this kid relent, the better Davis would feel. After all, this brat seemed like he was too far gone at this point to be saved.

With the conditions met, Nero seemed to disappear from the balcony. Davis on the other hand, sighed as the members of his crew circled around him. Already Davis could feel the swarm of nagging remarks and complaints that were going to come from those who surrounded him.

"Are you serious right now?" Rachel was the first to nag Davis. "How could you allow him to use us as future fighters in this messed up battle royal?" Rachel continued to spat in anger. "I hope you're not the type who will hold back on us now." She finished, her eyebrows seemingly knitting together to show how displeased she was.

"You know some of us can't fight, right?" Oliver started next. "Forty battles without losing. It's a lose-lose situation for us!" Oliver remarked, bring up a fair point. It was like this would be a never ending nightmare if Davis lost. But it wasn't like Davis was going to allow himself to lose. He'll find ways in making sure that he is going to win. After all, it wasn't just his life on the line anymore.

"Guys, relax." Chris remarked, being one of the few who was willing to step up for Davis. "He's one of the best fighters that we have." Chris continued as he placed a hand on Davis' shoulder in support. "If there was someone who is able to take down this kid, it would be Davis." A bit of poor choice of words, but the sentiment of what Chris was trying to say was apparent. "He has better training that all of us combined. Have faith that Davis can do this."

"Just be careful Davis. We don't need to lose you in this obviously rigged battle." Lizzie remarked, walking over with her arms crossed over her chest. "He'll try and cheat, so maybe try to out him for cheating in front of his people." Lizzie started to suggest as the crowd was starting to chant louder. "That way his pride wouldn't be the only thing to get hurt." It was clear that Nero was the type who liked to use dirty tactics in order to get the win. To be able to mess with someone's mind to catch them off guard to secure the win.

"What makes you think he'll cheat?" Mark asked, asking the question that seemed to be on everyone's mind as she brought it up. The question seemed to cause Lizzie to smirk a bit, bringing her index finger up towards her lips.

"It's really simple. He says that he has never lost a battle right?" Lizzie pointed out, taking some mental notes from their first interactions with the young leader. "So it only stands that he is cheating one way or another in order to win." Lizzie pointed it out, acting like she had solved some type of murder mystery even before it happened. "And with him being so young, it would only stand that he would want to keep that up." Lizzie continued with a small chuckle. "You know, look good in front of his peers. That sort of thing" The human ego could either make or break a person.

"If Davis loses, and we get put as prisoners, you better pray that we never have to fight. Because if we do, I won't hold back." Rachel snapped, clenching her fists as she wanted to simply fight Lizzie right there and then. It felt like the life or death situation was starting to bring out the bubbling tension in the group.

"What's that supposed to mean? You want to go right now?" Lizzie snapped back, not wanting to put up with Rachel's attitude right now. With the tensions being as high as they were, it was no wonder that some of the crew was already at each other's neck.

"Stop it you two!" Davis was quick to snap. "I won't be able to concentrate if I have to worry about the two of you fighting while I'm going against that brat." Davis scolded, watching as Mark and Oliver pulled the two women away from each other. At least he had some help, though Chris simply stayed out of it. Even when facing a literal life and death situation, the drama between the two women didn't stop.

"This day just needs to end already." Davis grumbled under his breath, rubbing his forehead to take the pressure of a headache that was already seemingly forming. He needed to keep a clear head if he was going to battle, and his crew wasn't making that easy.

As the two guards walked over to the crew with a spear and a small round shield, Davis glanced at the two weapons being brought out to him. The shield was much smaller than the large one that Davis and the crew were already wearing. "These will be your fighting weapons." One of the guards spoke, each of them handing Davis the spear and shield before they took the large shield off of the man.

Taking the items, Davis was quick to look them over. The spear was almost as tall as he was, allowing for the fighters to fight at a distance, but also be able to be deadly if they got some hits in. The tip of the spear was tied onto the wooden shaft by a dark red ribbon. The shield was large enough to give Davis some protection if he needed it, though there were some dents in the metal shield, showing that it had been used a few times in the battle arena.

After receiving the weapon and shield, Davis glanced up to see Nero wearing a similar outfit that the crew was wearing. It seemed like it didn't take long for the punk to get changed. Even though Davis didn't feel completely confident about this, he had to do everything in his power to save his crew. He couldn't allow them to become fighters in this rigged fighting arena. To watch them slowly devolve into mindless fighting machines, it was something that Davis wouldn't be able to forgive himself if he allowed that to happen. He'll fight with everything he had to protect the people who were the closest thing to family, even if it meant beating up a kid.

THE two fighters stood inside the inner circle of the arena. The cheering crowd echoed around them as both Nero and Davis stared each other down. The two referees were on standby, waiting for the two to start. After all, even though the two were using deadly spears and a small shield as their only means of protection, that didn't mean that the blows couldn't be devastating.

Shifting his foot ever so slightly to dig into the ground, Davis bent his knees to counter any attacks that could come his way. The crew stood by the gate, waiting with held breaths to see who would be the victor. They never got a chance to see Davis fight before, so they wouldn't know who would exactly be the victor of this battle.

"Think he'll be alright?" Asked Mark, giving Chris a light nudge. "I mean, we know that Davis came from a military style shelter, but it seemed like these kids have been fighting for most of their lives." Mark continued, earning a small glance from Chris before the male turned his attention to the two fighters. It seemed like Nero was looking for an opening as he shifted his feet to circling Davis who didn't take his eyes off of the kid.

"The military shelters aren't a joke Mark. They do this sort of thing on the regular." Chris started to explain as he watched the two. "You know how bad it can get with either food or water supplies being tampered with." Chris continued as he glanced towards Mark with a serious gaze. "It can cause some of the people inside to become loose cannons, ready to kill if it meant that their shelter would be safe from outside forces." Chris hated that they were seeing some of the side effects of what they were taught before being sent out to this shelter.

"Right now, that is what we are witnessing." The grim tone in Chris' voice was apparent. "We're the outside invading forces, so this kid is going to do everything possible to keep the people who look up to him safe." In some regard it was admirable. But in this case, it wasn't a good thing. "All the while Davis is going to give it his all in order to keep us safe." Chris remarked, crossing his hands over his chest. It felt weird to be dressed as some type of historical reenactor, but this was to decide the fate of the shelter and those who live inside of it.

When it seemed like Nero wasn't going to find a way to drop Davis' guard, the young male smirked as he tossed the small shield to the side. This caused Davis to raise an eyebrow before Nero ran towards the older male like a lion who had spotted their prey, pouncing on the unsuspecting prey with fangs and claws extended to bury into the preys' flesh for the take down. Before he knew it, the sound of the tipped spear head started to scrap against the metal shield took Davis by surprise, causing the older male to stumble back.

Keeping his guard up, Davis endured the brute force of the spear clashing against the metal shield being repeatedly slammed into the shield that pushed Davis back more each time the spear struck the metal shield. *"Damn, this cocky little kid has some strength behind his blows. It's no wonder why he chose to use the spear as the weapons."* Davis thought to himself as he made sure to watch where the tip was going to next. *"He's confident that he doesn't need the shield as long as he is on the attack."* Davis continued to think to himself as he could see some of the bits of metal being chipped away, threatening to get into his eye. It would be a cheap tactic, but an effective one if it was used right. Luckily Davis didn't get any of the metal shards in his eyes.

"What's wrong?" Nero spoke up in an attempt to try and distract Davis. "I thought that you were going to fight me?" Nero taunted, easily provoking Davis as the older male thrusted the shield to try and stagger Nero, but that only seemed to be what Nero wanted. A quick chuckle left Nero's lips as he used the shaft of the spear to throw Davis off balance by slamming it against Davis' knee, causing him to fall to the ground.

With a hard thud Davis landed on the dirt ground before rolling over to use the shield to block the spear from being thrusted into his gut. The crowd cheered as the referees pushed Nero back with a thick stick used to keep the fighters from killing each other. "Seems like you're not worried about your friends." Nero taunted as he glanced towards the worried group. "Or is it that you're the only strong among them?" Nero taunted one more as Davis slowly staggered to get up from the ground.

With a small growl, Davis got up back on his feet. It was true that he didn't have to deal much with the fighting aspect of his training as much as he would have in the real world, but he would be damned if he would allow this punk to make him look bad in front of his crew. Tossing the shield down himself, Davis gripped the spear's shaft tightly in his hands. "You have a lot to learn, kid." Davis spoke, a small smirk on his face as he watched Nero get into a more defensive position with his spear.

"Trying to attack him head on is suicide." Davis grumbled in thought as he kept his guard up. *"He demonstrated that he could easily move the spear around as if the shaft was made up of some type of bamboo shoot..."* Davis thought to himself, his right hand moving to brush the edges of the shaft to see if he could tell what material the shaft was made of. Raising an eyebrow, Davis glanced towards Nero as he studied the size and shape of the shaft. It seemed like there was a bit of difference between their two weapons.

An audible chuckle left Davis' lips as he moved to stand up, as if he wasn't going to fight anymore. "You thought that you were a sly one." Davis remarked, causing everyone to quiet down, the confusion seemingly spreading against the crowd and those who were in the inner arena. It seems that Lizzie was right about the kid cheating to ensure that he would win.

"What are you going on about?" Nero spat in an annoyed tone, not liking the fact that this adult was trying to trick him or something. The brows knitting together was a clear indication that Davis had gotten a bit under Nero's skin with that comment, it was like a sweet bitter taste of karma that was coming towards Nero's way, even if the younger male didn't have a clue as to what was going on. It seemed like Davis was onto something. There was a reason why Nero was able to win with his own personal weapon. Regardless if the boy knew it or not, but his spear was made up of something special that not most weapons could copy.

"The material that the shaft is made of for your weapon isn't like normal wood." Davis started out, bringing the spear that he had up as a bit of demonstration. "Not like this one at least." Davis continued, breaking the spear over his right leg with ease. The wood seemed to splinter off, destroying the weapon and in turn caused a bit of a ruckus in the crowd. "Your shaft is made up of a special type of wood that doesn't grow in this type of climate." Davis continued, walking over towards Nero and the two referees.

"It's made up of bamboo. Which makes it more flexible." Davis finished, placing his hands on his hips, only to move his right hand to be out stretched. "You've been cheating this whole time, haven't you?" Davis spoke, a smirk on his face as he twitched his finger tips in a 'give me' motion. "They are hard to break, which means you would have worn me down before defeating me. All for the sake of your little shelter."

The confused murmuring seemed to spread through the crowd, even Davis' crew looked a bit surprised when it seemed like Davis called out that the leader of this shelter was cheating. This only seemed to make Nero chuckle before he dug the end of the spear into the dirt rather than give it to Davis. "You think I would cheat in order to save the shelter?" Nero spoke seemingly grinning as he looked Davis up and down, though Davis didn't know if this was a good or bad thing.

The silence between the two warriors caused those in the stands to quiet down. It was only when Nero turned away from Davis and towards the crowd that the younger male started to speak. "If there are individuals who wish to venture out onto the surface where things are hectic and food is hard to come by, you're free to leave." Nero shouted, gaining everyone's attention. "Those who don't wish to lose their only home can stay. Secured in this shelter underground where, at any moment, it could come crashing down." Hearing this coming from Nero surprised Davis the most, seeing as how Nero accepted his defeat without any bloodshed.

"We've survived in the shelter even after being almost completely flooded…. by digging into the dirt that encased us in our coffin." Nero started to speak loudly towards the crowd. "We've survived the toxic mold that spread through our crops, causing many of the adults to either die, suffer from a brain infection that would leave them completely paralyzed, or caused them to go mad." Nero continued before looking back towards Davis and the other.

"Not like going up to the surface is going to kill us, but staying here very well might." Nero spoke, giving a bit of the inside information that the crew had sought out when they had gotten down to this shelter. "So, let's strike a new deal, saviors." Nero spoke, all eyes glancing towards Davis and the crew. "How about those who wish to go with you are free to leave without any type of punishment. Those who want to stay can do whatever they please from here on out."

This new revelation caused a bit of a surprise as no one figured that would happen. Even Davis was surprised at this sudden change, causing the older male to raise an eyebrow. "You honestly think that you can just change your mind and act like the whole battle that just happened," Davis started to speak up, his anger showing in his voice.

"You know, the one that you actively tried to kill me in, is just going to go away?" Davis spoke, raising both of his eyebrows up in disbelief that this punk had the brass balls for a power move like that. Maybe it was just a bit of a front, or an act so to speak, to make himself look good in front of the others. After all, Nero seemed like he was a pacing tiger, ready to get out of this cage and sprint back into the wild. "And that everything will be right as rain because you can't admit you were cheating…" Davis trailed off in disbelief. Not like there was much faith that Nero wouldn't try something after they left, but it was better than staying here a second longer. A win's a win to Davis.

Glancing towards his crew, he could see the mixed judgment in their eyes. Some of them didn't want anything to deal with the people here, figuring that it might be the best thing to let them stay and just fend for themselves, but there were some who figured that these kids just needed the right leader to guide them. If that meant that they had to release the tiger into the wild, they could do so with some conditions. After all, seeing what Nero did with mitigating the water levels to keep from having the shelter completely free of water, it seemed like this kid could very well come up with ideas to make their life easier.

With an exasperated sigh, Davis kicked the dirt as he knew that this could very well come and bite him in the ass. "Alright..." Davis spoke, nodding his head as if he was forcing himself to agree with himself that this was the right call that he was making. "Fine. If there are people who want to come with us, collect your things and wait by the entrance for us." Even if they don't get the evidence that would explain what happened to the adults, or any information that would help society grow, the very least that they could do was bring these kids towards the closest town so they could start learning a new type of trade.

"As for you." Davis spoke, turning his attention to Nero, who seemed to find most of this to be a bit amusing, Davis had a stern look on his face as he muttered the last part. "Don't make me regret this. You're going to come with us, and you'll have to use your skills for more than just helping those of your shelter. Got it?" Though during that time, Davis had no idea what would happen when he released Nero onto the world above. How much terror the kid was going to cause once he grew up to be a charismatic leader that would bring about the first war in over five hundred years.

AFTER the shelter had been long since abandoned, the doors had been opened once more for the first time in fifteen years. The dirty water above rushed in the blown up door and down the steep steps to the closed doors.. At the base of the shelters' door, a familiar figure pressed the pin to open the empty shelter, only to have the rest of the water trickle inwards like a bunch of rats fleeing a sinking ship.

The dark and empty hallways smelled of musk from the years of black mold creeping along the walls. The bit of fabric that was once reminiscent of a rug had been completely worn down by the water breaking down the fabric a little bit over time was easily squashed under the figures' feet. A familiar red cape was draped over the figure's right shoulder as a small group of elderly and weak citizens followed behind the older figure of Nero. All of them seemed to be wearing a gas mask as they made their way through the empty hallway towards the large opening that was once the market where the Colosseum stood slightly decayed.

Glancing around, it had appeared that nature took over the buildings with relative ease. Reaching up to take the gas mask off, Nero took a deep breath of the air inside of the self contained terrarium. The air was fresh and crisp, unlike the tunnel in which they had ventured through to get down there, meaning that those with even weak respiratory would be able to breathe without much problem. Well, as long as they do not enter through the tunnel towards the bed chambers.

Running a hand through his white medium length hair, Nero smirked a bit to himself as he knew that this would do perfectly. Everything was already set up, all he had to do was just leave these people here to take care of themselves while the war went on, and in no time, the Wrath clan will be on top.

Unlike his former self which was nothing more than a dirty child who wished that he could lead his people to be a powerful force, Nero was much older and wiser now. His hair seemed to graze his more stoic features that showed his maturity. Golden brown eyes that were once dead now seemed to be seething with the greed of power that would make him even stronger. His tan skin was a bit darker thanks to his time out in the sun. The slender form that he once had as a child was more well defined as he became an adult as he grew into his body with a more muscular frame.

Nero had learned a lot about fighting when he traveled with Davis and his crew, but now they weren't here. After the events that happened in this shelter the last time, they had decided that enough was enough. Though Davis was kind enough to take Nero in and teach him how to improve his fighting skills, Nero knew that there would be a point in which he would have to use those same fighting skills against the man who was like a father to him. But it was necessary in order to make this new society as a whole much stronger when the event of the Elites above could come down and try to take back what they once abandoned if they weren't careful.

"Welcome to your new home." Nero shouted, his voice echoing in the tunnels as he threw his arms up, collecting everyone's attention onto him. "For some of you, this is a very familiar place." He continued, seemingly to shout excitedly to put the ease of those who had doubts to rest. "Even after all the years in which we have been gone, our beautiful home still provides for us once again." It seemed like Nero was acting like some kind of preacher leading people to a promised land, but there was a reason why he brought the weak and feeble down to the place where many people didn't know the location of.

"Here you will be safe from the ongoing war above." Nero chimed up as people started to make their way pass him. "You won't have to fear the other tribes finding you here. You'll be safe from combat. You won't go hungry or cold." More promises coming from Nero as the grim looks on people started to lift. "Consider this the garden of Eden." Nero spoke, turning to the run down city that was covered in vines. Some of the buildings were a bit unstable for most people to be able to stay in for more than a few days, but this was the perfect place for what he had planned next.

Watching as people slowly walked past him, some even with their gas masks still on until they were completely out of the tunnels, Nero watched as some of the people collected towards the bottom of the steps with their back turned away from Nero. A sly smirk formed on his face as Nero slowly backed out towards the entrance, putting his mask on before heading back towards the entrance. He didn't have the time or luxury to really stick around and watch those in the shelter get used to their new surroundings.

Walking with a bit of haste, Nero made it back towards the entrance where he had two guards stationed to make sure that everyone was able to make it into the shelter, making sure that no one was left behind was the key to make his plan work and for his tribe to rise up above the others. If they wanted to take over the other tribes, they would need to set an example that would let the other tribal members know that those in the Wrath clan were serious.

"Is this all of them?" Nero asked, his smile leaving his face as he walked past the two guards who were holding something cylindrical under both of their arms. These metal cylinders weren't exactly light, but they were needed. Even though the labels had been worn down over time, Nero knew exactly what laid inside of them.

"Yes sir." One of the two guards spoke, giving Nero a small nod as they couldn't exactly salute the man. The two watched as Nero walked past the two of them, not really saying much of a word as he placed a foot on top of the bottom step of the worn down and soaked steps. There was a lingering smell of mold that escaped from the tunnel, but Nero couldn't smell it with his mask on.

"Good...." Nero trailed off before turning to glance towards the two guards while the shelter door was still opened. "Release the gas." Nero ordered as he started to climb up the steps. "Then shut the door and make your way up towards the surface." Nero commanded as he stopped close to the halfway point before glancing down. He wanted to make sure that the guards did as they were instructed before he went any further.

The two guards shared a glance between each other, knowing that if they don't do as Nero said, they would join those unfortunate souls down in the shelter. Hesitantly the guards gripped the nozzle of the tanks before tossing them into the darkness. Once the four cylinders were hissing, the two guards closed the shelter door before locking it. The gears slowly turned as a loud clanking noise could be heard from either side. With a heavy sigh, the two guards made their way up the steps as well, following their unstable leader.

Recently those around Nero had come to witness how ruthless the leader of the Wrath clan had been acting. First sending out a small squad towards the Sloth clan with their recent exiled member from said clan to lead the party, now this. It was concerning what else he was going to order next before heading to the meeting between the leaders where Nero was supposed to announce his war on the other tribes.

As they reached the top, Nero seemingly stopped the two guards who seemed to freeze in their movements. Both seemingly blinked in surprise when they noticed a little trigger device in Nero's hand. "You know, it's awful with what happened." Nero spoke, flashing a small grin towards the two before pressing the button. Both of the guards were unsure as to what Nero meant until they felt it. The ground below them started to rumble as explosive bombs that lingered along the dark were set off one by one, either trapping or killing those who were still in the shelter with no way in or out.

"Who could have guessed that there was actually a large gas pocket seemingly trapped under the shelter all this time." Nero chimed so casually, slipping the small trigger into a hidden pocket inside of his shirt. "Such a shame for all of those who were down there. Looks like we won't make it in time." Nero mused, watching in delight at the shocked and angered gazes cross the guards faces.

"You monster... " One of the two guards growled, the anger causing the guard to grip a hold of Nero's shirt as he pulled the insane male closer to him. "How could you-" The man continued, but seemingly stopped when he felt a sharp pain in his chest. Glancing down, Nero had been able to pierce the guards' gut with a hidden dagger that was well concealed by the long sleeves of his white shirt. The guards blood seemed to splatter a bit against Nero before the guard slowly took a few steps back in shock.

"I'm the monster?" Nero asked in almost a hurt turn before his brows knitted together in anger. "Weren't you two the ones who tossed the gas into the shelter?" Nero continued in an accusing tone before chuckling a little bit as he tilted his head back. "Then again....I did tell you to bring the mustard. So maybe I am partially to blame." Nero chimed in almost a haunting gleeful tone. The other guard was shocked to learn the truth as to what this mad man had ordered them to do.

"That was mustard gas?!" The uninjured guard shouted, causing Nero to slash the guard's throat. The man tried to speak, but anything he may have tried to say came out gurgled as blood filled his throat. The way that the man's life was slowly disappearing from his eyes brought a smile onto Nero's face.

Feeling the hot blood splatter onto his face, Nero brought up his red cape to wipe the blood from his face. Though there were still traces of blood lingering on the coins that dangled from the scarf wrapped across his forehead. The gurgling noises from the guard was rather pleasing to Nero at first, though it was quickly becoming annoying as Nero swiftly kicked the man down the steps.

"Y-You're sick." The first guard struggled to speak while he held onto his stomach. Nero let out an amused hum before leaning over the other male. Even though the sound of his partner landing on the bottom of the steps meant that he didn't have to hear the other suffering before dying, the guard couldn't help but feel the coldness of death while looking into Nero's eyes. There was no warmth in those eyes, just a cold and bleak death for anyone who stood in his way.

"Well, at least you could say that you were just following orders." Nero mused, shoving the man backwards. Watching as the guard struggled to stay upright was hysterical, but with the guard stumbling down the steps only to snap his neck halfway down was a riot to Nero. As their dying bodies laid on top of each other, Nero used his cape to wipe the blood off of his blade as he turned to walk out of the shelter.

Outside the sun was starting to set behind the mountains, meaning that the desert was about to get a bit colder. The tents that were used to house the injured, sick, and old were nothing more than metal bars with some of the lingering fabrics still burning, offering a bit of light for Nero. Peeling off his shirt, Nero wiped the lingering bits of blood off of him before using the knife to cut the blood soaked locks of his hair. It was much easier to burn everything rather than allow for people to find out the truth of his crime. Though it wasn't like there was much that they would be able to do. In Nero's eyes, those who weren't strong to fight in the upcoming war didn't deserve to live.

Tossing his blood soaked clothes into a small fire pit that had been made earlier, Nero was completely naked out in the open air. Of course he wouldn't be that way for much longer, having already planned ahead and packed a backup set of clothing, Nero yanked the old coins off as a bit of a souvenir. With the coins in hand, Nero walked towards the truck that was used to gather the weak and the sick. He collected the spare clothing that he hid under the passenger seat. Using small rocks to keep them in place, Nero set the blood soaked clothes on fire before heading towards the truck to drive back towards the nearest town, unaware of the consequences of his actions on that day.

In the end Nero would get what was coming towards him. By his own hands, Nero would bring about the events that would lead to his head being nearly decapitated by the Greed's clan leader in an ironic twist of fate, Nero made the path for a better humanity possible. His desire for power and to kill those who were unworthy was his ultimate demise.

From a struggling leader of a run down shelter, to a powerful force that almost seemed to be unstoppable, Nero would find those who, at one point shared in his dream to make the last remaining humans on the planet be a force that could take down the hovering elite bastards above them, would turn against him. To end the vicious violence once and for all, their own blood would eventually be spilled soon after.

Within that room, the amount of dead bodies would only seemingly pile on top of each other, one after the other, until only Greed was left. It seemed only fitting that his daughter would come to end the cycle of blood shed by the same method used on Nero. Thus ending the Wrathful cycle of human beings once and for all, allowing for humans to grow in a peaceful environment, rather than that of vengeance.

CHAPTER EIGHT: *Reflection*

WITH THE DISHES cleared from the table, two white ceramic mugs seemed to sit on the table that Felicia and Dean were at. A small plate of coconut cookies laid in a decorated pattern for them to enjoy. The smell of roasted coffee lingered around Felicia as she picked up the cup to take a small sip of coffee that was nestled half way in the mug. "So you're telling me, all of that really happened?" Dean started to ask as he grabbed a hold of the coffee mug of his own before taking a sip of the liquid inside of it. "That Nero guy going insane!" Dean continued as he set the mug down. "Killing innocent and defenseless people with a mixture of mustard gas and explosive bombs…" Dean trailed off in a disbelief tone. "For what? Because they were simply too weak to fight?" Then again, Dean was used to dealing with the Elite who would willingly use explosives to dislodge a pod to kill those inside, so it wasn't all that much different from that.

"Unfortunately." Felicia spoke, a soft sigh brushing against the dark colored water, her voice echoing in the mug ever so slightly as she took a sip. A soft hum of delight echoed in the mug as she finished her drink. The other mug in which Dean had been drinking was lined with specks of cocoa with a small trim of cream. Dean wasn't exactly fond of the taste of coffee, so he simply ordered some hot cocoa to wash the biscuits down.

"Frankly it seems like he had gotten what he deserved in the end." Dean remarked, a small shrug of his shoulders as he leaned back against the clothed seat. "He's just as bad as some of the Elites I had the misfortune of running into." Dean added, his eyes finding a clock that lingered above the doorway in which they had entered through their first time coming here. "Oh wow, we've been here for about two hours." It seemed like time had gotten away from him. "Guess I better go and check on Kane." Dean spoke up as he shifted towards the edge of the seat. "Poor guy will be stuck in bed all day at this point without much relief." Dean commented, slowly rising from the comfortable seat, finding that his legs were a bit stiff from sitting down for so long listening to the story Felicia provided to him.

"If you want to really help him," Felicia paused as Dean started to stretch a bit. "You should crawl into bed with him and rub his stomach or his back." Felicia continued, catching the curious gaze from Dean. There was a mischievous glint to Felicia's eyes as she placed the mug back down with a smirk on her face that made Dean wonder if she was actually being helpful or if she was simply toying with him. With a hesitant wave, Dean was heading towards the exit of the dinning hall. The lush carpet helped Dean to find his way back towards the staircase that headed up towards the bedroom quarters.

Walking past people who were now making their way down to get some food after they had put their own personal belongings away, Dean found himself stopping at the top of the stairs that led towards the leaders living quarters. There was a man who seemed to walk towards Dean who was dressed similar to Kane before they had left the hospital. Though unlike the dark clothing that Kane wore, this guy dressed in a light gray robe with dark squares slowly disappearing upwards around the hem of his sleeves.

As the man approached Dean, he could tell that the man was an inch shorter than himself. His long dark gray hair was a bit shaggy yet tucked behind his right ear. A clump of long bangs seemed to nestle over the bridge of the man's nose, parting perfectly so that the man's steel gray eyes gazed towards Dean. Long black eyelashes seemed to make his gaze even more pronounced. The man's ear seemed to stick out through the tusks of hair. His eyebrows were thin as his eyes looked tired, as if the man never had a good nights' sleep. The man's skin had more color to it than Kane's, showing that he had a bit of a light tan from working outside in the sun.

"So," The man spoke, his words seeming to carry a bit of confidence behind him. A small smile seemingly tugged against the corners of the man's lips as he stopped in front of Dean. "You must be the newcomer that everyone has been talking about." The man continued, though Dean watched a bit weary of the man. It wasn't like Dean knew who this guy was, but if he was up here in this section, that must mean that he was one of the other leaders. "Dean Torres, right?" The man asked as one of his brows raised.

"Yeah?" Dean answered, his weary showing as Dean watched the man reach out his hand as if to offer Dean a hardy handshake. *"Just who is this guy? He doesn't exactly look like someone who would fit the name Keaton."* Dean started to think to himself while his brows knitted together in thought. *"Then again, with that slender face and the way he seemed to smile, he resembles a fox more than a wolf."* Dean thought to himself as he let go of the man's hand. "And may I ask who you are?" Dean asked, as he retracted his hand. The other male certainly had a bit of a grip to him, almost like the male was trying to see how strong Dean was with his grip.

"Ah yes," The man started to speak with a smirk on his face. "My name is Miles Mayworth. I'm the leader of the Sloth tribe." The man introduced himself, the name clicking in Dean's mind. Dean was taken back as he was surprised that he would be meeting this Miles guy so suddenly. "I see that you have met my fiance Felicia, and little brother Kane." Miles continued, seeing the surprise in Dean's eyes at his last remark.

"Wait, Kane's your little brother?" Dean asked, a bit confused since neither Kane nor Miles seemed to look alike. Sure they both had similar hair color, though Kane's was lighter than Miles, but besides that there was no real connection that the two would have been related.

"We're not related by blood, or even marriage." Miles continued before crossing his arms over his chest. "But I did take him in when his family was murdered." It was a bit of a heavy bombshell that Miles seemingly dropped on Dean's head, but Dean was a bit distracted when he noticed that Miles had slipped one of his hands into the sleeve of his robes.

"Wait, murdered?" Dean asked, the concern showing in his voice as Dean's eyes went back to studying Miles' face. "Who killed his family, if I may ask?" Dean asked, curious as to how or why this Miles guy came across Kane if his family was murdered. But instead of getting any type of answers, Dean was simply presented a small bag of something that seemed to have a scent of ginger to it.

"Here, these are for Kane." Miles commented, tossing the bag towards Dean, resulting in Dean stumbling back a bit in order to catch the thrown bag as it bounced off of his chest. "The ginger will help to ease his stomach." Miles started to instruct as Dean looked back up at Miles with a confused look on his face. "But also if you want him to feel better, try giving his stomach or back a small rub." Again with that suggestion? "Usually it tends to help more than any conventional medicine can." Miles added as he walked past Dean, seemingly finding the confused look on Dean's face amusing.

"Though it would be up to you to decide if you want to. That is, if you're too afraid to be intimate in that way." Miles finished, only to head down the stairs passing Dean on the way down towards the dining room. It seemed like Miles was going to meet up with Felicia. Mentally shaking his head, Dean looked at the small bag given to him.

There wasn't anything unusual about the bag besides the smell. There was something round inside. They were hard against Dean's thumb as he stroked the texture through the bag. Glancing over his shoulder, Dean was all alone in the hallway now. "So that was Miles, huh?" Dean mumbled to himself as his fingers clenched onto the bag. Dean didn't know why, but there was something off about that guy. Mentally shaking his head, Dean figured that he should just simply check in to see how Kane was doing. After all, Dean had been away for a couple of hours now.

As Dean entered the room, he glanced towards the top bunk. The curtain had been pulled mostly closed, but Dean could see the light silver locks that belonged to Kane buried his head into the pillows. Closing the door behind him, Dean placed the small bag on the little side table before grasping the ladder. Pulling the metal ladder over to the opening in the curtain, Dean steadied himself as he stepped up on the first rung to peek in on Kane. There was a sound of a small groan that seemed to be muffled by the pillow, but it was reassuring that Kane was at least awake.

"So, how are you feeling? Any better?" Dean asked, watching as Kane shifted to look at Dean with a tired expression. With a slow blink from Kane, Dean glanced around the small enclosure to assess the situation. It seemed that there was a glass bottle of ginger ale that was at least half way gone. At least it seemed that he was able to keep down liquids. "So um...I ran into some guy named Miles out by the-" Dean started to speak before seeing Kane jerk up suddenly.

"Miles is on the ship?" Kane asked in a shocked tone of voice, taking Dean back by surprise. Just by the reaction alone, it was evident that this Miles guy was the one that Kane had been infatuated with in the conversation that the two leaders had while Dean was in the bathroom. Sitting up, Kane seemed to look for his robe to put on, but the feeling of nausea seemed to cause Kane to cover his mouth. As he slumped back down on the bed, a small groan seemed to leave Kane's lips as he stifled an upcoming burp.

"Yeah...his name was Miles Edgelord." Dean lied, watching as the energy that Kane did have started to slip away when he glanced over towards Dean. "He was a crew member. He sold me some cookies that have some ginger in them to help with nausea." Dean continued, feeling bad for lying to Kane like that, but he just didn't know if he liked the feeling washing over him at that moment. It was almost like he was resenting Miles. Feeling like Kane would simply ignore him if Kane knew that the very Miles that took Kane in after the death of his family was on board the ship.

This was the same type of feeling that Dean felt in elementary school when one of the little girls was nice enough to share some of her toys with Dean, only to completely ignore him the next day. Or how his so-called family straight up abandoned him after the death of his parents. Dean simply didn't want to be abandoned by the only friend he had now. To be tossed to the side like he was nothing more than a piece of garbage, it was a big blow to Dean's ego.

Sure he felt bad for lying to Kane, but right now the other needed his rest in order to get better. To not worry about someone being on the ship when he could barely move about as it was.

Pushing the feeling of guilt from the pits of his stomach aside, Dean reached down to grab the bag. Pulling the tied on ribbon off, Dean reached in to pull out a round and slightly cracked cookie. Bringing it up to his nose, Dean gave it a quick sniff before taking a bite out thick cookie. The overwhelming taste of ginger was cringe worthy, though it did remind Dean of the ginger cookies his mother used to make when Dean was feeling under the weather. "Very... chewy." Dean commented while chewing the cookie in his mouth, his brows seamed knit together as it was clear that Dean didn't exactly like what he was tasting.

"You don't need to torture yourself to eat it." Kane remarked through a groan as he reached out to grab one of the cookies from the bag. Bringing it to his mouth Kane took a bite of the cookie, sighing through his nose as he could taste the ginger. Closing his eyes, Kane didn't start to chew but to simply let the ginger slowly dissolve in his mouth. Nestling his head against the pillow, Kane looked as if he was ready to fall asleep. Dean on the other hand looked while he was forced to swallow the cookie, not wanting it to go to waste since he couldn't stomach letting food go to waste.

"Well, I guess I was a bit curious about how it tasted." Dean made something up to explain the need to taste the cookie. "My mother used to make ginger snap cookies when I was little and would get sick." Dean spoke up as he smiled a bit while talking about his mother's cooking. "It was actually quite often that I got sick, though sometimes I would fake it to get out of going to school." Dean continued with a soft chuckle towards the end. "But this one has a bit too much ginger in it for my liking. But I guess it would help your stomach out more, huh?" Not that Dean wasn't grateful that he was able to give something to Kane to help him out, but there were times in which Dean could show how much of a picky eater he could be, as he forced the rest of the cookie down only to lightly cringe at the end.

There was an awkward silence that seemed to linger in the room, making Dean feel uncomfortable. It seemed like he wasn't going to be of much use to Kane like this. It was almost like Dean was back in school, being paired up with someone for some project and feeling useless as he couldn't contribute much to the project over all. That familiar feeling of resentment he felt from the kid who was partnered up with Dean would rather be with his friend than that weird kid that nobody talked to.

Taking a small deep breath, Dean lightly tapped the wooden frame before stepping off of the ladder. "I'm....uh...." Dean started, letting out a small cough as he slowly backed towards the door. "I'll go and take a look around the ship." It was a lame excuse, but right now Dean just couldn't deal with this feeling that seemed to sit in his stomach, like he was the third wheel when it was just the two of the leaders known as Kane and Miles. Though Miles wasn't in the room, he might as well be. "I'll come and check up on you later." Dean softly waved as he moved to grab the handle on the door.

As Dean left the room, Kane let out a small sigh before peeking out from the pillow. There was a hurt gaze to Kane's eyes as his ruffled locks seemed to go this way and that. "Idiot...." Kane scoffed softly as he moved to roll onto his stomach. "These walls are thin." Kane mumbled to himself, adjusting to tuck his left arm under the pillow. "I know Miles is here. I know his voice anywhere..." Kane continued, mostly to himself as he closed his eyes. "He always makes the ginger cookies too puffy. The lingering taste of ginger is the only thing that helps my stomach." Nuzzling into the pillow, Kane groaned. "Why bother lying to me when you're such a bad liar?"

ROAMING the ship aimlessly for roughly half an hour, Dean couldn't seem to get that odd feeling out of his mind. It felt as if Dean was a fish that simply allowed the current to guide its way in a stream. Eventually through his wandering, Dean came across an observation room that was lined with different seats along the walls with enough room for most people to turn around in the chairs. There were windows that took up half of the wall, though most of them were covered up with blinds to protect the passengers' eyes from the blinding sun. The sunlight seemed to become more intense than normal as the light reflecting on the ocean's surface seemed to intensify from the sun's rays as it peeked through the clouds.

Walking over towards one of the seats, Dean sat down on the rather hard cushion. There was no backing for the seat, so it felt more like a place to rest for a bit. Hunching over as he placed his hands against his cheeks, Dean could over hear some gossip that seemed to come from a group of women. Each of the women looked to be around Dean's age, though the way that they conversed with each other made Dean feel as if he was listening to teenagers gossiping about the latest news on their peers rather than what was important.

"You got to see some of the leaders? Lucky!" One of the women spoke, her excitement evident from the way she had gasped before even speaking. Looking between the three women, Dean took notice of the first girl. She was rather thin with a slightly sunken face as if she didn't eat a lot. Either she was watching her diet, or she just wasn't getting nutrients into her body. Her hair was a bit short and on the curly side too, a light brunette by the bits of curled hair that seemed to stick out of her black hat with a small spider like veil that clung to her hair. The small beads scattered around the veil seemed to sparkle in the sunlight that caused parts of the wall and ceiling to form small circled rainbows that followed her movement.

Glancing down her to her outfit, Dean noticed that she was wearing black shorts that seemed to cling to her thighs. The corset that she was wearing seemed to be white with decorative belts that seemed like they would be able to adjust to help the woman keep her figure. The loose sleeves she wore seemed to mostly dangle while her hands were free to move about with little effort. She was wearing fishnet stockings that went from under the sorts she was wearing down to the boots that seemingly rested against her ankles. A jeweled choker was nestled against her thin neck while large hoop earrings dangled just above her shoulders. Her skin was pale white, completely different from the other two standing close to her.

"Oh yeah." Remarked the one girl who had commented on seeing the world leaders, making Dean pay attention to her next. She had a tad bit of color to her skin, though she seemed to heavily rely on makeup to make her stand out against the three. Her red hair was tucked back in a slightly messy braid with bits of flowers seemingly decorating her hair. Dean didn't know exactly what she was going for, but part of him believed that she wanted to be seen as someone who was pure yet knew what she was doing. The dark blue and black striped corset dress hugged her body tightly as the hem of the dress in the front stopped just shy above her knees.

Striped stockings added to the appeal as the thin high heels she wore accented her legs. Layered necklaces seemed to decorate her chest as the heavier decorative pieces fell down her chest. Her arms were completely naked, except towards her wrist where some heavy bracelets seemed to draw attention to her hands.

"I'm surprised to see Miles here. Wasn't he supposed to be getting the crops transported to the underground facilities as we're expecting a heavy winter?" She seemed to continue, the small earrings she wore dangled ever so slightly from her ears as they moved with her movements.

"I think he wanted to surprise Felicia since she had been missing him while she was busy with the yearly crops." The third girl seemed to chime in, her voice soft and almost sheepish. Her dark ebony hair seemed to barely brush past her ears, showing off the small silver earrings that would have been missable is it wasn't for the sunlight making them apparent. She was wearing something that appeared to be some type of sun dress that lightly hung off of her shoulders. It was a light ivory color with light pink ribbons that were etched into the sides of the dress, showing off her slender waist.

The hem of the dress seemed to brush down a little past her knees as she wore matching heels along with it. She had a bit of a tan on her, which really made the dress stand out more. A small silver necklace was delicately placed around her neck, again only being noticeable when the sunlight was on it. The only thing she was missing was a large sun hat that would match her dress with a large light pink ribbon wrapped around the base with a sunflower pinned to it to make her ideal for a summer time ad campaign during the times before the nukes were dropped.

"I'm so jealous." Remarked the red haired woman with a small sigh. "I wish I could nab someone as sweet and romantic as Miles." A small pout crossing her lips as she let out a whiny groan. "Most of the guys I have either dated or met have been self entitled jerks who only want to have a bit of fun on the side." She finished, earning small nervous giggles from her friends.

"Well, isn't he bisexual?" Commented the brunette, causing Dean to glance at her with a slightly puzzled expression on his face. It wasn't that Dean was the type to normally listen to gossip too often, especially when it was coming from sources that he didn't know if he could trust, but everything in him told Dean to listen to what these girls were saying. "There were even rumors that he hooked up with his little brother Kane." She continued, tilting her head as if she was trying to remember correctly what had happened and what had only been a rumor.

"No way, Kane only wishes he could be with Miles." The red haired girl remarked, though it seemed like she was teasingly saying that, but her tone was more taunting. The very fact that people would say something like that about Kane started to make Dean angry.

"You're wrong." Dean thought bitterly to himself, moving his hands to hold them together, trying his best to stay calm. The girls seemed to continue on, but Dean was trying his best not to listen. Whether or not these girls seemed to do it in order to piss Dean off didn't matter, he just didn't like these feelings swelling up inside of him. Feelings that Dean thought that he buried a long time ago after his parents death.

"It's sorta sad if you think about it." The girl with brunette hair chimed up, catching Dean's attention. "Miles took Kane in when he was, what? Fourteen?" The brunette spoke, tilting her head a bit as she crossed her arms against her chest. "That's a long time to carry a torch for someone who took you in and helped to raise you." She added, causing Dean to focus on their conversation again. Maybe when the time comes, Dean could ask Kane about this personally, but for now there was an awkward rift between them. Mostly due to Dean's own awkwardness that he never learned to get over, though acted like he did.

"I don't blame him though." The ebony haired girl dressed mostly in white added to the conversation once again. "To think that someone would take you in when you had no one else in the world. Who wouldn't be grateful?" That statement was something that Dean could never comprehend. No one took him in when his parents died when he was younger. If he had someone like that, Dean doubted that he would even be down on this forsaken planet.

"Grateful?" Dean thought bitterly to himself, glancing to the side as he wondered what that felt like. To be grateful that someone took pity on Kane and took him in. To raise a young orphan who literally had nothing left. Was Kane's admiration for Miles something that Dean could never really understand? Sure he was glad that Kane took him to the hospital and was teaching Dean about how their world works, but it wasn't like Dean would get so worked up that he looked like a flustered school boy who spotted their crush coming up towards them. At least, that's how Dean pictured the way Kane was acting when Miles' name was brought up. Even if it wasn't flattering, he wasn't exactly wrong.

Releasing his hands that were clenching each other tightly, to the point where it seemed like Dean's knuckles were ready to burst out of the skin as they were also whiter in color, Dean gently placed a hand on his stomach. There was that heavy feeling again. It felt like a rock was sinking in his stomach and someone invisible was pushing against his back. Knitting his brows together to show his discomfort, Dean slowly got up from his seat and made his way over towards the window. Perhaps a change in view, as well as distance from the gossiping girls, was what he needed right now.

Parting the blinds to peek out, Dean was surprised at the vast ocean landscape in front of him. Parts of destroyed skyscrapers seemed to linger in a pathway that was too dangerous for any boats to safely cross. Trapped metal vehicles from before the bombs being dropped seemed to pile up on the ocean floor that was visible even from how far up they were. The colors had long since been dissolved away, leaving nothing more than a metal frame. It was a shame that they were too far up as Dean wanted to see what kind of aquatic life was able to find its way into the empty streets of the once busy city life.

Leaning against the window, Dean simply stared out to admire the view below him. All this time Dean had watched the soft glowing planet slowly spin around in the vast and dark space. His reflection was barely noticeable on the reflective surface of the window, but his eyes went from being turquoise green to being that of a dark emerald from the sunlight. His pale skin started to have a bit of color to it, though just enough to make him not look like some type of glowing angel that descended from space. The surface of the window felt cold at first, but with the heat of Dean resting against it, the window started to fog up, making it a bit harder to look out casually. Dean gazed out as he was trying to figure out his own thoughts about what was going on in his head. Despite all his time alone, he could never escape his intrusive thoughts.

"What is wrong with me?" Dean started to scold himself as he paid no mind to the glass fogging up his vision, though it wasn't too noticeable as it seemed to only trace around where his body touched the glass. *"Lying to Kane like that.... I don't know what came over me."* He continued to think, a heavy sigh escaping his lips as it fogged up more of the glass in front of him. *"Actually I do know what is wrong with me..."* Dean started to reason with himself, taking a small step back from the glass so he wasn't pressed against it anymore. *"Just like Kane, you latched onto the person who took pity on you."* As much as Kane didn't want to admit it, he knew it was the truth.

"He was the first person to literally reach out to you..." Thinking back on the crash, Dean crossed his arms over his chest before bringing up a hand to brush back his bangs that lingered over his left eye. *"Since being abandoned by my family after my parents death, and being sent towards my own death, I guess it only makes sense that I latched onto the first person who showed some actual human compassion."* It wouldn't be the first time in history for this sort of thing to happen. It was natural for another person who had been neglected for half of their life to cling to the first thing to give them a bit of hope in their bleak life.

"It's still early enough to make amends for making myself look like a complete ass in front of him. Maybe I can do something to cheer Kane up. Or at the very least, apologize for being an ass." Dean audibly sighed as felt his bangs fall back in place. Looking back at his reflection in the window, Dean noticed that there were some people looking at him with odd or concerned looks on their face. It didn't bother Dean as he was used to those same gazes from his time on the station.

"Guess it's' time to head back." Dean muttered under his breath, turning to head out of the little observatory. Dean could feel the mutters as the people talking about him like he was some type of circus animal who didn't live up to expectation, it was best to ignore it. Let people talk. Not like Dean could change their mind about him.

HEADING back towards the tribal leader's sleeping quarters, Dean noticed a familiar figure finally walking about. Wearing a long dark robe, a tired looking Kane closed the door that was to his room. With a click of the door locking, Kane turned away from Dean before heading towards the deeper part of the upper level that Dean had yet to explore. Instead of calling out to Kane, Dean instead watched as the other slowly trekked down the hallway. The sun seemed to be setting, judging by the orange coloring in the windows, allowing for the lights in the hallway to flicker to provide some extra light for when it would get dark.

"When did it get so late?" Dean muttered to himself as he briefly glanced towards the window. Perhaps it was simply due to them flying towards the darker side of the planet that was always casted in a shadow. At least, that's how it seemed when Dean would often gaze down at the planet when he lived on the station. "Whatever..." Dean snapped to himself mentally as he focused his attention on watching Kane walk behind a curtain off section, causing Dean's interest to be peaked.

With careful footing, Dean made his way down the hallway. Dean's heart pounded against his chest as he felt like he was doing something that he shouldn't. Dean's mind seemed to race as to why Kane was up and walking around now when he seemed to be so sick earlier. Remember the look on Kane's face upon seeing him coming out of the door, it almost looked like the other had been tired despite sleeping for most of the day. Kane's hair was brushed back as there wasn't any evidence of the bed head on the tribal leader's head. Though Kane's skin was normally pale, there was still a small hint of green as Kane seemed to still be a bit under the weather.

"I knew Kane was stubborn, but this is just asinine. He should rest in bed. What could be so important that he would get out of bed and make his way down the hall for?" Dean thought to himself before it dawned on him. A small disappointed glance towards Dean's left side pretty much said it all. *"Oh right... him."* It would only make sense that the one person who Kane would get out of bed for was that Miles guy.

With a small slump of his shoulders, Dean let out a small audible sigh as he turned back towards the stairway. It didn't feel right to be up in the higher living quarters anyways, not like he was a leader of anything. All Dean was to anyone was just a strange man who fell from space. He wasn't charismatic or interesting at all. He didn't have a high Elite job aboard the Millennium. He was a boring orphan who struggled every single day of his life after his parents died working in the janitorial part of the Millennium.

Taking a few steps, Dean noticed Miles and Felicia making their way up towards the hallway in which Dean was currently standing in. Stopping in his tracks, Dean glanced around to see if perhaps there was a place where he could hide, feeling the wave of panic rushing through his body as it seemed that the two took notice of their space friend almost appearing to be in distress in the middle of the hallway.

"There you are Dean." Felicia called out, her arm seemingly wrapping tightly around Miles' clothed arm like a viper who was squeezing the life out of their prey. Her chest brushed up against the other tribal leaders' arm as she wore a rather loose dress that had both of the sides of the dress barely stitched together along the top portion of her dress. A golden belt wrapped around her waist against the ebony black dress that appeared to be tightly fitting.

Felicia's locks were pulled back into a rather large bun though her normally curled ends made the bun appear to be a bit more messy than anything else. Around her neck appeared to be a necklace with three pink pearls lingering against the silver linked yet sleek chain. If Dean was back on the station, he would have sworn that Felicia was one of the young trophy wives for one of the Elite members, or at least someone who was high Silver class.

"Ready for dinner?" Miles asked, his silver locks seemed to be slicked back. He was wearing something like a tuxedo, which was a bit surprising since he had only seen the other wearing a robe much like Kane. The suite was dark, much like his female counterpart. Though instead of expecting a bow-tie, it appeared that Miles was wearing a regular tie that was black with some golden blocks disappearing along the bottom of it.

"Dinner?" Dean asked, a bit confused since it didn't seem like time had passed that quickly while he was on this airship. If anything, it would feel a bit more like lunch than anything else. Perhaps this was just simply a side effect of being up in the station for too long. His perception of time was clearly different. Not to mention that Dean was used to eating only two meals a day, so eating roughly three or more times in a singular day was making Dean feel like his stomach was constantly full. A concept that he had only had the privilege of feeling when he was in the Silver class.

"Dinner on the ship often takes a couple of hours." Felicia started to speak, finally loosening her grip from Miles' arm as she went to explain how meals after breakfast would seemingly work. "As you saw, breakfast is a bit more food focused so that people could get something in them before going about and enjoying everything that the airship has to offer." Felicia spoke while Dean remembered that much of their meal was Dean eating while Felicia told him about Nero. "Those who might like to sleep in more towards the afternoon tend to enjoy lunch as their first meal." Even though that didn't seem to make much sense, Dean simply raised his left brow before giving a slow nod to her.

"Not everyone tends to wake up at the same hour." Miles politely interrupted Felicia before she started to get ahead of Dean. "So to compensate for the different times, meals are provided for those who wake up at different times." Miles continued to explain. "Whether they would want to wake up in time to catch breakfast, or if they would rather stay in and wait till closer to noon before getting up and grabbing a quick meal, no one goes hungry. After all, we want people to enjoy their trip." Miles finished, figuring that would make it easier for Dean to follow as he was new to all of this.

"Oh....gotcha." Dean mumbled more to himself than towards the two leaders in front of him. Just the way that Miles was able to control the conversation was a bit irritating, simply because Dean didn't even have to ask for a better explanation, but Miles could pick up that Dean wasn't quite understanding it the way that Felicia was trying to explain everything.

"Anyways," Felicia paused a bit, her smile slowly flat-lining before clearing her throat. "So for our dinner, it's a chance for people to come together as a whole and enjoy a nice gigantic meal." She chimed in a more eager voice while flashing a smile towards Dean who seemed to lighten up a bit at her explanation.

"You see, since there are a lot of new people flying, we wanted everyone to be comfortable and at ease." Felicia continued with her explanation before parting from Miles' side and clung onto Dean. "But there are some people who are too shy to want to be around strangers. So we have an option for people to dine in their rooms if they want." Feeling Felicia cling onto Dean and start to drag him towards the curtained off area made Dean feel uneasy since he wasn't prepared to have Felicia practically sweep him up.

A light smile formed on Dean's face, though the uneasy feeling continued to linger, but not to such a degree as earlier. Glancing towards the wooden interior panel of the hallway and away from Felicia as they made their way towards the back of the ship, Dean wondered how things would have been different if everyone could come together for a giant banquet on the Millennium. Instead they were practically forced to eat in their own makeshift homes, separated from everyone and in a sense isolating themselves. Thinking back on it, those of the Elite class were more likely to come together as a whole to wine and dine among themselves while laughing at those who were less fortunate. They would rather focus on how well they were as a class rather than want to come together as the last members of humanity.

"Well, we can't keep Kane waiting. I'm sure he's dying for us to come to dinner." Felicia chimed, the closer that they got to the curtain. As Dean looked back towards Miles, it seemed that Miles was simply finding this to be amusing. It was probably amusing that someone else was able to feel Felicia's beast-like grip that was the amusing part. Even though Felicia was a rather beautiful and slender woman, she had the strength of an ox behind her grip. Dean felt like she could choke him out or break his arm if he wasn't careful.

As the curtain was pulled back, Dean was able to see that Kane was seated at one of the chairs facing away from the door. With the sound of people shuffling in catching Kane's attention the leader turned to notice Felicia pulling Dean in through the open door. A small flat smile lingered on Kane's lips before Dean noticed the lifeless eyes seeming to sparkle a bit when Miles followed in afterwards. Not saying much of a word, Dean was guided towards his seat, which was next to Kane's.

"Look who I was able to catch trying to slink away from joining us for dinner." Felicia chimed happily, forcing Dean into the seat next to Kane. There was that same awkward energy that seemed to be growing between the small rift that was caused by Dean's foolish choices, causing Dean to laugh a bit nervously before looking away from Kane after taking his seat.

"Glad you could join us." Kane mused, the soft smile lingering on his face. The shift of expression and the direction of Kane's eyes was noted as they seemed to watch Miles more than pay attention towards Dean. Following the older male till he pulled a chair out for Felicia, Dean could notice the small hitch in Kane's breath as he stared at Miles.

"My dear." Miles spoke in a mixture of amusement and a flirtatious tone. Watching the interaction between the couple, Dean was reminded of the same type of interaction his parents used to do between each other. With witnessing the kind of behavior that Kane was expressing for Miles, Dean felt that same sinking feeling seemingly getting heavier in his stomach. It didn't seem fair that Dean was feeling this way when he had no reason to. There was not a single logical explanation as to why this ever growing heavy pit seemed to be swelling inside of him.

With a small mental shake of his head, Dean glanced towards Kane. Offering the other a small smile, Dean figured that he might as well start in a bit of light conversation with Kane. Though it might have felt like a sad and desperate attempt to get Kane's mind off of Miles, it was at least a step in the right direction.

"Seems like you're feeling well." Dean started after a quick clearing of his throat. "How's the nausea?" Dean asked, knowing that the first part was a bit of a lie. Kane looked like he would much rather still be sleeping in bed than to be sitting here at the table with everyone. But because of the knowing fact that Miles was on board, Kane seemed to be pushing himself to appear stronger than he was.

"It's gone down a bit thanks to the ginger." Kane remarked, placing a hand on his stomach to give it a gentle rub. "I think I might have some room for a light soup." Kane replied, a bit of a shrug from his shoulders as he looked forward. The feeling of being rejected was something that Dean was used to, but being brushed off so easily seemed to hit harder when Kane did it. It seemed that Felicia and Miles had taken note of the small exchange, causing them to glance at each other before Felicia picked up a glass of water to drink.

"So Dean," Miles paused for a few seconds, allowing for the attention to be directed more towards their outer worldly guest. "Why don't you tell me a bit about yourself? I've heard a few things, but I think we could all use this time to get to know each other better." Miles continued, seemingly moving to get comfortable in his seat.

"About myself?" Dean mumbled a bit, a little shocked that Miles would want to know about him already. "Eh, well." Dean swallowed a bit nervously, taking a small glance towards Kane who seemed to be glancing back at him. It always seemed like when someone wanted to know more about Dean, Kane would at least show a bit of interest. Maybe it was because Kane was trying to make sure that Dean kept his stories correct, or that maybe he really did want to know more about the other, but it did give Dean a bit of reassurance that he wasn't being completely ignored by the only person who was like a friend to him.

"As you probably could already guess, I came from the space station orbiting around the planet." Dean spoke a little meekly at first, used to there being at least two people listening to his story rather than dealing with three. "It wasn't exactly the greatest place to live." Which wasn't a lie, as the other two leaders had heard his story before as well. "I was originally born in the silver class. My mother was a teacher and my father was a mortician." Dean continued, grabbing one of the glasses. The glass was cold to the touch as it started to fog up ever so slightly from the heat coming off of Dean as he didn't get a chance to change out of his overly warm clothes.

"That must have been quite the odd couple." Miles spoke, seemingly to give back a bit of feedback to the story that Dean was telling. It was something that Dean wasn't exactly used to, but he was at least a bit relieved that there was some conversation going back and forth now.

"It really was." Dean remarked with a soft chuckle before he continued. "But my parents loved me more than anything. Well.... except for maybe each other." Dean mused a bit, a light smile flashing on his face before taking the sip of water to help cool himself off. "That's why when they were murdered, and I was left to defend for myself, it really turned my world upside down." Dean spoke after setting the cup down. "No one on either side of my parents' family would take me in after their death unfortunately. As a result, I was put in the Bronze class." Dean spoke, his upbeat tone started becoming more bleak as he continued.

"I was placed in a small pod as a living quarter. It wasn't all that big really. It felt more like a kennel when I was little." Dean continued with his story, his eyes trailing to gaze at the glass in front of him. "It was only when I had gotten older and taller that I realized that it was becoming less like a kennel...and more like a coffin…" Dean didn't normally like opening up about himself, but he didn't want to tell the same old story that he had told before, but he wanted to at least have someone like this Miles guy understand why Dean wanted to destroy the place that was once considered home to someone like Dean.

"Everyone was pretty much isolated from each other, and I never heard back from those who were once called family." Dean let out a small audible sigh towards the end before looking up towards Felicia and Miles, the two appearing to be interested in what Dean had to say. "Any time I would try to save up money, it seemed like something would happen that would make it hard for anyone to save. But that's how it was in the Bronze." Dean shrugged as if it was to be expected when living in that particular class.

"You lived to work until you died. All the while those in the Elite lived a much better life than the rest of us." Much like life on Earth before the nukes dropped. "Spending money on food just to be wasted away and burned for fuel, that would support the inner main core of the station first before being dispensed across the rest of the classes. Leaving the Bronze with hardly anything left to provide us with either heat or electricity." Dean continued, figuring that he could at least give a bit more information for Felicia to work with.

"But how did you get here?" Miles asked, causing Dean to be a bit thrown off by the question. Normally someone would at least want to know about the situation that would lead towards the actions that resulted in their current situation. But it seemed like Miles wasn't interested in that. It seemed like Miles was more trying to gauge if Dean was telling the truth or if he was trying to elaborate everything that happened.

"By my crashed shuttle?" Dean spoke in a slightly confused tone, raising his left eyebrow a bit as he didn't know how else to describe how he landed on the station. "It's not like we have the technology to easily land here if that's what you're asking." Dean continued, tilting his head as he softly glared at Miles. What was with this guy? It seemed like he was ready to jump and cut Dean's throat if he said anything wrong. Like a snarling wolf with a big deceptive grin on the leader's face.

"Did you even know how to land your shuttle?" Miles asked a bit more aggressively. "It seems a bit suspicious that you would seem to be able to land without being burned up like most of the rest of the unfortunate souls who seemingly crashed on our planet." Miles spoke, a bit more direct, his voice stern as if warning Dean to choose his words carefully.

There was a silence in the room that made it seem like one would be able to hear a pin drop. With a quick swallow, Dean didn't dare to look away from Miles' piercing gaze. It felt like Dean was frozen in his spot, unable to move or even breathe, he just simply stared into Miles' eyes. It was almost like staring at a giant silver moon that was creeping closer to the ground, crushing everything in its destructive fall. Dean felt like Miles would be able to see how fast Dean's heart was racing just by watching his jugular pulsating on his slightly exposed neck.

Another swallow to cool his throat, Dean took a deep breath in to steady himself with his explanation. "Frankly the trip down here wasn't exactly ideal." Dean started off, causing Miles to tense up a bit though he was sitting down. Dean could tell by the man's posture that this wasn't exactly an ideal way to discuss a sensitive topic when it appeared that the other two leaders might get in the way of Miles' decision; whether or not Dean was even worthy of meeting the remaining three leaders.

"But considering that the lady above me had no say in being dejected from the pod, and the corrupt Enforcement officers were behind the attempted assassination as they tampered with the guiding chip inside of the shuttle, I had no choice but to crash my shuttle." Dean spoke up in his defense. "I had to aim away from water. Otherwise, I might not have been able to get out." Dean spoke, his voice stern as he didn't break eye contact from Miles. It felt like Dean was a lone wandering hiker staring down a hungry wolf.

There was another wave of dead silence in that room, though the ship did creak as a small bump of pocketed air caused the table and its contents to bump. Miles and Dean were caught in a stare down to notice. Dean could feel his heart beating against his chest as he wasn't backing down from this type of staring contest. It was like they had shifted from being a human and animal staring at each other, to the two bucks ready to clash their horns against each other.

It was only when Miles had finally been the one to lean back that Dean could feel the tension lift from his body. "Hm..." Miles seemed to hum, glancing towards the other leaders as if he made some type of unvoiced opinion. "I guess that would make sense." Miles continued, seemingly relaxing his shoulders as he glanced towards Kane, who had been silent this whole time. "I may not trust you wholeheartedly, but I'll go with Kane's decision." Miles seemed to add, glancing back towards Dean. "After all, he is the one who will be traveling with you."

Dean didn't know rather he should be annoyed, pleased, or worried with that decision. Before the whole incident with the cookies had taken place, Dean would have been over the moon. But now, things were on the fence with Kane. Dean didn't like how things were going with the only friend he seemed to make on this whole journey as they were still up in the air with learning how to trust each other, but Dean had to make things right one way or another.

THE minutes felt like hours as the staff started to bring in the food. Upon the dishes were things that Dean didn't even know what half of it was. There was something that resembled pork chops mixed with a brown sauce with odd shaped vegetables that seemed to act as if it was there to absorb the juices. It was either that or it helped with flavoring. There were some small golden orbs that looked almost like edible bits of gold. Sliced fruit seemed to sit next to the golden orbs, seemingly arranged in a decorative art piece that appeared to be something you would rather admire than eat.

There was also something that looked like a salad that his mother used to make, though it seemed that they added bits of white meat, or was it cheese? There was a bowl of something that appeared to look like white clouds with a white golden square that seemed to sit on top. The heat from the dish seemed to melt the golden square as it looked like small yellow streams were slipping down the smooth white surface. Dean never saw so much food presented to him before, though he always had to witness the aftermath of the Elite's festive banquets, it took him by surprise.

"What is all this?" Dean asked, watching as some of the staff had started to arrange the plates for those present to eat. Well, all except for Kane who appeared to be given a type of liquid dish that had long golden noodles with small bits of meat in a golden broth. A glass of ginger ale that looked more like a fizzy drink than anything else seemed to sit close at hand.

"It's a broiled pork tenderloin cooked in its juices with some red potatoes and onions." Felicia started to speak, before moving her fork over to the other various dishes as she explained what they were. "We also have some corn, mashed potatoes with melted butter, and a salad mixed with some chunks of chicken meat and goat cheese." Felicia spoke before her fork moved towards the dish with the fruit inside of it.

"We have a fresh fruit salad for dessert. It's a good way to end the night with something sweet, but not overly sweet. Plus this fruit is from my clan." Felicia spoke, her excitement for Dean to try some became apparent. "The pork, chicken, and goat cheese came from Kane's tribe, and the vegetables are a mix of Miles and Kane's tribes as well." Hearing that, Dean was surprised at how everything seemed to come together for the different tribes to make a rather delicious looking meal.

"Well, it does smell delicious." Dean remarked, though he didn't know what he was supposed to expect. Perhaps remembering the sight of the mutated sea gull led Dean to believe that all animals had become some sort of mutated creature that was beyond recognition caused Dean to be a bit hesitant. After all, Kane had told Dean about how most of the people had been living underground for the duration of the time after the bombs fell. So perhaps the animals didn't change all that much over the hundreds of years since then.

When the dish was presented to him, Dean was surprised at how elegant it was presented.

The bits of pork were arranged neatly in a crescent shape along the edge, the mashed potatoes seemed to look as if Dean was hovering over a white volcano while gazing into the golden magma as the butter was nestled neatly inside the dip of the potatoes.

There was a neat pile of the red potatoes that had an appealing amber coloring to the inside of the exposed vegetable as the onions seemingly matched the amber coloring while some of the juices from the pork lightly cradled under the mixture. All the while the corn was its own beauty as it helped to fill in the gaps on the plate. A small bowl of the chicken and goat cheese salad was placed next to Dean, only to be lightly drizzled with some type of orange sauce that Dean had never seen before. There was a light smell of ginger that seemed to come from the salad, though Dean didn't know what it was.

"The ginger dressing helps to bring out more of the taste of the vegetables, all the while giving a little bit of a bitter and sweet texture to it." Miles spoke up, being able to see the puzzled look on Dean's face. It seemed to snap Dean out of his trance before his eyes met Miles. Dean could see the thoughts going through Miles' mind, seemingly finding it a bit entertaining that Dean wasn't used to such food. Considering that Dean had been basically starved for a fair number of years, it was no surprise that Dean found himself almost hypnotized by the food in front of him.

"Oh? I've never had ginger dressing before." Dean admitted, though he felt a bit embarrassed. Mostly because his stomach seemed to start growling just by looking at the food in front of him. The smell of the various foods seemed to melt into each other, seemingly complimenting each other in a well orchestrated scent that just seemed to make Dean's stomach growl uncontrollably. The last time he felt his stomach growl this badly was when he first had to fend for himself after his parents death. That was a time in which he had never wanted to remember. The constant desire for some type of food, but the lack of experience making anything was a dark part of Dean's remaining childhood.

Grabbing a fork in his right hand, and a knife in his left, Dean stabbed the pork with the fork before using the knife to easily slice into the meat. It was so tender that the knife looked like it was cutting into hot butter. Bringing the piece of meat up to his lips, Dean took a bite out of the juicy meat. The hot food felt like it melted against Dean's taste buds, the juices of the pork making Dean feel that same spark he used to have when his mother would cook his favorite food.

A small hum of approval left Dean's lips as he eagerly chewed the food. Even though Dean's first instinct was to practically devour the pork, he had to fight the urge as he wanted to try everything that was offered to it. The red potatoes with onions were a bit bitter, like the juices had a hint of vinegar and salt to it. Though it wasn't exactly bad, it just didn't appeal as much to Dean as he thought it would.

Moving to the golden pile that was corn, Dean was surprised when it didn't exactly have much of a taste to it. Though he didn't know what to really expect, there was a bit of a watery texture to them but otherwise, it tasted like corn that grew on the station only smaller. Dean didn't know if he should have been as disappointed as he felt by it, but with a small shrug he simply moved on to the mashed potatoes. Unlike the red potatoes, the mash potatoes were light and creamy.

The butter seemed to add to the flavor, causing a small hum of approval to leave his lips. The last thing that he needed to try was the salad. Taking a small stab of the sliced tomato, it seemed bits of the goat cheese and ginger dressing clung to the red thinly cut tomato. Opening his mouth, Dean slipped it into his mouth. It felt like it seemingly filled the void in Dean's mouth, allowing him to experience some of the flavor.

The tomato itself was juicy, seemingly sweet despite the lack of salt that his mother used to put on the tomatoes she cooked. The ginger dressing had a small bitter taste, but overall it was fairly sweet. The combination made it pleasing to one's palate. Though the taste of the goat cheese hitting his taste buds was something that Dean didn't really expect. It was a bit tart like in flavor, but it wasn't exactly displeasing. It was just something that he didn't expect. Swallowing the bit in his mouth, Dean took a stab of a bit of chicken and lettuce to get an overall taste of the meal.

With a bite from the bit on his fork, Dean was surprised at the crunch of the lettuce, indicating that it was fresh. There was a small watery texture, but it wasn't displeasing. When the chicken seemed to hit his mouth, Dean was surprised at how flavorful the bit of chicken was. It was tender, with a small taste of lemon and pepper that the chicken was cooked in. Overall the meal was delicious, and Dean seemed to be at least satisfied with the course that he was presented.

"Glad to see you like the food." Felicia mused, a light smile on her face as she glanced over towards Kane who seemed to be more absorbed into sipping the soup than taking notice that Dean was enjoying the food. Or perhaps he was just trying to avoid eye contact with Miles, considering that the male was right in front of him. A light frown crossed her features for a second before she turned to face Dean once more. "Speaking of food." Felicia continued, placing her fork down before she moved to lean against the table a bit. Her chest barely hovering over her plate.

Naturally Dean's eyes went down her chest to make sure that they wouldn't stain her dress, but seemed to glance back up when Felicia started to talk. "What kind of food did you guys have on the ship?" Felicia asked as she took a bite of the food on her fork. It was a question of curiosity, to which Dean could understand where she was coming from, but it wasn't really a question that Dean could answer fully. So he would just have to answer the best that he could with what he knew.

"Uh, well..." Dean started, clearing his throat as he glanced towards Miles, hoping that the tribal leader didn't think that he was trying to check out Felicia. "It really depended on your class." Dean remarked, telling the truth. It wasn't like he knew for sure what the Elite had as a whole, but he did know that most of the Elite got to enjoy meals similar to what he was currently eating right now.

"The Elite would often eat premium cut meat and the freshest vegetables." Dean started to explain before setting his own fork down, figuring that it would have been rude to eat while conversing. "Since they were the Elite, they were always first when it came to the variety of food that they would get." When Dean said the freshest vegetables, he meant it. Each vegetable that was perfectly ripped would be handed to the Elite first. Same for the best cut of meat. Only the best for those on the top.

"Meanwhile, those in the Silver class often got the leftover choices." It wasn't exactly fair considering that the Silver class was responsible for growing the cattle and crops to provide food for the station. "While the rest of the station was eating decently, those in the Bronze class often got the deformed crops and last pick of the meat." Dean finished, a small frown landing on his face as he hated everything that happened on that damn station.

"Oh, I'm sorry I asked." Felicia apologized. Though it wasn't exactly her fault. She was curious about what it was like to live on the station after all. Who wouldn't be? To have someone who came from the station be able to answer questions that many wanted to know about, it was understandable why she would ask. After all, when would they be able to get this chance?

"Don't worry about it. It's not like we had much of a choice anyways." Dean remarked, a soft sigh escaping his lips before his shoulders shrugged a bit. "If you weren't born into the Elite class, you were pretty much done for." Dean remarked, before glancing over towards Kane who seemed to be done with his food. Blinking a bit in surprise when Kane seemed to push back from the table, Dean parted his lips to say something, but the words didn't seem to come out.

"Going back to bed?" Miles spoke, earning a glance from Kane who looked back towards him. Placing a hand on his stomach, Kane was silent, wondering if he should even say something. At least, that's how it appeared to Dean. With a small tilt of his head, Kane glanced away from the three before taking a step towards the exit. This seemed to cause Miles to change his expression from concern to a tad bit of annoyance. Even though Dean didn't know what was going on, he could tell that something was off.

It was then when Miles seemed to turn his attention towards Dean. "You want to know a little something about Kane, Dean?" Miles asked, glancing towards Dean. This seemed to catch Dean's attention as the male looked towards Miles. Taking note of how the man's eyebrows seemed to knit together, and his once relaxed position was more straightened like that of a scolding parent, Dean remembered his father in that instance. It reminded Dean of how his father Max would appear right before scolding Dean for something wrong he did, like fail a test or was caught fighting back against his bullies.

The gaze in Miles' eyes seemed cold as he bore daggers into Kane's back. "Our little Kane here isn't the oldest of his family, which normally to be a leader you would need to be the oldest sibling in your family." Miles added, his voice seemingly normal though his facial expression showed his annoyance. As Kane turned around, Dean was surprised to see the look of bewilderment and betrayal lingering on Kane's face. The sickly green was gone as Kane looked ghostly white now.

"Why would you-" Kane mumbled, his voice trembling a bit as if the cat had been out of the bag. Normally this wouldn't have been a big deal, but considering what Kane told him about the oldest siblings being the ones put in place for the leaders, it would make sense that this information would have been a big deal to someone like Kane. Little did Kane know, Dean had heard that something happened to Kane's family that caused Miles to take Kane in and raised him like a younger sibling.

"You see, I took Kane in because his family was murdered." Miles continued, despite the news being something that Dean had already heard about. "Naturally as you know, his father was killed by the leader of the Greed clan, but you want to know who killed the rest of his family?" Miles asked, ignoring the panic that seemed to be setting on Kane's face. It was like Kane was left speechless that someone he thought that he trusted was going to spill a dark secret of his past in front of a random stranger.

"Please don't do this..." Kane whimpered, any color seemingly draining from the poor male's face as he took a weak step forward. The hurtful betrayal was getting to be a bit too much for Dean to stomach. It was like he was seeing a younger version of himself, glancing up to seeing the dead body of his parents. The anger, sadness, and painful memories come back, causing Dean to quickly stand up, resulting in the table jumping a bit and rattling some of the somewhat empty plates.

"I don't want to hear it from someone like you." Dean shouted, causing everyone's attention to go towards Dean. A scowl landed on Dean's face as he glared towards Miles, displeased that he would willingly hurt someone he supposedly cared about. "Can't you see that you're making him experience a painful memory?" Dean growled, clenching his fists. "How could you do that to someone you willingly took in? To someone who you consider to be like your younger brother?!" Dean continued, not exactly sure where this was coming from, but he didn't want to see his friend hurting.

All three of the leaders didn't dare say anything as they heard the sharp hiss coming from Dean. Watching Dean's fists shake as he stood in place, Miles leaned back in his chair, as if he was waiting for Dean to continue. *"Damn it....I went and opened my big mouth."* Dean mentally scolded himself. Dean had to say something. After all, this was his chance to mend the rift that was growing between the two.

"I don't care what happened to Kane in his past." Dean finally spoke after a minute or so of silence passed. Glancing towards Kane, it appeared that Kane was the most surprised by Dean's outburst. Despite the surprised look, there was still a painful gaze in Kane's eyes. "When he is ready to talk about it with me, I will only want to hear about it from him." Dean finished as he unclenched his fists. The only time that Dean was ever this angry was when someone spoiled a good book before he even got to the climax of the story.

There was a silence that seemed to linger in the room. The mood had been spoiled from his outburst, but Dean didn't care. Grabbing hold of Kane's hand, Dean wasn't willing to stick around for an argument to occur when he had already said his peace.

"Come on. You're full right?" Dean asked briefly in an angry tone, not even paying attention to see if Kane would answer him before pulling the male out of that room. "I'll take you back to your room so you can rest." There was no way that Dean would simply allow another person to bully another for entertainment or whatever Miles was trying to pull back there.

"What the hell is wrong with that guy? Why was he being such a dick to Kane?" Dean thought as his feet stomped on the floor. *"It makes no sense to me! If he acts like that all the time, why the hell would Kane be so head over heels in love with that asshole?"* Kane thought bitterly to himself. If you loved someone, weren't you supposed to try and make them happy? At least that's what Dean thought based on how his parents interacted with each other.

Once it seemed that the only ones left in the room were Felicia and Miles, the tension had slowly died down. The sound of a match striking broke the silence as Miles lit the pipe he tends to carry around. It was an elegant looking pipe with its' thin wooden casing. The small silver tray holding some type of crushed plant that was set on fire. Taking a small hit from it, Miles glanced towards Felicia who seemed to wear a sheepish grin on her face. "What?" Miles asked, raising an eyebrow towards her as white smoke escaped past his lips.

"Do you think it was wise to do something like that?" Felicia asked, watching as Miles blew out a small puff of smoke that still remained in his mouth. "To make Kane hate you for trying to let out his little secret of his past before he was ready to share it?" Felicia finished, slowly taking the slender pipe from Miles' hand, wanting to take a small drag for herself. Her red lipstick seemed to leave a small ring around the silver mouthpiece as she held the drag in.

"What can I say?" Miles spoke, glancing towards the door with a more relaxed expression lingering on his face. "It was about time that I stepped out of Kane's limelight." Miles remarked, slinking back into the chair. "He held me in such high regard. It's about time he stops thinking of me as his first love, and more like his brother." Miles continued, moving to wrap an arm around Felicia. "And with the way that Dean seemed to stick up for him," Miles paused, looking at Felicia who was smiling up at him. "It seems that those two are getting closer the more time they spend with each other. Who knows, maybe it will work out in the end."

"I can only hope that it works out for them." Felicia spoke, letting out the drag she was holding, making sure to blow it away from Miles. "They seem like a good pair." Felicia continued with a soft hum towards the end. "They could very well change this world for the better." Felicia spoke softly, seemingly like a mother who had approved of her child's potential lover. It wasn't like they would out right say it, but perhaps this was the right course of action.

ONCE Dean and Kane were inside the room, Kane slowly made his way over towards the chair that he had sat in prior to the launch. A small groan leaving his lips as he sunk into the seat. Dean walked towards him, a worried expression lingering on his face. Hopefully Kane didn't think that Dean was being rude, but seeing as how things were going, it felt like things would have ended badly otherwise.

Watching Kane hunch over, seemingly covering his face from the rest of the world, Dean felt his heart sink a bit. Without much of a word, Dean walked over to the other seat. Sitting down next to Kane, Dean sat there silently, wondering how he could cheer his friend up. Even though he wasn't good at comforting, he could at least be there to lend an ear. After all, sometimes that's all that someone really needed.

As the minutes seemed to pass, Kane finally spoke up a bit. "It was my brother..." Kane remarked, breaking the silence in the room. Slowly removing his hands from his face and sitting up, Kane looked at Dean who still remained silent, unsure of what to really say. "And no, I don't mean Miles..." Kane corrected any thought that Dean might get from the reveal of who murdered his family. "It was my older biological brother who," Kane paused before wrapping his arms around his stomach, like he was experiencing it all over again. "Killed my mother and my baby sister..." Dean didn't know how to deal with this new information. But it seemed like Kane wasn't done. Brushing a hand through his silver locks, Kane let out a small sigh as he looked at the reflection against the polished wooden door. "He also gave me this scar. When he tried to kill me..."

"Look, Kane....you don't-" Dean started to speak before Kane turned towards him. Blinking a bit in surprise, Dean was surprised to see the look of determination on the tribal leaders' face, causing Dean to stop mid-sentence. Even if Dean was going to argue that Kane didn't have to go into detail about what happened in his past, it seemed like Kane was going to spill it regardless of what Dean said.

Keeping silent, Dean listened to the younger man's story about the death and betrayal that happened to Kane when he was younger. It seemed that five years ago was when everything seemed to shake the foundation of the world as a whole. Whatever it was, something major happened that turned people crazy. Killing each other or their kin, making it hard for people to trust each other, it made Dean feel like he was on the station hearing the story. There was no trust between anyone, and it seemed that it took a lot of effort for things to become stable once more.

CHAPTER NINE: *Kane's Past*

THE SUMMER SUN had been beating down on a grassy hill side in the Gluttony clan. The hot breeze of the wind swept through the tall grass that led up towards a dirt road. Two figures walked along the path, a taller male standing roughly 5'9 with disheveled platinum blond hair with lingering traces of silver mixed in that seemed to swoop down over his right side. The man's locks were medium length as it brushed slightly past the middle of his ears. His hair was thick, unlike the boy that walked beside him who had thin silver hair that barely brushed past the boy's temples.

With piercing yellow eyes, the man's skin was sun kissed while the younger boy was pale. A permanent scowl lingered on the man's face as bags nestled under his eyes. On either side of his ears, two small silver hoops lingered together against his ear lobe, making them glint from the sun. A few bugs flew past their ears, the buzzing as they passed a reminder that they would need to wash up as soon as they got inside.

"Hey Lucas?" The boy called out, wearing a small t-shirt that had lingering bits of dirt that seemed to trail from his torso down to the hem of the shirt to reveal the shorts that were barely noticeable from the length of the shirt. Lucas glanced down at his little brother Kane, who had only been a couple years younger than he was. The two looked completely different from one another, but that was due to Lucas looking more like their father while Kane looked like their mother.

"What Kane?" Lucas asked in an annoyed tone. His voice a bit scuffed as Lucas didn't seem to pay Kane much mind at the current moment. Lucas was wearing a buttoned up shirt that seemed to match the dirt that lingered on Kane's clothes. With black suspenders, the hem of the pants Lucas was wearing seemed to be wrinkled, showing that his pants had been rolled up previously with small bits of water and dirt crusting parts of the legs.

"When do you think that dad will be back?" Kane asked, looking up at Lucas, his silver eyes seeming full of curiosity. The sight of the looming space station seemed to peek through the clouds, causing Kane to turn his gaze back at the road that was leading towards their house. "I want him to take me hunting again. The deer we had last time was really good." This seemed to cause Lucas to roll his eyes before letting out a small sigh, indicating that Lucas was frustrated at the question.

"I don't know Kane." Lucas spat, his voice carrying his annoyance. It wasn't like Lucas was really annoyed at Kane, he was just annoyed mostly at the way that the world had become. With the murmuring of people seemingly wanting to take more than what they already had, tired of working day in and day out to have everything that they worked hard to grow having to be shared with those who didn't want to work, and the fact that many people were choosing to share their crops only within their circle or community, it was starting to get on people's nerves. Plus the lack of sleep from their newly born sister was making it hard for Lucas to stay awake through the day when he would work the fields. It was just starting to get to him.

The two continued to walk down the road in silence, Kane pouting as he didn't like when his brother would lash out with Kane's questions. The day would have seemed peaceful, if it wasn't for the fact that the rain clouds over the mountains indicated that a storm was on its way. Which meant that it was going to be a sleepless night for Lucas once more. Unlike his little brother, Lucas would be able to wake up at the slight disturbance that seemed out of place.

Glancing down at Kane, Lucas could see that the other was visibly upset, causing the man to sigh before placing a hand on top of Kane's head, causing the younger male to stop and look up at Lucas. "Look," Lucas remarked, his voice still showing a bit of annoyance, but he was at least trying to be nice for the sake of his younger brother. "If dad doesn't get home by the weekend," Lucas paused as he tried to think if he was able to keep his promise to his little brother. "I'll take you hunting." Lucas had a slightly soft smile on his face, though it might not have been noticeable due to Lucas still having a scowl on his face, but it was there.

"But, you aren't that great at hunting…." Kane trailed off, his eyebrows knitting together, not sure why Lucas would want to take him out hunting. It wasn't like Lucas had a problem with killing, he just wasn't all that good with moving targets in general. But, like their father said, it was a sort of bonding experience that everyone has when they go out hunting.

"No, but I am good at butchering and tracking." Lucas remarked as a chuckle left his lips. "How else do you think I was able to find you all those times you would run away to the barn when you and mom would argue?" A light chuckle leaving Lucas' lips as he started walking again. Kane seemed to have a surprised look on his face at the realization that his brother had been able to track him all the times he would 'run away' to the barn. No wonder his parents seemed to know where he would run off too. Despite his best efforts, Kane could never escape his brother's sharp eyes.

"No fair!" Kane shouted, running to catch up to Lucas who was a bit further ahead. Thanks to his long legs, Lucas was able to get a bit of distance before Kane caught up to him. "You were the one who told mom and dad where I was hiding? They weren't supposed to know!" Kane grumbled, lightly hitting Lucas' backside in retaliation. Of course the punches weren't exactly all that hard, but seeing as how they were getting close to their home, Lucas lightly pushed Kane away from him since he didn't want to have their mother yelling at them for 'fighting'. Not like she hasn't yelled at them for less.

"Not my fault that they were worried about you." Lucas remarked, only to let out a small sigh towards the end. "Not like they would be worried about me though…." Lucas trailed off as he muttered to himself before Lucas shoved his hands in his pockets. It wasn't like there was any need for them to worry about Lucas being out on his own, but they had seemed to baby Kane and their new born sister more than Lucas. Maybe it had to do with Lucas getting closer to being able to set out on his own that they just didn't seem to bother with Lucas much, but that didn't mean that he didn't mind getting some attention from them. After all, he was their first born.

Glancing up the road from their position, the two boys were able to see their home in the distance. The home which once belonged to their ancestor had once been a fallen structure that was in need of much repair. At one time the roof had been caved in, allowing for nature to reclaim it with various plants making it their home. Patching on the roof was evident by the spots that weren't covered in moss or ivy, indicating that over the years that people had left the shelter they were able to build on existing structures.

The wooden roof seemed to help keep most of the outside out of the home, but there would arise some new problems that would require more patching on the roof. There were a few ladders that rested against the wooden panel that held bits of lingering white paint chips that refused to fall off. Thankfully most of the siding on the house was able to stay in place over the hundreds of years of being neglected, a good sign that the house was at least made up of good materials that seemed to last the test of time.

The foundation of the home had to be repaired with stone and concrete, making the house stable as it rested on bricks before being taken over by the Flores' family once more. The windows that were once broken had been repaired, allowing for the house to remain dry when it rained. Beforehand, the vines from the ivy had encased the wooden frames, the flowers seeking shelter under the slightly ruined porch roof. The very porch roof had been long since patched with a more stable wooden structure, though the vines could be seen still crawling up the side, bringing a bit of nature back to the home. Just outside of the home, resting in a small wooden chair with a woman who was enjoying a book while a little one seemed to rest beside her in an old bassinet.

The woman wore her hair fairly short. Her silver locks barely brushed against the edges of her shoulders. Her hair was thin, the ends curling away from her. Bright blue eyes glanced at the pages she was reading, her long eyelashes giving her eyes more depth while a small butterfly shaped gem hair pin pulled her locks back against her left side. The gem encrusted hair pin was a gift from her husband. Ivory skin barely seemed to be touched by the sun as the loose laced dress provided some relief to the hot temperatures rising outside.

The wind picked up a bit, causing a small sweat to trickle down from her temple, slowly making its way down towards the thin necklace that she often wore around her neck. The necklace was of a white flower, nothing too fancy, but it meant a lot to her as it was something that both Lucas and Elijah had made together when Lucas was only a small boy.

Elijah had been Celia's first serious boyfriend that had eventually gotten her pregnant. Since then, the two had decided to get married after they learned that she was pregnant with their first child. People often referred to Elijah and Celia as the sun and moon, as often their whole worlds would revolve around each other. At least, at first it was like that. But with the disputes on the rise and people still scattered, it seemed that Elijah was gone more often than he would have liked, causing a small rift in their marriage. Though Celia was a dedicated woman, it was hard raising two teenage boys and now an infant daughter by herself.

Elijah was a man who had stunning yellow eyes that were often referred to being as bright and blinding like the sun. His blond hair was more tame than Celia's hair, though it had more thickness to it. His skin was sun-kissed as he often liked to work out in the fields when he was home. He often refers to Celia as his blue butterfly in a field full of bright and glistening white flowers.

While at home, Elijah likes to wear a traditional kimono that sports dark flowers that often lead towards a silver background with gray hibiscus towards his shoulders. It was clear that Lucas looked more like their father as Kane took after their mother. All the while, the youngest and newest addition to the family Ava barely had any real visible hair on her head. Sporting a white bonnet with a loose white dress to keep the sun rays off of her delicate skin, Ava mostly slept through the day. Her eyes still blue while any visible light on her hair made it seem like she would have light blonde hair when she gets older.

"If you didn't want me to find you, maybe make it harder for me to find you." Lucas remarked, making his way past the wooden fence that lined the property in the past, though some of it had been falling apart from the years of neglect and weathering. "Hiding in the same hay fort of yours makes it obvious where your hiding spot is." It wasn't like Lucas was saying that to be mean, but to rather help his brother hide in case of an attack. Whether it was an invading force, a wild animal who has come for an easy meal, or something else that was yet to be foreseen; being able to hide meant the difference between life and death in some cases.

"But I worked hard on my awesome fort." Kane mumbled, passing by the worn down barn that housed a few cattle. The barn itself was just as in bad shape as the house when they were first rebuilding it. The worn down brown wood that was its original panels no longer had the bright red paint that gave it color when it was first built. The roof had been completely destroyed, forcing the family to use straw as a makeshift roof. It kept the hay upstairs dry, though it did make it a bit drafty in the winter. Thankfully the animals were back in the underground shelter, allowing them to be safe and warm during the hellish winters that often came as a result of the nuclear fallout.

Joining Lucas on the porch, Kane was ready to head inside before the voice of their mother seemed to catch their attention. "And where do you think you two are going?" Celia remarked, her voice stern as she slid a piece of paper into the pages of the book she was reading. Standing up, the hem of the laced dress she wore barely touched the top of her knees. Celia's shoulders were exposed as the dress she was wearing exposed her shoulders, making it easier for her to breastfeed Ava if the baby became too fussy.

The two boys had stopped their movements, the door resting against Lucas' side as they turned their attention towards Celia. The two looked as if they had been playing around in the dirt, when they had really been working in the fields for the last couple of hours, hoping to bring in a bit of food for their family home. Most children their age had agreed to work in the fields if it meant that their families would be able to get a bit more in the way of food. Plus, if the children of the tribal leader came to help them, it would leave a favorable impression on their people.

Not that Lucas really cared. He just needed to get away from Celia for a bit. Not wanting to deal with her forcing him to do more chores around the house that didn't need immediate attention. Since their father was away, Lucas had to step up as the man in the family, putting additional stress on the already worn down teenager.

"We were hoping to get up to our room to relax before supper," Lucas spoke, his annoyance carrying onto his voice as he glanced over towards Celia. "But let me guess, you want us to do something for you while you finish up dinner." Lucas finished his remark, his eyebrows knitted together, ready for a lecture from their mother about being the man of the house and doing the duties that Celia gives him since the two boys live under her roof. It seemed that the response that Lucas gave her didn't seem to settle well as Celia placed her hands on her hip, ready to dig into him. But seeing Kane grimace at the thought of hearing the two of them argue, she stopped herself.

"I just cleaned the floor..." Celia spoke, holding her anger back but her annoyance was noted to the two. "Instead of getting the house dirty, clean yourselves up in the water basin in the back of the house.." Celia softly ordered as she watched Kane head back first before Lucas started to follow him. "And take some of the clean clothes off of the line." It wasn't a request, but more like a stern order. Running towards the end of the porch, Celia started to call towards the two as they were slow to walk to the back.

"I made roast chicken with crispy potatoes. Figured that you would have been hungry by the time you got home... so I wanted to make you your favorite meal." Celia shouted as she held onto the sturdy railing. "I also made some strawberry lemonade for you guys." Kane glanced back to see Celia's softer expression, however Lucas paid her no mind.

"I know lately we've been arguing, and it has been causing us to drift apart, but I wanted to make it up to you guys." Celia finished, even though it felt like she wasn't heard. A soft sigh escaped her lips as a worried look brushed over her face. She knew that things couldn't continue to go on like this. She couldn't see how the tension was ripping her family apart as Elijah was away. Even though there was nothing more that she could do for her teenage sons. At least she had Ava.

Walking along the stone path, Kane's eyes focused on Lucas' back as they walked along the length of the house. The grass was already starting to get a bit taller as it brushed against Kane's ankles. Wild flowers seemed to stick up between the blades of grass, some even seemed to stick up from under the rocky path. The sounds of bees buzzing about was a common noise that often brought Kane enjoyment, as it meant that life was starting over on the once dead planet. The birds could be heard as they sang to one another, the dark clouds and threat of the storm creeping closer let out a dull roar as the wind picked up.

Once they had gotten towards the back of the house, Lucas stopped at the barrel of rain water to quickly wash off his face, hands, and feet. Kane followed his lead, wanting to make sure to get cleaned up properly before they would be able to have some dinner. The two seemingly peeled off their dirty shirts before heading towards the wash line that was tied up between two tall trees. Even though they got clean shirts on, Kane could sense that there was still something wrong. It was like there was something going on that both Lucas and Celia weren't telling him.

Once Kane's head popped out of the shirt, he cleared his throat to start to speak. "What's going on with mom?" Kane asked as he watched his brother quickly put on a new shirt. "Why is she sad?" Kane added, but noticed that Lucas was lost in thought. Seeing how his brother had a bit of a hundred yard stare, Kane sighed as he was finished slipping his arms through the sleeves of his shirt. "Lucas." Kane spoke louder, catching his brother off guard, causing the male to let out a small hum. "Why was mom sad?" Kane asked again, causing Lucas to reach down and ruffle Kane's hair a bit.

"It's because dad won't be able to come home for a while bud." Lucas answered, removing his hand to finish buttoning up his shirt. "Apparently there is a bad guy going around, making trouble for the tribal leaders." It wasn't like Lucas cared either way if Kane could at least grasp the situation that is going on in their world, but he wasn't going to cover it up either.

"See, the guy is going around convincing people that there should be a head leader who will look over all of the tribes, making important decisions and figuring out what people's roles should be." Lucas continued, bending down to be more eye-level with Kane as he continued to explain everything that was going on. "If it isn't done right, it could lead to a person getting a lot of power. Nothing would be equal." In a sense, it would feel like everything would be ruled over one dictator rather than having a fair and well balanced system put in place.

"How is that bad? Shouldn't we come together as the last surviving humans on the planet?" Kane asked, his innocence still apparent as he didn't understand the real gravity of the situation. Not like Lucas would really be able to tell him the type of horror stories he heard about this Nero guy. But with that type of government put in place, it would only lead people to be even further divided, rather than being brought together as a whole.

"Normally it shouldn't be bad." Lucas remarked with a soft sigh at the end. "But given how controlling and manipulative this guy is, it will only lead us to a destructive path." Lucas added. "Dad worked hard to keep peace in our tribe." With how little land they took back from nature, it was hard to explore more when one is always called away to deal with political matters. "We have a bit of land, but if we don't change something where our people can be brought in together, we'll never make it to being a real tribe.." Lucas continued slowly standing back up as he gazed moved towards the valley below them.

They have come a great ways since leaving the shelters, and this Nero guy has helped to make their advancements in technology in only a few short years. Keeping communication low with using the old communication towers that wouldn't breach into the atmosphere allowed for better communication than letters. They even brought back electricity with the form of crystals that could be used as a current. It was due to these types of advancements that allowed the people on the surface to communicate better than ever that caused Nero to get a following large enough to become a leader. That's why the tribal leaders were concerned with the man becoming the Head of the Leaders.

"But, isn't he the guy who gave us back electricity? How is he a bad guy?" Kane asked with a small tilt of his head. "After all, thanks to him, we can have food that won't go bad." Kane started to explain in an excited tone. "Plus we can actually enjoy cold drinks when it is hot outside." Kane remarked, not understanding the gravity of the situation. Sure they were able to get electricity outside of using a large generator, but at what cost? They were able to make a form of electricity that wouldn't be noticeable to those cowards up in the sky, but they had other things to deal with. Making the survivors passive with technological advances seemed to be Nero's way of giving people bread and circuses.

"He's bad because he has killed people in the past. He's not above killing people to get his way Kane. And if he isn't controlled or stopped, he could very well try and kill our dad." Lucas finally snapped, wanting his brother to understand the danger of one's' past. How someone may seem like they were some type of savior, only to turn around and be someone's butcher. Though it had appeared to be the type of wake up call that Kane needed to understand why the situation was bad. If this Nero guy did kill their father, then it would be like their sun dying out.

Glancing down, Kane bit his inner lip as he reeled in the information. "I see..." Kane mumbled, his hands subconsciously clinging to the hem of his shirt. "So mom thinks that dad will die?" Kane asked, however he didn't get an answer from Lucas. Watching Lucas glance away before standing up, Kane felt a sinking in his chest by the silence from his older brother.

Taking a deep breath through his nose, Kane glanced towards the sky overhead. The rain clouds seemed to be rolling in, meaning that they would need to hurry and get the cattle and laundry in. "I um....I'll get the clean clothes." Kane trailed off as he turned away from Lucas. "You know how to whistle to get the cows to come in. So you might want to hurry up before the storm hits." Kane finished before taking a step towards the tall trees where the wind was trying to pull the clothes off of the line. It would provide Kane with enough time for this information to sink in properly.

Lucas stood there for a few seconds, taking in the discouraged look on Kane's face before letting out a small sigh. Turning away from his little brother, Lucas walked towards the small path to the barn. They didn't have too much in the way of cattle. Just three cows and a few chickens that were usually kept in the coop. Taking a small glance back towards Kane, Lucas could feel the wind picking up. It wouldn't be too much longer until the storm hit. The sound of thunder in the distance meant that it would be a hellish storm. The clouds flashed with a light purple, meaning that there would be lightning that could very well strike the barn. If that happens, they could say goodbye to their cattle for good.

Mentally shaking it off, Lucas disappeared into the barn, leaving Kane to collect the laundry that was dry. Putting the dry clothes haphazardly into the basket before heading inside. The dirty clothes that they changed out of laid on the stone porch in the back, only to be collected by Kane and tossed in the small makeshift basket that they used to house dirty clothes in. The air was getting colder, a sign that it wouldn't be long before they would feel the first rain droplets. Entering from the back door, Kane made his way into the house before he sat down by the round dinner table that looked as if it came from the trunk of a fairly decent size tree. The chairs were seemingly made out of the same wood, though the carving in the wood work showed that a lot of attention went into each chair. After all, each chair was unique.

Crossing his legs against the plush seat of the chair, Kane glanced around the area. Everything was a bit more open than a traditional house, mostly due to the fact that most of the walls had crumbled over the years of neglect. It had taken a fair amount of years and a few changes of hands within the family to make it work to the point that there was little need for support in the bottom portion of the house. Most of the walls had the arch support, giving the illusion that the house was more open. The floor that once had any type of covering, rather it be from a carpet or tile, was replaced with a solid wood flooring. There were times in which the floor would creak, but Kane had avoided most of those patches of flooring.

The kitchen was similar to how it was before the bombs had dropped, though there was a replacement for the old oven that had been rusted to hell and back. Instead, they used a wood burning oven that had been made out of stone and concrete. Most of their meals were often cooked in a variety of skillets that Celia had mastered cooking in. The lingering smell of the chicken and potatoes filled the air as Kane could tell that it wouldn't be long before they got to eat. Despite all of the bickering that came with eating together, Kane loved the food his mother often made for them.

Taking a glance towards their living room, Kane was able to look out the large window that was almost as tall as his father. If all of the family stood close together, they would be able to look out of it with ease. Sure there were bits of ivy lingering along the wooden frame, it still gave anyone who looked out of it a perfect view of the town in the distance. The fireplace that was in the living room laid vacant of any wood. Seeing as how it wasn't going to get cold any time soon, there was no need for a fire.

During the winter months, they would sit around the fireplace in silence while the winds outside howled. It was probably one of the few times that Kane could enjoy a nice book without his brother giving him crap for reading the various books in Kane's collection. The couch that they had could sit three adults. The fabric was made out of horse hide while the inside was stuffed with a mixture of sheep wool and bird feathers. The frame was made out of wood with metal hinges on the joints of the frame to keep it in place.

There were different types of art that lined the walls to add a bit of decoration to the room, often mixed in with some lingering photos that Kane's ancestors were able to save before the day that everything went to hell. The coffee table was much like the dining room table, though with this tree, it was much smaller and made out of a white tree that Kane couldn't remember the name of. On the various furniture, a stitched blanket made from animal fur rested over the head rest. These were often made out of deer, wolf, or anything that happened to be killed by the family to provide variant meat for them to live off of. Along the window sills were various potted plants that were used for spices. They often gave off an aroma that Kane seemed to like, as it often reminded him of Celia.

Glancing towards what was once a den as he continued to fold the clothes, Kane was able to see the lush books that were neatly organized in the wooden shelves that his father made. Often Kane would use the desk for his school work. That was, when they weren't needed to help on the farm and with the crops, of course. It would have made sense for Kane to use the desk while he read, but Kane often liked taking the books he selected to read in the living room or his bedroom, it was never easy to read in the bedroom at night since he shared a room with Lucas.

There were times in which Kane would be so absorbed in reading, that when Lucas turned off the little oil lamp that he used for reading, Kane would nearly jump out of his skin since he didn't hear his brother walk towards him. Afterwards Lucas would often lecture Kane about being careful with the oil lamp as it could cause a fire if he knocked it over.

There was only a single window that lingered in the den, the view of it was towards the barn. When Elijah was home, he would have the window open so he could yell for Lucas and Kane to come in when lunch or dinner was ready. It was currently closed due to how hot the weather had been, though it wasn't nearly as bad now as it was a couple hundred years ago.

Thankfully the sudden drop of temperature from the rain storm coming in, the heat trapped inside of the house would be a welcome change for those coming inside. Kane could see a bit of the darkness that was looming over the town through the white see-through curtains. It almost looked like the night sky had swooped down in the form of a cloud, ready to devour the helpless town in a single gulp.

The sound of the door creaking from behind him caused Kane to tilt his head back and see Lucas coming in. A soft smile lingered on Kane's lips as he was glad that Lucas was able to make it inside before the rain started to pour. "Hey Lucas, did you see those clouds over the town? It's so massive! Almost like it could swirl into a black hole and devour the town!" Kane grinned, pointed towards the window in the den.

But Lucas didn't say anything. Instead, the male grabbed the clothes that were already folded and rushed up the wooden steps towards the bedrooms just outside of the den. Watching as Lucas' feet disappeared up the stairs, Kane couldn't help but frown a bit. Why did Lucas always have to be so distant? Sure they were a few years apart, but it seemed like each day Lucas would shut himself off from the rest of the family. Before the two were so close, now it felt like Lucas was more like a stranger than a brother these days.

After Lucas had seemed to disappear upstairs, the sound of the front door opened, causing Kane to glance towards the living room to see Celia carrying Ava inside. The sound of the rain seemed to finally hit the windows, sounding like small pebbles being thrown against the glass. The chill from the wind blowing inside of the house made the drop of temperature apparent before Celia closed the door behind her. "Hey honey. Did you and Lucas get the animals into the barn and the clothes off the line?" She asked, walking towards Kane with Ava in her arms. The book she was reading seemingly stuck out under Celia's armpit, making sure that neither the book or Ava had gotten wet.

"Mmhm. Lucas went upstairs with some of the folded clothes." Kane remarked, pointing towards the stairs, Celia glancing towards the direction Kane pointed, nodding mostly to herself. At least she didn't have to nag them any further. Ava had been sound asleep, though that might not be for much longer considering the thunder and lightning could cause her to wake up screaming. It would take up to a few hours to settle Ava back down if she woke up from the loud sounds.

"Good..." Celia trailed off, moving to the table. "Do you mind holding your sister while I check on the food? I don't want to burn it." Celia asked, her nerves seemed a bit frazzled as if there were a million things that she needed to do in a short amount of time. It wasn't easy taking care of a newborn while having to do a bunch of household chores, but at least her sons were able to help out. Celia was appreciative for the help, but it didn't feel like it was enough. Causing her to become stressed that led to the fights she would have with Lucas. He was a grown man now, bound to do great things in the world, but he stayed to help out with the family instead of following his own goals and dreams. Celia could only hope that they could be stable enough to allow Lucas the chance to leave and be on his own rather than stay behind to help them out.

"Sure mom." Kane spoke, getting up from his spot. It wasn't abnormal for Kane to help out with watching Ava. She was a baby after all. Unable to fend for herself. Having to rely on others in order to get what she needed. Only crying as a means to address an issue as she wasn't even able to use words. Kane always had a way of making her smile at least. Putting a bright bubbly smile on her face.

Celia would often make remarks that if Kane was born as a woman, he would have made a wonderful mother. Though Elijah would simply remark that Kane would make for a wonderful father, Celia would brush it off like a small grain of sand. Carrying Ava over towards the living room, Kane placed her down on the couch. Thankfully Ava wasn't at the age where she was able to move around much, making it possible for Kane to start the fire to keep the house warm as the house would get colder. It was going to be a cold night ahead of them, even after the rain would stop.

TOWARDS the end of the meal, Celia had taken notice that Lucas didn't eat his food. The chicken that was laid on the plate with the crisped potatoes looked as if they had been mostly pecked at. Glancing towards Lucas, Celia couldn't help but frown a bit. "Lucas, how come you didn't eat your food?" Celia asked, her brows seemingly knitting together as she didn't know if perhaps Lucas wasn't feeling well or if he didn't like the meal that she prepared. "Are you not feeling well?" Even Lucas' favorite drink was barely touched, leaving Celia even more worried than before.

The silence in the room seemed to be deafening, causing Kane to glance over towards Lucas now. It seemed like Lucas was a bit irritated, keeping his jaw clenched as small water droplets ran down the glass of lemonade that Celia prepared earlier. Even that was barely touched. "Lucas... honey... are you-?" Celia started to ask, only to have Lucas practically shout at her question.

"I'm fine!" Lucas growled, shooting Celia an annoyed glance before picking at the golden potato slice. "Just ... tired." Lucas added, a small scoff towards the end as he glanced towards Kane, taking note of Kane's worried expression. Swallowing a bit of the food that he had been working on, Lucas focused his gaze to the plate in front of him. He wasn't sure if he could really stomach the food in front of him. Lucas didn't know when it really started, but everything that he used to love seemingly tasted like ash in his mouth. There was no real flavoring to anything anymore, causing him to not want to eat. It wasn't Celia's fault, but yet it felt like it was.

"You don't need to shout at me Lucas." Celia snapped back reflexively. The sound of her utensils rattled on the wooden table, causing the two males to look towards her direction. "I don't know what is going on with you anymore Lucas." Celia started with a huff to her voice. "One minute you seem fine. Then the next minute, you're either snapping at me or lethargic." Celia continued, it was like she was at her wits end at the unstable mood swings of her oldest son. "You used to be a bright and happy boy…" Celia continued before trailing off. "But ever since you hit puberty, it's just been four years of constant unstable mood swings." Celia's hands were shaking a little from the frustration she felt. She tried to keep herself relaxed, but it wasn't working.

"I'll... just excuse myself." Kane mumbled, pushing back from the table. Kane didn't want to be involved in the constant fighting that would happen between the two. Oftentimes it would get to be physical with Celia often slapping Lucas, trying to end it by 'straightening' out her son. To teach him to respect his parents authority, but Kane knew what would happen in the end. It would result in Lucas backing down before coming back to the room that they shared. Often ranting about how unfair Celia was being, but he would never strike her back. Or at least, Kane never knew if Lucas ever did.

"Way to go Lucas." Celia scoffed with irritation. "You scared off your brother." Celia grumbled, crossing her arms over her chest. Watching as Kane scampered up the steps, Celia could feel her appetite disappear. Though she had worked hard on the meal, it seemed like it was just going to waste now that no one was going to eat it. An exasperated sigh escaped her lips as she crossed one leg over the other. "Well, are you going to answer my question Lucas?" Celia asked, her patience getting thinner by the second. To Lucas and Kane, it always felt like her patience was as thin as an unstable thin ice sheet on a slightly frozen lake.

"And what question is that mother?" Lucas asked, his tone of voice more on the bitter side, as if he was holding back his temper until he heard the sound of the bedroom door being closed, meaning that Kane was off to drown out the shouting he knew would be coming next. "The question of am I feeling well? Or the question as to what is wrong with me?" Lucas asked, leaning back to look at his mother with an irritated gaze, though he looked calm and collected. "Because I can answer both of those questions right now if you want me to."

The tension between the two was thick enough to be cut with a knife. The creaking of the door seemed to be louder than the thunder and lightning that was going on outside. As the door latched shut, Lucas took a deep breath in through his nose, as if preparing himself for an important presentation, calming his nerves and pounding heart that was beating hard against his chest.

"For the first question," Lucas started, pausing as he locked eyes with Celia at this point. "No, I am not feeling well. And you want to know why?" Lucas asked, his brows knitting close together. Naturally Celia didn't respond, but the look on her face was apparent enough to have Lucas continue. "Because I feel numb to everything that is going on around me." That remark seemed to perk Celia's interest as she tilted her head to the side with a confused look on her face.

"I can no longer taste anything but ash with everything that you make." The bewildered look on Celia's face as Lucas admitted that was only the start of it. "I can't feel the world around me. I can't sense anything." The bewildered gaze slowly turned into a sadden as Lucas tried his best to describe what was going on inside of his mind.

"It's like I am dead already, but still walking among the living like nothing is fucking wrong." Lucas growled, clenching his fists as he sat in his seat. "Day in and day out, it's the same thing." At this point there was a stinging in Lucas' eyes as he bared himself to his mother. "I lay in bed staring at the ceiling while the sound of the roosters cawing the morning kept me from getting any sleep." Lucas spoke, his voice starting to tremble a bit as he was going to break down how he felt for so many years.

"After peeling myself out of bed and helping my little brother get ready, I come down to a crying sister who doesn't even really allow me to get near her without screaming when she sees my face." Lucas spoke, bringing up his hands towards his face, his hands visibly shaking as he was continued on. "It's like, one look at me and she throws herself into a fit…" Lucas paused as he stifled a sniffle. "Like, I'm some kind of monster." Lucas cast his gaze down towards the gap between him and the table.

"It's like all of you view me as some type of monster. Someone whom you chose to distance yourself from, simply because you don't understand the thoughts going around in my mind." Lucas admitted as he clenched his hands into his hair. "The horrible thoughts that always seem to linger in the dark regions of my mind." Lucas continued, his shaky breath seeming to turn into quickened pants as if there wasn't enough oxygen in the room. "The thoughts of either hurting myself… or hurting my family…." Lucas trailed off in a shaky voice. It felt like his world was spinning out of control, and he could feel the darkness creeping in. As if it was starting to change him into something he didn't even recognize.

"Lucas… you're not a monster honey." Celia spoke, her voice seemingly softer as she could see that her oldest child was visibly hurting. All this time, she figured that he was just dealing with mood swings. That, if she didn't constantly coddle him, then perhaps he would grow up into a functioning adult. Though she couldn't exactly speak on the behalf of Ava or Kane, she knew that Elijah and herself often stayed up talking about how they could better raise Lucas to be a fine leader.

"We love you." She continued, standing up from her seat as she carefully walked over towards Lucas, who was currently cradling his face between his hands. "You know Kane loves you too. He always looks up to his big brother for everything." Celia continued to try and comfort Lucas the best she could without making it seem like her oldest was weak. It might not have been apparent to Lucas, but Celia believed that it was just the way that brothers tended to act like rivals when they got towards their adolescent years.

Carefully Celia approached Lucas. There was something telling her that it was not safe to touch Lucas, but she wanted to show her son that she wasn't afraid of him. That Lucas wasn't this monster that he claimed that he was. That all he needed was a bit of love and affection right now. Placing a hand on his shoulder, Celia offered him a warm and gentle smile, at least at first.

It was when she noticed Lucas staring at her with an intense gaze that she lifted her hand from his shoulder. The way that Lucas' eyes were shrunken in and the blood vessels seemed to be more apparent as they scattered like lightning around the whites of Lucas' eyes that caused Celia to move her hand away from the male. The way Lucas appeared to be more tense by her touch, it was like looking at some rabid wolf that had its' large mangled paw encased by a bear trap.

Taking a small step back, Celia instinctively brought her hand back towards her chest. She could feel the hairs on her neck stand up on end as lightning flashed close to the house, lighting up the room with a blinding flash of white light as Lucas moved to stand up. Celia felt frozen in fear as Lucas stepped closer to her, his movements jagged like he was some mindless creature. The fire roared in the fireplace with small sizzling hisses from the rain entering through the chimney.

Before Celia could even shout, she felt a hand wrapped around her neck. First it was one, then it was the other. A quick gasp of air seemed to be the only reaction that seemed to come from Celia as she looked up at Lucas. The way that Lucas started to tighten his grip around her throat, Lucas could see the fear in her eyes. The same fear that he delusional saw each time his mother would glance at him.

How often her gaze would drift away from her oldest son, how she would almost flinch each time that she was alone with Lucas. He could see it all. The sounds of her gasping weren't even registering as Ava started to cry upstairs from the loud noise of the thunder that followed after the lightning strike. The sound of footsteps indicated that Kane was quick to attend to his little sister's needs, all the while Lucas focused on squeezing the life out of his own mother. The way her body heat felt against his cold hands as he felt each choke from Celia's gasps. Watching her eyes tear up, an amused smirk landed on Lucas' face the more he watched their mother struggle in his hands.

KANE had been idle in the shared room he had with Lucas. His own bed rested neatly beside the right side of the room, while Lucas' bed was on the left side. The room was a bit cluttered, mostly books from their makeshift library that ranged from all types of genre from mystery to romance. As cliche was it sounded, Kane's favorite type of books were romances. There was just something about being able to find someone with whom you connected with right away that always made Kane smile.

Most boys his age were into adventure or science fiction, though there were some who always loved to play as the charming detective who was able to solve cases about underground criminals, Kane was often cast to play as the damsel because he was the closest thing to a girl that they had at the time. It never really bothered Kane much. He was often the odd one out.

As he was getting to the part where the handsome shirtless man was wooing the fair maiden whose dress was seemingly ripped in a slightly revealing fashion, the sound of the lightning hitting close by caused Kane to practically toss the book across the room. "Damn it!" Kane hissed, bringing his ears up to try and clear the ringing in his ears. The bright light from the lightning was just as blinding, causing Kane to close his eyes tightly. It felt like Kane was in some type of war where a flash bang was thrown, causing those around to become disorientated.

The red curtain that allowed for some privacy between the brothers was already opened, the edges of the curtain seemed to drape along the floor as Celia had been too busy to properly cut it. The mattress that Kane was on was made of the same stuffing as the couch, but was built more solid to keep it from sagging over time. "Ugh, where did my book go?" Kane mumbled to himself, tossing his legs over the side of his wooden frame of his bed, opening one eye to see if he could locate it.

Though his vision was a bit blurry, thanks to the brightness of the lightning, Kane was careful with his steps as he didn't want to knock anything else over. Slowly Kane's vision came back, the book seemingly landing on Lucas' bed as it knocked down a drawing that Kane had made Lucas when he was little. It was of two small stick figures with scribbled words that once read *I love big bro*. The words seemed to have faded, a big heart that occupied the space between the two smiling figures had ripped in half.

Picking up the picture, Kane sighed as he flipped the two broken sides between his fingers, wondering if it was salvage-able. "Hm, maybe if I make him a new one, maybe he might not notice?" Kane muttered to himself, figuring that it would be easy to fix. Not like his brother would really notice much of what Kane did.

Sitting down on Lucas' bed, Kane dangled his feet over the edge. The dark sheets were a bit messed up as Lucas never really made his bed. On the side of a bed was a small night stand that had a book that seemed too complicated for Kane to understand, but it seemed that his brother enjoyed reading it.

The letters on the hard cover book had been worn down over time, so Kane couldn't exactly remember the title of it. It had a bunch of scientific words that went over Kane's fourteen year old mind at the time, but it seemed that it was something that they enjoyed together. It wasn't long before Ava started to scream that caught Kane's attention. Tossing the ripped drawing towards his side of the bed, Kane stammered towards the door. With a quick turn of the knob, Kane rushed towards his parents room where Ava seemed to be occupied in her bassinet.

"Hush Ava. Big brother is here." Kane spoke, rushing towards the wobbling bassinet as Ava seemed to be throwing a fit. It was apparent that the lightning hitting close upset everyone in the household. Carefully picking her up, Kane made sure that he cradled Ava in his arms like how Celia showed him.

"Shh…" Kane hushed softly as he bounced her in his arms. "There's no need to fear Ava, because I am here." Kane remarked with a happy chuckle towards the end, trying to be like a super heroic big brother who could make anything right if his words were convincing and he wore a big smile. But it didn't seem to work. Tears seemed to stream down Ava's face, making Kane to wonder if perhaps she needed to be either changed or was hungry. Carefully setting Ava on the bed, Kane hurried towards the little dresser that held some clothed diapers and washed clothes in case she needed to be changed.

Kane's feet continued to stomp against the wooden floor as he rushed to get the wash clothes wet. Normally he would have waited for some warm water, but Kane was in a hurry. With the washcloth rung out in the sink, Kane hurried back towards Ava who seemed to be trying to curl in on herself. The sounds of her crying never ceasing as Kane started to change her diaper. But to his surprise, she was only a little wet. Perhaps the sudden crack from the lightning was enough to cause Ava to at least wet herself. With a soft sigh, Kane went to work changing the diaper to make Ava comfortable at least.

"It's alright Ava. I almost made a mess of myself too." Kane lightly chuckled, scooping Ava back up into his arms. "Let's go and see if mom could get you some nice warm milk to suckle on. I bet having a warm belly will sooth all your troubles." Kane mused, mostly to himself as he could see Ava slowly calming down. Watching her softly look up at Kane, it felt like she was looking into Kane's soul. The light smile that seemed to creep up, that toothless smile that she often gave to Kane, it made dealing with Ava's crying worth it. "See? You have nothing to fear as long as your two big brothers are here." Kane mused with a soft hum towards the end, giving Ava a gentle smile back.

But that wouldn't last for much longer. Walking down the hallway with Ava in his arms, Kane was careful where he stepped as he came down the steps. Lucas seemed to be sitting back at the table while it seemed that Celia was resting on the couch. The top locks of her hair was visible, indicating that she was probably laying down to try and nurse the headache she often got after the two of them argued. Kane didn't find anything about this off. Though Ava let out a small whimper as a sniffle caused a small snot bubble to grow against her nose, Kane smiled as he started to walk over towards the couch. "Hey mom. Can you heat up some mi-?" Kane started before he heard Lucas snap at him.

"Don't bother her." Lucas snapped, his eyebrows knitting a bit though the crack in his voice indicated that he had something in his throat. Kane grew a bit worried, not sure what caused Lucas to snap at him like that. It was like Kane had found a broken doll figurine that their mother used to collect. Fearing that Kane could cut himself on the broken pieces or something. Kane halted in his steps, a concerned look on his face as he wasn't sure what was going on, and he could feel like something was amiss.

"But... Ava needs some warm milk." Kane mumbled a little, only to clear his throat. "So, do you think you could warm up some milk for her? It'll help her sleep." Kane continued, figuring that perhaps if he could help Ava go back to sleep, then perhaps Lucas would be able to get some decent rest. Kane knew how hard it was for Lucas to fall asleep, which was why he made sure that he took the wall closest to the house, providing his brother a chance to be away from the noise of the house.

The silence in the room was a bit unsettling. The way that Lucas stared at him, it wasn't even like Kane recognized the man sitting before him. Swallowing the lump in his throat, Kane parted his lips to say something, but the words didn't come out. Eventually, Lucas pushed the chair back without a single word. Kane held onto Ava tightly as he watched Lucas' movements carefully. There was a sense of dread washing over Kane the more he studied Lucas' movement. It was like his brother's limbs were loose, like he had just gotten back from carrying a dead animal's body from the nearby woods. His brother was indeed strong, but even he got tired after using his strength.

Kane carefully took a few steps back towards the stairs, carefully watching Lucas who seemed to be making a bunch of noise that would have normally caused Celia to sit up and shout for the two of them to keep the noise down. The fact that his mother wasn't doing that was sending alarm bells through his mind. Ava let out another whimper, causing Kane to bring up a finger to his mouth to show that she needed to be quiet right now. But that didn't seem to pan out as Ava started with the tears once more while the whimpering seemed to grow louder. Kane almost jumped out of his skin when the sound of the metal pan was slammed on the counter top, causing Kane to look at Lucas.

"Kane," Lucas spoke calmly, his eyes narrowing ever so slightly towards his younger brother. "Where is her bottle?" Lucas asked, moving to crack his neck, the sounds of his bones popping ever so slightly. "If you want me to heat the milk for her bottle, I'll need to properly measure it." Kane didn't like the tone in Lucas' voice when he talked. It wasn't like his brother's normal tone. It was different. Like some sort of monster taken over Lucas' body and was trying to act like the older male.

Kane was caught off guard by the question, but seemed that this was his chance to either hide Ava or escape. "Oh, right. Sorry.." Kane started to apologize. "I must have forgotten it." Kane chimed with a smile on his face. Using his free hand to come up and lightly bump the side of his head. "Silly me. You know how I can be forgetful when it comes to Ava's bottles." Kane spoke, a bit out of character for him, but Kane figured that Lucas would see it as Kane trying to be goofy to ease a tense situation. That, or Kane was being unfunny in a sad attempt to be funny. Either way, the annoyance on Lucas' face was apparent that he didn't have time to deal with his little brother's foolish behavior.

"Whatever, just go and get it." Lucas growled, his tone was a mixture of annoyed and angry. Kane let go of the breath that he was holding, glad that his little act seemed to at least work. Turning and making his way back up the stairs, Kane steadily walked back towards his parent's bedroom. At first Kane thought about heading into his room and trying to block it from the inside, but he knew that there was no way to safely get out without Lucas seeing him. Plus Lucas knew that something would be up if the sound of his feet headed towards their room instead of their parents room.

Reaching his parents room, Kane took a deep breath before he went inside the opened room. As the storm continued to rage, causing the house to creak a bit more than normal. The roof seemed to stay in place, but it didn't exactly reassure Kane that he was able to get out of this whole thing unscathed. Ava had a better chance than he did, but it seemed clear that their mother was no longer with them. Or at the very least, she was unconscious.

At least Kane didn't see any blood that would indicate that Lucas slash their mother open or anything like that, but knowing Lucas, the man was the type who would break the neck to end an animal's suffering. Even though Lucas didn't look like the type, he was fit under his slightly baggy farmer clothes.

Glancing around the room, Kane took notice that the storm wasn't close to stopping. The trees outside looked as if they were going to break free from their rooted spot, threatening to fall over and damage the house. Even though that would have been something that Kane would have been concerned about, his focus was about surviving this night. He needed a spot to hide Ava. Otherwise, who knows what might happen to the both of them.

Spotting the closet being opened a bit, Kane got an idea. Carefully making his way over, Kane slid the door open. It was dark, meaning that he would be able to hide Ava inside the closet and pray that she didn't make any noise. Reaching up, Kane tore down his parents clothes to make a small bed to lay Ava down in. The smell of their parents should be comforting enough to keep her content until Kane did something to take his brother's mind off of their little sister.

Once the clothes were deemed safe to place her in, Kane gently placed Ava inside of the closet. "Ava, I know you can't understand me yet, but you need to stay quiet. Okay?" Kane started to speak in a hushed tone. "Big brother is going to protect you, no matter what." Kane remarked, giving Ava a soft smile before closing the closet doors. Resting his head on the door as he heard Ava starting to whimper, Kane had to steady himself. He couldn't take her outside while it was pouring rain, she could get sick. Taking a step back, Kane was a bit surprised when he bumped into something solid. Freezing in place, Kane's eyes widened as he slowly looked up to Lucas standing directly behind him.

"Ah! L-Luca-?!" Kane started to stammer as he moved to face his older brother. But before he could even finish his sentence, Kane was greeted with a heavy blow to his stomach. It felt like Kane was kicked in the gut by one of their cattle, causing Kane to stumble backwards and fall against the door that was protecting Ava from Lucas. Kane's vision started to blur a bit as he gasped for air, the distant sounds of Ava crying before everything seemed to go silent. The sounds of Ava crying, and the overwhelming feeling that he couldn't protect her was something that would haunt Kane for the rest of his life.

As Kane started to stir, the sound of a fire crackling was the first thing that Kane noticed. He found himself wondering if maybe he had fallen asleep reading a horror story or something, but found that the room he was in was the living room. There was a sharp stinging sensation against the back of Kane's head as well as a pain resentating against his stomach. Glancing over towards the couch, he saw his mother Celia still laying on the couch. She looked as if she was sleeping, so perhaps Kane did have a bad dream. But then the question reached Kane's mind. How did he get to the living room?

"M-Mom?" Kane spoke out weakly, his vision becoming a bit fuzzy as he tried to move. There was a dull ringing in Kane's ears as he felt restriction against his limbs. Looking down, Kane found that he was bound to the chair he was occupying. "W-What the hell?" Kane mumbled to himself in a distressed tone. Giving the ropes a few tugs, it seemed like they were able to come a bit loose. It seemed that luck was on Kane's side as he figured that he could break out, find Ava, and run into town and get some help. That was, until he noticed that his brother was sitting at the dining room table, seemingly motionless with his back facing towards Kane.

Kane could feel his heart sinking into the pits of his stomach. A cold sweat slowly trickled down from his temple as his eyes didn't avert from Lucas. Surely Lucas would have noticed that Kane was up when he started to speak, so why wasn't he coming over? Everything inside of Kane was telling him to escape right now. To slip out of the binds, run out the door into the storm, and never look back. But he was frightened. Scared out of his mind as he knew the type of things his brother could do.

Glancing down, Kane noticed a small trail of a white liquid that seemed to roll in his direction. Following it with his eyes, Kane noticed that there was a white liquid dripping down from the table. His eyes tried to focus the best that they could, only taking notice of a white dress that Kane had used as the first layer to clothe Ava to keep her safe. "L-Lucas?" Kane softly called out, his voice still weak as his head seemed to spin from the slightest movement.

Lucas turned his head slowly, turning to look towards Kane, a blank expression seemed to rest on Lucas' face as he picked up something that resembled a doll. "Ah, Kane." Lucas spoke, his voice cracking ever so slightly as he tucked the doll close to his chest. "It seems that you've finally woken up." Lucas continued, the sound of the chair sliding against the wooden floor sounded like nails to a chalk board for Kane at this point. It wasn't long before the sounds of Lucas' heavy foot steps started to creak against the floor, keeping Kane mindful of where his brother's location was despite the fact that Kane could barely keep his head up, the pain steadily growing the more that Kane was awake.

"It seems like Ava finally is letting me hold her." Lucas seemed to continue, walking along the edge of the couch that was facing the fireplace. "She's not even crying... or pushing me away with her weak hands... or anything that would make her seem like she sees the monster in me." Lucas finished, standing in front of the fireplace now, the light from the fire revealing that the entire right side of Lucas' face was covered in blood.

The sight alone caused Kane's stomach to churn. The pain in the back of Kane's head seemed to be gone as he got a closer picture of what happened to Ava when Lucas attacked him. How his sister's beautiful angelic face had been bashed in with what looked like a hammer. Kane was left speechless as he was witnessing his brother holding the deformed dead carcass of their little sister. It was taking everything in Kane's power not to throw up right then and there. Blood seemed to slowly drip from the edges of the now blood stained dress.

"It seems that babies can really sense the true nature of people, huh?" Lucas spoke once more, catching Kane's attention, as he knelt down in front of the fire. "That's why I can't stand them." The tone of Lucas' voice changed from someone who seemed to be disconnected from reality, to sounding bitter. "They're better off as fuel for fire." Lucas remarked in a monotone voice as he faced the fire. The embers were threatened to be snuffed out with the rain seeping down the chimney. Without a single word after, Lucas tossed Ava's dead body into the fire like she was nothing more than a heavy log that would burn for hours.

"Ava!!!" Kane shouted at the top of his lungs as his voice cracked towards the end, the shock apparent on his face as he sat helplessly as the fire started to eat up the fabric of the dress. "How could you?!" Kane shouted in disbelief, tears filling up his eyes as they stung. "What kind of fucking monster would murder his entire family?!" Kane asked as the tears continued to flow down his cheeks. "How could you fucking do this Lucas?!" Kane seethed with anger while trying to pull against the ropes but failing. Dropping his head, Kane closed his eyes as he wept silently.

The creaking sounds of Lucas' footsteps went unnoticed as Kane was still trying to figure out everything that was going on. It was only when the creaking stopped that Kane opened his eyes. Seeing Lucas' legs appear in his line of vision caused Kane to glance up, but it wasn't quick enough as Kane felt Lucas' fingers grab a hold of his silver locks. Tugging Kane's head back to look into Lucas' eyes, the older male reached behind him to pull out a knife that Lucas often used to go hunting with. The fire seemed to make the blade glisten like the sun reflecting against the water's surface. An audible gasp left Kane's lips as he watched the edge of the blade land over his right eye.

"I'm the kind of monster that won't feel any guilt for killing his so-called family." Lucas remarked, lightly tapping the edge of the blade against Kane's right eyebrow. "Though, you should be grateful little brother." Lucas started to reply as he pressed the edge of the blade into Kane's flesh, watching the blood slowly pool up towards the surface. Kane gasped and whimpered from the pain, knowing that he couldn't move without the risk of losing an eye.

"You didn't have to hear our mother's neck as I snapped it with my bare hands." The admission coming from Lucas caused Kane's eyes to widen in fear. "Of course I killed her after she passed out from being choked." Lucas spoke, jerking the blade back and forth, as if teasingly making Kane suffer in his dialogue. It was like a saw being pulled back and forth, slowly cutting deeper into Kane's skull. Lucas seemed to ignore Kane's screams as he continued his treatment. "And you really should be thanking me for knocking you out before killing Ava with the hammer." Lucas remarked, a small chuckle towards the end as he seemed to find it rather amusing.

"Then again, she was a baby. So she was still very squishy. Unlike our mother who was older and getting to be more brittle." A mused hum left Lucas' lips as he jerked the blade out from Kane's flesh. "But you little brother. I can't simply kill you quickly." Kane didn't know if he should have been grateful or worried about that remark. "After all, you were the only one who actually seemed to try and look past the monster inside of me." Lucas added, taking note of Kane closing his right eye to protect it from the blood that was trying to seep out from the deep wound.

"I-I never...thought you were... a monster." Kane panted out, only to take a deep breath as he felt light headed from the injuries he felt all over. "Until...today." Kane finished, collecting some saliva and spitting into Lucas' eye as he was at a perfect level to get spat on. A weakened growl left Kane's throat as he looked up at Lucas with hatred for the first time in his life.

"You can burn in hell for what you did to mother and Ava." Kane spat, his fingernails digging into the frame of the chair. "You best kill me Lucas. Because if you don't, I'll make sure that I kill you instead. Then I'll set this whole place of fire." It wasn't a threat but a promise. Kane was not going to allow his brother to go free after this. Even if the man did survive the attack, Kane would make sure that Lucas would be dead for certain.

It seemed that Lucas didn't exactly like the gesture of Kane spitting in his eye. The rage behind his eyes was evident as he pulled harder on Kane's scalp, bringing the knife's edge to rest against the bottom of Kane's eye. "Seems like you forget the old saying little brother. An eye for an eye." Lucas growled, pressing the edge of the knife under Kane's eye. As Kane could feel the blade starting to cut him. "It makes the whole world blind." Lucas remarked ready to make his little brother blind, but Kane jerked his head to the side, forcing the blade to miss the eye completely, and instead forcing Lucas to cut towards Kane's right ear.

This little act of defiance seemed to anger Lucas, resulting in him grabbing more of Kane's hair, forcing him up from the seat a bit. "You honestly think that you can do as you please Kane?" Lucas growled, forcing the chair to rise up with him. This seemed to allow Kane to slip his hands free from the ropes that were loosely tied, offering Kane a chance to turn the tides on his brother.

"Yeah Lucas. I can do whatever I damn well please!" Kane growled, using this time to punch Lucas in the groin. Normally Kane would never go for a low blow like that, but considering that this was life or death, he had no real choice in the matter. Watching as if Lucas had the wind knocked out of him, Kane could feel the locks that were once clenched in Lucas' grip loosen to the point where Kane was able to get free from Lucas' grasp. Without thinking, Kane shoved Lucas back onto the coffee table, causing the knife that Lucas held to fly off in an unknown part of the dark home.

With Lucas doubled over in pain, holding his groin from being punched, Kane took this chance to start to undo the other bindings. Once he was set free, Kane scrambled to get up on his feet. As Kane had more stable footing, Kane rushed towards the kitchen like his life depended on it. Jagged pants escaped his lips as he slammed his body against the countertops' edge, pulling the drawer with the knives inside to try and find one that was sharp enough to protect him. The groans coming from Lucas meant that he still couldn't move.

Rushing back into the living room with a knife in hand, Kane watched as Lucas continued to hold onto his groin, slowly rocking back and forth as soft grunts left his lips. The light from the fire seemed to grow brighter as smoke started to fill the living room, the fire finally reaching Ava's dead body, causing the crackling of the fire to get louder as it burned the clothing Ava was wearing that was covered in blood and milk.

Kane stood there, wondering if it was alright if he should kill his brother. After all, how ironic was he in the situation where he had to kill his brother? It wasn't out of jealousy, but out of a need to defend himself. Taking a deep breath, Kane took small steps towards Lucas, watching as his older brother finally started to move around. Lucas appeared to still be in pain but was moving to brace himself against the coffee table. Kane clenched his jaw tightly as the grip on the handle of the knife matched his jaw. Kane didn't have much of a choice now, it would only be a short time before Lucas would be able to over power him. With the knife securely in his hand, Kane was quick to rush towards his brother. Pushing Lucas down on the floor, Kane used his strength to stab Lucas through his heart.

The shock on Lucas' face was evident as Kane heard the sharp inhale from the knife piercing into Lucas' heart. But Kane didn't stop there. Watching Lucas' body slump backwards onto the coffee, the rage that had built up from Lucas' actions caused Kane to repeatedly stab Lucas' body. By the time that Kane stopped, it looked as if a wild animal had attacked the older brother. Even as Kane sat on top of Lucas' dead body, Kane still held onto the knife as the storm continued to rage on.

BY the time that Kane came to after blacking out from the mindless attack on Lucas, he found himself sitting just inside of the barn. The door was wide open as the water droplets from the storm slowly dripped down from the wooden door frame. The house, and most of his family, were dead inside, was now engulfed in flames. The dark purple sky was lit with a bright orange thanks to the fire that looked as if it could not be tamed.

The cold air chilled Kane to the bone, shivering as the damp clothes stuck to his body. Kane felt like he had just lost everything. It was only when the sound of a horse and buggy approaching caught Kane's attention that he glanced towards it. It was the Mayworth's coming to check and see what exactly happened. A young boy and woman were the first to approach the gates of the farm house. The horror on the faces was evident as they didn't know what caused this to happen.

"Oh no..." The woman gasped, covering her mouth as she wasn't sure what happened. The woman was Miles' mother Rosa Mayworth, a woman around Celia's age with long dark gray hair that was often tied back into a tight bun. She was wearing a long fitted rain coat to help keep her dress dry from the pouring rain. It had a flower pattern that rested against her slender body. "Do you think any of the Flores' were home when the fire happened?" She asked, looking towards her husband who had tied the horses up to keep the horses from running off before joining the rest of his family. It seemed that they were here to visit, only to have the storm prevent them from arriving earlier that day.

"It's hard to say." The man spoke, his large rim hat covering the hair on top of his head. Ryan Mayworth was a man whom the Flores' family could often count on for pretty much anything. His piercing gray eyes scanned the area of the house the best he could. But it seemed like he couldn't exactly see if there was anyone around that was still alive. It was apparent that they were growing concerned since they had only gotten to the house recently as many trees had been blown over, making the trip down the road take longer. "Miles, go and check the barn. Maybe they are in there. After all, you often play with Kane in his little hay fort." Ryan remarked, glancing down at Miles.

Miles had been a bit lost for words upon looking at the scene before him. Watching as the home that he often came to visit was up in flames with no way of saving it, not knowing if his best friend and his family were even still alive. He had only recently lost his own brother, and now to lose a friend who was like a brother to him, it felt too surreal right now. Glancing towards the entrance of the barn, there was a set of staggering foot steps that lead from the house towards the barn.

Following the trail, Miles could see a bloodied Kane seemingly curled up with his knees pressing against his chest, staring at them with a distant gaze resting on his face while leaning against the door while sitting on the floor. "Kane!" Miles shouted, causing his parents to glance towards Miles' direction. Running through the puddles on the pathway, Miles didn't care if he was wet or dry at the point, he needed to be there for his friend more than anything right now.

Stopping just shy of Kane, Miles was surprised to see the full extent of what happened to his friend. To see bits of his skull exposed just above his right eye, and how bloody Kane's right side had become, it was amazing that Kane could even make his way towards the barn with how bloody he was. It was like Kane was able to pull himself out of the house just from the sheer will power he had to stay alive. Kane would never see it that way. He was in a daze after he felt all of the anger that was inside of him leave. He killed his older brother in revenge or justice, if you want to call it that. How was Kane expected to explain all of this to his father?

Once Ryan and Rosa had joined Miles at the barn's entrance, they couldn't help but be taken back with how bloody Kane was. The two had passed a glance towards each other. It was apparent that they didn't need to say anything. They had to take Kane someplace safe while getting in contact with Elijah who was still stuck thanks to the storm that came in. There was no way that Kane could defend himself in the state he was in. "Let's get Kane the cart. He needs medical attention." Ryan spoke, walking over towards Kane.

Picking Kane up in her arms, Rosa headed towards the door. "Don't worry Miles, your friend will be staying with us for now while we figure everything out." Rosa remarked as she started to walk back towards the carriage. "I'm sure his father would want to know what happened..." Rosa softly muttered before looking down at Kane's shocked expression. Her heart bleed for Kane right now. Knowing the feeling of loss as the reality of Parker's death was still fresh in her own mind. Nuzzling Kane ever so slightly, Rosa closed her eyes, praying that Celia and the rest were safe.

Over the years, after that night, Kane kept quiet about the events of his family being murdered. Rather it was due to grief or his work, Elijah couldn't find time to be able to come back to the burned remains of their old home, and looking for a new place was time consuming. But it was clear that Kane needed to recover from this ordeal. Elijah gave permission to the Mayworth's to help raise his son at their place, which was far away from ghostly remains of the old home that could trigger Kane's flashback of that night. But this wasn't the end of Kane's tragedy. It was only a few months after that night that the leaders were killed. The news reached Miles, Kane, and Rosa, causing the three to have to look out for each other. But after certain events had unfolded, Rosa had ultimately killed herself out of grief for losing a child, husband, and being violated the same night her husband died.

As Kane only had Miles, and vice versa, the two needed each other now more than ever. Needless to say, Kane's confidence wasn't the greatest. Feeling more like a curse who only brought misfortune to those who tried to help him, Kane was grateful that Miles stuck around. Perhaps that was why it had been so hard to give up the lingering feelings Kane had for the man. But now that Miles had been so willing to give up Kane's guarded secret, causing him to feel all alone again.

Granted it seemed that Dean was at least willing to hear him out, as both of their families had been murdered, but it felt like Kane was completely alone in the world. But seeing as how Dean didn't show him the type of pity that everyone had shown Kane, though a lot of people didn't know the facts surrounding that night. It was a relief that Kane could at least count on someone else.

CHAPTER TEN: *The Amber Glow Of The Crater*

A s THE DAYS had passed on the airship, Dean had found it hard to get Kane to venture out of the room. Granted Dean didn't know how to feel with Kane's secret being revealed to him, but it was better to come out of Kane's mouth rather than some stranger that Dean didn't even know. Even though Miles was one of the leaders, there was just something about the man that threw everything off. The way that Miles could seemingly look through Dean, like he was searching for some hidden secret that even Dean didn't know about, it was just unsettling to be around the man. If anything it was like they were playing some sort of invisible chess and Dean didn't know the rules of said game. Regardless, it was another day in which Dean found himself gazing up towards Kane as he stood on the floor below. Kane was currently wrapped inside of a blanket on the top of the bunks, staring at the wooden panel in front of him and away from Dean. It was like Kane's whole world had been shattered.

Not that Dean could blame him. For a while, Dean was just like that when his parents died. How he had to pack a duffel bag full of his belongings in a short time before being kicked out of the only home he knew. Using the blanket off of his old double bed to keep him warm in the new place. The blanket had acted like some kind of shield for Dean when he was on his own. The comfort of something that he knew in a place that was new and unsettling, it was the only comfort afforded to Dean during that dark time in his life. But watching Kane suffer from the depression that was hitting him, Dean felt like he needed to make it right.

"So uh," Dean started to speak, hearing a bit of movement of the sheets as if Kane was turning to listen to what Dean had to say. "How about we go to the library?" Dean suggested, despite not being there just yet, he figured that it would have been fun to share in the experience. "You said that there was a library on the ship right?" Dean spoke up, remembering that Kane spoke about how he loved to read romance books. Even though Dean wasn't a hardcore fan of romance, it was better than simply staying in the room the whole trip. Besides, it was a bit lonely wandering around the ship on his own.

The few times that Kane would get out of bed, it was merely to use the restroom. Dean would have been worried about the other eating, if it wasn't for the fact that Dean would bring him food and just sit and watch Kane take the food and slowly eat it. Maybe Kane felt like Dean was like some type of loyal dog, trying hard to make their master happy and make sure that they were at least eating.

Silence seemed to fill the room as Kane didn't answer him. Moving towards the ladder, the sound of the metal ladder shifting back and forth seemed to fill the void as Dean popped his head up to see Kane turning away from him. "Come on Kane." Dean spoke up, reaching over to place his hand on Kane's covered shoulder. "I know it's not easy talking about the past, especially to someone that you just met." Dean paused as he heard a small inaudible murmur from Kane. "But you heard my story too." It wasn't much of a solid argument, but at least the two knew about their past.

"We're not exactly all that different when you think about it." Not that it really compared, seeing as how Dean didn't get scarred like Kane did, but he at least understood. Frankly the only one who might know the feeling of killing off a family member would be this Amelia woman that was the Head of the Leaders. "We were both left alone around the same age." Dean spoke up once more as he leaned in closer to Kane. "Having to struggle in order to survive....we both are strong because of it." Dean's voice may have been full of confidence, as if it would be enough to build up Kane. But deep down Dean felt like this was pointless. He couldn't cheer up Kane, not after the events that led up to this point.

Again, silence came from Kane. Watching as the tribal leader moved to curl up into a tighter ball once more, Dean's eyebrows knitted together as he pulled the male back to look at him. "Look!" Dean raised his voice as he studied Kane's face. The other looked as if he had witnessed someone killing his beloved pet or something. The redness to those silver glistening eyes that were once full of expression had turned almost lifeless. The redness around Kane's nose showed that he had been trying to keep everything inside, and the bags under his eyes seemed to indicate that Kane hasn't gotten full sleep since talking about the past after burying it for so long. It made Dean feel like an asshole for yelling at him now.

"You didn't judge me when I told you about my parents being murdered and sprawled out like gutted pigs. What makes you think that I would do the same to you?" Dean asked, his voice seeming to soften as he knew that Kane had already been through enough. "Unlike you, I didn't exactly have someone who was willing to take me in. I had to live by myself for so long that I even started to talk to myself like some crazy person talking to the wind..." Dean trailed off, closed his eyes briefly as he retracted his hand.

"I would have given anything to have someone willing open up their home to me. To make me feel like I wasn't someone who could be discarded so easily." Dean's voice wavered as he felt a hot ball growing in his throat. "But you can't exactly blame Miles for trying to bring up your past as a way to get me to understand you better. He was just-" Dean continued before Kane started to speak, cutting Dean's little speech off abruptly.

"It's not about my family's death..." Kane weakly spoke, turning his head to look back towards the panel. It was like Kane was struggling to talk with the built up mucus in his throat. "I got over that a while ago..." Kane slightly lied. Even though he would never say it, Dean knew that it took more than a few years for someone to get over the death of their whole family. "I'm upset," Kane paused to better collect his train of thought. "Because the only man who I thought I could trust, betrayed me more than my brother killing my mother and sister ever could." Hearing it put that way, Dean couldn't understand how Kane felt since Dean never had someone close to him betray him in such a manner.

Letting out a small huff, Dean moved to steady himself on the ladder a bit more as he climbed onto the bed a bit. Dean's hands were a bit shaky as he didn't exactly trust the weight of the bunks to keep from crashing down, but he at least got half way onto the bed before his torso was hovering over Kane's body with his arms supporting him. "Listen," Dean paused, moving to bend one of his knees to kneel on the ladder to better support himself.

"You should be grateful that you got to trust someone." Dean continued, watching as Kane moved to look towards him, though with a small confused look on his face. "On the station, I couldn't exactly trust anyone but myself." Dean remarked, a small frown lingering on his lips. "Trust means nothing on the station because it can easily be bought out by the Elite." Dean's eyes glancing down to the fabric of the blanket. "Hell, there are incentives for other people to rat each other out for their own benefit....Rather it's for a better home or more credits added to their account, trust isn't sacred on the Millennium...." Not like Dean really trusted anyone on that damn space station as it was, but at least here he could learn to trust Kane.

"I couldn't even trust my aunts or uncles on either side of my family to take me in." As silly as it sounded, it was the reason why Dean was abandoned to live in the Bronze Class. "I nearly had my hand crushed by someone of the higher silver class, and I couldn't trust the higher ups to punish the man who nearly broke my hand." Even when Dean pleaded with his superiors to do something about the man, they simply shrugged him off and said that there wasn't anything that they could do for him.

"Trusting someone.... it doesn't come easy. And oftentimes, we learned the hard way that not everyone that we trust in our lifetime is capable of keeping that trust." Dean added, a small shrug of his shoulders. Dean couldn't count the number of people that he could trust on a single hand while on the station. "But as long as you're able to build up that trust again, you will find that there are some people who would be willing to give their life for you." Dean paused, giving Kane a soft smile while the other male seemed to look up at Dean like a deer caught in headlights. "After all, I know I can at the very least trust you." Dean spoke in a soft almost quiet tone as he saw that shimmer of life coming back to Kane's eyes.

Dean could never trust another person on the station who wouldn't stab him in the back at the first chance that they could get. Everyone was out for themselves, or at the very least, they were loyal to the Elite. After all, getting into the good graces of the Elite has given people better perks the more one was loyal to them. Dean would never sacrifice his morals just for better living conditions or credits that could help him live a better life. Which was why he was quick to be placed on the slaughter hook, much like those who leaked what really happened on the day the bombs dropped. It was before Dean's time, but from what he remembered his parents talking about it. Those who tried to take down the Elite were quickly put in their place. When the only salvation one had was at mercy of a group of murderous individuals with enough power and influence to make everyone become docile, it was hard to break away from the illusion of the so-called paradise they lived in.

"You... just won't get it Dean." Kane spoke as life started to fade his eyes once more with a pout on his face. "I'm not just dealing with someone who simply betrayed me...." Kane trailed off a bit, only to close his eyes. "It was a clear message that he doesn't care about my feelings anymore if he was willing to spill it to a stranger..." Watching the soft pout lingering on Kane's lips, Dean grew a concerned look on his face.

"Not to be disrespectful or anything, but we aren't exactly all that close on an emotional level." Kane corrected himself, though they were very close on the bed with Dean hovering over him. "I just figured that I would tell you what happened as a means to patch a hole before it would get bigger." Kane pulled the sheet closer to himself, as if to shield himself off from the rest of the world. "Sometimes it is just easier to let people believe what they wanted rather than have them ignore the truth..."

Dean's facial expressions softened a bit as he kept silent while Kane continued. "For as long as I could remember, people believed that a would-be assassin from the Wrath clan came to assassinate my family as a means to send a message to the other leaders." Kane continued in a soft tone as he stared at the wood panel before him. "That the Wrath clan was capable of doing whatever they wanted to prove a point." Kane explained, moving a hand up to tuck some of his messed up locks behind his left ear out of habit.

"But that's not the point right now." Kane paused before clearing his throat. "Miles was willing to tell the truth to you against my wishes. That kind of betrayal felt like I was getting sucker punched in the gut." Kane spoke through shaky words, his eyes starting to tear up once more. "To break his promise like that unprovoked, it was like he didn't care about what it would do to me." Kane narrowed his eyes at the panel, whether it was out of anger, sadness, or tiredness was up for debate. "He hurt me more that way than just simply rejecting my feelings for him." Kane admitted, a small sniffle escaping him as Kane moved to sit up at this point.

Dean's brows furrowed together as he tried to rationalize this whole concept. It was clear that Kane had romantic feelings for Miles, but the other male just didn't feel the same. As Kane moved to sit up, Dean started to climb down the ladder a bit to readjust himself. After all, being half way on the bed wasn't exactly comfortable. "Well, who cares if he did that." Dean spoke bluntly, causing Kane to appear shocked at the statement as he reached the floor.

"W-What?" Kane stammered, moving to lean over the edge of the bunk down at Dean with widen eyes, though he scowled a little at how blunt Dean was after hearing Kane's sob story. "What do you mean who cares? I care!" Kane was hurt as a confused facial expression lingered on his face. It seemed almost heartless for Dean to say something like that. Biting his lower lip, Kane dug his nails into the wooden surface of the rail.

"Well, he didn't exactly say who it was, so therefore he didn't break his promise." Dean spoke, a small shrug of his shoulders as he looked up at Kane. Seeing the astonished expression take over Kane's expression caused Dean to smile a bit. "Sure he may have tried to say who it was that killed your family, but I didn't let him." Dean added, placing his hands on his hips, a small tilt of his head. Bringing up a hand to give the air a small dismissal wave, Dean continued to speak. "I don't want other people to tell me about my friend's past." Dean continued as he looked up at Kane.

"What kind of satisfaction would I have gotten from listening to some guy I don't even really know?" Dean continued as he moved to cross his arms over his chest. "If my friend wants to open up to me, and tell me more about himself, I want to hear it directly from the horse's mouth." Dean remarked before realizing what he had said may have sounded like an insult. "Not that I'm calling you a horse or anything, but I just want to hear it from you and no one else." Dean finished though a bit awkwardly. Gazing up towards Kane, Dean was watched as the tribal leader's expression softened a bit as the relief of Dean's words eased the weight off of the male's chest.

"So, how about it?" Dean asked, reaching a hand up towards Kane, watching the younger male studying him as if waiting for something to happen. "How about we explore this ship together?" Dean paused with his hand still reaching out, all the while Kane's right hand released the railing as he thought it over. "I feel like we could both have a better time if we enjoyed each other's company." Dean smiled up towards Kane. "Besides, I want to hear what kind of books that you would recommend." Dean continued, flashing a wide smile to Kane.

"I may not like romance, but I'm at least open minded." Dean lightly chuckled towards the end, though he was feeling a bit foolish as he stood on the ground while reaching a hand up towards Kane. Curling his fingers inwards, Dean retracted his hand when Kane didn't answer, and instead scratched the back of his head. "Or not..." Dean trailed off. "I mean, it's not like we'll be doing much for the next couple of days anyways." There was that nervous and awkward feeling back again.

"You're....really something else." Kane finally spoke, breaking the awkward silence as he reached over to grab the curtain. Pulling it closed all the way to get dressed, Dean seemed to watch helplessly. Watching as Kane disappeared behind a curtain, Dean took a few steps back as he gazed as the curtain shifted around a bit. Eventually, Dean rested his back against one of the wood panel walls as he heard the curtain pull back. It seemed that Kane had gotten dressed in that small space, which probably wasn't ideal, but at least it seemed that Kane was feeling better.

Not using the ladder, Kane easily jumped down from the top bunk with a small thud. Wearing his usual dark robes, Kane made sure that there were no ruffles that would make him look like the mess he was a few minutes ago. As Kane stopped in front of Dean, Kane brought a hand up to rub his own right arm as he glanced off to the side.

"Sorry," Kane started to speak a sheepish smile forming on his lips before he glanced up at Dean, taking note of the man's slightly puzzled gaze. "For not really being myself." Kane continued, before clearing his throat. "But you are right... Miles didn't spill my secret." Kane spoke, though it was mostly to remind himself more than anything at this point. "And that, well, you wanted to hear it from me. Like a good friend."

"Like a good friend?" Dean asked in a light teasing voice. "Come on, shouldn't it be like a best friend?" Dean spoke, giving Kane a light punch on his arm. "You know I'll have your back man." Dean reassured him, turning to face the door.

"Now, let's go and check out this ship together. I've only looked around the dining room and the observatory. I haven't really experienced most of what else this ship has to offer." Dean remarked, grasping onto the door handle before feeling Kane's hand against his arm, feeling the light tug coming from the tribal leader. "What is it?" Dean asked, facing to turn towards Kane. Needless to say Dean was a bit taken back when he saw a determined yet mischievous gaze lingering on Kane's face. "What's that look for?" Dean asked, feeling a bit confused before he watched Kane move closer towards him.

"How about we go and train your body?" Kane remarked, moving closer to Dean, breaking the space between the two of them. Dean was a bit surprised at this more assertive side of Kane, resulting in a small flustered blush to cross Dean's face as he swallowed the lump in his throat. It was almost like Dean had just unleashed a whole new side of Kane that was kept hidden for the sake of their friendship.

"W-What do you have in mind?" Dean asked as he was a bit nervous. Taking a step back, resulting in Dean's back resting against the door. It felt like Kane was towering over him as the light from the window surrounded Kane in almost a blinding light. Dean seemed to wait with baited breath as he watched the corners tug against Kane's lips into an almost cruel smirk.

"We're going to head down towards the cargo area to train. After all, I don't want my best friend to be breathless and weak on the journey. We have to train your body to handle the rough terrain between the different clans." Kane remarked, though Dean didn't trust that seemingly innocent smile that Kane was flashing towards him.

"After all, you're going to have your right of passage if you want Amelia to see you. So, I want to make sure that you can at least hunt." Even though Kane had talked about it briefly, it seemed that this right of passage was a big deal. Not like Dean could really argue. If Dean wants to be accepted, he'll have to do it, and what better teacher than one who knows about hunting than Kane?

AFTER a few days of training, Dean was grateful when they would finally be landing at their destination. Despite his appearance, Kane was a capable fighter. There wasn't a single time in which Dean was able to take him down. By the end of the day, Dean would be a sore mess from the blows that Kane delivered from the mixture of his hands to his kicks. It wasn't surprising when Dean noticed the patches of bruises on his body, but at least Kane would provide him with some pain medicine.

One could only imagine the surprise on Dean's face when Kane told him to try and actually attack him. At first Dean didn't take it seriously, but after getting his pride bent a bit when Kane could easily dodge or push his attacks back, that was when Dean started to get serious with his attacks. But no matter how hard he tried, Kane was as fast as a rabbit and Dean was always trying to catch up.

After each round, Dean would find himself struggling to get up from laying on the floor, his body covered in sweat as his lungs felt like they were on fire. Even when the airship would get bumpy, Kane was able to move swiftly while Dean looked like he was a newborn calf, struggling to stand up straight. There was only so much that they could do with the training. All that Kane was able to teach Dean was self-defense techniques and how to take down opponents using their weight and momentum against them.

Strapping himself into the seat, Dean felt like he could just simply melt into the fabric with how exhausted he was. His hair was slightly wet from the shower he took before they would land. Changing into a spare robe that Kane had, Dean could feel some of his muscles twitching as his bones felt like they were like sandpaper.

The robe that Dean was wearing was a light green design that had black trimmings as there was a lining of white fabric under the robe. It was a bit breezy, but considering that they would be landing in an area that was tropical, it only made sense for them to wear something light. Apparently this was the main area of Felicia's clan. They would only be able to be here for a day or so before moving onto the next location. This would be the perfect time to take in some of the sights for himself.

It didn't take long for Kane to join him in their seats, though Kane's face did look a little sickly. Seems like it was the rough patches that tended to get the better of Kane, so perhaps Dean could take the tribal leaders mind off of the bumps since it appeared that during their practice matches Kane didn't seem to be bothered with the bumps. "I was a bit curious," Dean spoke up, causing Kane to look towards him with a soft hum of curiosity leaving the tribal leader's lips. "What is the island like? The one we're going to?" Figuring that at least an explanation could help ease the tension.

"Oh, the island?" Kane repeated, a faint smile landing on his lips as he was glad that Dean was asking him about it rather than Felicia. "It's a place where a lot of people who love studying machinery and engineering tend to flock." Kane started as he moved to face Dean a bit more. "It's set on a cluster of tropical islands. They have bridges that connect to each other through a series of draw bridges. That way, when there is a storm, they can easily raise them up so they won't get damaged from the debris still lingering in the waters." It seemed that was an issue in the past, but seeing as how they were able to solve it, it showed how they were problem solvers at least. "They are also the ones who are surrounded by a giant crystallized wall thanks to all the salt water around them. This allows them to be protected by the harsh waters surrounding them and also provide enough energy to keep the machines going." Kane explained, his eagerness from their first meeting seeming to be resurfacing.

"Machines?" Dean asked, a bit unsure as to what they could use machines for if the sole purpose of being undetected by the Elite made it hard for them to advance their progress. Wouldn't that make them simply stick out more? "What kind of machines are we talking about? Aren't they afraid of getting caught by the Elite?" Dean asked, knowing that if the Elite knew about the survivors, it would ruin their chances of getting the element of surprise. But seeing the knowing smirk on Kane's face made Dean wonder what the tribal leader had in store for him.

"Well you see," Kane started to speak, only to feel the ship hit a pocket of air, causing the ship to become a bit bumpy. Dean grew a slightly concerned expression as he wondered if Kane's motion sickness would cause the male to stop with his explanation. After a few minutes, it seemed that Kane was able to regain a bit of his composure. This was a bit relieving since it meant that Dean's idea was actually helping the other. "O-Okay," Kane mumbled a bit to himself as he took a shaky breath in. "T-They were able to make the collapsed cave look like a volcano." Kane finished, only to place a hand on his stomach.

"Like a volcano?" Dean asked, a bit surprised that they would be able to make something like that seem possible. Then again Dean didn't know the difference between a volcano and the top of a mountain that peaked out of the clouds. Maybe if he didn't know the difference, then perhaps the Elite didn't know as well? Who knows, maybe Dean was able to see the islands and just paid it no mind. Either way, Dean was interested in learning more about this island that they were heading towards.

"They use a mixture of orange and yellow crystals for the street lights to make it appear as if the volcano is still active." Kane explained, flashing Dean a bright smile as if it was his idea in the first place. "It was a bit risky at first, but since it didn't seem to draw attention, it was worth the risk." Kane finished, causing Dean to chuckle a little bit. "What's so funny?" Kane asked, seeming to be a bit offended that Dean laughed at him.

"Nothing. It's just," Dean started to speak, moving to relax in the chair a bit. "Seeing how eager and happy you look explaining it makes me think of an eager and excitable dog." Dean explained, seeing the slightly flustered look on the male's face after the comment. "Like, right now, if you had a tail it would be going wild." Dean teased, watching Kane's face get a bit red from the mixture of being flustered and embarrassed at the same time.

"That's not something that you should say so easily to someone." Kane grumbled a bit, straightening himself up a bit. "Someone would get the wrong idea." Kane added, a small glance towards Dean as he gripped the straps more. It wouldn't be much longer for the ship to arrive, and Dean was excited to see how the crystals looked like lava. Dean had never seen lava before, but he could imagine how the glow from the crystals looked at night. After all, while they were walking along the countryside, the stars were vast in the patches he could see through the parted clouds. Dean could only imagine how it would look lighting up the whole area.

As the ship had finally landed, those inside could feel the loud thud of the bottom of the ship landing on the anchoring dock. Slipping the straps off, Dean was relieved that he could actually move again after sitting for so long. With a long groan, Dean stretched his body, feeling his bones popping and cracking in the process. Collecting the pouch of poker chips, Dean grasped the satchel in his hand before grinning to himself. He'll finally be able to get something for himself with the chips that Kane gave him. It still felt a bit off to have a visible source of currency on hand, but it was better than nothing.

"Well, ready to check out the Pride Clan?" Kane asked, his hand resting on the handle of the door. It was apparent that Dean was ready for whatever the island had to offer. But one of the things that Dean wanted to see would be sought out after nightfall. To see the mixture of orange and yellow crystals that would be bright enough to make it seem like they were inside of a volcano. Dean could only imagine that they would need to be up higher for it to be noticeable. Who knows, maybe Kane could pull some magical strings for Dean to be able to see it. Either way, Dean was ready to get off of this ship. It was starting to feel like the Millennium after a while of being cooped up in the room.

Exiting out of their shared room, Kane carefully scanned the hallway to make sure that there wasn't a chance that he could bump into Miles. Though Dean wouldn't know it, there used to be a time in which Kane used to purposely look out for Miles. It was funny how things could easily change over the course of a few days and the circumstances forcing the two of them to drift apart so easily.

Most of the crew had been hard at work making sure that the docking had gone without a hitch. So needless to say, the hallway had been pretty bare. "Alright, let's go." Kane had given the all clear, moving out of the room first as he waited for Dean to exit the room so he could lock up. "Good thing about being the one of the Clan leaders, we get to exit the ship first." Kane lightly mused, tucking his key into a hidden pocket, before making sure that the door was securely locked up.

"Guess I should count myself lucky then." Dean mused a bit, ready to follow Kane's lead like he did the first time that they had gotten on the ship. The sound of the empty ship was a bit unsettling. Not for the fact that it looked abandoned or anything like that, but purely for the fact that the wind surrounding the boat made it sound as if the ship was breathing. When they were flying it wasn't much of an issue since the sounds of the engine were reminiscent of the Millennium's hum, but the fact that it sounded like lungs inhaling and exhaling was the fact that creeped out Dean the most.

As they got off of the ship, there was a soft ringing sound that seemed to fill the air, like the wind was singing to those who got off of the ship. Glancing around the area, Dean was surprised to see a large tree that seemed to stick out over the rest. Unlike the natural green leaves that most of the trees had, this one seemed to glisten with a variety of colored leaves. Upon further inspection, it appeared that this tree wasn't natural, but rather artificial. The large tree appeared to be see-through in texture as Dean could clearly see people walking around the tree to head towards their next destination. Looking further up the length of the tree, Dean noticed that the leaves that appeared to be multicolored at first were actually crystals shaped like leaves. The way that the sunlight reflected against the individual leaves, it seemed to make the individual leaves glisten, welcoming newcomers to gaze at the beauty of this structure in awe.

"Wow.... " Dean spoke with awe as he stood in the shade of the makeshift tree. "I've never seen anything like this." He continued, listening to the footsteps of Kane who was amused that Dean took in the sight of a tree that a whole team of collective artist and craftsmen worked to make such a structure possible. "The only thing remotely close to this beauty was the fountain on the level I worked on as a janitor." Dean continued, glancing towards Kane for a second before looking back at the crystallized tree structure.

"Oh yeah? What kind of fountain design was it?" Kane asked, a bit surprised that there would even be some type of structure on board of the station. Though it would make sense if you remember that the ego of the Elite and the most powerful would want to make something grandiose and expensive looking. In Dean's eyes, it was in poor taste the way that they designed it. Reflecting on how the Elite thought of those left behind as nothing more than unwanted faceless creatures of what were supposed to be human.

"Yeah, it was made out of solid gold." Dean started, shrugging his shoulders a bit as he felt an odd sense of peace standing by the tree, listening to the crystals chiming as they softly rubbed against each other as the leaves were connected by thin lines that were once used for fishing lines. "It was a replica of the Millennium with a rocket swirling towards it. The smoke from the rockets spiraled downwards to a bunch of figures below that looked as if they were crying despite the fact that they were faceless. But with the way that the water rolled down their faces, it gave off the eerie vibe of people crying while displaying the anguish they felt for being left behind." Dean spoke, his tone indifferent about the statue. "It always made me wonder," Dean continued. "Why would anyone find that fountain to be beautiful? I found it revolting that they would glorify something like that." He finished, glancing towards Kane who seemed to look upset at what he heard.

"They really found our pain and suffering to be amusing?" Kane spat, clenching his fists as he couldn't help but take in what Dean had said. Dean couldn't help but look and be a bit surprised that everything that Dean had told the tribal leader had no effect on him, yet the news of the glorification of the destruction of the human race was what sent him over the edge.

As Dean turned to face Kane, the tribal leader closed his eyes before taking a deep breath through his nose. It appeared that Kane was trying to calm himself down, knowing that if he got upset over something like that, he wouldn't be any better than Felicia. It took a few seconds before Kane cleared his throat.

"Well... at least they would have to remember how inhumane they were. That their actions will forever immortalize their crime of leaving us as they escaped from the bombs that they launched." Kane remarked, seemingly hiding the anger swelling up. He had to keep a poised appearance since they were people around. "Well, shall we get going? We need to get you some more clothes before we visit Ashley's tribe." Kane flashed a fake smile on his face, heading towards a direction that would leave them to walk around the crystal tree.

It wasn't like Dean didn't know how the other felt. Every day Dean had to walk through that station, shifting his feet mostly in place as he used muscle memory to head towards his next location. Every day felt the same, like he was just a small cog in a large complex wheel that functioned as the pinnacle of human ingenuity. But now that he had been on Earth, he felt more free than ever. Every day was something new and exciting. It was something that he had longed for since he was left to simply rot in the prison of the Bronze Class.

Looking around, Dean took notice of how greenery the island was. There were a couple of different plants that he couldn't figure out what it was, so he simply figured that they were just some type of mutated flora thanks to the radiation and passage of time. Seeing a punch of people roaming around dressed in fairly light clothing reminded Dean of some old magazines that featured people wearing clothing a bit similar to what most people were wearing now. The smell of sand and rich soil seemed to be abundant as they reached a large opening of the cave that led towards the collapsed cave. Stepping inside and walking further in behind Kane, there wasn't much that Dean could see as it was a bit dark. But once he noticed the light up ahead, the sight before him was like he stepped into a fantasy world.

The interior of the cave looked like Dean had stepped back into the rings of the Silver class once more. The way that the roads had seemingly spread in a chaotic yet organized mess that allowed people to grow food in and around their homes. The streams of fresh water trickling through the town to allow for clean water despite being surrounded by an ocean. People were walking around with arms full of fresh fruit from their garden, seemingly passing them out to their friends to try out the result of their hard work. Some of the pathways leading towards the higher elevations of the cave were replaced with a wooden road that made it easy for those pulling carts to go up and down without much trouble.

Glancing up towards the opening, Dean noticed that there were a bunch of orange and yellow crystals that looked almost like they were woven into a design that could look as if the makeshift volcano was active if there were enough lights from underneath to give it that illusion. Frankly Dean was looking forward to seeing the place alive with the different crystals all lit up. It would be quite a show for him since he never got to see so many crystals lit up at once.

Making sure that he didn't get separated from Kane, Dean caught up with the other in no time. Around the center of the town seemed to be a large community hub where all kinds of shops seemed to land. The amount of clothing boutiques, restaurants, and bars seemed to make this place the first stop for anyone who was looking for a good time. Heading towards a shop with a little hanging sign that had something that resembled some fabric and a needle seemed to hang above the door. The design of the wooden sign had started to show a bit of its age by the paint that had been chipped away, it was still evident that this was some type of clothing shop.

Upon entering through the wooden door with a familiar stained glass design of the loose fabric and giant needle on the door, a little bell rang above the door to signal that there were some new customers. Dean didn't exactly know what to expect, but the walls seemed to be covered in what looked like old book shelves full of clothing material. There were some displays of their current product already out. There were plenty of sizes for people to be able to purchase the different clothing right then and there. There were a few patrons in there already, but it wasn't like much of them paid attention to Kane or Dean. Then again, Kane was already heading towards the cashier by the time that Dean stopped looking around. Though he couldn't tell what Kane was talking to the lady behind the cashier's counter about, Dean could only assume that it had to do with clothing.

"Wow, I can't believe the different types of clothes that they have here." Dean mostly talked to himself, taking a look at the designs that they had for women first. If Dean's mother was still around, he knew that she would want to try on everything if she could. Of course Dean and Max would slowly shuffle towards the men's section while she would go ham over this or that being cute before finally picking something out that she would love. Too bad that they would never get a chance to experience this, but at least Dean was able to.

"Hey Dean, I need you to come here." Kane called out, raising a hand up and waving towards Dean, hoping to catch the man's attention. Naturally, Dean glanced up from the clothing that hung towards the front, only to make his way carefully around the different displays. The last thing that Dean needed was to knock something over and break it. When Dean successfully managed to squeeze through the displays, Kane seemed to be waiting with a woman who wore a tape measure around her neck. Her brunette locks were short, barely grazing over her ears as she wore a red pair of glasses. She looked to be around Dean's age, all the while wearing a white sundress that hung off of her shoulders.

There was a thin belt that had yellow gems encrusted in a flower pattern around her waist as the hem of the dress caressed against her knees. She was wearing white sandals that had a similar flower that was on her belt, though it was a singular flower that had a few of the gems seemingly missing thanks to either age or the gems becoming loose and fallout out.

She seemed to greet Dean with a light pink lipstick covered smile as her blue eyes barely peaked over the rim of her glasses. Three slender white crystals laid against the nape of her neck, seemingly separated by small metal beads. "It's very nice to meet you." She spoke with a small bow towards the end, throwing Dean off by her politeness. Normally if Dean had gone into a shop for clothing on the Millennium, the shop keeper would have been snarky.

"Oh, yeah. Pleasure to meet you too." Dean returned the bow, causing the woman to chuckle a little bit. The way that she seemed to find Dean's return bow to be amusing only made Dean feel a bit self conscious. He didn't know any traditions, so he was only trying to make her a bit more at ease, or at the very least, not seem like he was being disrespectful.

"This is Mia. She can help you with some clothes that would be more suited to your style. She'll want to take your measurements of course. That way she'll know what to work with as well as keep it handy in case you want something tailored made." Kane explained, figuring that this would help to ease any tension that Dean could be feeling at the moment. Granted it was appreciated, but Dean had a feeling that Kane was enjoying Dean making a fool out of himself. "Once we're done here, we can head over to another store to pick you up some stuff to help with our journey towards Ashley's clan." Not that Dean was really looking forward to it, but it was better than going unprepared.

"We don't normally get people who are courteous enough to give us a polite bow back. Sorry if my amusement caused you a bit of distress." Mia spoke, wanting to dispel any unwanted stress from Dean. It seemed to work as Dean's shoulders started to relax, helping to change his posture. "Now, if you'll follow me." Mia finished, giving a small nod before bypassing the two men and heading towards a section of the store that was only for employees and clients.

It was a desk that had all types of measuring tapes decorating the dark wooden table top. Books with various pages opened allowed for one to see that page had different design sketches of different styles, making it seem like they came from other artists. Rather it was from decades prior, or if it was from a collection of recent artists, the level of detail was astonishing on the faceless figures.

"Mia was one of Ashley's top students for the arts. If you ever want to have an amazing outfit, Mia is one of the most recommended seamstresses you could ask for." Kane remarked, causing Dean to be caught off guard by the statement. Was she really the one who had been able to make a vast majority of the clothes here? "Actually, once we get your measurements, I'll place an order for you. Think of it as a gift for around the holidays since it should be done by that time and sent out before the weather gets too bad." Kane suggested, though Dean didn't understand what Kane meant at the time.

"What? You don't need to do that." Dean spoke, feeling himself become a bit flustered. "I mean, it's not like you know me all that well to get me a gift." Dean stammered a bit, reaching a hand up to scratch the back of his head. Casting his gaze down a bit from the embarrassment he was feeling, Dean noticed the white sandals coming into view as Mia stepped a bit too closer to him. Stumbling back, Dean felt the measuring tape wrap around his neck, causing Dean to stiffen his posture.

"Relax. I can't take proper measurements when you're all stiff." Mia spoke, a soft chuckle leaving her lips as she tilted her head up to read the measurements. "But I don't mind. It's been a while since I was able to make a special formal outfit." Mia continued to speak as Dean felt her warm breath close to his neck. "Being on an island, you rarely get the chance to make someone look amazing in a tuxedo." Mia spoke, a mused hum leaving her lips towards the end.

"Well that settles it then." Kane remarked, crossing his arms over his chest loosely. "Besides, you'll need one anyways for the end of the season banquet." Hearing about a banquet was something new to Dean. Sure there were holidays in which people would come together and take in feasts, but to have a banquet was something unheard of. Plus with the fact that Kane was willing to pay for a formal outfit for him, Dean felt like he was taking advantage of the tribal leader. Kane was being a real friend to him, and yet Dean felt like he didn't offer anything in return.

"I'll pay for it." Dean finally spoke, relaxing his body a bit as Kane looked at him a bit surprised. "I don't want you to feel like you have to get me something as expensive as a formal outfit." It was better off this way as it was. The less that Kane had to pay for him, the better. That way if they parted ways down the road it wouldn't feel so awkward. "And besides, we still have to collect other things while we're here, right? So don't worry about it." Dean added, giving Kane a reassuring smile. Though it didn't seem like Kane liked the idea, it wasn't like Kane could argue.

The rest of the time spent at the shop was in relative silence. Not that Kane didn't try to make some type of conversation, but having a stranger this close to him didn't put Dean in a talkative mood. He would rather get the measurements done and get out. After all, feeling another person touching his body through his clothes was a rather unusual feeling. Mia's grip was rather strong with her slender fingers wrapping around his legs. They felt very bony, only a small step up from feeling like a skeleton was caressing his body, but the scent coming from Mia smelled faintly of lavender.

"Alright, let me write this down for you." Mia spoke up as she took a step back from Dean. "Make sure to memorize it if you can if you're going to the other shops." Mia instructed as she walked towards the table. "I'll make sure to adjust the clothes in case there are some changes between now and the banquet." She finished, taking out some paper to write the measurement notes on it. It took only a few minutes before she extended a hand back to let either Dean or Kane grab hold of the paper. Dean gingerly took the paper before watching Mia flip a page towards a new blank page in a sketchbook. "I'll make sure to send the finished project towards Ashley's estate. Is that where you two will be staying for the winter months?" Mia asked, glancing towards the two.

"Yeah. We'll be staying there for most of the winter. Don't want to do any traveling in the snow." Kane remarked, earning a slightly puzzled glance from Dean. As he caught the glance, Kane smiled as he faced Dean. "Around the first couple of days when the snow starts to fall and stick, that's usually the indication that everyone will have to start settling in for the winter months. It's far too dangerous to head out when we're in winter months." Kane started to ex-plain, figuring that since Dean had been stuck in the Millennium all of his life, he didn't know the dangers of snow. After all, why would he? It wasn't like the Millennium could actually experience seasons in a normal sense like they would on Earth.

"Oh? Is the snow really all that dangerous?" Dean asked, unsurprisingly confused since it seemed that all they had to deal with was the cold of space that surrounded his pod. Surely they could just bundle up and keep going, right? Sure they would need to find food, but if they went from town to town, they should have a steady supply. If it got too cold they could always make a type of shelter and make a fire.

"Dean, you can't be serious." Kane spoke, his surprise apparent that Dean would even sug-gest that the snow wasn't all that dangerous. "I don't know how the weather was like during the colder months of the year on the Millennium, but there are a lot of facts that make the snow dangerous here." Kane started out, moving his fingers to be in front of him to start listing some of the problems that they could face while out walking during the cold.

"For one, if we get trapped in a snowstorm without any shelter, we could easily freeze to death. Second of all, during a blizzard, we could be caught in a white out and become con-fused and lose our way." Kane started, his voice almost in a scolding tone that was like Dean's mother. "And even if we find a shelter, we might be buried inside, and unable to dig our way out. Which leads me to point out that if we're trapped, we could run out of food long before spring arrives." The more that Kane described what could happen to them, the more that Dean got the picture. "Third-" Kane started before getting cut off by Dean.

"Alright alright! I get it. Traveling in the snow is a no go." Dean relented, not wanting to hear a whole list of reasons why something like the snow was dangerous to travel in. When it seemed that Kane was able to relax as Dean got the message, Dean took this as a chance to at least ask some questions about the subject of the estate being brought up earlier. "So what is the deal with the estate then?" Dean asked. "Do all of you live there or is it just for that Ashley chick that we're going to meet?" With the word like estate, it was easy to think of some type of large lavish building that they would collect in for the winter season.

"Well, each year we rotate which clan member will house the banquet for the year. This year we're going to have it at the Envy's clan. Next year will be my clan's turn." Kane explained, taking a quick glance over at some of the notes that Mia was writing. "It started out as a way for everyone to come together after the sin wars." It must have been hard on the leaders after dealing with this war. "There, if anyone has any concerns or issues from the year, they are able to address it to us more directly." It seemed like a more stable way to make sure that people's needs were at least being addressed.

"That's really amazing." Dean chimed in amazement, his response seemed to be a pleasant surprise to Kane, seeing as how the tribal leader was taken back that someone actually thought that the idea was amazing. Oftentimes people would keep quiet, just glad that they were able to go through a whole year without much incident, but there was a feeling that most thought that they being 'ruled' over still meant that they weren't completely free to live the way that they wanted. Sadly they would never know how bad it could really get. The people living on the Earth should be grateful that no one is trying to control every single aspect of their life. Unlike those who lived on the Millennium.

"I'm glad you think so." Kane admitted, glancing down a bit as a soft smile crept on his lips. "It's not like we get to hear people say that it's a good idea very often." Kane added, rubbing the back of his neck before he realized that they had some people looking in their general direction. "Well, let's get you settled with the payment up front before we head out and get some more supplies." Kane shifted the subject, his uneasiness was noted, though Dean didn't comment on it. Instead, he just figured that it was best to get everything done before the night. That way, when they headed out later in the night, he could take in the sights with Kane by his side.

What seemed like hours of shopping finally out of the way, Dean was just glad that they were able to make it towards the inn that they would be staying the night in. Granted it would have been easier to go back to the ship and sleep, but the two agreed that they wanted a change of scenery as they would be on board the ship the following day. It was one thing to sleep on a bumpy airship where it was hard to get a restful night sleep, it was another to actually sleep on solid ground.

The room that they were currently in was certainly an interesting one. The walls had a mixture of a wooden design that had different parts of wood woven into each other in an articulate way that Dean had never seen. That section of the wall seemed to be placed behind the two beds while the rest of the walls were mostly white, except for the different types of leaf prints that lined the walls in patches of a dark blue and light green. There was a woven carpet under each bed that had a similar style to that of the wall. The rest of the floor had a white coloring to it, to which Kane had pointed out that the wood came from some type of spruce tree. The ceiling had a bit of a darker coloring to it, as the exposed wooden beams seemed to add to the flair, it gave the illusion that the room was bigger than it already was.

The bed sheets were a light gray with white trimming, tucked under a thin blanket that looked as if it had been dyed with blueberries. It looked as if there were patches of dark blue where the berries had been crushed, leading to the conclusion that was how they dyed some of their clothes. Not that Dean minded it. He actually thought that it was creative. He just never seen it before. Sitting on the bed, Dean let out a small groan as he still felt a bit tired from the training they did on the ship, not to mention the long walk they took in order to get to their hotel room in the first place. Though the lobby was a bit more elegant than their room, that was pretty much a given.

"I feel like my limbs are going to fall off." Dean groaned, letting his back slam onto the top of the bed as gravity took over. "Why did you pick this inn over all the others that were closer to the entrance?" Dean grumbled, feeling like he could barely lift his arms up from the bed. Laying on the bed Dean could feel every muscle aching from the climb. Even though they had taken in a bit of the sights, at the end of the day, Dean would just be too exhausted to see anything else.

"Well, you did say that you wanted to see the lights at night." Kane reminded him, setting his own bags down on his bed. With a swift movement, it didn't take long for Kane to sit across from Dean, seeing as how Dean didn't appear to want to move a single inch, Kane started to study Dean more closely. Watching his chest slowly rise and fall with just a small key notice of Dean's heart beating against his chest from their hike up. Moving his eyes over towards his arm covered by the robes, a bit of his arm sticking out of the sleeves and his fingers gingerly curled inwards. Kane's glance moved to look at Dean's stoic face next. The parting of his lips as he took sporadic deep breaths, the way that Dean's lashes curled as he closed his eyes, it made Kane wonder what Dean's parents looked like.

"Yeah... don't remind me." Dean groaned through a few pants, finally catching his breath. Opening his eyes, Dean glanced up at the ceiling before his eyes moved downwards to see Kane watching him closely. "So," Dean started to speak up, shifting to sit back up once he felt like he wasn't dying. "Guessing this place gives you an amazing view of it?" Dean asked, watching Kane glance away from him when it seemed Dean caught Kane staring at him.

"You got it." Kane admitted, a coy smile flashing across his lips. "The places we stopped at earlier made it easier for us to get here faster than going around the edge." Kane explained through a small groan as he stretched his body. Seeing as how Kane was used to making long treks across the hilly land of his clan, the long hike up to the inn didn't bother him as much.

"The trek down will be a lot easier than the one going up." Kane spoke in a slight teasing tone before he glanced at the glass door behind Dean. There was a single door that led out to a balcony, from there they would be able to see the cavern with minimal lights around them to give Dean the view that he was waiting for. The window along the single door had more of that similar design that Dean noticed on the airship. Etched into the windows was the scenery of the jungle. The large broad leaves towards the front while vines dangled against two trees with some type of hairy beast peering through one panel of glass while the other panel seemed to trail off towards a cliff-side with a waterfall in the distance.

"Just put me in a barrel and wheel me down. I'm done." Dean groaned, letting his body slump onto the bed once more before seeing the elegant design on the window behind him. "You know, I've always wondered this," Dean spoke as he rolled onto his stomach to look at the door's design. "But how is it even possible to make such elaborate designs on a window even possible?" Dean asked, figuring that since they had some time, he might as well ask the question while it was right in front of him. It was like a painting made out of glass. No one on the Millennium could pull something like that off, not in a million years.

"It's actually done with a very fine needle that was once used for tattoos." Kane started to explain, figuring that it would be something that would interest Dean. Sure enough, Dean's interest peaked. It was like seeing an excited child being taught about something that perked the child's interest. It at least made Kane chuckle a bit as he moved to stand up and walk towards the door.

"What?! How could a needle make such an elegant design like that without breaking it?" Dean asked, unsure how this would even seem to be a realistic explanation to how someone could even be able to sketch on glass as if it was paper without the glass breaking. Using crystals was one thing, but using something as fragile as glass, that took some major skills. "I mean, I could understand if it was using crystal, but glass? How does it not break?" Dean asked.

Kane couldn't help the chuckle that seemingly left his lips. Seeing Dean trying to figure it out through logic was amusing to say the least. "Well, technically it's through layered glass instead of a single layer, allowing for the needle to puncture the surface at high speeds in order for it to cut into the glass without actually breaking it. Plus the needle they use is very thin." Kane started to explain, kneeling down in front of the window. "It takes some time, but the artwork that they are able to come up with is simply amazing." There was a lot of talent that had been literally buried away in the shelters for years. After all, without the use of technology, how else was one to keep from being bored all the time? If they had the skills, why not try and master it?

"Wow." Dean remarked in amazement. "So do the artists live here? Is this part of the clan or something?" Dean asked as Kane who simply shook his head. "Really?" Dean asked, raising an eyebrow as his mind couldn't wrap around this whole clan thing. Since it seemed like everyone was spread out, it was hard to really keep track of it all. "Then how would I know who belongs in what clan if people are spread out over the lands?" Dean asked, realizing how rude that must have sounded as he quickly added towards the end of his question. "Not that it's wrong to have different clans mixing with each other. It's just, I'm still a bit new to this."

"It's quite alright. We're so used to having our tribes mingle with one another." Kane reassured Dean with a small wave of his hand dismissing any crudeness to Dean's remark. "It's not like people are usually born into one tribe and simply stay there. Since we're free to move around before settling down, people tend to go through different phases to help them learn about who they really are as a person." Kane added, knowing that he would have to explain how one would settle towards a particular tribe over all.

"Oftentimes people tend to gravitate more towards one of the clans than the others. Those who are more artistic will gravitate towards the Envy clan, while those who want to learn more about medicine and healing people will lean towards the Sloth can. People who are usually sexually inclined and want to learn how to better use their assets will go towards the Lust clan, while individuals who are more into being financially richer will head towards the Greed clan." Kane explained, figuring that using two different extremes will help Dean better understand.

"But what if people want to mix things up? Learning from two or more clans?" Dean asked, not sure what he should really expect for an answer. After all, not everything was as clear as black and white. There were many issues in which they had to address something as important as being able to be in a particular clan. "Don't get me wrong, I really do want to understand, after all…" Dean paused as he moved to sit up and face Kane. "Since I find myself here and unable to really get back to the place that I once called home, I'll have to figure this out if I am welcomed to live among you." The thought of being able to settle down on the planet was oddly comforting. For once, Dean felt like he actually belonged.

"It's not like we have some sort of citizenship here or anything like that. People are free to move about as they pleased, remember? There is always a place for someone to live." Kane continued to explain. "Though there are some people who never want to leave their birth place." The way that Kane explained it felt more like how people who were in the Silver class never wanted to leave their class. To move upwards rather than down.

"After all, my folks took over my ancestors farm house and started to remodel it with the tools and material they had at the time." Kane continued to explain. "Not like they could just simply knock the whole thing down. They had to work around the original frame of the house in order to make it function." It sounded like a lot of work went into the home that simply ended up in flames. "There were some buildings that were completely unsafe to live in, which would result in the doors and windows being blocked off to prevent people from venturing inside and getting hurt without any chance of someone rescuing them." Listening to Kane, Dean was getting a better picture of what the survivors did in order to have a place they could call home.

"But I'll describe what kind of skills and services that each clan provides and maybe it might help you figure out where you would tend to fall in line with." Kane remarked as he could see the wheels turning in Dean's head. "Just as a way for you to figure out what makes each clan special. Then whichever clan seems to suit your skill, you're always free to explore it and change it later." Kane finished, a joyful smile landing on his face, seemingly excited to talk about the other clans so freely.

Starting out with the Gluttony clan, one tends to usually find farmers who grow crops and herd cattle, but there is much more to it than that. Typically those who are able to track wild game, forage for different edible flora, and butchering said game are some of the most common practices of the Gluttony clan members that you will see. However, there are those who tend to practice using leather or animal hide in their designs to make clothing warm for the colder seasons. Not only that, but some often migrate towards a mix of being in the Gluttony, Pride, and Envy clan. However, sticking towards the more open areas of a region leads those of the Gluttony clan to live nomadic lifestyles.

Next is the Envy clan, the area which would be their next stop on the journey to get approval from the leader. Those who find themselves with more of a creativity type will usually flock to the pursuit of their passion in this clan. Whether it is through artwork, novel writing, or simply creating fashion from the available materials at hand, many of the different tribal members will spread out to the various other tribes to help make the world seem to be more alive. As noted with the various outfits that wasn't for one particular style over the other. Though most of the members of the Envy clan that find themselves using their hands to craft their artwork would often find themselves working with those of the Pride clan.

Speaking of the Pride clan, it is easy to see why those who tend to want to work either on the open seas or are able to work well with machinery are often transfixed on becoming part of the Pride clan. With their help, Nero was able to move around the fact that most of the electrical appliances were destroyed from the electrical grid being taken out by some of the nukes exploding in the air. With a bit of hard work, those in the Pride clan had been able to help rebuild some of the old structures that needed repair, making housing livable for the surviving members of the human race.

Those who come from the Lust clan tend to be more adept with the human body. Often being the course of educating people from a wide range of subjects dealing with puberty, sexual orientation, to safe childbirth with the use of cattle as a demonstration of what to expect with labor. Though most of what the Lust clan focuses on has to do with the sins of flesh, there is more to it than just focusing on the primal desires that many wish to feed upon. Those who are from the Lust clan seem to combine their knowledge of the body, they often head towards the Sloth clan in order to help make medicine that was once lost.

The Sloth clan has been the clan that most of the Gluttony and Lust clan aim towards when it comes time to wind down from their excited youth. Focusing on herbal crop growth that helps numb pain and relaxes the stress of both the mind and body, those of the Sloth clan are more down to Earth and are some of the best cooks out there. Often coming up with odd combinations that surprisingly work well together, those of the Sloth clan tend to be easy going compared to their neighbors of the Greed clan.

The Greed clan is often known as more of a beehive as business oriented or high profiling members of society. Often out to overachieve, they are able to spread throughout the other tribes to make for better trading practices so that no one would feel as if they were taken advantage of. Those who come from the Greed clan don't find themselves working the land, but rather strategically divide sections of crop to make for a higher yield or are able to set prices that would be deemed fair in a particular region. Though with the demolishing of the Wrath clan, the Head of the Leaders took it upon herself to incorporate training people how to defend themselves from either human or animal, all of which is necessary in the world they currently live in.

"Seems to me the Greed clan and the Sloth clan really are opposite of each other." Dean remarked, crossing his arms over his chest as he took everything in. "And if everyone is working together, you're completely different from those living on the Millennium." Dean could only wish for things to be that easy, but those in charge never allowed it. "After all, you don't exactly get much of a choice on where you are able to live on the station." Dean continued, bringing up one of his legs to be bent on the bed towards him. "Hell, I didn't even get much of a choice when I finally got myself a job. It was either maintenance or cleaning duty." After all, since he wasn't able to get an education thanks to the unfortunate circumstances, Dean had simply chosen the easier path that wouldn't lead to an early accidental death.

"Well, given that you're free to start your life over here, what would you want to do?" Kane asked, bringing up an interesting point to Dean. This was his chance to really start over. After all the years of isolating himself in the confinement of his pod, Dean was able to finally be free to explore his own endless possibilities that he had only dreamed of. Sure he may not know exactly what his skills are, but here, Dean was able to actually have the tools at his disposal to know who or what he was.

"What would I want to do?" Dean asked, mostly repeating it to himself. "Well, when I was growing up, I loved reading and helping my mother with her garden." Dean spoke, thinking back on the days in which he had fond memories of getting his hands dirty. Being able to watch the small patch of green sprouts flicker in the man-made wind, and watching them bloom over time to produce delicious vegetables that would be collected and disputed over the different classes. Dean often wondered who ended up eating the ones he planted. Of course, he was a naive child then. Now, he couldn't care less what happened to those on the station anymore. "There were times in which I would sneak into my dad's study to read up on some of the medical papers that he would bring home to finish. I often thought about being a mortician like my father." Dean spoke, feeling a bit silly with talking about this sort of thing with Kane.

"I just couldn't take the smell of opening up a dead person. Having to pull out their organs after examining their body thoroughly, it always made me a bit squeamish." Dean continued, a small chuckle leaving his lips as Dean remembered something he had almost forgotten about. "The first time that my dad brought me into the morgue, I actually fainted when he started to pull the guts out." Dean spoke, a lingering smile spread across his face as he remembered the panic look in his father's eyes. "I was there to learn about what my father did for his job, since my mother was a teacher, I figured that his job would have been more interesting."

"Wasn't your mom a bit upset that you would rather learn about your dad's job rather than hers?" Kane asked, his brows knitting together as if he was concerned about the woman's feelings. It was sort of sweet that Kane was interested in learning about Dean's past. Not like there was any way that either of them would be able to meet their families, it was still a sentiment that Dean took notice of.

"Quite the opposite really." Dean remarked, a grin landing on his face as he remembered how excited she was that Dean was wanting to learn more about his father's line of work more than anything else. After all, Emily would often drag Dean to school early in the morning to help her out with setting everything up for the day.

"I knew what she did for her job, since she was a school teacher after all, I had to spend a majority of my weekday mornings helping her to put everything together. Once I was done, I would take a nap in the reading corner." The smell of the carpet and books always brought back those simple times to Dean when used to read in his room. "She would come and wake me up before school was about to let the kids in. Fix my hair up if it got messed up, and send me on my way." Dean remarked, the faintest memory of the time he spent surrounded by books often helped him feel safe in those early mornings.

"At least your mom was supportive." Kane remarked his shoulders dropping ever so slightly. It seemed like a hard subject to talk about, but the two were bonding over talking about their parents. It was a step in the right direction. Though from what Dean had gathered, it seemed like Kane's mother Celia wasn't into the whole nurturing her children past a certain age, unlike Dean's own mother who seemed to want to show her son as much of her motherly love as she could, but in a healthy way.

"What? Your mom wasn't?" Dean asked raising an eyebrow before he heard the exasperated sigh coming from Kane was a clue as to how the other felt about his mother. "Was it really that bad? I mean, what could she have done that was really bad?" Dean asked, though remembered how Kane's mother and brother constantly argued before that fateful night, Dean felt a bit foolish for asking.

"It's not that it was really bad, but it could be a bit overwhelming." Kane remarked, letting out another exasperated sigh as his eyes moved towards the floor as he pressed his back against the wall. "I never told anyone this, but I think my brother had a bit of a split personality." Kane remarked, not even sparing a glance towards Dean.

"When he would go out and hunt with father, he would often change." Kane continued, clasping his hands together as he could feel the heavy guilt weighing on him. "I never went out with him, but I did overhear my dad talking to someone about it." Kane moved his gaze to the side as he thought about it more. "How, my brother would turn into this bloodhound who was set to kill anything out in front of him. It scared my dad, and he never told my mom about it either. But I guess when he heard about what happened, he wished that he had spoken up about it."

The smile that Dean once had slowly disappeared. There was nothing that he could really say to something like that. Moving to rest his feet against the floor, Dean shifted to move against the edge of his bed. "It's not like you could really change the past Kane." Dean finally spoke, his voice holding no emotion as he couldn't even think of what would be appropriate to feel at a time like this.

After all, Kane didn't know what would have happened that night where they argued. "Even if you told your mother, it's not like she would believe you." Not that Kane wanted to hear the blunt truth, but Dean was telling him. "You even said it yourself, you didn't go with him, so you would have not known. Only your father did, and he kept quiet about it too." This seemed to be more or less a way to lessen the guilt that was weighing on Kane's mind.

Watching as Kane's shoulders dropped a bit more, it seemed like Dean was making some headway with the tribal leader. Just like Dean, Kane had a lot on his shoulders that he would have not been able to get off of his chest otherwise. They both have been dealing with a lot since they were out on their own. Even if Kane had Miles, there were probably things that Kane wouldn't be able to tell him.

"So don't blame yourself for what happened." Dean spoke up once more, catching Kane's gaze. Seeing that Kane was at least looking at him now, Dean offered him a soft reassuring smile before continuing to speak. "After all, I'm sure they would want you to live your life the best way that you can, right?" A bit more encouragement was probably what Kane needed at the moment.

Smiling at Kane, Dean braced himself as he slowly stood up. The room had started to get dark, meaning that they would be able to take a look over the city. "Think it's time for the lights to be on?" Dean asked, trying his best to hide a bit of excitement. But it seemed that he wasn't all that great at hiding it. "Not gonna lie, I might crash after taking in the sight." Dean remarked, earning a small chuckle from Kane as the tribal leader joined him. Despite his legs feeling like jelly, Dean was ready to head out onto the balcony to gaze out at the city below them. Already the two could see a faint orange glow like that of a fire piercing through the glass panels.

"I might just be there with you. The hike up the sides is never easy." Kane remarked, moving to walk out to the balcony door. Placing his hands on the wooden guard rail, Dean took his place beside Kane, the two looked over the edge towards the crater in the center of town.

The orange and yellow crystals that decorated the various lamp posts often seemed to mix together to give the streets below them an amber like red glow to it. It looked a bit more like honey that his mother used to put in her tea. Watching as some of the crystals slowly flickered here and there, Dean was amazed that the wind that blew through the crater made it appear as if the crystals were swimming in the air, making the colors shift around like it was moving lava. It was stunning, unlike anything he had witnessed.

"Wow, this is amazing." Dean awed, letting his body move to be pressed against the railing of the balcony. Crossing his arms over the banister while leaning forward to feel that warm wind brushing past him, Dean took in the sights around him. It was hard to believe that they would be on the move once again after tonight. Was it so bad to want to stay here and simply enjoy this bit of peace for a little while longer? To simply take in the sights in the warm humid air despite his body wanting to slump over. This was an experience that Dean never imagined he would be able to see in his life.

Glancing over towards Kane, Dean could see the shimmer in Kane's eyes as his pale skin started to softly glow in the light. There was an odd sensation that swept over Dean, it was subtle at first, but it felt almost like his soul was at peace. It didn't make much sense, but Dean brushed it off for now. He just wanted to enjoy this beautiful scene with no lingering regrets on his mind.

Chapter Eleven: *Meeting The Lil' Princess*

FOLLOWING THE LONG trip to their next destination, the moment that Dean and Kane got off the airship to the central capital town of the Envy clan, Dean was taken back by how well persevered everything had appeared. Normally Dean was used to seeing homes that were either overgrown with plant life or made out of some type of rock and concrete with wood mixture. But here, everything looked like it belonged to a setting of an old Victorian story. The buildings were made up of brick, as well as the roads, and there were some type of vehicles being driven around.

There weren't many of the cars around, but the fact that there were some type of automobiles in this particular area showcased how they were able to overcome the obstacles that once faced the wasteland of the world. If it wasn't for Kane's weakness of getting sick when riding on some type of transportation, they could very well make their way to the next clan by vehicle. However, being able to see the change of the world would be worth it in Dean's eyes.

"Whoa...." Dean's voice trailed off as the heat from his breath formed into a small cloud from the cold air. "I've never seen vehicles like these before." Dean remarked, watching a car that had a sleek design that one would find from the roaring twenties drive past them. Though, unlike those cars at the time that used to have pure black smoke trailing from the engines, it seemed that these cars were modified to run on some type of fuel that didn't have some type waste coming out of it. But the purr of the engine was unmistakable.

"Yeah, the Pride clan had a lot of fun refurbishing old cars and making a whole new engine that ran on large crystals that could easily be charged." Kane remarked as he joined Dean's side. "You can't exactly take them out of the city unfortunately. But slowly we're working on making some new roads when we don't have to hide from the cowards overhead." Kane explained as another car drove past them. Unlike on the island, the two were wearing actual clothing that helped to keep them warm.

Kane was wearing tan slacks that tucked under a white buttoned up shirt. A pair of suspenders seemed to lay loosely against his hips while his tan vest rested open on him. A pair of black loafers kept his feet warm as they seemed to match Dean's. Though unlike Kane, Dean was wearing black slacks that hugged his body. A dark blue buttoned up shirt that hugged Dean's torso as a black vest that hid a pair of suspenders.

"Seems like you're finally on board with helping me blow up the Millennium." Dean lightly teased, glancing over Kane as he was surprised that the other male didn't get completely suited up like himself. It wasn't like Kane was as opposing as he was when the two had started out, so perhaps Dean may have gotten the leader on board with his plan afterall.

"It's not that I exactly agree with you completely," Kane remarked, pulling out a long trench coat that was a light tan color to complete his outfit. "I'm just a bit curious to see if you are able to get the others to agree with you is all." Kane remarked, a light shrug of his shoulders as he started to work on fixing up his coat to keep from getting too cold. The clouds overhead were a dark gray as the ground was a bit damp as it showed signs that it had rained the night before their arrival. Dean was at least glad that the ground wasn't frozen over to the point where they would have to about the streets being slick with ice.

Grabbing his own black coat, Dean followed Kane's actions in getting his coat on to help keep him warm. The last few nights on the ship were rather cold, so it was simply best to bundle up while they had the chance. There was one thing that Dean had noticed on the airship when they were heading over towards the Envy clan. The fact that Miles wasn't around as much after they landed on the Pride clan's island was a bit peculiar. Whether the male had gotten off or was making sure to avoid being seen was something that Dean couldn't exactly say, but Dean respected Kane's feelings as to not bring it up. After all, with the fight that they had, it would just make things more awkward than it already was.

"Well, hopefully I can convince the other three leaders to join my cause, but then again.... Miles didn't exactly show that he was willing to join in the cause just yet. So my work will still have to be at four..." Dean grumbled a bit, more to himself than anyone else. Miles was a bit of a wild card in Dean's plans. With spilling Kane's secret, or at least trying to, it made Dean wonder if he could trust Miles.

"So this Ashley girl, the leader of the Envy clan; what's she like?" Dean asked, a bit curious as to who he was going to meet. It seemed that Felicia was easy to get on board for the mission of revenge that Dean was on, but Miles was hard to read. Frankly it was a bit scary dealing with Miles. That cold hard stare still unnerved Dean.

"Ashley... is," Kane started to speak, pausing as if he had to figure out a good way to describe the youngest of the tribal leaders. Picking up Dean's bag, Kane handed it to the other to carry as they needed to head towards their next destination. "Well, she can be a bit abrasive. A bit blunt and straightforward. A real princess type who is very cold on the inside and the outside." Kane explained, a small nervous chuckle escaping his lips as he lightly scratched the side of his face.

"She doesn't exactly care for your opinion and isn't above physically hurting you if she doesn't agree with you." Kane knew from past experience just how blunt Ashley could be, and would rather warn Dean ahead of time so he knew what he was dealing with. "She is known as the ice princess, and for good reason." Kane paused as they stopped at light while some cars drove past them. "She doesn't like people touching her. Her temper is as short as she is. But once she opens up to you, she softens her blows a bit." Not exactly reassuring, but it was the best that Kane could offer in terms of advice. "After all, she has a good reason to be cold towards strangers..." Kane trailed off the end, figuring that he would simply let Dean experience it for himself.

"Geeze, how could someone like that be the leader of a clan?" Dean remarked, his pace keeping up with Kane's as the two walked down the street together once the roads were clear. One would expect that she was someone who came from one of the Elite families with the way that she acted. After all, it wasn't like the Elite were above physically abusing the help. They actually got off on stuff like that. Or at least, that's what Dean told himself to help his hatred for the Elite to never cease. Could this girl be as cruel as the Elite?

"She never used to be like that." Kane spoke up, not really coming to her defense, but figuring that if Dean knew a bit of her history, it would help Dean understand her better. "Before the Sin wars, she was a bubbly girl. Often smiled all the time too." Kane explained, pausing a bit as they stopped at a corner of a street that had some cars driving by.

"She loves to draw, and she has a pretty big sweet tooth. Pretty much she's still a little girl, but a certain traumatic event caused her heart to close off. Not that I can really blame her..." Kane trailed off, a soft frown lingering on his face as Kane's eyes casted downwards on the puddle in front of them before the car driving by splashed the water onto the street, barely missing the two men standing on the corner.

"What happened to her?" Dean asked, his voice showing his concern. It seemed that most of the leaders had some type of traumatic event happen in their life that caused them to practically force these leaders to grow up quickly. Well, except for maybe Felicia and Miles. Then again, he never really asked them what happened to either of the leaders if anything happened to them when they were younger. But from what happened to Kane, Dean had no idea what he would be in store for when it came to the other leaders.

"That's not my story to tell you." Kane remarked, shaking his head a bit. It wasn't like Kane could really do the story justice as Kane couldn't explain in details of what happened. This was due to the fact that Kane had only heard bits of what happened through the rumor mill. Ashley was never the type who openly admitted what happened on that night. Not even to the other leaders.

"Besides, wouldn't you feel better if she told you?" Kane asked, glancing up towards Dean with a genuine smile on his face. "Once you break down her walls, I'm sure she will be more than happy to tell you what happened to her." Kane remarked, though even he was doubtful that Dean would get the whole story from Ashley. She was rather protective of her past.

The rest of the walk seemed to be fairly quiet, outside of the idle chit chat of people around them, it gave Dean time to think. Passing by the sturdy iron barricades that decorated the sidewalks' edges to keep the pedestrian safe from any of the cars that might slip and crash, Dean wondered what he had in store for him over the next couple of months. They would have to live under the same roof with all of the other tribe leaders during the winter months. Or at least, that is what Dean imagined would happen. Dean had no idea that two leaders would share a household based on their age or relationship. They would be stuck with Ashley in her place while the other would be scattered to the other buildings close by. That is, if the little princess tribal leader would allow Dean the chance.

As they stopped by three houses that were close by to them, Dean noticed that the houses were blocked off by a large gated fence, Dean took notice of the letters on top of each of the homes. *ENVIOUS GLUTTON* on one building, *PRIDEFUL SLOTH*, and *LUSTFUL GREED* on the others. Dean was taken back a bit since he was unsure what that all meant. It almost looked like these were simply three houses that were either turned into an inn, bar, or brothel. As the gates creaked when Kane pushed on the gates, he stopped to notice the questionable look that seemed to linger on Dean's face.

"What's wrong?" Kane asked, standing inside of the gate as he tilted his head a bit. The wind started to pick up, the chill from it caused Dean to snap out of his hesitant stance as he was more than ready to head inside where it was warm. After all, he could see smoke coming out of the chimney on top of the buildings, which meant it would be much warmer than where they were standing.

"It's nothing. Just the names took me by surprise." Dean remarked as he joined Kane's side. "I didn't think that I would find myself staying at a place called the Envious Glutton." Dean spoke, shrugging his shoulders as they walked along a stone path. At least it wouldn't be a long walk towards the building. Considering that most people were already heading inside for the day as the cold wind wasn't enticing to stay out for long periods of time, there wasn't much activity on the ground. Though there was some movement coming from inside the buildings, Dean didn't pay any attention to them.

"Well, we didn't exactly come up with the name for it. It was put up to the members of a tribe to come up with the names. And this is what they came up with." Kane explained, his feet landing on the first steps that lead up towards the door. "Though I guess it is kind of fitting since Amelia and Keaton are in a relationship, same with Miles and Felicia." Kane mused a bit as he grabbed the door to open it. "Ashley and I are kinda the odd balls out of the group. Considering that Ashley is asexual and I'm gay, it's just fitting that we share a place. No need for the adults to worry about the two of us hooking up." Kane half joked, a small red coloring appearing on his cheeks as he waited for Dean's response.

"Wait, she's asexual?" Dean asked, his surprise seemed to be completely different than what Kane was expecting. To think, Dean seemed to more focused on the fact that someone was asexual rather than focus on the fact that the guy he was traveling with was gay? "So that means that she gets no enjoyment out of sex, right?" Dean asked, wanting to make sure that he at least got the terminology corrected. Not that Dean knew the pleasures of sex either, but his own sexuality was still up for debate.

Kane couldn't help but feel relieved when Dean wasn't repulsed by the fact that he came out to Dean. "Y-Yeah. She doesn't exactly like the idea of anyone being intimate with her." Kane explained as he closed the door behind them. "She says something along the lines of 'Why should I care about someone pleasuring me when I can just do it on my own and be done with it? Sexual intimacy isn't a factor needed when you are supposed to love someone'." Kane spoke in a girlish voice before a small chuckle left his lips.

"I can understand to an extent of what she meant by that." Kane paused as he watched Dean start to take off his shoes. Biting his lower lip, Kane clenched onto the hem of the trench coat while fiddling with it. There was a question that was on Kane's mind, and perhaps now was the best time to ask it. "But you...you really don't mind that I outed myself as being gay, Dean?" Kane asked sheepish.

"Well, yeah man." Dean started to speak up, wondering why it was an issue. "Just because you like people of the same sex doesn't mean that you're revolting or anything like that." Dean spoke, giving Kane a reassured smile as he stepped closer to him. "I mean, I kinda figured it out when you were freaking out over Miles being on the ship." It wasn't like the other was hiding it well, though it did earn a small chuckle from Kane when that memory was brought up. "Besides, you've been a good friend to me. Why should I ruin a good friendship simply because you were comfortable enough to tell me the truth? Seems counterproductive you know?" Dean finished, giving Kane a light pat on the shoulder.

"I mean, it's not like I really know what I am." Dean remarked, crossing his arms over his chest. "But I do know that I want to connect to someone on a more emotional level." Dean paused as he tried to figure out the right term for it. "Sort of like a soulmate." Dean continued as he tilted his head to the side. "Like what my parents had." If there was ever such a thing as a soulmate, it would be Emily and Max.

"They loved each other uncontrollable. Nothing could separate them." Dean continued with a big smile, before it started to fade the more Dean thought of his parents. "I want that same experience they had." Dean paused before crossing his arms over his chest. "It might not happen right away, but one day I'll have that same feeling. Being with someone whom I can be myself with, and get through all kinds of hard situations that life will throw at us." Dean trailed off as he shrugged his shoulders with a daydream like smile on his face. It may not be a reality that Dean could experience yet, but he had plenty of time to find true love now.

"You don't know how much of a weight that lifted off of my shoulders." Kane remarked, letting out the held breath with a sigh of relief. "I was honestly scared to tell you." Kane remarked as he moved a hand over to his chest before digging his fingers into the fabric of his trench coat. It seemed that Kane visibly hunched over as he caught his breath. Dean was a startled that Kane was holding so much in, and to see the relief was a little worrisome. But seeing that relieved smile on Kane's face, Dean was glad that he was able to take that burden off of Kane's shoulders.

As they entered the foyer from the mud room, Dean was surprised by the décor of the room. The sound of a distant song seemed to be playing upstairs, something that was a bit jazzy and something that Dean never heard before. The wall paper may have seemed to be a bit faded, but among the dark navy blue of the paint, Dean could see small white faded flowers seemingly in a pattern that spread across the surface.

The wooden banister looked freshly polished as the dangling crystal lights that hung between the two stories reflected against the wooden surface of the stairs and floor. There was a lingering scent of cinnamon and burnt firewood that Dean had come to recognize through his travels. The inside of the foyer looked like it was stuck in time, long before the bombs had dropped. It was amazing just how different each of the leaders had made their tribes.

"Whoa. It's almost like we went through time going through the door." Dean remarked, watching as Kane brought his coat over towards the hanger in the corner of the room. "What kind of music is that?" Dean asked, following suit, the coat getting to be a bit to warm on Dean.

"Ashley tends to like to listen to jazz for some reason." Kane remarked, collecting his bag from the ground. "She probably hasn't noticed that we're here yet, which may be for the best." Kane continued, taking a couple of steps up the stairs. Small creaks against the floorboard could be heard under Kane's feet. "Knowing her, she'll demand that you sleep outside like a dog or something." It might have seemed like a joke, but the tone in Kane's voice didn't seem to imply that.

"Woof." Dean half joked in order to lighten the mood, but the sound of heels clicking against wood and the creaking of the floorboards above them seemed to catch both the men's ears. Kane had straightened up as he braced himself while Dean looked a bit more curious since he was not sure what he was going to expect.

According to Kane, Ashley was a short girl with a temper to match, a real princess type. Sure enough, over the banister Dean had seen for himself what he was dealing with. With a bobbing cow lick curl on the top of her blonde locks, a short girl wearing a white wrap dress that that was a low cut seemed to barely brushed against her thighs, a black long sleeve wrap crop top that seemingly wrapped around her chest to give herself a bit of a lift stood on top of the clearing.

With her hair draped behind her back, the ends of Ashley's hair seemingly curled this way and that as it seemed to rest down towards her waist. Her emerald green eyes looked at the two men with a mixture of disdain and annoyance. Her pink lips were flat, though the corners did seem to fold downwards into a frown. With one of her hands being placed on her hips, Ashley tilted her head up as she glared down at them.

The white stockings she was wearing seemed to lead down towards a white pair of house shoes that she often wore to keep her feet warm. Around her neck was a black choker with a green gem in the shape of a crescent moon. Her fingernails were neatly trimmed. A small black head band seemed to stick out of the blonde locks as the side had a little skeleton made out of the same green gem as her necklace.

"Oh great, you brought in a stray." A cold yet sneering tone came out of the short girl's mouth. Dean was a bit taken back by that remark, though it did make Dean wonder if she might have heard the remark about a dog, which would lead to that snarky remark. "And just where do you think he's going to stay? We only have so much room in the house as it is." The disdain on her voice indicating that Dean was nothing more than a dog was insulting to say the least.

"Ashley, could you at least attempt to be nice to my friend." Kane remarked, letting out an annoyed sigh as Kane crossed his arms over his chest as he stood up from his spot. "I'm sure that Dean wouldn't mind sleeping on the couch or something. That is, if he doesn't want to share a bed with me." It wasn't like there was much that Kane could do about the short notice of bringing someone along with him. But it wasn't like Kane could just simply allow Dean to be kicked out with no place to really go.

"You honestly think I would let someone I don't know sleep on my furniture?" Ashley snapped back, a cold glare shot towards Dean. Just seeing that coldness towards him in her eyes, Dean felt like he was back on the Millennium, being stared down by that older man who almost crushed his hand. Gently shaking his hand that was starting to shake from the memory, Dean had to keep his head strong when dealing with this little wanna-be princess.

"Then he'll sleep in my room if it bothers you that much. I'll set him up with something. I'll even pay for it." Kane quickly spoke as he didn't want there to be a big issue about where someone would sleep. "The room is big enough that we can find a spot for Dean to rest on. It's not a big deal Ash." Kane continued, only to see the anger growing on Ashley's features.

"Oh no you don't." Ashley snapped as she pointed her sharp index finger towards the pair. "If you insist on him sleeping in your room, you'll have to share your bed Kane." This had completely taken both Dean and Kane by surprise with her bold statement. Share a bed? Wasn't it a bit weird for two guys to share a bed together?

It might have been worse if they were strangers, but this would be the first time that they would be sharing a bed. "Otherwise, he can use what little money he has to buy a room at one of the inns in town. That is, if they aren't already full by now." She finished, a bit of a joyous grin on her face as she watched their reaction.

Kane's expression showed that he was worried about the idea that Dean would be left out in the cold. Considering that he didn't know if Dean was even comfortable with the idea of sharing a bed with Kane, maybe he could pull some strings and ask either Felicia or Miles to take Dean in if he couldn't find a place to stay for the night.

Meanwhile, Dean had a bit of an annoyed look on his face. They were talking about Dean as if he was some kind of stray animal that seemingly followed Kane back to the house. Plus the way she was so demanding and off putting made the picture of what Kane meant about how abrasive Ashley was made abundantly clear what Kane meant.

"I'm fine with it." Dean remarked bluntly, catching the two leaders off guard by his remark. "What? We have been sharing inn rooms together. It's not like we haven't slept in the same room. So sharing a bed isn't all that different." Dean added, giving a small shrug of his shoulders.

"Besides, we're friends, right? Friends used to sleep in each others' bed if they were close enough on the Millennium. So it wouldn't be any different to me." Dean added, giving Kane a reassured smile. Though he had never had a friend on the Millennium, he simply went by what his classmates had said while they talked about what they had done for the weekend. Little did Dean know, this was not how sleepovers actually worked, and therefore had no idea what he was saying.

Kane seemed to part his lips to say something, but simply closed them as he lightly shook his head. "How can I really say no to something like that?" Kane remarked with a small chuckle. Not like he could really say no to Dean when he didn't seem to see a problem with it. But then again, it was bound to happen one of these days. Whether it would be at some random inn along their way to see the other leaders home, or have it happen now. Unlike the journey on the airship, the last two leaders had a bit of distance between them from the Envy clan's capital.

The smirk on Ashley's face seemed to disappear as the annoyed expression seemingly landed on her face once more. Crossing her arms across her chest, Ashley cocked her head a bit with a small 'hmph' noise leaving her lips and echoing against the walls a bit. Dean felt like she was assessing him more than anything. Whether or not Dean would be just a simple annoyance or if he was going to try and pull something. Looking up at her, Dean waited in silence for her judgment to be decided. Even though Kane had every right to have someone there, it seemed like Ashley was the type to force her opinions on anyone who got in her way.

"Fine." Ashley seemed to remark in a snippy tone, placing her hands on her hips as she couldn't exactly deny Dean from staying. "But I don't want him thinking that he gets free range around here." Dean had no idea what she meant by that, it seemed that he was able to stay.

"You just better keep an eye on him Kane. I don't want him sniffing around in places he doesn't belong." Ashley finished, narrowing her eyes at Dean before she headed back towards a closed off section of the house. With Ashley gone, it seemed that the two could finally breathe easier.

Before making any remarks, Dean listened to hear if he could still hear the pitter patter of heels against the wooden floor. When he heard the sound of a squeaky door open and close, followed by the stomping sounds of the petite tribal leaders entering her room and walking about, Dean felt like he finally had some room to speak.

"How can you put up with someone that high strung?" Dean asked, jerking his thumb towards the upstairs a small perplexed scowl on his face. To think, Dean thought that he was able to get away from individuals who thought of themselves as higher on the social scale than others.

"You learn to put up with it." Kane remarked through a small chuckle. "But she's not always that bad." Kane added with a small shrug as he walked up the staircase. "Once she gets to know you, she will be more tolerable towards you." It wasn't exactly reassuring that Ashley would become tolerable towards Dean the longer that he stayed there, but perhaps that was just her way of keeping people at bay.

Dean could understand the need to keep people at a certain distance in order to keep from being hurt. After all, he was like that to a degree on the Millennium, but his circumstances were different than Ashley's. Who knows, maybe after some time, Dean would get to learn a bit more about Ashley and what has caused her to be so distant from everyone.

As they collected their belongings and headed up the steps, Dean took the time to look at the decorative art that seemed to linger on the walls. Many of the art pieces seemed to be portraits of people that Dean didn't know, but seemed to follow a particular pattern. The paint seemed to be that of oil, consistent with the paintings looking a bit faded over time. As they went further down, it seemed that there were some spots along the wall that appeared to, at some point, once hold a portrait. In its place, the wallpaper was lighter in color and looked almost brand new compared to walls that appeared darker in color, meaning that there were some pictures here that were removed at some point not too long ago.

"So what happened to the pieces that were here?" Dean asked, causing Kane to stop in his place to turn and look at what Dean was referring to. Studying Kane's expression, it didn't seem like the other male actually knew. But considering that it must have been a while since he was there last, it appeared that Kane didn't really know what happened to whichever portrait was there last.

"I'm not sure." Kane remarked, simply shrugging his shoulders before heading back down the hallway. "My room is just around the corner." Kane pointed the way before disappearing around the bend. Dean hurried up and made his way towards the area that Kane had vanished. Seeing as how there was only one door and a single window at the end of the hallway, it was clear where Kane had gone.

Upon entering into the room, Dean looked around to see what Kane often slept in while in the Envy clan. There was a metal framed bed that appeared to be at least large enough for two people to sleep in. The sheets that rested under the rather heavy looking dark blue comforter was a dark gray that seemed to have crisp corners as the sheet was tucked under the mattress. Dean glanced towards the floor under the bed to see that there were some books laying underneath in small stacks.

It perked Dean's curiosity, but he would respect the other's privacy, for now at least. But it was interesting that Kane had some books hidden under his bed where anyone would be able to come and read them. It wasn't like there was anything wrong with that. After all, Dean loved to read some books before bed as well. It felt like a lifetime ago since he was able to actually read a good book while lounging in bed.

Hearing the sound of a door creaking open, Dean turned his attention over towards Kane who seemed to be opening up a small closet with some clothes lingering just inside. There wasn't much inside, maybe except for some robes that Kane was so fond of wearing, but seeing Kane put the clothes away reminded Dean that he didn't exactly have a place to put his clothes. Then again he didn't have many to begin with.

"Guess I should at least try to rotate the clothes I have." Dean mumbled to himself, swinging the bag off of his shoulders and onto the ground. This seemed to catch Kane's attention, realizing that there wasn't much room for someone else to place their clothing in the closet. With a small look at his closet, it seemed that Kane came up with an idea before stepping away from the closet.

"I do have an old trunk with some of my dad's clothes in it." Kane remarked, walking towards an old looking trunk that had a small bit of dust in it. It was seemingly hidden away from sight with the lack of light in the room that helped to hide the trunk in the shadows. There was only one curtain open to allow light inside of the room. It was just enough light for the two of them to be able to see without any of the lights being turned on.

"If you want, you can use some of his old clothes." Kane continued, picking up the trunk and carrying it over towards the bed. It didn't seem to be heavy for the tribal leader to carry, but the way that the trunk seemed to creak against the bed had given away that it had some weight behind it. Just how strong was Kane?

"I know we don't have much in the way of clothes for you, but if you want, I'll find a way for us to share the closet." Peeling open the trunk, Kane popped the top of the trunk to reveal some of the clothes that he never thought that he would ever use. Considering that most of Kane's family belongings were burned up in the fire on that horrific night, Kane didn't have much in the way of personal items that could have been saved. "I will probably end up donating my old clothes that I grew out of to some of the local seamstresses to use for fabric for future designs." Kane remarked, a lingering smile on his face as Dean walked closer to see what sort of clothing Kane had in the trunk.

"Are you sure it's alright for me to wear your father's old clothes?" Dean asked, feeling bad that he would be walking around in someone else's clothing. It wasn't like Dean would ever get to know the man, considering that the man had been dead for a couple of years now, but Dean couldn't help feeling that perhaps he was treading on ice. Wouldn't it be painful for Kane to see someone wearing his old man's clothes?

"I don't see that it would be an issue." Kane remarked, turning his attention towards Dean. "After all, you are about my father's height. I'm sure he would say the same thing if he was here." Kane added, though there was a small hint of sadness in that last remark. "Besides," Kane paused as he turned to look at one of the pieces of clothing that Kane held in his hands. "I don't think I could picture myself giving his clothes away to the seamstresses to use. I would much rather hold onto his old clothes and cherish the fond but few memories I have with him." Kane finished, pulling the fabric close to his chest and closing his eyes.

Hearing that brought a small ping of remorse to Dean. Unlike Kane, Dean would never be able to go back and collect his father's clothing to be able to hold onto for remembrance. Hell, he didn't even have their portraits anymore considering that everything was destroyed by the

Enforcement officers who came into his pod to 'move' them to their new location. It showed that Dean could never reclaim those old sentimental objects that gave him some concrete evidence that he had something to live for on the Millennium. All he had was his memories now.

"Well, if you don't mind." Dean remarked with a small shrug of his shoulders. Not like he could exactly reject an offer to have a bit more clothing. Plus it showed that Kane trusted Dean enough to be able to wear Elijah's clothing. "I'll make sure to take good care of them." It was a little reassurance that Dean could give to Kane. "You know, we've come a long way." Dean remarked, sitting on the side of the bed, his arm resting on the curved metal corner.

"What do you mean?" Kane asked, a bit confused by Dean's statement. Not like there was much pretext to the remark, and it had seemed to come out of nowhere, but that didn't mean that Kane wasn't interested in learning what Dean meant by that. After all, they had been traveling together for a little over a month. They still had a long way to go, and with everything that could or would happen, at this point it didn't seem like they had really come all that far along.

"I can't exactly describe it." Dean started out, feeling the awkwardness build up since he didn't exactly know where he was going with that remark. "I got to learn about you, and in a way you learned a lot about me." Dean continued, shrugging his shoulders a little bit before gazing over towards Kane. "You trust me with your past, telling me everything that happened to you." Dean added, a small shrug of his right shoulder. "It's frankly surprising how quickly everyone else is so easily on board with trying to find a way to get revenge on the Elite. And yet you were thinking of your tribe first." It spoke volumes about what was more important to Kane than anything else. All of the other tribe leaders were ready to spill blood, all the while Kane was the only one so far who wanted to try and keep the peace.

"It's not like I don't know what the other leaders are feeling." Kane spoke, keeping his hands idle by pulling out the clothes from inside of the trunk one piece at a time. "There was a time in which I would have done anything to see those cowards fall from the sky. To watch as pieces of the station broke apart and fell into the acidic sea... and just let the Earth devour each and every single one of the cowards body without remorse." Kane spoke, his eyes seeming distant as if Kane was remembering the scenario in his head. Silence seemed to fill the room before Kane snapped back to his normal self and continued his remark. "But that wouldn't exactly change anything now, would it?" It felt more like Kane was trying to convince himself of that rather than Dean.

"But causing others pain won't change anything. It won't bring back the people who died so many years ago. It won't ease the pain, but it would feel like a momentary victory." Kane remarked, a light faded smile lingering on his face, but Dean could see the pain in those silver eyes. "It would just be a hollow victory at the cost of decent human lives. And for what? To kill off the descendants who haven't done anything wrong to us? That don't even know that we're here?" The smile from Kane's lips was gone now, his train of thought seemingly causing a look of disappointment at the fact that there was no need to kill the innocent on board the Millennium. Kane's tone of voice gave away how he was feeling about all of this. Sure it would have been nice to make the great grandchildren of the Elite assholes pay, but they didn't do anything to the planet. They simply kept their sadistic tendencies to those unfortunate enough to live on the station.

"Kane," Dean spoke in a serious tone, his face reflecting his voice to show that he was going to say something to demonstrate that what they were going to do was for the best. "In order for everyone to advance on the planet, you have to destroy the Millennium." Dean spoke in a stern yet gentle tone. "Otherwise you will always have to be hiding." Dean was trying to implore Kane that this was a necessary step that they needed to free themselves. "Don't you want to broaden your growth as a society?" Not like hiding would benefit them in any way.

Sure it would keep them safe, but for how long? How long until one of the other clans slips up and makes the return of humans on the once dead planet apparent enough for the Elite to decide to take action once again? "It's more than spilling blood Kane." Not that Dean was wrong about it, but he had to be direct with Kane. "Unlike revolutions in the past, you won't have to work hard to recover from it once the station crashes back down to Earth. You'll be ending human suppression entirely."

"We're not ending anything Dean." Kane quickly snapped, slamming the top of the partially emptied trunk down. "It'll eventually pop back up. There is no ending human suppression. It will always come back." Kane raised his voice, slamming his hands on the trunks as he hunched over it. "Humans are prone to suffer and be suppressed." Kane continued in a weak and weary tone. "Whether it's through famine... or war... or greed. Humans can never get a break from the day to day life being a constant struggle. As long as we continue to live, there will never be an end to the constant pain that we call a life." Kane finished, lowering his head while his shoulders tensed up.

Watching Kane tremble and twitch, Dean glanced away. He didn't mean to upset Kane, but they needed to get rid of the evil that lurked above them. The vast majority of people were being oppressed on the station. Being worked to death by the fat cats that ruled over the gigantic beehive like station. Sure there were plenty of things that could easily kill off humans on the planet now, since radiation forced everything to evolve into deadly creatures, but they didn't have a government that was trying to suppress them. They were far more liberated than anything Dean could ever dream of.

A soft sigh escaped Dean's lips as he stood up from the bed. "It may not go away completely," Dean spoke, placing a hand on his hip as he kept his gaze away from Kane. "But it's up to this world's leaders, their tribal leaders, to make life easier for everyone." Dean paused, figuring that he would let that statement settle into Kane's mind.

"If the people didn't believe in you, do you honestly think that they would work hard to make sure that they could advance the technology to be better?" Dean paused once more as he watched Kane lower his shoulders in thought. "You're breaking free from your oppressors. You'll have a chance to make everyone come together more than you already have. To give them a fighting chance to no longer hide in fear, but to branch out from the shadows and reclaim the glory that they so rightfully deserve."

After a few minutes of silence that filled the room, Dean brought up a hand to ruffle some of his own hair, Dean felt like he could take a shower after the long trip on the airship. "Listen, I'm going to head for a shower. Take some time and relax a bit. I'll join you later for dinner, alright?" Not like Dean could really say or do anything else for Kane, so he might as well take this time to sit back and think about everything that happened. Heading out of the room, Dean closed the door behind him, allowing Kane some time to reflect and think things through on his end.

AFTER a bit of guessing which door led towards the bathroom, Dean found himself in a rather large bathroom with a wooden soaking tub with the faucet appearing as if it barely hovered over the tub. There was a large folding screen close by to allow for some type of privacy. Taking a look at it, it appeared that on the thin white cloth was a well drawn out portrait of a garden. Linger flowers that have long been since dead seemed to be elegantly placed around a white table with a small tea set on it.

There was a little girl in a pretty white dress, though her face had been painted over to make it appear like she didn't have one. The blonde curls showed that her hair was short with only the ends curling this way and that against the side of her face. A light green ribbon rested on her exposed temple. A cross from her was a little teddy bear with a white ribbon wrapped around its neck. A small trail of pink butterflies lingered against some of the flowers. The detail on the cloth was amazing, like an expert painter took their time making sure that everything had been put in its place perfectly.

Moving behind it, Dean placed down a pair of clothing that he would wear for the night, considering that the sun would be setting before too long, Dean didn't have much planned out for the rest of the night. After the long travel between the islands, he was ready to settle down for the night after the bath and a nice hot dinner. Stripping down to nothing, Dean walked past the folding screen with a washcloth in hand to help cover himself up while getting the bath set up. Dean's body still had small bruises on it thanks to the training Kane gave him, Dean wished that Kane would have gone a bit easier on him. The marks were slowly fading though, which was a good thing.

Turning the handles for the faucet on to the perfect temperature, Dean placed the plug into the drain so he would be able to let the water fill up. It wasn't much longer before Dean was dipping his toes into the hot water. Dean slowly emerged himself into the water with a small groan escaping his lips. The water rushing in seemed to slightly vibrate against the wooden tub, which didn't bother Dean in the slightest. It was only when the water was above his bent legs that Dean turned the water off, allowing himself to simply linger in the bathtub without much care in the world.

With his back resting against the smooth surface, Dean took this time to look around his settings. The wall paper had bits of tears here and there in the dark fabric, exposing a bit of the drywall underneath, but there were some hand drawn paintings that seemed to be neatly framed. Some of them were colored, while others weren't. There was a fireplace to his right and the folded screen to his left. Behind the screen was a large paneled window that had looked over the garden. One could only image the view from it once the flowers were in complete bloom. Glancing up towards the ceiling, Dean was greeted with a white crystal chandelier. The light coming from outside caused the crystals to reflect the light, causing slender small rainbows to spread across the white ceiling while the setting sun cast an orange glow on the floor.

Closing his eyes, Dean allowed the hot water to work its magic. Feeling the rough texture of the washcloth cling towards his groin, Dean blocked out any ambient noise that might have disturbed his peace. Further sinking into the tub, Dean stopped short of the water resting below his nostrils.

A bit of the water seemed to splash out as he did so, but he could always clean that up later. Resting his feet just a bit over the edge of the tub. The sides of his feet looked a bit bruise and dark from the long trek. Slow deep breaths through Dean's nose caused the water underneath to lightly ripple. The water helped to numb the aching pain in his back that Dean had pushed off of his mind for too long. He never wanted Kane to worry if he was being pushed too far since they had a long way to go, but being able to relax in peace was what Dean truly needed at this moment.

Before he knew it, Dean had started to drift off to sleep from the hot water relaxing him. By the time that Dean started to come to, he started to feel something trickling onto his stomach. It was sand like in nature as it gently poured onto his stomach, causing Dean's eyes to slowly flutter open. It was a bit blurry at first, but a figure standing beside the bathtub caused Dean to jolt forward, causing some of the water to splash over the edge of the tub.

Taking a second to adjust to his surroundings, Dean glanced at his arms and noticed how his once light skin was now that of a lightly boiled lobster. "W-What the?" Dean asked audibly as this was the first time that he had seen his skin becoming such a shade of red that it looked like he had been baking out in the sun.

"You sat in the bath for too long stupid." A familiar female tone caught Dean's attention, causing Dean to look towards his right. There, kneeling over the edge while holding a white bag that seemed to be pouring out some type of white looking sand material into the bath was Ashley with her usual annoyed frown on her face. She was wearing something that looked like a woolly white robe with her hair seemingly pulled up into a messy bun. Instinctively Dean reached both of his hands down to cover his groin.

"Relax, not like I haven't seen some guy's dick before. And before you even ask, I tend to draw in my spare time and I've had to draw a few males nude before." It wasn't a comforting fact, but this was the first time that a girl had seen Dean naked.

"But it is rather cute that you think I would be embarrassed about you exposing yourself to me." Ashley commented, putting the bag down before standing up, a coy smile seemingly lingering on his lips as she moved towards the fireplace that had a small fire going. Ashley must have started the fire considering that Dean never started one when he first got into the bathroom.

Dean didn't know how he should really take that comment. On one hand it was surprising just how cocky this girl seemed to be, and on the other hand she was so abrasive that Dean was not used to this sort of situation, it left him wondering what he should do. Not like he could be mean to this girl, but it seemed that she was trying to get him angry. The sound of the chopped wood being added into the fire seemed to catch Dean's attention as he looked over towards her.

"Despite your sharp tongue, I guess I should thank you." Dean started, figuring that he should at least be a bit grateful that Ashley was able to stir Dean before he fell asleep thanks to the hot water and almost drowned. "If you didn't sprinkle that stuff in the bath, I might have been a goner." Dean continued, as he reached forward to pull the metal cord that connected to plug to the tub. With a quick tug, Dean could feel the water starting to spiral down the drain.

"Whatever." Ashley spoke, moving to turn her back away from Dean. The sound of fabric coming undone caught Dean's ear, causing the male to turn his head and see the fabric of her robe starting to slide down her backside. With her usually long locks tied up, her rosy skin was noticeable as well as her slender frame. Dean was practically frozen in place as his mind started to panic as to what he should do in this sort of situation. Despite having a rather nasty attitude towards everyone, Ashley was rather beautiful.

Grabbing the wash cloth that Dean was using earlier from almost being sucked in by the draining water, Dean covered himself up as he stood up. The water splashed about as he did so, but with Ashley's back turned towards him, he used this as a chance to get behind the folded screen to get dressed. Sure there were some watery foot prints from his hasty retreat, but it was better than risking the tribal leader thinking that Dean was some kind of pervert for staring at her. Feeling his heart pounding against his chest, Dean sighed as he felt better being out of sight. At least his clothes were still there, though hanging up on a little hanger was a thin white nightgown.

Placing the wet washcloth in a white wicker basket, Dean collected the towel to start drying himself off. The silence between then was almost deafening. Not like there was much to talk about. After all, most of the time Kane would be there with him to talk about his plan to get back at Elite for everything that they had done. But now, Dean was alone with a girl who clearly didn't seem interested in anything that Dean had to talk about.

"Why did this have to happen to me?" Dean thought to himself as he brought the towel up to start drying himself off. He was careful where he placed the towel as his skin was still hot and irritated. *"I feel like some kind of pervert. Granted she came in after me, but it will seem like I'm trying to take a peek at her."* Not that anyone would believe Dean's innocence, expect for maybe Kane. *"What can I even say to her right now? I can't even bring myself to say anything in fear that she will take it personally and hate me even more."* The very thought caused Dean's eyebrows to knit together as he focused a little too hard on his own thoughts that he didn't notice how hard he was drying himself off until he noticed the thin layer of skin trying to peel back on his arms.

"So how come you haven't tried to do your little pitch to me?" Ashley asked in her sharp tongue, catching Dean by surprise. Pitch? Ashley must have been referring to asking for her aide in trying to take down the Elite. But then again, who told her about it? Did Felicia or Kane tell her about it? Well, Kane couldn't have because Dean was with him the whole time. Perhaps Felicia had mentioned the plans before they had even arrived to Ashley? That made more sense than Kane talking to her about it.

"Do you think now is the best time to talk about that?" Dean asked, glancing down at his reddened chest in a bit of disbelief that she would want to talk about the mechanics about their makeshift death ray while they were both naked in the same room. "I mean, I would rather talk about this in a better setting than in the bathroom where we only have a folded screen between the two of us." Was that too much to ask for?

Collecting his underwear to slip on before Ashley could do something as brash as pull the screen back before he could get some kind of covering that wasn't the small wash cloth. But to his surprise, Ashley didn't do something as reckless as the worst case scenario that played out in Dean's mind. Instead, she started to run the water. Perhaps this meant that Dean was just starting to over react?

Blinking a bit in surprise, Dean kept silent, as if he was waiting for Ashley to speak up. But yet she didn't. Grabbing the loose pajama pants, Dean quickly pulled them on before collecting a loose shirt that was darker than the pants he had on. "Uh, hello?" Dean called out placing his hand on the edge of the folded screen.

"Stay behind there until I'm done pervert." Ashley snapped, causing Dean to almost jump out of his skin. Retracting his fingers, Dean let out a small exasperated sigh as he wondered back towards the window. Not like he could really defy her and peek his head out. She was the only one naked right now. The very thought made Dean feel a little flustered. He has never been in this situation. To be trapped by a younger girl who was currently getting ready to bathe with a single screen between them.

Glancing towards the ceiling, Dean could hear the light splashing of the water as Ashley got inside of the tub. There was a smell that seemed to linger in the room, almost smelling like lavender and vanilla mixed together. Slumping against the windowsill a bit, Dean crossed his arms as his back rested against the cold glass. The window started to fog up from the steam rising from Dean's body. Right now he was glad to have something cold resting against his hot skin.

"You still haven't answered my question." Ashley snapped as there seemed to be some bubbles rising overhead. It caught Dean's attention as it felt like a lifetime ago since he had last seen bubbles. The last time he was able to see the clear reflective orbs was the last time he took a bubble bath on the Millennium.

"Like I said, I feel like it would be better for the both of us if we didn't do it in here." Dean seemed to snap back towards Ashley, getting a bit fed up with her snappy attitude. "Besides, I'm not trying to sell a pitch." Dean continued, shooting a glare towards the folded screen. "What I'm trying to do is get the other leaders on board to help take down the eyesore of the space station known as the Millennium." Dean huffed a bit, figuring that Ashley wouldn't understand just what Dean was trying to do. After all, this leader was the youngest of them all. What could she possibly know about revenge?

"So you want to take down the cowards' ship?" Ashley asked, her voice seeming to change from annoyed to actually having a bit of interest in what Dean was trying to do. Taking note of this change, Dean couldn't help but raise an eyebrow. Pushing off of the windowsill, Dean watched the bubbles to see the distorted reflection as to what Ashley's posture was like. It seemed that Ashley was leaning back against her tub, bubbles covering her body as a single knee was sticking out of the surface. Her small chest was covered with the bubbles. A small tray-like table rested beside the right side as the fire continued to burn the logs. The smell of burnt wood mixed in with the lavender and vanilla scent that already seemed to fill the room.

"Yeah. They killed my parents and made my life a living hell with their rules that they set in place." Dean remarked, figuring that he should be honest with Ashley. Not like she had any sympathy towards anyone else, so why mince words and try to get on her good side? "They made it so those who were in the lower classes didn't have any chance to branch out and reach their true desires. Making each day a living hell while trying to kill us when we stepped out of line." Dean continued, his brows knitting together as he despised the treatment he had gotten from the Elite.

"They will literally crush your hand with no remorse afterwards." Dean knew from experience what that was like. He could still clearly remember the look in the man's eyes as he looked down on Dean like he was nothing more than a worthless cockroach, staining his perfectly expensive shoes as if they were fresh out of the box. Hearing a mused hum leave Ashley's lips, Dean was a bit surprised his statement had caused that reaction from her. In fact, Dean was expecting her to make some remark that he shouldn't be so pitiful. But instead, her next words left Dean speechless.

"Alright, I'll help you." Ashley spoke as her amusement lingered in her tone. Dean blinked a bit in surprise as he wasn't sure if he should be happy or weary of receiving her help. Letting his hands move down towards his sides, Dean was left with his mouth part slightly as he couldn't find the right words at first.

"Why?" Dean blurted out in shock. "Why would you agree to help me so easily?" Dean asked, shocked that he was able to make this little princess help him instead of forcing him to jump through hoops. Realizing how inconsiderate it may have made Dean sound, he was quick with his followed up remark.

"Sorry to make it seem like I'm not grateful or anything. But it does make me wonder why you would be so easy to convince." Dean continued, taking a few steps closer to the edge of the folded screen before stopping in a small puddle of cold water.

"It's simple." Ashley spoke, her coy smile lingering on her lips. "I'm the tribal leader of envy." She spoke in a matter-of-fact tone. "Unlike the other leaders who simply fight against their sins, I embrace it." She continued, slowly raising her right leg out of the water, pointing her toes towards the white barren ceiling. "I want to destroy the things that I'm envious of." A small chuckle left Ashley's lips as she placed her hands on the edges of the tub. "And those bastards deserve to die for making the rest of us suffer. Wouldn't you agree?" Ashley asked, her voice sounding almost singsong like towards the end.

Dean could understand where she was coming from, but the part about the other leaders fighting against their sins did raise a few questions. "What do you mean the others are fighting against their sins?" Dean asked, taking a small peek from behind the screen, only to be greeted with a bar of soap being tossed at him. Thankfully Dean ducked back behind the screen, only to fall and land on the puddle of cold water that rested on the floor from him rushing behind the screen earlier. "Shit that's cold!" Dean grumbled under his breath, though he was slow to get up with a now wet butt mark on his pants.

"Serves you right for trying to peek." Ashley remarked with a small huff, crossing her arms under the water. Not like Dean was trying to peek or anything like that. He was only curious and wanted to make sure that she wasn't trying to lie to him. "But to answer your question, most of the other tribal leaders try to fight against their sins because they don't want to end up like their sin." Ashley remarked, her tone sounding a bit sad.

"They don't want to end up like Nero." Ashley paused for a few seconds. "After all, he was the Wrath Clan leader." Ashley continued after sighing while her leg slipped back into the water. "He was angry at how the rest of the world had ignored his shelter's cries for help and how no one came to rescue them when things were at their worst." Ashley continued as she closed her eyes.

"He was angry that the other leaders weren't trying to fight back. He was angry that women only wanted him for power and fame, nothing more." The more that Ashley spoke about Nero, the more that Dean was able to understand where Nero was coming from. "So he kept himself distant and made everyone hate him. Or at least, that's what my mother told me." Dean wondered if maybe the other leaders would have acted differently if they knew this. "Cursed to hate everything and everyone because they are always out to get you in the end." Ashley finished, slowly sinking down into the tub a bit more while looking up at the bubbles that floated upwards.

"That sounds more like it should be in a fictional story than it being real." Dean argued as he took his towel to try and drive off the wet spot on his butt. "It makes as much sense as someone saying that they killed someone because their zodiac sign led them to be unstable enough to do something that horrific." Dean continued, rolling his eyes at the thought that someone could easily lose their mind simply because they allowed some type of title control over their actions. Then again, Dean had seen how those in the Elite or the higher Silver class treated those around them like they were nothing more than garbage. So perhaps what Ashley was saying wasn't too far off from the truth.

"Believe what you will, but don't come crying to me when you start to notice that some of the other leaders are acting like the sin of their tribes." Ashley remarked before glancing towards the folded screen with a scowl on her face. "After all, I'm envious with how close you and Kane have gotten." Ashley continued, causing Dean to raise his eyebrows in surprise at her statement. They were friends, nothing more.

"What? We're just friends." Dean remarked, taken back a bit by Ashley's comment. "Don't you have any friends?" Dean asked, raising an eyebrow as he didn't know how to take that comment. "I thought that you and Kane got along." Though considering how horrible Ashley tended to act around other people, it wouldn't surprise Dean if she didn't have much luck in the whole friends department.

Then again, Dean was the same way on the Millennium. The silence after the question was proof enough that Ashley was lacking in the whole friends department. A soft sigh escaped Dean's lips as he slowly nodded his head, figuring that perhaps he would be able to relate to Ashley in this regard. "I wouldn't let it get you down." Dean remarked, reaching a hand up to scratch the back of his head a bit. "I mean, Kane's been the only real friend I've made so far in my whole life and I'm 24." As embarrassing as it was, it was the truth.

"Wait, you're 24 and have only now gotten a real friend?" Ashley asked, her voice seemed to be more taunting than thankful for someone knowing what she is going through. "That's hilarious!" She cackled, the sound of the water splashing as she moved to hold her sides, her laughter filling the room. The only sound that could really be heard among the mixed sounds of the water splashing and Ashley's laughter was the sound of Dean's annoyed groan that the little princess was laughing at him.

"Listen here you little princess," Dean snapped, grabbing the screen and pulling it back with a scowl on his face. "You don't know what it was like on that damn space station." Dean growled angrily as he watched Ashley sink into the water, quickly covering herself in the bubbles that filled the bath tub.

"Every day was a living hell in that place! Especially when you don't exactly conform to the standards on the station." Dean yelled as he reached the side of the bathtub. "Being a pudgy little boy meant that I was constantly picked on. Only to be completely alone as no one was there for me when my parents died." Dean growled, grabbing Ashley's hair and pulling her hair back.

The shocked and scared look on Ashley's face seemed to knock Dean back to his senses. Quickly realizing his mistake, Dean let go of her locks as he stumbled back a bit as Ashley whimpered while covering herself the best that she could after Dean let go of her. He blew it. Dean had just blown the chance to get the leader of Envy to join him, and now he would be labeled a pervert for what he did.

"S-Sorry...I..." Dean quickly apologized, his eyes averting from Ashley and towards the door as he started to take a few steps back. "But you have no room to talk since you have a problem with communicating with people that aren't in a demoralizing way." Dean lightly scolded Ashley. Though Dean would never say it, it felt good to make that prissy princess a bit afraid of him.

Dean would never hurt a woman, especially a vulnerable girl who was naked in the bathtub, but she needed to be knocked down a few pegs. "I'll be leaving now." Dean excused himself, figuring that Kane would probably be worried that he was taking so long. Besides, Ashley needed some time to think about how she came across people.

UPON entering the room that he was to share with Kane, Dean made his way towards the bed where Kane had been currently sitting and reading a book. Flopping onto the bed with a groan, Dean pressed his face into the sheets. The sound of a page turning caught Dean's ear as it became a bit harder to breathe from the thickness of the blanket he was currently laying on.

"You sure took your time in the bath." Kane remarked, not bothering to look up from his book. "I almost thought that you fell asleep in there and drowned." Kane remarked in an attempt to make a joke, but he had no clue just what happened in that bathroom, nor how right he would have been if it wasn't for Ashley coming into the bathroom and pouring something on his stomach to wake Dean up.

"Frankly I would have rather drowned than what I just went through." Dean remarked, though some of it was muffled thanks to the blanket. This seemed to perk Kane's attention as the sound of something sliding against the thin paper and the small clasp of a book closing resulted in Dean looking up and seeing what exactly Kane was doing. Upon seeing the tribal leader place the book down on the small table beside the bed, Dean brought his arms up to cross them on the bed in front of him, only to nestle his head against his still warm arms.

"What happened?" Kane asked, raising his left eyebrow as a curious yet puzzled expression crossed Kane's features. Where would Dean even begin to explain the hell he had just gone through? Not only was he continuously teased and made to feel less like a man and more like the pudgy child he once was in school, but that he let the anger get the best of him and he actually caused a bit of harm to the petite leader. Sure Dean felt bad about it afterwards, but in that short time, it felt amazing to bring her down a few notches.

"I fucked up." Dean groaned, moving to bury his head into his warm arms. All Dean wanted to do was to hide away from it all. The darkness his arms provided was a welcoming distraction from the turmoil that was going on in his head. "It started with falling asleep in the tub and waking up to see Ashley pouring something on me that seemed to wake me up." Dean continued, figuring that he might as well skip Kane asking him what happened.

"Then it moved to her demanding that I stay behind the folded screen while she took her bath, only to have our conversation lead towards her asking why I didn't ask for her help." Dean continued to explain as he peaked up from his arms towards Kane.

"Surprisingly she actually agreed to help with the plan to take down the station." Dean paused, still trying to wrap his head around it all. "Then she made the conversation weird by saying how all of the leaders are fighting against their sins," Dean paused, not sure how Kane was a glutton or how Felicia was prideful. "Then Ashley started remarking about how she was jealous of our friendship." Dean spoke, slowly lifting himself up the more he prattled on.

"Eventually, I said that I was like her and didn't have friends for most of my life. That's when she laughed at me and called me pathetic...." Not that Dean was trying to sound whiny about it, but being called pathetic by someone who didn't have any friends didn't sit well to his ego.

"Not like I am not used to being called horrible things like that before, it's just..." As Dean knelt on the bed, he could feel the weight of his actions resting on his shoulders. "I got upset and grabbed her hair before saying some mean things to her." And there it was. Dean felt like a puppy who made a mess on the floor, and was waiting for his master to scold him. But surprisingly the scolding never came. Instead, Dean could feel Kane moving closer towards him.

"Well, you probably shouldn't have pulled her hair for one thing." Kane remarked, his voice seemingly tender as if he could understand what Dean was going through. "But, it did get her attention." Not like that would really help Dean at this point. If it wasn't for Kane, Ashley would have demanded that Dean be thrown out right there and then. But it got Dean wondering why she didn't say or do anything after he let her go. "Knowing you, you probably felt bad, and apologized right away once you snapped back to your normal self, right?" It was scary just how accurate Kane was with all of that.

"Yeah..." Dean nodded with that simple statement. The guilt hasn't exactly gone away, but at least Kane seemed to be understanding and level headed considering that Dean could have hurt Ashley if he didn't control himself. "I left after I apologized, though it wasn't like I could just stay in there after what I did." Dean continued, his shoulders dropping a bit as he wondered if she was still in the tub, thinking about what just happened. "Maybe it might be better if I find an inn to stay at. Better than staying here with the little princess who might try to find a reason to kick me out." There was no need for unnecessary drama after all.

"Give it a day." Kane remarked, causing Dean to look up at him with a curious gaze on Dean's face. "Tomorrow we're having a meeting about the rate of crops and other inessential things." Kane continued, moving back to rest against the pillows as he laid back into a reclining motion. "If you want, I could talk things over with Ashley. Tell her that it was just a misunderstanding." Not like that would help much, but it would at least take some of the stress off of Dean.

"I guess it wouldn't hurt." Dean groaned, moving to get off of the bed. Standing up, Dean glanced at the window that seemed to be closed off by the curtain. If the leaders are out with their meeting, Dean would have to find something that he could do as he waited. Not like he could come along.

"Guess I could find something to read tomorrow while you're out." Dean remarked as she walked towards the window to peek out of it. " It would be something that would take my mind off of things. But I doubt it will help anything between me and Ashley.." Just like Dean often did when he was bored on the Millennium. When he didn't have any friends he could play with. Books were something that he often turned to in his times of boredom.

Moving back to the bed, Dean crawled into the bed, though curled up against himself the best he could. He didn't like this feeling of hurting Ashley, even though she sort of deserved it. Dean's mind started to think of ways in which he could have changed that situation all together, but nothing came to mind. It seems like Dean would just have to wait and see how Kane could handle it tomorrow. Hopefully this wouldn't be the only night he would get to sleeping at the estate.

CHAPTER TWELVE: *Tribe Meeting*

C LOSING THE GLASS side door that was slightly frosted over, Kane peered through the glass to see a blurred version of Dean sitting at the table in the kitchen. Wearing a white buttoned up shirt with some black suspenders that connected to the formal pants, Dean was sitting at the table with a warm white mug in hand. His hair was pushed back a bit, the ends seemingly ruffled from the night of tossing and turning in his sleep. There were still some bags under Dean's eyes, but they were at least better than the first time that the male had arrived. Kane could remember how exhausted Dean looked. Almost like he was a walking hollowed version of a man. The very thought of how frail Dean looked brought a small frown to Kane's lips. It was like looking at an older yet different version of himself. If Kane had allowed the darkness in his heart to take hold of him, he might not have recovered so easily.

With the bulky deer mask in hand, Kane sighed as a hot puff of air escaped his lips. Wearing an old navy style outfit that looked as if it once belonged to a high commander of a vessel from a long dead country, the white fabric hugged Kane's body tightly. The top of the uniform felt more like a dog collar than anything else. The black stripes that were horizontal across his torso went downwards like largely spaced out buttons on a trench coat. The long black ornamental shoulder piece looked a bit out of place, but with the silver rope draping down from his shoulders and connected to the top bar towards the collarbone, it seemed to look good on him.

Though the uniform had long since lost its meaning thanks to humanity being wiped out, at least with Kane wearing it, it made him look like a proper leader more than anything. He may not have been the commander of the seas like Felicia, but even she wouldn't dare to try to wear something that covered her completely. The end of the sleeves had ended towards the elbows where the edge was covered by black coated gauntlets that were used for protection in case of anyone getting any ideas of attacking him. The end of the gauntlets revealed the black gloves that barely kept Kane warm due to the fabric being thin.

The edge of the hem for the top coat landed just shy above Kane's belly button, revealing the second shirt that was a normal buttoned up shirt that was also white in nature. It was always hard to keep the white outfits clean, so Kane was always self aware when he wore it to not get it stained. The black suspenders that Kane was wearing only seemed to reveal the last bit as they clasped against Kane's black formal pants. The belt that was tied around his waist was black with a silver trimming. His pouch that carried his chips were hooked into one of the belt loops, making it hard for anyone to nab it.

There wasn't much of a design to the pouch that was on Kane's waist. Frankly it was just a white deer against a black background, making it easy to identify. The pants Kane wore were tight, but then again they needed to be to help with keeping in heat. The black boots that Kane wore came up to his mid calf, his pants legs tucked into the black boots to keep them from getting soiled. He hated having to dress up so tightly like this, but it was the burden he had to face when dealing with the other leaders.

Turning away from the door, Kane carefully stepped down the icy rock stairs. The cold night had allowed patches of ice to form, adding in the factor that the tall buildings blocked out the morning sun, making the trek towards the meeting hall tricky. One wrong step and Kane could be looking at a soiled uniform. Slipping his deer headdress on, Kane made sure to secure the small strap to keep the headdress from falling off. With a deep inhale of the frosty air through his nose, Kane ventured along the stoned path towards the back of the buildings.

There was a thin layer of fresh snow that seemed to be untouched by any living creature. The wind gave a gentle blow, causing Kane to shiver as he cursed how cold it was under his breath. If there wasn't the threat of slipping against the hidden black ice, he would have simply ran towards the building. *"Seems like Ashley had already gone ahead of me this morning."* Kane thought to himself as he was surprised to see her dark green coat already heading towards the building when the two men had come down for breakfast.

"I guess she was still angry at Dean for what he did to her." Not like Kane could blame her. *"But to act completely avoidant, that isn't like Ashley that I know. I just hope that she'll be alright after this."* Letting out a deep sigh that caused a large puff of white smoke to leave his mouth, Kane continued on his walk as the sound of the snow and ice crunched under his feet. *"As long as she doesn't demand that Dean gets thrown out, I'm fine with whatever."* Kane continued to mostly think to himself as he walked down the barren pathway. It seemed no one would be joining him, leaving Kane alone in his thoughts. He hasn't felt this way in a long time. Kane should have figured that he would have gotten spoiled having Dean by his side, always there to listen to Kane with whatever he said, it was a pleasant experience for the lonely leader.

Glancing to his side, Kane felt a bit empty that Dean wasn't there to smile towards him, or to perk up with a question that Kane could easily answer. There was no one there to keep him going, causing Kane to look a bit defeated as he strolled the area by himself. Without realizing it, Kane was lowering his head as he couldn't help the feeling of emptiness wash over him, like when Kane had lost his family. Or when Miles had plain out rejected him after Kane painstakingly poured his heart out to him.

It wasn't long before the sound of rock crunching under someone caught Kane's attention, causing the leader to turn his head and noticed a familiar figure walking towards him wearing all black. Kane's eyes widened as he noticed how the white snow behind said man caused him to stand out with the help of the snow that lingered on the ground. Standing just an inch over Kane, Keaton, who was the leader of the lust clan, was wearing his own formal attire.

With large curved horns that had small chains trailing down the edges of his ox skull, Keaton had made sure to have the long nose of the ox skull cut off as it was a little too long for his liking. Keaton's untameable hair seemed to rest neatly against the edges of the skull. The skull's eye sockets nestled against Keaton's temples, his piercing golden eyes seemed to be amplified by the decorative pure black mask that made it seem like one would be looking into the depth of the long dead beasts' soul. The edges of the cut off nose were sharpened to curve around Keaton's eyes. The only color visible seemed to be the bits of his cheeks that peaked through between the base of the skull and the top of the black mask that he wore, showing that Keaton's natural flesh color was a light peach.

As Kane's eyes glanced down towards the outfit that Keaton had picked out, it appeared just as punk-like as Kane would have figured the other would wear it. With everything being black, it was almost hard to know what Keaton was wearing. The first thing that Kane noticed was the spikes that rested against Keaton's left shoulder as his singular epaulet. The epaulet had been attached by a thick rope that seemingly tied to a small black furred sash. The black leather trench coat bound the Lust's leader frame, making it easy to see his movements as Keaton walked down the path towards Kane.

"Well, if it isn't our glutenous deer." A deep but slightly rough voice called out as hot puffs of air appeared to be disturbed from the fabric of the mask. The silver earrings that normally decorated along Keaton's ears were covered from the pressure of the mask. "See you're running later than usual. Something happened between you and Miles?" Was it really that noticeable? How clingy Kane was to be able to be near or to see Miles that he would get to the meetings earlier just to have some time with his long time friend? But now that Miles betrayed his trust, it seemed to have disrupted Kane's normal schedule.

"Eh, not really." Kane lied, reaching up to lightly scratch the bit of scalp free from the deer's skull. "I wanted to make sure that Dean got everything settled before we started our meeting." Which wasn't exactly a lie, but it was best to not get Keaton involved with Dean right off the back of the bat. Knowing how the other tends to act around people, with Keaton's flirty nature, it was best just to avoid any awkward scenes that might drive Dean away.

"Dean huh? Is he your replacement for Miles?" A light jest towards Kane, but it wasn't like that was really the case. Keaton could see the hesitation on Kane's face, the way that the shorter male's lip trembled before parting a bit. Raising an eyebrow, though it wasn't visible, Keaton waited to see the lie that Kane would give him.

"No way. He's just traveling with me." Kane started to speak as Keaton reached the smaller leader's side. "We don't really have that kind of relationship. We're just friends after all." Not exactly a lie, but it wasn't the whole truth. "You'll meet him soon enough Keaton. After all, he has a bit of a proposition for everyone." Kane continued, glancing down to make sure that he wasn't at risk of slipping on a patch of ice.

"You'll hear about it soon enough. Just have a bit of patience." Kane remarked, a bit of a huff towards the end before glancing away. "But since we're waiting out the winter here, then perhaps it would be best if you and the other leaders don't come around." Hearing that remark coming from Kane caused Keaton to look down at the shorter male with a puzzled gaze. "Considering that right now Dean is working on trying to get Ashley's approval for his idea, I want them to get closer." A convenient excuse for the meantime, but perhaps Kane was simply stalling for his own needs. "Sure she may have already agreed, but I want her to get to know Dean better to see what he has to offer us." Another convenient lie for Kane. "So until then, would you mind keeping your distance?" Not like Kane had much of a chance at stopping Keaton if he wanted to, but perhaps with the excuse of Dean getting to know Ashley, then perhaps the Lust leader would stay away from the manor.

"Big talk for such a frail deer." Keaton remarked through his mask before a chuckle left the leader's throat. "Afraid I'll try and make a move on your little boy toy?" Keaton remarked in a teasing manner as he knew how Kane could get. Before Kane could argue that his relationship with Dean wasn't like that, Keaton grabbed a hold of Kane's shoulder to twirl the shorter leader towards him. Clasped his thumb and index finger around Kane's chin Keaton leaned in close to the other male.

"But don't worry, I'll be spending my winter with Amelia. So I won't be stopping by and trying anything on your new little pet." Keaton remarked with an amuse chuckle escaping his lips. "After all, it's the only time I get to have some fun time with her. Makes me feel like we're some sort of married couple and she doesn't have to attend to more pressing matters that involve the clans." It was hard for most of the leaders to find time with any romantic interest, especially when they had to check in on the different parts of their clan to make sure that everything was going according to plan. "This is our only free time that we get through the year." Keaton added, only to watching Kane pull himself out of Keaton's grip.

"It's not my fault that she decided to name herself Leader of the clans." Kane huffed a bit as he took a step back from the taller male. "She put that responsibility on herself." Kane snapped. It wasn't that Kane was jealous of the position that Amelia put on herself, but there wasn't room for debate at the time.

"I bet that your sister isn't happy that you're spending the whole season with Amelia though." Kane muttered in a snippy tone as he glanced away from Keaton, his anger only seeming to grow. "Guessing she went and hoarded some of your clothes away before you made the big trip here? That would probably explain why your clothes look a little wrinkly." Kane continued as he could see the anger starting to rise in Keaton's eyes. "Then again, those two don't exactly get along, huh?" Kane finished, narrowing his eyes at Keaton who seemed to find this whole ordeal amusing. The two were often at odds with each other, more so when Keaton invaded Kane's personal space.

"How about you keep Maiti out of this," Keaton paused as some anger showed in his tone. "After all, not my fault she has the same illness as you. Then again, she is my sister and we have a habit of having weird sexual fantasies." Keaton retorted back, tilting his head to the side. Kane knew that Keaton was smirking under that mask, the twinkle in his eyes was always a dead giveaway.

"What the hell do you mean by that?" Kane snapped his voice showing his displeasure at the remark, narrowing his eyes at the other. Kane didn't know where this was going, but Kane knew that he wasn't about to simply let Keaton get away with it. Not like Maiti was into other females, but it seemed like the only other 'illness' that she would have is loving her brother in more than a family friendly way. But bringing up that remark meant that Keaton didn't exactly approve of how Kane felt towards Miles all these years with wanting to be more than the so called brothers that Miles placed on the relationship.

Just seeing that smug twinkle in Keaton's eyes irked Kane like no other. "You know exactly what I mean." Keaton spoke in a taunting tone as he leaned down to be eye level with Kane. "You both want to have your older brother, but they just aren't interested in you that way." The singsong tone didn't make Kane like the remark any less, but the way that Keaton said it, it seemed to spark a small fuse in the smaller leader's mind.

"And here I thought that you fucked anything that moved." Kane bluntly spoke with the anger lingering in his tone. "But I guess even a perverted masochistic fuck like yourself has standards." The cold angry glare on Kane's face was like he was shooting daggers at the taller male. "Though it must be rather tempting with how slutty your sister dresses from time to time in a sad attempt of getting you to notice her. At least I haven't gone that far." Kane may have loved Miles more than he should have, but they weren't related by any normal standards. "Then again, maybe mental illness runs in your family." Kane snapped back, glaring up at Keaton who only seemed to find the remark more amusing than anything else.

"My, didn't know our little deer had such fangs." Keaton chuckled as he started to walk ahead of Kane, who was clenching his fists so hard that they were shaking. "Glad to see you still have some fight in you after all." Keaton remarked with an amused chuckle as he moved to circle around the large fountain that rested just before the banquet hall. The fountain had been long since turned off. Kane stood there for a few minutes, trying his best to calm down. But the way that Keaton always taunted him, it always made Kane see red.

After Kane started to move, he took a second to look up at the statue that lingered in front of the building. Green algae from the years of trapped moisture had clung to the once bronze metal. The head of the figure lingering on the top had been broken off , the jagged ends showed that the head was broken off by young teenagers who had broken into the estate when the place seemed abandoned. There was only one wing sticking out, and the chest that once revealed the statue to have been a female angel had been destroyed. It was a shame that they never got the fountain to work. It would have made for an amazing piece of art otherwise.

The rim of the enclosed circles of the fountain had been broken off in bits, mostly due to normal wear and tear. Some of the pieces rested against the base of the large circle. There had been talk about it being repaired, but no one could seem to figure out the right design to replace it with. Not to mention it had a bit of history behind it, so it would have been seen as disrespectful to replace it with something better. So the leaders who were currently in charge decided to just simply leave it as it. Unless, however, something happened to completely destroy the fountain than it already was.

Upon entering the building and feeling the warmth thawing him out, Kane was greeted with the familiar red carpet that seemed to drape the floor. The lingering smell of the burning firewood and the idle chatter of the other leaders collecting together in the room towards Kane's right. The large broad staircase in front of him led towards the ballroom that was often used for banquets before the destruction, but seeing as how the banquet was still a little ways off, it was currently closed off.

Glancing down, Kane noticed some of the shoe prints leading towards the meeting room. It appeared that everyone had finally arrived. Kane must have been the last one in considering that he could already see everyone taking their seats in their masks on. As he walked through the sliding doors, Kane's eyes seemed to notice that Ashley had seemingly cut her hair. No one would have ever imagined Ashley cutting her hair to such a short length after she had grown it out to be past her waist. Yet, here she was, sitting all prim and proper like nothing happened.

With the elk skull adoring her head, the long stick like antlers pushed back and curled inwards as the curled ends of her newly fresh cut hair brushed along the edges of her jawline. The curls twisted this way and that, as the small free feathers that hooked along the bottom tips of the horns nestled against the sides of her face. The dress that Ashley wore was a long sleeved Lolita dress that one would almost expect someone to wear at a tea party. Which considering that she was enjoying a cup of tea made it all that more ironic.

The ruffled breast piece covered her chest had an emerald encrusted decorative pin resting against the middle of Ashley's collar bone. With a glance, it seemed that the bits of the dress were white in color, the jacket that she wore above it looked like some type of Gothic jacket that had a lace trimming that went over the sleeves perfectly. The torso of the jacket wrapped around Ashley's slender figure as the edges brushed against her waist. The coat parted to have the long sides brush over the dress that seemingly puffed out thanks to the petticoat giving the dress more of a rounded look. The stocking Ashley wore were white in color as the boots she wore had a small heel to give her some height.

Felicia sat close to Ashley, seemingly studying the small petite girl's hair in awe. Unlike her normal clothes, Felicia's outfit resembled the type of style that one would expect Ashley to wear. With a tight knit jacket wrapping around her frame, the black shirt she wore was short sleeved as it wasn't visible against the hem of the sleeves of the jacket Felicia wore, as the hem barely brushed her elbows. The jacket rested just shy above Felicia's waist was the shirt seemingly ruffled against the pinstriped bustle gray skirt that went down to Felicia's knees. The metal right leg she often kept hidden was exposed as the high heels she wore wrapped round her ankles. The tiger skull rested on top of Felicia's head as her long hair had been braided to one side and draped over her shoulder. Reaching her fingers out gingerly, Felicia couldn't help but gently play with the trimmed locks with a big smile on her face.

The tiger skull had a rather unique design to it. The part of the large incisor that was broken seemed to be replaced with yellow crystals. The nostrils were encrusted with black crystals as the eyes were mixed with both orange and black to make it seem like the skull still had the eyes of the once living beast. There were parts that were painted black like stripes, while some of the other stripes were only visible in the dark.

On Felicia's left was Miles. Wearing a cleanly washed and pressed white long sleeved top that seemingly stuck out against dark gray vest and striped necktie, Kane was always surprised to see Miles in anything other than his typical long robe. With the wolf skull seemingly nestled on his thin silver locks, Kane was finding it almost hard to simply look away from the man. There was always something about Miles that made it hard for Kane to look away. Despite the number of heartaches from the continuous rejection had on him, Kane could never stop the longing gaze he had for the man. The wolf mask was oddly plain in comparison to the other leaders. Miles wasn't the type of person who often put much work in if he didn't need to.

Having to mentally shake himself out from staring at Miles, Kane moved to take his seat next to Ashley. Amelia was still collecting things from the other room, as her cursing could be heard only when she would raise her voice. "So what caused you to cut your hair after all this time?" Felicia asked, her hand still gently brushing her fingers against the curled ends of Ashley's hair like it was some sort of dangling cat toy.

Kane had an idea as to what caused the youngest of the leaders to cut her hair, specifically Dean grabbing it and pulling her head back to yell at her, but he was interested to know if she would divulge that information. Though the look on Ashley's face was more annoyed than embarrassed, not showing that she was willing to give an inkling to exactly what caused this sudden hair style change. "I got tired of brushing it every day." It was an obvious lie, but she sounded so convincing that Felicia seemed to buy it.

"Really?" Felicia asked, her eyes going wide as she never expected Ashley to simply grow bored of grooming her long hair every day. Kane couldn't help but give a knowing glance towards Ashley, only to have the blonde haired girl glance away from him before taking a sip out of her cup of tea. For an instance it seemed that there was a small flustered gaze on the usually stoic princess' face. It was quite a show for certain, but Kane wasn't going to make a big deal out of it just yet. "I must say, it looked really good on you. Makes you appear a little older." Felicia chimed in with a bright smile on her face.

"Older?" Kane asked, his eyes widening a bit as he felt like he was told that his friend was trying to get together with his crush or something. "You're seriously trying to go for an older look Ashley?!" Kane asked, standing up and slamming his hands down on the table, causing the others to look towards their way. "Is that why you-" Kane continued to talk, only to have Ashley interrupt his train of thought.

"No." Ashley quickly defended herself, snapping Kane a glance before setting her cup of tea down. "It has nothing to do with that." Ashley continued, her voice straining as if the two were trying to keep some sort of secret from the others. "I just thought... it was time for a small change." Ashley continued, bringing up a hand to twirl her fingers against one of the curled locks. "After all, it's not like I would even..." Ashley continued, though the flustered appearance seemed to peek its head back up as she gave a small tug on the ends. Judging by the way that Ashley was biting her lip ever so slightly, it was clear that her words were empty.

"Seems like the two of you are trying to hide something from us." Came a more commanding female voice. In walked the leader of the other tribal leaders, Amelia Park. Carrying in her right hand was a bunch of folders with different papers peeking out of them. Instead of her usual punk outfit that showed off her curvatures, Amelia was wearing something similar to the other two females in their group. With a white long sleeved shirt that appeared to be a bit more wrinkly than what everyone else was wearing, Amelia wore a tight vest that covered her entire torso while the edges pulled up towards the nape of her neck. A ruffled collar covered Amelia's neck with a silver ring in the middle. The buttons on the vest were in two perfectly straight lines as the hem of the shirt seemingly parted against her hips. Though her sleeves did appear to be a bit loosened, the cuffs were tight against her wrists. Unlike Felicia or Ashley, Amelia wore pants that had a few thin strips that traveled down her legs until they seemed to meet the edge of the boots she was wearing. The boots traveled halfway up Amelia's calf as the edges were covered in small decorative spikes.

"Because if that is the case, I would find it in your favor to disclose the personal matter right here and now." Amelia finished, her piercing light silver eyes glanced at the two like a scolding mother. Unlike the others who were more fairer skinned compared to Amelia, her skin seemingly glowed with an over all tan. Her brunette hair was pushed over towards the right, exposing her left ear that was decorated with different piercings. The skull of a bear seemingly rested against her straight locks. Much like Felicia's, the fangs' large incisors were made out of a white crystal while blue marbles surrounded by white crystals make it appear like the bear had eyes. "Well? Speak up." Amelia commanded, resulting in Kane easing back to stand up properly.

"Well, it's about a subject that we'll be discussing in the meeting ma'am." Kane remarked, figuring that they would just simply have to bring it up eventually, especially if Amelia was going to be meeting with Dean for her approval. "It's about my traveling companion Dean Torres." Kane spoke up a bit more, causing Ashley to glance towards Kane with a pleading look on her face, as if begging him not to bring up what happened last night.

"What about him?" Amelia asked, her stance indicating that she was wanting to hear what Kane had to say, and was going to punish him if he were to try and lie to her face. The way that Kane was trying to figure out what details he should include was apparent as he looked like a deer caught in the headlights. He glanced towards Ashley as if to ask if it was alright to say something, but the look in her eyes indicated something else.

"Well, it seems that Ashley..." Kane started, giving a small glance towards the smaller leader who gently shook her head, causing the curls to jiggle with her every movement. "Has developed a bit of a crush on him." It wasn't exactly a lie, considering the way that she was acting, but it seemed like the fastest way to go around the whole ordeal about what happened in the first place. Of course this seemed to cause Ashley's face to get as red as a tomato, but if Amelia learned about someone putting their hands on one of the tribal leaders, she would have forced the male out of the housing and to parish in the winter that was approaching.

"W-Why would you make up something like that?" Ashley stammered as she stood up, spilling the tea that she was drinking onto the large wooden table. Thankfully there weren't any documents in front of her, but the need to clean up the tea became apparent as Ashley backed up to keep the tea from spilling onto her dress.

"Seems like someone's embarrassed." Felicia chimed in, a little devious grin on her face as she could see right through the facade that Ashley was trying to put up in front of everyone. "Though I can't blame you, Dean does have a way about him." Felicia added, moving to lean back in her chair a bit. "The man knows how to pull the strings to get you to understand what's driving him."

"Is that why you were so quick to agree to his little plan?" Miles chimed in, glancing towards the three before Keaton got up to go and fetch a towel to keep the rug underneath the table from getting stained. Luckily the male didn't have to go far as there was a small closet that some of the helpers used for cleaning the dust that would settle over the seasons.

"You've met the man." Felicia cooed towards Miles, the grin still lingering on her face. "You can't deny that the way he sticks up for Kane is rather sweet. Like a galactic knight in tight armor." It seemed the focus of the conversation shifted towards Kane's 'relationship' with Dean, causing the others to glance towards the silver haired leader at this time. "Wouldn't you say so Kane?" Felicia mused with a preppy hum leaving her lips.

"W-Well of course he would stick up for me. I'm his friend after all." Kane muttered a bit, his own fluster seeming to pick up. It seemed that all of this talk about Dean was starting to bother Amelia as she slammed a hand down on the table as if to bring order from the chaos of this unknown man to her. The others turned their attention towards the woman.

"We're getting off track and the meeting hasn't even started." Amelia raised her voice, placing a hand on her right hip as she scanned the leader's faces with a scowl on her face. "We'll get to the subject of Dean later." Amelia remarked as Keaton finished cleaning up the spilled tea before tossing the stained towel into the fireplace. "For now I want everyone to get in their seats so we can start already." An exasperated sigh escaped Amelia's lips as she moved towards the door. "Worse than a bunch of kids before class starts." Amelia grumbled under her breath as she could hear the others starting to get into their seats after the mess was cleaned up.

The sound of heels clicking against the bit of exposed floor board by the door filled the room as Amelia closed the sliding doors. The other leaders sat in their chairs. Some seemed to be bored while others looked like they had something on their mind. Kane couldn't really tell what the other leaders could have been thinking right now, but he wondered how the conversation would go when they talked about their mysterious space man who fell from the stars.

As the meeting went on, the discussion for crop rotation wasn't as long as it usually was. Considering that they actually had a good harvest this year, they would simply have to use the previous year's designs and make small improvements in order to have another bountiful harvest. The rest of the other details weren't of much concern to Kane, so he was able to tune out most of what was being said, as he normally did in the first year or two when he was the leader. Before he would often think about Miles and how he would try to win the other over, but now he had to think about how their plan to bring the station down to Earth would go. How they would be able to try and recover survivors, what to do with the Elite, or if they should fail what their next course of action would be.

"Now for the last topic of discussion." Amelia spoke, closing the last folder that held the information that she gathered since last year's meeting. "Who is this Dean, and why has he been meeting with a majority of you guys already?" The tone in Amelia's voice showed that she was displeased with the course of actions that lead to her just now finding out about this mysterious man who didn't have the decency to come and meet her right off the bat.

The room seemed to fall silent as four of the leaders who had met Dean exchanged glances. It seemed that it would have to fall on Kane to be able to start things off with this discussion. "I'm sorry Amelia." Kane started off by speaking, causing Amelia to cast her gaze towards the male. "You see, Dean had crashed his shuttle in one of the nearby fields in my clan." It was for the best that Kane started to talk about how Dean got there in the first place.

"Normally when the bodies of those from the station crash to Earth, they're already dead thanks to the vacuum of space. But Dean was the first person to survive in a long time." This notion seemed to cause Amelia to lean back in her chair as she was ready to interrupt with questions as the need would arise. "We took him to the nearest hospital by the bay where I oversaw his recovery." Granted the news of a living person landing from the station should have reached Amelia before they even got to this point, but Kane didn't feel the need to let her know at the time. "In time, once he was up to talking, I started to get to know him." Kane spoke up, his voice trailing off a little towards the end.

"Why didn't you grill him for information?" Amelia started up with her questions. "What if he is a spy for those cowards Kane?" Amelia remarked, starting to grill Kane for answers why he was being lax on someone who came from the station. "Why did he survive while others died trying to come back?" As much as Kane would have answered Amelia's questions, he simply didn't have the right answer for her. "We need to know in case they try to come back in droves to take back the planet from us." It was a valid point, one that Kane had thought about himself, but seeing the way that Dean appeared, it was apparent that the time in space had left those aboard the Millennium weakened to Earth's gravity.

"If he wanted to attack us he would have already done it by now." Kane remarked, leaning a bit forward in his chair as he was more than ready to counter Amelia to have her understand that Dean was no threat. "Besides, if the Cowards attacked us, they wouldn't be able to simply land and take over." Kane spoke up, knowing how weake Dean was when he first arrived. "It took weeks for Dean to be able to walk." Kane was quick to point out before he would continue. "Dean survived his shuttle exploding, but he was still injured when he fell from a tree. I couldn't exactly let him lay there defenseless." Though Kane could have mentioned how the heavy seat landed on Dean's back, he figured it wasn't a major detail that needed to be shared.

"We don't know what technology they have, Kane. They could use some sort of blaster that could very well vaporize us." Amelia pointed out, causing Kane to slump back with a small roll of his eyes. "Or they could have developed some kind of illness that can spread to us, making us weak in the process before they come down and take over." Amelia spoke, though that seemed to be more of a science fiction trove than anything else.

"From what I have gathered," Kane spoke up for Dean's defense. "It seems that the ones in charge use a police force to maintain the order." Kane sat up as he kept his attention on Amelia before he continued. They control resources in order to keep people in line." Kane remarked, remembering the conversations that the two had in their time spent together. "Even if they did come and try to attack us, it's not like they would be familiar with the planet. We have ways of hiding ourselves if they were to try and attack us." Kane added, a small chuckle leaving his lips. "And we have been keeping track of the station's movements, Remember?" Kane spoke with a small huff towards the end. "Not like they would be able to land without anyone noticing." One could thank their ancestors' paranoia for that.

"Did you not think to look at his personal belongings to make sure he didn't have any type of weapon when he was brought into the hospital? What if it was in the shuttle? Did you check the wreckage?" It was another good point that Amelia made, but it made Kane wonder if she even thought that Kane was capable of being a leader if she asked novice questions like this. It was rather insulting if Kane took it personally.

"Do you really have that little bit of faith in me Amelia?" Kane asked, his brows lightly knitting together. "He was striped down at the hospital while he was unconscious. We didn't find anything on him. Not even an identification." Though they didn't realize that the little circular harness was the identification that had Dean's initials and ranking when he was on the Millennium. "Besides the shuttle was completely destroyed in the fire when it landed on the field." Kane added, watching Amelia sigh in frustration while trying to find something else to argue with Kane about Dean.

"Look," Kane spoke up, his voice firm as he caught Amelia's attention. "Here's what I can honestly tell you about Dean." This whole twenty one questions game wasn't going to get them anywhere. "Dean wants revenge on the ones in charge for killing his parents. Those people sent Dean on a one way trip to his death when he found out something about the leaders." Considering that was what seemed to be driving Dean, it made sense that he wanted revenge. "They made his life a living hell up there." Kane didn't want to give out too much information as he wanted Dean to tell the others his own story. "They would work people to death if they were in high rankings. So, Dean just wants to make them pay for not only what they did to him, but what they are doing to everyone on board the ship." Kane remarked before a small sigh left him before the next part. "Even if it means killing everyone on the station.."

It seemed like Amelia wasn't exactly moved by the statements that Kane made, causing Kane to wonder if he should just let Dean speak when they would make their way towards Amelia's clan. "I can't exactly talk on Dean's behalf, but he isn't someone who is going to try and betray us." Kane may not have evidence behind him, but he knew Dean well enough to know his true nature. "If he wanted to attack us, he would have already done it when he was able to walk around." Kane spoke, his facial features and tone lighted as he wanted Amelia to trust him. "I've been by his side this whole time Amelia. You honestly think I wouldn't know if he was planning something?"

Amelia was silent for a couple of minutes as she thought over the information. Seemingly weighing her options before she spoke up once more to try and argue her distrust of the unknown man. "What if he does betray us Kane? Would you be willing to kill him yourself if he does?" Amelia asked, crossing her arms as she waited to see how Kane would react to such a thing. It was one thing to say that they would be willing to kill someone that might betray them, but Amelia was looking for Kane's body language and tone to speak the truth where his words might lie.

The question caused Kane to pause in thought. The room seemed to be filled with tension as everyone wanted to know if Kane was up to the task. Sure the other might have killed his own brother, but that was in self defense. But to be willing and able to kill someone who was like a best friend, someone that Kane willingly allowed himself to care for, it would take some time to be able to honestly say if he could or not.

Parting his lips to speak, Kane seemed to fall silent in the process. Glancing towards the others, Kane knew he was alone in the decision. Not like the others could understand what he was going through, but ultimately, Kane knew what he had to do.

"If it turns out that Dean really is working for those cowards," Kane spoke once he found his voice. "And seems to be giving them information, then I'll kill him with my own two hands." Kane spoke, though he was a bit reluctant in his statement. Closing his eyes, Kane took a deep breath in. "Of course I would want evidence first. I won't simply kill him because you ordered me to do it." It was only reasonable since Kane wasn't about to be a jury, judge, and executioner. "I know deep down Dean is a good guy. He just wants some type of closure for what happened." Kane continued, a sadden expression crossing his face. "Not that I can really blame him..." After all, Kane didn't really get the type of closure that he wanted when dealing with his brother.

With that remark, it seemed that Amelia was a bit satisfied with the decision. "Alright." Amelia spoke, turning his attention to Ashley. "Since it seemed that Kane is willing to keep an eye on this Dean, I want your honest opinion on him." Amelia remarked, moving to rest her head against her fist as she would take in consideration what the other leaders thought of him. "Of course Keaton and I haven't met him, so you are free to leave dear." Amelia spoke towards Keaton who seemed to perk up a bit.

"Are you kidding? I want to know what this guy is like." Keaton chimed up, his own curiosity getting the better of him. It wasn't every day that they got to hear about a survivor from the station walking about their clans so freely. "Especially if some of the other leaders have become fond of him." Keaton remarked, a devious smirk forming on the male's face under his mask. Seemed like even when Dean wasn't there, he was still the center of attention.

"Ashley," Amelia spoke, causing everyone's attention to be focused on the petite princess of the group. "What are your thoughts on Dean?" Amelia asked in a stern yet soft voice. Kane felt like this was going to be a shit show, but there wasn't anything that he could do to help out Dean. If Ashley's brash nature was going to be apparent, it would be now.

"My thoughts?" Ashley asked, only to get a small nod from Amelia as if to encourage the youngest to continue. "Well," She paused, leaning back in the chair and crossing her arms against her chest. "It's not like he is someone who would willing harm someone," Kane was a bit surprised by that statement considering what Dean told him last night. "And he could be a lot worse compared to those other cowards." Considering that would be a compliment compared to how Ashley treats people. "He hasn't treated me like a princess like most people do, nor is he a suck up." Ashley continued, surprising Kane mostly. "At the very least Dean seems to tolerate me, and yet he doesn't seem to back down when I put him down." She continued, closing her eyes as she turned her head in a small huff. "He isn't afraid to get rough when he gets angry, and he at least tries to be friendly towards someone like me."

"He must be a saint if he's getting high praises from a spoiled princess like you." Keaton remarked, seemingly interested as most people wouldn't get such praise from the princess of the leaders. "But I do wonder what you meant about him getting rough when he is angry. What happened between the two of you that would put you in a risky position?" Keaton asked, raising an eyebrow. Kane felt his breathing stop short after hearing that question. But it seemed that Ashley was able to quickly recover from the remark.

"T-That's none of your concern perverted ox!" Ashley stammered, grabbing the cup and throwing at Keaton's head, only to have the glass cup bounce off of Keaton's ox skull, causing the cup to shatter on the floor when it landed. "At least he doesn't try and creep on everyone like you tend to do." Ashley snapped as her face became a darker shade of red. "Groping them through their clothes and passing it off with some lame excuse." Ashley stammered with small pants towards the end of her mini rant.

"Careful," Keaton remarked in a taunting tone. "Don't need you blowing a blood vessel because you don't know how to have fun." Keaton added, leaning back in the chair with his arms resting against the back of his head. "It's always fun when people can explore their bodies in a natural setting." Keaton added as he closed one of his eyes. "To hold your lover in a tight embrace and make them feel amazing is the duty of any lover." Seemed like the conversation was starting to go off the rails if this kept going.

"Don't be disgusting. Why do you people always seem to so interested in sex anyways?" Ashley huffed in her defense. "It's gross, and you get hot and sweaty. It's repulsive." Ashley snapped, standing up and knocking the chair over in the process. "I figured with your nose you would find the smells of the human body disgusting. Like raw and decaying onions." A small gag came out of Ashley towards the last bit, causing her to cover her mouth. "There is no way you could get any pleasure out of something that smells disgusting like that."

"That's where you're wrong." Keaton remarked as he tilted his head to the side. "Being able to smell your lovers scent is one of the best things after sex." Keaton chimed up as he leaned back in his chair a bit. "Given if they make sure that they have a proper pH balance of course." Keaton added, wiggling in his finger at Ashley as if he was lecturing her. "Plus, it makes you feel like you're one being when you're connected. You no longer are two people, but one." The more that the two went on, the more irritated that Amelis seemed to appear. "To bring your lover to ecstasy is like allowing them to experience the creation of life in a big bang."

"Enough you two." Amelia interrupted their discussion, giving them both a hardy glare. "We're getting off track with your mindless bickering about sex." The discussion seemed to be trying Amelia's nerves. "Felicia, you're more likely to be honest. What's your opinion on Dean?" Not like Felicia would talk about wanting to bang Dean, unlike the two previous leaders were.

"Well, let's see." Felicia spoke up, bringing a finger towards the edge of her lips. "He does seem to have a lot of pride, and he seems to be eager to get revenge on the Cowards." Short and to the point. "Though I notice that he often relies on Kane for a majority of the time." Felicia continued, a small grin forming on her face, practically throwing Kane under the bus.

"The way he eagerly looks to Kane for advice is like a puppy waiting for his master to give a command." Felicia continued, a big smile appearing on her face the more she talked about it. "And the way that the two smile at each other, it's really precious." Felicia teased, a small chuckle leaving her lips in the process. "He even stood up to Miles. Saying that he wanted to hear Kane's background story from Kane himself, it made my heart flutter just hearing him say that." Felicia continued, almost brimming with joy.

"Stop trying to put me and Dean in a relationship! You're making it sound weird!" Kane quickly spoke up wanting to make Felicia stop, his face becoming flustered out of embarrassment. The way that Felicia kept going, it would give Amelia the wrong idea about what was going on between them. "Besides, he's not like that at all. I don't even think that Dean is gay. After all, he gets flustered around anyone who gets up close to him." Kane remarked, not appreciating being put on the spot like that.

"But he doesn't seem to be actively seeking them out." Felicia rebuttaled, causing Keaton to chuckle a bit. "I saw him around the ship while you were recovering in your room." Felicia commented, causing everyone's attention to focus on her. "He seemed more distant around people that he doesn't seem to know. Like no one else could seem to catch his eyes the way that Kane does." Hearing this for the first time caused Kane's eyes to widen. Did Dean really not look at anyone the way he often gazed at Kane?

"Oh?" Keaton asked as his interest peaked from that statement. "Seems like he may very well be pansexual then." Keaton remarked, moving to lean against the table a bit. "If he doesn't seem to be perverted around Ashley, and he doesn't actively look for someone, he might want to connect to someone on a more emotional level." The look on Keaton's face indicated that he seemed to be plotting something, but it seemed like now wasn't the time for it.

"Whether or not he is trying to get with one of the leaders doesn't concern me. I just want to know if he is even worth meeting with." Amelia snapped once more, the constant change of the subject seemed to be wearing her down a bit. Not that Kane could really blame her. Even he was getting a bit tired of the subject seemingly being drifted towards romance opinions on who should be with Dean.

"I'd say it would be worth your time to listen to him." Miles seemingly spoke up, causing everyone to be surprised by the sudden remark. Even Kane was surprised that Miles would even suggest that Amelia should listen to what Dean has to offer her considering that they didn't spend too much time together.

"I'm surprised to hear this coming from you Miles." Amelia remarked, her interest seeming to be perked. "Normally you wouldn't even suggest someone who would waste their time coming to meet me." Amelia continued, moving one leg to rest over the other. Studying Miles' face, it wasn't clear if Miles had already made up his mind on if he should help out with the plan or not. "What made you decide that it is worth the time to come and see me about his plan?" Amelia asked, interested in knowing what was going on in Miles' head.

Miles glanced towards Kane for a brief second before turning his attention towards Amelia once more. "I figured that it would be fun to listen to what Dean has to offer." Miles remarked with a small shrug as he leaned towards Keaton. "Besides, Dean has already told Ashley, Kane, and Felicia about his plans and what is driving him to want to get revenge. So why not see if Dean still feels that way the longer he spends time making his way towards the rest of us? To have him win our final decision on his terms with his words?" Miles remarked, a coy grin on his face like Kane had never seen before.

Kane didn't know how he should feel when Miles made it sound like that. What was the man thinking? It seemed to raise some flags, but it wasn't like Kane could really do anything about it. All he had to do was escort Dean to the other leaders and let them figure out if they would still support him or not. Granted it might have been easier if Dean collected the leaders in one room and talked about the plan to them while they were in one location, but it might not go very well. Considering how hard it was to get through one meeting as it was, getting to talk about a plan to destroy the Millennium would have been disastrous in one meeting place.

"I didn't hear the plan myself." Ashley spoke up as she crossed one leg over the other. "I just simply told him to ask me and I would be on board no matter what the plan was." Ashley remarked, seeming to catch the other leaders by surprise. "What? I'm the leader of the Envy clan. Of course I was going to say yes as long as he asked me." Ashley continued, though it seemed that there was a bit of disbelief that still lingered on the other leaders' faces.

"I don't imagine why you would agree to something when you don't even know the details of the plan." Amelia commented in a nagging tone, wondering if she needed to teach the other leaders not to fall for lies from someone who was on the station. "That's something that I would have expected out of a child, not someone who is the leader of a clan, Ashley." Amelia remarked, her disappointment was evident, but the damage had already been done.

"What do you expect, Amelia?" Ashley snapped. "I was envious of Kane for having someone he could count on like Dean. Of course I wanted to have the feeling of someone being able to count on me." Ashley remarked, though her voice sounded a bit pouty with the explanation. This seemed to make Kane realize that Ashley must have felt a bit left out considering that the only other leader like her was Kane, and it wasn't like they could ever become romantically involved. Not to mention Kane didn't exactly make friends with the other leaders. It certainly made Kane feel like an asshole for not realizing sooner what was going on with Ashley sooner.

"Amelia, you haven't even met Dean." Kane chimed in, figuring that he could set things right. "I'm sure if he wasn't traveling with me, there would be no way that Ashley would have agreed to help him as quickly as she did." It wasn't like he knew what was going on in Ashley's mind, but he was certain that she would have agreed if Kane asked her. "She knows me. After all, we spend all winter together so I know if I were to have pulled Ashley to the side and tell her that it was a bad idea, she wouldn't have agreed to help him like she did."

"Kane..." Ashley softly called his name, seeming to be touched by what he had said. No one liked getting lectures from Amelia, considering that it often made those being scolded feel like a bug once Amelia was done, it was nice to know that at least Kane had her back. "I know that it might seem like a mistake to simply go with the flow, but once you meet with him, I'm sure you will see that he stands by his words to take down those who abandoned us to rot on the destroyed world." Ashley continued, her voice showing her new determination to stand by Dean's side.

Once again the silence seemed to fall in the room. Everyone's eyes were on Amelia as she took everything in. Sparing a glance towards Keaton, she could tell that her lover would also be wanting to meet with this Dean. Though she didn't like it, she would be out voted by the others who had the luxury of already meeting the man. "Fine. Bring him to the Greed clan." Amelia relented. "Of course you'll have to bring him to meet with Keaton beforehand." Amelia continued before a soft sigh escaping her lips as she gave into the pressure of seeing what Dean had to offer.

"I'm sure you'll want to stay a bit in Miles' clan for a bit before you make your journey to see me." Amelia continued, sitting up right as if she was prim and proper. "Once you arrive, I'll have a private audience with him." Amelia spoke, making a plan of action for the other leaders to follow. "If he is able to convince me that his cause is to help us and even does the ritual to become one of us," Amelia paused as she didn't like the idea that would soon follow.

"Then I'll even give him my backstory." The other leaders were surprised that Amelia would willingly tell a stranger the truth about her past after all these years. "Not that it would really do much good, but I'm willing to promise you that much." Amelia continued, shooting a glance towards Kane at this time. "I'll expect you to give me a full report about him before I make the decision to see if we will go with his little plan. After all, I don't want to see our progress squelched because of one man. Is that understood?" Amelia finished, sounding more like a leader in her commanding tone.

"Yes ma'am!" Everyone spoke in unison. It seemed that they just might be able to pull this off. The question that seemed to remain, would Dean be able to successfully convince Keaton and Amelia to put everyone's lives in danger if it meant that they could finally get rid of the Elite for good? If they did, this would make all the sacrifices that everyone endured worth it. At least in Kane's mind it did.

"Now that the meeting is over with, I think it's time that we have our own little celebration." Amelia spoke, a small lingering smile landing on her face as they were finally done with the official business. "We will be coming up with ideas for the banquet and what to serve. If you don't feel like partaking in this discussion, you are free to leave."

It would be a couple of hours of working out the details, but eventually Kane and Ashley started to walk back towards their building first as the rest of the adults started to indulge in some liquor as they often did when they got together. The walk seemed to take a bit longer as some snow had started to pile up on the ground. The bitter wind didn't help matters either, but at least this would give the two some time to talk. The crunching of the snow seemed loud as the clouds overhead darkened. The silence between them was deafening, almost making one wonder who would talk first about what happened in the meeting. Sure they were able to convince Amelia to meet up with Dean, but what if she didn't agree with his plan? Then what?

"You didn't have to do that for me." Ashley finally spoke up, seemingly causing the two to stop walking in the cold. Kane seemed to be a bit surprised that Ashley was the first to say something, but he was also relieved as the whole conversation is a bit awkward on both of them. "I'm sure I should have received the lecture for what I did to Dean." Ashley continued, her eyes glancing down towards Kane's boots as she couldn't look at him directly. "I pretty much trapped him like a rat after spotting him in the bathtub." Kane remained silent, figuring that he would allow Ashley to speak her mind, even if it might have seemed to be a bit scattered.

"I didn't mean to walk in on him." Ashley continued, her face becoming a bit flustered as she recounted what happened. "But seeing him turning red, I used some of that special salt from the springs, the ones that are used for common aches and pain." Hearing that, it seemed to dawn on Kane that the salt bath was what Dean felt that woke him up while he was still in the bath.

"You know how I tend to get when put into an awkward situation Kane... I become this cocky little princess that everyone is used to seeing." A small grunt left Ashley's lips as she clenched her fists. "So I sort of lashed out on him." By this time Ashley had small warm tears stinging her eyes. "And now... Dean probably hates me because I don't know how to interact with other people." Ashley continued as a small sniffle escaped her.

"That's not true." Kane finally piped up, moving to place a hand on Ashley's shoulder, causing the short female to look up at him. "In fact, Dean felt bad about what he did." It was best to let Ashley know now before things get worse between the two of them. "He figures that you hate him for it." Not like Ashley would have known, but it was nice to see that Ashley was actually more than just some uptight princess that didn't care what people thought of her.

"Hey, I have an idea." Kane remarked, figuring that there was a way in which all of this could work out for the better. Sure they may have had a rough start, but things could always swing around. "Since we have a couple of weeks until the banquet, why don't you try to get along with Dean." It wouldn't be exactly easy, but knowing Kane, he would be able to come up with something.

"How? We don't have anything in common." Ashley spoke, a small scowl forming on her face, almost like she was doubting Kane's plan even before hearing it. "I don't know anything about him." That was the problem with getting to know someone. Always trying to get around the small points of interest. "Like, what his favorite color is, or what kind of animal he likes, or anything that might be used to start a conversation." Ashley started to list off small talk pointers that she got from Miles a few years ago when she was still trying to make friends.

"Then why not simply ask him?" Kane remarked, flashing Ashley a smile. "The best way to get to know someone is by simply asking them." Kane continued before he started to walk back towards the house. "Besides, I think that you and Dean could get along if you tried." Ashley didn't know if she could really believe that, considering that they were already bumping heads as it was. "I know he does like books. Plus he used to help his mother grow plants while they were on the station." These were only the few things that Kane had learned simply by talking to Dean.

"Well, I guess it wouldn't hurt to at least try." Ashley remarked, glancing back down with a small pout as she continued to follow behind Kane. "I'll find him later and try to apologize in my own way." At least that was better than nothing.

"Good idea." Kane nodded, glad that he could at the very least help to clear this whole miscommunication between the two. As they got closer, Kane glanced down to see that Ashley was starting to return to normal, which was a good thing. "So, care to tell me the real reason why you cut your hair?" Kane asked, a small smile tugging on the corner of his lips. "I know it wasn't because you wanted to look older." That was a bull face lie on Ashley's part.

"If you must know," Ashley spoke up, her defiant voice seeming to return. "It's because I realized that I would be at a disadvantage if someone grabbed a hold of my long hair." Whether or not she was being serious is still up for debate, but considering that Dean was able to startle Ashley by using her hair against her, it did make sense. "Sure he may have scared me and made me feel weak and vulnerable, but it made me think that perhaps a bit of change is what I really need." Ashley continued as she reached up to play with her hair once more. "To stop acting like a spoiled brat if I want to make friends." A faint smile seemed to grow on Ashley's face as she took the words to heart.

"Seems like Dean was able to get through that thick skull of yours, huh?" Kane lightly teased, earning a sharp jab of Ashley's elbow into his rib cage. "Ow! What was that for?!" Kane yelped, moving to hold his side. The pain felt like it was slowly spreading with each throb against his side. Despite being so short, Ashley never held back her punches.

"That's for being an idiot." Ashley huffed, moving to walk ahead of him. Not that Kane could simply run after her, he took the time to glance up at the house and see the smoke slowly rising from the chimney. At least it seemed like Dean was keeping the place and nice and warm for them. Seeing the lights shining in the building, how full of life it felt, it was like coming home after being away for so long.

"To think, by this time next year, we'll be able to see if those cowards will finally disappear for good." Kane thought to himself, keeping his hand on the side where Ashley elbowed him. *"I just hope that Ashley and Dean can work things out before too long. After all, she's dealing with her first crush after everything that has happened. Not like I can really blame her. Dean has a way of speaking to your soul. His words make you feel like you could actually achieve anything you set your mind on. Which is why I believe in him and will back him up."* Kane took a jagged breath in, feeling the cold air give him a bit of energy, before he headed into the warm house. In a way, this was the closest thing to feel like home to Kane, and he wanted to treasure the moments for as long as he could.

CHAPTER THIRTEEN: *Scorned Love*

A s the weeks had passed from the meeting, things had started to become stable in the house that Ashley, Kane, and Dean were currently staying in. Even though Ashley would find herself acting like she was on a high horse, Dean had learned to simply walk away from her small tantrums. With the help of Kane, the house became more pleasant to stay in. The nights were getting colder by the day as the snow started to settle down in the streets. There were no longer any vehicles that roamed the streets as it was still too risky to allow people to drive on unstable roads. But that didn't mean that no one was wandering around the streets during the day. There was still much to do after all with the end of the year banquet approaching. However it was rare to see a single person out and about at night when it was the coldest.

With a small groan leaving his lips, Dean's eyes started to flutter as he stared up at the familiar ceiling he had gotten used to waking up to. Dean struggled to lift his head as his body refused to escape from the warmth the bed offered him, but he was able to eventually sit up as his wrinkled top helped to trap some of his body heat to keep him warm. Glancing down, Dean noticed that Kane's arm had been draped over his chest but had slid down as Dean sat up.

It seemed that during their time sleeping in the same bed, the two had started to seek each other out for warmth. There was heat that could be easily felt escaping from the space between the sheets when either one of them would move. Shifting his gaze to see Kane laying on his stomach, Dean could feel the others' knee slightly poking him. With Kane's hair disheveled, and a bit of drool drying against the corner of his lips, Dean couldn't help but feel the corner's of his lips tug back. It wasn't every day that Dean got to see Kane looking vulnerable.

The coldness of the room was quick to greet Dean, causing him to shiver as the warmth of the blankets was calling to him. "Cold." Kane grumbled, reaching down to grab the blankets to wrap up towards his shoulders. With narrowed eyes, Dean could barely see in the darkened room. It must have been still early in the morning, though Dean didn't have a possible way of telling without any light. Reluctantly Dean reached out to turn on the small light against the bedside. The room seemed to brighten up, causing Dean to close his right eye. It seemed that the heat must have stopped during the night as the room felt as cold as the outside temperatures.

Shifting out of the bed, Dean placed his bare feet against the rug underneath the bed, saving him the dreaded shocking sensation of bare feet on the ice cold wooden floor. By this time Kane seemed shifted towards rolling over on his side, wrapping a bit of the blanket around him to keep the heat trapped inside the large comforter. Reaching down, Dean pulled the slippers they had gotten a few days prior to the snow falling down and sticking, slipping them on to keep his bare feet safe from the frigid cold.

"Waking up freezing sucks." Dean grumpily thought as he forced himself out of the bed. His feet shifted towards the closed wardrobe that had a fuzzy bathrobe that would at least keep Dean warm. At first Dean was against getting the bathrobe since it was a bit bulky as it was made out of black sheep wool, but now it was his saving grace with the freezing temperatures that was greeting them.

Taking a step forward, a small splashing sound reached Dean's ears, causing the groggy man to look down to see that there was a water puddle that hadn't frozen over yet. *"So that's why it's freezing."* Dean grumbled, mentally glad that he wore the slipper to keep his feet from not only getting wet, but to make him even more cold. Apparently the radiator in the room that was keeping them warm had broken, causing the frigid temperatures to take over.

Looking towards the radiator, it appears that there was a small leak dripping from a pipe. Considering that there wasn't much lighting, Dean wouldn't be able to successfully tell where the leak was coming from, but figured that he might as well find Ashley to let her know about the leak. He could wake Kane up and explain his finding, but the tribal leader was seemingly happily sleeping the morning away. It was a rarity considering that Kane often woke up early to get breakfast started. But seeing as how Kane had been getting to bed a bit later than normal, Dean took this chance to see if he could make them something for once.

Reaching a hand up, Dean started to lightly rub the back of his head before glancing around to see if there was anything he could use to stop the dripping. Spotting part of the towel that Kane had used during his bath last night, Dean was quick to snatch it before shoving the fabric under the radiator. "Hopefully that will keep the damage from getting worse. I'll inform either Ashley or Kane once they get up." Not like Dean could do much about it right now. He didn't understand how the radiators worked, so he left it to those who were used to fixing it. That way he wouldn't mess things up more.

With a small huff, Dean stood up before walking towards the door. With a twist of the door knob, it didn't take long before the warmth from the hallway started to seep into the room. It felt like a warm wave from the ocean sweeping over Dean's body, helping to thaw him. *"Well, at least I know it was just our radiator, so maybe if I keep the door open it should warm up the room in no time."* Dean thought to himself before glancing over his shoulder towards the bed.

"At least then Kane won't have to worry about waking up to a cold room." Dean didn't appreciate being cold, but what could he really do? Sure he may have gotten used to waking up cold in the pod, but now that he was used to waking up warm, he didn't want to be cold ever again. Stepping out of the room, Dean kept the door halfway open before walking down the hallway. Glancing out of one of the windows, Dean took notice of the snow falling ever so gently onto the snow piles that had built up during the night.

Even though this wasn't the first time he was watching the snowfall, it still was amazing to watch the fragile flakes fall from the sky. The first time that the snow had started to fall, the three housemates were just about to settle down for dinner. Kane was the first one to notice that it was snowing. The tribal leader looked as joyful as any child seeing snow for the first time. The eager twinkling in Kane's eyes, the bright smile that seemed spread wide across his face, and big puff of hot air leaving his lips as Kane looked up towards the sky without any type of protection on was something that Dean couldn't exactly ignore. Ashley may have seemed to be a bit indifferent to the falling snow, but Dean was able to catch the sparkle in her eyes as she looked up to see the snow falling.

"Guess Kane was right about watching the snowfall." Dean mumbled to himself, moving towards the window as he placed his hand on top of the cold surface. "It's really fun to watch." A small tug formed on Kane's lips as he pulled away, watching the outline of his hand linger on the surface as he pulled the warm hand away from the cold surface.

Kane didn't exactly have much to do today as everything was being wrapped up for the banquet, meaning that he was allowed to sleep in. As Dean made his way down the stairs, it seemed that Ashley was already up and about making something for them to eat. Guess she was a morning bird regardless of her age. Since breakfast was already being taken care of, Dean headed into the den that had some books in which he would be able to read. Since Dean was stuck inside the house all day, he used the time to read some of the old books that lingered on the shelves. There was still the issue of the radiator needing to be fixed, but Dean would bring that up later.

THE rest of the morning wasn't very eventful. The first one to greet Dean was Kane, who seemingly noticed the towel under the radiator. The tribal leader decided to take it upon himself to fix the radiator as this wasn't the first time it had broken down during the winter while Kane was there. After a quick breakfast, Dean was in the living room with the woolly bathrobe no longer draped over him. Instead Dean was wearing some slacks and a regular dark blue buttoned up shirt with the black undershirt sticking out as the two top buttons were undone.

With his sleeves rolled up, Dean found himself sitting comfortable on the couch that was centered in the living room with some books he picked out resting beside him. His feet were propped up on the coffee table, the house slippers covering his feet as they rested close to the roaring fire. With his right arm propped up against the arm rest, Dean held the light novel he was reading with his left hand. The look on his face indicated one of two things, he was either absorbed into the book or he found it boring.

The living room was fairly big compared to the other rooms that Dean had the fortune of exploring. The walls were a faded aquamarine blue with bits of brick exposed in various patches around the room. The fireplace had specks of black soot sprinkled against the ivory frame. Against the right side of the room rested four bookcases with various books that the previous owners had left behind. The left side provided a window towards the gated fence, only allowing for the buildings that peaked over the fence to be visible.

"Do you really have to put your dirty feet on top of my good coffee table?" A familiar angry voice seemed to call out from the door. Dean placed the folded piece of paper he was using as a bookmark on the page that he was reading before he glanced over his left shoulder. Ashley seemed to be wearing a ruffled gray top that seemed to tuck into some dark pants that draped close to the floor. Small white socks poked out against the hem of her pants, showing the edges of her rather small toes. She wore a headband with her green jeweled encrusted skull that always rested on the left side as her one long cowlick bobbed in place as she walked towards Dean.

"I'm sorry," Dean spoke in a rather dull tone before turning to move his attention back to reading his book. "I have long legs. Therefore I need to put them on the coffee table in order to get comfortable." The dull sarcastic tone was evident as Dean didn't see the need to really argue about whether or not he should have his feet up on the little wooden table or not. It seemed like they were at least being civil around each other, though they were both making snide remarks when given the chance.

"I didn't expect you to disrespect another person's property. Is that how you were raised by those cowards?" Ashley harshly remarked as she reached the other side of the couch, making sure to be away from Dean. "No wonder you felt no remorse when nuking the planet." Ashley grumbled under her breath before moving towards a chair that seemed to linger closer towards the window. It was close enough to the fireplace where she could feel the heat coming off of the fire to keep her warm.

"That might have counted for an insult if it wasn't for the fact that I hated everything about the station and would rather see it blown up than spend another second worrying if I can see it while looking up at the sky." Dean retorted, moving his feet off of the coffee table. Shifting his body to lay on the couch, Dean figured that he would find himself more relaxed if he used the book to block out having to see Ashley.

As it stood, Ashley had positioned herself to sit sideways in the chair. Her back resting against the right side of the chair while her legs dangled over the left. It seemed that her sketchbook rested neatly against her lap as she stared at the blank sheet with a pencil resting in her right hand. "That makes two of us." Ashley huffed a little, turning her head away from Dean. Silence fell in the room as the two went about their own activities.

An hour had passed before Dean's eyes grew tired of scanning the pages. Finding a good resting spot in the book he was reading, Dean slid the bookmark into the crease. With a groan, Dean was quickly up from laying on the couch. His joints were a bit stiff, but at least he wasn't having as much trouble with moving about since he was released from the hospital.

Glancing towards Ashley, Dean noticed that the figure in the sketch she was drawing was a woman. Even though he couldn't see the features right away as the sketch was drawn in pencil, Dean removed himself from the couch to see if maybe he could get a better look at it. Walking towards the window to watch some of the snow fall, Dean glanced over his right shoulder to take in more of the details.

The woman had soft curled hair with a single bang that seemed to rest between her eyes. Her eyebrows were thin as her lashes were thick. Soft cheek bones seemed to show off the woman's slender cheeks as the edges of the woman's hair brushed against her right shoulder. A soft pout seemed to show a lifetime of sadness while the eyes almost seemed to be hollowed, as if the woman was a prisoner. Her jaw seemed to be clenched as if the words she tried to speak out couldn't flow, as if her own mouth was a dam. Scattered freckles almost looked like stars on her face. The figure through her clothes was slender, almost bony, like she refused to eat as food seemed to taste like ash in her mouth.

For someone that appeared to be sad, the portrait could easily draw you in. "Whose that?" Dean asked, seemingly causing Ashley to jump in her seat. It would have been hilarious if it wasn't for the fact that Dean had no intention of scaring Ashley. He was just simply curious as to who Ashley was drawing. It wasn't Felicia that she was drawing, perhaps it was this Amelia that Dean heard about?

"What is wrong with you?!" Ashley snapped, pulling the sketch book close to her, seemingly guarding it from having Dean see what she was drawing. The flushed cheeks was an indicator that Ashley seemed to be a bit embarrassed by either what she was drawing or that she didn't like people seeing her sketch.

"Sorry." Dean quickly apologized, walking over towards the couch. Sitting down on the end closest to Ashley, Dean watched as the flushed princess started to erase the small mark she made in the corner when Dean startled her. "I was just curious about the woman you were drawing." Dean continued, tilting his head a bit to get a better look at it from the angle he was sitting in. "Who is she?"

At the question, Ashley let out an agitated sigh as she gripped the pencil in her hand. "She was my mother." Ashley remarked, twirling the pencil around to continue working on the sketch. "And before you ask," Ashley was quick to snap. "She died by that bastard's hands for the crime she committed." This news was something that Dean wasn't expecting. Considering that he didn't know anything about Ashley, it made sense that one of her parents died during the incident involving the leaders.

"What crime did she commit?" Dean asked, a bit interested to know what happened. By the way that Ashley was behaving, Dean doubted that he would really be able to get a good answer from her. Ashley appeared to be guarded like she wouldn't dare to speak about the incident. Dean could have asked Kane about it, but Dean was the type of man who would much rather hear it from the source than anything else.

Ashley seemed to remain silent at the question. Her pencil was not moving at all, as if she was trying to figure out if she should trust Dean with the history of what happened. After all, they were in the room where her mother committed the crime. After a few minutes, Ashley set her sketchbook down on her stomach. Tilting her head back, Ashley stared up at the ceiling. "... She murdered my father in cold blood before trying to kill me five years ago..."

***

It happened five years ago, the night that Ashley's mother had killed her father. Ashley was only thirteen at the time, playing with her little brother who happened to be three years younger than her. Her brother's name was James, a silent boy who had dark brown hair with piercing green eyes. His hair was thick as his bangs seemed to swoop over his eyes. Ashley loved her little brother, often doing what she could to protect him from their mother's wrath. She never hit them, but after learning about their father's affair, she started to grow cold towards her children. They had learned about their father's affair on a cold rainy night a few years prior.

A woman dressed in a cloak appeared one night. After knocking on the door repeatedly, Ashley's father Michael had finally grown irritated and answered it. Ashley didn't get a good look at her face, considering that her father was in the way, but she did see the shocked and hurtful gaze that lingered on her own mother's face when the evidence of the affair came to light in the form of James. He was barely a month old and the woman couldn't take care of James anymore. Deciding to leave their child with James, the woman left shortly after, never to be seen again.

After that night, things started to grow worse. Ashley took care of James and barely allowed anyone near him without being close by. Around the tenth year anniversary of the incident, the arguments stopped altogether. Ashley's parents started to live in separate rooms on the other side of the house. Michael's drinking seemed to get worse to the point where he was hardly sober anymore. Ashley's mother Lily had started to take down any portraits that they had together and burned them in the fireplace, erasing any happy memories that were once associated with the portraits.

THE night was quiet, except for the sound of the rain pounding against the glass. The dull roar of the fire seemed to heat up the room as Lily stood in front of the iron bars that lined the fireplace. A white rose shawl draped around her arms as her blue eyes gazed into the fire. The black silken nightgown she was wearing barely dangled over her feet. Her face looked sunken in from her refusal to eat. The bags under her eyes showed the sleepless nights that she went after discovering her husband's affairs. Apparently the woman from that night wasn't the only one. Apparently she was just one of the more recent women that her husband had messed around with, or at least that was what he admitted to during one of his drunken ramblings.

Crossing her thin and frail arms over her torso, Lily watched as the last portrait that she made was burning against the logs. It took much longer to burn thanks to some of the rain getting in through the chimney. Lily's hair was parted to the right, her locks seeming to bunch together into a messy bun. A small creak in the floor boards caused Lily to turn towards the entrance, ready to scold the children to head back to bed. "Ash, James, go back to-" She stopped, seeing the mess that Michael had been the one standing in the doorway rather than one of the children. "What do you want?" Lily sneered, turning to look back at the fire.

"Is that any way to treat your husband?" Michael spoke, his words a bit slurred as he stammered forward into the room. Michael appeared to be wearing a white buttoned up shirt that had buttons either missing or in the wrong hole. One side of his shirt was tucked into his dark blue jeans while the other half hung outside. His blond hair was all over the place, like the locks couldn't figure out which direction they wanted to go. His beard had become just as untameable. Before everything seemed to go downhill for the family, Michael often kept his hair slicked back with maybe a single strand of hair that lingered almost like a cowlick between his eyes as he would sport a cleaned goatee. Now he just looked like a wild man that was living in their home.

"My husband?" Lily seemed to scuff as she turned to face the man who used to be her husband. "My husband was supposed to love only me." Lily snapped as she glared daggers towards the mess of a man Michael was. "My husband was supposed to help me raise my child. Not go around sleeping with countless women like he was some young spry rooster!" Lily growled, her eyes glaring at Michael as he continued to stagger forward.

"And wives aren't supposed to be the leader of a whole clan." Michael rebuttaled as he made his way over towards the chair. Slumping down in it, Michael let out a loud groan as he tilted his head back, the booze he had consumed earlier made his head feel heavy. "And yet here we are." Michael remarked, tilting his head to the side as he glared towards Lily. The glossed over eyes reflected Lily's slender frame as a silhouette against the fire.

"You can't even possibly expect me to believe that the reason you cheated on me, with countless women, was because I'm the leader of the Envy clan." Lily couldn't even believe that Michael was making that assumption straight to her face. "Were you using my title as a way for you to get into a bunch of girl's pants?" Lily accused as she clenched her fists in anger. "That you could get any girl to spread their legs for you because your wife is the leader of the Envy clan? Is that really the excuse you're going with?" She continued with disbelief in her voice.

"It worked, didn't it?" Michael chuckled, raising his arms as he shrugged, as if it was no big deal. "The beautiful ladies over the land seemed to take quite the notice of me once I came in with you wrapped around my arm." Michael chuckled as he could see how angry Lily was getting the more that he talked. "Making all the girls envious...making them want a piece of me." Michael reminisced as he closed his eyes with a smile lingering on his face. "After all, you had so many male suitors who were there chatting you up, so I figured that I might as well indulge in some company as well." Lily's eyes widened at the accusation that Michael was trying to imply, her mouth gaped open at his remark.

"I never cheated on you Michael!" Lily snapped, grabbed the bit of fabric of her nightgown to keep from throwing something at the man's head. "And those gentlemen were the other leaders of the clan! I had no interest in any of them!" Lily continued, feeling the sting in her eyes as she failed to see who Michael was before she married him. "You ....were the only man I loved..." A small sniff escaped Lily as she admitted it. Even through everything that Michael had put her though, she still loved him. "To me, you were the only one that I ever found the desire to be with. And yet you...." Lily trailed off as a whimper escaped her lips.

"Don't give me that teary act." Michael snapped, sitting upright in the chair now, a scowl landing on his face as he gripped the end of the arm rest. "I saw you walk off with that Nero guy plenty of times. The uh, leader of the Wrath clan." Michael growled, his mind a bit foggy from the amount of liquor he had consumed. "I saw the way you two looked at each other. Always seeming to communicate without words as you would saunter off as if nobody noticed." Lily looked at Michael with a bewildered gaze at the accusation. "But I did!" Michael raised his voice as he started to stumble forward a little.

"We talked about who I was planning on taking over for the leader position if anything were to happen to me." Lily responded in her defense, watching as Michael stumbled towards her. "With the clans at each other's throat, I was trying to make a deal with him that would benefit all of us." Lily continued as she let go of her nightgown. "If we had to choose sides, I wanted to make sure that our child would be safe." Lily continued, her arms moving to wrap around her body before taking a few steps away from Michael who got closer to her.

"Oh?" Michael started to ask as he raised his right eyebrow. "So you only cared about Ashley's safety, huh?" Michael spoke in an accusing tone as he started to close the gap between the two of them. "But what about James' safety? Or are you a cold and heartless bitch that you don't care about a defenseless child?" Michael spoke, steadying his steps as he moved closer to Lily. Despite being inebriated, Michael was closing the distance between them rather easily.

"He's not my child." Lily snapped, glaring at Michael who was closer to her now. The stench of booze was almost overwhelming. "If I had given birth to James, I would do anything for him, like a proper mother would." Lily continued, her glare intensifying. "Unlike his mother, I never would give him up." Lily snapped with a sharp hiss at the end. "But then again, she's nothing more than some whore who likes to have men warm her bed while all she does is spread her le-" Lily started to speak before feeling the sharp sting of Michael slapping her across the face.

"Don't you dare act as if you know her." Michael growled, his displeasure apparent as he glared down at Lily. The shock on Lily's face reflected in Michael's eyes as she looked up at him. There was no love or warmth in his eyes anymore. It felt like he loved the woman who gave him James more than he loved Lily. This was the reality that Lily had tried to ignore for so long, but knew that it was always going to be there.

"You son of a..." Lily seethed under her breath as she placed a hand over her cheek that was smacked. "If you want to play this game, then I should tell you something." Lily grumbled, slowly removing her hand from her face, though it didn't seem to take the stinging sensation away. Taking a deep breath in, Lily did her best to compose herself like a true leader should.

"Oh? And what is that?" Michael asked, trying his best to hold in a burp that was trying to escape him. He was quite interested in hearing just what Lily had to say that would perk his interest.

"Well for one, there is no way that you'll ever be the tribal leader if something ever happens to me." Lily spoke, a small devious grin landing on her face as if she had been waiting years to tell Michael something. "Because I already told Nero who I want for the leader of the clan way before you started your cheating spree." Lily studied Michael's face, ready to see the anger that would rise once she let him in on the secret.

"So who will get it if it isn't me?" Michael asked, almost a bit skeptical that anything Lily could say or do that would surprise him. Not like he couldn't figure out what she was going to say. She was probably going to say that nobody gets the position or that the tribe would be absorbed into the Wrath clan.

"I decided that Ashley gets it." Lily giggled as she witnessed the change of facial expression on Michael's face go from amused to confused, only to finally shift towards anger. "And the rest of the clan will vote for her as well." Lily continued, only to start to cackle a bit. "While you were busy with your sluts, I made sure that you would never be able to get your hands on being the leader." The look of devious pleasure rested on Lily's face while the fire snapped the frame, causing a loud crack in the room.

"You little-" Michael growled, reaching out to grab Lily's throat with both of his hands. "You honestly think that a child who just barely became a teenager could handle the responsibilities of becoming a leader?" Michael spat, his grip only seeming to get tighter as he watched Lily's face getting redder by the second. The sounds of her struggling to breath mixed with choking almost echoed in the room. "If you expect me to stay back and watch this clan become nothing more than the train wreck it already is, you're sorely mistaken." Michael continued in an angry growl as he watched Lily's eyes starting to tear up as she frantically beat on his arms to get him to loosen his grip around her neck.

The more that Lily seemed to struggle, the more intensely Michael stared at her. He was waiting to watch Lily's life be squeezed out of her eyes. All the resentment he felt in the years after his affairs became public, the hatred growing in his heart for the ones he was supposed to love, and the sneers and gossips that people spread about him seemed to keep his hands tightly around Lily's throat.

Michael could feel how quickly her heart was beating against his hands. The way Lily's throat seemed to close more and more with each gasp she tried to gasp for more air. Watching the beads of tears roll down Lily's cheeks before the cold salty water reached his knuckles. It all felt like it was worth the last ten or so years he had to put up with this. That Michael was finally getting the payback for putting up with all the bullshit that came from marrying the leader of the Envy clan.

"What are you doing to her?!" A small voice shrilled, causing Michael to glance over and see James standing there. James' mouth was agape in horror witnessing his father strangled Lily. It wasn't long before the sounds of someone's footsteps coming down the stairs reached Michael's ears, causing him to let go of Lily's throat.

Falling to the ground, Lily gasped and coughed for air. "This doesn't concern you James." Michael spoke in a stern tone, though any emotions behind it were gone. "Go back to bed. I'll deal with you in the morning." Michael ordered, but James wasn't the type to listen to him.

James stood in the door frame, seemingly frozen as he didn't understand what was going on. "Jay, what's wrong?" A voice called out, causing James to flinch. With a quirk turning of his head, James' eyes started to water up as he spotted Ashley in her light green nightgown with her hair tied back in a ponytail. With a shaky hand, James raised his finger to point into the room. Ashley didn't waste any time running towards the doorway to make sure that her brother was alright.

"James! What did I say?" Michael growled out, his voice booming against the walls. "Go to bed this instant young man!" Michael didn't have the time to deal with his children becoming upset at the sight of their parents arguing.

"What the hell is going on here?" Ashley shouted, grabbing James' hand and tucking the boy behind her. Glancing behind Michael, Ashley could see her mother still gasping for breath as she held her throat. "What did you do to mother you bastard?!" Ashley quickly snapped, glaring at Michael who moved to step in front of Lily, blocking Ashley's view of the woman.

"Is this what your bickering has resorted to now? You physically assaulted my mother?" Ashley yelled, her grip tightening on James' arm. "Do you have any ounce of humanity left in you?" Ashley asked angrily. "What kind of example are you giving James?" Ashley yelped, her voice shaking as she could feel the anger swelling inside of her. Despite the fact that James was clinging onto her, Ashley was still able to move around a bit.

"Ash... just take your brother back up-" Michael started to speak in a stern tone, only to have Ashley quickly snap at him. Cutting the man off, causing Michael to growl under his breath while his brows knit together to show his displeasure.

"Don't you dare call me that!" Ashley growled, taking a step forward, only to stop as she felt James' small hands wrap around her waist. The small trembling of the boys' arms was evident that this whole ordeal was upsetting him.

Taking a deep breath in, Ashley closed her eyes as she placed a hand on top of the small frail limbs. "You've lost the right to be able to call me Ash." Ashley remarked in a stern tone as she raised her head. "Your constant abuse of liquor, the endless bickering that you cause with my mother, and now physically abusing the woman who has allowed you to stay in this house instead of kicking you.... you've lost all of my respect as my father." Ashley spoke, her eyes continuing to glare at the slob that was Michael.

"I couldn't care less if you lost respect for me." Michael remarked in his scuffed voice. "Because no matter what, I will always be your father." Hearing that caused Ashley to growl under her breath while Michael walked closer to the two siblings. "You, your brother, and your mother have seemed to think that I have no right to control what goes on in this house." Michael paused as he steadied his steps towards the two children. "All because your mother has a damn title that makes it seem like she is better than all of us." Michael stopped just a few inches in front of Ashley. Staring down at the young girl, Michael had no warmth left in his eyes. "I'll be damned if I am treated like a simple pet in this household. I am your father, and you will respect me, or so help me...." Michael trailed off as he raised a hand as if to threaten violence towards the children.

"That you'll assault us as well?" Ashley asked, her voice more stern as she kept her head held high. "We're both children you asshole!" Ashley snapped in an accusative tone, her brows knitting together. "Really? You're going to go that far just to prove a point? To prove that you're man enough to take control by physically assaulting your whole family?" Ashley barked, taking a step back while feeling James' grip tremble more. "You're not a man at all if you think that will work on us!" Ashley challenged him, only to see Michael's fingers twitch in the air.

"If need be." Michael bluntly spoke, his eyes staring into Ashley's. As his hand started to ball up into a fist, bringing it down with a staggered movement. Ashley closed her eyes, flinching as she waited for the impact of the fist to her face. But it didn't come. Instead, Ashley felt warm droplets splattering against her face, followed by the sounds of Michael gasping.

Slowly opening her eyes, Ashley found a blood caked end of a poker stick sticking only a few centimeters from her face. The black pointed end dripped in blood as Michael braced himself against the door frame. A sharp gasp left Ashley's lips as she looked up to see the surprised look on Michael's face. Opening her mouth, Ashley wanted to scream, but her voice seemed to be locked up. It was when Michael's legs gave out, that Lily was standing in his place, her nightgown splattered with blood. The white rose shawl started to soak up the blood, causing some of the white petals to turn red.

Stepping closer to Michael's slumped body, Lily pulled the poker out of the male's body. Bringing up to her face, Lily studied the poker for a few seconds, almost like she was admiring her work before kneeling onto Michael's back. Raising the poker stick over her head, Lily started to plunge the poker stick repeatedly into the male's back. Ashley stood there in horror, her voice unable to come out as she guarded James' sight to prevent the male from witnessing the horrific as the vision in front of Ashley. The sounds of the poker piercing Michael's body over and over again still lingered in Ashley's mind.

Slowly Ashley started to back away from the door, though it was harder with James still sticking to her back. "J-James...." Ashley whispered as she finally found her voice. "Head up to your room... don't look back, just go and hide under your bed." Ashley instructed when they were in the hallway. The sounds of the poker piercing into the flesh with the grunts coming from Lily in the living room seemed to echo into the hallway loud enough that Ashley could feel James' face move from being pressed against her back to shyly moving to see what was going on. Ashley didn't know how much James had seen, but it appeared to be enough that he understood why he had to run.

With a heavy sigh after James started to run upstairs, Ashley peeked past the door frame to watch the puddle of blood creeping towards her. It didn't take long for Ashley to see herself in the blood. Her green eyes carefully moved to see her mother still on top of her father's dead body. The blood soaked through the messy shirt, staining it a deep red while Michael's muscles and bones were visible. Lily appeared to be equally covered in blood. Her blonde hair slowly turning red, her green eyes almost vacant as if she was no longer there or in control of her actions. The blood weighed the silky black nightgown down as it clinged to her skeleton frame while the shawl Lily was once wearing fell onto the ground, soaking up the blood that pooled on the floor.

"M-Mom? A-Are you alright?" Ashley asked, her voice a bit timid as she stepped out from behind the door. Watching as Lily stopped what she was doing, Ashley felt a tingle run down her spine, as if her body was trying to tell her to run. Except her legs were frozen. She didn't want to run away from her mother. She loved the woman and idolized Lily. But it didn't seem to matter. This woman that was standing up before taking a step on top of Michael's head wasn't her mother anymore. Ashley stepped back away from her mother as Lily moved closer. The poker stick was still in Lily's blood soaked hand, droplets of blood made their way onto the floor as Lily moved with grace.

"Y-You're scaring me mom... stop it." Ashley pleaded, her voice wavering as she walked backwards in the hallway towards the kitchen. Ashley's hand braced the wall as she waited for the perfect time to run. "Come on mom, wake up! Snap out of it!" Ashley continued with her plea, only to see that it had no effect. Hitching her breath, there was only one thing that Ashley could do in the situation. That was to run.

With a quick turn of her body, Ashley started to run down the hallway towards the kitchen, to which Lily started to run as well. Keeping up with Ashley who felt her socks slip against the floor, almost causing Ashley to fall, the young girl recovered enough to avoid any swings from the poker stick her mother was swinging. Turning the corner, Ashley bound towards the dining room in hopes that she could make her way towards the front and head to the police station. However she wasn't that lucky.

Lily reached towards her and grabbed Ashley's ponytail, pulling the young blonde down onto the hardwood floor with a loud thud. Glancing up, Ashley's eyes widened as she saw her mother raise the poker stick up in the air. "You took everything from me..." Lily muttered, the blood on her face slowly dripping down and onto Ashley's face. "My youth... my beauty... and the man that I love. And for what?" She continued to mutter, her grip on Ashley's hair getting tighter. "All because *he* could see how much better you are. That you will be the one to replace me." Ashley looked up at her mother with fear in her eyes as Lily continued with her mumbling rant. "You will all replace us. And your price... is the blood of the elder... " Lily growled lowly as she continued to hold onto Ashley's hair.

"W-What are you talking about?" Ashley asked, her panic raising as she brought her hands up. But Lily went silent, bringing the poker stick down to pierce Ashley's chest. But with some quick thinking, Ashley brought her leg up as a means to protect her body and kick the poker stick away. However not without a price. The end of the poker stick pierce through Ashley's leg, causing a blood curdling scream. The pain that shot through Ashley's leg was intense, causing her to visible shake as the metal stick remained stuck in place.

Feeling Lily tug the poker stick, it seemed to cause Ashley more pain. Reach down, Ashley grasped the stick to keep her mother from pulling it out and doing more damage. "S-Stop it mamma... stop!" Ashley cried out, only to be caught off guard when the sound of something metal striking Lily from behind, causing her to slump over. Looking up, Ashley saw that James had one of the pots in his hand. "J-James..." Ashley weakley spoke, though she was relieved that he came to her rescue. Knowing that she should have scolded James for not listening to her, Ashley was thankful that he didn't.

"Come on, we need to get you some help." James spoke, trying his best to help Ashley up, but found that Lily was still clutching Ashley's hair. Stepping on Lily's hand, James knelt down to unclenched her hand, helping to free Ashley from her captive. With James there to help walk her out, Ashley was able to recount the events of what happened that night to the police officers, causing her mother to be faced with the punishment by the tribe leader's death. Her own mother who had tried to kill Ashley would end up being the one to die only a short few days later, along with the other leaders.

As Ashley finished her story, Dean could understand why she was so cold towards other people. Her father didn't feel like he was respected in his own home, the mother was dealing with the fact that the man who had claimed he loved her actually fooled around on the poor woman. At least Ashley still had her brother, though Dean hasn't seen him around. "Seems like you and Kane both went through some real heavy stuff." Dean remarked, though his voice was weary as he didn't know what the right thing to say to all of that was. "But what happened to your brother after that? I don't believe I met him yet." Dean remarked, his curiosity seemingly to get the better of him.

"He's dead..." Ashley spoke, her voice monotone as she stared ahead. "He felt like he was the cause of it all...That everything that happened was because he was born..." It seemed that the death of her parents didn't seem to phase Ashley, but recounting the death of her brother did. "He killed himself last year..." Ashley continued, her voice hitching as she tried to keep it together. "I found him in the bathtub...." Dean noticed the tears that started to form in Ashley's eyes, The quivering of her lower lip before a tear fell down. "He had cut his wrist...and simply allowed the blood to seep out." The quick sniffle didn't go unnoticed as Ashley tried to keep it together. "He was cold by the time I came to check up on him. There was no way that I could have gotten to him in time to save him…" Ashley's voice trailed off, as if she could recount the scene before her.

Dean watched as Ashley moved to sit up right in the chair. The tears in her eyes as she recounted the last of her family dying, leaving her behind to cope with it all. "He saved me, and yet... There wasn't a goddamn thing that I could do to save him." Ashley snapped, her voice cracking as she brought her hands up to try and stop the tears. "How am I supposed to feel knowing that the one person I cared for more than myself, who I loved with all of my heart, decided that it was best to kill himself than to live another day with me?" Ashley asked, her voice straining while the tears continued to flow down her cheeks.

"That he felt like he was sick in the head... that he was nothing more than a freak who didn't deserve to live." Ashley continued as her body shook. "That I would be better off not having a curse of a human like him around me. When all I wanted was to be able to spend my life with my brother?" Dean knew the feeling of loss, but not like this. "I loved him like I was his mother... he was my whole world Dean. And I failed him..." Ashley started to softly sob in front Dean.

How is anyone supposed to react to something like that? Dean slowly got up from his seat, figuring that there was only one thing that he could do for Ashley. As Dean reached Ashley, he could see her covering her face while trying to stifle her sobs. Small droplets of tears ran down her cheeks before making small round puddles on the sketch book, seemingly ruining the paper.

Placing a hand on her head, Dean started to slowly stroke Ashley's hair before kneeling down to her level. Ashley reminded Dean of a younger version of himself. Being left alone in the world with the only people who loved you seemingly disappearing from the rest of your life. That was a pain that Dean knew all too well.

"Ashley…"Dean started to speak in a gentle tone. "I know what it is like to go through being completely alone." Dean spoke, watching as Ashley slowly looked at him through red teary eyes. "To wonder how you're even able to make it day to day without the people you care about the most." It pulled at Dean's heartstrings seeing the young leader like this. "It makes you want to barter to whatever god may be listening to bring them back, or to simply take you too." Dean couldn't even count how many times he wished to join his parents on the bad days of working on the station.

"But that's not what they would want." Dean spoke, offering a kind smile to Ashley before he continued. "It sucks being left alone in the world." Dean continued to lightly pet Ashley while seemed to be calming down. "Not knowing what kind of hardships are out there waiting for you, it makes you want to give up on life." Dean paused, allowing Ashley to wipe her eyes with her sleeves, but the tears wouldn't seem to stop. "To just simply lie down and wait for your last breath so that you won't be alone anymore…it's an overwhelming feeling when you're all by yourself." Not exactly comforting, but it was the truth.

"To be envious of the dead, it's not a good mindset." Dean knew all too well how envious he was that those who had died were able to escape the hell that was known as the Millennium. "Dying won't solve anything." Dean paused as he retracted his hand. "It might seem like it will put a stop to the pain, but wouldn't that just prove that you weren't strong enough to continue pushing through the pain? That everything that you had worked for simply ended in vain?" Dean asked as he kept kneeling in front of her.

"You want your clan to see you as a tough leader right? Which is why you put on that persona where nothing tends to phase you, right?" Dean asked, only to watch Ashley's eyes widen as if her secret was leaked out. Despite the front that Ashley had, she was still a young girl full of emotions that she hasn't been able to freely explore.

"How did-?" Ashley asked in a stunned tone of voice, only to see Dean smirk a bit. As if Dean was able to read her like the book he was reading earlier, but he was simply talking through his own experience and how Dean had tried different personas himself. From trying to be the helpful neighbor to being distant and off putting, Dean went through it all.

"Because if you were really an emotionless, stuck up bratty princess, you wouldn't be sitting here crying over the death of your brother." Dean remarked, a soft chuckle leaving his lips as he closed his eyes half way. "I frankly don't envy you guys." Dean spoke bluntly. "Having to think about your tribes over your own personal gain or wants, it must make you feel as if you never had much of a childhood." Considering that most of them were barely over twenty, it made things harder on the leaders. "Nor did you have time to properly grieve over the loss of your brother, am I right?" Dean asked, keeping his eyes on Ashley's facial reaction to either confirm it for himself, even if she didn't say anything.

"Just because you're a leader, someone that the members of your tribe looks to for guidance, doesn't mean you have to keep your emotions locked up." Dean continued, even though he didn't have the slightest clue as to what it took to be a leader. After all, Dean spent his whole life listening to other people tell him how Dean should live his life. With the very few freedoms he was granted, Dean didn't have what it takes to guide people into a better way of life. "You're allowed to show your emotions on your own time." Dean remarked, giving a small shrug of his shoulders at the last comment.

"That much is obvious." Ashley remarked in her usual snarky tone, causing Dean to be taken back a bit. "I know I'm allowed to have emotions on my own time. I'm not always in the public spotlight." Seems like Ashley's usual 'better than you" attitude was making a return as well. Watching as Ashley reached a hand up to wipe away the tears that rolled down her eyes only a few minutes ago, Dean was relieved that she was feeling well enough to make quick witted remarks again.

"See if I ever try to give you an emotional lift again." Dean grumbled in annoyance as he stood up to back away from Ashley. As Ashley stood up from her chair, she started to brush the wrinkles from her clothes. It was nice to see that the young leader was able to bounce back so easily. "So guessing you're back to your normal self now?" Dean asked, raising his eyebrow as Ashley cast a glance in his direction.

"I guess you could say that." Ashley remarked with a small huff. Reaching up, Ashley brushed her hair behind her ear before looking at the sketch book in her other hand. "You know, you're bad at comforting people." Ashley remarked, a small chuckle leaving her lips as she started to walk towards the fireplace. "Just like Kane." Ashley finished, a small sniffle leaving her as she started to feel a bit better now.

"What's that supposed to mean?" Dean asked, not sure if he should either be insulted or find it odd that Ashley compared Dean to Kane. "I know I'm bad at comforting people, but I'm sure Kane is better at it than I am. After all, he puts his heart into everything he does." It was admirable in a way how Kane put himself in other people's shoes. Dean lacked the social cues to be able to properly pick up the mood of a conversation.

"Exactly." Ashley quickly remarked, reaching the fireplace. "He tries his hardest to be able to make everyone happy." She spoke, her voice uncharacteristically soft. "He knows better than anyone else how hollow it can feel to lose everything around you in an instant." Ashley paused as she looked down at the sketch. "To feel as if your heart is an endless void that can never be filled... no matter how much love is poured into it... it can never be filled..." Ashley trailed off as she gazed at the fire burning the cut log into it was nothing more than a thin strip of burning wood.

Dean listened to Ashley carefully. Knowing a bit about Kane's past, it made Dean realize that he had the similar void from his own parents dying and being abandoned to survive on his own for ten years. Even if Dean had tried to get out and socialize on the station, he could never fill that empty void that seemed to linger in his heart. How relationships didn't feel as if they could satisfy a need that would never come. Glancing to the side, Dean wondered if he could even find someone to be able to fill that empty pit in his chest. If he could, maybe he would be able to help Kane fill his void as well.

"Each of the leaders of the clans are broken Dean... we don't get the right to be able to be human anymore." Ashley spoke in a monotone voice, bringing up the now closed sketch book, looking at the worn down cover that had small doodles etched into it. "Nero pretty much cursed all of the leaders with their sin titles." Ashley continued, grasping the book in her delicate fingers before tossing the sketch book into the fire.

"I'm forever envious of others as I can find no pleasure in the company of my fellow humans." Ashley remarked while watching the fire start at the corners of the sketch book. "Kane is forever a glutton, his desires never quenched as he craves more than he should." Ashley continued to speak, as if reciting a curse. "Keaton will forever be a lustful beast who can no longer feel himself emotionally attached to a single lover." Despite the fact that Keaton was bound to Amelia, he could never really feel that desire that a single lover could provide him.

"Miles, the lazy sloth who can no longer find the drive to pursue his dreams. Amelia the greed, always seeking out power and wealth, neither one quenches her desires for more." Ashley paused before taking a deep breath to finish the last part of the curse.

"Lastly Felicia, a beauty with scars from a beast so foul, she hides her deformity in order to protect her vanity, her pride as a strong woman that many wish to be or lust after..." Ashley finished while watching as the fire engulfed the sketch book like a school of piranha in the river with some fresh meat in the water. Turning towards Dean, Ashley's face showed a type of sadness that Dean never seen on her.

"As long as the eye in the sky forever watches us, our sins will never be washed away. That is the curse that Nero placed on the new generation of clan leaders." The look on Ashley's face made it seem like she was waiting for Dean to say something, but he couldn't. "The blood that was spilled from the elderly leaders, it will spill a path for the new leaders to find peace for the remnants of humanity, but at the price of satisfaction, and an unquenchable thirst for their sins." Ashley sighed at the end, her face becoming flushed from the crying she did earlier.

"Is that some type of tome? Or was that his curse?" Dean asked, raising an eyebrow as he wasn't sure what to make of it all. It felt more like a long winded curse or warning that one would find in a medieval setting book. Maybe he could talk about this whole thing over with Kane later. Perhaps the two would be able to brainstorm some type of solution to this riddle. That is, if Dean believed in curses.

"Who knows." Ashley remarked, shrugging her shoulders before moving a hand to cover her mouth as she yawned from being emotionally spent. "Anyways, I'm heading to bed." Even though it felt a bit more like an excuse to get away from Dean, Ashley made her way towards the door empty handed.

It was only when she stopped at the door and looked over her shoulder to see Dean pondering the odd poem. A small smirk formed on her lips as she felt lighter telling Dean a bit about her past. Though she didn't exactly care too much about the man, she at least could understand why Kane was quick to defend him. Maybe Dean's plan could work, provided that Amelia approves of it in the end. There's a lot one can do within a year. Ashley was interested to see just what Dean could do for them. Especially if it meant that they got rid of that eyesore hovering in the sky.

CHAPTER FOURTEEN: *The Banquet*

THE BANQUET WAS only in a few hours, Dean and Kane were looking at the scattered clothes that Ashley had thrown onto the bed. It seemed like she had a particular style that she wanted to see the two men wearing if they were going to be seen in front of her clan. The sound of the metal hangers gliding against the metal bar had always become ear shattering to Dean as he winced as the curl of the hook grated against the metal bar. It wasn't like there was much on the rack left since most of the clothes the two males had were now on top of the bed seemingly discarded into an ever growing pile.

"No... no." Ashley muttered, flinging the clothing only to have it bounce off and land on the floor. "Honestly Kane, don't you have anything else besides robes?" Ashley scoffed, looking over her shoulder at the two. The dress she was wearing looked like a vintage swing kleid that had a dark mesh covering that had peacock feather designs scattered around neatly. Thanks to the mesh over top, the green strapless dress looked complete. Ashley's fishnet covered legs stuck out under her dress that had a laced petticoat underneath. The dark emerald heels she wore didn't have much length on the heels themselves, but it did give Ashley a bit of height to her short appearance. The mesh topping was sleeveless, as a small black ribbon dangled from behind the dress.

The hair clip that pulled the side of Ashley's blonde locks back was a rather elegant design that had a large emerald square that was lined with blue sapphires only to have three peacock feathers lining the sides and top of the emerald. As the hair clip rested tucked behind Ashley's left ear, it made the darkened emerald skull earrings she was wearing more noticeable in appearance. Draped around her shoulders was an elegant shoulder necklace that had been crafted to look like an assortment of roses and leaves that spanned across Ashley's slender back, only to have the rhinestone chains to connect to the pins that attached to the top corner of the dress' seams.

"I can excuse Dean for not having much clothes, but you should at least branch out more than just wearing the same old thing." Ashley remarked, her green eyes glancing at the two with disapproval. Dark blue eyeshadow decorated with thin black winged eyeliner seemingly brought out the green in her eyes while a light red lipstick looked as if Ashley took her time to get the right shade to rest on her lips. Her eyelashes were curled, almost looking a bit feathery, making it seem like the petite princess spent hours making sure that she stood out more than usual.

"I don't know what I can tell you Ashley. I just don't really like to wear a bunch of clothing when I don't have to go outside." Kane remarked, lightly scratching his cheek as a nervous smile appeared on his face. "Besides, you know I don't like the color of orange. It doesn't fit my look at all." Kane continued, a soft defeated sigh leaving his lips. Dean was a bit confused as to why the tribal leader would have to wear a certain color to an event. "It might have looked good on my dad, but not me."

"So I'm guessing orange is associated with gluttony?" Dean asked, glancing over at Kane who was wearing his dark robe with some of his old accessories on. The topaz earring on Kane's ear seemed to be sticking out against his silver locks.

"Unfortunately." Kane mumbled, a defeated sigh leaving his lips as it was clear that the other wasn't a fan of the color choice. "It would be one thing if I could wear some ceremonial robes with some type of black and orange design, even one with just simple squares could do." Kane spoke, crossing his arms in thought as he didn't have a problem with something like that. "But wearing actual formal wear just doesn't suit me. I hate wearing pants." Of course hearing that remark, Dean couldn't help but chuckle a bit. "Well, not tight pants anyways." Kane corrected himself, a faint smile lingering on his lips from Dean's small chuckle.

"Since we're having the banquet at my clan this year, I get to set the attire." Ashley spoke up, placing her hands on her hips as she often did when she was ready to speak her mind about a subject. "You and Miles often have your kimono style robes with elegant designs. Do you know how hard it is for women to get out of those kimono robes?" Ashley asked seemingly ready to give up on her search for something decent for the men to wear. "We have to wear so many layers, so it's only fair that you have to wear what I say, and this year I want to have women wearing beautiful dresses and men looking sharp in tuxedos or at least wear a nice pair of pants, shirt, and a vest." Was that so hard to ask for?

"You know, you sort of sound like my mother that way." Dean remarked. If his mother was here, she would be looking high and low for the perfect dress that would bring out her sunny personality while also making sure that Max and Dean looked sharp in their tuxedos that would match the color scheme of her dress. "She would argue that we need to look our best to impress those around us." Dean continued, getting the attention of Kane as he continued.

"My father would just want my mother to be happy, so he would go along with it. After all, he always wanted to see her bright smile. Often said it could brighten up a whole sector." It was hard to deny that his parents loved each other. The way that their eyes would glisten with pure love as they looked at one another was something that Dean wanted in a partner.

"Sounds like your mother had a very bubbly personality." Kane remarked, a soft chuckle leaving his lips. It made the leader wonder how their parents would have interacted with each other if they were alive. It was hard to tell since Kane had no idea what Dean's parents were like or even what they looked like. Perhaps their fathers might have gotten along, considering that Elijah was a reasonable man. It might be a hit or miss with their mothers though.

"Yeah, she always looked for the good in people." Dean shrugged, knowing that it didn't help her now. Hell, it didn't even help him get a home after she was dead. "But that's not here or there." Dean lightly shrugged his shoulders as he knew it would do him no good to focus on his past. Glancing towards Ashley, he looked at the pile of clothes on the bed before sighing.

"Guess I have no choice." Ashley grumbled to herself as she left the room, leaving Kane and Dean there to start picking up the clothes that were tossed onto their unmade bed. Thankfully a lot of the clothes still lingered on the hangers, making the clean up process that much easier. It wasn't long before Ashley came back with two gift wrapped boxes in her hand.

The boxes were rather thin, each wrapped with a ribbon. One was wrapped with a red ribbon that looked like it had some type of red rose decoration on it while the other had a dark orange wrapping with an orange cosmos flower. Both flowers were neatly tucked in the upper corner of the boxes. "I figured that this would be an issue. So I went ahead and got you two a pair of outfits that I would find suitable for the banquet." Ashley explained, a small smirk on her lips as she nodded to herself.

Both of the men were a bit surprised that Ashley went ahead and actually got them something. Not only that, but she had it gift wrapped. Opening the gifts from the side, the two glanced at the clothing choice that Ashley had picked out for them. Pulling the outfit from the box, Dean was surprised that she had gotten him not a suit, but rather a regular outfit.

There was a blood red long sleeved shirt, a pair of black formal slacks, a black tie with a small pattern of ivory roses at the bottom of it, and a black vest with a similar design on the back. The ivory roses seemed to dance against the lower part of the vest. It was simple yet seemed suitable to Dean's everyday look with a formal twist to it.

Glancing over to what Ashley had gotten Kane, Dean was surprised to see an actual suit resting there. Though it wasn't what he had thought she would have picked out for the male. As most suits were black, this one had a dark orange coloring to the jacket. The shirt and vest were black in color, while the tie was black with orange butterflies that appeared to be flying up towards the top while a collective remained at the bottom. The vest had elegant orange and black monarch butterflies fluttering against the black background. The black pants were similar to Dean's though shorter in length.

"I figured that you would have had a hard time picking out a suit since you don't like the color orange. So, I made sure that you would be able to stick out without looking like the other guys and still showing off your tribal colors." Ashley remarked, slightly beaming as Ashley placed her hands upon her hips. "So, do you like it?" Ashley asked, peering at the two with a small excited twinkle to her eyes.

"I do, it's just..." Kane started to trail off, causing Ashley's excitement to waver. "What happened to the garments that we ordered? Did they not get here in time?" After all, they had paid for their outfits in advance in hopes that they would be able to wear it to the banquet. Seemed like a waste of chips otherwise. Not like it was a short trip since it was coming from the Pride clan.

"It did, but since the banquet is at my place this year, I took the liberty of getting everyone outfits that would suit them." It seemed that Ashley had already planned this in advance. Since Dean was the only one that seemed to be unlike the others, she must have gone out to buy it before the banquet. "So no need to thank me." Ashley remarked, placing the tips of her fingers gingerly on her chest with a beaming smiling.

This only made Kane sigh as he placed his hand on his forehead, covering his eyes. It wasn't exactly like Kane could be angry at Ashley, considering that she went out of her way to look out and make Kane look decent, he could at the very least be a bit irritated. "So what did you do with the package that was sent?" Kane asked, the annoyance evident in his voice.

"Relax, the package is in the trunk in the corner." Ashley remarked, pointing to the trunk that had some of the old clothing that once belonged to Elijah. "I'm not so much of a monster that I would open it." She continued, crossing her arms against her chest, a small annoyed scowl lingering on her face. "Anyways, I'll be heading out. Don't keep the rest of us waiting. It's an important night after all." An excited giggle left the younger leader as Ashley made her way out of the room.

Closing the door behind her, this allowed for the two men to change without any onlookers. Dean noticed the small look of relief on Kane's face as he walked over towards the trunk to make sure that Ashley was telling the truth. Inside the trunk was a neat boxed package with the address written on the upper corner. For whatever reason Kane didn't take it out. Instead, the male closed the trunk before glancing over his shoulder at Dean. "Guess we should get dressed for the party." Kane remarked, though it seemed like he had something on his mind.

"Is something on your mind?" Dean asked, figuring that since it was just the two of them, they had more liberty to speak. The two have grown closer over the months that they traveled together, they were pretty much family at this point. "Are you nervous about the banquet?" Dean asked, moving to sit down on the bed that had been cleared of the clothes that were once sprawling over the edges.

"I guess..." Kane spoke, his voice seeming to be a bit disappointed as he slumped onto the bed as well. Kane's hands idly caressed the fabric of the suit, feeling the silk lining of the jacket, only to have a bit of it snag against his rough hands. "It'll just be a bit awkward sitting next to Miles." Kane remarked as he glanced towards Dean.

"We would always talk a bit during the dinner portion before we would start meeting our clan members to talk about any concern that they had going into the next year." A small frown seemed to form on Kane's face, casting his eyes downward towards the messed up bed sheets from the night prior. "But I won't be able to have that this year. Not after what he has done." The two leaders haven't been able to really make up since their incident on the airship.

"What would you guys talk about?" Dean asked, figuring that perhaps Kane would want to open up about that sort of thing. "That is, if you don't mind me asking." Dean didn't want to step on any toes that would make Kane feel uncomfortable. Slowly Dean was learning to skate around the blockades that Kane would have up, allowing for a more nature approach to learning about Kane.

Kane glanced towards Dean, his facial features showing that Kane was debating on rather or not he should tell the other. Kane closed his eyes, only to open them back up after a few minutes. "It's not like we really talked about much." Kane started to speak as he leaned back into the smaller pile of clothes with an audible sigh. "Just catching up with what happened in our clans over the year." Kane remarked, his eyes gazing up towards the ceiling as a small frown landed on his face.

"It was just that small amount of time that I got to have time with him. Just the two of us and no one could interrupt us." Dean figured that Kane must have looked forward to that time since it meant that Felicia wasn't around them. "It felt like time had stopped when it was just us, and no one else mattered." The look in Kane's eyes was almost longing, like he wished he was able to continue that tradition. "But I don't know what I'll do now." Kane finished, closing his eyes as if he was still figuring out the whole situation in his mind.

"Well, despite the fact that you can't have time to catch up with Miles, we could always hang out and chat." Dean suggested, though he could already tell that it wouldn't be the same. "Sort of like what we're doing now." Dean watched as Kane lightly shook his head. It was clearly not that simply because Kane was deeply in love with Miles. Dean would feel more like a cheap replacement more than anything. Even if Kane didn't say or think that, that's how it felt to Dean.

"I appreciate it Dean... I really do." Kane trailed off with a faint smile on his face before letting out a small sigh. "But it just wouldn't be the same." There it was, that little statement that showed that Kane simply wanted that bit of time to be with Miles. The year long distance longing was all that Kane had going for him. The endless hopes of being able to see the man Kane cherished close to his heart, was now crushed by said man's actions. It was apparent just how crushed Kane was in his eyes.

"I think I'll go and change in the bathroom." Kane spoke up, not being able to look at Dean as he grabbed the box that held the tuxedo inside. Kane left the room without a single glance towards Dean. It felt like the mood had soured from the talk of the banquet. If it wasn't for Ashley or Kane, Dean doubted that he would have gone. Not with the unease tension in the room.

AFTER a bit of time fussing with his clothes and hair, Dean finally left the room he shared with Kane. The black undershirt poked out against Dean's collarbone, the top button undone as Dean didn't like how the tie felt like it was trying to choke him. Whether he had it on too tight, or not tight enough, it just didn't suit his overall look. The vest hugged his torso tightly as the shirt was tucked into the pants neatly. The shoes that Ashley had given him were simply too tight, so Dean opted for the loafers that he had been wearing around the house. It wasn't like they were dirty or worn out. They just fit like a glove compared to the other shoes that often pinched his feet. Dean's hair was pulled back on the right side, leaving his bangs on the left side to lightly drape over his left eye.

Walking down the steps, Dean noticed that Kane at the bottom of the steps looking himself over in the mirror. Despite the slight redness in his eyes, the other male looked ready to have this whole night simply put behind him. Kane didn't do anything different with his hair, which seemed surprising to Dean. The same long silver bangs covered the scared right eye.

The lingering sadness filled Kane's silver eyes that seemed to glance down to the ground as if Kane was ashamed to look at himself. His whole stance just screamed that Kane wanted to curl up from head to toe in a blanket. To shut out the world. The black pants seemed to be loosely clinging to Kane's slender frame. The black shirt seemed a bit too big on Kane, while the vest wasn't even closed. The air around Kane felt like he had simply been defeated. As if Kane had just given up all hope. Dean couldn't simply stand by and see his friend go out and greet the world with an air of depression surrounding him.

Knitting his brows together, Dean turned back to head towards the bathroom. Glancing around for the box, Dean was able to see it discarded into the trash can. Though the box looked as if it had been stomped on, the flower surprisingly remained intact. Plucking it off, Dean went back to the foyer. It seemed that Kane didn't exactly move much as his hands were gingerly resting on the small cabinet under the mirror. It was only when the floorboards on the steps creaked under Dean's feet that seemed to make Kane look towards the other male.

"Hey...ready to go?" Kane asked, his voice seemingly deprived of emotions. The side glance away from Dean made Kane seem to be submissive, almost like he wasn't even worthy of looking at Dean. "If we're late, Ashley will be mad..." It was like Dean was looking at an abused dog or something. The once liveliness that Kane used to display was now gone.

"Not quite. There's something that I need to do first." Dean remarked, heading back upstairs to collect a small comb since he had gotten an idea on how he could lift Kane's spirits. It would only be a few minutes before Dean was back down the steps with the flower and comb in hand. "Now, time to clean you up." Dean beamed as Kane looked up to the taller male with a confused look on his face.

Putting the comb and cosmos flower in his mouth, Dean's hands reached out to start buttoning the black vest. Kane was taken aback as he shifted backwards. However instead of fighting it, Kane allowed Dean to do what he wished as the tribal leader simply didn't have the energy to make an effort for tonight.

Once Dean had finished with fixing the vest, Dean removed the flower from his mouth to pin it to the vest against Kane's left breast pocket. Next was to use the comb to brush back Kane's bangs till the scared eye was visible. Tucking some of Kane's hair behind his right ear, Dean smiled as he was pleased with himself for helping to make Kane look a bit more like himself. "There. Now you look more presentable as the leader of the Gluttony clan." Dean spoke in a more chipper tone of voice.

Kane was a bit beside himself. He didn't expect Dean to really care for Kane's appearance since he wasn't part of any of their clans. It was rather moving, though Kane wouldn't voice it out loud. "Why did you do this for me?" Kane asked, glancing up at Dean with a somewhat confused look. It wasn't like Dean was expecting anything in return, so why would he go this far just for someone like Kane?

"Because you're my friend." Dean remarked bluntly. "I can't let you be seen looking like a hot mess in front of your people." Hearing that remark caused a faint smile to appear on Kane's face. "You have to be strong for your people. Even if you feel like your whole world is crumbling," Dean paused as he reached out to readjust the flower that was starting to fall from the pocket.

"When you are going to face them, you need to be the strong leader that they see you as." Dean continued, moving his hand to brush back some of Kane's hair back that tried to part from the rest of the locks. "After this evening, you can let your world crumble around you when it is just the two of us." Dean's voice was softer at that part, knowing how much Kane just wanted to simply give up even before the banquet would start. "After all, if you don't give your arms a rest from holding up the world for so long, eventually you'll be crushed by the weight of it all." Kane wasn't Atlas after all. "Let me help to take care of some of the burdens, alright? Even if it is just for tonight." Dean continued, moving back to take a better look at Kane since he was fixed up.

The faint smile seemed to grow a bit more, the corners of Kane's lips tucking back some as a spark seemed to come back to Kane's eyes. "Thanks Dean, I really needed to hear that." Kane remarked, bowing his head a bit before feeling something warm against his head. Dean had placed his hand on top of Kane's head, giving it a small yet gentle caress. Surprised, Kane glanced up at Dean to see the gentle smile resting on Dean's face.

"Don't worry about it. That's what friends are for." Dean reassured him, only to remove his hand from Kane's head. "We should probably head out now. Don't want to be the last ones to arrive, right?" It seemed that the air of doubt and unease seemed to be lifted from Kane, even if it was for tonight. It felt like the two of them would be able to get through anything, as long as they simply had each other. Even if one let their world crumble, the other was there to pick up the pieces.

As the two men walked along the shoveled pathway, the sun was just starting to set. The purple and orange mixture against dark clouds were barely visible against the skyline of the buildings surrounding them. The small rustle of the branches surrounding their path lightly scraped together as Dean and Kane reached the building where the banquet was being held. Two figures seemed to linger just inside of the doors, keeping warm while waiting for the last of the guests to arrive. The two figures were that of Felicia and Miles. Seems that either Ashley or the head of the Clans had ordered them to either wait for the two stragglers to either show up or go out and retrieve them.

Felicia was wearing a beautiful off the shoulder mermaid style gown that clung to her figure. The torso of the dress was a deep violet purple that slowly trailed down an ivory white. Dark crystallized shoes poked out as a large slit gave Felicia room to move about as she didn't like the concept of being trapped in her dress. With Felicia's hair pinned up in a french twist braid, the amethyst hair pins that looked like small lavender flowers were visible against her dark platinum blonde hair. She seemed to be smiling the brightest as she stood next to Miles, her blood red lipstick accenting her dimples as dark purple eyeshadow made her silver gray eyes stand out against her lightly tanned complexion. Small purple earrings rested against her ears while an amethyst necklace dangled against her chest.

Felicia's arms seemed to be wrapped tightly around Miles' left arm, though the man didn't seem to mind it one bit as he seemed to be enjoying a quick smoke. With his normally messy hair pushed over to the left side, exposing the small light blue gem earring that dangled from his right ear, both Kane and Dean were surprised that Miles was wearing a tuxedo like on the airship. With the jacket and pants being a dark shade of gray that seemingly boarded on black, the baby blue vest and matching tie seemed to stick out against the white buttoned up shirt that had been neatly pressed the night prior. Glancing down, Dean could see the small beads of water from the melted snow still clinging onto the smooth surface of the shoes that Miles was wearing.

"Seems like you two sure took your time." Miles remarked, a puff of smoke snaking out of his mouth. His eyes glanced towards Kane, an eyebrow lifting as the leader of the Gluttony clan actually seemed to wear a tuxedo. The jacket that Kane was wearing covered the cosmos flower that was pinned to his vest, the silky interior keeping Kane and the flower warm. "I'm surprised to see you actually wearing a tuxedo, Kane." Miles remarked, bringing the pipe that he was smoking out of up towards his lips. "I figured you would have fought tooth and nail to be able to wear a ceremonial robe instead." Kane remarked, though there was some laughter coming in from behind him.

"Yeah, well Ashley was able to find something that was suitable for him." Dean butted in, figuring that with how tense Kane had been prior to coming to the banquet, the male might not be up for some casual conversation at this point.

"I wasn't asking you." Miles quickly snapped, his sharp gaze glancing towards Dean. The sound of Miles' teeth against the steel end of the pipe was evident that Miles wasn't exactly pleased with the stunt that Dean did, but at this point, Dean just simply didn't care for the antics that Miles was trying to pull on Kane.

"It's alright Dean." Kane mumbled, lightly grasping onto a small piece of fabric of Dean's sleeve, just enough to give it a light tug as if to indicate that Kane could handle himself. With the little hint taken, Dean took a small step back.

With a small clear of his throat, Kane flashed Miles a soft smile. "Well, you know how stubborn Ashley can be Miles." Kane spoke up in a friendly manner. "If Ashley doesn't get her way, she won't let it go until the next banquet." The statement in itself may have been true, but the smile didn't hold much kindness to it. It was more like a pleasantry type of smile than anything else.

"You do have a point." Miles remarked, his eyes glancing Kane over once more before a side glance was made towards Dean. "We're about to serve dinner." Miles spoke before blowing the smoke out from his lips. "But before we go, you'll need to introduce Dean to Amelia and Keaton." Miles continued, his gaze glancing between Dean and Kane as he spoke, seeming to gauge their reaction. "They've been waiting for a chance to meet with him briefly. Exchange a few pleasantries, and then head towards the balcony for dinner."

"Thanks for the heads up." Kane was polite, but he didn't show his usual longing that he once had from the previous year. It seems that Miles' little plan was starting to take effect, even if Kane didn't exactly realize it. "Come on Dean, guess we should get the introductions out of the way." The tone of voice that came from Kane was one that wasn't of excitement, but rather a hint of dread. There was no way that this could end well. But perhaps this little introduction could help Dean grasp an understanding of who he is dealing with.

"Just head on up through the double doors, you can't miss it." Miles instructed, only to watch as the two men started to leave. After they were out of earshot, Miles sighed as he turned the pipe upside down to tap the ash that had collected at the bottom. "Seems like those two are getting closer each time I see them." Miles mostly mused to himself, offering a glance towards Felicia.

"You worried? That you'll lose him forever?" Felicia asked, pulling back a bit from Miles to be able to see his face. "After all, you two were so close. After you lost your family, Kane was the only one you had left." Felicia's concern was noted as Miles gave her a simple nod. It wasn't enough to satisfy Felicia, she simply sighed as she grasped his hand. "I know you're the leader of Sloth, but think this through. I don't want the both of you to be hurting." Felicia remarked, gently placing a hand on Miles' cheek, causing him to look into her eyes. "Once this is all done, just make sure you don't ruin your relationship permanently with Kane."

Miles stared at Felicia for a few seconds, only to reach up and grasp her fingers gingerly. "I appreciate your concern." Miles started with a soft sigh at the end. "But being distant from Kane isn't going to make him hate me forever." Miles spoke in a soft but stern voice. "It'll be just enough to give Dean an edge in overcoming Kane's high barriers and expectations. That's all." Miles reassured her. But in the end, Felicia couldn't help but worry for everyone's sake that this wouldn't blow up in their faces.

As they entered through the doors on top of the stairs like Miles had instructed, Dean was surprised to see two large crystal trees much like those on Felicia's island to greet them at the door. However the petals on the crystalized tree were blue instead of multicolored. The dim lights above the tree gave them a soft glow while the current from the open doors caused the crystalized leaves to sing a soft enchanting tune. The sound of people laughing could be heard as Dean glanced around the further that the pair entered the banquet hall.

Passing through the small arch between the sculptures, the large room they entered looked almost like a fairy tale. The ceiling lights may have been dimmed, but it seemed that they were able to use the crystal lights to fade in and out as if they were outside and able to gaze at the stars. Circling the room was a soft dark green light, almost making it seem like they had some type of protective barrier that would keep those inside safe from whatever dangers lurked past the walls. There were plenty of circular tables that looked like miniature islands on a raised platform. There were people on the large dance floor seemingly enjoying their time here at the banquet as a band played music that Dean never heard of.

The main dance floor had a fair amount of people either struggling to keep up with the music, or they looked as if they had been dancing for years. Some small children either danced with each other in their formal outfits, or they were busy running around. Being able to see an abundance of people in one room was rather reassuring.

The last time Dean had a chance to see this many people in a single room, it was when his grandparents on his mother's side were still around. It was around the last Festival Day where some of the extended family members came for the day. It was one of the few times that Dean had a chance to hang around children his own age that didn't push him away for being abnormal in their eyes. It brought a smile to Dean's face being able to see everyone coming together like this.

Glancing around the room, Dean's eyes came across a man who he had seen coming and going from one of the other houses that was for the other tribal leader. Wearing a black facial mask, Dean noticed that the tall looking male's hair was pushed back, unlike the other times when it was rather messy and seemingly went everywhere. A few of the locks of the man's hair nestled between his yellow eyes, those same eyes made Dean think of a wolf who was always on the prowl.

The man looked somewhat uncomfortable wearing a black tuxedo with a dark blue vest pressing against the white buttoned up shirt. The tie that matched his vest appeared to be loosen, as if he couldn't stand the thought of something being against his neck. Glancing down to the man's feet, Dean noticed that the man was wearing dark boots, which was an odd choice if you asked him. But then again, Dean didn't know anything about Keaton as he never met the man.

Standing next to the uncomfortable male was a rather beautiful woman. Though her dress was strapless, the black and golden sequin dress made the woman sparkle in the light around her despite the room being rather dim as the sun had set for the night. Her dress stopped just shy above her knees as the black and golden heels she was wearing that matched the dress showed off her long tan legs. Her dark brunette hair was put into a simple side braid that made her hair brush against her right shoulder.

A metallic black shawl with golden specs wrapped around her elbows as she carried a wine glass in her right hand. A black collar with small golden flakes rested perfectly against her neck as her lips looked like a blood soaked rose. Piercing silver eyes scanned the roam as smoky black eye-shadow made her appear like a goddess. Small golden rose pins helped to keep Amelia's hair in place as the small golden hooped earrings decorated her ears.

"Looks like they're waiting." Kane softly mumbled, taking note that Keaton's eyes seemed to be glancing towards them, only to have the man turn to speak to the woman standing beside him. Though the man's mouth was covered, it didn't take long for the woman's gaze to find them in the dimly lit room. "Just a couple of rules when meeting Amelia and Keaton," Kane started off as he turned to face Dean.

"Don't try and be funny." Kane started off bluntly. "Amelia isn't the type of person who finds jokes to be amusing. Not unless she knows you." Dean didn't understand why anyone would want to try and make jokes when meeting with the head of the Clans, but it must have happened enough times that Kane felt the need to warrant the warning. "Be curt, don't break eye contact, and don't interrupt her." To Dean, it felt more like he was dealing with someone who was in the hierarchy of the Elite class than anything, which might help him in this regard. "Most importantly, don't try to say anything snarky as she leaves." Hearing that caused Dean's eyes to widen a bit.

"Why is that?" Dean asked, his curiosity seeming to get the better of him. Of course it would come as no surprise what Kane would say next, but Dean still wanted to hear it for himself.

"Because the last guy who uttered the word bitch when she started to walk away," Kane spoke, pausing almost for dramatic effect. "He found that most of his property had been bought out by the bank and he was left with nothing but his house and an empty farm." Dean couldn't help but blink in a confused disbelief at how that would impact him in any regard.

"What does that have to do with-" Dean started to speak before Kane placed a finger on Dean's lips, cutting off the question mid sentence. Dean leaned back a bit, unsure of what he should really expect next from this so-called horror that is Amelia's wrath.

"He didn't have any means of being able to get more animals because everyone refused to sell to him. Seeds, food, animals, nothing." Kane continued, leaning in closer to Dean as if to whisper a secret to Dean, low enough to where only the two of them would be able to hear it. "Because he couldn't buy anything, he came begging back to Amelia to let the shops in the clans sell him some supplies." Hearing that, Dean realized that he could very well end up like that man. Not being able to buy or sell anything without getting other people in trouble.

"The man was on his hands and knees, begging Amelia to lift the ban on him." The more that Kane told the story, the better picture that Dean got of the head of the clans. "Now Amelia normally would let things slide, but this guy had a history. So, Amelia told this man that if he wanted the ban lifted that badly, he needed to cut off both of his middle fingers right there and then." Dean couldn't believe what he was hearing. That was something that Dean would have expected something that the Elite on the station would have done. But to see it here, it was the first time that Dean heard about it.

"Wait....why did she have him cut off his middle fingers?" Dean asked, a bit confused on that part, only to see the wavering smile on Kane's face as if he couldn't say the next part without finding it to be a bit comical. It took Kane a few seconds to regain his composure from fighting the urge to chuckle at the next part, but he was finally able to get it out.

"Because, she said that if he wanted a field of fucks to give, he needed to give her the few fucks he had in this world." It seemed like Kane couldn't help the small laugh that came out from remembering Amelia tell the story the first year that they were the newest leaders of the clans. Dean couldn't exactly see why that was funny, considering that he didn't know the outcome of the rest of the story yet.

"He didn't exactly need the middle fingers to be able to do field work. So he needed to give up his middle fingers in exchange for the ban to be lifted." Dean glanced towards the two leaders, watching as Amelia took a small sip of the wine in her hand. She looked as if she would be anywhere else other than here, making Dean a bit worried as to how he should approach her.

"Did she really have him cut his fingers off? Or are you just messing with me?" Dean asked, a bit skeptical that someone who wanted to bring everyone together would simply be that cruel. To make a man cut off his fingers to be able to get supplies? That was a type of evil that Dean expected from the Elite.

"Well, it's not like the guy actually did it." Kane remarked, crossing his arms over his torso as he glanced towards the two leaders. "He refused and left. Simply storming out of the office cursing her name in the process." Kane finished, a small smile lingering on his face. "Though to be honest, I don't think she would have really made him go through with it." A small shrug of Kane's shoulders seemed to make Dean wonder what the other meant, though didn't voice it. "After all, if he truly wanted that lift and her forgiveness, she would have stopped him as soon as he grabbed the knife." Amelia wasn't as cold hearted as she appeared, but she did have to make people believe that she wasn't at all weak.

GETTING through the crowd wasn't exactly easy. With children darting between or around Kane and Dean, it was hard not to almost trip on a few of the children who wanted Kane to play with them. Eventually they had reached the other side, only to have to brush themselves off to rid their clothing of wrinkles or speck of food off thanks to some of the children snagging a couple bits of snacks while waiting for the dinner to be done. Walking up towards Amelia and Keaton, Dean could already feel that familiar judgmental gaze coming off of two leaders. More so coming from Amelia than Keaton.

"Sorry we're late." Kane apologized quickly, that familiar fake smile that Kane had offered Miles earlier was now being presented in front of Amelia and Keaton. "But I would like to introduce to you our special visitor." Kane started off, glancing towards Dean who was to his left. "This is Dean Torres. He is the only one to survive breaking through the atmosphere from the station." Even though that might not seem like it was much of an accomplishment, not many individuals were as fortunate.

"Hello, it's a pleasure meeting you." Dean responded to the introduction by extending his hand out. It seemed that Keaton was the first one to grasp a hold of Dean's hand, giving it a firm shake while Amelia stood back, simply watching for the time being.

"Pleasure to meet you Dean." Keaton remarked through his facial mask. Dean felt those golden eyes glance down him, sending an unpleasant chill down Dean's spine for a split second, but appeared unphased by it. "We've heard a bit about you, but not enough to make a proper assessment." Keaton spoke, letting go of Dean's hand before tilting his head to the left.

"So why don't you do us the pleasure of telling us a bit about yourself." If this Keaton guy was smiling creepily under his mask, Dean felt like he would have been unsettled by it.

Dean blinked a bit in surprise at the comment at first, but he figured that the leaders would want to know more about Dean to make sure that he wasn't exactly a threat. "Well," Dean started to speak, clearing his throat a bit. "Guess you already heard that I came from the station, though not by choice." This remark seemed to get Amelia's attention as her silver eyes seemed almost fixated on Dean.

"My shuttle was on the course towards my new pod that was relocated on the other side of the station, when the controls were suddenly hijacked. Forcing me towards Earth." It wasn't a lie, but Dean didn't want to go into specifics as to what led towards his relocation. "Somehow, I was able to survive the crash, where I was rescued by Kane." Dean continued, his eyes glancing back and forth between the two leaders, the feeling of unease still lingering. Dean couldn't get a proper reading on if he was making an impact on them or not.

"So you don't have much to your personality other than the story of how you got here?" Amelia spoke up, seemingly unimpressed already. Bringing up the glass to her lips, Amelia took a sip of the drink before her eyes glanced over towards Kane, the look of either disapproval or doubt lingering in her eyes. The frown on her face wasn't much of a confidence booster either.

"Eh, no. I just figured that I would start off with how I got here before continuing." Dean remarked, his eyebrows knitting together as he showed his own displeasure in how Amelia was quick to judge. "For all I know, you might think that I am an enemy. Especially with how hostile all of you have been acting towards me." Dean huffed. "You barely got to know me for more than five minutes, and already you have decided on not giving me a chance." Dean was usually a patient man, but with the constant hostility towards him at every back and turn, he wondered how anyone could stand to be pushed around by those who wouldn't take the time to get to know him. Sure even Kane was a bit weary, but he at least helped Dean get medical attention.

"Forgive me," Amelia snapped with a hint of bitterness to her tone, implying that she was not asking for forgiveness, but rather she was going to tell Dean off. "But what makes you think that we should act friendly towards the group of people who left the rest of the world to die?" Amelia spoke, causing a few heads to turn in their direction. "Of course we're going to act hostile towards an invading force that tried to literally nuke the world from outer space." Amelia remarked, the grip on her wine glass tightening, threatening to snap the fragile glass in half.

"Amelia, please don't start this here." Kane begged, reaching out to place his hand on Amelia's right arm. With a small squeeze of Kane's hand, Amelia reluctantly relaxed her tense muscles as an exasperated sigh left Amelia's lips. "How about we get the dinner started? I'm sure that you're probably just really hungry right now." Kane continued, his eyes glancing towards Keaton, as if to cue the man in to helping him out. They didn't need to make a big scene in front of everyone right now. Not when they were supposed to be enjoying the banquet.

"We'll talk later." Keaton remarked, his eyes focused a bit more on Dean as he said that. "Hope you'll continue to make the rounds with Kane and pay my clan a visit." Keaton remarked with a soft chuckle towards the end. "I would be very interested in getting to know you more, Dean. But right now we have a hungry leader who needs to learn not to drink so much before having a proper meal." Again the way that Keaton spoke sent chills down Dean's spine. He didn't know what about the man that gave him the creeps, but Dean didn't know if he could trust the man entirely just yet.

As Keaton lightly took a hold of Amelia's hand, the tall male led Amelia towards the stairs that spiraled up towards a balcony section, leaving Dean and Kane surrounded by some onlookers who seemed to catch a bit of the interaction between the four. "Sorry for the bad impression you might have gotten from Amelia." Kane started to apologize, offering Dean a light smile to help lift the males' mood. "But you should understand something." The smile seemingly disappeared from Kane's lips as he looked Dean in the eyes.

"Amelia has come to loathe and despise those who came from the station ever since any of us could remember." Kane started to speak as he moved closer to Dean. "Mostly because her grandmother was one of the few people that was part of the Elite of that station that was outcasted." This was news to Dean as he never heard of Elites outcasting their own members. Then again, why would they make that public?

"Wait, for real?" Dean asked his astonishment apparent as he gazed at Kane with an almost bewilder stare. "Seems like the Elite love to keep their secrets..." Dean trailed off, his mind reeling in this new information that Kane had provided for him. "If they really did outcast one of their own, I'm sure it would have been kept quiet." If the Elite were bold enough to banish one of their own, just what else did they keep quiet about?

"I shouldn't say much more, considering that Amelia doesn't like to talk about it much." Kane remarked, a light sigh escaping his lips as Kane wished he could simply tell Dean everything that he needed to know. But Dean was the type of guy who would rather hear it for himself after all. "But it's a good little fact to keep on the back burner. Maybe you should ask her about it when you meet with her." Kane suggested with a small shrug and devious smirk on his face. "Anyways, the banquet will be starting. I'll make sure that you get a nice plate full of our delicious food." Kane gave Dean a soft pat on the shoulder before heading towards the staircare to join the other leaders, a place where someone like Dean wasn't welcomed.

UNLIKE the leaders, Dean had found an extra seat that was close to the balcony so that he could easily glance up to see the other leaders. Dean's eyes drifted over towards the two leaders who had already excused themselves. It wasn't long before Felicia and Miles joined them. Ashley had been there, seemingly drawing rather than socializing. Not that Dean would have been surprised either way, but it seemed that the princess really didn't like talking to people.

It was only when Dean noticed that Kane came back to sit next to Ashley that he noticed that the two had switched seats. A small frown seemed to linger on Kane's face, causing Dean to wonder if he should stay down with everyone else. He didn't have a right to be up on the balcony, but that didn't mean he couldn't worry about this friend.

After the leaders were settled down in their seats, the guests had started to make their way towards the tables. A couple and their child, as well as two other gentlemen seemed to sit next to Dean. There were a couple of quick greeted smiles as people took their seats, though it seemed that the only lady of the table felt the need to make some idle talk.

"Hello gentlemen." She greeted, flashing a smile towards the males closest to her. "How is everyone?" She asked in a chipper tone, though Dean felt a bit out of place. Thankfully the large centerpiece in the middle helped to hide Dean from her gaze. The woman was a bit older than Dean, she had small wrinkles around the eyes, making one wonder if they were from years of fake smiling or from old age.

She was wearing a green strapless dress, indicating that she was part of the Envy clan. Her dirty blonde hair was pulled back into a ponytail as her locks seemed to curl together. Her blue eyes were deep, as if they had seen a lot in the course of her lifetime.

"Oh, I see that our dear Kane isn't sitting next to Miles this year." The woman observed, glancing up at the balcony. "I wonder if something happened between the two." She continued on with her small observation. The rest of the males at the table didn't seem hardly interested in the casual talk, simply keeping to themselves and glancing elsewhere.

Seeing as she wasn't going to get any conversation out of the men, the woman turned towards the ladies behind her who seemed to be in the midst of their own conversation. Dean really hated how rumors were spread. Not like she knew the situation, but it seemed like this is what people often did to pass the time apparently. Just like on the Millennium.

When the plates of food had been placed on everyone's table, Amelia cleared her throat as she stood up. "I want to take this time to thank you all for making it to the banquet this year." Amelia started off, her voice loud enough so everyone would be able to hear her. Those who had been talking before she spoke stopped, all eyes were on Amelia as she waited patiently for everyone to gaze at her. "As you know, we've had a bit of a tough couple of years." Amelia continued, pausing to allow people to hear her in the back. "Whether it was from failure of crops being able to grow due to the lingering effects of radiation, or the slaughter of cattle from the wild life seeking out a source of food." She continued, letting the echo of her voice settle towards the back of the room. "But since the years after the senseless bloodshed of our former leaders, we have come a long way since we crawled out of the shelters." Amelia continued, pausing once again, though interrupted by someone from the back.

"Says the one who slain her father after he killed the other leaders." A male voice called out, causing everyone to glance around, either in surprise, shock, or awe. The crowd started to mutter to themselves as the one who made the remark seemed to keep silent for now. Dean kept his attention on Amelia, gauging what her reaction would be. Would she be upset? Shocked? Or maybe angry at the remark that someone made?

Surprisingly Amelia appeared to be a bit annoyed, but not to the point where she would have had the man escorted out, that is if he was found. "Not by choice, as I have stated time and time again." Amelia spoke, an exasperated sigh leaving her lips at the end. "But that is neither here nor there." They had more important things to talk about. Amelia looked like she wanted to get through this as quickly as possible, without much more interruption. "Thanks to the farms in the Envy clan, and those who worked around the clock to make the banquet possible, we toast to the future of success of all the clans." Amelia spoke raising her glass, though no smile seemed to appear on her lips.

"Hold up." The sound of the same man who spoke out finally stood up. The man looked like a hot mess, as if he had drank a bit too much of the free wine that was being served earlier. There were a few red stains that lingered on the white shirt he was wearing. The vest that had once been buttoned up, appeared to only have one button keeping it closed, as it wasn't even perfectly lined up. The dark blue tie he had was loosened to the point where the man could easily lift it over his head. The corner of his thin lips had some red stains that seemingly stained his light blond mustache. The man's bushy brows knitted together as he struggled to stand up.

The man pointed towards the balcony, though his finger swayed more than his body did. The man's thin hair seemed to be slicked, however it almost appeared as if the man was bald in the dim lights. "How are we supposed to enjoy our feast when our so-called leaders aren't even happy when addressing us? She looks like she would rather be somewhere else." The man remarked looking around to see if anyone was willing to join him. However, everyone seemed to be looking away, as if they would be disassociating themselves from the man. "Come on! She's not even smiling. She doesn't want to be here. How can we allow someone like that to be the head leader?"

"Are you quite done?" Amelia asked, her voice scolding the man for his disruption. "Because I would rather not have to eat a cold dinner before we have a meeting to discuss your grievances." It seemed like everyone's attention was between Amelia and the man, waiting to see if the man would either continue to stand up, or if he would tuck his tail between his legs and simply sit. For a few seconds, it appeared if the man was going to defy Amelia as he stood up, but eventually he sat back down with a hard thud. Perhaps his drunken state caused his knees to buckle, possibly even saving the man from any type of scolding or punishment that came his way.

"As I was saying," Amelia cleared her throat before grabbing her glass. "Raise your glasses in cheer. To the newest days ahead of us, and may the troubles of our past and future act as challenges we can overcome." Amelia practically shouted with a flustered look on her face. A side glance was noted as Amelia's lips trembled to say the last part with a straight look on her face. "To the rise of humanity, and the downfall of the Cowards." Amelia cheered, raising her glass high into the air as everyone in the room cheered. Dean wasn't expecting the last part. After all, Amelia didn't say that she was on board with taking down the Elite. Did Ashley put Amelia up to it?

It seemed everything had settled down by the time that Amelia was done downing her wine that everyone was able to peel off the little tray covers that kept their food warm while Amelia gave her speech. Peeling off his silver tray, Dean was greeted with a rather large amount of food on his plate. Glancing to those closest to him, it seemed like they didn't get quite as much as he did, making him feel rather guilty since Kane remarked about how he would pull some strings to get him some of the better selection of food they had to offer. But the smell coming from his plate was simply divine.

On the upper part of the plate rested a beautiful chicken breast. The skin was baked to the perfect golden brown with a layer of breadcrumbs to give it an audible crunch once bitten into. To the right of the chicken rested in a neat pile that smelled of garlic and butter cut up pieces of red potatoes. Even in the dim lighting Dean could see that the potatoes had additional seasoning like salt and pepper as droplets of a golden butter slowly descended against the cut slices. Towards Dean, on the lower section of the plate rested some type of mashed breading that was similar to that of stuffing his mother used to make. Bits of chopped yellow onion stuck out of the lumps and thin slices of celery. The scent of chicken was apparent in the stuffing, almost making Dean's mouth water.

To the left of the plate were various types of vegetables that Dean remembered seeing on the station. Bits of corn, broccoli, cauliflower, and green beans were arranged neatly on the plate, the steam still raising from the vegetables as it caused the candle lighting to waver a bit. In the middle rested two pieces of an egg that had been cut in half. The core had been scrambled into a pasty texture that filled in the gap with some type of red seasoning sprinkled over top of it with bits of black pepper resting on top. Beside the plate was a basket with at least three golden buns that could fit into his hand. There was so much food that Dean didn't even know he could finish it all.

"How am I supposed to finish this all?" Dean mumbled a bit to himself, looking at the food in front of him. Even when Dean was rather pudgy he could never eat all of this. Glancing over to the child, who must have been at least six or seven, it seemed that the child had a fraction of what Dean had. Scooping up the one of the pieces of egg, Dean casually slid it onto the kids plate as he seemed to go for it first. It seemed like the child didn't exactly notice, but was rather glad that he mysteriously got a new piece of egg that could easily slide into the boys' mouth. Next was to figure out what to do with the buns. They were so large that Dean felt like he would only be able to eat one of them.

With a small clearing of his throat, Dean glanced towards the two gentlemen. "Hey guys, would either one of you like another bun to eat?" Dean asked, holding out the basket that had two out of the three buns. Dean would at the very least have one of the buns. Without a single word, the two men easily took the buns without hesitation. Either they were really hungry or the food was just that good that they didn't mind eating more. Placing the bowl back down, Dean looked at the food, there was so much that he had to try. With a small inhale through his parted lips, Dean grasped the fork, it was either now or never.

Stabbing the fork into the chicken, Dean could see some of the white meat already sticking out just from penetrating it and he hasn't even brought the chicken up to his mouth. With a small tug, Dean broke a piece off before bringing it up to his lips. With a quick bite, Dean's taste buds were met with a new taste he never tried before. It was similar to that of the sunflower seeds his mother would offer him as a snack around the early fall time, except in an oil form. On top of that, there was a lemon and honey flavoring that seemed to resonate on his tongue. The steam from the meat made it rather hard to collect more flavors when his mouth felt like it could burn his mouth from the steam alone.

Glancing towards his left, the vegetables seemed like they were calling his name, however the heat from the chicken still lingered. Grasping the wine cup, Dean took a small sip of the red liquid inside. It was a rather strong taste, but it wasn't half bad. It helped to wash some of the heat from his mouth, and in a sense cleansed his pallet. Sticking the sharp prong of the fork into some of the vegetables, Dean was able to sample the vegetables from the Envy clan while comparing them to the vegetables he had on the ship. As the vegetables passed his lips,

Dean took notice that there was a certain garlic, lemon, and buttery taste to the vegetables in his mouth. It was certainly an interesting combination, but it wasn't exactly all that bad. It certainly caused Dean's brows to lift as he thought about the taste. Thankfully the heat didn't almost burn his mouth like the chicken did.

Speaking of chicken, Dean was quick to wash his pallet with the red wine before taking hold of the egg that seemed to try to slide away from the rest of the food that lingered on the plate. Popping the hardened white yolk of the deviled egg into his mouth, Dean started to sample the yellow pastry on top. It was certainly a unique taste that Dean never tried before. It was like a honey mustard flavoring mixed in with yellow yolk that once resided in the egg. The red specks mixed in pepper gave it a small sweet kick to it. It certainly made him almost regret giving the young child the other half of the egg.

Needing a small break from the food on his plate, Dean grabbed the bun he had left before pulling the hot bun apart, opening up to white flaky interior. In a small circular dish rested a semi melted butter that smelled oddly of honey. Grabbing the knife provided to him, Dean started to spread the butter against the parted bun. Upon setting the knife down, Dean took a bite of the bun with a small hum. The bun had a sweet taste to it. Whether it was because of the butter that was currently spread on it, or that it was the natural taste of the bun, it was hard not to want to put down. With another sip of the wine, Dean picked up his fork that rested against the plate. Deciding on what he should go for next, it seemed that he should try the potatoes as they called to him as the steam raised up and the smell was mouthwatering.

Gently stabbing one of the red potato skinned pieces, the heat of the potato brushed against his lips as he took a bite. The taste of garlic was overwhelming. There was some lingering taste of butter afterwards, but overall it was still very good. The potatoes were soft, making it easy to either eat as it was, or to simply smash it up and enjoy it that way. Glancing around, Dean noticed that there were some people using a bit of the butter he used for the bun to mix it up into the potatoes.

Either Dean was eating them wrong, or perhaps those around him have learned how to make their meals taste even better than originally intended. Using his fork to scoop out the butter, it didn't take long for Dean to mash the potatoes up into a small pile with the honey butter blending into the mixture. Taking another sample bite, Dean was surprised at how much better it tasted. Plus with the added bonus of pieces of the chicken skin collected underneath the mashed potatoes it seemed to mix into a perfect harmony in his mouth.

The last bit Dean had to try was the stuffing. With a small huff leaving his lips, Dean took the fork that lingered in his hand before collecting some of the crumbling bread onto the fork. Bringing the fork up to his mouth, Dean took a bite, only to be met with the honey chicken flavoring from the chicken he was provided. With a bit more chewing, Dean was able to taste the soft crunch of the celery and onion combination that he could somewhat make out in the lighting. There was some extra seasoning that had a bit of lemon and garlic in it, but it wasn't as overwhelming as some of the other dishes.

Reaching out to grab the wine glass, Dean took another sip of the wine to help him rinse out the garlic taste that was on mostly every dish. Before too much longer, Dean found that his stomach had become full, his mind slightly buzzed from the wine warming his body, and the plate completely empty, so for a few small crumbs that even a mouse wouldn't be able to eat. All in all, the food from the banquet made up for rudeness Dean experienced earlier.

With his stomach full, Dean felt like he could fall asleep right there in the chair. But sadly, he wouldn't get the chance to do so. As some of the guests had started to make their way out the door, Dean noticed that a lot of them were those who had some children. Just what time was it anyways? It didn't matter either way. Dean just wanted to be able to see if he could collect Kane so that they could head back to the manor now. With the one glass of wine in his system, Dean wasn't exactly at his best as this was the first time he had anything alcoholic. Sure Dean could have made his way to the space equivalent of a dive bar while he was on the Millennium, but that meant that he had to go out and be around people.

Taking it rather easy with getting up, Dean glanced around to those who were still in the banquet hall. Those who weren't still eating had started to either idly chat among each other, or had headed towards the dancing area as the band had come back from their break. The music that filled the air was a light jazz that people could slow dance to. It reminded Dean of the times he would try and sneak down for a snack when he was out of school, only to see his parents slow dancing in the living room. The way Emily would rest her head against Max's shoulder as they slowly danced in a small circle. The smile lingering on his mother's face as she looked as if she was in heaven. It made Dean ache to be able to experience something similar, though he never got close enough to anyone to try it out.

Making his way over to the steps, Dean noticed that Felicia and Miles were the first ones down the steps. The same type of smile that Dean's mother used to have was seemingly spread across Felicia's lips. Dean couldn't help but notice the similarities when it was right in front of him. Felicia was really head over heels in love with Miles. The couple resembled Dean's parents so much, it almost hurt.

Keeping out of their way, the two passed Dean with a small nod of their head. Next down the steps were Amelia and Keaton. Though Amelia kept a stoic gaze, she did glance towards Dean as the two of them passed Dean. Seemed like the couples were heading towards the dance floor already. Nothing like music to bring couples closer together. A faint smile lingered on Dean's lips as he figured that this would be the perfect time for Ashley, Dean, and Kane to head on back to the house.

Each step felt like it was a bit heavier than the last, like Dean's shoes were slowly becoming filled with cement. Using the railing to help guide his way up, Dean reached the top in the steps in no time. Ashley and Kane seemed to be sitting at the table. Kane glanced over Ashley's shoulder as she was using the light from the candles to draw. They seemed to talk a bit, or rather Kane was the one doing the majority of the talking, all the while Ashley was focused on the sketch pad in front of her.

Slipping his hands into his pockets, Dean made his way over to the two. As he got closer, Dean gave a small wave in order to get the two leaders' attention when Kane looked over towards him. "Hey, you two. Ready to head back?" Dean asked, calling out to the two leaders. Kane seemed to be the only one to get up from the table while Ashley kept on drawing on her newly bought sketchbook.

"Oh, Dean." Kane called out, causing Ashley to glance up to spare Dean a small glance before going back to her sketch. "How did you enjoy the banquet?" Kane asked, making a bit of idle conversation while getting out of his chair. Unlike Dean, Kane didn't have much to drink, but then again Kane didn't exactly like the taste of wine to begin with. It always left a bit of a sour taste in his mouth.

"Yeah, it was really great. Filled me up and then some." Dean lightly joked, a small chuckle leaving his lips. "Though there was a noticeable amount of garlic, lemon, and honey. But over all, it was good." Dean remarked, shrugging his shoulders a bit. Not that he minded the taste, but it did leave an odd aftertaste in his mouth. He'll just have to make sure to brush his teeth and scrap his tongue to get the garlic taste out of his mouth. "I'm ready to call it a night if you guys are." Dean commented, earning a small sigh from Ashley as she gave Dean a rather annoyed glance as she stopped her sketching. "What?" Dean asked, a bit confused as Kane joined his side.

"Ashley has to stay and help clean up everything." Kane remarked, noticing the annoyed scowl on Ashley's face. "Part of the rules for the hosting Clan's leader to have a banquet at their place. They get to dictate what they want to do for the end of the year banquet, no matter how big they want to have it," Kane continued to explain as he collected his jacket from behind his chair. "But on the condition that they help to clean up at the end of it." Kane explained as he slipped on the jacket. "I even offered to help her out, but Ashley was insistent that she do it herself." Kane continued, slipping his hands into his pockets before turning away from the two.

"Don't phrase it like that." Ashley snipped, a small scoff leaving her lips as she closed her eyes and tilted her head away from the two. "It's not like I am going to be the only one to pick up after everyone. I'll have some volunteers to help me." It seemed like Ashley wanted to make that point clear to the two. "Anyways, you two should get going before the snowstorm hits."

"Snowstorm?" Kane asked, his voice indicating a bit of concern, though Dean didn't know what the big deal was. Not like it would completely bury them, right? They had some of these snowstorms in the last few days, or at least that was what Dean thought. "What level are we talking about?" Kane asked, a bit concerned now that Ashley spoke up about it.

"A level three." Ashley spoke in a 'matter-of-fact' type tone. "I'll be sending everyone home shortly. Perhaps Amelia and the others would be kind enough to help me out since Amelia doesn't like snowstorms either." Ashley kept talking before side glancing at the two.

"You go ahead and go home. Just prepare a fire by the bathtub. I'll want to get the smell of booze off of me when I get home." Ashley instructed as she moved a wine stained napkin off to the side. "Some dumb ass spilled their wine glass over me and now I simply reek of it." Not that Dean had seen it happen, as he was absorbed into sampling the food when it happened, but there was a small lingering smell of wine that seemed to be coming from her.

"You got it Ash." Kane quickly remarked before grabbing a hold of Dean's arm. "Come on, we can head out the back. No need to go the long way around when we have a direct pathway to the house." It almost seemed like Kane was in a hurry to head back home, though it could just be Dean's imagination. "Ready?" Kane asked, giving Dean's sleeve a small tug as he started to head towards the stairs. Dean silently followed Kane, figuring that it would be better to not argue or linger more than he should have. After all, Dean wasn't exactly thrilled with the idea of walking back in the cold.

Reaching the bottom stairs wasn't much of a problem for Dean, nor was skirting around the rooms' walls to either avoid other people or to slip out undetected, but it was the cold air hitting his thinly covered body that caused Dean to stiffen. He didn't imagine that the wind would be a big deal, but the thin air around him felt like he was being stabbed by invisible ice shards that were cutting into his lungs.

"F-Fuck it's cold out here." Dean remarked through chattering teeth. Wrapping his arms around himself, and sticking his hands into his armpits to keep them warm, Dean moved to curl into himself a bit. Unlike Kane, Dean didn't have a jacket offered to him to keep him warm.

"Of course it's' cold." Kane remarked, a soft chuckle leaving his lips as the hot air puffed out into a visible ball in front of him. "No sun means no heat." Kane lightly taunted as he started to lightly jog down the pathway, turning to move around the broken fountain. "Keep moving and you won't freeze too badly." Dean seemed to resent that remark. One would figure that someone who lived on the space station would be used to the freezing cold atmosphere of space. With his sector being furthest away from the sun, Dean was used to the cold. But this was a whole new level of cold Dean never experienced before.

"Come on, if we jog towards the house, we'll be able to warm up faster." Kane remarked with a soft mused chuckle towards the end, his body seemingly bouncing to keep his body temperature up. Even though Dean didn't like it, he knew Kane had a point. Better to keep moving than to stay and freeze.

By the time they had gotten inside, Dean felt as if he was a giant popsicle. The house was warm thanks to the radiators spread through the house to keep it warm in the winter. It didn't take long for Dean to find the radiator that was located by the table in the kitchen. The heat coming off of it was simply heavenly to Dean at that moment. "I feel like meat being put out to thaw." Dean cooed as he felt like his skin was starting to sweat the cold off.

"That's one way of putting it." Kane remarked, peeling the jacket off of him. The small cosmos flower seemed to fall to the ground as it became loose when he jogged towards the house with Dean. Stepping over the flower, Kane headed towards the foyer, seemingly ready to just crash for the night. The tone in his voice made it seem like there was something bothering Kane, but perhaps he felt like he needed to keep it to himself? Was Kane trying to simply get this night done and over with already?

Peeling himself away from the radiator, Dean followed Kane upstairs. The silence in the house was rather eerie as the winds were picking up. Since there wasn't anyone in the house, it felt like every board that was stepped on creaked under the smallest pressure. As Kane got up to the top of the steps, he glanced back to see Dean walking a few steps behind him.

"Are you heading towards the bathroom to take a bath? Or starting up a fire for Ashley?" Kane asked, looking at Dean briefly before he started to walk down the hallway, seemingly in a hurry to get away from Dean.

"I just figured that I would check up on you first." Dean remarked, continuing to follow

Kane. "After all, you seem like you are in a big hurry to get out of the banquet." Dean spoke as he kept his attention on Kane's back, watching Kane's body language since the leader wasn't going to be honest with him. "I could have shared the radiator you know." Kane didn't say anything.

Instead, Kane's foot steps seemed to get quicker as he rounded the corner that led towards the room they shared. A sigh escaped Dean's lips as he followed Kane, though his footsteps were normal. Rounding the corner, Dean went inside before closing the door behind him. Kane seemed to already be working on the buttons of the vest to peel it off of him. Tossing the jacket in some random corner of the room, Dean watched as the articles of clothing were flung against the wall. "In a bad mood?" Dean asked, raising a brow as he glanced at the jacket that was thrown.

An exasperated sigh seemed to leave Kane's lips as he stood in front of the bed. Lowering his head, Kane's shoulders dipped as he clenched his hands. "I don't really want to talk about it right now Dean." Kane spoke, bringing up his right hand to cover his right eye with the palm of his hand while Kane's fingers gingerly rested over his left eye. "I don't exactly have a right to complain...but I don't think that it's fair that I always get the short end of the stick." Kane muttered, slowly shaking his head as he didn't care if Dean heard him or not at this point.

"What do you mean?" Dean asked, his concern showing on his face as he walked over towards Kane. It seemed that Kane would keep quiet as he simply didn't answer. Placing a hand on Kane's shoulder, Dean pulled the other back to have Kane look at him instead.

Slowly dripping down Kane's face was the tears that Kane was holding back that night. Dean tightened his grip on Kane's shoulder, feeling a need to comfort the smaller male. Without saying another word, Dean wrapped his arms around Kane's neck as Dean embraced him tightly. It wasn't long before Dean felt Kane's hands tightly grip Dean's arms as if to make sure that Dean didn't leave him as well.

"Listen Kane," Dean spoke softly close to Kane's ear, ignoring the fact that his own heart started to pound against his chest from having another person so close. "No one deserves to put themselves through hell." Dean rested his own head against Kane's before he continued. "Life itself isn't exactly fair... but that doesn't mean that you should always feel like you are getting shafted simply because you are the leader of the Gluttony clan." Dean remarked, bringing his hand up to place on the back of Kane's head. With small soft strokes, Dean lightly petted Kane's head before continuing to speak. "Right now, it's just us in this room. You don't have to worry about titles or what other people think. You're my friend Kane, so naturally I care about you."

It wasn't long before Dean felt Kane loosen in his arms, causing Dean to let go in case he was suffocating Kane. Luckily that didn't seem to be the case. It appeared that all the tension that Kane had seemed to fly out the window. Though Kane's eyes were a bit red from crying, Kane reached up to wipe them away before an audible sniffle could be heard. "I know Dean." Kane spoke, before taking a deep breath to help calm his down a bit more.

"I appreciate it. I really do." Kane continued, taking a small step back. "It's just... the last couple of years have always been the same." Kane remarked, moving to the bed to sit down, hunching forward and seemingly draping his arms over his legs. "We would have a banquet, everyone would be paired off except for Ashley and myself, and we would sit there and watch other people have fun." It seemed that perhaps this repeated behavior was getting on the last of Kane's nerves. "Amelia and Keaton would usually be the first to pardon themselves, and then it would Felicia and Miles. But it seemed that they have really grown closer over the years... and I have been left behind."

Before they were leaders, Miles would often spend a majority of his time with Kane. But it appears that as they got older in age, the rift had been getting gradually wider. Now Kane was left by himself, watching as the man Kane loved for so long practically ignored him. And for what? Simply because of an ideal that Keaton put in place? Those who were brought into a family, regardless if they weren't blood related or married into a family, they were considered sick if they had more than family love for one other? It didn't make any sense, but Miles seemed to play along with it. Not like Kane had a choice when his brother slaughtered his mother and sister, only to have his father killed off shortly after. Perhaps it would be a completely different story if none of that happened.

"Being a Tribal leader is overrated... I just want to be done with it." Kane muttered, lowering his head even more as his feet shuffled together. "People will only try to use you in order to get power. So it's not like I'll be able to get a real connection to someone." Kane continued, the defeat seemingly sinking in. Not like Dean could blame the male. It was just like that on the station. No place seemed to be safe for those in power to make real connections. It was either people were going to use you for their own personal gain, or to feel like they had no control over what happens to those under the Elite.

Moving to sit down next to Kane, Dean placed a hand on Kane's back. Softly stroking his hand up and down on Kane's back, Dean took some time to think about what he was going to say. He didn't know if there would be anything he could say or do to cheer Kane up, but at the very least, he could at least try something, right?

"People can be both the greatest thing to happen to you, as well as the worse." Dean remarked before pausing. "You just gotta let the right people in is all." A small smile seemed to linger on Dean's face as he glanced at Kane. "You're doing everything in your power to be the greatest leader for your clan, and so far from what I can see, you're doing an amazing job." Dean wasn't the type to know for certain how Kane did when it came to doing his actual job, but Kane was at least trying his best. "You're a lot better at being a leader than the Elite. That's without a doubt since you actually care about the people you lead." Dean continued, a little chuckle leaving his lips towards the end.

That comment alone seemed to make Kane chuckle a bit, meaning that Dean was on the right path to cheering the male up. "But as a person, without titles behind your name," Dean paused, taking notice of the small head tilt from Kane, as if the male was hanging onto the words that Dean would say next to determine if Kane was at least a decent person worthy of being Dean's friend or not.

"You're probably the only one whom I can trust." Dean continued, watching as Kane lifted his head to meet Dean's gaze. "Sure you may have your small flaws, but that's what makes you human." Not like the leaders on the Millennium who felt the need to hide their own flaws. It was as if the Elite wanted themselves to be seen as gods to the remaining human survivors. "You could have very easily left me to simply die on the planet. To be engulfed in the meadow by the fire that came from my shuttle, but you helped me out."

"Well, to be fair, the meadow was close to my house." Kane remarked, the corner of his lips seeming to tug back as his gaze moved to the floor. "It was just a good thing that we didn't have any important crops that were going to be yielded. Otherwise we may have charged you to pay for the damages..." Dean softly chuckled towards the end of Kane's remark, removing his hand from Kane's back in the process.

"I would have hated to see what you would have done if I did crash into your place." Dean remarked, this time earning a soft chuckle from Kane. "You made sure to get me medical attention before I passed out." Dean continued as he moved to rest his hands behind him on the bed. "You came pretty much every day to check up on me. You could have simply left me to rot in a jail cell or something. But instead, you treated me as one of your own, and I can't thank you enough for it." It wasn't like that on the station. It was always every man for themselves.

"Hell, you've even allowed me to come with you to meet with the other leaders after you heard about my plan to bring down the space station." That was probably the most surprising part of the whole ordeal if you were to ask Dean. "You really don't deserve the shit that you're dealt Kane. You deserve to be happy." Dean remarked with a smile before bringing up a hand to lightly ruffle Kane's hair. "I'll do whatever it takes to make you happy."

"Anything?" Kane asked, a hopeful gaze to his eyes as the male glanced towards Dean. The way that Kane's silver gray eyes shimmered with hope, Dean could only ponder as to what Kane had up his sleeve. A nervous smile grew on Dean's lips as he lightly nodded, praying that this wouldn't backfire on him. "Alright..." Kane continued, moving to stand up from the bed. "I think I will hold onto your promise and cash it in later." Kane remarked, his back facing Dean, leaving him to wonder what kind of look Kane had on his face right now.

"For now, I'm just exhausted." Kane finally spoke after a few minutes of silence filling the room. "I think I'll take a bath before Ashley gets back." Kane added, moving to face Dean with a light flustered look on his face. "That way she'll have hot water when she comes in." Kane finished as he moved towards the door. It felt more like a reasonable excuse to get out of the room to Dean, but it was probably for the best right now.

Dean was unsure of what to make of what he agreed to, but it seemed to cheer Kane up. Surely Kane wouldn't make Dean do something that he would regret later on, would he? Watching as Kane left the room, Dean was left alone with his thoughts. His mind was swirling from everything that seemed to happen, as well as curious as to what Kane would ask for in either the near or later future. Laying back against the bed, Dean gazed up at the ceiling. Bringing his hands to rest against his stomach, Dean closed his eyes. It seemed that their relationship could get to be a bit more complicated in the future, but for now, at least Kane was acting more like himself. Or so, that's what Dean told himself.

CHAPTER FIFTEEN: *The Long Journey*

MONTHS AFTER THE banquet seemed to roll on by. Before too much longer, the snow that had once been piling up to the windows was completely gone. The buds on the trees were growing greener by the day as the season turned into Spring. Walking out of the house was Dean and Kane, followed by Ashley who seemed to stop by the entrance of the estate. Dean was wearing a new type of outfit that had been put together for the long journey ahead of him. The shirt that Dean was wearing was a type of tunic that he could only imagine someone in the medieval wearing with a warm long john shirt that was colored white to keep the cold away as the tunic itself was black with the edges silver in color. The gauntlets he was wearing were changed out for ones that covered his fingers, as well as be lined with a type of fur to keep him warm. The pants were rather thick in material, allowing Dean to remain warm as the temperatures were still a bit cold, only to get colder when they had to head through the mountains.

The boots Dean wore clung tightly to his calves, allowing for his body heat to be trapped and the fur inside of the boot to keep Dean's feet from getting cold or frost bitten. A dark poncho was draped over Dean's shoulders with a rather large pin with deer antlers kept the fabric held together. The hood rested against his back with the hood lined with white fur to stick out more easily in case of hunters in the area. On top of his head was a wool cap that covered his ears while a warm scarf was neatly wrapped around Dean's neck. As they were going to venture towards the mountains, it was best to dress in layers.

"Do we have everything that we need?" Kane asked, walking behind Dean with a large backpack in either hand. Kane was wearing something completely different than Dean, seeing as how the male was needing to stick out more while wearing his decorative headpiece of the deer antlers. Wearing a dark blue cap underneath to keep his ears warm, Kane had a small scarf that was neatly tucked away that had some deer figures etched into the woolly fabric. With the white and blue poncho pulled open, Kane's outfit was available for people to see. The dark blue tunic top was rather loose on Kane as the dark gray long sleeved long john ended at his wrist. The gauntlet gloves were finger-less, but there was a pouch that dangled against Kane's right hip that had regular gloves to help keep him warm when they got up to higher and colder regions of the mountains.

Tight shorts with bits of black long johns peaked out against Kane's legs as the knee high boots with white fur trimming against the bit of exposed edges showed that Kane would at least still be comfortable walking around in the mountains. Setting the bags down with a small groan, Kane didn't waste any time as he started to do some basic stretches.

"What are you doing?" Dean asked, a bit surprised to see that Kane was doing the same type of stretching as if they were getting ready to do some training. Speaking of which, Dean had noticed that his muscles were getting to be a bit more defined as Kane started to help train him. Mostly it was a precaution if anyone were to try anything with them on the open road or if a wild animal were to try and attack them. Even Kane admitted that there were rumors of some people giving travelers' a hard time in some of the villages along the way.

"I'm getting my muscles ready for the long journey. What else?" Kane mused as he continued with the stretching. "You should probably do the same." Normally Dean would have made up some excuse as to not need to stretch, but given that they were going to be walking for what could be a few weeks, Dean was not going to argue.

After a few minutes of awkward stretching grunts and groans, Ashley let out an exasperated sigh. With a white shawl over the dark green dress she was wearing, Ashley's usual frown seemed to rest on her face. "Are you two done yet? The sooner you leave, the sooner you can make it to Keaton's clan." Dean still wasn't sure about how he felt about Keaton, but he wouldn't let the other leaders down now that they were already halfway done with meeting everyone. "I'm sure he'll be thrilled to get to know our little visitor here." Ashley remarked, crossing her arms to keep warm in the slightly chilled air. There was a bit of dew still lingering on the grass as the sun was barely peeking out over some of the buildings in the distance.

"What do you mean?" Dean asked, his curiosity seeming to get the better of him. Dean had only seen this guy around the estate and only got to talk to him once properly at the banquet. Dean would much rather forget about how he had practically bumped heads with the Head of the Clans. Eventually Dean would have to sit down with the other leaders and have a deep discussion with them. Whether Kane was present or not, Dean had to at least talk to Miles alone and ask him why he was so set on making Kane distant with him. If not for Kane's sake, but for Dean's own personal curiosity.

"You'll just have to wait and see." Ashley spoke almost in a sing-song tone with a hint of mischievous in her eyes. That was never a good thing. Perhaps Dean could ask Kane more about it when the time comes for the two of them to get closer to the Lust clan. "Now, do you want me to send your belongings back to your place, Kane? Or are you just going to store them here?" Ashley asked, her usual uppity voice returning.

"Good question." Kane remarked as he placed his hands onto his slender hips. Leaning back for the last bit of his stretch, a long groan escaped his lips before stopping. "You can send the remaining items over by the end of summer or early fall. Anything that you would want to be set up in your room as well send with it." Kane remarked as he picked up his bag.

"That way you'll have something to wear when you come for the next banquet." Seemed like this was their usual tradition after the winter months end. "Let the others know to do the same. And to label it too." Kane continued before slipping his backpack on. "I don't want Amelia to get angry at me simply because I thought Felicia's clothes were hers and vice versa." Rather this has happened before or not, it seemed like Kane was covering all of his tracks before leaving Ashley to pass along the message.

"I still don't see why you couldn't just take the airship over to Keaton's place. Even if you had to take it later in the evening. It would be better than trekking through the mountains just to get there." Ashley remarked, knowing that she wouldn't be able to stop Kane once his mind was set. The two men looked like regular explorers now, though Ashley never got the appeal of walking the long distance between the other clans near her. They made plenty of advancements since coming out of the shelters and reforming humanity, it was a shame that the two males were ready to make the long trek just to get to the next clan.

"I uh," Kane started to speak, trying to find the right words to explain the situation. After all, it wasn't easy to deal with being able to see the person you longed for seemingly flirting with someone else, much less risk having to share the same airship ride with them.

"I asked Kane to take me." Dean lied, stepping up to help the male. "I always wanted to see nature in the purest element. Considering that we don't have anything real on the station besides the crops that we grow, I figured it would be nice to see how much has changed since the bombs dropped." Which wasn't exactly a complete lie. Dean had always been curious about how the world changed by comparing the images he had seen in old books and magazines. Sure he may not be able to see everything, but being able to at least go out and see it for himself, that was worth the long trek they would deal with.

"Fine... not like I can really stop you." Ashley huffed, side glancing the two males as she turned as if to head back inside. "Just make sure you don't get lost. Or get eaten. We don't have anyone that could replace you Kane." Ashley remarked, though she was showing a bit of her concern for the other leader. "Stay at the inns when you can. If you need extra money or anything, sell what you can and get reimbursed later on." As she headed inside, Dean pulled the hood of the poncho over his head, signaling that he was ready to head out. It was nice knowing that Ashley at least cared for them, though showing it in her own nagging way.

It was a bit unsettling walking past people who seemed to be staring at them like the two males were crazy to walk the path that led towards the Lust clan, but this was the direction that they had to go, so why not make the best of it? Once they were far away from people, Dean felt a bit more at ease. As they kept to the dirt path that had been worn down by time, Dean couldn't help but take everything in as they walked.

As the sun started to warm up hillside that they were walking up, the cold air that once felt like shards of glass being pulled into his mouth or nose started to warm up. It made walking that much easier, despite the amount of items that they were carrying. Dean figured that Kane had gone a bit overboard with collecting supplies the moment that the snow started to melt, but it seemed like a sound investment now. The pains that once ached Dean's back had seemingly faded the more that he worked out with Kane. It showed that even Dean was able to adjust to his new surroundings, despite not being born on Earth like the other male.

The grass that seemingly grew on the sides of the road was a dark shade of green that Dean never saw before. Or rather, he never saw it on the station. Compared to the grass close by, the grass on the Millennium was fake. The fence posts on either side of the road were made out of rocks with a spaced out board that were being held up by some type of barbed fence. The cattle that seemed to be grazing out in the field indicated that the fence was used to keep said cattle in. Sadly they were too far away from Dean, keeping him from seeing how much the bovine had changed over the course of the generations since the bombs had dropped.

The hills in the distance were colored different shades of green from the mixture of the clouds that hung overhead, casting shade on the field in front of them. The clouds were a thin gray, but there wasn't any type of dark coloring that would indicate rain, so at least they didn't have to worry about getting poured on so early on in their journey. The sound of the stones crunching under their feet reminded Dean of the first time seeing the Millennium from space for the first time.

Remembering that the red lights that once indicated the housing pods for the Bronze class encircled the edges of the station to make it appear like some type of glowing red eye was casting its gaze down onto the Earth below. How menacing it appeared. It's crazy to even believe that it would look like anything other than some type of judgmental eye of god peering down to see if there were any survivors when the bombs had dropped.

The place that was once home looked completely terrifying on the outside. How could Dean even comfortably say that he came from such a place? How often did Kane look up and wonder just what those on board were like. Surely those on the station must have been seen as nothing more than heartless monsters to these people. Dean had to take that damn station out of the sky, even if it was the last thing he ever did on this planet.

***

After walking what felt like hours, Dean felt as if his legs were about to fall off. Walking in silence wasn't exactly something that Dean thought to be ideal, but at least they made some distance. Finding a stump that seemed to be lingering years after the tree had been cut down, Dean peeled off the backpack with a small groan. This seemed to catch Kane's attention, who probably would have kept going if it wasn't for the groan. Backtracking a couple of steps, Kane walked up to Dean who looked to be exhausted. "Finally need a break?" Kane asked, a faint smile on his face as he stepped over the bag that Dean placed on the ground before taking a seat next Dean.

"Yeah. My stomach is running on empty." Dean explained as he moved to lean back against the stumps' surface. The tree was cold, no life seemingly coming from it, like it was completely hollow at this point. While laying there, Dean could feel bits of his muscles twitching from the long hike they had already taken. The cool breeze of the spring air helped to cool off bits of Dean's face, feeling a bit overheated since they stopped walking. "Can we make something to eat? I'm starving." Dean asked with a light pat on his stomach that had a low growl escaping afterwards.

Instead of saying anything, Kane set his backpack down in front of him before starting to shift around in the bag. Pulling out some tightly wrapped bars, Kane tossed one on Dean's stomach before fetching out a container that had some water in it. "Eat up." Kane chimed, bringing the container close to his lips before drinking out of it. Dean seemed to be fumbling with the package before finally tearing it open."It has some protein in it, so it will help with your sore muscles. It's not much, but the town we'll be staying in is at the foot of the mountain." Kane pointed down the pathway, causing Dean to turn his head to see where Kane was pointing.

Dean's eyes seemed to widen in awe as he didn't even realize that they were heading towards a mountain. Dean had thought that perhaps his vision was playing tricks on him. The powder on top of the mountain looked like clouds. There were small bits of rocks visible even from the distance that they currently were, but being able to see where the green tree tops stopped and the rocky edges began. The snow on the very top stuck out against the pale blue sky as the actual clouds nearby were heavy with water. The ravine at the base of the mountain showed a fairly decent size town, making Dean wonder how the people could stand living so close to the large mountain.

"Whoa..." Dean gazed in awe before taking a bite of the bar. "I...always saw what a mountain looked like in the books I read," Dean started to talk, a bit of food in his mouth as he chewed. "But I never thought that I would actually witness just how beautiful it looks in person." Dean finished, only to take another bite out of the bar as a soft hum left his lips. Seems like Dean was hungrier than he originally thought.

"Yeah." Kane agreed with a small nod of his head before starting to unwrap the package of his own protein bar as well. "It's been so long since I had seen the mountains this close, that I forget just how amazing they are." Kane remarked, only to take a bite out the bar himself. "The way that forest surrounding the mountain seems to flourish is something that I was always interested in." Kane continued after swallowing the food he had in his mouth.

"How only particular ferns and trees can grow in a cold and harsh environment....I will need to take some soil samples and see what we can grow around here." Kane mostly noted to himself as he never got the chance to be able to do so in the past. It made Kane feel like he was slacking in his role since he wanted to find the right types of crop growth for various regions so produce the best type of produce for the Envy clan.

"I was curious about something." Dean remarked, causing Kane to glance over to him with one of Kane's cheeks puffed out ever so slightly with the bit of the protein bar in his mouth. "Do you enjoy growing crops?" Dean asked, moving to sit up a bit so that the two of them could actually talk about this in depth. "You seem to like researching different types of soil and the way that certain crops are grown. Is that something you enjoy?" Not that it was a bad thing, but it was just something that Dean seemed to notice about the other and had some questions about it.

"Well, I guess you sort of get used to it after a while." Kane remarked, a small shrug of his shoulders as he lightly grasped the wrapper. "My father taught me everything I knew before he died." It might have been a sore subject in the past, but it seemed that Dean had been around him so much and knew the dark history that haunted Kane that it only made sense to be able to talk about this subject more freely with the male.

"My big brother and I would always help out the other farms around our place. Though my father knew a bit more than the farmers around us. So it's sort of like second nature now. Like an old habit." That was the best way that Kane could really describe it. He often did things revolving around vegetation growth that came as second nature and wouldn't notice until someone pointed it out.

"So what was your dad like before and after the incident?" Dean asked, a bit curious if Elijah had changed much since everything happened before his untimely death. If Max had lost Emily and only had Dean left to be with him, Dean could only imagine just how overprotective the man might have gotten. It would be even worse if Emily was the one who was alive. She would become overzealous with wanting to protect the only thing she had left to remind her of Max. Considering that Max was her one true love, it was only because of Dean that she was able to remain strong enough to put Dean to bed without him catching on that something wasn't right that night.

"Well," Kane paused, bringing up the container to take a sip to wash away any of the protein bars that lingered in his mouth. "Before the incident, my dad was rather relaxed most of the time." Kane paused as he took a sip of the cold water. "But there were times when he had to be tough on us. Especially when my mom got on his case." A small faint smile seemed to linger on Kane's face before the frown took over when thinking about how much Elijah changed.

"But afterwards, he got to be really protective..." Kane trailed off with a small sigh at the end. "Sort of like a protective owl that has a nest with one egg surviving in it." It was a sad thought, but losing all but one of your offspring can really change a parent. "I went to stay with Miles afterwards when dad would have to do business with the other leaders." Kane lowered his head as he clenched onto the water container for the next part.

"I could barely go outside and play, or really do much of anything else without letting him know." The tone of voice in Kane's remark was sad, like he hated recalling the hard memories associated with his father. "But, it didn't last long since only a few months after my brother went crazy and killed my mother and sister, that dad's life was taken as well." If Kane would have known what was about to happen to his father, then perhaps he could have stopped Elijah from leaving that day.

Dean sat there, trying to think of what to say that could change the mood from something as depressing as the death of Kane's father, but nothing came to mind. Finishing their snacks, they started to pack up their items and head down the pathway once more. Dean felt like an idiot for bringing it up, but he was just curious as to how Elijah had changed after the traumatic event. It wasn't like Dean would ever get the chance to know how such an event could cause the mental shift in a parent since Dean's parents died one after the other. But it did make Dean wonder if his parents had thought about him in their dying moments. Did they regret the choices they made? Did they wish the best for him in a life without them around? Not that Dean would get the chance to know, but it was something that often weighed heavily on his mind when the subject matter of family came up.

As they entered the town, Dean was surprised that most of the people there seemed to ignore the two men. There was an overwhelming smell of dead meat close by to a butcher shop, it was a rather unpleasant smell that reminded Dean of the time spent at the morgue. It seemed that this town was able to get fresh meat that would result in most of the people around to be either plump or fit. It was an interesting concept from everything that Dean had seen so far.

Not that this was his first time seeing people that weren't rather slimming, but it gave off the sense of a community where one would have expected to be in the Bronze class. A bunch of hard working individuals who would come together in order to make the best out of a bad situation. Kane wasted no time in walking over towards the inn where some people seemed to be enjoying a midday drink. Following behind him, Dean stepped into a rather worn down brick building with its' french style doors opened to allow for better traffic.

As they headed inside, the smell of burning wood and a lingering stench of cheese filled the air. It wasn't exactly bad, but certainly not what Dean was expecting when he walked in. There were a few patrons lingering about as they sat down to large circular tables that looked as if the tables used to be the trunk of various trees, much like what Dean had seen at the inn he met Felicia in. The wooden floor was a bit dusty with bits of caked mud in various locations. The crackling of a fire and the murmurs of the patrons sounded a bit distant with bits of clinking glass from the beer mugs that still had bits of beer foam resting at the bottom.

A barmaid with red hair that was twisted into a french bun wandered around the tables to collect the empty glass mugs. Her uniform was a bit dirty from the various stains from the greasy food she served mixed with bits of frost from the beer mugs. Bit of her red bangs were scattered from dealing with the first rush of customers to come in. It seems as though Dean and Kane had just missed the lunch rush.

Kane headed towards a section of the inn that was separated from the tavern area. Following Kane up the single step that led towards a more relaxing lounge area, Dean looked around at the wooden interior. There were plenty of stuffed trophies of creatures that Dean had never seen before, all of which were animals that had been mutated after the bombs dropped. There was something that must have been a deer considering that the antlers were much like the ones that Kane was currently wearing as his head piece.

The eyes were obviously fake, but the fur was different from the original tanned coloring. In the place, patches of the fur appeared to be spotted with bits of white, almost like a fawn. There was another creature that looked like an albino moose. The blue eyes used made the stuffed head look like it was some type of mystic creature that could hold the spirit of a god. Dean could only imagine what the hunter thought when they had seen this beautiful creature gazing beside a lake, drinking the water before ultimately meeting its death. Certainly looked heavy from the size of the head.

"You can't be serious." Kane's voice remarked, catching Dean's attention as he walked over towards the leader. "That would be all of my chips!" Kane continued, seemingly making Dean even more curious as to what was going on. As Dean moved to stand next to Kane, the tribal leader looked up at him with a rather worried expression. "They want to charge 500 chips per person to stay just one night at the inn." The disbelief in Kane's voice wasn't unwarranted.

"What comes with it?" Dean asked, glancing towards the innkeeper who looked rather bored. Like he had heard this whole speech about the unfair price a million times before. "Does it come with meals? A hot bath or shower? Or would we have to pay that separate?" Dean asked, figuring that the cost should at least cover something other than a single night in a bed.

"Aye." The man remarked, his voice monotone as he picked up the book he was reading before the two had come in. The man was rather scruffy looking with a long bushy beard. Wrinkles creased his eyes as his rather large belly seemed to be poking up on the edge of the counter. The book he was holding seemed to be rather worn out. Bits of red leather was missing, exposing the white binding underneath it while the words had long since faded.

"To which part?" Dean asked, rather confused since he didn't seem to get his question answered. The man wasn't quick to reply. Dean couldn't make heads or tails if it was simply because the man was thinking about the response or that he was still looking at the book he was reading.

"Aye." The man repeated, not even bothering to look up at the two men.

It seemed that Kane was a bit at a loss of what the two should do. They had just started on their journey and this man was already taking most of their chips. Dean glanced around to see if perhaps he would be able to come up with a solution. Even though he hated the idea, he knew what must be done.

Reaching under the poncho, Dean pulled out the satchel he was carrying and handed it to Kane. "Here, pay the room with my chips. I think I have an idea in which we can get a bit more." Dean remarked, making his way towards the french doors that led outside. Kane didn't even get a chance to argue before Dean was out the door.

Heading out into the cool air, Dean made his way over towards the butcher shop. Though he didn't like the lingering smell of the dead carcasses, it did give Dean an idea. "Excuse me." Dean called out, glancing around to see if perhaps there was someone around who may help him. It took a bit, but the sound of creaking wood made it apparent that at least he was heard.

The creaking of a door revealed a woman coming around the corner that caught Dean's attention. There was a bit of blood soaked into the woman's apron, her hair pulled back by a red bandanna, and her face a bit oily but her bright green eyes caught Dean's attention the most.

"Sorry to be a bit of a burden, but I have a question for you." Dean spoke, a nervous smile on his face since he wasn't exactly the best at talking to women who looked like they had enough strength in their arms to chop him up and feed him to the pigs.

"Yes, how can I help?" She asked, a bit surprised that someone wasn't demanding that she either cut this animal up or they would take their services elsewhere. Not like there were many butchers around that could easily chop up animals the way she does, but it was a nice change of pace.

"I was wondering," Dean started to speak, though he wasn't exactly sure how he should ask the question. "If I were to kill an animal, how much could I sell the meat for?" It probably seemed like an odd question, but it was something that he needed to know. After all, it was about time that he started to earn some money for himself instead of always counting on Kane to lend him some money.

"I usually pay about two credits per pound worth of meat. So if you get something big and heavy, you could make a decent amount. But if you want a cut of the meat, I could pay you with how much I can sell it for." She remarked, her green eyes glancing up at the prices she had set above the board with the different meat she had to offer. "But then again, it varies from the type of meat as well." The woman took a step back to make sure that she was able to give Dean the rundown of her prices.

"If you get a bear, I'll pay twenty credits per pound since they are rather dangerous to kill." The woman remarked, causing Dean's eyes to widen. Who could kill a bear? "If you kill something easy like a rabbit, it's one credit as they are rather small and most people tend to keep the meat anyways." The woman remarked, knowing how much the villagers loved their rabbit stew. "But if you get something in the middle like a deer or elk, I could offer you perhaps five credits considering that they are a bit heavier but their meat sells pretty fast." Dean couldn't believe his luck! Of course Dean couldn't very well kill a bear, he wouldn't have the means to transport it after the creature was dead, let alone be able to kill something that would ultimately kill him with one swipe. So if he got something smaller, and in bulk, he could very well make out like a bandit.

"Yeah?" Dean asked, a bit of excitement in his voice. "Thank you. You've been a big help." Dean thanked her, turning and heading back towards the inn. Just as he was about to enter, Kane was coming out, resulting in the two of them bumping into one another. Dean had only backed up slightly while Kane wasn't as fortunate. With a loud thud, Kane fell on his butt with a small groan. "Shit..." Dean grumbled, only to step forward and reach out a hand, offering to help Kane back up. "Sorry about that Kane." Dean quickly apologized, helping the poor tribal leader up to his feet. "You alright?"

"Yeah," Kane grumbled as he was pulled to his feet by Dean. "Just didn't expect to literally have you run into me." Kane finished, reaching behind him to dust off any of the lingering dust or mud that might have stained his shorts. "Why were you in a rush?" Kane asked, his curiosity peaked since it had been a while since he had seen Dean this excited. It wasn't every day that Kane got to see Dean act like an overly excited dog who was seeing their master come home for the day.

"Oh, well I found a way for me to earn credits is all. It might be able to help us out on our journey." Dean remarked, as if he had solved all of their problems from here on out. It made Dean seem rather cute in Kane's eyes, so the tribal leader would at least humor the male for a bit.

"Oh yeah? And what's that?" Kane asked, a small coy grin landing on his face. It seemed like Dean's excitement was rather contagious. Not that Kane could really blame Dean, considering that it seemed like Dean was struggling on how he could contribute to their little journey to meet with the others, besides coming up with a plan on defeating the Elites that literally hoovered above them. It was refreshing to see this of Dean again.

"Well, I figured that you could teach me how to hunt. That way we can trade in the meat for chips." Dean remarked, placing his hands on his hips, almost making a triumph stand. Kane gave him a rather inquisitive look. "Well, you said that people are taught how to hunt, so why not teach me?" Kane was taken back about the question, not sure if Dean was even ready to move to hunting. "Plus then I'll get to make a cool head piece like yours." Not that Kane could really blame Dean for wanting to make money, but maybe there was another way to go about it than hunting. But it gave Kane an idea if Dean was willing to do this.

"So does this mean you officially want to be one of us?" Kane asked, arching his right brow with an amused smirk on his face. "Because you won't be able to go back to being a coward. You'll have to take a lesson from one of Keaton's classes on reproduction, and figure out what clan you want to be a part." If Dean wanted to be part of them, Kane would be more than willing to help the other out. After all, it might even make for a stronger argument that Dean was really wanting to work with the tribes rather than against them.

"Yeah. Are you kidding? I would be more than willing to be one of you." Dean remarked, before catching himself from sounding excited. "I mean, it's not like I have anything back on the station anyways." Any evidence of Dean's existence had been burned months ago. "Everything was already taken away from me." Not like Dean could get any of it back. The credits he had would go back to the Elite, his personal items would either be burned or distributed among the Elite, and he didn't have any family members or friends that would care about him being gone. So what did Dean have to lose with siding with the tribal leaders over the Elite?

With a crossbow in hand, and a quiver of bolts at his side, Dean walked behind Kane down a trail that led towards the mountains. They were able to barter some food they brought with them as a means of acquiring the cross bolt and some regular bolts that Dean could use to take down an animal while being stealthy. Making sure that they didn't rustle much of the foliage underneath, Dean was careful where he stepped. The clouds above them were starting to collect overhead, though the sun was still out. They had a couple of hours to hunt, making it prime time for them to find something for them to hunt.

Stopping only when Kane did, Dean glanced around to see if there was anything that he could spot. When Kane crouched down, so did Dean. The whole experience was certainly something that Dean never thought that he would be a part of. Getting down into the grass, the rich scent of the soil was apparent. Not that it was a bad smell, but it was something that was oddly relaxing. The cold grass reacted to the warmth coming from Dean, seemingly heating up just from being close to him.

"There's a herd of mountain goats up ahead. We need to be quiet if we want to get one." Kane whispered, making it almost hard for Dean to hear him. Keeping low to the ground and crawling on all fours, the two made their way closer to the herd. It was only when Kane stopped moving that Dean glanced up. "Go ahead and line up the shot." Kane whispered as he slowly and carefully moved to the side. With a deep breath, Dean made his way past Kane while keeping his eye on the herd.

Bringing the crossbow up to his face while laying on the ground, Dean glanced through the metal hole used to aim just like how Kane showed him. Taking a few deep slow breaths Dean placed his finger on the trigger once one of the mountain goats was in sight. Trying to keep his aim steady, Dean squeezed the trigger with all of his might, sending the bolt flying through the air, only to miss the mountain goat that he was aiming for.

"Damn it." Dean cussed under his breath as he reached behind him to try and get another bolt to put on the crossbow before the goats had time to scamper away. As Dean stumbled to grab the bolt, he failed to see that there was one of the mountain goats starting to rush towards him. It was only when Dean felt the ground starting to shake close to him that he saw the rather large beast rushing towards him that Dean sat up.

The beast was close to five feet tall when it was on all fours, its fur a mixture of brown with patches of white along its underside. The horns curled in towards its face. The hooves were about as big as Dean's hands, and the eyes were a bright golden color. As it got closer, Dean instinctively rolled out of the way, feeling the brush of power that the mountain goat had as it ran by. Slowly and steadily, Dean moved to stand up, watching the goat circle around, ready to try and attack Dean once more.

"Fuck! What is that?! A goat or a fucking train?" Dean spoke in a mixture of awe and horror. Watching the goat kick up from the bit of Earth as it lowered its head, Dean knew that it wouldn't be too much longer before the goat would charge once again. Taking the bolt and putting it on the crossbow, Dean's hand slipped, causing the bolt to stumble into the grass below. "Shit..." Dean cussed once more, bending down to try and grab the bolt, the goat took it as a challenge and stamped towards him. As the goat got closer, Dean was able to grab a hold of the missing bolt, only to look up and see the goat approaching him even faster.

"Dean! Just dodge it!" Kane shouted as he stood up from his current location in the grass. The goat didn't seem to take notice. Dean on the other hand, felt like he was frozen in place. He couldn't believe that this creature had almost doubled in size from their original size before the bombs dropped.

Moving his feet to plant themselves in the soil, Dean braced for impact before the goat slammed into his body. Much like how Kane taught him to use the enemies' body against themselves, Dean was ready to use those lessons now more than ever.

It felt like Dean was hit by a rather large and bulky football player. The wind felt like it was literally taken out of him, but Dean grabbed a hold of the antlers. Using the goat's force against it, Dean was able to slam the mountain goat onto its side while still holding onto it. As the goat kicked against the ground, it let out a deep and gut wrenching call. With the bolt still in his hand, Dean was able to pierce the goat's neck, hearing a bloodcurdling scream. The more the goat trashed around, the further the bolt went into its neck. Dean struggled to keep the goat still, all the while wheezing as he tried to catch his breath. It was only when the goat went limp that Dean finally let go of the lifeless creature.

By this time, Kane had rushed over to make sure that Dean was alright from everything that went on, Dean slumped over on the grass beneath him. Panting heavily as his heart raced, Dean laid his hands against his chest while catching his breath. He couldn't believe that he just did something dangerous to take down a rather large mountain goat the way he did. Though his chest did hurt from taking a direct hit, he never felt more alive.

Closing his eyes, Dean could feel the pain throbbing through his body, but he didn't mind it for once. The sound of the wind rushing down from the mountain brushed against Dean's ear as he laid in the tall grass. The sun above was warming his body as the overwhelming feeling of victory filled Dean with a new sense of bliss he never felt before. The sound of Kane shuffling around the now dead mountain goat reached his ears, causing Dean to slowly lift his head to see what Kane was doing.

"What are you doing?" Dean asked, his voice a little groggy from his adrenaline wearing off. Thankfully they had some medicine in their bags that was back at the inn, though Dean hoped that he wouldn't slow them down if he was injured after all of this. He couldn't wait to see the look on everyone's face when they walked in with the huge creature in toe.

"I'm just securing the animal so we can drag it back. If it had only passed out from the initial pain, it could very well escape and we'll be out of the meat, therefore we won't get the credits." Kane explained as he started to tie the hooves of the goat. "There have been many rookies who made that mistake." Kane started to explain. "It allows the animals to escape because they weren't properly tied up. It's a survival tactic." Kane finished tying the knots in the rope he brought. "I'll help you drag the goat back to the town. Don't need you getting too tired before the sun goes down." Not that they had to go too far, but it was just far enough that carrying it by yourself would make the trip not even worth it.

By the time that they reached the town, the sound of thunder started to roll in from the distance. The clouds weren't coming their way thankfully, but it meant that their way forward would be slick. Upon reaching the butchers shop, the woman was upfront as she heard that there were two people with a large mountain goat heading towards the shop. The man from the inn's registry was there as well. Walking up to the butcher shop, there was a large scale already set up in front where they would be able to weigh the heavy kill. As they lifted the dead animal up to the scale, Dean found himself having a bit more trouble than Kane, but it turned out that the goat was far heavier than Dean expected. It weighed a massive six hundred pounds. Needless to say it was worth the possibility of getting seriously hurt, at least in Dean's mind it was.

"So at five chips a pound, I owe you 3,000 chips. Good haul today hunter." The woman praised Dean, heading inside to collect the money for him. Dean couldn't exactly stop the smile that crept on his face. If it wasn't for Kane, Dean would never even get this far. Surely he should do something as a way to repay the other. Not like Dean could buy Kane anything, so maybe he would have to come up with another way to repay Kane.

"I still can't believe that you took that mountain goat head on like that!" Kane excitedly remarked as the crowd started to disburse. "Some people might call you foolish or insane for that stunt, but I call it impressive." Kane remarked, placing his hands onto his hips while looking over the goat. Dean figured that he might as well take a look at his prize as well. Sure there was a bit of blood seeping from the wound, but for the most part, the coating could always be reused in some kind of outfit or furnishing. "Since you paid for the room, how about I pay for you to be able to keep the skull and antlers?" Kane suggested, catching Dean a bit off guard.

"Wait, really?" Dean asked, a bit in disbelief that Kane would offer to do something like that. After seeing the other tribal leaders with their own decorative headpieces on, Dean always wondered what he would look like with one of his own. It wasn't too surprising that a goat would be most suited for him, considering how hard headed Dean could be, but to think that he could actually have his own was rather thrilling.

Dean couldn't show his excitement, considering that he wasn't a kid, but it did put a small spring in his step. "I mean, I would actually...love that." Dean's words trailed off towards the end as he chuckled in disbelief. Watching the woman come out with three golden chips with $1,000 written in black italic letters. Dean couldn't help but look at the chips with awe as he had never seen something like it before.

The chip practically glistened in the sunlight. "Feels like the first time I got an allowance for doing some chores around the house when my parents didn't even ask me to." It was the same type of feeling that he had back then. The euphoria of being rewarded for doing something on your own without being told to. It may not have been the best example, but it was pretty damn close to that feeling.

"Be proud of yourself Dean. You earned it. I didn't even have to do anything to help you." Kane remarked, giving Dean a pat on the back. Turning towards the woman as she was heading inside, Kane trotted over towards her before she closed the door. "Excuse me ma'am." Kane spoke up, causing the woman to stop and turn to Kane.

"Can you keep the head and antlers together after you skin it?" Kane asked, knowing that it might seem weird, but it was for a good reason. "This is actually my friend's first kill. So we would like to keep the skull and have it bleached." Kane continued, reaching into his pouch to pull out the chips to pay for it. "We'll swing on by in the morning to pick it up before we head out. If that's alright." Without much of a fuss, the woman took the chips before heading inside. Now all they had to do was wait for the morning for the finished product.

After a full night of rest, along with some pain medicine to help Dean's sore torso from his encounter with the mountain goat, the two picked up the freshly bleached skull of the mountain goat and proceeded towards their next stop. Dean held the skull in his hand, surprised at how big it was. The skull itself seemed to be as wide as Dean's abdomen. The horns that were ridged crossed just below the area where the ears could have stuck out. This all still seemed to be a bit too surreal for Dean. He went from being on the bottom of the social ladder to living on the planet he had longed to see for himself what happened, to actually making a friend while exploring said planet. If someone were to tell Dean that this would happen to him, he would have thought that the person was insane.

"So how does it feel to be a big game hunter now?" Kane lightly teased, giving Dean a light nudge against his arm. It wasn't enough to bump the skull out of Dean's hands or anything, but enough to help bring Dean out of his head space.

"I wouldn't exactly call myself a big game hunter." Dean remarked sheepishly. "More like, trying to get us some fast cash kinda guy." Dean remarked, a small shrug of his shoulders as he stopped to grab his backpack. The road was about to get a bit wet, so Dean wanted to make sure he didn't trip or fall, resulting in the skull getting dirty.

With the use of a bit of twine, Dean was able to loop the thin string around the eye sockets and connect it to the backpack physically to keep it from moving around too much. "Thanks for paying to keep the head. I really owe you one." Dean spoke up once he put the backpack back on. "Honestly, I never thought that I would meet someone as amazing as you Kane." Dean added, adjusting the backpack to be more comfortable.

"Don't worry about it. It's what friends are for." Kane remarked, making sure to wait up for Dean before they continued down the path. "Besides, you paid the expensive fee for the room, so it was only natural that I pay for something." Kane continued, walking beside Dean, trying to keep in line with the other's steps.

The storm from yesterday seemed to have been long gone as they walked against the wet path that had small bits of branches and leaves lingering around the path. With the smaller ones left to rest on the path, the two would clear off much larger branches that would cause problems for other people walking the trail. There may not have been many people there, but it was better than risking the chance of someone getting hurt.

When they reached a small shop close to a waterfall, Dean found a spot close to the raging waterfall while Kane grabbed them something quick to eat. Looking over the waterfall that had a small barrier around it to keep people from jumping over the edge to either be daring or to be stupid, Dean took in the beauty of the rushing water. He had always seen still photographs of various waterfalls that people used to visit, but now he was here to enjoy it in person. To think, on the station the closest thing he would have gotten to this was his shower head, which always seemed to leak even after he was done with it.

Now here he was, sitting on a chair that was made out of some type of white wooden trunk, looking at a natural waterfall as if he was looking at a nature book. As Kane sat down next to him, the silver haired male offered Dean half of a type of sandwich wrap he never had before. Picking it up from the wooden plate, Dean glanced at the rather full wrap. The outside was pale, but on the inside there were bits of chicken, lettuce, white rice, and tomato with some type of yellow or golden sauce dripping from it.

Taking a bite out of it, Dean hummed as the combination of the filling felt like it wanted to simply burst into his mouth. Kane seemed to be pretty content with sitting close to Dean and eating the wrap in peace. The lingering scent of the water and rocks seemed to fill the air. Glancing around, it seemed like many people were taking this time to enjoy the sights of the waterfall. There were people there with their children, watching them point towards the rainbow that appeared in the mist from the waterfall.

The way that the children seemed to exclaim about seeing the various rainbows in the water brought a smile to Dean's lips. How would his parents react to seeing a real life waterfall? Well, for one thing Emily would have been excited enough that she might almost fall over the barrier, but at least Max and Dean would have caught her and pulled her back. The three of them sharing a small laugh, making memories of it all, it was something that Dean would never be able to experience now.

"If only I was born here on Earth instead of on the station." Dean spoke, almost in a daydream tone. This seemed to catch Kane's attention, causing the male to look over at Dean with a slightly puzzled look to his face as the food lingered against his mouth. "What I mean is," Dean started to correct himself, feeling a bit flustered that his thoughts were audible. "If I was born here on Earth, I'm sure my parents would be alive." Dean remarked, lightly bouncing the sandwich in his hand.

"They would be the type who would want to venture out and see what kind of beautiful things the world had to offer. But now, they won't ever get that chance." It wasn't normal for Dean to wish that his parents were still alive, but felt better talking about the possibilities of what would happen if his parents were still around or lived on the surface. "Maybe it's wishful thinking, since my parents died in a horrific way, but I just can't help thinking about all the wonderful things they are missing because they are dead."

Kane swallowed the bit of food in his mouth, letting Dean get the last bit out before placing a hand on Dean's shoulder. "I don't think it's something that you need to be ashamed of Dean." Kane remarked, only to let out a small sigh out towards the end. "I mean, I've wished for my parents to be alive so I could have grown up as a normal teenager." That's right, Kane was still in his early teenage years when the incident happened. It was hard to remember that fact when Kane acted a bit more mature for his age.

"I didn't really know what I was doing in those awkward years, and it was a miracle that the people kept me as their leader for as long as they did." Kane continues, releasing Dean's shoulder before looking up towards the sky. "My birthday will be in a few weeks, so this will be the last of my teenage years. And it's only now that they get to be interesting." Kane mused mostly to himself with a daydreaming smile on his face.

"What do you mean?" Dean asked a bit curious as to what Kane meant by that. Surely things must have been exciting for someone who was the leader of a whole clan. Then again, Dean didn't know what Kane did in his free time. They may have been getting closer, but the two of them were still getting to know each other.

"Well, what could possibly top meeting a man who literally fell from space?" Kane asked, a playful smile lingering on his lips. "Not to mention, this same man happens to be very interesting." Hearing that remark caused Dean to stiffen a little, a flustered look crossing his features.

"The smallest thing he does has a rippling effect that shakes up the people surrounding him." Kane continued, a genuine smile lingering on his face. Dean felt that perhaps Kane was giving him too much credit. "I don't think I've ever met someone as interesting as you Dean. And I should know, I've met plenty of people in my travels between the other clans." Kane finished, a soft chuckle leaving as he glanced away from Dean.

"I-," Dean started to speak, though he was starting to feel a bit embarrassed that Kane could say those things so naturally. "You said your birthday is in a couple of weeks right?" Changing the subject seemed to be the best course of action right now, considering that Dean felt his heart was beating against his chest as if he had climbed up a mountain. "What day is your birthday?"

"It's March tenth." Kane said rather proudly. "That means I'm a spring baby. Unlike Ashley who is a summer baby with being born on July seventh." Not that it really meant anything to Dean, but he was just glad that he could change the subject a bit. "What about yours Dean?" Kane asked, figuring that if they were going to share personal information like birthdays, Kane should at least be able to know what the other males' birthday was.

"Oh mine?" Dean asked, feeling a bit on edge at the question being redirected towards him. "I was born October third. So we're pretty much matching but our numbers are reversed. What are the odds?" Dean commented, a nervous laugh leaving his lips before he took the rest of the wrap and shoved it into his mouth, helping him to keep quiet before he said anything else embarrassing. Just being able to enjoy this time with Kane was enough to make Dean glad that he was sent to his death.

As they traveled the long and winding paths that lead towards the Lust clan, Dean and Kane had found themselves having to hold up in a cave as the sudden downpour outside was preventing the two from advancing further. Having to sleep under the stars wasn't a new experience for Dean as he was practically raised surrounded by the vast growing galaxy, but being able to sleep under the stars on Earth was a whole new sensation. There were times in which he would sneak out of the tent just to be able to gaze up at the sky when the weather permitted. But considering that they were in a cave, they couldn't exactly set up the tent as the ground was too hard.

Small cans rested by Dean's feet as the skull from the mountain goat rested in his left hand. In his right was a small brush with a semi clear white paint. Keeping the brush tilted at an angle to keep the paint from dripping, Dean's eyes glanced over towards Kane who was busy stirring a clear liquid that would be used to protect the special paint.

"So how will I know if I did a good job with the paint?" Dean asked, bringing the brush over towards the teeth to paint over them. It was hard to tell if he was able to do it correctly, but he wanted to make the design on the skull simply but a bit elegant, if that made sense. Whether or not it did, didn't exactly matter but Dean wanted to make it his own.

"I'm making sure that the resin doesn't start to get hard. So I'm stirring it." Kane remarked, sitting across from Dean. The poncho looked a little worn from the bits of climbing that they had to do since their time at the waterfall, and Kane's hair was starting to get a bit longer as the edges of his locks rested just below Kane's earlobe.

The head piece that Kane wore rested beside him, half of the mask seemed to be glowing as it wasn't completely exposed to the small fire pit that kept them warm. The lower tips seemed to glow a bright blue, as if there were thorns sticking out along the step of a rose. The skull itself had the same coloring of blue that matched the tips. The center of the skull had an elaborate design that looked like some kind of tribal art, but from that far away it wasn't something that Dean could make out perfectly.

"How come this is the first time I've noticed the coloring of your skull to be so bright?" Dean asked, moving to set the brush into a small dish with murky water in it. "And only in the dark does the blue light seem to show up." Dean noticed as Kane picked it up, the blue fading in the light. Kane had previously told Dean about the special type of paint, but seeing it illuminate the skull made it stand out more than anything.

"Well, the paint we use is special." Kane started to remark, looking at his skull with a smile on his face. "Since we've been traveling out in the sun, the paint has been able to collect sunlight and make it shine brighter in the darkness." Kane could have used a bit more scientific jargon, but it was just best that he keeps things simplified for now. It was getting rather late and the rain always made Kane lethargic. "Most of the time we don't wear our skulls out, but since mine has the long antlers, it's just easier to wear it instead of trying to stuff it into my pack." Kane commented with a small shrug of his shoulders, placing the skull back down before collecting the can with resin inside of it.

"Why don't you just tie it to your backpack like I did with mine?" Dean asked, picking up the skull and brush. Picking out the red color, Dean turned the skull to its side before working on the tips and rims of the horns. He wasn't exactly sure how it would turn out, but he was doing his best to make the skull his very own. It was when Dean heard Kane gasp that he looked up to see the light bulb in Kane's mind go off.

"Ugh... I'm so stupid." Kane grumbled, bringing up a hand to cover his eyes. "Why didn't I think of that." It was a common mistake that people made, but it was rather amusing to see Kane call himself stupid. Not that he was, but it was just the younger male showing that he was capable of making human mistakes. "I really feel stupid now." Kane seemingly continued, a defeated chuckle leaving his lips. "All this time I was wearing it because it couldn't fit into my bag." Not that Dean needed an explanation, but it was at least making Kane feel a bit better as he explained himself.

"We all make mistakes Kane. It just shows that you're human." Dean remarked, going back to painting the edges of the grooves of the horns. "You sorta remind me of my dad when he would mess up." Dean continued, a faint smile on his face as he continued to paint. "There was one time he was trying to get this rug to fit in the foyer of our house. And no matter what he tried, he just couldn't get it to fit." Dean paused, moving to brush some of the excess paint off as the droplet started to trickle down the side.

"Then my mom remarked about how he had it the wrong way." Dean rememenced as he moved to the second layer of the horns. "He tried to fit it in the narrow section when all he had to do was turn it to make it fit." Dean continued on with his story as he dipped the brush into the paint again. "They eventually got rid of the rug, but they had a good laugh at it. Even bringing up that memory when they were tossing it." It may not have been the greatest of stories, but it was a fond one that Dean had.

"You know, hearing about your dad reminded me of this one time, my dad tried to cook dinner for us." Kane started with his own, leaning back against the cave wall. "It was when mom was feeling under the weather because she was pregnant with my sister." Kane spoke, his hands going back to stir the resin in order to keep it in its liquid state. "My dad, for the life of him, couldn't figure out how to make the oven work. So mom dragged herself off of the couch and turned it on for him." A soft chuckle left Kane's lips as he stopped stirring the resin.

"She looked a bit annoyed, but found it comical later on and often teased him about it." A daydream-like smile formed on Kane's face, seeming to remember the good times that he had with his family, rather than the darkness that loomed overhead. Then again, it had been a couple of years since the tragedy happened, and Kane seemed like he had moved on from the horror that plagued him. Or at the very least, Kane was more than willing to share more stories of his family with Dean.

The silence between them was evident as the sound of the fire crackling and the storm just outside of the cave was the only noise that could be heard. It would be a while before either one of them could be comfortable talking. Mostly because it seemed like the two males thought about their families. Seems like the more they talked about it, the unpleasant memories would soon follow. It was only when Dean was finally done with the red paint that he placed the brush down into the murky water to clean off the bristles. "Man, this feels like it is taking forever." Dean groaned, only to hear an amused chuckle leaving Kane's lips.

"Yeah. Usually one would do this in their house to let someone take their time with decorating it. But we don't have that luxury." Kane remarked, knowing that someone who isn't really artistic might find it to be rather dull. "But since we have time before the storm passes, I figured we could take this chance to do it now. " It seemed like the storm wasn't going to settle down for a couple more hours as it was, leaving the two of them stuck inside the cave with a fire roaring between them.

By the time that Dean got done painting the last bit of the yellow lines to make it appear like the skull was cracked, Kane was busy cooking them some seaweed wrapped potatoes with bits of meat they picked up from their last stop over a small fire. In between rotating the food, Kane kept stirring the resin. "Finally... it's done." Dean remarked, carefully setting the skull down.

Resting his head against the wall, Dean looked down to see that there was still a bit of white, red, and yellow paint. Looking around the cave, the walls looked a bit barren. It seemed that not many people probably stopped in this particular location, giving Dean an idea. With a small smirk, he grabbed the yellow paint and started to go to work.

Using his finger tips, Dean would pull back the bristles and flick the paint against the barren wall. Kane watched with a curious gaze before reaching over to grab the skull. It didn't take long for Kane to paint the resin over the horns since the paint had long since dried as Dean decided to paint thin cracks along the skulls' base. Once Dean had used the yellow paint up, the next paint to be used was red. Dean worked on splattering the mixture on the wall as if he was making the night sky.

There was still a bit of red and yellow paint left, but getting an idea for the white paint,

Dean washed off the brush before using the while paint to mix in some clouds among the red and yellow painted wall. After a bit of time with the paint being fussed with, Dean was able to create a small memorial of the night sky with lingering clouds drifting by.

It wasn't exactly something that would be a work of art, but it was something that Dean could focus on and use up the paint so he wouldn't go to waste. Stepping back, Dean looked at his hands to see the fingertips were covered in paint, making him realize that what he did was a bit foolish.

"Crap..." Dean groaned as he turned to face Kane. "What am I going to do about this?" He asked, showing the other the bits of paint that still lingered on his fingertips. There wasn't much of the paint visible on his hands at the moment, but Dean could feel it starting to dry. "I'll be a glowing freak tonight." Dean remarked as he turned the palms of his hands towards himself.

"Well, lucky for you the paint comes off fairly easily." Kane remarked, putting the last touch of the resin on the skull before setting it down beside him. "Just use a bit of the water from the canteen. We'll share one until we reach the next town. That, or get some from the river." Kane suggested before standing up from his spot.

Dusting off some of the dry soil under him, Kane made his way over to Dean before taking notice of the painting on the wall. It wasn't exactly visible yet, but there was some color in Kane's shadow for the male to see what Dean was trying to do. "Hm, reminds me of the other night when we found a safe space to put up the tent." Kane commented on it before glancing over at Dean. "You really do admire the stars, huh? Though considering that you were born in the stars, it shouldn't be that surprising." Kane remarked, putting his hands on his hips.

"Well, it was just something that I rarely get to see." Dean replied with a small shrug of his shoulders. "I guess my eyes tend to gravitate over towards things that I find to be either beautiful or appealing." Dean remarked, glancing towards Kane briefly before his eyes went back to the wall.

"While I was living on the station, the only real beautiful thing that caught my eye was the Earth." Dean admitted as he felt an awkward sensation rise inside of him. He never told anyone how often he would gaze at the large blue marble that was Earth, wishing to explore it some day. "It was just so bright and beautiful, I could barely take my eyes away from it." Not that there was much else to see, and people often ignored Dean. So he often found himself gazing towards the only beautiful thing that Dean could think of.

In Dean's eyes, the Earth was like an ever spinning complex marble. The way that the various clouds would often change color depending on if there was a storm or perhaps the clouds were simply building up moisture that would trickle down over valleys. Watching bits of blue and green meshing together as if both land and sea mixed together in harmony. If the surviving humans weren't so afraid of being found out, Dean would have been blown away by the lights on the surface of the planet.

How it would look brighter than any star close by while showing where the roads merging into the cities before scattering out like a river of light. The closest thing that Dean got was seeing the street lights glowing at night was when they were in Felicia's clan for the night. Sadly they couldn't stay longer, but just seeing that bit was enough to make a lasting impression in

Dean's mind that he wanted to see the lights in the street shine brighter than any star could.

"Didn't you get to see the galaxy from the station? I'm sure it was far more impressive than anything you could see on Earth." Kane asked, tilting his head a bit as he watched Dean's reaction. There was a lot that Kane wanted to ask Dean, but it wasn't like there was a right time to be able to ask such questions. In Kane's mind, Dean had seen and experienced so much that he was far more interesting to talk to rather than just be the man's guide.

"It usually depended on the position that your pod was in. Mine was usually facing the Earth, so I didn't get to see much of anything else." Dean remarked, probably sounding disappointing to Kane. "Not that I minded it of course. The Earth was a luxury compared to being positioned close to the sun or moon like some people got." Even though it was warmer to be in a pod close to the sun, and the moon was hauntingly lonely, the Earth made for an interesting view to fall asleep to. "So when they were moving me, or at least that's what they claimed to get me into my shuttle, I was disappointed." Dean continued, letting out a small disappointed sigh towards the end. "I wouldn't be able to admire the beautiful glow of Earth anymore." After all, the Earth has been the only comfort that Dean had in his bleak times.

"So who lives in the rings?" Kane asked, figuring that if those who were in the Bronze class, Dean's class, Kane would be able to figure out more of the layout. It wasn't like there was some type of blueprint that would be left behind once the Elite members were in outer space. If it was on a computer, the aftermath of the bombs dropping and the years of radiation in the air would wipe out any evidence of what was on the station.

"On the rings are the Silver class. They are usually people who grow food to share with the station." Dean started to explain as he poured the water on his hands to scrub off the paint. "Some people specialized in livestock, while others had a small garden and worked different jobs around the station." The more that Dean explained, the harder the paint seemed to get off.

"I used to live towards the middle section of the ring layer. Mostly because my father was the only mortician in the Silver class." Dean paused as he moved to try wash the other side of his hands with the canteen. "He had assistants, but ultimately they would answer to him. My mother was a teacher, so she had more time to tend to raising me and working the garden." Dean had it rather good compared to most. Probably why a lot of the kids picked on him for being rather pudgy.

"In the middle or center of the station is the Elite class." Dean started to explain with a huff to his voice. "They get protected by any space debris, unlike those in Bronze class that often had to worry about various space debris knocking our pod loose." Dean continued, rubbing his hands harder to get the paint off, though it was coming off in small bits.

"If anything happened to the station, they would be the only ones who might be able to survive." There was the lingering anger that Dean had for the Elite. "The Silver and Bronze classes are disposable to them." It was simply easier to answer the next question in his explanation rather than play twenty questions.

"Disposable?" Kane repeated, a bit surprised that even on the station there were plenty of people who were considered disposable enough to sacrifice their lives for the Elite's sake. "Maybe it would be best just to have the whole station crash and burn then..." Kane trailed off, his voice hinting at his disappointment. It wasn't like there was much that they could do to save people in the Silver and Bronze class. If any of the Elite were to survive the crash, they would simply try to take over and mess everything that those left behind worked hard to re-establish.

"As much as I would hate to kill off innocent people, there would be no way of saving them." Dean added, an exasperated sigh leaving his lips as he walked over to the backpack that lingered by the wall where Dean was once sitting after he was done washing his hands off. "We'll try to help any survivors that we can, but they would have to go through a lot of rehabilitation in order to be able to function on Earth. Sort of like what I went through."

The first couple of times that Dean tried to get up and walk around was rather painful. It was like pure torture for the first couple of weeks that Dean had to learn to get use to walking around. "Do you think you'll have enough medicine to help everyone out?" Dean asked, pulling out a small bit of soap to use in order to get more of the paint off before he started to wash off the paint once more.

"I'll talk to Miles about it." Kane started to speak, watching Dean carefully. "Even if things are awkward between us, I know he'll send us supplies if it means that it would help to gain more people to help out in the long run." Kane remarked, though there was a hint of hesitation in his voice.

"I know Felicia would be ready to take measurements if there is a need for people to get artificial limbs. And Ashley is good enough to paint the limbs to make them look real despite being made out of metal." Seems like the leaders already had a bit of a system put in place before they would even make their first real attack against the station. It took a bit of the stress off of Dean's shoulders. It wasn't easy to mentally think about killing off so many people to bring down the station that was the eyesore of the sky.

"Seems like you already thought of everything before I even got the okay from Amelia." Dean spoke with a soft chuckle, his eyes focused on water pouring over his left hand that held the soap before Dean started to rub his hands together in order to get the paint off.

"Well, we did have a meeting about it..." Kane's voice drifted off as he moved a bit closer, the sounds of his feet shuffled against the dirt floor caught Dean's attention. "All you would really need to do is convince Amelia that this would be the right direction for everyone." Kane spoke, his voice softer than normal. "Only when you talk to her about what you plan on doing afterwards, that is when she'll make her decision." Kane continued, stopped behind Dean who placed the soap down on the ground and let the water pool up in one hand before washing the soap off.

The sound of the water splashing against the rocky soil caught Dean's ears as Kane stood still behind him. It was only when he felt pressure on his back and watching Kane's arms wrap around his waist that Dean glanced behind him. Seeing only the smallest bit of silver locks over his shoulder, and the warmth that Kane offered made Dean's cheeks warm up a bit.

"Uh, w-what are you doing Kane?" Dean asked, feeling his body freeze up. As Kane seemed to tighten his embrace against Dean, the brunet male could feel his heart seemingly picking up once more, as if they were walking up a hill against a wind storm. The tight arms wrapped around Dean's waist made him feel conflicted. It wasn't the same as his parents hugging Dean from behind, but it made his whole body tingle unlike anything Dean felt before.

The feeling of Kane's cheek against Dean's body, it felt solid enough but there was a softness to it. The longer that Kane held onto him, the faster Dean felt his heart pound against his chest. Especially when Kane remained silent the whole time.

"I just...wanted to know what it felt like to hug you." Kane remarked, though his voice was a bit muffled. "Since we're going to be heading towards the Lust clan, it would just be easier for us if you just let me hug you." Dean had no idea what Kane was going on about, but the longer that Kane held him, the more conflicted that Dean felt. He wasn't the best at social awareness, nor was he able to read people as well as Kane did, but it wasn't like Dean hated this feeling. It was like Kane was starting to let himself push the boundaries between them, feeling out what was right in their current relationship status.

"So, how does it feel to hug me?" Dean asked, moving to place his cold wet fingers against Kane's arm. It seemed that Kane didn't appreciate it as he retracted his hands quickly and stumbled back. This allowed Dean a chance to stand up with a small groan from being hunched over in a weird angle thanks to Kane's need to hug Dean from behind. His hands were still a bit wet and smelled faintly of the soap he used, which was still on the ground collecting the dirt as the water rolled off the soap's edge.

"Well," Kane paused as he turned away from Dean. "It felt a bit bony." Kane mused with a light chuckle towards the end. It seemed like Dean wasn't the only one who was embarrassed in this situation. The way that Kane acted was as if he was alone with his crush, and finally got the nerve to act on said crush. "But besides that," Kane paused, clearing his throat a bit as if to collect himself from the embarrassment Kane put himself through. "It was rather nice..." Kane admitted through a mumble, hoping that Dean didn't hear him.

Dean took the way that Kane was looking at him and found that it was similar to the way that Kane often looked at Miles. There was a curious gaze to Kane's silver eyes, and there seemed to be a faint hint of dimples on either side of Kane's lips. It made Dean want to clench onto his poncho where his heart rested and give it a squeeze, but now wasn't exactly the right time. Besides, it wouldn't help his own heart calm down. It would only make things worse or make Kane just as uncomfortable as Dean was feeling right now.

"Well, of course it would be bony." Dean stammered out in a flustered mess. "You were pressing yourself against my back after all." Dean remarked, his own face seeming to get equally as red. Clearing his throat, Dean used his poncho to dry off his hands. "Perhaps, in due time, you'll come to appreciate giving me a normal hug where we face each other. None of this sneaking up to hug me from behind." Dean continued, as if lightly scolding Kane. The lingering warmth of Kane's body heat still rested on Dean's back and torso, though thanks to the cold air from the rain, it was quickly fading.

There was a small awkward silence between them, the sound of the fire still crackling behind them. The food was done, leaving both Dean and Kane to eat in an awkward silence. It was clear that they were unsure of how to proceed after the hug. Even if Kane wasn't thinking about it as he ate, it was on Dean's mind. As they ate, Dean would flick his eyes to Kane, who seemed a bit unbothered by his actions of hugging Dean from behind. But it was still lingering on Dean's mind as he tore into his food.

"How can he just sit there and act like it was no big deal to hug me from behind?" Dean thought to

himself as he glanced towards the fire pit. "*I mean, my parents used to hug me all the time when I was kid because they cared about me since I was their kid. But this is the first time that someone had actually held onto me. As if they were afraid that I would simply disappear on them...*" Dean continued to think to himself, chewing on the bit of meat as he thought about the times his parents gave him a hug. He could still remember their quick but tight embraces. But this was on a whole new scale, and Dean didn't know how to feel. Seems like it would be a partial restless night sleep for Dean.

CONTINUING through their journey, Dean took in the sights as much as he could as they walked. Along the pathway, they were able to see old towns submerged under water thanks to a broken dam that acted like a waterfall. Peering over the edge, Dean was taken back by the clarity of the water. Though the roads and streets had been long since covered in settled broken rocks and sand, the buildings that appeared to have been made out of stone appeared visible. The various lengths of fish swimming through the broken windows and open doors was like Dean was looking at a large fish tank from above.

The grass that once provided food for cows that would graze in the barb-wire fence gently swayed in the current as some fish used the grass as hiding places from the large fish. A single church seemed to be sticking out from the water as bits of bubbles escaped from the holes along the steeple, providing the water with enough oxygen to make the ecosystem possible for the underwater town.

As the days passed, Dean followed Kane along an abandoned railroad. The wooden tracks had long since decayed, leaving only the metal rods to act as a guide. There were bits of metal sticking out against the mossy surface as flowers lined their way. Various blue and white flowers that Dean had never seen before gently brushed against their ankles. Making their way towards an old building that must have acted like a station, Dean took in the green vines that encased the old buildings.

Glancing above where the lines connecting some of the old power lines to the train, Dean was met with vines crossing over them, giving them a type of tunnel experience as they walked underneath the power lines. The platform that used to see hundreds or thousands of people a day now looked completely taken over by nature. The wooden floorboards had long since broken up, exposing the space below the floorboards. The metal benches rested partially inside of the platform as it gave way years ago. The old vending machines that used to house snacks and drinks looked rusted over and the glass long gone as well as the snacks that it once housed.

"We're getting close to the dangerous part of the route." Kane spoke up as he turned towards Dean. "So you might want to get the gas mask out." Kane remarked, stopping by the platform to put his backpack on top of it. Not even waiting for Dean to ask why, Kane started to shift though the pack until he landed towards the bottom where his mask was nestled down.

"How is it dangerous?" Dean asked, following Kane's example of getting out his gas mask that he borrowed from Ashley. She was allowing Dean to use it on the grounds that she never walked the dangerous route anymore, and that they were 'foolish' to go on the journey in the first place. Even now Dean could hear Ashley's nagging despite the distance between the two.

"We'll be above a large crater where one of the few nukes that actually touched the ground landed." Kane spoke, inspecting the gas mask to make sure that nothing was loose. "It no longer holds any radiation, however there have been dangerous flora that have grown in the radiated pool." Kane continued as he connected the ties to his belt.

"The flowers themselves aren't exactly dangerous, but the gasses that seep through are deadly to humans." Kane continued in his explanation before he took Dean's gas mask away from him to inspect it. "The crater is deep enough that the gas can't be carried off by the wind towards the towns surrounding it, however we can't take any risks. We'll be skirting along the edge as it is the fastest way to get to Keaton's place." Just hearing about this place perked Dean's interest. He always wondered how radiation affects an enclosed area.

"Why do we need to cut through it if it's so dangerous?" Dean asked, a skeptical look on his face as he didn't exactly like the idea of going through something that sounded like it could very well get them killed in the process. "Or rather why don't we go around it?" That would have been the simpler choice between the two.

"It's not that easy." Kane's words were muffled thanks to the gas mask. "There are a couple of unknown pockets of the gas that can seep out along the way. Those areas are forbidden." Kane handed Dean his mask before closing his own backpack up. "So it's the only pathway that is the safest route for us. At least that we know of." Kane continued his explanation as he put his backpack on.

"It won't take long, and we can run if need be. Once we get a bit away from the crater, we can take the masks off and cross the lake by boat." Dean was following what Kane was saying so far, but was confused on the boat part. "Then, we'll just have to navigate the city till we find the entrance towards the underground city, and finally we can deal with Keaton." It seemed like Kane had this all figured out, but Dean could still feel the knot in his stomach of unease about this.

Looking at the mask, Dean audibly sighed before he followed suit and attached the mask. The shuffling of their feet continued as the two walked with Kane in front of Dean. Staring at the headpiece attached to Kane's backpack, Dean couldn't help but find it amusing how Kane's eyes lit up at the suggestion. Or how good it felt to feel Kane's arms wrapped around his torso.

The more that Dean thought about their time in the cave, the more that Dean's focus shifted to the hug. How Dean could feel the warmth of Kane's chest against his back, or the faint beating of Kane's heartbeat close to Dean's back. The lingering scent of the fire and meat being cooked in the cave. The way that Kane covered the scar over his right eye in the beginning, and how now the silver locks brushed against Kane's pale shoulders. Physically shaking his head, Dean had to snap himself out from thinking about that moment in the cave.

Despite how nice it felt, it was probably due to being so touched starved since Dean often pushed people away from him. Yet, he couldn't exactly push Kane away. After all, Kane was one of the few people who treated Dean like he was actually a person rather than someone who ruined his life. It was hard to think of Kane in any bad light.

The silver haired male did so much for Dean that there was no way Dean would be able to pay Kane back in his lifetime! Perhaps that was why Dean was so quick to stick up for Kane. Even if Miles knew Kane longer, he didn't treat Kane like an equal. Rather, Miles often treated Kane like how an older brother would. Yeah the man was protective of Kane when anyone else tried to put him down, but there was always a boundary.

By the time that they had reached the crater, the sound of their heavy breathing was all that Dean could hear. An eerie blue and white glow seemed to be coming from above the crater. The hill was covered in grass with a faded path that people must have taken before they had the airships. As they reached the rim, Dean couldn't believe the sheer length of the crater. It was as if he was standing on the top of a football stadium and gazed down at the field of white glowing flowers as far as the eye could see. At the center of the crater looked to be some body of water with white glowing water lilies that had dark blue tips.

Small hisses of gas escaped through small cracks in the soil, causing the white flowers nearby to gently shake. In the middle of the body of water was a single white glowing tree. The bark was pure white like the snow that fell when they stayed at Ashley's place. The tree branches dangled from weight as small creatures seemed to cling to the stems.

At times there would be small flashes of a light blue from the creatures that quickly flapped their wings. Even though Dean couldn't see them with the goggles of his gas mask starting to fog up, he learned that they were actually butterflies who have evolved to be able to survive in the gas as it ward off any potential predator.

Walking along the edge, Dean made sure to mind his step. One false move, and either one of them could tumble down into the crater, making a rescue pretty much impossible right away. If the gas wasn't so dangerous for humans, Dean would have loved to stay and gaze at the sight before him, taking in the beauty of the gentle glow of the flowers and watch the butterflies move between said flowers to collect the pollen. Which was a shame considering that it showed that something so beautiful could be so deadly.

As they were getting towards the end, Dean felt a small rumble underneath him. Before too long, the ground started to crack, forcing Dean to leap forward and bumping into Kane, causing Kane to fall forward. Breaking his fall with his hands, Kane glanced back to see bits of rock tumbling down into the grassy meadow below. "Dean, you gotta be careful." Kane lightly scolded, though his words were a bit muffled thanks to the gas mask.

"Sorry about that. I just didn't want to end up falling." Dean quickly apologized as he reached a hand down to help Kane up. It wasn't long before Kane was back on his feet, dusting himself off once he was back on his own two feet. "You alright though?" Dean asked, a bit concerned since he did feel bad about knocking Kane over, but he didn't want to fall into the crater.

"Yeah..." Kane trailed off, letting out an audible sigh. "We're almost at the other side. Then we'll be able to take these masks off and breathe the fresh air." Kane remarked, starting to move ahead as they didn't have much time to waste. The sooner they got through the other leaders, the sooner they could get rid of the eyesore that currently hovered over them.

"We can rest on the boat ride when we get there." Kane spoke up, looking over to Dean from his shoulder, making sure to mind his step. "It'll be a twenty minute ride one way. The boat runs on the hour, so by the time we reach it, it'll be on its way back." It was nice to know that they would be able to rest, after all they had been going nonstop for a while now.

"Every hour?" It was almost hard to believe that a boat could run that long, or that people were riding it even late at night. "Don't they need to make sure that the engines aren't over worked?" Dean asked, raising his eyebrows under the gas mask. Surely it wouldn't be too busy when it was later in the night.

"Save your questions and breath for later Dean. The oxygen here is thinner here." Kane remarked over his shoulder, his breathing getting a bit heavier. Dean was starting to feel it as well. It wasn't like they were up high, but the gasses being released certainly made it hard to breathe for anyone.

Keeping quiet, the two made it to the other side with only that small scare to be the only incident. By the time they reached the base of the crater, the two men were more than eager to pull the gas masks off. With a deep breath, Dean closed his eyes as he caught his breath. Kane on the other hand was gently panting, causing a bit of concern given that Dean didn't know if Kane's mask had come loose when he fell. Surely Kane would have reacted differently if that was the case, right?

"Are you alright Kane?" Dean asked, looking over the other, seeing a bit of sweat visible on Kane's forehead. The lines from how tight the mask was was apparent that there was no way that the mask came loose, so what was the reason behind Kane panting so heavily?

"Y-Yeah. I'm fine." Kane remarked, using the hem of his poncho to wipe his forehead and face. "I just get to be a bit claustrophobic when I have to wear the gas mask." Kane brushed it off as if it wasn't anything to be worried about. "Guess it was a good thing that I was born outside of the shelter. I could only imagine how bad it would be if I was stuck inside one." Kane half heartedly joked about it, clearing his throat in the process.

It seemed like Kane didn't want to talk about it, but Dean would have to remember that bit of information if there ever came a time in which he would need to comfort Kane. Not like that would actually happen, but it was best to avoid certain situations that may trigger it. So far it seems that wearing a gas mask that restricts breathing was one factor that could trigger it. But what caused the initial panic attack from closed quarters? Dean would have to come back to it later.

FINDING a seat on the boat was rather easy considering that there weren't many people who would be out around the time. There was a small nip in the air, causing Kane to move a bit closer than normal to Dean. Resting their bags in front of them, Dean covered his mouth as he let out a small yawn. Seemed like their journey was starting to take effect on him. Dean's legs felt like jelly from all the walking and climbing that they had to do in order to get to the boat after walking along the edge of the crater. Each muscle was twitching and felt like there were small bits of pop rocks in his veins. One thing was for sure, thanks to Kane's training, Dean was able to survive this long trip.

Feeling the bit of facial hair on his cheeks, Dean couldn't help the small groan escaping his lips. "Maybe we should find a place to stop for the night. Give ourselves a small rest you know?" Dean suggested, knowing that he clearly needed to shave his face. Plus he would need a small hair cut before they reached the clan leader known as Keaton.

"By the time we reach his place, it will be late right?" Dean continued as Kane looked up at him with a confused look on the leader's face. "So we might as well at least find a place to sleep and wash up." Dean could still feel a bit of dirt lingering on his body, meaning that he would at least need to scrub himself clean before they got to properly meet with Keaton.

Kane let out a small audible sigh at the suggestion. "I guess you're right. Not like it would hurt to sleep in a nice bed again." Kane softly grumbled. "I don't think my body could handle another night of sleeping in the small sleeping bag or on a hard surface." Kane remarked, placing a hand on the back of his neck and giving it a good crack. Seems like the two of them needed to rest somewhere comfortable.

Not that either of them were complaining, but it certainly made Dean appreciate just how much Kane was willing to slow down and help him out. There were plenty of times where Kane could have simply gone ahead and been at the Lust clan in no time, but he was willing to take it much slower as Dean wasn't used to long distance hiking. "Besides, we're close to enough that one more night wouldn't hurt us." Kane remarked, a faint smile on his face. "We can even order some food and just enjoy the rest of the night."

"I like the sound of that." Dean chimed in, stretching out his legs with a long groan. "A hot shower, delicious hot food, and good company. What more could you ask for?" Dean continued, moving to rest his arms on the top of the bench. Leaning his head back, Dean looked up at the canopy that protected the passengers on the boat from any type of rainy or bad weather.

The small stuttering of the engine was a bit worrisome, but the captain driving the boat didn't seem worried too much by it. The water caressed the side boat as it made its way over towards the other side of the lake. There was hardly much noise outside of the boat as many insects were still in their hiding holes from winter.

It was oddly relaxing on the boat, not that Dean ever rode one before, so this was a pleasant first experience for him. To think, he would meet Keaton and talk to the leader more in depth and learn what it takes to be part of their society. Things were still a bit conflicted between Kane and himself, but they could work it out, eventually.

CHAPTER SIXTEEN: *The Fox's Den*

B Y THE TIME the sun was starting to set, Dean and Kane stood above the edge of a ramp that led down into the inner city. The metal rebar frames of buildings that indicated that they were what remains of a city that was devastated by the blast from the bomb that dropped close by surrounded them. The two men stood peering down into the darkness that looked as if it was swallowing the ramp. There were a few people who lingered up top close to the entrance, making Dean a bit cautious when he followed Kane. The two had gotten a late start, sleeping in from the long journey that had worn them out for starters. Of course they also had to visit a barber so that the two could get a trim since they were going to be meeting with Keaton. Dean figured that a change in his own look would probably do him some good as well. In a way, he was slowly discovering who he was as a person.

The style that Dean went with had the right side had been slicked back and cut shorter, exposing his ear that was bare of any piercings. It was unusual as most people around them often had multiple piercings decorating their ear. As Dean's hair curled a bit towards the left side, the longest strands of Dean's new haircut barely brushed against the edge of his eyebrow. It helped to expose more of his features, even if Dean wasn't exactly used to having such short hair after all this time. He was used to medium length hair that seemed to help hide his face when he had to look away from the Elite.

With his jaw clenched, Dean placed a hand on the dark red buttoned up shirt with black buttons that rested tightly against his body. The first few buttons were undone with the black muscle shirt peeking from the top. With the sleeves rolled up to his elbows, Dean wore the tight leather gloves that were finger-less. The black pants rested neatly on Dean's legs as the hem of the pants hung loosely over the boots he was wearing.

As for Kane, his haircut was shorter than he had originally wanted. With the back end of his silver locks tucked just a centimeter behind his ear, Kane's bangs brushed against the bottom of his right eye. Normally Kane would have kept his hair to at least brush against his cheeks, but it was better than nothing. His earrings were more exposed, making Kane look a bit more like a punk than anything else. Wearing a tight white shirt, Kane left the top two buttons undone. Wearing a black jacket where the hem of it seemed to nestle against his mid-torso, Kane adjusted the straps on the sleeves to tighten them. The pants that Kane wore were rather tight, showing off his slender body as he wore two belts. One was loosely on his hips that hung over his left leg while the other belt nestled just under his shirt. The boots Kane wore trapped the hem of Kane's pants.

"Ready to properly meet Keaton?" Kane asked, resting his hands on his hips. It was unusual for either of them to wear something so tight or revealing, but it was a must when meeting with Keaton, the leader of the Lust clan. Not that Kane minded it so much, but he knew how Dean was when it came to wearing rather tight clothing.

"Not like we really have much of a choice." Dean grumbled as they started down the ramp towards the dark howling cave. The sound of the footsteps wasn't as loud as Dean had originally thought it was. Small crystal orbs helped to guide their way towards the entrance, a low rumble could be felt, making Dean feel uneasy, as if there was going to be some sort of cave in. Was there gas trapped underneath the city as well? There were a few buildings that had been caved in under the ground. Bits of broken windows seemed to still linger, though they had been coated with dust over the last couple hundred years, making any type of reflection distorted or hard to clearly see one's reflection.

If it wasn't for the small crystal orbs, Dean wouldn't have been able to see much in front of him. A dull roar echoed through the cave from time to time, putting Dean on edge the further they ventured in. Before too long, they finally saw people. Not only that, but there were some lights that flashed different colors the closer they headed towards the entrance. There was an unknown scent that Dean couldn't even describe, it was a bit fruity with a hint of musk, or at least that was the closest thing that Dean could even think about what he was smelling. The people ahead of them seemed to be forming some kind of line, as if they were being led to some sort of slaughter house without even realizing it.

Taking a small gulp, Dean got in line behind Kane, seeing as how the other male was already in the line, Dean might as well follow suit. Glancing around as they waited, Dean noticed that there were some people who seemed to be wearing revealing outfits that left little to the imagination. What the hell were they going to? A large brothel?

There were some girls who seemed to be wearing skin tight outfits that showed off their curves. It appeared that their outfits seemed to be more leather based with some fishnets that decorated their legs and boots that barely reached their knees. The corset tops they wore accented their breasts while the skirts they wore barely caressed against their mid thighs. Around their necks were chokers with little hoops.

Dean could feel his face getting a hotter the longer that he gazed at them. *"What the hell is going on? I feel like I am being escorted to some type of crazy orgy party!"* Dean mentally panicked to himself, but he wouldn't voice it out. Dean could already feel his cheeks getting brighter the more he glanced at the girls, but they didn't seem to mind it.

"You alright?" Kane asked, giving Dean a light jab. It was a small subtle hint that Dean had been looking at the small group of girls a little bit too long, making it not so obvious that what they were wearing certainly gained attention. "I didn't picture you being into bondage." Kane lightly teased, causing Dean to stiffen a bit before quickly looking over at Kane.

"It's not like that." Dean started to interject with the reddened cheeks, averting his gaze from Kane. "I was just taking notice of their clothing choice." Dean lied, mostly trying to make it seem like it wasn't something he often did. Admittedly the girls did look outstanding. Deep down Dean wondered if perhaps the Elite would have made those who survived on the station wear something similar when they were going through their "revival of mankind" parties.

"Sure..." Kane spoke with a hint of sarcasm. "But you know, if those outfits got you hot and bothered, I know that some light bondage will really get the blood flowing south." Kane continued, a devious smirk on his face. "Just picture it," Kane started, bringing an arm up and around Dean's neck before pulling the taller male down.

"You get one of those beautiful girls in a hotel room with you," Kane whispered close to Dean's ear as the taller male looks forward at the girls. "She has you tied up on the bed while slowly crawling towards you. A small lick of her lips as she snakes a hand along your chest.

You arch your back unwillingly as your body quivers." As much as Dean didn't want to imagine it, Kane was painting a clear picture for him.

"You playfully struggle against the bonds against your wrists, meanwhile she sits on top of your lap. You can feel the body heat from between her thighs as she pulls at the buttons. A devious chuckle leaves her throat as she bites her lower lip." Kane continued, watching as Dean's eyes widened. "You ready? She asked almost innocently as she reached up to unzip her top. Your throat hitches in your throat, ready to see what comes next before you realize that she pulls out a blindfold." Kane continues on with the little story before Dean pulls back with a small grunt.

"Just stop." Dean lightly whined, feeling his face getting to be bright red the more that Kane went on. "I just," Dean started to speak in his defense. "Never got a chance to really experience my youth in ways that are usually normal." After all, when you always felt like you had eyes on you, it was hard to really get horny after working yourself near to death on top of it.

"It makes this whole scene a bit uncomfortable and a bit confusing." Dean continued as he straightened up. "I mean, I don't know what the point of wearing such revealing outfits is supposed to do for the on-lookers." Dean spoke trying to shift the attention towards something else. It didn't help that Kane had whispered that stuff in Dean's ear and it wasn't a girl that Dean was picturing doing that sort of thing with him. "I mean, one wrong sneeze and everything will be exposed." That was the focus that Dean was going with, no need to out himself so fast, right?

Hearing that remark, Kane couldn't help but laugh a bit. "Oh Dean," Kane remarked, sounding as if Dean was some child who made a comment that he didn't fully understand to a bunch of adults who were about to open his eyes to a world he never thought possible. And boy, was that an understatement. Then again, the education system on the Millennium wasn't the best about talking about sex. Not to mention when Dean's parents tried to bring it up, Dean would get embarrassed and try to change the subject.

"They are wearing those clothes to attract people whom they find to be attractive." Kane continued, wrapping an arm around Dean's neck and pulling the other closer to him once again. "The fishnets are used to give a lush peek of how tasty their legs and thighs are. Most people would love to be squeezed between a pair of thick thighs like those." Kane started to explain, keeping an eye on Dean's facial expression. "The skirt would make it easy for a quickie. Taking a potential lover into a dark alleyway and letting them go down on you, it's like a rush of excitement you never felt in your life." Kane started to whisper, his eyes closing half way as he could only imagine what was going through Dean's head. Dean's eyes wavered, half trying not to gaze at Kane the more the other male went on, and the other not trying to stare at any of the girls in particular.

"The corset is nice and tight, allowing for her breasts to look bigger than they are." Kane continued, forcing Dean to look at the girl closest to him that was wearing one. "See how they are pushed together? It makes them look bigger as a lot of men like big breasts." Kane paused before an amused chuckle left his lips. "Are you one of those types of guy Dean?"

"What?" Dean yelped, causing some people to look towards them. "O-Of course not!" Dean stammered, moving to pull away from Kane. This seemed to amuse Kane more as the young male leader covered his mouth to keep from busting out in laughter. Dean felt like he wanted to bury himself in a corner under the rumble close by and simply die. It seemed like Kane was getting a good laugh at his expense. "Honestly, I think you're enjoying this a little too much, don't you?"

"Maybe." Kane remarked quickly as he gave Dean a soft pat on the back. "But at least it's good to see that you aren't completely dead when it comes to lusting over someone." Kane teased as he glanced down, causing Dean to reflexively hunch over a bit. "Do you want to go over and ask those girls how long it takes for them to get dressed up in layers?" Kane asked in a taunting tone, watching the flustered Dean try to come up with some type of rebuttal.

"No.....no...." Dean trailed off as he averted his eyes from Kane back to the girls. "Seems like they know how long it takes for them to get dressed. So we don't...need to bother them." Dean cleared his throat as he noticed the girls looking towards the two of them now.

A jolt went straight down Dean's spine as he turned to look away from the girls. The line wasn't exactly budging right now, which was a bit concerning since Dean didn't know how to explain himself for gazing at the women for so long. Placing a hand on his chest, Dean was trying his best to steady his racing heart but to no avail. Dean wasn't used to the change in his appearance just yet, but it seemed to get him a couple of looks. Whether those looking for good or bad were still on the table.

"So, how much longer until we enter?" Dean asked, looking slightly above the heads of the people in front of him. Dean glanced to the side, noticing that a few of the girls from earlier were making their way over towards him. The way that they seemingly smirked in a knowing way, it sent a chill down Dean's spine. *"Great, now I'll have to explain why I was staring at them! This is all Kane's fault..."* Dean panicked in thought as he felt like his head was swimming.

Averting his gaze forward, Dean tried to simply ignore the girls. But their overwhelming presence was unavoidable. Turning his gaze back towards the women, Dean was greeted with the one who seemed to be wearing the skimpiest outfit of all. The slits in her skirt went up all the way towards her hips as she wore some black laced stockings that nestled into some belt laces heels. A thick white belt with a golden latch trimmed her slender waist. The black crop top she wore may have been long sleeved, but the edges of the crop top barely covered her chest.

A small mused hum escaped her lips as the redden colored lips formed a smirk. Long eyelashes curled upwards against black smokey eye shadow that accented her golden honey eyes. A few thick black locks of her hair delicately ivory colored skin. The woman's hair seemed to be tied back in a messy bun as golden hooped earrings dangled against her jawline. Parting her pouty lips, the woman looked as if she was about to speak before a man's voice seemed to catch a Dean's attention rather quickly as he called out Kane's name.

"Kane." A deep voice called out, that sounded a bit familiar. The man who had approached the two was a bit shorter than Dean. Bright golden eyes, much like the woman standing close by. The man's hair seemed to go this way and that, like the edges were on non-speaking terms. The man's ears seemed to be decorated with a few silver earrings that seemed to trace the edges of the black surgery mask the man was wearing. It was the same man from the banquet, the leader of the Lust clan.

Keaton was wearing a black buttoned up shirt that had some silver looking buttons with a silver tie loosely hanging over them. Dean took notice of the suspenders that the man was wearing, which seemed to connect to some dark gray slacks with a black belt. Wait, did this guy seriously have suspenders and a belt on? This detail seemed to make Dean raise an eyebrow. The jacket the man was wearing seemed to rest on his shoulders while the man's hands seemed to have rested in his pockets. "Glad you could make it." Keaton continued, finally approaching the two men.

As Keaton stood still, staring at the women close to Dean and Kane, it wasn't long before Keaton turned his back towards them, causing a puzzled look to wash over Kane and Dean's faces. It seemed like Keaton was giving someone the cold shoulder, but to who exactly? Kane glanced over towards Dean, as if to ask if the male did anything to upset Keaton, to which the only reply that Dean could honestly give was a simple shrug of his shoulders.

"Hurry up. We don't have much time to waste." Keaton barked as if ordering them around. Dean and Kane followed behind Keaton as they started to head towards the front of the line, but in a direction that was to the side of where everyone else was heading. There seemed to be something odd about the whole situation. Not like Dean could put his finger on it, but it could be addressed later on.

As they stood outside of a large metal door away from the main gate, the three men stood with Keaton's hand just on the door knob. There was a loud bass that rattled the door ever so slightly, giving a preview of what Dean was about to experience when they crossed over the threshold. There was only one thing preventing them from venturing further, and that was Keaton.

"Before we go in, I want to let you know that we won't be able to make idle talk when we go inside. As you can tell, the night time is very loud, making it impossible to hear." Keaton spoke in a louder tone than normal. "Kane, keep a hold onto Dean the best way that you can." Keaton instructed, making Dean wonder how large this place was. "If we get separated, just make it to the large fox that is pressed against the tallest building that stands above all of the other buildings. That's where my office is." Keaton explained briefly. With the door opening up, Dean seemed to be transported into a new world that he never thought that he would ever experience.

At first the lights were blinding to Dean, but eventually his eyes adjusted to the bright pink and blue mixture of lights that gave off a dark magenta glow when the two colors melted together in the middle. Feeling the warmth of Kane's hand as the male grabbed a hold of Dean, it wasn't long before Dean was pulled into the crowd of people that made their way into the large neon glowing city. Glancing around, Dean was amazed at the different cultures mixing together as if they were animals ready to mate while the music blasted in the air. Some people wore their skulls as the paint glowed various colors, as if the skulls were masquerade masks that complimented the outfits.

Glancing above the crowd, Dean was able to spot the tall skyline in the distance. Sure enough, in the middle of the towering buildings, there was a smirking fox that glowed a bright orange with a white tip with the words 'Fox's Den' in flickering white letters, that was to be their destination. There were so many people starting to crowd around them, Dean felt like he was going to be swallowed by the sea of people encroaching around them. If it wasn't for Kane, Dean probably would have been swept away into the world of debauchery and sin.

Letting his eyes scan the side areas around them, Dean mostly saw X's in bright neon letters with either an outline of a girl or lipstick prints lingering along the design. There was a lingering scent of strawberries from one store that was called Strawberry Kisses with a fair amount of women with unnatural red hair and bright red skin tight outfits on them. Even their lips were red. Glancing towards the other side of the street, it seemed that there were some rather fine looking men who were roaming around without shirts. The men looked rather fit, as if they were trying to attract mates with their well fitted bodies. Above on particular store was images of blue neon bubbles with the name 'Bubble Pop Inn' over top of it. A couple of the guys seemed to eye Dean as the three men passed by them, making Dean shuffle a bit closer to Kane since he wasn't exactly sure what he was supposed to do around these sorts of people.

The further they ventured forward, the fruity smell seemed to fade, only to be greeted with savory smells of food. Who would have guessed that they would pass by the sex shops and brothels only to land towards the food section of the city. They were still a bit off from the fox building, but at least it wasn't as packed as it was in the area they were just in. At least here Dean could feel himself breathe easier. As Dean gazed down, he was relieved to see that he still had a hold of Kane. Dean was almost afraid of what could have happened if Kane wasn't holding onto his hand. Frankly, Dean could have been pushed in either direction and find himself in a flustered mess trying to get away and make his way to the Fox Den. Dean never was good with people pushing up on him. It gave him an anxiety attack just thinking about it.

As they were stopped, Keaton handed the two men some ear plugs, causing Dean to become a bit puzzled as Kane let go of his hands. "You're going to need this." Keaton started to speak as Kane quickly grabbed his pair. "It can get to be a bit overwhelming with the music, especially for new members entering." Dean picked up his pair as he started to follow Kane's example. "You'll feel it more in your body than anything, it shouldn't be too concerning for you, but better to have you prepared." Keaton finished as he put his own plugs in his ears.

Dean wasn't sure what the Lust leader meant, but as the large clock above one of the clubs hit the hour mark, it wasn't long before Dean could feel a rumbling in his body. It pulsated his body in a way that Dean never felt before. It was like his heart was beating at the same pace of the music. Even with Kane's hand in his own, Dean could feel the music even pulsating through Kane's body as they walked. Placing a hand over his heart, it felt almost like he was back on the station when he stopped in the middle of the corridor. Remembering Keaton's words, Dean now understood what the leader meant by that.

As they continued to walk through the crowd behind Keaton, Dean felt a small tug from Kane, who started to pick up his movement. With a sudden jerk, Dean was pulled to push past Keaton, causing Dean to look back and watch as Keaton was swallowed up by the crowd of people. Unlike Dean and Kane, Keaton was more at home here, therefore he didn't need to stick with the two men in order to find his way around the city. Not that Dean was sad to leave the loud music behind him, it did make him wonder what had gotten into Kane. Why did they brush past their host? Did Kane know something that Dean didn't? Or perhaps Kane didn't want to be around the music anymore than Dean did?

Breaking through the crowd as the music got louder, the two men were able to breathe freely. For a while it felt like Dean was going to suffocate in the sea of people walking around. As more people made their way towards the central hub, the skyscrapers looked empty. There were a few lights that still lingered, but overall the buildings were completely dark, making the lights behind them glow brighter.

Reaching an area that was safe from the pulsation feeling, Dean reached up to take out the plugs. There was a small ringing in his ears, but at least it was just the two of them. Glancing behind him, Dean couldn't see Keaton anymore. The two stood in front of the large building with the fox on it, but it appeared to be locked. Hearing a soft groan from Kane, Dean shifted his attention over towards Kane, watching as the other male started to rub his ears.

"Sorry if I pulled you away too fast." Kane was quick to apologize before tossing the plugs into a nearby trash bin that was metal in appearance. "I just wanted to warn you about Keaton before we go up to his office." Kane added, fussing with his short hair as it got disheveled as they moved in the sea of people. "After all, I don't know how much longer he'll be…" Kane trailed off with a soft mutter, as if talking to himself.

"Warn me about what?" Dean asked, pocketing the earplugs for now. As he waited for Kane to walk back towards him, Dean took this chance to look around. It seemed like this area was a housing section. There were a couple of lights on in brick buildings that had shadows of the occupants moving about in front of the lit up windows.

As Kane closed the gap between them when he got back, Dean's focus shifted to Kane's face. Seeing as how close Kane was, Dean could feel the same tensions that he felt when they were in the cave. With everything that they had walked through, Dean felt his heart picked up once more as he couldn't stop gazing at Kane's face. Not to mention what happened earlier, the flustered look on Dean's face made an appearance once more.

Dean stared into Kane's silver eyes as he raised his eyebrows. "Well," Kane started to speak, reaching up to button up Dean's shirt a bit. "Keaton is the type of guy who will try and push your buttons." Kane spoke up, his eyes lingering on Dean's chest. "He'll gauge your responses... see if perhaps he could read you... understand what your preference is." Kane remarked, his fingers gingerly lingering against the last button, his expression showing that Kane was thinking of something. Like it was something that Kane didn't want to talk about.

"He'll get in your personal bubble." Kane continued, moving to look up at Dean. "Invade your personal space, and he might try and coax you into something that you might not understand what his ulterior motive is." Kane finished, though his voice was rather low, causing Dean to swallow the lump in his throat. "So, you really should be on guard when he's around you."

"Guard?" Dean started to stammer with a small squeak. "Ulterior motives?" Dean asked, trying his best to calm his beating heart. "What sort of thing would he try to pull?" Dean continued to ask as Kane took a step back with a small huff. Not like Dean could understand what was going on, but it seemed like Kane was on.

The last time that Dean felt this much pressure was on the night of the banquet. Perhaps it was due to the fact that Dean had gotten used to most of the leaders being friendly that put Dean into a dangerous lull. Miles' decision was still up in the air, and Dean didn't know much about Keaton and Amelia that would suggest that the two would be willing to work with Dean. If he was going to survive this and get his revenge, Dean needed to start learning to keep his guard up around the other leaders.

"I'm not exactly sure..." Kane spoke, his shoulders dripping as his gaze moved down towards the street. "But, considering that Keaton is the type who likes to press others for information, I wouldn't put it past him to make you uncomfortable enough to slip up and say something that you might not actually mean." Not like Dean could really say that he knew what type of character Keaton was. The man was always so mysterious that it put Dean off. Not to mention he got a weird feeling from Keaton that was unlike anything Dean ever felt before. "If he tries to find an excuse to make me leave, promise me that you will not let your guard down around him." The pleading gaze in Kane's eyes caused Dean to step back, a feeling of uncertainty seemed to wrap around him.

"Y-Yeah. I will." Dean nodded in agreement, though he could see the doubt in Kane's gaze. "Look, if there is anyone who is able to make it seem like they don't know anything, it's me." Dean tried to reassure Kane with a half hearted smile. It seemed like Kane wasn't going to take Dean on his word. A soft sigh passed Dean's lips as he placed a hand on Kane's shoulder. "I promise on my life that I won't allow Keaton the chance to pressure me into something that I don't want to do," Dean paused as he looked into Kane's eyes, seeing his own reflection in those silver orbs. "Nor will I say anything that I will regret. You have my word on that." Dean spoke, keeping a firm gaze as he looked into Kane's eyes. "Just, trust me, okay?" Dean spoke in a more direct tone as he didn't take his eyes away from Kane.

Kane kept his gaze with Dean before slowly backing down. "Fine..." Kane's voice trailed off as his shoulders relaxed. It may not have been ideal, but it seemed like Kane put his trust in Dean. "Just, make sure he doesn't try anything with you either." Kane spoke, crossing his arms over his chest. "Keaton can be a bit handsy with people that he finds to be interesting." Was it Dean's imagination, or was there a hint of jealousy in that remark? Not like Dean could further inquire about it as the sound of someone approaching them got the two mens' attention.

"I figured something was up." Keaton spoke as he casually strolled towards the men. Keeping his hands in his pockets, Keaton started to fish for something in his pants while keeping eye contact with the two. "It's not like you to skip past me Kane." Keaton remarked, his gaze shifting to Kane. "Usually you like to stay and feel the beat of the music pulsing through you. Or to get a contact buzz through the lounge area. To make it here before me, well..." Keaton continued, his yellow gaze drifting towards Kane as he spoke. "Makes me think you wanted to talk to our precious visitor about something without me around." Talk about hitting the nail on the head.

"It's not like that..." Kane lied, his voice trailing off before a grunt escaped him when Keaton grasped Kane's jaw in a vice grip. Pressing his right thumb and index finger into Kane's jaw, Dean watched as Keaton practically forced Kane to gaze up at him, yellow eyes gazing into silver. Dean could see that Kane was trembling as Keaton seemed to hold the shorter male in place, causing Dean to clench his jaw. He had to save Kane from the other, even if he had to deal with Keaton violating his space. But what could he do to break Keaton's hold on Kane without getting in trouble? Dean's mind started to race before he came up with a plausible excuse.

"Kane was worried about the condition of my heart when we went through the club section." Dean spoke up, catching Keaton's gaze as he let go of Kane. Instantly Kane stumbled backwards, lightly rubbing his chin afterwards with a disgruntled look on Kane's face. Seeing that Kane was at least free, Dean let out a small sigh of relief, only to have Keaton step closer to him. There was that Elitist air that Dean felt back when his hand was almost crushed. It was cold, like he was looking at a large sheet of ice as a barrier. The shaking in Dean's left hand started, causing Dean to clench his hand to stop the shaking.

"Since I never had to deal with anything like that, I gave his hand a quick squeeze to signal that the music was causing my heart to palpitate." Dean continued to explain before he felt Keaton grabbed a hold of his chin. It felt like a crab had gotten a hold of his chin and wouldn't let go. No matter which way Dean tried to shift his head, he couldn't get out of Keaton's grasp. "So he figured getting me to the building faster was the best course of action." Dean continued to explain through some grunts from the pain of Keaton squeezing Dean's chin.

Staring into those yellow golden eyes, Dean could see that Keaton was searching to see if perhaps Dean was lying, which he was. But did Keaton realize that? It was almost like looking into a void, no emotion behind those golden eyes as they wavered ever so slightly. The tight grip never releasing. It was only when Keaton couldn't find the answer he was looking for that he finally let go of Dean.

As he was free from Keaton's grasp, the Lust leader brushed past the two men as he headed up the stairs to unlock the door to the building. Dean reached up to gently massage his chin as well as Kane joined his side. It seemed that Kane's chin was starting to bruise as red dots appeared on Kane's pale complexion *"The hell is wrong with this guy? He's as strong as an ox. Felt like he was going to crush my jaw."* Dean mentally grumbled as his eyebrows knitted together angrily. Now Dean could see what Kane meant about Keaton getting into his personal space to make him uncomfortable. Though Kane failed to mention how strong Keaton was.

With the creaking of the door, Keaton moved to the side. "Well, shall we go upstairs?" Keaton asked, raising a brow as he gazed down to Kane and Dean. It didn't take long for Kane to start heading towards the stairs, passing Dean with a quick glance. Dean was quick to follow, side eyeing Keaton as they walked through the opened door. Inside the foyer was rather empty. In the distance was a desk that had some fake flowers in a glass vase. A long worn down red carpet guided them towards the desk that would normally have someone seated behind it. Considering that it was rather late, that meant that the building was closed off to the public, how convenient.

Heading towards the elevator that would lead them up towards Keaton's office, Kane pressed the button since he was the first to reach the elevator. The building seemed to be rather quiet as they heard the mechanics of the elevator as it slowly descended from the upper floors. This was a chance for Dean to ask a few questions that had bubbled up in his mind when they had passed the gates.

"I was curious about something." Dean spoke, gaining both of the leaders' attention as they turned their gaze to him. "How is it you guys have so much electricity?" It seemed like the Lust clan was able to produce more electricity than those of the other clans. "The other clans are struggling to not be noticed by using soft crystal light, yet you have retrograded neon lights. It's like living in the future yet you're underground." That was the best way to call it out in Dean's mind. The city was like a large amusement park meets a brothel city. Not that Dean wasn't fascinated by the concept, but it was unfair for the Lust clan to use so much electricity while the other clans had to be cautious.

A small smirk formed on Keaton's face as his eyes narrowed with amusement. "That's fairly easy to answer." Keaton started out, turning to face Dean more directly at this point. "It's because we're underground that we don't need to fear those cowards finding us." The statement alone seemed to click in Dean's mind as he understood what Keaton meant by that. "We bring in members of the pride clan who want to focus on using crystals and electricity in order to make it easy for those on the surface to get their homes powered up without alerting the cowards in the station." Keaton finished his explanation just as the elevator reached their level. "We have to remind some of the other leaders that too much light will give us away. Resulting in the need to use more primitive sources of light in order to stay under the radar."

That would explain the small lights littered through Kane's clan, the large collection of yellow and orange crystals to make it appear like lava in Felicia's clan, and the spread out fire lamps in the countryside while the city had crystals in Ashley's clan. But here, it was like going further into the future with the advancements made while they stayed underground in Keaton's clan. Not only that, but the disguise of the rumbling from the music appearing as if the dangerous gasses made it easier for those in the lust clan to stay hidden.

"Gotta say, that's pretty ingenious of you to come up with that plan." Dean remarked, following the leaders into the elevator. "Seems like you have been building this place up for a while. So tell me, who came up with the concept?" Dean asked, a bit curious since this seemed like it took more than a few years for the clan to branch out like they did. But Keaton stayed quiet, seemingly pressing the button that would take them up to the floor his office was located on. Blinking in surprise, Dean cast a look towards Kane to see if maybe the other would chime up with the answer. But it was a no go. Seemed like the leaders were going to stay quiet on this matter, though Dean had a suspicion as to who it was.

Once they were inside of Keaton's office, Dean was a bit surprised with how different it was from his intestinal first impression of what Keaton's office would have looked like. Seeing how Keaton acted, Dean was expecting something with a bunch of leather covered sexual devices or something. Instead, Dean saw a beautiful library that seemed to have long vines weaving against the bookshelves. Glancing up at the skyline ceiling, it seemed that bits of plants dangled from the edges of the skylight. Small white crystal lights shined just bright enough to help give the plants some light without being overpowered in brightness to the human eye. Some places on the shelves were decorated with handmade crafts that slowly improved from one craft to the next. Sketches in frames clung the walls, almost like a proud parent displaying their child's work. There were a couple of chairs resting in a neat circle with a wooden coffee table in the middle.

As Dean's gaze shifted to the left, he noticed that there was a larger garden that seemed to rest below a balcony. There was a soft orange glow stemming from the rather large window, indicating that they were above the fox display. Even though Dean was a bit curious as to what was over the inner balcony, Keaton and Kane had moved towards the tables. Cautiously making his way towards the two, Dean sat down in the seat that nestled between Kane and Keaton. It wasn't long before Keaton reached his hands up to pull the black facial mask off, showing his face for the first time to Dean. To Dean's surprise, there was nothing wrong with the other. Instead, Keaton had a pretty decent face on him. It seemed that Keaton took notice of the stare and developed a smirk on his face.

"What? Were you expecting some type of hideous scar?" Keaton asked, though he seemed to flash a glance towards Kane when he said that. Dean had never once thought that Kane's scar was hideous in any regard. After all, it was hard to see it that way after what Kane had been through. But it seemed to be enough of a hint that it caused Kane to glance down and away from the two, resulting in Dean's brows furrowing together.

"No. But I guess your hideous attitude counts for something that I was expecting to encounter with you." Dean snapped, not at all liking what was coming out of Keaton's mouth about Kane. "Do you get off being a sadist to those around you? Or are you just usually a giant prick?" It was clear that Dean was annoyed at the remark, but seeing that Dean was quick on the remarks to defend Kane brought a smug look to Keaton's face.

"The only person who was as quick to defend Kane has usually been Miles." Keaton paused as he glanced towards Kane. "Nice to see that Kane is traveling with someone who he can get close with yet again. So long as you don't become like brothers." Keaton remarked, leaning back in his chair as he kept that cocky grin on his face.

Dean wanted to punch Keaton in the face, mostly due to the fact that the male resembled one of the Elites who enjoyed pushing some of the other Bronze members down when they were simply trying to work. One could almost argue that Keaton had a face one would expect to be a villain. "Speaking of which," Keaton continued crossing one leg over the other as he focused most of his attention on Dean. "How do you feel about Kane?"

This question seemed to come out of nowhere, surprising both Dean and Kane at the same time. "Well," Dean started to speak, only after being flabbergasted by the question since his mind started to think back on the cave and how the current events made Dean re-evaluate just how he saw his traveling companion. Not to mention needing to calm his heart that was currently beating against his chest from being put on the spot like that.

"I... like Kane very much." Dean admitted, feeling his cheeks starting to flare up a bit as he couldn't bring himself to look at Kane at the moment. This caused Keaton to grow a cocky grin on his face, as if the lust leader wanted to hear more about it. "He's someone who is very important to me." Dean added, this time his voice sounding a bit more confident in his answer as he briefly glanced towards the silver haired male before looking back to Keaton.

Keaton tilted his head back as his eyes glanced back and forth between the two. He stayed mostly quiet while Dean and Kane glanced at each other with uncertainty in their eyes. The silence felt awkward for Dean as he was not completely prepared for these questions. "Kane," Keaton finally broke the silence as he looked over at the silver haired male. "I'm running out of some scotch. Mind going down to the basement to find it for me? It's stored in its' usual place." Keaton remarked, watching as both Dean and Kane stood up.

"Not you Dean." Keaton spoke up quickly, catching the two men off guard. So this was what Kane was trying to warn Dean of. That he would break the two of them up before interrogating Dean for answers. "We have more important things to talk about." It was a subtle way of separating the two. Dean would have to keep his distance from Keaton, or at least put up his guard so he wouldn't slip up. But Dean had to show Keaton that he couldn't get under Dean's skin.

"Uh," Kane paused as he gave Dean a quick glance of uncertainty. "Sure. Is there any flavor that you want?" Kane asked, watching as Keaton brought up a hand to stroke his chin in thought. A small hum echoed in Keaton's throat as the male tapped his foot. A slightly worried expression lingered on Kane's face as he looked towards Dean, wondering if perhaps it would be wise to leave Dean by himself with the likes of Keaton. Not that Kane could have injected having Dean come with him. After all, Dean had to get Keaton on board with his plan.

"I'm in a mood for something fruity with a light vanilla texture. So how about looking for something like Heavenly Hills? Can't go wrong with that one." Keaton remarked, a cheshire smile on his face. Watching Kane turn and walk towards the door, Keaton's eyes were instantly glued to Dean who was busy watching Kane walk to notice that he was being stared at. It was only when the sound of the door closing behind Kane echoed in the room that Dean turned to see Keaton staring at him.

The way that the leader was staring at Dean gave the male the creeps. Like being watched by the Elite type of creepy. But perhaps that was Keaton's plan. Either way, Dean had to shrug off the unease he got from Keaton, and focus on the task at hand.

"So I guess you probably already know why I'm here." Dean started to speak as he sat down. "Considering that we just had the banquet and all..." Dean trailed off in an uncertain tone, but noticed that Keaton wasn't really reacting to him. Instead, the dark haired male had his head turned ever so slightly as if he was listening for something. "Uh, hello?" Dean spoke, only to have Keaton hold up his right index finger. Blinking in surprise, Dean felt like he had no control over the situation.

It was only when Dean noticed the sound of gears turning that he realized that Keaton must have been holding off in case Kane was trying to eavesdrop on their conversation. When Keaton seemed to be satisfied that Kane was doing as he instructed, the smile faded from his face and a different type of aura seemed to be coming from Keaton. "Now then, before we do our little back and forth, I want to know something about you." Keaton spoke in a more serious tone, his eyes fixated on Dean with coldness to them. It was the same type of coldness he felt when talking to Amelia. Dean stayed quiet, but his eyes were focused on Keaton. "Do you see Kane to be like a brother to you?"

This question had taken Dean back a bit. "Like a brother?" Dean repeated the question, but seemingly got no answer or response from Keaton. Pausing for a few seconds, Dean had to seriously think about this. Especially from what Kane told him, if Dean answered wrong, that could be it for him. "Well, I never really had a brother to be honest. Considering that those of the Elite were able to have a bunch of children while the most that the silver class were able to have was two..." Dean started to explain, but it didn't seem to satisfy the answer that Keaton was looking for. A small disgruntled groan left Dean's lips as he moved to sit a bit more on the seat. It was clear what Dean had to say in order to get Keaton to work with him rather than against him.

"Listen," Dean spoke, his voice more serious as he could feel the confliction in his mind already starting to race, but it seemed to get Keaton's attention. "Kane is far more special to me than someone who I would consider to be family." It was strange to hear it out loud, but it had to be said. "He's someone that I would do anything for to make sure that he's happy." Dean admitted, despite the flustered tingling Dean was getting in his cheeks.

"Kane's been hurt a lot in his past, and I can see it just by being near him." Dean continued, his hands gripping onto his pants. "I'll be honest," Dean paused, glancing down between his legs at this point. "The way he longs to be with Miles, only to look as if his heart has been ripped out when he sees how Miles looks at Felicia. It really hits me in a way I didn't even think was possible." Not that Dean could put his feelings into words so easily, he wanted to let the leader of the Lust clan know what Kane meant to him.

"Frankly, it makes me jealous." Dean admitted as he lowered his head a little. "But that doesn't mean I'm not grateful to Kane for everything he has done. But he's not a brother to me." To put a label on their friendship, it would only taint or sour it in Dean's mind. "Kane is always there to help out the other leaders, as well as helping me out." Dean continued before shifting his gaze to look at Keaton, his focus more serious than anything else.

"Kane is the type of guy who will put everything he has into something." Dean added, relaxing his hands as his knuckles were trying to turn white. "I mean, he's been there to bat for me when he didn't have a reason to." Dean continued, his voice more stern as to send a message to Keaton. "I'm grateful that I get to see that. I'm grateful that he's on my side and wants to destroy the station, even though it goes against everything that he believes in." Dean spoke, watching as Keaton softly nodded.

"So to answer your question, I care for Kane in a way that I could never see myself caring for a brother." They didn't have any sort of label on what they were, except for best friends after all. But with all that has happened, it was hard to simply ignore the fact that there was something going on between the two of them. "Kane's my best friend and I cherish him in a way that I don't know to handle." Dean admitted, his cheeks tingling from embarrassment. "To be honest, it's probably because I never felt this way towards someone in my life." It wasn't exactly something as intimate as love, but he did hold Kane close to his heart.

"So are you gay?" Keaton asked, causing Dean to sit up with wide eyes. By the surprised look on Dean's face, Keaton couldn't help the little chuckle that escaped him. "Okay, so if you're not gay, then what is your sexual preference?" Keaton asked, seeing the look of confusion washing over Dean's face. Dean wouldn't even know how to go about saying what his preference was due to the isolation he had on the ship.

"I-I..." Dean stammered, not exactly sure how he could even answer that question. Here he was, spilling his gut out in front of Keaton about what he thought of Kane, and now Keaton wanted to know if Dean was gay? "Well I don't find most people to be attractive." It was the truth. There weren't many people who made Dean aroused just by looking at them.

"Well tell me, who is your ideal partner. Does their gender have anything to do with your attraction towards them?" Keaton asked, seemingly trying to figure out what caused Dean to tick. This whole ordeal seemed to take Dean back as he slumped back into his chair. Bringing a hand over his face, Dean let out a small groan as he couldn't believe he was doing this. Just what was Keaton going to gain from this sort of information?

"Look, I just want someone to like me for who I am as a person." Dean spoke bluntly as he knew that a person's gender didn't matter to him. "I don't care what their sex is as long as they just care about who I am as a person rather than what my sexual preference is." Dean remarked, figuring that was the best answer since he didn't find it in himself to say if he cared much for men or women. Thinking back on it, he did think that Felicia and Amelia were rather attractive, but they didn't get his blood flowing. Both Miles and Kane were attractive too, but if he had to choose between them, he would much rather lean towards Kane since the other understood him better.

"Hm, seems like you belong in the same category as me." Keaton remarked, leaning back in his chair as his posture seemed to be more relaxed now. "But, you're still rather picky when it comes to finding the person that you want to be with." Dean was taken back by that remark. How could Dean be picky when all he wanted was to love someone for who they were as a person, and to have them love him back?

"What? How am I picky?" Dean asked, his brows seemingly knitting together as he took offense to that comment. Did Keaton think that he was better than Dean or something? Love wasn't supposed to be some type of competition. Frankly, all Dean wanted was something like his parents had. To be able to make each other feel like all they had was each other and that was all that they needed in the world to survive. There was no distrust in each other. They could simply gaze at one another and feel like they were in heaven.

"Because I see beauty in everyone." Keaton started off, as if bragging. "No matter what their size, shape, or even gender. They all seemingly shine in my eyes." Keaton remarked, a coy smile on his face. Dean clenched his fists as he felt like he really wanted to punch this guy in the face. Just what was his deal? Every muscle in Dean's body tensed as he stared Keaton down, not a single word seeming to leave him. It seemed like Keaton noticed this and let out a small agitated sigh. "Seems like you're not going to make it easy for us to get along, are you?" Keaton spoke as he appeared to be more serious. The silence coming from Dean was an indicator that he wasn't willing to say another thing to Keaton.

Resting his elbow on the arm chair, and crossing one leg over the other, Keaton placed his hand on his cheek as he tried to think of something that would break the tension. "I'm not a bad guy, honestly." Keaton started to defend himself with a small pout. "I guess a bit of Amelia's standoffish mannerism had rubbed off on me, but I have to be above those in the Lust clan for a reason." Keaton spoke, his voice seeming to be rather monotone as he lightly bounced his foot. "I have to teach sexual education and teach others how to properly deliver a child in an era where we don't have the proper medicine that we once had to ensure that both the mother and baby are delivered without risk of death." Keaton continued, but it wasn't exactly relaxing Dean any.

"In part of my education, I teach my students what their sexual orientation or preference is." Keaton continued, though Dean didn't see a reason as to why the male was continuing to ramble on. "It's one of the factors that helps a person understand themselves." Keaton paused, studying Dean's face to see if the other was at least trying to understand what he meant by all of this. "I'll be holding a lesson tomorrow in the afternoon. If you-" Keaton started to speak before Dean interrupted him.

"Why should I care what you're doing tomorrow when you have done nothing but insult Kane and myself?" Dean snapped, raising his voice a bit louder than he originally intended to. This seemed to make Keaton a bit angry, as shown by his clenched jaw and furrowing eyebrows. Dean should feel a bit ashamed to raise his voice at Keaton, considering that he was the leader of the Lust clan and needed his help, but screw that. Dean felt like he didn't need to hear a word of what Keaton had to say.

"Because you need this class in order for Amelia to take you seriously." Keaton spoke in a blunt tone of voice. That's right, in order for Dean to be able to make this plan succeed, Dean would need to make sure that he showed Amelia that he was willing to put in the effort to be like one of the clan members. Considering that Keaton was her lover, his influence could very well either make or break the whole plan. It seemed that this little match's winner was Keaton, leaving a rather hollowed feeling to linger in Dean's body. He was used to being able to win the other leaders over, but he was failing right now.

The sound of the gears seemed to rattle the floor a bit, meaning that their time together was cut short. Dean's shoulder dropped ever so slightly as he slumped into the chair. It felt like a weight had been placed back on his shoulders. Dean had been so worked up that he forgot how tense his muscles had become. Maybe Dean was becoming a bit blindsided at what his initial goal had been. He was caught up in learning about himself and learning about this world, that he forgot the plan.

As Kane entered the room with the bottle of whiskey in his hands, Kane's eyes scanned the two men to make sure that there wasn't any distress from Keaton trying something on Dean. The way that Dean's body posture showed defeat meant that something did happen, but not like what Kane had worried about. Honestly Kane figured that Keaton might try to get physical with Dean, but there was not a single shred of evidence to support it.

"You know, you could have told me that you moved everything down there." Kane spoke in a rather scolding tone as he set the whiskey bottle down on the little coffee table. "I almost got lost looking for this thing." Kane huffed making his way back over towards the chair. There was a concerned look on Kane's face as he noticed the defeated posture that Dean was exhibiting, but he could ask what happened later on in private.

"Sorry. It was a rather recent change. But I'm glad that you were able to find it." Keaton spoke, picking up the bottle to examine it. Kane took this as a chance to glance over at Dean to better assess the situation. Dean's clothes weren't disturbed, nor was there any type of physical marks that would indicate that they fought, so why did Dean look as though he lost a bit of himself? "Here, take it as a little peace offer." Keaton spoke as he placed the bottle back down on the table, sliding it closer to the two.

Kane was surprised at the generous offer, on top of the remark about a peace offer. Just what the hell happened while he was downstairs? "Peace offer?" Kane asked, only to grow a scowl on his face. "What did you do to Dean?!" Kane asked, his voice stern with a hint of accusation that Keaton had done something to Dean while Kane was gone.

"Nothing." Keaton was quick to reply, but the scowl on Kane's face showed that he didn't believe the leader. "I was trying to establish what kind of friendship the two of you have." Keaton spoke, as if he was innocent of any wrongdoing. "After all, we can't have a repeat of-"

Keaton started to speak before Kane stood up angrily, glaring at the Lust leader as if Kane could stab daggers into the man.

"The company I keep and my relationship with them is not for you to decide!" Kane snapped, clenching his fists as he glared at Keaton with a rage that Dean had never seen before. "You can't keep telling people who they can and cannot be with Keaton!" Kane continued his speech as Keaton stood up now. Keaton crossed his arms over his chest as Kane pointed a finger at the man as he continued to speak. "If someone isn't related to me by blood or marriage, then I should have a fair shot at them. We don't have the luxury of playing it by your rules." This remark seemed to get Dean's reaction as he looked up at the two.

"Rules? What rules?" Dean asked, a bit taken back that there would even need to be rules regarding who people could be with or not. Besides the whole blood relation, did it really matter if people were able to fall in love with an individual if they cared about them? But thinking about the way that Kane said it, Dean knew he was referring to his feelings for Miles. After all, Miles was the one who took Kane in when his family died. Being that close to someone for so long, it was no brainer that Kane developed strong feelings for Miles in their time together.

"You'll find out tomorrow." Keaton was quick to interrupt Kane. Knowing the male, Kane would have quickly spilled all of the rules that those of the clans must follow. Before Keaton took over, the rules were a bit more relaxed when it came to how people conducted themselves. Ever since Keaton took over, there were more rules added to make it seem like there was some type of structure in place.

"What is he talking about?" Kane asked, his attention being directed towards Dean. It seemed like there was a lot that Kane had missed, making him wonder if perhaps the two made some sort of deal behind his back. Naturally Dean had no idea what was going on, or at the very least, what Keaton was planning.

"In exchange for me helping out with your little plan, I told Dean that he had to take one of my classes." Keaton convincingly lied as his posture seemed to relax a bit. "After all, you helped him hunt and get his first skull, right?" The look of disbelief seemed to wash over Kane as he looked between the two men. Dean didn't agree to take any class, so he was the most blindsided by all of this.

"How did you-" Kane started to speak, only to be cut off by Keaton once more. It seemed like Dean was stuck between a power struggle between the two leaders, confused as to what was going on anymore. But the fact that Keaton knew about the hunt even before seeing the skull, it was concerning as to what else the Lust leader knew.

"I have my ways." Keaton spoke in a bit of a cocky tone as he glanced towards Dean. "Nothing goes on in this city without my knowledge. That includes the little inns outside of the city." This news shouldn't have been as shocking to Kane as it was, but it meant that they couldn't exactly do anything without Keaton finding out. If they did something that might go against Amelia's wishes, she may not allow them to follow the plan. "But as I was saying before the interruptions," Keaton paused, as he glanced over towards Dean.

"Dean will be taking my next available course for those seeking to become a member of the clans, isn't that right Dean?" Keaton asked, flashing his cocky grin towards Dean while keeping an eye on Kane. Dean, however, didn't say anything. He simply glanced away from the two, feeling as if he didn't have a right to say anything at the moment. Keaton was right though, he needed to go to the lecture so that he could show Amelia that he was with them rather than against them.

Kane brought a hand up to cover his eyes, as if he couldn't believe what he was seeing or hearing at the moment. "Fine..." Kane trailed off, his voice sounding as if he was defeated. It wasn't like Kane could blame Dean for not saying anything. Plus Kane said that he couldn't exactly make it easy for Dean to convince the others, but it was better than nothing. If Dean was able to get through the lecture, he would be fine to handle anything else. Kane glaring at the leader before swiping the bottle of whiskey from the table. "Come on Dean, we're heading out."

Following behind Kane silently, the two made their way out of the room. Glancing behind him, Dean took notice of the rather bored and irritated gaze that crossed Keaton's face before closing the door. Dean couldn't put his finger on it, but he felt like this was just nothing more than a simple game or a type of theatrical being played out before him. Not that Kane was part of this whole show, but he was more like an unknowing participant. Either way, Dean had to keep a close eye on Keaton. Perhaps this whole lecture was a good way for Dean to get to understand a bit more about Keaton, though Dean will keep his distance.

STANDING outside of an old looking brick building, Dean was surprised to see that there were so many people seemingly going into the building. Standing there with a piece of paper in his hand with the room number the lecture was going to be in, mostly due to the fact that Keaton personally handed it to Dean while he was having breakfast in the inn they were staying in, Dean sighed as he slipped it into his pocket. Wearing a pair of black slacks, the black muscle shirt he was wearing yesterday, Dean borrowed the jacket that Kane had worn yesterday though with the belts along the sleeves being adjusted, Dean followed the group of people ahead of him.

The chatter among the people was much like what Dean was used to when he was on the station. The idle chatter of every day didn't seem to differentiate from either location. Keeping his mind occupied, Dean glanced around to take notice of the interior of the brick building that seemed to have been some type of college before the bombs dropped. The windows had been long since repaired over the years, but the wooden frame seemed to show its age. There were plenty of cracks along the marble flooring that had been obviously patched over the years as well. There were some parts in the floor that showed bits of the wooden foundation, but at least there wasn't any type of creaking that would make Dean worry if this place was safe for so many people being around.

Upon entering the room that had the lecture in it, Dean walked down the rows before finding a seat close to the middle section of the lecture room. It didn't take long for some of the younger people in the group Dean was following to surround him. Keaton seemed to be busy writing something on the rather big green chalk board that was something similar to what Dean's mother used in her lessons.

One of the girls from the other day seemed to be standing in the corner. Unlike yesterday where she seemed to be practically nothing, this time she wore her hair back in a short ponytail with bits of her bangs resting against her forehead. Wearing a light blue tank top with a short mini skirt that peaked out of her lab coat. Her legs were covered by her pantyhose that led to a pair of black short heels to give her height. The look on her face wasn't something that Dean was expecting when he glanced towards her.

Her eyes were much like how Kane often glanced at Miles before the whole airship incident. The woman's lips were a bit pouty as if to show how upset she was that Keaton wasn't paying any attention to her. Though she crossed her arms, her stance was telling that she was ready to hop to the man's side in order to help out with anything that he needed for the lesson. Dean didn't know who she was, but it was clear that she was aching to be with Keaton. Why? Dean couldn't understand it. But then again, there were plenty of people who seemed to like people who were natural assholes. All Dean could do was visibly shake his head for the poor woman. She looked youthful and ready to show Keaton that she would practically do anything for him. But Keaton simply ignored her. So much for finding everyone to be beautiful, huh?

"Alright class, shall we get started?" Keaton spoke loudly in the room, causing many of those we were seemingly goofing off to land themselves in their seats. Wearing his usual face mask, Keaton was wearing a black shirt and slacks with a lab coat over top of it with a loose red tie dangling over his chest. He frankly looked less like a wanna be mafia leader like yesterday, and more like an actual teacher.

"As you know, you must take this class before you can move on to choosing a clan in which you want to be affiliated with." Keaton spoke in a more firm tone as he reached under the table he was currently standing behind. Pulling out pointing stick, Keaton glanced over towards the woman before motioning for her to join him. "As always, my little sister Maiti will be joining us. She will be assisting me." The woman took this as her cue to happily join Keaton's side as she walked with a spring in her step.

The woman from the other night was Keaton's sister? The one who looked as if she could get with any guy, who longed to be with Keaton, was his very own sister. Dean had to do his best not to let his jaw hit the floor. Did Kane know about this? There were so many questions that were going on in Dean's mind that he was pretty much blanking on anything else that Keaton was currently saying. It didn't really matter at the moment anyways since Keaton was simply going over different clans and what their roles were. Dean had already learned that much thanks to Kane explaining everything on their journey up to this point. But keeping his eyes on Maiti, Dean couldn't help but wonder if maybe the reason why Keaton was so cold towards her was due to the fact that they were related.

As the lesson went on, Dean leaned back in the wooden seat as he observed the interaction between Keaton and his sister Maiti. She seemed to keep her distance, yet she couldn't take her eyes off of the male. Dean brought a hand up to cover his mouth subconsciously. So far most of the lessons that they were covering were things that Dean already knew, but there was an interesting question that Keaton asked that related to his clan in particular.

"Does anyone know the real difference between lust and love? Or how you would know which one you are feeling?" Keaton asked, his eyes scanning the crowd. Most of the people looked among each other to see if perhaps anyone else knew the answer, but when Keaton spotted Dean sitting there, a small curl on the corner of his lips landed under the mask, indicated that Keaton was interested in knowing what their outer space guest had to say on the matter.

"What about you Mr. Torres?" Keaton asked, causing most of the people to look around as they never heard of that last before. "Do you know what the difference is?" Keaton asked, raising an eyebrow while placing his left hand onto his hip. It seemed that Keaton was rather confident that Dean might not know, or that Dean would at least have an interesting answer.

"Masturbation." Dean spoke bluntly, causing some of the people around Dean to burst out in laughter. It seemed that even Keaton had a small chuckle at the answer, but Dean didn't seem to be phased by this. With a loud clearing of his throat, Dean stood up from his seat, making all eyes shift over towards him.

"If you think about someone when you masturbate to them, if those feelings die out after you reach your climax, you were simply feeling lust towards that individual." Dean continued to explain, resulting in people still laughing at his answer. There was an annoyed look on his face, but Dean wasn't done there. "However, if you still have strong feelings for someone once you have finished, that means you truly have something stronger than lust for them." This answer seemed to be surprising to most, especially to Keaton.

"No way that can be right." A male spoke up, catching Dean's attention as he turned his head to listen to what other people had to say. "How can masturbating help to know if you love or lust after someone?" The male continued to ask, causing his friends to chuckle around him. "This person clearly has a couple of screws loose up there." The more that Dean listened, the flashbacks he had of the time he was in school on the station. Dean could still hear his bullies' voices despite the many years in which he hasn't seen them.

"Interesting choice." Keaton spoke, seemingly to be impressed with the answer Dean came up with. This caused a fair amount of students to become confused. Even Dean was rather surprised that he got a positive response from Keaton that wasn't demeaning "And where did you learn this? On the station?" Kane continued to ask, causing Dean to frown in anger. "I'm surprised that they would even teach you the difference in a manner that would seem to be rather fitting." Keaton continued, placing the chalk down on the metal bar that was used to collect the chalk bits that fell off.

"Actually my mother told me about it before she was brutally murdered." Dean spoke, causing the shift in the room to change from being rather silly to awkwardly serious. "She was a teacher, so she put it upon herself to teach me a bit about the difference between love and lust after I turned 12." It was a rather embarrassing talk, but considering that Dean was going to become a man in only a few short years, she wanted to cover all the basics. Even when Dean would cover his face and shake his head out of embarrassment, but yet some of it stuck with him.

"She didn't hold anything back. She made sure that I at least learned it because the school on the station wasn't exactly the best at covering sexual education." Considering that there were restrictions put in place for the station as there wasn't much room for people to branch out, it seemed that sexual education was something that wasn't a primary focus. Or at least, that's what Dean told himself since he didn't get a chance to dive more into that aspect due to his parent's death.

"Interesting." Keaton muttered as he moved to lean back against the chalkboard. "I've always been a bit curious as to how a station full of the so called last survivors of the human race was able to have such a wide variation of a gene pool." Keaton remarked, looking up at Dean with a cocky grin under the mask. "I'm sure probably in the beginning there were plenty of women who were used as breeders. Sort of like livestock for fucking." Keaton continued in a crude tone. "I'm sure that there were plenty of men on the station in order to have a well diverse community up in space. Right?" Keaton remarked as pushed off of the board and casually strolled around the front of the desk.

"Of course that was well before your time I'm sure." Keaton continued, before pulling out a chart. "You can only stretch a human gene so far without there being a risk of family members getting together and having abominations running around." The phrasing of that remark didn't exactly sit well with Dean. Did Keaton just call him an abomination?

"Surely the case of the last survivors on earth are much like the Elites and hierarchy of our own history." Keaton continued on with his lecture as he set up a chart on the blackboard. "How medically and genetically messed up they are, that is." Keaton pointed to the diagram, showing off how incest produced horrifying genetic mutations for the whole class to see.

"Family breeding with other members of the family often brings out mutants and freaks of the medical world." Keaton spoke with disdain in his voice, as if Dean was nothing more than some genetic freak. "Frankly, they won't need to be destroyed as they are slowly killing themselves off with their interstellar breeding practices." Keaton's remark caused a fair amount of the other students to chuckle at that remark, but Dean knew he wasn't a mutant.

Dean was taken back by the remarks that Keaton made. It was one thing to suggest that most of the women aboard the Millennium were nothing more than cattle being used for breeding purposes, it was something that Dean couldn't exactly argue, but it was another thing to call Dean a mutate. There were hardly any family records after what happened when the nukes were dropped. It was as if the Elite would rather keep the populace docile without thinking about the fact that they were in a way, all related to one another. But that didn't mean that Dean was some type of freak that should be experimented on. He was just as much a human as those currently surrounding him.

"Your genes are very unique as you would be considered a product of the chosen few who left us to rot." Keaton remarked, making Dean feel a shiver down his spine. Keaton wasn't exactly wrong either. Sure he may have some type of linear with one of the few pioneers on the Millennium, but he never lived like an Elite. The closest he came to living a better life before the death of his parents was living in the Silver class, and even that was still a bit rough compared to how others lived. "I'm sure that anyone who ends up having your children will have a very interesting offspring in the means of a gene pool." The way that Keaton worded that, it made Dean feel as if he was going to be hunted down. That he had special sperm living inside of him.

"I guess it does." Dean remarked, a fake smile landing on his face though Dean's voice was a bit monotone in nature. Dean wasn't looking for just anyone to be in a relationship with. He would much rather get to know someone rather than mindlessly sleep with any woman who came his way. "But getting back on the topic before the whole discussion about my sperm," Dean spoke up, figuring that he would just turn this burning ship back around before it made its way into uncharted waters. "I wouldn't be able to tell you how the Millennium went about their birthing practices." Dean hated this whole subject matter, but he needed to talk about in order to pass this portion of the ritual. "Since the room was rather limited, it wasn't like we were able to pop out kids left and right." Dean continued keeping his focus on Keaton as he spoke.

"Not to mention, the limitation on food in the early part of their 'breeding' session would have made it hard for people to even have many kids with their supplies being limited from what they brought to Earth, but I'm sure they had to spread it out." Dean was pretty much talking out his ass on this, he didn't know exactly what happened, but using a bit of logic and reasoning he came up with a pretty decent argument. "But what's your point? Surely you're not trying to make me seem like I'm some rare catch just for the sake of genetics." Dean asked, a small amused smile lingering on his face.

"No. But at least it seems that you're not some mutated genetic freak like some people." Keaton remarked, a subtle glance towards his sister which caused the girl to look down and frown. "Relationships between siblings, offsprings and their parents, cousins, and anyone who considers each other family, always leads to problems. Rather it is genetic or relationship wise." There it was, what Kane and Keaton often butted heads with their arguments. "It's best to simply keep a barrier between any relationship that is considered to be of the family nature." Keaton spoke in a firm tone, locking eyes with Dean.

Seeing the disappointed look on Maiti's face, Dean couldn't help but feel sorry for her. Being in love with a jerk like Keaton was something that no one should be put through. He seemed like the type who would make anyone feel bad about themselves no matter what they did. "What the hell kind of answer is that anyways?" Dean spoke up, causing some of the students to look at him with a rather awe look at them. "Actual blood relations is one thing, considering the ramifications that would cause a lot of health issues, but if you don't have a type of shared genetic, why should it matter?" Dean asked, not for himself, but for Kane's sake.

"If someone said that I was like a brother to them, I would take that with pride." Dean continued, knowing that if Kane remarked about being like a brother to Dean, it would make him happy. It would mean that they shared a friendship that wasn't like lovers, but more like family. "It means that they care for me in a way that it breaks through the barrier of friendship and pushes me that much closer to being intimate with them." The look on Keaton's face showed that he was rather displeased with that answer. But Dean didn't exactly care.

"I've never had any siblings, but if someone that I knew told me that they cared about me in a way that meant they wanted to be like family, I would treasure them wholeheartedly." It may not have been the answer that Keaton wanted to hear, but Dean was giving the leader a piece of his mind in front of all the students. "Sure it might mean that I might not be attractive or be to their specific liking, but it's better than getting angry at them and leaving them confused and hurt."

Dean wouldn't know how he would have felt if Kane liked him like a brother, but at least then Dean would know where he stood. "If I love someone, I would never want to see them hurt." Dean continued, moving to support himself on the table in front of him as he leaned over the desk. "Do you really think you're helping them by telling people that don't have any blood relations that they can't still carry a flame towards the person they genuinely love?"

"Yes." Keaton spoke bluntly as he took a few more steps forward. The students seemed to be interested in this debate between the newcomer and Keaton. "If you cross the line of being more than family, you'll get nothing but heartache." Keaton audible growled, taking everyone by surprise. Dean wasn't sure what he was going to expect, but it certainly wasn't what was about to come out of the leader's mouth.

"Do you understand what it is like to venture into one of the shelters and see the genetic nightmares that come out of them?" Keaton asked, his voice shaking ever so slightly. "To see young children with mismatched limbs who can barely move on their own? Struggling to even breathe?" Not like Dean would ever really understand that remark. He was never a father. If there were such genetic 'mutants' as Keaton claimed, the most likely thing the Elite would do is to simply kill the child out of the sight of the parents and claim that the baby died. Not like that was possible in the shelters. "It's best for everyone to simply keep lovers and family members apart." Keaton spoke, as if that was the final word on the subject. But Dean wasn't exactly the type to simply let someone have the final say without any real evidence.

"So you would rather people be miserable?" Dean started up his side of this debate. "To spare them heartache or pain because of the child that they were going to raise may have health issues? Despite the fact that they are not at all related?" Dean asked, his brows knitting together as he didn't believe a word that Keaton was saying. "I don't blame you when it comes to people actually being blood related," Dean paused, trying to collect his thoughts for a second. "But that doesn't give you a right to keep people apart simply because they say that someone is like a brother or sister to them. It doesn't automatically make them share the same DNA Keaton!" Dean commented, not understanding Kane's rational thinking.

"Okay Dean," The challenging tone in Keaton's voice made Dean a bit nervous as to what would come next. "If I were to say that it was alright for people who considered each other like family members to get together, don't you think you would be left heart broken then?" Keaton asked, causing Dean to become more confused in the process. Seeing the confusion on Dean's face, Keaton audibly sighed as he rested his hands on his hips.

"Because then Kane would continue his pursuit on Miles. Leaving both you and Kane heart broken." Hearing that explanation caused a red tint to grow on Dean's cheeks. It wasn't like they had that sort of relationship, despite what others had to say. "Kane would continue to pine for Miles, while you silently watch him struggle to be with someone who can't find it in himself to be with Kane." Keaton remarked, causing a couple of the students to gasp or start to gossip between each other.

Dean's face practically became a dark beet red when Keaton spoke so bluntly like that. "I-I don't have those types of feelings for Kane!" Dean stuttered, feeling himself become embarrassed that most of these students will get the wrong idea about the two of them. "We're just friends. Nothing more!" Dean panickally remarked, glancing around as he could already hear the whispers of gossip coming from those surrounding him.

"Right..." Keaton trailed off before a quick chuckle left his face. "The way I see it, and most of the other leaders see it as well." Keaton continued, finding it amusing to torture Dean this way. "The two of you are just too dense to realize how you feel about each other." Keaton continued, moving his way back towards the chalkboard.

"Aw, no fair. Kane gets all the cute ones." One girl said in earshot of Dean, causing him to glance towards her. Dean stiffened hearing the comments coming in. No matter what Dean could say, it seemed like everyone's minds were already made up about the pair.

"I know!" Another girl seemed to remark, causing a jolt to run down Dean's spine. "But they would look so cute together." The girl continued with a soft giggle. "Maybe the two of them could adopt some kids and actually grow the Gluttony clan more." A pair of girls on the other side of Dean spoke, giggling together as their fantasies were going wild.

"I always knew that Kane was a fruit, but this guy too?" Came a male voice close to Dean. "I guess there can even be those types of people on the station, huh? Guess they aren't as perfect as they claim to be." A man spoke, seemingly surrounded by a couple of his friends, only to have his head fling back when the chalkboard eraser hit him square in the face. A white cloud of chalk splattered around his face, causing the man to cough. "W-What the hell was that for?" The man asked, letting the eraser fall to his crotch.

The laughter and idle chatter seemed to stop as they noticed the angered look on Keaton's face. Though the mask didn't show his lower half on his face, Keaton's eyes said it all. "Looks like we have a volunteer to clean up the board once class is over." Keaton spoke in a firm yet angry tone. "Now then," Keaton continued, opening a drawer of the desk to pull out another eraser to use in the meantime.

"There's nothing wrong with loving someone of the same gender. But Dean here is pansexual." Way to call Dean out like that, but what was he supposed to do? "He's like me, but on the smaller side of the scale." Keaton continued, all the while Dean slowly sunk into his chair and using his hands to cover up the redness in his face. "Speaking of which, let's continue the lesson on sexual orientation." Keaton continued, moving to erase the ledger on the board. Just how much longer was this class anyways?

As the lesson went on, Dean hardly paid attention to what Keaton was saying. Even though Dean wanted to continue the debate, he was too embarrassed to keep going. Not only that, but Keaton was able to take charge of the class once again to continue with the lesson. Before Dean knew it, the lesson was finally over with. As the other students around him got up to leave, Dean remained in his seat. The boy who made the rude comment was summoned forth to clean up the large chalkboard, leaving only four people in the room.

As Keaton was lecturing the boy about his rude comments, Maiti made her way over towards where Dean was sitting. The sound of her heels hitting the floorboard underneath didn't seem to even stir Dean out of his thoughts, but rather her soft voice was enough to cause Dean to glance at her. Glancing up at Maiti, Dean was surprised that she looked just as beautiful in normal clothes as she did in her other outfit.

"Hey." Maiti greeted Dean as she sat down next to him. "I'm Maiti." She introduced herself before pulling out a chair next to Dean. "You're Dean, right?" She asked in the softest and gentlest voice that Dean had ever heard coming from another girl. She was completely different from Keaton in every way. She had a type of soothing aura about her, making it almost easy to let your guard down.

"Oh... hi." Dean spoke up, the flustered look on his face lingered. "Yeah, I'm Dean. Dean

Torres. Nice to meet you." Dean collected himself as he reached out a hand, offering Maiti a handshake. As she shook his hand, Dean noticed how much smaller her hand was and how soft it was. It wasn't like Kane's hand at all, the complete opposite actually.

"Likewise." Maiti remarked, a small chuckle leaving her lips as she turned to face forward. "Listen," She started to speak, her tone seeming to change from her friendly tone to a more sadden one. "I'm sorry about my brother." Maiti apologized, as if she was used to doing it to new people who simply didn't understand Keaton. "I know he can come off as a jerk most of the time, and he can even be cold towards me." A soft sigh escaped Maiti's lips as she gazed down at Keaton scolding the rude male. "It always breaks my heart when I see that coldness in him, but frankly I understand why he does it." Dean raised an eyebrow upon hearing that remark.

"You do?" Dean asked, a bit surprised that she has come to realize something that Dean never thought of. Frankly Keaton seemed to come off as someone who seemed like they knew what was good for everyone. It often gave off an Elitist type of mindset, something that Dean just couldn't stand seeing in other people.

"Yeah," Maiti spoke with a quick bob of her head. "He was never really like this, you know." Maiti started to explain while Dean listened to her intensely. "He used to let people do whatever they wanted because we needed to repopulate." Which made sense considering it was exactly what the Elite did once they tried to destroy the world. "But, there was one shelter that really changed his mind. After all, he was there to see it for himself." Maiti took a deep breath in, as if to steady herself for what she was about to say next.

"The shelter was full of rather sickly looking people inside of it." Maiti spoke, sadness lingering on her face as she kept her gaze on Keaton. "Apparently, the tunnels that led towards the other communities had caved in, leading the family to be stranded in their shelter. They couldn't exactly let all their hard work go to waste, so what other choice did they have but to grow their community with each other?" Hearing that, Dean could understand to a point of where this was heading.

"Over the years the family didn't really think twice about it, but as the babies being born were coming out deformed, they didn't have it in them to simply kill their children." What parent could be so cruel to ever kill their child after all? "So you had a community of deformed people who barely were able to understand basic human speech trying to keep their shelter afloat." Maiti continued, only to pause as she gazed at the back of Keaton with a small frown on her face.

"There was a small baby laying in a makeshift and broken cradle by the time they reached the shelter." Maiti spoke, holding out her hands as if she was holding onto a real baby. "She was so small when my brother picked her up. Her head was deformed to the point where it seemed like the large massive lump spilled over her left eye. She could barely see out of it, and she looked deprived of nutrients." The more detail that Maiti provided, the clearer the picture that Dean got. "She barely had any baby fat on her, and she was so small and frail that you could see her bones." Maiti continued, tearing up a bit as she recounted the memory. "Her left arm and leg were much shorter than her right side, making the chances of her being able to survive to be about a year old practically impossible." Maiti continued, though it seemed a few tears had started to escape down the side of her face.

"As my brother picked her up, he couldn't believe how badly it had gotten. She cried in his arms, her lower half basically dangled as she had no muscles to move her body. But she continued to cry in his arms, making him remember how he would hold me in his arms when I was a baby." Dean felt his heart sink hearing more of the story. "He swore right then and there that he couldn't allow this to happen to anyone else. He couldn't allow future children to suffer the same fate as this little girl in his arms." Dean glanced down at the desk as Maiti continued with the story. "Because it would have been much crueler to have her suffer the short life span she had simply because Keaton was selfish in his desire to have the human population grow." Maiti continued, though she pulled out a handkerchief from her pocket to wipe off the tears before a small sniffle left her nose.

"So what happened to the baby? And to those living in the shelter?" Dean asked, almost afraid of the answer. If Keaton was anything like the Elite on the station, he would have told them that they were better off being killed. To simply destroy the shelter and to be completely rid of the mutates. After all, that was the inclination that Dean got from Keaton. That he was so selfish in making sure that people never crossed the family boundaries, that he would rather make people be miserable than let them follow their heart.

"They rescued them." Maiti remarked, clearing her throat afterwards. "He gave the baby the best life that she could really have." Hearing that surprised Dean than it should have. "Unfortunately, she died a year later. Her poor heart wasn't the strongest, and she passed away peacefully in her sleep." Hearing that, Dean started to wonder if perhaps he was being too cruel on Keaton without getting to know to know the man.

"My brother was hit the hardest by her death." Maiti continued, letting out a soft sigh as she clenched onto the handkerchief. "That's when Keaton decided that family members, and those who consider themselves family, should never cross the line of intimacy. In fear that the future children would suffer as a result of it." Dean was surprised that Keaton actually let them live, and considering how badly the death of the child affected him, Dean felt a bit like a jerk for judging Keaton so harshly because of how worried Kane was.

"So if he is being cold towards you because of that?" Dean asked, surprised that Maiti would open up to someone like Dean like this. "Why do you seem to put up with it? Don't you think he may be going too far with saying who is allowed to be with each other?" Dean asked. He couldn't understand why Maiti would do that sort of thing. Did Maiti have some kind of brother complex or something?

"Because underneath it all, I know he is doing it because he loves me." Maiti remarked with a loving smile on her face. "He cares so much about me, that he would distance himself from me so that my love for him would be only family." Maiti remarked, letting out a small sigh towards the end. "I've never met another man like my brother. No one has been able to live up to his example, which makes it hard for me to really give other men a chance." Maiti continued, her gaze moving towards Keaton once more, the same longing gaze that Dean witnessed on Kane matched perfectly to how Maiti was looking at her brother.

"He's strong, brave, and handsome on top of it." Maiti continued with a small giggle at the end. "He still cares about me even though he keeps his distance, and he gives me the cold shoulder which only makes me ache for him more." Maiti continued, crossing one leg over the other as she seemed to have a more heated look to her now. "Maybe it's' the whole forbidden side that makes people ache for those that they shouldn't." Hearing that comment coming from Maiti was unnerving for Dean to hear.

"Where did that come from?" Dean asked, his confusion becoming notable, which only seemed to cause a small giggle to come from Maiti. *"Seriously, what is with this girl? She wants to bone her brother?"* Dean thought to himself as he gave Maiti a sideways glance. *"Guess this was why Keaton wanted to keep siblings away from each other if they behave like her."*

"Well, Kane is a lot like me. We're both the type of people who like forbidden things." That comment caused Dean to look at Maiti with a surprised look on his face. How were they the same? "Rather its' a lust for someone whom we think is like a sibling to us, or to want to savor the taste of forbidden fruit that is the same sex. We simply go for what catches our eye." Maiti spoke, her voice almost purring as she leaned in against Dean.

"But unlike me, Kane restricts himself. Mostly because he doesn't want to get hurt." It made sense if Dean knew Kane as well as he thought he did. "But you're completely different." Maiti continued, making Dean uncomfortable in his seat. "You say that Kane is only a friend, but the way you two interact, it says something a bit more. You're just too dense to realize it." Maiti continued, only to lightly poke Dean's temple.

"What is up with everyone?" Dean asked as his brows knitted together. "You guys think that just because two people are good friends, that there is more to it? Two guys can be friends and not be sexually attracted to each other." Dean practically shouted, causing Keaton to glance back and see the two. There was a small glare as he watched Maiti seemingly cozying up to Dean, but it seemed that Dean's words were more important at the moment.

"You honestly think that you're not attracted to Kane?" Keaton asked, moving towards the two. "Because I would say otherwise." Keaton spoke as he stopped in the front row of desks. "You got defensive when I bad mouth Kane. Your eyes barely leaves Kane when there are other people around, and you don't shrug him away when he gets close." Keaton started to list off a few observations from the time that he saw the two interact.

"Not to mention, the whole time that you were at Ashley's, you would smile at Kane the way that a lover would at someone who was their whole world." Dean stiffened in his seat when Keaton made that remark. Did Dean really smile like that towards Kane? "You're quick to make sure that Kane is happy, which is why when you saw how upset Kane was, you pulled him out of the banquet." Seems like they didn't go unnoticed after all. "If that isn't something you would do for someone you loved, what would you call it?" Keaton asked, seemingly putting Kane on the spot.

Dean was rather blown away by how blunt Keaton was describing things from purely observing the two. "He's just my best friend." Dean defended the friendship status. "Two guys can care for one other without there being more to it." Dean practically lied to himself. But it seemed that Keaton wasn't buying it. Nor was Maiti, and she wasn't even there. "I don't look that way to Kane all the time, do I?" Dean asked, mostly to himself as he tried to think back on all the times that he was with Kane. The time they were together in the kitchen, just simply talking and having a good time, did he really simply look at Kane as if the male was his everything? Like the way that his father would gaze at his mother? He was doing that with Kane, his best friend?

"Yup." Maiti and Keaton spoke in unison, causing Dean to nearly jump in his seat. This talk about feelings and his relationship with Kane was starting to feel overwhelming. They were just friends traveling together. Nothing more....just....nothing more.

"How would you know? You weren't even there." Dean was quick to snap towards Maiti, before seeing the knowing grin on her face. There was no way she was there, right? After all, Dean didn't see her at the banquet at all.

"A girl just knows when someone is in love." Maiti remarked, moving to stand up and stretch. "Anyways, I'm off to get ready to hit the clubs." She spoke through her grunts. Peeling off her lab coat, Maiti tossed it to Keaton who grabbed it with ease. "Don't think about it too much Dean. But sooner or later, you'll realize how much you'll only want Kane to yourself. Just like how I want my brother only to myself." Maiti continued with a soft chuckle.

"Not going to happen." Keaton spoke in a more irritated tone before letting the lab coat drape over his arm. It wasn't long after that Maiti left that Keaton glanced out the window to see the lights for the clubs starting to flicker on. "Guess you've been making him wait long enough." Keaton mumbled before taking a pencil from his pocket. Popping the eraser off, Keaton flicked it off of his thumb, causing it to hit Dean in the forehead.

"Ow, what was that for?" Dean asked, watching as the eraser bounced on the desk before rolling towards the ground as it slipped off of the edge of the table desk. Despite the eraser being somewhat soft, it still left a small bruise on Dean's forehead.

"To help snap you out of your thoughts for one." Keaton spoke, walking over to the small balled up erased to pick it up. "And for two, to let you know that I'll help you convince Amelia that your plan should get the green light." Dean was surprised to hear that Keaton was willing to help him out after all. With their debate and arguing, Dean thought that he messed it up big time.

"After all, if anyone would love to watch the mighty Elite empire fall, it's her." Keaton remarked as he turned his back away from Dean. "The next person you're going to have to convince is Miles." That wasn't much of a surprise, considering that they met with everyone else besides Miles and Amelia. "Word of warning," Keaton paused as he looked over his shoulder at Dean. "He thinks of himself as Kane's older brother. If he feels like you're not thinking of Kane's best interest, he'll work against you." Keaton's warning seemed rather ominous, but so far it seemed like Miles was trying to help them. Or was he merely observing Dean?

"Um... thanks for the warning?" Dean remarked, rubbing his head a little bit as he moved to stand up from his seat. But Keaton didn't seem to reply back. Dean didn't understand what was going on anymore. Glancing out the window, Dean could see the neon lights starting to paint the walls of the skyline. Despite it being underground, this place was truly beautiful.

It seemed like everything was going smoothly on convincing the other leaders to be on board with him. But Dean still didn't understand his feelings when it came to Kane. The more he thought about it, the more Dean's head and heart seemed to fight. Dean didn't exactly have time for this. What they needed was to meet with the other two leaders. And the closer they got to meeting up with Amelia, and getting her approval, the closer they were to giving everyone a happy ending. At least, that's what Dean hoped for. After all, his goal was in his reach. All he had to do was reach out and finish it.

CHAPTER SEVENTEEN: *Conflict Between "Brothers"*

WHEN IT CAME time to leave the Lust Clan, Kane had presented Dean with a pair of tickets that would allow them to leave via the train system that had just finished connecting the Lust Clan to a province that was only an hour away from the next destination, the Sloth Clan. Apparently the train ran on steam and would run back and forth between the two connected stations to test out whether or not they could rework the old systems to make for easier transportation with the old railroads. It was a little farewell gift from Keaton, or at least that was what Kane explained to Dean. It didn't matter at this point to Dean. They had to meet with the last two leaders, and then they could take down the Elite and the Millennium.

Sitting down on one of the red seats with golden trimmings, Dean found a spot next to a window so that he could gaze out any time that he wanted to. With Kane sitting down next to him, Dean stretched out his feet a bit as the other passengers were getting on. It seemed that there were a few people who wanted to experience the train ride for the first time, while others stayed behind since they didn't know what they were going to expect on the train ride. Dean would be lying to himself if he said that he wasn't nervous. But having Kane by his side, the two would be able to do anything. With their backpacks resting close to their feet, Dean was certain that they would be fine.

After everyone was settled down, the train jerked ever so slightly as it started to move. Holding his breath for the first few seconds to calm his nerves, Dean stared ahead to the wooden interior as the train started to gain momentum. It felt a bit strange as there were a few bumps that Dean could feel underneath him. It reminded Dean of the first few times that he rode the elevator on his own to his job on the station. There wasn't much to see when they were still in the underground portion of the Lust clan, but once they reached the surface, it felt like the whole cart they were in seemed to light up from the sun shining overhead. There was a small green tint, causing Dean to look out the window once his eyes adjusted to brightness, only to see them traveling through a tunnel that had vines climbing up the metal rebar. As the train rushed past, the leaves seemed to shake as if waving the passengers good luck on their ride.

Once the train left the plant covered tunnel, the train seemed to skate through the ruined city that had been taken over by nature. As Dean glanced out the window, he noticed how well covered most of the broken metal buildings were. Some buildings looked as if they were completely green from the vines that crept up along the sides, seemingly swallowing the buildings whole, leaving only the outline of the building to be seen.

There were a few buildings that one could see that it was either a business or a home that once held family members inside before the bombs dropped, then then there were some buildings that were nothing but rumble. In brief instances Dean could faintly make out roads that waved their way around the buildings that once held hundreds, if not thousands of people. As the train started to pick up speed, Dean wouldn't be able to make out much more than that. The clanking of the rods was something that Dean would have to learn to register as white noise, but it was interesting to hear the way that the train snaked along the rails that were long forgotten.

Feeling a light thud against him, Dean turned his gaze to see Kane seemingly slumped up against Dean with his eyes closed. "Wake me up when we get there…" Kane softly groaned, moving to place a hand on his stomach. Seeing how Kane didn't exactly like flying on the airship, it made sense that the male would also hate traveling by train. Dean wasn't exactly thrilled with it, but his stomach wasn't as sensitive as Kane's. Who knows, maybe growing up on the station helped Dean to have a more hardened stomach thanks to the artificial gravity he was used to.

"Alright. If you need to throw up, let me know." Dean remarked, a faint smile on his face as he turned to look out the window some more. The more that Kane got his rest, the more that Dean would be alone with his thoughts. And frankly, Dean needed to have this time to sit and ponder just what was happening in his life. After all, he had only met Kane roughly five months ago, and already Dean was living a more exciting life than he would have ever expected on the station.

Going from the daily grind of waking up and working a stressful twelve hour shift every single day for practically pennies on the credit, to actually living an adventurous life where Dean is able to discover new places and meeting exotic people, Dean couldn't have ever imagined living such a life. It was like he was living through one of his books that he used to read. Even if this was not real, it was much better than being alone in that isolated pod for the rest of his life. The warmth coming off of Kane made this feel more real than anything Dean could have felt on the station.

Whether it was the gentle bumps of the train tracks, or the dull roar of the train combined with the warmth of the sun on him, Dean found himself drifting off at some point along the trip. It was only when the train started to slow down and the small screech of the train brakes caught Dean's attention that he started to wake up. It seemed like nothing happened while he dozed off, so that was at least a good sign. Seeing that their bags were still next to their feet, Dean glanced over to see that Kane was passed out. Seems like the leader didn't mind sleeping on Dean. Once the train pulled into the station, Dean started to lightly shake Kane awake.

"Mm…" Kane protested, only to slowly open his eyes before shifting to sit up. "Are we there?" Kane asked through a yawn, though Kane tried to cover his mouth before asking, but failed to do so as he stretched one of the arms over Kane's head.

"I guess so. Unless we both slept through the stops." Dean seemed to suggest with a small shrug of his shoulders. It seemed that Dean's little joke didn't settle too well with Kane considering how fast Kane was to look out the window. Leaning over Dean's lap, Kane peered out the window to see that they were facing a field that had a couple of farmers already tending to their crops. A small sigh of relief left Kane's lips as he pulled back from the window.

"Don't scare me like that." Kane grumbled as he reached down to grab his bag. With a small groan, Kane raised his arms before bending the left arm over to grab his right elbow. With a small bend to the side away from Dean, Kane started to stretch his muscles from the long train ride over. The sound of people shuffling off of the train or grabbing their stuff seemed to fill the cabin. As some people seemed to lightly jump off of the train to get to the platform, it caused the cabin to shake ever so slightly, making it unsettling when one wasn't prepared to feel the shift of the weight.

"Sorry, I guess the ride was just so soothing to me that I thought we both might have slept through it and made our way back to Keaton's place." Dean spoke, a little apologetic tone to his voice as Dean grabbed his bag as well. Shuffling towards their nearest exit, Dean let Kane go first before hoping off to the little station platform.

The warm sun peaked out from the clouds as the sound of the wind rushed through the valley they were in. The hills parted this way and that way around the station, tall green grass waved through the wind as the smell of rich soil with a mix of sand filled Dean's nostrils. In front of them was a rather sandy and clay path that seemed to lead towards the hills. It was a bit far off, but there seemed to be a large building that almost looked like some type of temple in the distance that stood out over everything else. To the right of him Dean seemed to notice that a lot of the people they were on the train with seemed to be gathering together. Did they come here as a group? Or was there something else going on? It didn't really seem to concern Dean as they were here to meet up with Miles. From what Dean had noticed, the male wasn't there to greet them.

"Alright, we're almost there." Kane spoke up and glanced over to Dean. "From here it should be about a twenty minute walk if we don't make any stops." Kane remarked, putting on his backpack with his headgear still attached to his bag. Dean followed suit as he quickly put his backpack on as well. Though Dean was surprised that Kane didn't take a chance to change into something else, like he normally did before meeting up with a leader. Kane was wearing a regular buttoned up white shirt with a pair of black and orange suspenders connecting to his black formal pants. The sleeves were rolled up, showing off Kane's pearly white complexion. As Kane gripped the straps of his backpack, it seemed that Kane was struggling with some inner thoughts that he would rather not talk about right now.

As Kane started to walk ahead of him, Dean made sure to stay relatively close by. The pathway seemed to be clear, no obstacles to keep them from their current destination, but Dean got the feeling that Kane wasn't going nearly as fast as he did when they were walking towards Keaton's place. Dean felt like the pace had become rather sluggish, making Dean contemplate whether or not he should say something. Seeing Kane keep his head held high, it was a bit of a reassurance that maybe Kane was doing better with the betrayal of Miles trying to spill his secrets. Perhaps Kane felt like he could do anything as long as he had Dean by his side. At least, that's what Dean could only hope for. After all, Dean was able to overcome so much just by having Kane by his side.

THE walk towards the town was rather uneventful. Kane didn't say much as they entered the town. To Dean it felt as it seemed like Kane was walking with autopilot on or something. Dean on the other hand took this chance to look around a bit as they walked. The hills that they passed seemed to have been dug into, making them into smaller fields that grew various plants that were starting to sprout. There were various cattle that seemed to move freely as the only thing that seemed to be fenced off was the areas where the plants were growing. Seeing the farmers working hard to tend to their crops was something that Dean couldn't exactly get over. Just like on the station, the farmers here put their heart and soul into making sure that the crops were well taken care of.

By the time that they reached the village, a fair amount of the people were already walking around, doing their normal routines while some of the children were playing in the streets. There was a man in a cart that was slowly being pulled by a horse with some bits of fruit heading towards the large looking temple towards the center of town. Everyone was wearing the same type of robes, similar to the one that Kane was wearing when Dean first came to Earth, making the pair stick out like a sore thumb. The closer they got to the temple, the more detail Dean could see.

There were a bunch of bright red pillars that looked a bit faded from the years that it was abandoned. There was golden decoration on the top and bottom of the pillars with a golden circular middle with faded designs etched into it. The railings stuck out the most as they appeared to have been recently painted red to match the exterior of the building. There were a few people on the roof working to patch it up. As the temple seemed to rest on top of a rather steep hill, Dean took notice of the rather worn and ancient looking steps that had bits of it gone. It seemed that at one point this used to be a place where many people would come, but after the bombs hit, there wasn't anyone around in order to maintain the temple.

"So what was this place used for?" Dean asked, stopping close to the large stoned fence that seemed to surround the temple's base. Even the wall seemed to be full of cracks with the lingering smell of Earth seemingly wafting from it. There were a few gaps that looked as if they needed to be patched, with some areas surrounding the gap that had been recently renovated.

Kane seemed to be slightly startled from the question. Turning to see Dean stopping by the fence, Kane looked up to see that they were by the temple. "Oh the temple?" Kane asked, before his attention went back to Dean. "It was used for worship or festivals." Kane spoke before turning back around.

"We were going to use it for Miles' banquet hall one year, but it was in desperate need of repair." Kane explained as he moved to head towards a certain direction, allowing for Dean to follow after him. "We brought people in from Felicia's tribe to build a separate building for the banquet that year." Kane continued as he walked, clearing his throat before he continued to speak. "One year there was a bad storm and lightning hit the building and burned it to the ground. So they decided to try and rebuild the temple." Kane paused before glancing back to the temple with a faded smile on his face. "Glad to see that it's nearly done. Who knows, maybe when it is Miles' year to host the banquet, it'll be amazing."

Dean seemed to notice that there wasn't any lingering longing in Kane's voice. Usually Kane would have his head held high whenever he would talk about Miles, but now it seemed that Kane no longer seemed to idolize the man he once held so dear. Perhaps it was just Dean's imagination, but he felt like maybe Kane wasn't putting Miles on such a high pedestal anymore. Whether it was a good or bad thing that was still yet to be determined, but Dean would just simply keep an eye on the other until he figured this whole thing out.

After a bit more walking in silence, they came across a bamboo forest with a single path leading inside of it. Kane had no problem making his way inside, but Dean was surprised to see such greenery presented before him. Catching up to Kane, Dean glanced up to see just how tall they were. It was unlike anything Dean had seen so far. The sound of small birds echoed in the distance, similar to what Dean heard when he had first arrived on the planet. When they arrived at a split in the cross road, Dean wondered what either side of the pathway had to offer, but kept quiet as they continued heading straight.

As they finally reached the end of the forest, they appeared in a clearing with a singular house in the middle of the meadow. Just behind the one story house appeared to be a cliff, but it wasn't like it led towards the sea or anything. Dean couldn't exactly make out what could be laying at the base of the cliff. The house itself looked a bit like the temple they had passed, only the exterior was white with bits of green moss seemingly resting on the slanted roof. There was a wrap around porch that surrounded the whole house. The wooden front door was closed, but Kane wasn't heading in that direction.

Following the path towards the back, the two stumbled upon Miles resting on his side on the wooden floor. With a pipe in his mouth, and that familiar lingering scent of a skunk blowing towards them in the wind, Miles seemed to rather zoned out as he stared at the strange bamboo device that poured water into each other before one of the bamboo shoots slammed down on a rock. A small chime could be heard as Dean took notice of the little chime that dangled from the overhead roof.

Miles' robe was slightly open, showing off his legs that seemed to be rubbing against each other as Miles struggled to stay awake. The torso portion of his robe was opened as well, showing off the man's well toned chest and torso as the fabric of his robe was loose enough that it appeared that it could fall off at any moment. Miles' dark gray hair seemed to spill onto his left side as he glanced towards them. "I was wondering when you two were going to get here." Miles spoke, his voice sounding as if he was in a daydream state. Getting up, Miles was rather slow in the process of moving, making Kane appear concerned for the man's well being.

As Miles stood, it was clear that the robe was worn loosely around Miles' body. It took a few minutes for Miles to fix it, but once he had slid the hem of the robe back into place, Miles went to work gliding his fingers through his dark gray locks, pushing them back in the process to keep them out of his face. Steely gray eyes glanced at the two with a small tint of red on the sclera of his eye. Dean glanced towards Kane with a slightly concerned look as Miles stumbled a bit on his feet. Once he was stable, Miles headed inside without so much as a single word to the two men. Kane followed behind the Sloth leader, leaving Dean no real option but to follow behind them.

The house seemed to rather open, not closed off at all, as if everything shared a space. There was hardly any walled off sections. The interior furniture seemed to be made out of the same bamboo that was currently resting outside of the gate. There were a couple of pillows on the couch and chairs, adding some comfort to the hard furniture. The walls seemed to be smooth and made out some type of concrete material as there wasn't any type of décor that rested on the walls. Seems like Miles liked to live a very minimal lifestyle for someone who was a leader of the Sloth clan.

"So how did your journey go?" Miles asked, reaching what Dean could have guessed was the kitchen. There were a few counters along the wall, a small sink, and some kind of fire stove used for cooking. "Guessing from the little addition on your backpack, you decided to join us and abandon your old ways, Dean?" Miles asked, getting Dean's attention. Miles flashed Dean a small smirk as he noticed Dean giving Miles a rather quizzical look.

"Hm?" Dean hummed in response as he walked to join the other two. Seeing Miles' eyebrows knit together didn't seem like it was a good sign. As Miles took a peach from the small basket of fruit on the counter top, Dean could see those steely gray eyes pierce into Dean as the tribal leader waited for an answer.

"Of course." Kane quickly interjected as he placed his hands on the table. "He was able to take down a mountain goat by himself. The thing was gigantic too." Kane spoke eagerly with an excitement to his voice. "Guess I know how to train them, huh?" Kane boasted on Dean's behalf, catching Dean a bit off guard by the comment. "He did an amazing job painting the horn too. I think it looks intimidating." The last bit made Dean wonder if maybe Kane was forcing these praises to make it seem like Dean was doing more than he actually did. After all, Kane was there to help drag the heavy goat back to the village. Plus Kane was the one who coated it with resin to keep the paint from being washed off. If anything, they did it together.

Miles' focus seemed to shift towards Kane when he spoke. A faint smile appeared on Miles' face as he brought up his free hand to gently pet Kane's head in praise. "You sure do. Making your big brother proud." Miles spoke in almost a coddling tone as his fingers brushed through Kane's silver locks. It didn't take long for the smile to be replaced by a look of shock as it just dawned on Miles that Kane's hair was shorter than he remembered. "You cut your hair! Why?" Miles asked, letting the peach hit the floor as Miles brought his other hand up to cusp the locks between his middle and index fingers.

"Just as I thought." Kane muttered, moving his hands to lightly grip onto the sleeves of Miles' kimono. "You're really stoned right now, aren't you?" Kane asked, before he felt Miles wrap his arms around Kane's face. Seemed like Kane wouldn't be able to get much of a word in edgewise with how far gone Miles seemed to be.

"Mm, maybe just a bit." Miles chimed in happily as he buried his face into Kane's hair. "Not that your haircut doesn't look bad…" Miles trailed off a bit. "But, I'm just used to being able to bury my face into your long locks." Miles continued, a small pout on his face as he tilted his head to rest against Kane's. "But now that's gone." Miles' tone of voice with that little statement almost sounded sad to Dean, like he was hoping to be able to keep things the way that they used to be. "You're really growing up into a man. I'm proud of you." Miles commented before shuffling his Kane's hair around a bit, causing Kane to groan before pulling away from Miles.

"What has gotten into you?" Kane grumbled like a younger sibling being annoyingly coddled by their older sibling. "Great, now I have to go and fix it." Kane continued with his grumbling as he headed towards what could be assumed to be the bathroom. This left Dean alone with Miles, who was currently watching Kane leave with a soft smile on his face.

Dean could see the way that Miles looked at Kane was completely different than how Kane would gaze at him. There was affection there, but it was more like a brother or best friend type of affection. Nothing more to it than that. Miles looked more satisfied in their relationship while Kane seemed to be looking for something more, but it would never happen.

As Miles reached down to pick up the peach that had fallen on the ground, he seemed to act as if Dean wasn't there. Pulling out a knife, Miles went to work cutting out the pit for the peach. Carefully tending to cutting up the pieces of peach, it seemed that Miles would give Dean some passing glances before finally speaking up. "Seems like you and Kane have gotten close since the airship incident." Miles remarked bluntly, catching Dean off guard by that statement.

"What makes you think that?" Dean asked, finding his voice rather quickly as to not seem to be blindsided. This whole mess was getting to be a bit confusing. Mostly due to the fact of how Miles was acting with Kane versus how he was acting with Dean.

"Normally Kane would be happy to have me embrace him as tightly as I did." Not that Dean would have known the way that Kane acted before he got there, but if Kane still had those lingering feelings for Miles, Dean knew that he would be able to see the invisible tail wagging happily behind Kane with Miles holding onto him and pampering him. "Considering he was like a wet noodle in my arms, I could only guess that something happened between you two on your journey."

What was Dean supposed to say to something like that? *Kane hugged me from behind, so maybe he got over you with me*? It wasn't like they kissed or anything like that. They just traveled together and saw a bit of the ruined world being taken back by mother nature. "I wouldn't exactly say that something happened." Dean remarked, glancing away from Miles. It was only when Miles had seemingly slammed the knife that he was using into the cutting board that Dean looked at the leader with a surprised look on his face. It seemed that Miles wasn't satisfied with that answer, and it showed crystal clear on Miles' face.

Bringing a hand up, Dean started to scratch the back of his head as he tried to figure out how exactly he was going to explain it to the Sloth leader. "The only thing that happened was Kane hugged me from behind. Not that I didn't mind it or anything. But it was something that I wasn't expecting." Dean explained, though he could feel himself getting a bit flustered thinking about it. "But other than that, we haven't done anything." This seemed to make Miles a bit more relaxed when Dean finally told him, but Miles still didn't seem to be too happy about it.

Miles glanced off to the side, as if he was in deep thought about the information that Dean had given him. There was a sound of something sliding open, causing Dean to glance over in the direction of the sound to see Kane changed into something a bit more suited to his personal taste. It was a dark blue robe with a silver pinstripe design to it. The sash was black, tied up neatly around Kane's waist. It was almost a relief to be able to see Kane wearing something a bit more normal for once. Sure it was nice seeing Kane wearing different kinds of clothing as they traveled around, but seeing Kane wearing a robe, it made things feel normal, as if Dean was able to relax more.

"What are you doing now, Miles?" Kane asked, sounding a bit annoyed as he narrowed his eyes at Miles. The other male had seemingly snapped out of his thoughts as Miles poured the sliced peach with the pit into a wooden bowl. Meanwhile Dean looked a bit flabbergasted as to what happened.

"Well, I can't let the peach go to waste, now can I?" Miles remarked with a small cheeky grin on his face as he carried the bowl off. "I'm going to get a planter so the tree can start growing without being disturbed by the animals." Miles' voice was growing distant, but the two males were able to still hear him.

Kane softly shook his head before turning his attention to Dean. "Why don't you go and get changed as well?" Kane softly suggested with a lingering smile on his face. "I'm sure you'll want to be in something relaxing before the last stage of your ceremony begins." Kane suggested, giving Dean a small nudge in the process.

"My ceremony?" Dean asked, not sure what kind of ceremony that they two would be celebrating. There was a bit of concern lingering on Dean's face, but seeing the reassured smile on Kane's face was enough to put Dean at ease.

"Well, it's the last stage of it you becoming one of us." Kane spoke in a matter-of-fact tone as he leaned against one of the counters. "You see, normally you would go to Keaton's lecture first so you would start to understand what the different clans do." Kane started to explain while making an invisible diagram on the counter.

"Once there, you get a basic idea of what you would like to pursue depending on your skill set." Kane continued with his explanation as he crossed one leg over the other to balance himself a bit better on against the counter that he was resting on. "Then you will go out on a hunt. The first animal you kill that has a skull big enough to fit your head will be used to make your headgear." That part Dean already knew. Considering that he had the mountain goat on his backpack, Dean was able to be a bit head of the curve.

"Afterwards, when you have completed those two requirements, you can either decide on what clan you want to visit and try it out, or come to Miles' ceremony to decide where you want to go." Dean was surprised that there were more options when it came to deciding what clan one wants to align with. "If you're not completely sure, you can do a counseling session with him where you will partake in a smoke session that will help you decide what your calling is." Even though Kane had explained it, it wasn't making any sense. Smoking session? Deciding where he would want to stay?

"What do you mean?" Dean asked, his brows knitting together as his confusion was apparent. It wasn't like Dean didn't completely understand what Kane meant, but he didn't understand how a type of smoking session would help to determine where you would want to land. Leaning on the other side of the counter, Dean waited patiently for Kane to explain it.

"Well, instead of describing it to you, how about you ask Miles for guidance." It wasn't the answer that Dean was looking for, but it seemed like Kane would rather have Miles explain it. "Usually that means that you want to do a smoke session that helps make things a bit more clear for you." Kane remarked with a smile on his face. Seeing the confused look on Dane's face, Kane couldn't help but let out a small chuckle. "You'll see. Now, go and get changed. Those clothes won't help to keep in the warmth when the sun goes down." Kane remarked, moving around the counter towards Dean before lightly pushing him towards the room where Kane had emerged from.

Taking the subtle clue, Dean headed towards the room with his backpack still lingering on his back. Sliding the door closed, Dean noticed that it was a small bathroom that was a bit similar to the one he had on the Millennium, except there was a bit more room to move around. The sink seemed to spread across the small wall with a cement like counter. There was a single mirror that rested against the wall as there was a bit of sunlight seeping in through the circular window that rested above what appeared to be a shower head. The floor had a small indent towards the middle where there was a drain hole with a protective grid resting on top of it. The toilet looked as if it had just been recently cleaned in preparation for guests.

Setting the bag down on the counter, Dean unzipped the flaps before shifting through the bits of clothing that he accumulated over the trip. The smell coming off of them was a bit pungent, but nothing like a quick wash in some warm water couldn't fix. Shifting through the bag, Dean was able to find the right section with the clean clothes that had been neatly and tightly rolled up into what resembled a rather large burrito that was meant to be able to pack more clothes to fit into tight spaces.

Pulling out a dark green set, Dean went to work changing his clothes in the bathroom as the voices of Miles and Kane seemed to be muffled just on the other side of the door. It was hard to hear what the two could be talking about, but that didn't mean that Dean didn't find himself subconsciously listening in as he shifted about changing.

"So tonight then? You'll help out?" Came a muffled voice of Kane, his voice seemingly sounding excited but with a hint of worry mixed in. If this was going to be for the smoke session, why did Kane sound so nervous? Moving to press his ear against the door, Dean held his breath as he concentrated to understand what was being said.

"Of course. You know I could never say no to you." Miles spoke, his muffled voice sounding as if he was praising Kane. Dean could already imagine Miles reaching up and lightly ruffling Kane's hair, the invisible tail on Kane's back wagging wildly at feeling Miles stroke his hair even though he complained earlier about the male messing it up. Dean dug his nails into the door ever so slightly before he caught himself. Back up from the door, Dean reached up to clench the fabric over his chest.

"What am I getting jealous for?" Dean mentally scolded himself as he visibly shook his head. *"Miles is probably just going to do whatever he needs to do to help with this ceremony. That's all."* Dean reassured himself before he got a look at himself in the mirror. His eyebrows were knitted together rather tightly. His jaw was clenched tightly as a displeased scowl lingered on his face. It was only for a second, but it was enough to snap Dean out of his thoughts. "I really am getting jealous, aren't I?" It was an odd sensation when reality hit. Since Miles didn't even bother to care to explain the hugging aspect of what happened between the two males, Dean was simply left with his own thoughts.

With an audible sigh, Dean finished putting on the robe and fastened the sash to keep the robe from simply sliding open. He didn't want to be like the way Miles had presented himself when they had first arrived. Shoving his dirty clothes into his backpack, Dean fastened it up before sliding the door open. He saw Miles and Kane still lingering in the kitchen, though this time it seemed that Miles was mixing dirt into a pot while Kane leaned forward against the counter, watching Miles closely.

It didn't seem that Kane's hair had been disrupted, causing Dean to glance to the side as he felt the stinging sensation of guilt washing over him. Clenching one of his fists, Dean stood still as he looked somewhat disgusted with himself. This feeling of jealousy, it was as if a new monster was crawling around inside of him. Snapping out of his thoughts once more, Dean slid the door behind him before making his way over to the two men. Clearing his throat to get their attention, the two males glanced back at Dean.

Wearing a dark green robe with a light design on small lily water pads that dangled above Dean's left leg, the rest of the robe was a solid color. "Are we going to stay here tonight or should we find an inn?" Dean asked, forgetting about where they were going to sleep tonight. Dean didn't want to be rude and just assume that they would be staying at Miles' place, but a part of him would rather pay to stay someplace else.

"Oh, we'll be staying here for now. I have to go over a few things with Miles in regards to the rotation of the crops." Kane remarked, turning to face Dean while leaning against the counter still. "Come, I'll show you where we will be staying." Kane remarked, pushing himself off of the counter before making his way towards Dean. Grabbing Dean's hand, Kane gave the other a reassuring smile before guiding him to a long hallway that led out towards a garden area.

The garden itself wasn't much to really look at. There were a couple of bamboo trees in the various corners of the garden that was surrounded by a stone fence. A rock path seemed to guide towards a large pond that looked as if it was taken care of. Even though Dean didn't get a chance to see what sort of fish swam around it, there was no doubt about it, the lingering scent of fish seemed to reach his nose. Gazing up past the slants of the roof, the clouds appeared to be dark, as if it was going to rain. Not like they had to worry if the two men were going to sleep here for the night. As they turned a corner that led to the bedrooms, it seemed that Kane pulled Dean into the first one on their right.

The room was rather spacious, though there weren't any beds that were visible. As Kane let go of Dean's hand, Kane wandered towards a section of the wall before sliding open a door that had a spacious bottom section where Kane's bag had already been placed down. "Here, you can put your stuff in here while we eat." Kane explained, watching as Dean walked towards him with a rather confused look on his face. "Worried about where we'll sleep?" Kane asked, almost as if he was reading Dean's mind.

"Yeah, guess I expected there to be some beds for us to sleep on." Dean remarked with a small shrug of his shoulders as he peeled off the backpack. Handing it to Kane, Dean took this chance to look at the contents that laid hidden in the panel. There was at least one large white clothed item that Dean had never seen before that was visible in the one panel in front of him. Were they going to share a bed again?

"This is our bed." Kane remarked, standing up and placing his hand on the clothed item that Dean had taken notice of. "We place these on the floor, make up the futon the way that we like it, before we would get some sleep." Kane explained as he showed with his arms how they would lay out the futon. "In the morning we strip the sheets and fold the futon back up for the day. It saves on room for when you don't have a lot of guests over." Thinking it over, this would have been a bit handy in the pods on the station, but it seemed that they didn't have the materials or the know-how on how to make a futon.

"Since Miles has two, we can each have our own bed. Isn't that great?" Kane continued before he noticed how distant Dean seemed to appear, causing a small worried expression to take over Kane's face. "Is something wrong Dean?" Kane asked, his voice showing his concern as he stood up and slid the panel closed.

"Hm?" Dean hummed as he was pulled out of his thoughts. "Oh, nothing's wrong." Dean lied, whether it was to himself or to make Kane not worry, Dean could feel this hollowness in his heart. Dean didn't like the way he felt when he was getting jealous by watching Miles and Kane interact with each other. Dean didn't like the bitterness that seemed to linger in his mouth. It felt like it made it hard to swallow even just the smallest bit of spit. The way the jealousy felt like a hand gripping Dean's heart and making it hard to breathe. Dean hated it all, and yet, there wasn't anything he could do about it.

"Liar." Kane was quick to remark, causing Dean to almost jump in surprise at how fast Kane was able to call him out like that. "Look," Kane started to speak as he closed the distance between them. "You don't have to tell me what is wrong now, but when you're ready to talk about it, come to me. Okay?" Kane smiled softly up at Dean, the sincerity in his voice was evident. The guilt of not telling Kane was weighing on Dean's mind, but he couldn't exactly speak about how he was feeling. Not that Kane would really understand. It was a crushing feeling nonetheless.

"Yeah..." Dean trailed off, his eyes glancing away from Kane, which in turn caused Kane to frown a little. The room felt as if there was a rift growing between the two men once more. It wasn't as bad as the rift on the airship, but it was still apparent that something needed to be done. Maybe not now, but sooner or later it needed to happen.

As the day shifted to the evening, the sun was barely reaching the hills as it was setting for the night. As the three men had finished their meal, Dean found himself sitting in the living room alone while Miles and Kane were helping each other wash the dishes. The bit of light that was apparent left the sky with a small golden glow as the night started to creep in. Dean's focus was on his hands as he wished he had brought a book with him, but since they were still traveling, it wouldn't have been a good idea. Flexing the tips of his fingers, Dean looked as sad as a lost puppy with how much he was moping.

With the last of the plates being washed, Kane made his way over towards Dean before taking a spot next to him. With a small little nudge, Kane was able to cause Dean to look up at him. "Hey, you ready for your ceremony?" Kane asked, a lingering smile on his face. But he didn't exactly get an answer for Dean.

Only receiving a simple nod before Dean glanced back to his hands, Kane audibly sighed. "Come on Dean." Kane remarked, sounding a bit annoyed in the process. "You've been really quiet all day. Tell me what's wrong." Kane spoke, placing a hand on Dean's shoulder before giving him a small shake. "Did I say or do something to make you upset?" A concerned expression lingered on Kane's face as he didn't like the way that Dean seemed to pull away from him.

"Of course you didn't." Dean remarked, though he was unable to look at Kane. "I just want to get this ceremony done with so we can head to Amelia's place." Not that Dean was looking forward to seeing the woman. He just wanted to be away from Miles who was now walking in on the conversation. "We need to defeat the Elite before they hurt anyone else. I can't just sit around like we did at Ashley's place." Dean remarked as he stood up from the couch. The way that Dean seemed to be on edge was concerning to Kane, but for now the leader kept his mouth shut.

"What good would it be to rush ahead of yourself?" Miles spoke bluntly as he walked towards them. "It's not like we've all been sitting on our asses Dean." The scowl on Miles' face showed that he wasn't amused with the little temper tantrum that Dean was trying to pull on Kane. "Felicia is putting everything into making sure that the death ray will be built in time." Miles continued, crossing his arms over his chest as he gazed at Dean. "Do you have that much doubt in us that you want to start getting reckless after all the work you've already put in?" Miles asked, raising an eyebrow towards Dean.

Dean couldn't exactly argue back at Miles as he made some good points. While Dean was busy simply wandering around and meeting the leaders, Felicia was already ahead of him and working on the device. If he stopped now, it would be all for nothing. Then again, Felicia may very well end up using it regardless in order to take down the Millennium. An audible sigh left Dean as he reached up to scratch his head.

"When you put it that way, it makes me feel like an asshole." Dean remarked, glancing off to the side as he felt a little bit better about the situation. Moving to look at Kane, Dean could see the worry that still lingered on Kane's face. "But, I'm fine Kane. I just need to work some things out, is all." Dean remarked, figuring that he could at the very least lessen Kane's concern over him. "Guess probably now would be the best time to do the ceremony?" Even though Dean's heart wasn't exactly in it, he knew that it was better to get it done now rather than wait.

"If that's what you want." Miles remarked slightly annoyed still, though it didn't seem like he was completely interested in it. "Come, I'll show you where we have the smaller ones." Miles added as he stepped away from the two men. "Seems fitting since it's just you this time." Miles spoke, walking towards one of the open side doors. Dean didn't exactly know where they would be going, so he stayed relatively close behind Miles as they left Kane alone in the house.

Walking down a path towards a small steep hill, Dean noticed that there was a small square looking hut that looked as if it couldn't hold more than five people in it. Just how often was this building used? Dean had to mentally shake the thoughts from his mind as he needed to focus. Instead of making Kane more upset, Dean felt like he needed to make the other smile once more. Or at the very least, not make Kane worry so much about him.

***

As they got to the building, after nearly slipping and falling down on his ass, Dean was able to get a better look at it. The outside was white with a red tile base. There weren't any windows that he could see. The roof had some black tiling that looked as if the panels were arched. If it was raining, it might have been relaxing to hear from inside. The fence was made out of brick and cement, which was different from what Dean had seen around Miles' home. Perhaps it was the foundation on an old building from before the bombs dropped?

As Miles went to the door and unlocked it, the leader headed inside and turned on a light, this allowed for Dean to have a small peek inside. So far he could see a decorative piece in the middle that was like a dragon. Wandering towards the wooden frame, Dean cautiously placed a hand and foot against the threshold before peeking his head inside of the building cautiously. Despite the interior being rather plain, Dean noticed that the centerpiece of the room was what graviated his attention. It was the dragon piece that Dean barely got to see from the outside. Moving closer to it, Dean took in the details the closer that he got to it.

The dragon itself was golden with its wings ever slightly spread open. The tips of its wings and the chest's scales were as red as a polished ruby. The tail of the dragon seemed to wrap around the base of what appeared to be a chunk of rock that had green crystals inside of a clear orbital casing. Taking a closer look at the crystals, it almost appeared like he was looking into a portal that led to the inside of the cave. There was a soft glow to the crystals that made Dean feel oddly relaxed.

Glancing up at the head of the dragon, Dean noticed that the dragon had similar green eyes as the mouth was parted. The level of detail on the dragon was amazing. The way that the dragon had scales all over with different shades of gold and red, it made Dean wonder if it could even come to life. Even the claws looked sharp enough to be able to penetrate a person's skin as it rested on the rocky surface. Seemingly anchored into place.

Once they were both inside, Miles turned and closed the door behind Dean. With a small click, Miles locked the two of them inside of the small building. There was still a bit of shuffling behind Dean, but once it seemed that Miles was able to collect what he needed, the Sloth leader made his way over towards Dean who was solely interested in the dragon piece. Feeling another presence near him, Dean glanced up to see that Miles was moving a small tray out from underneath the dragon statue. It looked as if something had been burnt, leaving nothing but ashes.

"Go ahead and lay down on one of the couches." Miles started to instruct Dean, causing the taller male to glance back at the couches. "Since it's just the two of us, you can get comfortable." Miles spoke, a lingering smile on his face, as if he was trying to reassure Dean that he didn't have anything to be worried about. "You're getting the VIP experience." Miles softly mused as he slid a new tray into the center piece. "It's not often I get a chance for a little one on one with someone." Miles finished, taking the burnt tray with him as he left Dean to settle down for the ceremony.

A light scowl formed on Dean's face as he watched Miles head off towards a small table that had some type of equipment on it that Dean had never seen before. Turning his back to the man, Dean moved towards a couch that was behind the dragon, sighing to himself as Dean looked up to see square ceiling tiles. Each tile had little dots that didn't exactly have a type of pattern to them. The pillow that Dean rested his head on was a bit comfortable. Not something that he could see himself falling asleep on, but it didn't hurt his neck at least.

The sound of something being ground up seemed to reach Dean's ears as Miles was rather busy with doing what he needed for their little ceremony. If you could call it that. This felt more like counseling than a ceremony. Closing his eyes, Dean put his feet up on the couch like he often did when his father and himself were waiting for his mother to be done getting dressed and they waited in the living room. Why was Dean thinking of those memories right now? It didn't seem to bother Dean, but he thought he was done comparing life on the Earth with his old life back on the station.

Hearing the sounds of Miles' footsteps, Dean opened his eyes to glance over to the leader, who was starting a small fire on a pile of ground up herbs before blowing out the flame to let the leaves slowly simmer on the clean plate from earlier. Pushing the plate under the dragon decoration, Miles turned the dragon to face Dean. As the smoke started to slowly engulf the clear crystal opening, it wasn't long before the smoke started to seep out of the dragon's open mouth. Watching Miles pull out a long stick from inside of his robe, Miles was quick to light it as well before blowing out the fire, leaving a more pleasant smell to fill the room other than the herbs being burned under the dragon. Placing the stick some place behind the dragon that Dean couldn't see, Miles made his way towards one of the other couches before sitting down with a piece of paper in hand.

"Let's start off with something rather easy." Miles spoke as the sound of a piece of paper rustling could be heard. The room was slowly filling up with a thin smoke from the center of the room, making it a little bit harder to breathe at first without coughing. At least on Dean's end that is. "Your name, age, gender, and sexual orientation should be something that you could easily describe right off the top of your head." Miles spoke, watching as Dean got comfortable on the small bamboo couch.

What did Miles mean that those should be easy to describe right off of the top of Dean's head? Dean's brows furrowed together as the overwhelming sensation of his mind becoming clouded felt as if he had some sort of invisible wave rushing over his body. Even though it was an odd sensation, Dean felt a bit more relaxed, almost giddy even.

"My name is Dean Torres and I'm twenty four years old, though I'll be twenty five later on this year." Dean started off, though he was feeling a bit silly discussing something like this with the likes of Miles. Why did he agree to do this?

"I'm a male and I guess pansexual from what Keaton told me." Dean continued, not sure if he was exactly comfortable saying what his sexual orientation was, but as long as this was to help him discover who he was, the faster he would be able to get on with the ceremony before he talked to Amelia one on one. Then again, Dean wasn't too sure where his sexual preference rested. All this time he figured that he would not be able to become attracted to anyone, and yet, he was finding himself thinking about Kane the more time he spent with the man.

"Good." Miles remarked, a faint smile on his face as he waved the paper a bit before clearing his throat. "So you prefer to be with someone regardless of their gender?" Miles started to ask before commenting more on the question. "Not often you hear that. But then again, that might be a common thing on the station." Miles commented, a small chuckle leaving his lips.

"So how about you tell me a bit about where you're from." Miles continued with his questions, all the while Dean closed his eyes as his breathing started to slow down. "Did you have any hobbies on the station? What about friends? Did you have any?" Miles asked, his tone of voice seemed as if he was interested in knowing for himself about how life was on the station. Not like Miles would ever get to see it for himself, but with the smoking session, it would give the leader a better idea of what the station had become over the years.

"Don't pull back any punches, huh?" Dean lightly joked his sour mood slowly lifting the more they talked. Though this was just a means to help ease Dean up to talk about what life was like on the station. "Well, as you know I came from the United Space Station Millennium." No surprise there, considering that it felt like most of the planet knew who he was through word of mouth. "Growing up on the station was rather isolation-like. Not because it was a common practice, but because I always seemed to find myself in some form of isolation."

Dean was rather surprised when he bluntly stated it, like he didn't have much of a filter to shift out what Dean wanted to keep secret. Was this the smoke causing him to be honest? "I didn't have any friends growing up there," Dean paused before letting out a cough. "It was mostly because people thought that I was an atypical kid." Dean continued, bringing up a hand to cover up his eyes. "I liked to read more complex books than most kids my age. I didn't like to go out very often. I always felt unwanted by everyone on the station....except by my parents. They had always encouraged me to read." The loneliness has always been something that Dean was used to. To feel so out of touch with those who surrounded him was a constant feeling that Dean had to deal with on his own.

"I took it as a sign that I didn't belong...." Dean trailed off, a frown forming on his face at the bitter thoughts. "I started to isolate myself the best I could after the failed attempt to help the Bronze section grow their own food. Since everyone involved got in trouble, I just figured that it would be best if I just became a ghost." The despair in Dean's voice was evident as he talked about his past like this. "I was suited to be more like a background character rather than be someone who stood out in the crowd." Something that never seemed to die down until years later after Dean tried his best to avoid certain individuals who harassed him afterward the garden failure.

"With no family willing to take me in, and having no friends to begin with, I didn't feel like I could ever belong there." There was an uneasy tone in Dean's voice towards the end, as if he could never allow himself to forget what happened and how badly he messed things up. "Guess that would explain why I'm not the greatest at dealing with others..." Dean mostly mumbled the last part to himself, seemingly inaudible to Miles.

Miles seemed to be silent after Dean was talking, causing Dean to wonder if maybe Miles was taking down notes or was contemplating on what to ask next. Moving his head to look towards Miles, Dean saw that the other male was staring at the piece of paper. When Miles glanced up as if he sensed that he was being watched, Dean glanced away before shifting his focus to the ceiling once more.

"Usually self isolation is used as a way to keep from being hurt, you know?" Miles commented, before adjusting a bit on the couch he was sitting on. "But you couldn't exactly do that after you landed here, huh?" Miles asked, mostly as a bit of an afterthought. "So tell me, since you've been traveling with Kane, how have you enjoyed it? Was Earth how you expected it to be?" Miles asked, his interest perked as Dean was being open and honest with him.

"Honestly, it's been amazing." Dean remarked with a small smile seeming to tug on his face as his eyes started to get heavy. "Being able to see everything on Earth has been a far better adventure that I could have ever asked for." Dean spoke, closing his eyes as he moved his arms to lay across his arms over his chest before Dean continued to talk.

"Being able to gaze up at the clear blue skies with the biggest clouds I could have ever imagined myself seeing, to gazing at the changed landscape across the world has given me a new lease on life." Dean spoke, his voice showing the wonder he felt during their travels. "I never felt as free as I do right now when I was living on the station." Dean remarked in almost a bliss like state. "If I have died and this is some type of afterlife, I never want to be reincarnated." This caused a small chuckle to leave both of the men.

"This right here, in this moment, is something I would often dream of while stuck on the station." Dean finished, slowly opening his eyes almost expecting to see the bright sky above him, but was saddened when all he saw was the familiar ceiling he had been gazing up at. But that blissful feeling never seemed to fade away.

"What do you feel when you're around Kane?" Miles asked a question that seemed like it wouldn't really have been asked to anyone else but Dean. But in his current state of mind and the relaxation he felt, Dean didn't mind answering it one way or another. It felt like Dean had butterflies walking on the back of Dean's head, his arms felt a bit heavy as his left hand slowly slid down to rest at Dean's side.

"I feel something that I could only explain as something that my parents had." Dean remarked, only to let out a long and audible sigh at the end. "Since traveling with Kane between the Envy and Lust clan, I felt like time didn't matter." Dean paused as he thought back on their travels. "Each new sight was better because he was beside me. Helping me up when I would struggle climbing up a hill. Cooking amazing meals out of things I would have never been able to think of, and just feeling as if I was complete." Dean continued, his fingers moving to lightly drum against his chest as he spewed on while Dean's left hand gently gripped the fabric of the cushion below him.

"It makes me worry about what would happen when everything finally comes to an end and I might end up alone once more." Going back to isolation was something that Dean was secretly fearing for a while now. "How would I be able to face each new day without him there by my side?" Dean asked, a frown tugging at the corner of his lips. "I spent so much of my time alone, that now that I have someone that I find myself looking forward to spending my days with, that I'm afraid of losing him." Dean never expected himself to become emotional, but the thought that Dean wouldn't even be able to see or hang out with Kane, it weighed heavily on his chest.

"So it's like that, huh?" Miles spoke, a smile seemingly tugging on the corners of his lips. "Who would have guessed..." Miles trailed off, moving to get up from the couch he was sitting on. "Well, I just have one question left for you Dean. And then I think I have everything I need to know to put you exactly where you belong." Miles spoke, making his way over towards Dean who felt like his whole body weighed much heavier the longer he stayed laying on the couch.

"And...what question is that?" Dean asked, a bit confused as Dean felt his mind becoming a bit more clouded with the smoke that seemed to pour out of the dragon's mouth. Dean was struggling to keep his eyes open at this point. Dean's whole body became numb as his breaths were getting shallow, like he was fighting the sleep that was washing over Dean's body.

"Do you want to be one of us?" Miles asked with a brief pause, moving closer to Dean before shifting to sit down on the couch beside Dean. "To give up ever getting a chance to go back to the Millennium if you had a chance?" Miles asked, leaning in a bit closer to Dean while supporting Miles' upper body with his left arm braced against the top of the couch. Gray steel eyes peered down at Dean, waiting for an answer.

Dean's eyes widened as he heard the question, though his mind seemed to be a bit more preoccupied with just how close Miles was to his face. Getting a better look at Miles as the male leaned in close to him, Dean was surprised at just how similar Kane and Miles resembled one another. Though Kane's hair was shifted towards the right, Miles' hair was shifted to lean over his left side. While Kane was as white as one could be, Miles had a beautiful peach coloring to him. Miles' eyes were a dark gray like the color of a lone wolf. It was like the two leaders were yin and yang to one another. How did Dean never notice it before? Though Miles had a bit more of a pointed nose than Kane, if the two matched the others' skin tone, they could very well look like brothers.

"I..." Dean started to speak, forcing himself to snap out of his thoughts and clearing his throat in the process. "I would like to join you. I don't have anything left back there anyways." Not like Dean would say that he wanted to head back to the Millennium. If there was even a remote chance that he could, Dean still wouldn't take it. "Now, if you'll excuse me..." Dean mumbled, trying his best to get up from the couch, only to find his body wasn't corroborating with him. "Why... can't I-?" Dean started to ask, but a yawn interrupted his question. It wasn't long before Dean's eyes fluttered shut. Slowly fading out of consciousness, Dean felt like the world was shutting down around him as everything faded to black.

"Sorry Dean. Guess I used a little bit too much." Miles remarked, though his smile didn't seem to fade. "You should wake up in the early morning. I'll come and get you then." Miles muttered under his breath, getting up from the couch with a small groan. Placing a blanket over Dean's body, Miles left the building after turning the lights off. With the last bit of the smoke tapering out, Miles closed the door behind him, leaving Dean alone in the room to sleep undisturbed. With the heavy clouds swooping in to pour down during the night, Miles headed back inside to get some rest himself.

It felt like only a few minutes had passed by the time that Dean finally opened his eyes once again. Bracing himself with the back of the couch, Dean groggily sat up with a groan. His body still felt a bit heavy, but not paralyzing like before, meaning that whatever Miles burned no longer had an effect on him. Weakly Dean was able to pick himself up as he stumbled to his feet. Once stable, Dean reached his right hand up to touch his temple. Dean was struggling to keep his eyes open at this point, but he couldn't very well stay where he was. For one thing, it was getting colder the longer he stayed there.

Looking around the room Dean noticed that it was pitch black with only a small bit of light seeping in from the outside. Dean walked slowly towards the light, using the bit of light to adjust to the darkness in the room. With the use of his arms outstretched to help make sure Dean didn't bump into anything, and shuffling his feet to get his bearings, Dean reached the door without knocking anything over. As he gripped the hook for the door, Dean was half expecting the door to be locked from before. Thankfully Miles wasn't cruel enough to lock Dean inside of the building like he was some sort of dog who was literally in the dog house for behaving badly.

Heading outside, Dean noticed that it was eerily silent. The wind felt cold as it brushed against Dean's warm skin. "Damn. Why is it so cold all of a sudden?" Dean muttered to himself as he crossed his arms over his chest. Stepping onto one of the stones that led up to the small building, Dean noticed that the surface of the rock was rather wet. Looking around, Dean noticed some of the blades of grass had bits of water droplets still lingering on them.

Did it rain and Dean just now notice? The surface of the rock made Dean's feet feel cold the longer he stood on it. Unfortunately Dean didn't think ahead and wear shoes to the ceremony since he figured he would only be there for a short time.

Turning around long enough to close the door to the building, Dean started to hop from one rock to the other. Though his muscles didn't feel as if they could support him, causing Dean to stumble before finding a balance. "You know, I didn't think that there would be some type of obstacle course associated with this counseling or ceremony or whatever they want to call this." Dean grumbled to himself as he made it towards the path that led to the steep hill.

Knitting his brows together, Dean groaned as he knew this was going to be a problem. Bending down to pull the edge of the robe up, Dean tucked the extra fabric under his belt to keep the hem from getting dirty as he had to climb up the hill that looked and acted like a large green slip-n-slide. "Now then, how am I supposed to go up this hill without getting dirty?" Dean asked himself, lifting his sleeves up to examine them. Feeling the cold wind hit him, Dean shivered from the heat leaving his legs. Dean had to reach the house soon, otherwise he might get sick if Dean stayed outside in the wet and cold air for much longer.

"Fuck it. There's only one way I can get up this damn hill in my condition." Dean growled to himself as he started to slip the top of the robe slide off of Dean's shoulders. Letting the sleeves start to dangle around his waist, Dean slipped them into the sash to bind everything together to keep the robe from getting dirty. After the quick adjustment, Dean knelt forward, his fingertips digging into the soft soil as his toes sank into the soil ever so slightly.

Bracing himself, Dean studied the hill the best he could before he started to make his way up the hill with his hands grabbing onto clumps of grass and his feet tried to keep Dean from slipping. The further that Dean got up the hill, the harder it felt for Dean to reach the top. There were a couple of times where Dean had to brace himself from slipping by using his knees, resulting in Dean getting muddier than he wanted.

By the time that Dean reached the top, his feet were covered in mud and grass. Both of his knees were caked as well, his fingernails were basically black from the amount of dirt that had pushed under his once clean nails. His fingers felt almost raw as they shook from the cold ground. Bringing up one of his hands to wipe away the sweat that was dripping from Dean's forehead, he smeared a bit of the dirt on his forehead. But now was not the time to stop, he needed to head inside the house.

Gazing at the house, it seemed rather dark, like everyone had already gone to bed by this point. Looking up at the sky, Dean could vaguely see the moon as it hung up in the sky. The clouds passing over it were dark, with only bits of silver lining, indicating that it could possibly rain more. Just what time was it? If Dean wasn't so tired, he would have easily jogged over to the house, but his legs still felt like they were full of lead from his stumble up the steep hill.

Slowly shuffling towards the house, Dean noticed that there was something that resembled an old water pump hanging on the side of the house that faced the small building Dean had just come from. Underneath it was a pail that seemed to filled to the brim with water. Dean couldn't believe his luck! If he could clean himself off and slip into the bed, Kane wouldn't have been the wiser with how long Dean was out for.

Using what strength he could, Dean softly jogged towards the water pump, his breaths coming in as soft pants. As he reached it, the first thing that Dean had to do was work on cleaning off his hands. Even if he couldn't get the bit of mud out from his finger nails, it was better than nothing. The water might have been freezing cold, but at this point Dean didn't care, he just needed to get clean.

With a quick splash of cold water that could fit in his hands, Dean was quick to rub the dirt off of his face. It felt like sharp ice shards were being rubbed on his face as the water droplets ran down Dean's chin. Bits of the rain water clung to the brunet stands of Dean's hair and eyebrows as the water that fell from Dean's chin landed on the ground below him.

As the water started to drip down the sides of his face, Dean was quick to use the depleting water on his knees and feet, cleaning off any lingering bits of grass and mud that showed his struggle up the hill. No matter how hard Dean scrubbed, it was slow to come off. Dean's body shivered with the cold wind blowing against his moistened body, making Dean become a bit impatient as it led to Dean pouring the remaining water on each leg while using his opposing hands to clean off the last bit that clung to his feet now..

There were spots on Dean's body that seemed to feel as if it was burning in order to warm up his freezing body. Now the question was, how was Dean supposed to get back while still wet? He would probably drip water over the house if he tried to go through the front door. Plus there was the issue of not wanting to get his freshly semi-washed feet from getting dirty once again. Spotting the pathway of large stones that lead up to the house, it gave Dean an idea.

Using a type of leap frog style tactic, Dean was able to skip or jump onto each of the stones to prevent his feet from getting dirt on them. Eventually Dean was able to make it towards the front door. With a quick grab of the knob, Dean tried to rattle the door to see if perhaps it was opened. Unfortunately for Dean, it seemed that the door was locked and there wasn't anyone who would be up at this time. Glancing towards the moon, Dean tried to see if perhaps he could tell what the time was with the position of the moon. Thanks to the clouds in the sky, it seemed like that idea was thrown out the window.

Sighing heavily, Dean was able to see his breath for a quick second before it faded in front of him. "Gotta get inside." Dean grumbled through his chattering teeth as the wind made Dean feel as if he was stuck in some sort of refrigerator that stored meat. Seeing as how Dean was clean, now would be a good time for the male to undo the fabric that was tucked into the sash, giving him some kind of protection from the cold to keep from getting sick. Releasing the belt long enough to let the hem of the robe fall towards the ground, Dean quickly slipped the sleeves back over his bare arms as the numbing sensation was starting to travel from his fingertips down to the palms of Dean's hands.

Walking along the wrap around porch, Dean didn't realize that the bit of water that clung to his feet pooled onto the wooden surface as he walked towards the area where the bedrooms were. Pulling open the door, Dean was surprised that Kane wasn't sleeping in one of the beds that was laid out on the floor. Though upon closer examination, it seemed like the blanket was a little messy. At least compared to the bed that Dean was supposed to be sleeping in, which only had a white robe resting on top of it that he would have changed into for the night. "That's strange, wonder where Kane went to?" Dean muttered to himself.

As Dean lazily walked towards the bed, watery footsteps following behind, there were some rather muffled noises coming from the room next to this one. Following the voices, Dean was careful where to step. There were a few spots where the floor started to creak, but Dean was able to keep from making too much noise as he got closer to the door where the voices were coming from. Slowly peeking into the small crack in the door, Dean was able to see that it was Kane and Miles seemingly lingering in the Sloth leader's room.

Moving down to sit on the floor just outside of the small crack of the sliding door, Dean held his breath to make as less noise as he could while he spied on the two leaders. On top of the bed that had a wooden frame around it, Miles was sitting up with Kane nestled between the man's legs. Kane's arms wrapped around Miles' waist in an awkward angle as Kane's legs looked as if they were buckled under his weight.

Resting his head against Miles' stomach, Kane sighed as he gazed towards the wall facing the bedroom that Kane and Dean were sharing. Miles stroked Kane's hair with the top of his robe peeled down to rest on the messy bed sheets. Kane wore the matching robe that was left out for Dean, though there were a few wrinkles that rested on the back. Kane's hair was a bit disheveled, making Dean wondered if something happened between them while he was passed out.

"It's not fair." Kane softly grumbled, closing his eyes as nestled into Miles' lap more. It seemed that Kane's body went limp when Miles continued to gently stroke Kane's hair. "Why can't we just be more than what we currently are? Why does everything have to be so damn complicated?" Kane asked himself out loud as he opened up his eyes. It seemed that the two leaders didn't even notice that Dean was listening in on them.

"In what regard?" Miles asked, using his free hand to support himself as he leaned back. Keeping his eyes on Kane, Miles didn't even notice that there was another person who could be listening in. "Does this have to do with your relationship with Dean? Or are you talking about the relationship between you and I?" Miles asked, a gentle smile on his face as he looked down at Kane who shifted to stare up at him.

"It doesn't even matter anymore." Kane was quick to remark as he pulled back from Miles' lap. "Not like I have much of a chance with either." Kane spoke, sounding dejected as he buried his face against Miles' abdomen. "I'm just too much of a coward....I don't want to be hurt yet again." Kane continued, though his words were a bit muffled against the fabric of Miles' robe, causing the Sloth leader to chuckle briefly.

"I wouldn't say that." Miles commented, still stroking the top of Kane's head as it seemed to soothe the other male. "I think you've been making great success in your advancement." Miles encouraged the younger male like the brother figure Miles saw himself as. "You just need to give it a bit of time. Remember, you need to learn to be patient if you want to catch the fish on the hook." Miles reassured Kane with a smile on his face.

"After all, you did hug him from behind, didn't you? That's quite the bold move of you. Considering that you're not the type to be the one to take the first step unless you really like someone." Mile's commented, watching as Kane jerked his head up in surprise that Miles knew about it. This caused the faint blush on Kane's face to brighten while a look of embarrassment and astonishment crossed Kane's face as the younger leader tried to find his words to make a retort.

"W-Who told you that?" Kane asked, stuttering a bit as he pulled back from his current position between Miles' legs. Kane avoided Miles' gaze as he sat up on his knees. A soft pout landed on Kane's face as he clenched his hands against the fabric of the white robe while his mind could only figure out one person who would tell Miles what had happened. "Was it Dean?" Kane asked, his eyes slowly drifting towards Miles as if he was a puppy being scolded. "You're not going to hate me, are you?" Kane asked in a concerned voice.

"And what if it was?" Miles asked, moving to cross one leg over the other. Sitting up straight, Miles shifted to slip the top of his robe back on before adjusting himself into a more comfortable position. "Would it be a bad thing if he told me?" Miles asked, raising an eyebrow. Kane remained silent, leaving Miles to let out a small annoyed sigh as Miles crossed his arms over his chest.

"I can't exactly be mad at you since I want you to move on." Miles spoke bluntly, though there was an agitated tone to Miles' voice. "After all, you can't keep clinging to the past." Miles spoke in a stern voice, a soft frown replacing the smile that Miles had. "You wish for nothing more than for you to have your cake and eat it too." Miles paused as he loosely crossed his arms over his torso. "Despite everything that you tried, you know that I could never find myself loving you more than a brother. After all, you resemble Parker..." Miles' voice seemed to fade a bit towards the end, as if he couldn't finish the sentence.

"You can't hold me accountable for that." Kane spoke softly yet defensively, knowing the pain that Miles felt. "But I'm not him....I'm not your real brother Miles." Kane spoke up, almost yelling. "I could never replace Parker." Kane continued, shifting to meet Miles' gaze.

There was a silence in the room that was caused by Kane's little outburst. The more that Dean listened, the more confused he got. Who was Parker? It felt like there was more to this than either one of the leaders would have told Dean, but then again he wasn't of importance that would allow him to know this sort of information. Just as Dean was about to get up and head back to bed, Kane's voice reached Dean's ears once more. What would break the silence next felt like it would shatter Dean's world altogether.

"I'm capable of being more than a replacement for you brother. If only you give me a chance." Kane started to speak, his voice almost hitching as he held back the tears. "I could show you that we could be happy. Just like when we were younger!" Kane begged as he moved forward and placed his hands onto either side of Miles' legs. Hearing this, Dean pressed himself against the crack more, his heart beating against Dean's chest while letting small shaky breaths.

"All I want to do is to see you happy, Miles…" Kane started to speak, a soft annoyed sigh leaving his lips. "When you look at me, I don't want you seeing me as Parker, but as Kane!" Kane continued, his voice filling up with determination at this point. "I don't see why you refuse to look at me in any other way." The tension in the air could be felt. Dean found himself feeling even worse to hear how much Kane still longed to be with Miles, only to get rejected yet again. It left a heated hole in the pits of Dean's stomach that he couldn't shake away, no matter how hard he tried.

"Kane…" Miles spoke softly, reaching a hand down to lightly caress Kane's cheek with his left hand. "I'm sorry… but," Miles tried to speak, but was interrupted when Kane lunged forward to close the gap between them. Dean couldn't believe what he was witnessing! Even though the kiss didn't last long, Dean felt himself pulling away from witnessing any more of it. What Dean was witnessing wasn't meant for his eyes. Despite the urge to slam into the room and demand to know what was going on, he didn't have that right.

Instead of confronting the two, Dean quietly moved to stand up. Making his way back to the bedroom, Dean closed the sliding door behind him, trying to be as quiet as possible to keep the two leaders from knowing that he was back. Sluggishly Dean made his way to the neatly made bed before slipping off the wet and slightly soiled robe. Letting it fall in place without a single care where it landed, or how it was resting in a small puddle of the water that was lingering in place from the first time that Dean came in to check on Kane, all Dean cared about was getting that image out of his mind.

Grabbing the white robe, Dean lazily slipped it on. He didn't care about the sash not being tied on properly, Dean didn't care about how cold the sheets felt from the cold temperatures from outside. Dean just simply didn't care about anything right now. It was like Dean had become numb in that instance.

The ringing in Dean's ears didn't help anything as he rested onto the cold pillow provided for him. Turning to lay on his side away from the door that Kane would eventually find himself walking through to get back to the room, Dean closed his eyes tightly as he curled up into himself. It was best that Dean spared himself from seeing anything more than the kiss that was shared between the two leaders. Dean just wanted to feel like this was just all a bad dream. To slip away into the darkness fade around him and hopefully forget everything that happened.

CHAPTER EIGHTEEN: *The Story Behind A Leader's Scars*

A FEW DAYS had passed since that night. Dean had spent most of his days away from the house, only coming back to get a change of clothes or to sleep. Kane was starting to get worried as he didn't know that Dean had witnessed the kiss between the two leaders. Kane had figured that something else must be preoccupying Dean's mind, but putting a finger on what it could have been was out of Kane's reach. Dean was avoiding Kane, making it feel like everything was falling apart. Kane couldn't find it in himself to ask Dean what was going on, nor could he talk to Miles about it since Kane's heart and hopes were shattered from being rejected after their brief and fleeting kiss.

Miles could see the rift between the two males grow, causing concern over the future between them. Despite knowing that he shouldn't step in, it felt like it was Miles' duty to help those two. After all, if all goes according to plan, they would still be able to watch the destruction of the Millennium. Freeing everyone from the Elite's grip once and for all. If Dean had abandoned the plan, this would have been for nothing. There was no way that the two would be willing to sit down and talk about it, after seeing how avoidant Dean had been by just seeing a brief glimpse of Kane making his way towards the spaceman, Dean would duck out of sight and hide from the man who was supposed to Dean's one and only friend on Earth.

As Miles rested against the wooden floor of the wrap around porch, the garden to his left and the opened slide door to his right, Miles gazed up at the cloudless sky as the sun appeared to be drifting over the roof portion of the porch. With the shadow providing him enough shelter from the sun's harmful rays, Miles laid sprawled on the hardened wood floor. The light gray robe he was wearing seemingly barely covering much past his mid thigh. His pipe rested just out of reach, his current herbal intake already spent for at least a few hours. The sound of the insects buzzing around the few flowers showed that they were going from plant to plant to collect their nourishment, spreading the pollen to the spring flora.

Closing his eyes, Miles could feel subtle vibrations from the floor board. He was waiting to see if he could catch either Dean or Kane for a chance to converse about the recent developments, hoping to amend the rift between them. In a sense, Miles was like a fisherman. Casting his bait into the water in hopes of catching a decently sized fish. Much like any fishermen, Miles was about to catch one of the fish that would nibble at his lure soon enough. But which fish would be the first to nibble? Dean, or Kane? The Goat or the Deer?

As Miles opened his eyes, he felt the vibration of cautious feet, moving before stopping, as if the person was looking around. It must have been Dean, trying to make sure to avoid seeing either Miles or Kane in an attempt to collect his belongings and head out without the two. Sure enough, as Miles tilted his head back, he saw Dean turn the corner and freeze, looking like a deer caught in the headlights. A smile crept on Miles' face as he gave Dean a small wave. "Just the man I wanted to see." Miles remarked, slowly groaning as he got up, though albeit slowly.

"Great..." Dean grumbled, an exasperated sigh seemingly leaving him. It was clear that Dean wasn't exactly amused to see Miles at this point in time, as indicated by the frown that seemed to nestle on Dean's face. "I was just coming to grab my bag." Dean started to explain, walking closer to Miles as he watched the leader slowly get up from his spot. "Figured that

I could start to make my way to the Greed clan to meet with Amelia before it gets to be too late." Dean remarked, trying his best to walk past Miles who seemed to fiddle with his robe. Dean barely spared Miles a glance as he brushed past the leader, only to stop dead in his tracks by Miles' question.

"Without Kane?" Miles asked with a small lift of his eyebrow. Miles waited for an answer, or at the very least some type of reaction from the male, but the small flinch from mentioning Kane's name indicated that Dean was at least a bit hesitant. "You know that wouldn't look very good to Amelia, right?" Miles continued as he faced Dean before walking up to the man before placing a hand on Dean's shoulder.

"It would appear like you're impatient to her, you know?" Miles' words were more filled with caution than scolding. "Recklessly putting yourself and everyone in danger because you want to get things done now rather than strategize. It won't boost your score with her." Miles continued, causing Dean to finally turn towards Miles in an attempt to shrug the leader's hand off of Dean's shoulder, looking at Miles with an unimpressed expression resting on Dean's face.

"Then what do you expect me to do?" Dean spoke defensively. "Just smile and pretend that everything is alright? Pretend that I would have a place here once everything is done?" Dean asked in a fury of questions in a defensive tone. "How do I know you guys won't kill me as well once the Millennium is destroyed? After all, that's where I came from. That's where I belong, right?" Dean clamored in frustration. Miles didn't know where this was coming from, but he could at the very least sympathize with the way that Dean was feeling. "After all, I'm just an exiled coward!" The way that Dean looked right now was like a cornered animal. Ready to snap at anyone who was trying to help the poor male out.

"Not sure why you think you don't have a place here." Miles spoke, slipping his hands into each sleeve of his robe. "You killed a beast, and you went through Keaton's class. You even had your own private ceremony with me." Miles continued with a small shrug. "As far as I know, you're one of us now." Miles finished as he watched Dean's tense shoulders start to lower at the comment. It was clear that there was more to this than what Dean was saying, and Miles was going to get to the bottom of this.

"I'm not exactly sure what is going on through that head of yours, but maybe we should head to my office and find one of the clans that you might be interested in joining." Miles continued as he started to walk past Dean. "After all, if you're bent on seeing Amelia, you'll need the last piece of documents to take with you to be approved." Miles added as he glanced over his shoulder.

"If there's anything that you want to get off of your chest, we can do it in my den." Miles was offering Dean a place of solitude, allowing for the male to talk about any grievances that he may have. "No one really bothers me while I'm in there anyways." Even though Miles' voice sounded friendly, the tone of his voice was more commanding Dean to follow him than anything else.

Dean was a bit taken back by Miles' willingness to help him despite Dean suddenly snapping at the leader. Dean nodded in agreement, lowering his head a bit as he walked behind Miles. There was still a heavy cloud over Dean, but he would simply brush it off for now. No need to really bother Miles with it, despite the fact that it involved the man. But if it meant that Dean could get the piece of paper that he would allow him to talk to Amelia without bothering Kane, then so be it.

Glaring down at the wooden porch as Dean followed behind Miles, the negative thoughts started to build up in Dean's mind. The kiss replayed so many times that it felt like there were times in which the kiss was slowed down. It made the hot knot in Dean's stomach burn hotter each time he thought about it. Dean figured that perhaps the best course of action for him at this moment was to simply try and do as much as he could without Kane so that it would make their parting easier. That way when Dean disappeared from Kane's life, it would be easier for the both of them. Even though this may have seemed to be childish, it was better than knowing that Dean could never be good enough in Kane's eyes.

As they walked past the bedrooms, and around another corner, Miles entered into his make-shift den with Dean following close behind him. In the den rested a single desk that seemed to linger just a few feet off of the floor as it appeared to be almost like a smaller floor table than an actual desk. In the middle of the three sections of the desk was a singular large pillow that was used as some type of seat. On one section of the desk rested a couple of books that had the binder facing away from them with the pages revealing themselves to the two men in the room.

The lettering on the top book had long since faded. A single oil based lamp with some thin paper books rested in the middle section of the desk. Dean couldn't tell if they were documents or just some random papers that had been collected over the years, but they rested in a weird yet organized pile. There were a few pencils and pens that had been scattered around, as if this was where Miles would come to take down some notes about the plants that were harvested recently. It made Dean wonder if they were used in the collaboration Miles did with Kane. What kind of produce did they grow in this region?

The third section of the desk that rested on the right side of the pillow had some jars with green plants stacked on top of each other. Around the room were a few books that ranged from medical practices to plants species and where they would best grow in certain regions. The few windows that allowed a bit of light into the room were covered by a thin white paper, making it rather hard to see either in or out. The floor was different from the rest of the house as it appeared to have some type of mat that lingered on top of what could only be felt as an empty space. It was an usual feeling for Dean, but he watched Miles walk over top of it without much concern.

Miles had walked over to one of the shelves before kneeling down. Sliding a small door on the base of the shelf, Miles pulled out a similar pillow that was currently resting by the desk. Giving it a small toss to Dean, Miles closed the door before making his way towards the desk to seat himself on the large pillow. Flopping down on it, Miles waited for Dean to follow suit with putting the large pillow on the ground before sitting on it. It took a bit of time for Dean to get comfortable enough on the pillow while Miles braced himself against the desk with a small wince.

"Before I start with writing the paper work for you to see Amelia, I have something that I want to talk to you about." Miles remarked, his left hand grabbing one of the jars beside him. Dean watched as Miles collected two bits of the plants that resided in the jar before placing the fished out product on the wooden surface. Just what was Miles trying to do with the plant?

"And what do you need to talk to me about?" Dean asked with an agitated tone to his voice, a quick glance towards Miles before carefully watching the process that Miles went through in order to grind up the herb. "After all, I'm sure you want to get rid of me just as quickly as I want to get out of here." Dean finished speaking bitterly, clenching his jaw tightly as his brows knitted together in anger. The knot in Dean's stomach felt as if it was trying to burn through the lining of Dean's stomach.

"Well to start off, I wanted to apologize for the guidance talk. Or rather, your ceremony." Miles spoke, palming the grinder in his hands before he started to rotate it as if it was putty in his hands. "I'm used to consuming a large amount of the herbal medication that we use for the ceremony. It tends to help with the pain I feel on a daily basis." Miles remarked, seeming to catch Dean's interest. All this time Miles had been suffering, and Dean didn't know about it?

"What daily pain?" Dean asked, more in a skeptical tone than anything else. With the way that Miles seemed to carry himself, it didn't seem as if the male was any sort of pain. Miles just seemed to smirk at the comment as he reached over to the left side to pull out his classic pipe, though it seemed like this one was much smaller in length than the one Dean was used to seeing Miles carry around with him.

"Surprised Kane didn't tell you." Miles remarked, a soft chuckle leaving his lips as he poured the ground up herbal into the pit of his pipe. "Then again, Kane told me how you would rather hear something from the source. Which I can appreciate with how often people tend to love to gossip." Miles continued, bringing the end of the pipe to his mouth before pulling out a match stick from the same drawer he got the pipe from. "Too many people out there now and days who want to spread rumors about people rather than asking directly." Miles paused as he watched the fire start to consume the top portion of the match. "Guess some things never change no matter how much time has passed." Miles remarked, a small shrug of his shoulders before he lit the herbs on fire.

"Well I know how it can be dealing with people spreading rumors about you, rather than coming to you directly." Dean remarked, a light scowl on his face as the smell from the pipe hit him. It was the similar scent from the ceremony, making Dean's stomach churn a bit as he was already getting lightheaded. It simply reminded Dean of what he had seen between Miles and Kane, and how Dean wished he would have simply gone back to the room instead of watching the scene play out before him. Despite the fact that it might have just made everything worse, even if it could make Dean feel better, it wouldn't change what happened.

Miles seemed to take a long drag from the pipe, watching as the herbs quickly burned into a small ash pile with the ember's were still glowing bright red. Miles held his breath for a few seconds before blowing the smoke towards the ceiling. "The daily pain I feel is something that I've been trying to recover from for the last five or so years now." Miles spoke up, placing the pipe down onto the desk beside him carefully, making sure not to knock it over. "It's not something that I really tend to go around showing off, but it's better that you see it while Kane is out. Even he hasn't seen the extent of my injuries in full." Miles remarked, standing up from the cushion with a small groan.

Dean looked up at Miles with a slightly confused face. Watching as Miles's hands reached up to peel the torso section of his robe down, Dean couldn't see a single scratch on Miles' fit body. However, when Miles turned around, it was unlike anything Dean had ever seen before. Along the curvature of Miles' spine spelled out *S L O T H* that went deep into the skin. Around the shoulder blades and down towards his waist were lash marks and small indents that looked as if Miles had been poked and prodded with something rather sharp. There were still bits of pink indents from the skin healing, but it would take a while for the words to fade. The look of shock quickly took away the angry scowl on Dean's face, unsure on how he was supposed to process what he was gazing at.

Miles lowered his head as he could feel Dean's eyes scanning his back, taking in everything as if it told a story that Dean didn't even know the details to. "Out of the six leaders, three of us were unfortunate enough to suffer from physical scars, while the other three have the nightmare fuel that is the mental scars that keep them up at night." The tone in Miles' voice indicated that he knew all too well how often the other leaders suffered as much as he did. It wasn't right to have a pity party when Miles wasn't the only one suffering. But perhaps seeing these scars gave Dean a better picture that each of the leaders suffered in their own.

"Kane used to wake up in a cold sweat, covering his right eye as he begged his brother to stop." Miles continued, grasping onto the bits of robe in his hands. "He would remark about how he could still feel the blade piercing through the skin to the bone. How he could feel the edge of the knife digging into his skull just above his eye. Feeling helpless while being tied up." Miles' voice dipped the more he continued, wavering as if he was recounting the memories as well.

"Watching his dead baby sister's body burn in the fire," Miles trailed off gritting his teeth as he swallowed the knot in his throat. "All the while his mother laid dead on the couch." Miles continued, swallowing a bit of spit to moisten his drying throat. "Then there's Felicia." Miles continued, glancing back at Dean whose mouth hung open a bit. "She wakes up in a nightmare feeling the same pain she felt when the tiger tore into her leg." This part would probably be the most gruesome, but Dean needed to know.

"She could still feel the tigers' hot breath against her skin," Miles paused, lowering his head while closing his eyes. "The rough texture of the tiger's tongue, making it feel like her flesh was being caressed by a mixture of spikes and sandpaper." The level of detail that Miles was explaining, causing Dean's stomach to squeeze as he could only imagine the pain Felicia went through. "The way her bones snapped and the feeling of her flesh being torn apart." Miles could still picture seeing Felicia on the hospital bed, a breathing mask wrapped around her nose and mouth, slowly fogging up as her breath finally stabilized.

Miles had been able to find some morphine that was recovered from a shelter before hand, making it possible for Felicia to be knocked out as they patched up her leg the best they could at the time. "There are times in which those memories flare up for her, and the best thing I can do is just be by her side and hold her." Miles continued to explain as he gathered the courage to finish his story. "I have to always reassure Felicia that it was all over....that the tiger was dead." Not that it would matter anyways, the damage was done and Felicia would never get that leg back.

Slipping his robe back up, Miles quickly changed the subject since he didn't want to talk about Felicia's anymore as he couldn't stomach the memories. "Ashley still has nightmares about feeling her father's blood being splattered on her face." Miles continued before turning to face Dean with a somber expression on his face. "The sight of fire pokers used to be overwhelming for Ashley, but she was able to overcome it with the help of her brother." Miles paused, moving to sit back down on the pillow. "However, he too passed away just recently. Making Ashley close off her heart to anyone getting close to her." Dean knew all too well how much Ashley had been holding in. Just remembering how much she cried to Dean showed that Ashley had reached her limit.

"I'm sure you got a bit of backstory about Keaton through his sister Maiti, right?" Miles asked, though Dean glanced off to the side with a matching somber expression at this point. Seems like these leaders did go through more than Dean could have ever experienced in his own lifetime. "Bet she told you about how messed up the poor child's body was in the shelter that Keaton's team had explored, right?" Miles continued, causing a soft disgruntled noise to escape Dean's lips as he clenched his fists against his legs.

"I bet she even told you how shocked Keaton was when he saw the condition of the child, right?" Miles continued, making Dean grimace at the recollection. "In a way it was a good wake up call for him." Miles paused as he moved a hand up to brush back some of his locks towards the left side of his face.

"Though how he handled it wasn't exactly the best." Miles paused, taking a deep exhale to calm himself down. "Putting restrictions on people who were not blood related or married into a family..." By the sounds of it, even Miles didn't agree with Keaton's choice. "It made people reconsider their relationships, which is something that Kane hates...making it hard for him to ever agree with Keaton on the matter." Miles finished, only to grab the pipe once more to take another drag from it.

"It's probably because you see Kane as a replacement for your little brother," Dean spoke up, his voice wavering slightly as he steadied his nerves a bit. "That's why you put a barrier up between the two of you, right?" Dean asked, earning a small scoff from the Sloth leader. "So that Kane wouldn't get too overly attached to you?" Dean asked, a bit bluntly but it seemed warranted.

"You know that Kane has feelings for you, but yet you don't let him." Dean paused, his tone getting defensive once more as he wanted answers to the burning questions inside of Dean's mind. "Why is that?" Dean continued to ask, moving to lean forward towards Miles who sat idly by in front of Dean. "Why hang on a notion that you only see him as a brother when it is clear that he yearns to be with you?" Dean finished, his heart pounding loudly against his chest as his hands started to shake ever so slightly.

Miles looked at Dean with a somber expression once more. Averting his eyes, Miles placed the pipe back down on the desk once more as the small bits of lingering ashes continued to burn. "Let's get one thing clear." Miles spoke, glancing back at Dean who seemed to be hanging on every word that came out of the Sloth leaders' mouth. "I love Kane with all of my heart. He's everything that I could have asked for..." Miles started to speak before Dean interrupted him.

"But as a brother." Dean remarked, causing Miles to pause, letting out an exasperated sigh. "Like Parker?" Dean continued after a few seconds of silence on Miles' end. Miles didn't answer right away, instead Miles picked up the pipe to dump some of the ashes into a small tray that had old soot ashes collected at the bottom. Despite the calm expression that Miles was showing, it seemed like there was a storm building up in Miles' eyes.

"Guessing you overheard something that you weren't supposed to?" Miles was quick to remark, not even glancing towards Dean who swallowed the lump in his throat. "Or rather, you witnessed something that you shouldn't have?" Dean was taken back by the remark, forcing Dean to lean back as a guilt expression formed on the man's face. "Forcing you to regret what you say that night?" Miles continued to ask, watching Dean recoil a little into himself. "Is that why you have been running away and hiding like a guilty pup who took a shit on the floor?" Miles snapped, crossing his arms over own chest. It was clear that the Sloth leader was not amused by Dean's actions, and with reason.

Dean had become quiet, knowing that what he said next should be carefully worded. It felt like hours had gone by as the two men sat there silently. *"Guess I might have just jumped to conclusions…"* Dean thought to himself as he could barely glance at Miles without the overwhelming guilt forming. After all, Dean didn't know what happened last night, he only caught the tail end of their conversation. Not to mention how blinded Dean was acting because he couldn't outright admit that he saw the two leaders kissing. Eventually one of them had to speak up.

"So who is Parker?" Dean asked, a bit curious as to who Parker was. "Was he a sibling?" Dean asked, raising his right brow. "Perhaps he was a younger brother since Kane said he was the same age." Dean continued to inquire. Carefully Dean watched Miles for any clue if he was going to make any headway with the leader. Watching Miles seemingly bite the top of his lower lip, resulting in a small sucking noise as the leader was lost in thought, it wasn't long before Miles sighed as he relented to Dean's questions.

"Parker was my little brother, if you must know." Miles relented. "He was killed by a hunter….though it was an accident." Miles continued to speak, his eyes glancing away from Dean as he was recalling a painful memory. "Since food was pretty hard to get at the time, especially for fresh meat, it wasn't unheard of for there to be hunters out around that time." Miles started to explain before clearing his throat. "My brother and I were out playing in the snow after the snow storm had passed." Miles continued with his story as he leaned back against the desk. "It was our usual bonding time since he was still rather young at the time. He couldn't be outside unsupervised for long, so I was outside with him while our mother was cooking stew." Not that Miles felt like that was a major factor in his story, but he figured it would help Dean understand what would happen next.

"As Parker was rolling up the base of our second snow man since the first one was rather small, he wanted to make bigger ones to resemble each of the family members. Like any little kid would." Miles continued, a faint smile landing on his face as the leader closed his eyes a bit. "I was in charge of getting supplies to decorate the first one with, as well as the others." Miles added as he reached over to gently brush the pipe that was still warm from the earlier drags. "At the time we didn't have twigs or branches, so the snowballs looked pretty small at time…" Miles' face slowly disappeared as he stopped caressing the pipe to look over towards Dean.

"Now keep in mind that this time, we had a lot of fur to use for the winter time….after all, it kept us warm…" Miles trailed off, letting out a sigh from the breath that he was holding in. Seemed like these memories were just as hard for Miles to talk about as it was for Dean to hear about. "So you can imagine how a little kid would look from the distance as a deer or something rolling on top of the snow ball to grow it to be bigger." Miles remarked, figuring he would include that part before he would get to the more gruesome part of his story.

"I was gone for maybe five or so minutes… and by the time I rushed back out there, I noticed that Parker was slumped over the large snowball. I thought that perhaps he was playing a joke like he was going to try and scare me." Miles continued, a sadden expression landing on the leaders face. "That was just the kind of idiot he was..." Miles paused with a small chuckle as if he was remembering the better times he had spent with Parker. All the jokes that Parker used to play on Miles to get the older male to laugh, it didn't dawn on Miles that something tragic had occurred.

"But he wasn't moving…" There was a subtle hitch in Miles' voice as he told the story. "Even when I lightly kicked his foot... he still didn't move." Dean watched as Miles' eyes started to tear up at the next part that was coming up. "It was only when I actually lifted him up to try and tickle his sides that he was limp in my hands." Dean felt his heart sink just picturing it. "It was only when my eyes noticed the red stain dripping down to the snow, and the arrow that pierced my brother's skull from the front, that I realized that it was too late for him..." Miles tried his best to swallow the hard lump in his throat from recounting that memory.

"I called out to my mother as I kept his head in my lap after I turned him over. I couldn't leave him there after all." Miles continued, shifting his gaze towards his pipe now. "Sadly by the time she heard my cries, it was too late." Miles remarked, a soft shrug as he knew that even if he carried his brother to the house, there was nothing that he could have done to save his brother.

"My father found out who the hunter was and had the man moved to another clan. After all, he couldn't stand the idea of spilling more blood." Despite all the protesting from both Miles and his mother, Ryan wouldn't allow himself to have more blood spilled in his clan. "It wouldn't bring my brother back, and it would just be another life lost." The notion of simply leaving a killer alive and only moving him didn't make sense to Dean, but he wasn't there and it had already been decided.

Dean remained silent as he listened to Miles' story. Even if Miles couldn't look at him while telling the story, Dean felt like Miles was telling him the truth. After all, what motivation would Miles have to lie to him? Relaxing his shoulders, Dean sighed as he glanced off to the side, the feeling that he was being an asshole seemed to wash over Dean. "Your dad seems like a good leader if he didn't straight up want to murder the man for killing his son. Accident or not." Dean remarked, reaching a hand up to scratch the back of his head, the overwhelming guilt seemingly to take over. "I couldn't blame your father from wanting to kill the man though. I know my father wouldn't have been as forgiving." Dean remarked, knowing how protective Max was to his family.

"I wish my father would have had the man executed frankly." Miles spoke up, his voice a bit dark, catching Dean a bit by surprise. "After all, it's not like my brother did anything wrong. He was just playing out in the field, minding his own business." Despite the fact that winter has always been the hardest time to find food, there shouldn't have been any hunters near the town.

"How any hunter could mistake a small child as deer is something that I will never be able to understand." Miles continued, his gray eyes seemingly hollowed from any type of emotion. "After all, the man came back later on with a couple of people from the Wrath clan a few months later." This part of the story was something that Dean wasn't expecting. "Two of his people held me down while the asshole carved the sloth into my spine. Though they didn't exactly leave unscathed.." Miles trailed off, a dark tone lingering in his voice that seeped with hatred from the normally smiling leader. "I did what my father should have done to that man." Miles spoke in a deep tone as his eyes showed no sympathy.

Dean's eyes widened at the remark as Miles stared at him with an expressionless gaze. "Do you want to know the story Dean?" Miles asked, moving to rest on the desk with his elbow helping to hold Miles' head up. "Of course, with everything that happened on that night, you'll understand why I am not exactly quick to forgive, unlike my father." The harsh tone and angered expression on Miles' face sent a sharp shiver down Dean's spine.

"Not only that, but why I can't allow Kane closer to me since he would never accept the monster that I am. How truly cruel I am to those who cross me. And why I keep Kane at bay no matter how hard he tries to break through the barrier." Dean was left to be a bit speechless with a curiosity of knowing more about Miles. With a small nod of Dean's head, Miles would tell Dean the horrors of the night that Miles got the scars on his back.

As the spring was turning into summer roughly five years ago, Miles had been taking care of Kane, who was still recovering from the incident where the majority of his family were slain in cold blood. With their house destroyed by the fire, and the Mayworth's moved to another location for Rosa's sake after the death of Parker, the rest of the Flores family had been staying with them while trying to find a new place to relocate to. Seeing as how the Mayworth's lived closer to the city where the head of the clans would often meet up, Elijah was trying to find a place that they could call home. It was made apparent that the clan leaders needed to establish a better way of communication thanks to the events that had unfolded.

Gazing up at a rather cloudy sky, Miles was planted on the floor with the side door wide open. The pitter patter of the rain drops started to trickle down on the clay roof top. Softly tapping his toes that rested out before him, Miles glanced over to Kane who seemed to curl up inside himself and faced away from Miles. The bandages still clinging over Kane's right eye while the green and yellow checkered robe clung to Kane's smaller frame. Miles was eighteen at the time, while Kane was only fourteen. Their difference in height and age was much more apparent. Miles was wearing a black robe with a gray cloud design towards the hem of his robe. The sound of the rolling thunder in the distance made it apparent that it would be raining soon.

"Still afraid of the lightning?" Miles asked, a small smoking pipe lingering in his right hand, the smoke coming from it started to waver ever so slightly as it drifted from the metal ring. Kane shifted ever so slightly, the sound of the fabric shifting as the silence was apparent. "If you want, I'll get your safe space prepared so that you can wait it out." Miles spoke, his voice sounding concerned though in a bit of a monotone voice. Despite the gentle smile on Miles' face, his concern showed on Miles' face the more that Kane kept quiet. It wasn't until Kane finally spoke up a few minutes later that Miles was able to relax a little.

"That would be nice....thank you..." Kane softly mumbled, his thin arms wrapped around his legs. Kane rested his chin against the top of his knees while still resting on his side, his long gray hair was pushed over the right side of his face as if to hide the bandages to no avail. Miles could tell that the unease that still lingered on Kane's face, despite Kane facing away from him. Miles had struggled to get Kane to eat recently, causing Kane to lose weight. It was concerning since Kane was rather thin to begin with, but seeing his best friend wither away into nothing felt like it was also killing Miles. Seeing how sunken Kane's cheeks were, it felt like Kane was recoiling into a literal husk on himself in front of Miles. The older male would be lying if he said that he wasn't worried for his friend.

"Very well." Miles started to speak as he placed his hands on the floor, shifted himself to be able to stand up. "But you need to promise me that you'll at least eat some apples." Miles remarked, slowly getting up from his spot on the floor. "I'll also get some earplugs so you won't hear the lightning when it strikes down. Don't need to hear your pathetic whimpers under the mats." Miles lightly teased as he took his time getting up, a small groan leaving his lips. "If you want to get in before the rain comes down, you can start by getting the spare blanket and a pillow. You're thin enough to sleep in the storage without a problem." Miles finished as his feet started to stomp on the floor, making his way out of the room, leaving Kane alone to do as he asked.

The house seemed to be rather quiet the further that Miles had gone inside, which wasn't surprising considering the atmosphere that Miles had to put up with. First he had to deal with his best friend suffering from trauma from the recent events, and also dealing with his own mother who was still holding herself up in her room, grieving over the loss of her youngest son. It wasn't easy having to fend for himself, but Miles was doing a pretty decent job at it. Besides, Miles had to take care of Kane now on top of taking care of his own mother. Seeing Kane wearing Parker's old clothes reaffirmed just how much the two boys were similar. Miles couldn't help but grow a soft side for Kane because of it. In a way, Miles still hasn't come to terms with the fact that his little brother was still dead.

After seeing Kane look so far gone when they came to rescue any surviving members of the Flores family, Miles was worried that Kane had been killed. Imagine his relief when they saw Kane in the barn that had been untouched by the fire. Naturally Elijah had become over protective of Kane once he saw the state of their families' house after the fire was finally put out. Unfortunately Elijah would never be able to hear the events of what was to happen, as it was during this time that the present leaders would eventually lose their lives as well.

It was after those events that Miles was put in charge of the task of looking after both his mother and Kane. Not that it was ideal, and Miles learned to brush up on reading some books that seemed to cover various trauma cases from materials that were collected from various explorations of the accessible shelters. There were many suggestions in the medical books that seemed to fail, but with enough determination, Miles was able to help Kane become a bit more independent. Now if only those tips and tricks could work to help Rosa out, Miles would be in business.

Glancing out the window in the kitchen, Miles took notice of the rather pitched black clouds that would flash bits of purple lightning here and there, as if it was some type of dragon or snake slithering around in the clouds. As the rain droplets had started to hit the glass, the windows began to slowly fog up. "Seems like it'll last for a few hours." Miles mumbled to himself as he steadied himself from the herbs he inhaled. "Once it starts to die down, I'll check on Kane to see if he needs anything." Miles spoke out loud, mostly to himself as he grabbed two apples from the little fruit bowl on the counter. Thanks to the generations before them, people were still able to eat out of seasoned fruits and vegetables that were still being grown down in the shelters.

Unbeknownst to those in the house, a small group of people were gathering just outside the property. A couple of yards away from the house rested withered trees from the dying forest thanks to the lack of nutrients that have been stripped from the soil. With the cover of darkness from the storm, the small group waited with baited breath as the scout hid in the bushes. Armed with a pair of binoculars, it wasn't long before the man emerged from the bushes with some news for the men.

"So, anyone inside?" One man asked, covered in a mixture of mud and fur, wearing a bear skull on his face to help cover his identity. Most of the people had mud splattered on their skin with patches of their clothing seemingly infused with fur from the animals that they slaughtered. They looked like some type of barbaric outfits, which seemed to be fitting for the nature of the Wrath clan. Each individual had an animal skull on their face to hide their identity from anyone who saw them. But with the way they carried themselves, it was very clear that these people belonged to only one specific type of clan.

"So far I only spotted one person walking around. Looks like the leader's kid." The man spoke carrying the binoculars. He was wearing a large predatory bird skull on his face as the beak curved downwards. "If we flank the house on either side, we should be able to take him down without much hesitation." The male continued as he shoved the binoculars into his side sash.

"How do you know it was him?" The male with the bear skull asked. It didn't seem like a lot of these men were comfortable with the idea of taking out a child, but this was to prove a message that the Wrath clan was tired of being represented as the outcasts simply because they were not wanted by the other clans.

"Because I watched that kid hold his brother as he bled out." The man spoke up, his tone bitter as a scowl landed on his face. "He cried for his mother like a little bitch, all the while he could have carried that kid inside so he didn't have to die." The man with a bird skull remarked, pulling out a large knife that had an ivory handle that he got around the time that he was forced to leave the Sloth clan. "If that damn kid wasn't so slow, I could still be with my wife and kids." He grumbled, turning away from the group.

"I don't know about this guys." A woman seemed to speak up, wearing the skull of antelope over top of the fur hood she wore to protect her from the cold. "Going after kids? It doesn't seem right." Clearly she wasn't the only one who thought this through either. There were a few individuals who felt her concern. "I know Nero said that in order to prove the point that we are the better clan, we should make an example of how the leaders are weak. But to go after their families, do you think that is the best decision?"

"Of course it is!" The man in the raven skull snapped, quickly turning around to face the group. "After all, that dick head took me away from my family. So he deserves to have a scare or two of his own." The man spoke in a bitter tone, catching a few people off guard by his remark. "Besides, if you can't handle the idea of wronging those who hurt you, you might as well crawl back into shelters where you belong."

"That might have gone a bit too far man." The man with the bear skull spoke up, his voice showing his disgust for the way that the man with the raven skull remarked. "Even you can agree that Nero went too far with what he did to his own people." The man continued, reaching his hand forward to grab the collar of the raven skulls' shirt.

"He killed the people of his own clan who were considered weak. They were innocent men, women, and children who couldn't defend themselves that he killed!" The man wearing a bear skull continued, jerking the raven skull man forwards to him. "Locking them up in the shelter, gassing them with flammable gasses and then blowing the shelter up! You really think that is the type of leader that we want to be following?" The man with the bear skull growled, shoving the man with the raven skull back into the bushes.

"You don't agree that the weak should be wiped out?" The man with the raven skull asked with a scoff to his question, his brows knitting together as the man pushed himself back up from the bushes. "Then maybe I should gut you right here and now?" The raven haired man spoke, holding out his knife while standing in a guarded position. It seemed like the man with the bear mask was about to say something before they were interrupted.

"Knock it off you two," The woman with the antelope skull spoke up. "We should just get this done and over with." Just thinking about hurting children never seemed to settle with the woman. But they had to prove those who abandoned them for making mistakes. "Though I don't like the idea of hurting kids, Nero put you in charge of this since you were so quick to lick his boot." She continued, glancing towards the man with the raven skull.

"So just tell us what you want to do." The woman continued in a stern tone, averting her gaze from the raven skull man. "I'd rather not get sick from the damn rain because you were trying to have a dick measuring contest with Bear here." It seemed like tensions were getting high within the group. If they weren't going to act fast, they might slaughter each other before they even get a chance to try assaulting the Sloth leader's new home where his family was waiting for the leaders' to return home from the meeting.

Walking back to the room where he had left Kane, Miles looked around for the other. The rain was starting to hit harder at this point, to where some of the droplets even started to bounce once they hit the hard wooden floors that were exposed outside. Seeing a small bump in the floor mat, Miles smiled as he knelt down to peel the mat up. In the space rested Kane who looked like he had wrapped himself up into a tight little burrito with the blanket. A pillow was already nestled close by, along with a book and a small gas lantern that Kane would be able to use to read in the dark. It seemed like Kane didn't notice that Miles had opened the mat up before feeling the rush of cold air from the storm swooping into the room when the wind picked up.

"Here. I brought you an apple." Miles spoke as he placed the red apple close by to Kane.

"Figured you would be able to eat it to help drown out the sound of the storm." Miles remarked, flashing Kane a smile. "I'll let you get some rest. Don't strain your eye too much from reading." Miles commented, moving to close the floor mat more securely. Even though Miles often teased Kane about straining his eyes, Miles was still worried about the younger male. Despite the fact that Kane had a lighter shade of hair color and eyes, it was still uncanny how much Kane looked like Parker. It was almost like Kane was the ghostly reminder of Parker, and how Miles let his younger brother die in his arms.

What was Miles supposed to do? Carry Parker back to the house only to have him die on the way there? No matter how many times it seemed to play out in Miles' mind, the end result was that he was just too far from the house to make much of a difference. Miles could have screamed his lungs out for his mother to come, or have anyone come at that point. It still wouldn't have been enough. Parker was just simply too far gone by the time Miles had reached him. Miles would be damned if he would let anything happen to Kane. Miles could feel the guilt building up inside himself. Even as he sat down and sliced the apple open with a little sharp knife, Miles' mind always went back to the 'could of, would have, and should of' mindset.

As the rain picked up, Miles sighed as he slowly chewed the apple slice in his mouth as Miles sat on the floor, his back propped up against the small table in the room. Kane was safely protected underneath him. If the other needed to get out, all he had to do was simply tap on the mat, allowing for Miles to get up and help Kane out. The pitter patter of the rain drops seemed to get heavier as the trees started to rustled against the strong winds that picked up. As a deep sigh escaped him, Miles glanced down at the half cut apple. It seemed that Miles' appetite was lost in his over thinking about the past. Tossing the remaining apple out the door, Miles stretches out his right leg as the small blade he used to cut the apple was brought up to his lips. As his tongue slid along the sharp edge, Miles collected the bit of juice that still clung to the blade.

Tilting his head back, Miles closed his eyes as he heard a rumble from the thunderstorm. A long groan left Miles' lips as he felt like he could fall asleep right there and then. With the cold air sweeping into the room, it made Miles want to wrap himself up in a blanket as well to sleep through the storm. Moving to lay down on the floor, Miles started to feel his eyes getting heavy, his body slowly becoming numb and desensitized to his surroundings. That was, however, except for a tapping sensation against the floorboards like someone was running. Or rather, a bunch of people were running when everyone in the house was resting.

Snapping open his eyes, Miles saw a group of people standing in front of the side door. A large flash of lightning illuminated their silhouettes in that brief instance where Miles couldn't move fast enough. Miles didn't get much of a chance to react as one of the three individuals had taken a hold of Miles' legs, pulling him close to the group. As he was pulled closer to them, Miles used his free foot to kick the skull off of the person who grabbed him. The sharp end of what felt like a beak dug into Miles' foot. Despite the pain that this caused, Miles was able to get a good look at the man's face.

To Miles' surprise, it was the man who had killed his little brother, causing Miles' eyes to widen in terror. The man's dark brown sunken eyes, the scruffy beard that seemed to grow in patches and was already graying in certain spots was all too familiar to Miles. There was a small cut on the man's upper left lip from when someone threw a broken bottle at him for killing Parker. The man's dark brown hair looked as if it hasn't been washed since the trail. Why was he here? "You..." Miles spoke in almost a husk tone as he froze in place. "Why are you...?-" Miles was about to ask before the man interrupted him.

"What are you waiting for? Pin him down!" The man yelled, causing the man with the bear skull and the woman with the antelope skull to rush in and pin down Miles' arms. Upon hearing this, Miles started to thrash his arms before a fourth person came in from behind the man whose raven skull mask was broken. "Help to hold him down before you bind his hand." The man barked angrily. "We can't have him overpower the others." The man finished as he wiped his mouth from the kick Miles gave him. Seems like Miles was actually able to make the man bleed a little bit, which resulted in the man getting angry.

With each step, it felt like the floor shook. As Miles gazed up at the man, it felt like he was looking up to a giant. With a gorilla skull covering most of his face. Despite the size of the skull, it seemed that the teeth and fangs seemed to dig into the man's flesh. He was a rather burly man who looked as if he could crush Miles' skull with just one hand. Swallowing the lump in his throat, Miles failed to realize that the other two had grabbed a hold of Miles' arms, pinning him down with their knees.

The large man with the gorilla reached down to pull Miles up by his locks, putting some strain on Miles' body. "L-Let go of me." Miles groaned out, feeling as if his arms were going to be pulled out of his socket. "Y-You're going to snap my arms." Miles was able to force out, resulting in the large man letting go while the other two kept Miles' arms down. As a result, Miles' head flung back into the mat, causing it to crack ever so slightly before a loud yelp escaped from Miles' mouth.

Miles' head felt like it was on fire as he laid there, his arms felt like they were on fire from being nearly pulled out of their sockets by the gorilla man. Slowly opening one eye, Miles watched as the larger man turned to the side, allowing the man without the skull to step closer. "Turn him over." The man spat as he glared down at Miles. "And make sure you keep him pinned while I check on the others. Surely they must have found the wife by now." He spoke, stepping over Miles as he walked towards the door that led to the rest of the house.

"No wait!" Miles yelled, the look of panic washed over his features as a cold sweat started to form on Miles' temple. "Please spare my mom! I'll do anything you want." Miles spoke, trying to figure out if there was a way he could appeal to the man. "I'll give you all the money I have." Granted it may not have been much, but it was the start of Miles' bargaining chip. "I'll give you all of my prized possessions." Miles continued, gauging to see if this was some sort of robbery or if it was something more. "I-I'll even try to work out a deal with my old man to give you whatever you want. Just leave my mom alone." Miles pleaded, his body jerking up as he had to look up at the man at an awkward angle.

"Hm..." The man hummed, reaching up to rub his chin as he glanced off to the side. Miles looked up at the man with an eager and pleading gaze. If he could protect his mother, it would be worth whatever they decide to do to him. It wasn't like she had anything to do with the clan's decisions anyways. She was tucked away in her bed, still grieving the loss of her youngest child. Not like she was in any type of position to fight. "As tempting as it is, I feel like it's my duty to make sure that your father knows what it feels like to lose everything he ever held dear." The man remarked with a wicked smirk on his face.

"Wha-" Miles was left practically speechless as he watched the man slide the door open, disappearing into the darkened house. Miles couldn't believe what was happening. First he was helpless when it came to saving his brother, and now something bad was going to happen to his mother. It felt like everything was crashing down around him. All he could do now was pray that Kane would stay safe under the floor mat. Pressing his forehead against the mat Miles could hear himself breathing a bit too hard. He was panicking, which would result in hasty decisions that could risk all of their lives.

"Think Miles... if you're going to keep anyone safe in his current situation, it'll be Kane." Miles thought to himself as he gazed at the pattern below him. From the feeling, it didn't seem like Kane took any notice of the thrashing around above him. Which meant that perhaps Kane was sleeping through the storm.

At this point, Miles could only hope he knew the younger male well enough by now to guess what Kane was doing in the storage space. *"I'll have to apologize to mom.... letting her get eaten by the wolves....but at the very least I can protect Kane."* It was a saddening thought, but Miles wasn't able to get away any time soon. Not with the people holding down his arms. "I'm sorry mom..." Miles whispered in a whimper, the hot stinging sensation of tears coming to his eyes, only to shut them tightly as if to shut out the world as the ringing in his ears didn't stop.

IT felt like hours had passed, when it had only been half an hour. The man seemed to be more than satisfied with himself as he walked in with a big grin. Miles quickly stared up at the man to see if there were any lingering sights of blood on his clothing. Thankfully there wasn't any. But if that was the case, then what did the man do?

"There we go." The man remarked, walking over towards the table where Miles had been resting prior. Miles was quick to clench his teeth while looking up at the man. Studying him, Miles could see that the man's clothes were disheveled as a bit of sweat still lingered on his forehead. There were a few scratches against the man's cheek and neck. In the right light there was a darkening ring around the man's left eye.

"What did you do to my mother?!" Miles growled, glaring up at the man with anger in his eyes. Struggling against the people holding him down, Miles wanted answers from this man who was clearly leading the group. However, the man didn't say anything at first. Instead the man reached down to pick up the knife that Miles had used to cut the apple, only to inspect the blade as it showed a clear reflection of himself.

Gazing at himself in the blade, the man chuckled a little bit. "I made everything better." The man continued as he walked over towards the four, staring down at Miles with a bit of a cocky grin on his face. The aura coming off of this man was of a cruel and vengeful type that loved seeing other people suffer.

"What do you mean made things better?" Miles asked in a snapping angrily tone, his brows knitting together, not liking the idea of exactly where this was going. The way that the man talked made things even worse, causing Miles to grit his teeth to the point where it felt like they were going to break just by the pressure alone.

"Well, in about six to nine months, you'll have a new little brother or sister. Though I guess," The man paused as he knelt down. Grabbing the back of Miles' head, the man tilted his head to the side. "They'll be more like a half sibling than a full blooded one. Lucky you." The man chuckled darkly as he tapped his lips against the blade of the knife. "You'll certainly have your hands full afterwards." The man sneered vindictively. "After all, there certainly are a lot of bitches in my family." The man finished, a cocky smirk on his face as he could see the color draining from Miles' face while a burning hatred shone in Miles' gray eyes.

"You sick son of a-!" Miles growled, using his feet to try and lunge himself forward at the man, only to have the man punch Miles back down. The man's friends used a bit more force in order to keep Miles in place. "I-I'll kill you....I'll fucking kill every single one of you." Miles continued to growl, his feet were trying their best to find some type of dent in order to prevent his feet from sliding. "I'll wrap your guts around your neck as I strangle you with them." Miles threatened, sounding more like a rabid animal who was trying to fight against the hunters that trapped him.

"Now we can't have that." The man remarked, standing up as he watched Miles wither under his crew's grip. "After all, you didn't act fast enough to protect your brother. If you did, then perhaps he might still be alive." Hearing that forced Miles to freeze in place. The memories of his brother's death still lingered in the back of Miles' mind, and this man brought them back to the surface as if adding salt to the wound. "And now you are simply laid there the whole time I violated your mother. Talk about being a lazy sloth." The man taunted, moving towards Miles' back before straddling his legs to be on either side of Miles.

Slamming Miles' head forwards with a loud thud, the man brought up the knife once more while Miles continued to struggle against the people holding him down. "Lazy boys such as yourself need to be taught a lesson. Wouldn't you agree?" The man continued, bringing the knife up to the top part of the backing of Miles' robe. Gripping the fabric in his left hand, and the knife in his right, the man started to saw into the thick fabric with the jagged edges of the knife.

"W-What are you doing?" Miles asked in a panicked tone, feeling the man tugging against the fabric of Miles' robe. It didn't take long before Miles could hear the fabric tearing behind him. The cold air from the damp atmosphere started to cool off Miles' hot flesh as the man continued to tear into the robe, exposing the younger male's back to him. "What are you doing?!" Miles shouted this time, feeling the robe becoming looser on him before noticing the torn fabric dangling over his shoulders.

"Teaching you a lesson, what else do you think I'm going to do?" The man remarked, pressing the edge of the knife into the top section of Miles' spine. The way that the knife seemed to pierce right into Miles' flesh was as if the knife was cutting through hot butter. At first Miles didn't feel it thanks to herbal medicine he had less than an hour beforehand, but soon Miles would start to feel a deep burning sensation in his back.

When the man started to glide the ridged edge of the knife across Miles' spine, the male could feel every bump from the sharp knives' edge. The way it easily tore into the muscle felt like a saw against Miles' spine, leaving Miles speechless. Feeling the curves of the S as the man took his time with the curls felt like the knife was tearing into Miles' muscles even deeper, like the man could puncture an organ. "Oh, looks like we'll have to make sure to clean the edges off." The man sneered as he spoke in a taunting tone.

Bringing the knife up to Miles' shoulder blade, the man started to saw the knife back and forth, as if that was the best way to clean off the blood while still torturing Miles. Each movement caused Miles to shout horrifically as his feet slammed against the mat below. At least at first since it was an uncontrollable reaction when someone was being literally sawed by the jagged knife.

Next the man started with the L, working the vertical part first as he pushed the blade into Miles' skin. Biting onto his lower lip to the point that it filled Miles' mouth with a metallic flavor from piercing the skin with teeth, it was Miles' best way to fight against giving the man what he wanted. Which was to make Miles cry out in agony as he carved the poor male up. If Miles was going to protect Kane, he had to endure this torture.

Next was the O, something that Miles wasn't looking forward to was the curves on the S were just as bad. Miles dug his toes into the mat as the man circled the blade slowly into Miles' flesh in an agonizingly slow circle, as if he was trying to make it perfect. Just like with the other finished letters, the man made sure to slash Miles' back each time that he was done with a letter. However instead of simply keeping it at the shoulder blades, the man worked to make long marks resemble claw marks on either side of Miles' back.

The T was the worst of it. Not so much for the dash that went across, but like the vertical section of the L, the longer section that spanned across the disks hurt the most. Each stroke had Miles' legs curling inwards as Miles struggled to keep from crying out in pain. At this point, Miles could feel his back was on fire. Each nerve in his body was telling him to pass out. But the fact that they could find and possibly harm Kane caused Miles to stay awake through it. He couldn't allow them to hurt Kane, not after losing his brother and being helpless as the man raped his mother Rosa.

Finally it as the H, the last part of his intense torture. As the man dug the blade a bit further into Miles' body, all that the young man could do was hiss as Miles felt his whole back flaring up like a Christmas tree from the burning sensation of the knife repeatedly being etched into his back. It was only when the man finished that Miles was thankful for being able to endure the pain. His body felt heavy and sticky from the blood that was sweeping out of his wounds.

Miles' breathing felt shallow, his body seeming to be unresponsive as the man got up. The cocky grin didn't seem to go away either. "Good boy. Now, maybe if you're lucky, you'll have someone close by to rescue you." The man taunted, sneering at Miles and watching the red pool of blood seem out of Miles' back. "Who knows, maybe your little brothers' spirit is close by. Perhaps he'll welcome you to hell as he drags you there." The man cackled, taking in his artwork.

"You can let go of him now. Not like he'll have the strength to move much after that." The man instructed his lackeys as they reluctantly let go of Miles' arms. "His body will more than likely go into shock if he tries to move." The man instructed his men, dropping the knife as it was covered in blood. The knife bounced against the mat, landing close to Miles' left hand.

"Let's go and find this storage area that bitch was talking about. Apparently the leader of the Gluttony clan's kid likes to hide there." The man's words seemed to be distant as he walked away with the group of people. As Miles tried to move, his body was unresponsive.

"*Not....Kane...*" Miles thought to himself, grunting with each movement as he reached out his hand to try to get the knife that was close to him. Miles' body had been beaten and battered, his spine was throbbing and felt like it was on fire, but yet Miles could still move.

Carefully Miles moved to push himself up with his arms, determined to move and make these people pay, Miles was trying his best just to get up as he grabbed the knife. Even just using his arms, Miles could feel his body wobbling as Miles carefully steadied himself to be on his hands and knees. The bloodied knife clenched tightly in Miles hand, fearing that if he were to let go of it, he would allow these guys to kill Kane in the process.

As the four had their backs turned towards Miles, the younger male figured that this would be a good time to strike where they least expected it. "*If I'm going to die like this, I'm at least going to kill a couple of them first.*" Miles thought bitterly to himself. Steadying his breath, Miles knew that he had to strike first while their defenses were down.

Placing one knee down, Miles' brows knitted together as he scanned the area where he could strike the larger man who wore the gorilla skull. There could be plenty of spots where Miles could strike but would they be enough to cause the man to be down long enough for Miles to take out the others? The man was wearing plenty of armor around his torso and upper thighs, but the back of the man's legs were free from any protection.

"*Perfect...*" Miles thought to himself as he took a deep breath. With the adrenaline rushing through his body, Miles pushed off of his feet, darting on his hands and legs to quickly cut towards the man's ankles, gashing the man's Achilles' tendon, resulting in the larger man to shout out in pain as he quickly fell on top of the man who wore a bear skull and the woman wearing the antelope skull.

"Get off of me you big ape!" The woman shouted, being pinned from her waist down by the larger man's arms. She was trying her best to punch the large man off of her, but all they got from him was grunts before he spoke up.

"I-I can't get up." The man with the gorilla skull groaned in his deep voice as he felt as if he was immobile. The pain against his ankle was preventing him from being able to move, let alone put pressure on his leg to be able to get off of the two he trapped.

"You've got to be kidding me." The man with the bear skull remarked, glancing over his shoulder to see a pissed off Miles. "How can he still move?!" The man continued to shout as Miles rushed towards their leader. It seemed that the man was also taken back by the fact that Miles was able to get up despite his injury, but in a brief instance it felt like he watched as a wolf was lounging towards him, ready to kill the man for what he did.

"How did you-" The man started to speak, but the feeling of the knife he had used to torture Miles with had sliced through his neck, cutting the off mid sentence. The rest of what the man was going to say seemed to be filled with gurgling noises. It didn't take long before he fell to ground in front of Miles, holding onto his neck as his body started to thrash around a bit. The two who were pinned under the large man couldn't believe their eyes.

As Miles turned towards them, he could see the fear in their eyes. Walking towards them, Miles still had the blade in his hand, staring down them with such an intense stare. "Please don't kill us..." The woman pleaded, her voice cracking. She dug her nails into the ground under her. The overwhelming feeling of fear caused her to visibly shake as she looked up at a bloody Miles.

"Kill you?" Miles spoke, a small coy grin forming on his face. Kneeling down, Miles made sure to pin down her hand as he brought the knife into view. "As much as I would love to kill you for simply holding me down while your prick of a leader raped my mother and then proceeded to take his time into carving my back up like I was his personal pumpkin," Miles paused as he knelt down by the woman. "It would just be more work for me to clean up your disgusting bodies once I'm done with you." Miles remarked, moving to slam his knee down on the woman's palm.

"Instead of going through all that hard work, perhaps I'll just do something else to make you remember what you did." Miles added, a dark chuckle leaving his lips as he felt the woman's hand trying to unwedge herself from Miles' knee. "A constant reminder if you will. Perhaps I shall carve up the arm you used to pin me down. That seems like a much better punishment, wouldn't you agree?" Miles spoke, his voice almost husk as he brought the knife to the woman's forearm. "Hm... what should I carve into this pretty little arm of yours?" Miles asked, lightly tapping her arm with the edge of the knife as a curious hum left Miles' throat.

"Slut? Nah, that's too generic." Miles suggested before lightly shaking his head in disapproval. "Bitch?" Miles asked, raising an eyebrow before visibly shaking his head once again. "No. That would be insulting to dogs." Miles lightly chuckled to himself as he got an idea. "How about compassion? Since that seems to be what you're lacking." Miles remarked, rather pleased with himself as he started to dig the tip into the woman's flesh, causing the woman to whimper.

"Hey, can you move at all?" The man with the bear mask asked the larger man who was pinning them down in a whispered tone. "If you can roll off of us, it'll give us a chance to break out of here." The man didn't know if the woman would be able to get away without a scratch as Miles was already working on the C of the compassion carving, but if he could get free, the man might be able to knock Miles unconscious. This would allow them to carry the larger man with him as it seemed that Miles was still moving by using adrenaline alone.

"If you think I'll let you get away, you have another think coming." Miles quickly snapped, glancing towards the pinned down man with an intense gaze. "If the big man even sneezes, I'll plunge this knife into each eye socket and stir it while you watch helplessly." The look on Miles' face showed that he wasn't messing around.

"Take your punishment like the good little boy you are." Miles hummed in a more chipper mood as he moved onto the o. "The sooner you simply let me carve into your bodies, the quicker you will be able to drag your large friend out of my clan." Miles added, ignoring the whimpers from the woman as she felt the blood slowly dripping down her arm. "Do that, and you'll be lucky enough to leave here alive." Miles stated in a matter-of-fact tone, digging into the woman's arm with enough force to make her cry out in pain, sending a message that Miles was not one to be crossed.

By the time that Miles was done with the woman, Miles had his sights on the man with the bear skull. There was a small puddle of blood just below the woman as she gently held onto her shaking and freshly carved up arm. As she softly sobbed, Miles spared her no glance. "You're really crying because I cut your arm?" Miles asked in disgust as he walked over to the man with the bear skull. "Are you really that much of a weak bitch that you can't handle a bit of pain? I thought the Wrath clan was tougher than that." Miles spat towards the woman, only to pin the man with bear skill down by his foot, giving it a small twist as if to crush the man's hand.

"How do you think I felt during all that time? Do you think I'm a masochist who enjoys being carved up like some kind of pumpkin?" Miles remarked, kneeling down and grabbing the man's skull mask before ripping it off. "My back is absolutely killing me at this point." Miles snapped, screaming at the man's face as he brought the knife up to the man's right eye. "Your dumb ass leader really carved me up good. I could almost pass out any second. But knowing that you shit heads will try and kill me or my little brother is the only thing keeping me going." Miles growled as he pulled the knife back from the man's face.

"We won't...I swear it." The man pleaded, his black hair disheveled from Miles' yanking the mask off. Blue eyes met gray, the man's lip trembled as he glanced over towards the woman. She was still silently weeping as she tried to cover the wounds with her other hand as if it would stop the bleeding somehow.

"Like I can believe anything that you would say." Miles quickly snapped in a cold emotionless tone. "You're nothing more than outcasts now. You should be glad that I'm at least showing you some mercy. Unlike what you showed me." Miles remarked bitterly. "Yeah, compassion and mercy. That seems like a perfect fit." Miles remarked to himself as he started to work on the engraving. "It's a shame I'm not good at writing with this hand." Miles toyed with the man, purposely messing up on the man's arm, watching as the man tried his best not to yell. The vibration of the man trying to kick the floor was rather amusing to Miles, knowing that he himself was in this very position.

Once Miles was done, he let out a small relief as he studied the words, though the woman covered hers up, making it hard for Miles to enjoy his hard work. "Now, I want the three of you to get the fuck out of my house and out from my clan. If you ever try and dark in my door or clan ever again, I'll gut you like the beasts you are. And I will proudly display your entrails all over the clan to prove a point." Miles was not the type to use violence, but he wasn't about to stay silent while those around him were being threatened.

Backing away, Miles watched with the knife in hand to see if the three would get up. Of course the knife was pointed towards them, ready to be used if the three tried anything. Slowly the three started to hobble off, like wounded animals with their tails between their legs. It wasn't like Miles was in any position to simply kill them, but he felt better knowing that out of the three in the house, at least Kane wasn't injured.

Glancing over towards the body of the leader of the people who attacked them, Miles sighed as he felt bad for taking a life, but the man raped his mother and left Miles to bleed to death. "Now to check on mom..." Miles mumbled to himself. But as Miles took a step, his body started to feel heavy. Miles' knees were weakening as he slowly turned to head inside. With his bloody hands, Miles used the wall to help guide his way back inside, leaving a small trail of blood behind him. It wasn't long before Miles' vision started to get fuzzy, resulting in him slipping on a puddle of blood, crashing to the ground and passing out.

"By the time I came to, I was in our little shed that was used for gardening. My mother was sobbing in the corner, holding onto herself while rocking herself back and forth from the trauma she endured." Miles spoke, bringing the pipe up to his mouth to take another drag from the smoking pipe, the embers slowly glowing in the metal ring. "My wounds were treated and my body was wrapped up, though the bandages were still a bit bloody." Miles continued with his story, a small hum of amusement thinking back on that night.

"There was a distinct smell of smoke blowing in from the breeze that I can still remember to this day." Miles continued , almost fondly before blowing a bit of smoke from his mouth up towards the ceiling. "Apparently Kane heard a bit of the commotion and came out of his hiding hole to see me completely bloody. He says that he must have knocked over the lantern and it caught the blanket and his book on fire." Miles continued with his explanation before he moved to get rid of the ashes in his smoking pipe.

"But you don't believe him?" Dean asked, raising an eyebrow as he took everything in. Miles simply smirked at Dean as he adjusted a bit in his seat. Dean could see the wheels turning in Miles' mind as if to try and figure out what to say next. "After all, it's not the first time that Kane has been a part of a burning house. Is that what you're thinking?" Not that it wouldn't have been a stretch, but the fact that this was the second time a place was burned down around Kane couldn't have been a coincidence.

Miles didn't say anything. At least, not after a few seconds of silence. "Whether Kane was behind it or not, it doesn't matter." Miles continued with a light shrug of his shoulders. "Because soon after we learned about what happened to our fathers. How they were killed in a struggle with Amelia's fathers after Nero killed Ashley's mother for her crime, it was only a matter of time before the inevitable happened." Miles commented as if it was no big deal.

"My mother ultimately couldn't bear the fact that she was violated, her youngest was killed, and now her husband was dead. She became overwhelmed by the grief and loss, that ultimately she ended up killing herself." Hearing that was surprising to Dean, though in thinking about it, Emily might have done the same thing. "Telling me, I was strong and capable enough to live my life. Though at the time I thought she was full of herself, spouting off some bullshit.." Another shrug from Miles' shoulder as he gazed towards Dean. "But I guess she was at least right about one thing." Miles finished, leaving the rest up in the air for interpretation.

"How can you go on each day after dealing with that?" Dean asked, feeling a bit sorry for everything that Miles had to go through. It felt like everything went to shit for the leaders at such a young age. Did people keep them in the leadership positions out of sympathy? Or perhaps people wanted to live their own lives and didn't want to deal with the hassle of problem solving every little issue? After all, the only one who held any power over everyone seemed to be Amelia.

"You just have to keep on living for yourself." Miles wasn't exactly wrong. If you couldn't live for someone else, you had to live your own life for yourself. "Both you and Kane are like lost souls right now. Trying to find an ending to a journey that would lead to some sort of happiness." Dean lowered his gaze as he took that to heart. It wasn't like Miles was lying. After everything that they've been through, Dean was still trying to figure out where he belonged.

"What makes you happy Dean?" Miles asked, bringing Dean out of his struggling thoughts. "Walking around and seeing the planet? Or perhaps helping others?" Miles continued while raising an eyebrow. "Or maybe seeing the death and destruction of your own people is something that would bring you happiness?" The last remark from Miles caused Dean to look at the leader with a bewildered look. "Relax, I'm just teasing," Miles chuckled as a soft smile rested on his face. "Or is it, maybe with Kane?" Miles finished, only after a few moments of silence between the two of them.

An audible sigh left Dean's lips. Not like Dean could deny the fun he had walking around with Kane. Meeting all of the leaders and getting them on board with the plan to destroy the Millennium. Nothing really made Dean the happiest than when Kane was right next to him. With avoiding Kane, Dean didn't feel like himself. He felt hollowed, as if Dean was back on that empty station. "What am I supposed to do? Not like I can go back and erase what I had seen that night." Dean remarked, lowering his head.

"Well, it's not like you're official or anything." Miles spoke bluntly as Dean looked up the male with a rather surprised look on his face. "Does Kane even know how you feel about him?" Miles asked, slipping his arms into the sleeves of his robe before resting his arms against his chest. "You don't exactly have a right to be angry when Kane is just as oblivious to your feelings as you are of his." Hearing that remark caused almost a light bulb to click in Dean's head. Miles couldn't even hold in the chuckle from seeing the epiphany register in Dean's mind.

"And there it is." Miles lightly chuckled as he reached to the side drawer to pull out some papers. "Seriously, I don't think I've met two dense idiots like the two of you." Miles muttered under his breath as he shifted some documents between his hands while Dean was reeling in his thoughts. "But as long as you finally realize that you at least have feelings for another, it should be easy enough to work it out. Though I think only one of you realizes it." Miles remarked under his breath as he turned himself around on the pillow.

"What?" Dean asked, a bit surprised by the remark, only to have Miles wave the back of his hand to Dean. It seemed that Miles didn't want Dean to hear that last part, so the leader simply brushed the question to the side.

"Nothing." Miles quickly retorted, dipping the pen into the little ink bottle. "Go ahead and get some laundry done. By the time that the ink is dry on the document, you should be able to head out." Miles remarked, brushing Dean off as the sound of the pen scribbling against the paper and desk filled the room. "Besides, it'll take a day's journey to get there by cart. However if you walk there, it'll be around three or so days." Miles spoke up as he glanced towards Dean. "You'll want some fresh clothes when you leave. I have a washer and dryer you can use. But for now, get some rest. You're on the last leg of your journey after all." The smile that landed on Miles' face was reassuring, though Dean felt like he still had some things to work out by himself still.

Dean got up with a small groan, his legs becoming slightly numb from sitting on the pillow all that time. It took a bit of convincing, but eventually Dean was able to leave the room, leaving Miles to go about his business. Now if only he could find the courage to tell Kane how he felt. That was much easier said than done. After all, with the realization that they weren't officially a couple, Dean felt a bit of the weight lifting off of his chest. Perhaps if they ran into each other, maybe Dean could work up the nerve to apologize. But then again, with Kane seemingly avoiding him as well, Dean would have to sit on that apology.

CHAPTER NINETEEN: *The Clock Tower*

T HE NEXT MORNING was a rather humid one. As Dean walked out sporting a buttoned up white t-shirt with a white muscle shirt underneath, a loosen red tie dangling from his neck as the jacket he was going to wear hung over Dean's right arm. The black formal pants he was wearing had the shirt tucked into them, allowing for the dark belt he was wearing to become visible. The pair of loafers he was wearing had a small bit of dirt already clinging to them as Dean walked the dirty and rocky road towards the carriage he was going to be using to get to the last clan on his adventure. Amelia's clan, or the Greed clan which was the center of power for the six leaders. Miles had been up early already brushing the horse that was connected to the carriage. Wearing a dark gray robe, Miles was busy making sure that the horse was ready to travel before he heard the scuffing of Dean's footsteps as he got closer.

"Morning sleepy head." Miles remarked, turning to watch Dean open the side door of the carriage. Already there was creaking from the carriage as Dean leaned in long enough to put his bag on the seat he would take for the rest of the journey. "It's going to be a rather hot one. Sure you'll be cool enough wearing that on the last leg of the trip?" Miles asked, giving the horse a light pat as a sign that he was done with grooming the horse.

"I'll survive somehow." Dean quickly remarked, already feeling the effect from how humid the morning air was. "I figured that Kane would be with you by now. Is he not coming with us?" Dean asked, glancing around to see if perhaps Kane might be trying to sneak up on the two men. But it didn't appear that way. The two friends haven't even gotten a chance to talk since the incident. Dean had been hoping that by this time the two would have at least made an attempt by now.

"Sadly no." Miles remarked, moving to put the brush into a little makeshift pack that rested on the front of the carriage where the driver would sit. "He went on ahead a few hours ahead of us. Figured that you two needed a bit more time apart." Miles remarked, moving to lean against the side of the carriage. "Lucky you. I'll get to keep you company." Miles added, a small chuckle as Dean didn't seem to share the male's enthusiasm as Dean formed a light scowl of disappointment as he climbed into the carriage.

Did Kane really not want to talk to him? It wasn't like it was Dean's fault for overhearing the conversation a couple of days ago. Surely Kane had time to think about everything that happened since then. Granted Kane wasn't mad at Dean as the leader didn't even know that Dean witnessed everything that happened that night, but what could Miles have said to Kane to make the other not even want to stay together on the last leg of their adventure together?

Once he settled in, Dean grabbed his bag with the goat skull still attached, and rested the rather heavy bag on his lap. Moving over just a little bit, Dean expected Miles to sit beside him while the two rode towards the Greed clan, only to be surprised when Miles took the seat in front of him. As a result, the window that was in front of them was blocked, making it rather hard for Dean to be able to see the way that they were going. Was this on purpose? Either way, Dean just wanted to head out and finish this last leg of the journey already.

Feeling the creak of the carriage as the driver got on board, Dean took this chance to glance out of the side window. A small frown lingered on Dean's face as he appeared to be bummed by the fact that Kane didn't want to join him. Miles seemed to take note of this, causing a small hum to leave his lips. "You seem to be really disappointed in your travel partner. Sorry I'm not as young and good looking as Kane." Miles remarked, the playful smiling indicating that he was clearly messing around in order to lighten Dean's mood.

"It's not that," Dean quickly remarked as he glanced briefly at Miles before he turned his attention on the road as they were starting to move. "I just wish I could have at least gotten a chance to talk to Kane on the trip." Dean continued, a small shrug of his shoulders as he figured that it was too late to get a chance to talk to the male. "I'm used to having him by my side. So with him not here, it makes me feel rather hollow." Dean's eyebrows lightly knitted together as the sunlight was starting to get to be a bit too much on his eyes, causing Dean to close his eyes rather than closing the blinds. *"After all this....I still have to travel without him..."*

"Is that so?" Miles remarked in a pondering tone. It seemed that the wheels were starting to turn in Miles' mind as he studied Dean. After a few minutes of silence, Miles crossed one leg over the other. The sound of the fabric shifting caused Dean to peek towards the noise. "Tell me Dean, what kind of relationship do you hope to have with Kane?" The question seemed to come out of nowhere, but it caused Dean to wonder what he wanted with the kind leader who helped him get through the harder parts of the journey. Friendship? Kinship? Or romantic? Dean didn't know what he wanted with Kane, nor how the Gluttony leader felt after all of this.

"I....don't know honestly." Dean remarked, the uncertainty seeming to rest in his voice. It wasn't like there was an easy way of saying what Dean felt when he didn't understand most of the more complex emotions that humans had. Or rather, Dean knew that he wanted Kane to always be by his side, but he never expected anything more than a type of friendship with male. Dean didn't have much of a physical attraction towards anyone, but he found himself looking forward to having Kane by his side every day.

"Alright," Miles remarked, the knitting brows on his face showing that Miles was trying to figure out a way to better word the question to make it clear what the leader was asking. "If you don't know what kind of relationship you want with him, then how about you tell me how you feel about Kane." The loaded question seemed to make Dean wonder how he was around Kane, as if the gears were starting to turn in Dean's mind. Shifting his gaze to the other side of the cabin, Dean lightly scowled in thought.

"I..." Dean trailed off once more before pausing as he reminisced about their time together. The feeling of being able to explore the new lands that were completely new to Dean, and how he felt recently now that Kane wasn't exactly by his side. "When Kane is with me, I feel like a part of me that I have been missing is filled in." Dean started off, his eyes wondering back towards the window.

"I guess, it makes me realize how my parents felt when I would watch them slow dance in the kitchen or living room." Dean continued, knowing that it was a weird example to use in the first place. Not everyone liked to dance after all, and no one but Dean could see the love that his parents had for each other. "The way my mom would smile as she rested her head against my father's shoulder, and how he would tilt his head to lightly rest it on hers. They had each other, and that's all they needed." Dean spoke, remembering the few good times he could recall of his parents. "And now that Kane isn't here with me, I feel rather empty." Dean didn't understand what his parents had, but this was the closest feeling that Dean had to understanding what love was.

"You feel empty? Huh..." Miles repeated as he trailed off towards the end, moving to slip his arms into the sleeves of his robe before resting them against his chest. "Hm, guess I can see why Kane and the other leaders are falling for your charm." Miles lightly teased, causing Dean to sit up right from his slouched position. "Surprised?" Miles teased as an amused chuckle left his lips. "I wouldn't be." Miles remarked, a light chuckle leaving his lips. "After all, you are a very interesting person Dean. It's not every day someone from the station comes along that is as entertaining as you." Miles remarked, fiddling with something in his sleeves before pulling out his long smoking pipe.

"There were others who survived like I did?" Dean asked, his voice and facial expressions showing his disbelief. It was hard to believe that the woman above him survived the crash as some of her personal effects were floating around in space. Not to mention the large hole where the door was. Even if she survived being hurled towards the Earth, the amount of heat against the pod's outer shell and the lack of air from the vacuum of space would have been the factor killing the woman off for good.

"Of course." Miles stated as if it was a matter-of-fact remark. "Though most of the time the people we find are on death's door if they survived the impact." Hearing this news caused Dean's heart to sink. So there were actual survivors that survived the trip? "By the time we get them to a medical station, it's up to them if they want to survive or just end up as another victim of those cowards execution attempts." Not that Dean could blame the survivors who landed on Earth. Some of them probably still believe the rumors that the planet was not safe, and therefore felt it was simpler to just give up. "You're one of the few handful of people who actually crashed without much injury. Guess lady luck really has a thing for you." It wasn't luck that saved Dean, but rather quick thinking.

"Yeah?" Dean remarked, a bit surprised that there were people like him who were able to survive the crash. "What happened to those who crashed landed and were able to pull through the wreckage?" Dean asked, his curiosity perked since Miles seemed to bring it up. Maybe Dean would be able to meet some of the survivors and talk about their own personal experiences on how they ended up on Earth as well. At least if they saw the destruction of the Millennium, then would they cheer or cry themselves?

"Well, usually after they would be enrolled into our society. If their limbs were badly damaged, we would amputate them before fitting them with a prosthetic one." Miles spoke as he prepared his pipe with some more of his herbal medicine. "Once we get them evaluated, they are free to choose to go to whichever clan they wish to be a part of. Though oftentimes they will tend to stick around the clan that they crashed near." Miles finished before taking a small drag of the pipe. "Which reminds me, you're going to stick with Kane's clan, am I correct?" Miles asked, raising an eyebrow as he waited for Dean's answer.

"I'm not sure." Dean answered, feeling a bit unsure of if it was wise for him to join the Gluttony clan. After all, if Kane didn't want anything to do with Dean, then what was the point? Where could Dean even go? "I feel like Kane doesn't want me to be a part of his clan." As much as it pained Dean to say that, it was what Dean's mind told himself.

"After all, what can I really bring to the table that Kane could find in someone else." Dean remarked with a small shrug of his shoulders as his eyes went down to gazing between their feet. "It makes me worry that I might not have a place to go if Kane doesn't want me. I have no place to really call my own since I'm originally from the station. I'll be completely alone on this planet without a single clue as to what I'm supposed to do." The worry in Dean's voice was apparent as he hung his head down.

"Well, you're always free to join my clan if you want." Miles offered, causing Dean to look at him with a rather surprised look on Dean's face. "Aw, don't look so surprised." Miles spoke with a smile on his face. "Like I said, you're a very interesting person Dean. Plus you do know a bit about medicine, so that would come in handy when making the medicine we provide for the other clans." Thinking about what Miles said, Dean wondered if he could find it in himself to go to one of the other clans.

Dean wasn't exactly well off in his creative skills to join the Envy clan, nor was he a type of person who could find himself surrounded in the loud underground city of the Lust clan. He wasn't mechanically inclined enough to join the Pride clan, so really it would leave the Gluttony and Sloth clans where Dean might be able to work in the fields. Not that Dean knew much about the Greed clan, but it didn't feel as if he would be as welcomed as he was in Kane and Miles' clans. But then again, he had never seen what the Greed clan was like, only knew a bit from what Kane told him.

"Thanks but, I feel like I would still want to stick with Kane's clan." There was just something about the idea of being able to work in a place where he felt comfortable being around Kane that Dean would find it easier to settle down in that clan. "I just hope that I can get a chance to talk to Kane and sort everything out before we destroy the station..." Dean trailed off at the end, feeling like a bit of the fog had been lifted from his mind, though there was still a lot of uncertainty that lingered. "I just hate the idea that Kane isn't talking to me because I might have said or done something to make him mad." Dean admitted out loud, not caring that Miled could hear him. "That's the last thing that I would want to happen."

"Kane's not really angry at you." Miles remarked, leaning back against the seat of the carriage as they went over a small creek. "He's just mad at me because I lied to him." Hearing this caused Dean to gaze at Miles with a rather puzzled look on his face. "Nothing worse than having the person you long to be with lie to your face in order to spare their feelings." Miles spoke, a small sigh leaving his lips as he didn't think lying to Kane would have such a ripple effect towards Dean.

"Though seeing you running away from him the next day made it seem like you were completely avoiding. Perhaps it had to do with something you heard or saw the night before?" The comment made Dean stiffen a bit since that was exactly what happened. Miles kept his gaze on Dean, spotting the bewildered and guilty expression that Dean showed, even if it was for an instant.

"Thought so." Miles muttered to himself, bringing the pipe closer to take another drag from it. "I don't know how much you had seen or heard, but I can guarantee you that my feelings for Kane will always be that of a brother." Even though Miles was sure that Kane's feelings would die down, Dean knew that it wasn't easy to squelch feelings like that. Kane would always pine over Miles since he was willing to destroy evidence and bodies to protect Miles. Or at least, that's what seemed to have happened with the story Miles told him.

"How could you just ignore his feelings like that?" Dean asked bluntly. "You know that Kane is crazy about you, so why just brush him off so easily?" Dean spoke up, his brows knitting together though it was out of concern. "I've seen the way he looks at you. How much he wishes that he could be the one that you are with instead of Felicia." Not that Dean would ever understand why Kane would want to be with someone like Miles, but he was conscious enough to know that there was no way that Dean could ignore how Kane felt.

"Let me tell you a little something Dean." Miles started off, moving to open the window up as the carriage was starting to fill up with a bit of smoke. "All of the leaders have been through a lot over the last five or so years." Miles started off in a scolding tone, a serious expression landing on Miles' face as he continued. "Each of us are going onto different paths that we didn't exactly want to follow through. We all had to make choices back then that may seem to be a bit unfair, but that doesn't mean I don't love Kane in my own way." Miles continued before clearing his throat.

"I love Felicia for everything that she is." Miles continued, wanting to make Dean understand his own point on why he could never find Kane to be more than just a brother. "Her whole being is what makes me happy. From her smile that shines brightly when we're together to her bad flirting when she is drunk. She makes me feel fulfilled in ways I never thought possible." It seemed almost like Miles and Felicia had the similar type of relationship that Dean's parents had. The more that Miles went on, it was clear that Miles was head over heels in love with Felicia as she was to Miles.

"What I get from her is completely different than what I get with Kane." Miles continued, clearing his throat once more as a light scowl landed on his face. "Honestly it's better if I stop stringing Kane along like Keaton often does to those he finds to be attractive, and let Kane be with someone who he can actually have a real relationship with. Frankly, you're a better person to make Kane happy then I ever could." The response was oddly welcoming to Dean as he didn't think Miles knew what he was doing to Kane for all those years.

"Wait..." Dean spoke up, a bit surprised that Miles had put it that way. "String along? But isn't Keaton in a relationship with Amelia?" That comment from Miles caused the last part to fly over Dean's head. "Wouldn't she be angry that he is flirting with other people while he is with her?" That type of relationship would never work on the Millennium. More often than not people would tend to get to be jealous, ruining a long standing relationship simply because the other person felt insecure with themselves that their partner even hinted at being interested in someone new.

"It's not that Amelia doesn't get angry when Keaton flatly flirts with other people, but they have an arrangement." That was an easier way of describing the leader's relationship to an outsider like Dean. "It's not up to us to judge how their relationship works. If it makes them happy, then just let be." Miles remarked, moving to rest his elbow on the armrest of his seat. "I may be bisexual and Felicia is straight, but we can both agree on when someone is attractive despite their gender, or lack of one." Miles finished, taking a small drag from his pipe as the opened window helped to ventilate the carriage.

"I guess I just come from a place where that sort of thing isn't common." Dean admitted, knowing that people were often insecure in themselves to accept that another person may not be the loyal type. "I just can't wrap my head around it. How could they simply be happy with an arrangement that would make it seem like one of them is cheating?" Dean continued, reaching a hand up to scratch the back of his head in thought. It seemed like people on Earth were more open about themselves than those on the Millennium. Then again, it seemed like nothing had changed on the station since the day the bombs were dropped.

"It works for them, and they're happy." Miles continued in a blunt tone. "It may not be for everyone, but controlling another person isn't healthy for anyone. It puts a strain on the relationship." Miles remarked as he took a small drag from his pipe once more. "Let me put it in a way that I think would make it clear on how everyone is different and how they tend to adapt to change." Dean was a bit intrigued with what kind of metaphor Miles could come up with to explain something that Dean couldn't clearly comprehend.

"There are some people who like to be in a small boat with only two people on board, while others like to have a few more crew members on board. There are even some who like to be solo, and that's fine too." Miles remarked, as he pulled his pipe back from his mouth. "The key to making any boat stable enough to brace any seas or obstacles," Miles paused as he guided the pipe out of the window to tap some of the ashes out of it.

"You have to work together to make sure the boat doesn't sink." Miles continued, watching as Dean nodded his head as the male seemed to follow the logic. "People need to let each other know if there are holes that need to be patched up, or if it is alright to build onto the ship." It seemed simple enough, after all communication is the key to any relationship. "If you can't even do that much with your crew, how are you supposed to get along?" Miles asked rhetorically. "You might as well stay in your solo boat and explore the sea yourself until you come across the right crew who you can easily rely on if that's the case. Right?" The way that Miles spoke, it oddly made sense. Not everyone was cut from the same cloth after all.

A relationship is like a boat huh? Whether people are just simply two boats passing in the night or they collide into each other to make for an odd but functional boat strangely brought a smile onto Dean's face. "I guess you're right." Dean started to speak, a light smirk on his face. "When you put it that way, it makes a lot more sense." Dean remarked, moving to lean back in his seat. The road started to feel a bit bumpy, as if they were going over some type of rocky road that the carriage wasn't exactly used to. If Kane was here, he would probably need to have the carriage pull over so he could empty out his stomach from the motion sickness. Either that, or lean against Dean for support.

Glancing to his left shoulder, Dean felt like he could see the miserable look on Kane's face as he would suffer from motion sickness. With a small stretch of his feet, and a groan escaping from his lips, Dean took this chance to rest his head against the side of the carriage, allowing for the rocking of the cart to put him to sleep. They had a long way to go after all, so why not catch a few winks in. It was better than having his eyes strain from the sunlight coming in.

***

By the time that Dean had finally opened his eyes, he could hear the small pitter patter of light rain against the top of the carriage. Glancing out of the window before him, Dean noticed the small bits of water pressing against the glass. A bit of the window had been fogged over from his hot breath, distorting some of the scenery before him.

Moving to lightly wipe away the white fog, Dean noticed a large field with tall grass waving ever so slightly in the wind. Yellow and light pink flowers seemed to peek through the bits of tall grass as the clouds overhead were a light shade of gray mixing in with black. The overcast was too thick to tell what time it was, but it appeared that there was still a bit of sunlight that would peek out from the clouds from time to time.

"Well, good evening sleepy head." Miles greeted Dean with a smile as the carriage seemed to shift from a slightly bumpy terrain to a smoother surface. "I take it that you slept well?" Miles asked, handing Dean something that seemed to be wrapped up in a red and white flannel cloth. "Got you a little sandwich to go since you were so passed out that you didn't even wake up when we stopped to get something to eat." Miles explained as Dean took the wrapped sandwich from the leader.

"Really? I didn't feel that tired." Dean remarked, his voice a little groggy as he started to peel the fabric back from. "The only time I got this groggy was when-" Dean stopped, shooting a small glare at Miles who was looking out of the window to see how much longer they had until they reached their destination. "Was when you did that whole smoke session with me. That herbal medicine you use always puts me to sleep." Dean snapped, clenching onto the fabric tightly. If Dean wasn't so groggy, he would have grabbed the leader by his robes and shaken the man out of anger.

An amused smirk popped onto Miles' face as he could see the annoyed yet slightly angry look that was on Dean's face. "Oh right. I tend to forget that not many people can handle the smoke from my pipe." Miles half joked, knowing that his own tolerance was higher than most. But Miles took this as a chance to get to toy with Dean while it was just the two of them. "Then again, you have a rather low tolerance if it always puts you to sleep for hours on end." Dean didn't know if he was being insulted or not, but Dean figured that it was an insult if it was coming from Miles.

"Anyways, we're still on the way to the capital of the Greed clan. By the time we reach the clan, it will be close to closing time." Miles remarked, all the while Dean finished unfolding the meal's container to eat. "I'll have the driver stop at the inn so you can get your room and a hot meal before crashing. After all, Amelia isn't going to stay in her clock tower all night just for the sake of you." Miles remarked, his tone still rather playful as Dean took a bite out of a sandwich that looked a little questionable.

"Clock tower?" Dean asked, his mouth a bit full from the sandwich. By the taste and texture of it, it seemed to be a type of pulled chicken sandwich with some type of mayo and barbecue taste to it. It wasn't bad, but it wasn't exactly something that Dean would find himself eating cold very often. Not like there was some type of device that could warm it up in the carriage.

"Yup. It's in the center of town, by the world water fountain." Miles chimed up, moving to close the window as a cold breeze started to pick up. "It's a fountain that was donated by the Envy clan. It's made up of crystals with different colored crystals from each region to act as a guide." Miles continued to explain, already visualizing it in his mind. "It showcases the islands and which of the clans the islands belong to. It's rather an amazing work of art if I do say so myself." The way that Miles described it, it was almost like it was something that he came up with. But if this fountain was true, Dean would like to see it for himself.

"Why do you say islands? I thought that there were plenty of land masses like how the Earth originally was before the bombs dropped?" Dean asked, followed by a quick lick of his fingers as some of the sauce was trying to trickle down onto Dean's clothing. It was a good thing that he used the fabric from the package to act as a type of barricade to keep the sandwich from falling down on his clean clothes. Though could you call it clean if his back was completely wet from sweating in his sleep.

"Well, with the impact of the bombs dropping on some of the cities, and the natural course of the Earth breaking up and shifting over the past couple of hundred of years, it's only natural that the original landscape will change." Miles remarked, sounding almost like a professor. Not that Dean was in the mood to be lectured, but it was interesting to learn that Earth actually shifted in such a way because of two different types of variables that caused the land to change so much.

"I'll check it out then. Seems like I might be able to learn a couple of things by studying it." Dean remarked, a small nod of his head as he often liked looking at various art that he was able to see in the different clans. It was a shame that Dean didn't get a chance to see what kind of beautiful structure the Envy and Lust clan had to offer. Maybe he could accompany Kane on another round trip and be able to see them once more. After all, the two had been in a rush to meet with the leaders before moving onto the next clan that they didn't get a chance to look around like they did on Felicia's island.

UPON pulling up to a large gate, Dean glanced out of the side window to see that they were on some sort of bridge that was made out of brick with a large river gently flowing underneath them. So the Leader of the clans' place had a fresh supply of water nearby? Looking a bit further out, the trees surrounding the area were rather large with a mountain in the distance. Was that the one they traveled to while heading towards the Lust clan? Dean couldn't exactly tell, but it was still an amazing sight to see. Scanning the river as the carriage was stopped, Dean could see some areas that had been cleared out for farms, making it seem like this area was rich with all kinds of resources.

As the cart started to move again, Dean nestled back in his seat before looking at Miles who was currently shifting around the chest of the robe for something in particular. Dean's eyes traveled to Miles' chest as an envelope started to peek out from the folds of Miles' robes. Blinking in surprise, Dean watched as Miles pulled it out before handing it towards him. "What's that for?" Dean asked, his voice showing his interest being peaked. Taking a look at the envelope, it was silver in color with a red wax seal on the back.

"This is for you to hand over to Amelia." Miles explained, watching as Dean looked it over a bit more. "It's the last bit of paperwork you'll need when seeing Amelia." Miles continued, earning a skeptical glance from Dean. "Don't give me that look." Miles spoke, a reassuring smile landing on the leaders' face. "Make sure that you make up your mind about what clan you would want to stay with." Miles instructed like a nagging wife.

"Decide on a clan, huh?" Dean mumbled to himself as he still felt conflicted about it. Sloth or Gluttony? Which one could Dean honestly find himself being happy in? The conflict appeared to become evident as Miles took this as a chance to speak up, reassuring Dean to take his time in the decision the man will ultimately make.

"Don't worry about your first choice." Miles spoke, catching Dean's attention from his internal struggle. "If you decide later on that you want to explore the other clans, all you need to do is get in touch with the leaders after you've been approved and we'll help you." Miles remarked with a smile on his face. It was better than having to come all the way to the Greed clan in order to change their current situation. But if Dean wanted to move from the Gluttony clan to the Sloth clan, wouldn't that make Kane sad? Dean figured it was best to set aside his decision until the time came. After all, he would be alone with his thoughts at the end of the day. He could just decide then what he wanted to do.

"Really?" Dean asked, wondering if it was possible for him to settle down in the clan of his choice without worrying too much about it. "I'll keep that in mind." Dean finished as he looked over the envelope. Glancing at the wax seal it had an only had the initials M.M with each letter pressed into each other. "Do I open it up and fill it out? Or..." Dean started to ask, figuring that if he needed to open it up, he might as well do so while he was resting in his room.

"No, most of it is filled out. You can just hand that to Amelia once you see her." Miles instructed Dean, figuring that he would save Dean the trouble of worrying about. "We'll be stopping by the inn that is only a few blocks away from the tower. That way you should be able to make it to her place in no time." Miles spoke, glancing to the window to see that they were inside the city. Dean could feel the sinking feeling in his stomach as soon as they went into the city. Being here without Kane by Dean's side felt wrong.

"You should try some of the wurst." Miles remarked, catching Dean by surprise. "It's a bit on the spicy side, but paired with the melted cheese and buttered bread, you'll be full through the rest of the night." It was an odd thing for Miles to bring up, but considering that it was getting late, Dean would probably at least get a bit of something to eat before hitting the bed. Though the thought of sleeping alone the first time in months without Kane by his side did put a small damper on things.

"If you say so..." Dean trailed off, holding the envelope in the curve between his thumb and index finger on both hands. The gentle rocking of the carriage made Dean feel like a pendulum, swinging back and forth. It was only when they rode by some people walking on the street that it dawned on Dean to ask the question. "By the way, why did you decide to ride back here with me? Shouldn't you have been up in the driver's seat?" Dean asked, the lingering thought through this whole ride being brought to light.

"Well, I wanted to see how my new driver handled being able to make their way from my place to Amelia's clan without any guidance." Miles quickly retorted, a suspiciously smug smile landing on his face. "I figured I would see how he did considering that it's been a while since he drove anything." The remark seemed oddly phrased, causing doubt to fill Dean's mind. Why on Earth would anyone let a person, who hasn't drove in a while, drive the cart?

The look of doubt must have been evident on Dean's face as Miles was quick to add onto his statement. "Don't worry, the horses know their way to Amelia's place like the back on their hooves, so to speak." Miles' pun wasn't being appreciated as Dean was getting to be suspicious of the male. "I wouldn't have allowed the driver to get behind the reins if I didn't think that they were capable of driving. At least have that much faith in me." Hearing that excuse left Dean feeling annoyed as it didn't answer his question.

"Your driver has me concerned when you put it like that." Dean remarked, his voice showing that he wasn't exactly impressed by the way that Miles was talking. Thinking back on it, Dean pondered if this was how his father Max would have handled teaching Dean how to drive the shuttle. Since there was no adult capable of teaching Dean how to fly it, he simply read the manual front to cover multiple times, taking notes on what each part of the shuttle did and how to avoid crashing into the planet. Perhaps that's why Dean was able to escape the shuttle before it crashed without much injury.

Eventually the carriage arrived at the inn, allowing for Dean to exit out of the carriage when it came to a stop. Opening the door, Dean was met with a brisk wind that chilled him to the core. Stepping out the carriage, Dean noticed that most of the town had been completely covered in brick. From the walls to the roads, to even the chimneys that currently had smoke seeping out from the top, everything was covered in bricks. The smell of burnt wood swept through the street along with a slight Earthy smell from the rain that collected in small puddles through the street. The sound of the carriage creaking and the horse neighing came from behind Dean as the streets were slightly empty.

"You did a decent job Kane." Miles called out, causing Dean to turn around to see Kane on top of the drivers' seat. Seeing Kane sitting up on top of the carriage left Dean feeling frozen in place. So Kane was here this whole time? And Miles just let Dean think that he left the other leader behind like that? Dean felt furious at Miles, wanting to punch the male. It was like Miles got off teasing or torturing Dean. "Are you suffering from the usual motion sickness?" Miles asked, helping Kane down from the carriage.

"A bit, but not as bad as normal." Kane remarked, a soft nervous chuckle leaving his lips as his feet landed on the ground. Kane was wearing a light trench coat with a large brimmed hat to keep him dry from the light rainfall that washed over them on the way to Amelia's clan. "Your coat is still a bit baggy on me. But it at least kept my clothes dry." Kane continued to talk to Miles, his hands moving to undo the trench coat before handing it to Miles. With a pair of normal black slacks with matching loafers, Kane was wearing a baggy beige cardigan sweater with a white buttoned down shirt underneath.

Dean was silent for a few minutes as the two talked. It was only when Dean found the strength to move his legs again that he walked towards the two leaders. "Kane," Dean's voice was weak to pick up before he cleared his throat. "I thought that you had already left before I got up." Dean spoke up, a bit surprised that Kane was the one driving. Considering that Kane could barely stand being able to ride on the train, it was impressive that they didn't have to keep stopping so that Kane could empty out his stomach. Or for that matter, need to rest inside of the carriage where Dean would have surely seen him when he was awake.

"You can blame that one on me." Miles quickly spoke up, figuring that he should squelch any type of tension that may result in his choice. "Normally I would have been the one to drive the carriage, but I wanted to be a bit selfish and have a little bit more time to talk to you." Miles added before glancing over towards Kane. "Besides, Kane was still a bit angry with me, so I figured some fresh air would do him some good." Miles remarked, lightly patting Kane on the shoulder.

"I have every right to be upset with you." Kane quickly snapped at Miles, clenching his right fist as if he was ready to punch Miles in the face. "You lied to me and made up some lame excuse about Felicia being pregnant. Can you blame me for being mad?" Kane continued in a nagging tone as he frowned thinking back on that night after they kissed. Hearing that remark, Miles had a small scowl on his face as he was quick to put Kane in the place.

"I wouldn't be so quick to judge Kane." Miles spoke up in a stern voice. "After all, I could let Amelia know what you did." Miles was quick to throw it back in Kane's face, seemingly adding insult to injury with his next comment. "You remember what the punishment of sexual assault an another individual is, don't you Kane?" Miles spoke bluntly, his tone having no emotion behind as if this was Miles' one and only warning to Kane.

As Kane seemed to unclenched his hand and quickly look down, it was clear that Miles had made his point. With a small clearing of his throat, Miles brushed past Kane as he started to climb into the driver's seat as the horses were starting to get restless. "Now then, do you two have everything you need?" Miles asked, seemingly ignoring the fact that he threatened blackmailing Kane into submission, before feeling something against his foot. Reaching down, it seemed to have been Kane's bag. "Ah, can't forget this now." Miles spoke, lowering the bag down to Kane, but the male refused to budge.

Seeing the look of shame and hurt on Kane's face, Dean couldn't simply stand there and let the other sulk. Slipping on his backpack first, Dean walked up to the two before grabbing Kane's bag. "I got it." Dean called out, holding it in his left hand before gently grabbing one of Kane's hands into his right. "Come on….we better head off to the inn and get something to eat." Dean softly spoke to Kane, trying to catch the other's attention.

When it seemed that Kane had been pulled out of his thoughts, Dean glanced up towards Miles. "Are you sure it's not too late for you to head back?" Dean asked, making some idle talk while Kane collected his thoughts, despite the fact that Kane was hurting, Dean wasn't going to let Miles win with hurting Kane in front of him again. Not like on the airship.

Feeling a gentle squeeze from Kane, Dean glanced towards Kane who sheepishly looked away. Whether it was in disgust or shame was still up for debate, but at least Kane didn't break down completely right then and there. A gentle smile landed on Dean's face, knowing that at least Kane was willing to work with him once again. Despite their time apart from avoiding each other, they could still come together and be there for one another.

"I'll be staying the night somewhere else, and then I'll be heading back home in the morning." Miles commented as he made himself comfortable on the seat. "I have a dinner meeting with Amelia though. So I'll be informing her of your visit tomorrow." Miles remarked, reaching for the reigns as he spoke. "Take care you two. Best to get inside before the rain picks up. Don't need to have the two of you getting even more wet." Miles teased in his playful tone, grabbing the hat that Kane was previously wearing and placing it on top of his head. With a small crack of the reigns, the horses were off, leaving Dean and Kane alone on the slowly emptying street.

"Come on, let's get inside before it gets too late." Dean spoke in a soft tone, a light tug on Kane's arm to coax the male into walking. It was clear that there was something lingering on Kane's mind, occupying his every thought as they made their way towards the closest inn. Dean had no right to ask what was on the other male's mind at the moment.

Glancing up at the inn in which they would be staying in, Dean noticed that the inn had a horse shoe sign that was made out of iron. The words were a bit too small for Dean to read, but it's better to head there and get settled in for the evening than stand out in the cold where either of the two males could get sick. It was clear that the two men needed to talk, especially if Dean was going to decide where he was going to stay, but Kane was shivering from both the cold and betrayal. It was more important to get the smaller male warm than to have the heavy topic laid out before them.

***

Once they had settled in for the night after a quick meal that they shared, Dean was growing worried for Kane who barely ate anything at dinner. After taking a quick shower himself, Dean was able to coax Kane into a shower to help warm him up. Dean hated seeing Kane look as if his puppy was just run over in front of him, which is exactly the expression that Kane wore after the little incident earlier. Even some of the staff noticed it, pulling Dean aside and asking him what was wrong with Kane. Dean came up with an excuse by saying that they received news that Kane's pet had passed away, easing the concern that many had watching him.

With a pair of red baggy sweat pants and black muscle shirt, Dean sat down on one of the beds with a sigh. He could still hear the shower going as the rush of water in the pipes along the wall seemed to drown out any outside noise that could be heard. Taking this time to look around, Dean took in the interior choice of the room. There were no tears in the silver and blue diamond pattern wallpaper, unlike the other places which had a bit of exposed wall in them, it seemed that this inn took care of the structure, or at the very least had the resources to take care of it.

The bed underneath felt much softer than Dean expected, almost as if the mattress was made out of some type of foam. The sheets felt as soft as silk under Dean's hand. There was a rather pleasant scent that filled the room, making Dean feel a bit relaxed the more he could smell it. Looking around, Dean was able to spot the two small vases that rested by the window that had lilacs stems from the clear water. The curtains were white with translucent coloring to allow the occupants to gaze out to the street below. The street lights underneath seemed to be the type that were gas lights, offering sporadic lighting on the street.

The white blanket that rested on the silver colored sheets felt as if Dean was resting on a cloud. How could something be this soft? Dean laid back on the cool sheets, closing his eyes as he felt some of his bones pop as if the tension was being released. Focusing on the sound of the water, Dean wondered if Kane was alright. They had been traveling together this long that it seemed like Kane was taking too long in the shower. Just as he moved to sit up, the sound of the water stopped, shortly after the sound of the shower curtain was pulled back. Even though there was steam coming out from the cracks of the bathroom door, there was a heavy cloud that could be felt coming from the bathroom.

When Kane finally emerged from the bathroom, Dean quickly stood up from the bed. Noticing that Kane was wearing a baggy t-shirt that exposed some of his shoulder. The shirt looked like it was almost two sides too big on him as the hem barely covered the bottom of his boxers. It wasn't the outfit that Dean took notice of first. It was actually the lack of piercings that once decorated Kane's ears. There were no silver small hoops or large square earrings that rested on Kane's lower earlobe. They were just completely bare. The disheveled look of the still wet locks that went this way and that showed as if Kane simply gave up. The way that Kane shuffled his feet across the floor before eventually collapsing on the second bed had Dean worried about the male. With Kane's face literally face planted into the pillows, Dean moved to sit down on the edge of the bed, his back facing away from Kane.

"Want to tell me what's wrong?" Dean asked, only receiving a small shoulder shrug from Kane. How was Dean supposed to work with that? Kane was completely shutting down, making it nearly impossible for Dean to communicate with him. Moving to sit sideways on the bed, Dean reached out to softly rub Kane's back. The heat from the steam shower seemed to linger on Kane's back as Dean softly rubbed along the spine. "Don't let what Miles said get you down Kane. You're not someone who is some type of sexual predator if that's how he made you feel." Dean was mostly taking a stab in the dark as to what was wrong, only to have Kane glanced towards Dean before sighing.

"It's not that." Kane softly spoke, moving to rest his chin against the pillows. "I've never seen him or heard him talk so harshly towards me before. Like he is disgusted by my very presence." Kane admitted, his fingers digging into pillow casing. "It's like he was someone that I didn't even know anymore. Like he was finally showing me the real person he was all this time." Kane remarked, his eyes still staring at the wall. "After everything I did for him, how much I risked for him, and he treats me as if I was the one who..." Kane couldn't even find it within himself to finish as he buried his face into the pillow once more.

Dean listened, trying to follow Kane's logic, but he couldn't find the right thing to say at this moment. The whole 'reading the room' concept wasn't exactly easy when one person knew what they were talking about and the other was lingering in the darkness. "I can't exactly speak on Miles' behalf, but I think he was trying to do you a favor." Though what that favor could be was something that Dean didn't even know himself.

"Doubt it...." Kane's reply was muffled as he pressed into the pillow. "He acts like I forcibly pinned him down and had my way with him without his consent." Kane finally spoke clearly as he turned to look at Dean. Slowly sitting up on the bed, Kane placed his finger tips against his clothed chest. "I mean, look at me! Do I look like I could push someone down against their will?" Kane asked, his eyes widened with a mixture of fear and sadness.

"I caught him off guard with a kiss once... and then he treats me harshly." Kane added, his voice wavering as he started to remember it all. "I tried to apologize to him, but he kept shutting me out. So I tried to look for you... but even you were avoiding me..." Kane continued, his gaze moving down towards the bed. "And then he goes and lies to me because he wanted to spare my feelings after all this time of stringing me along. I just don't get him." The agony on Kane's face seemed to make sense the more that Kane explained everything that was going on, resulting in Dean feeling guilty for not being there for his friend.

"Well you are pretty strong. You've been able to kick my ass during training." Dean remarked in a bit of a light hearted nature, trying his best to cheer Kane up. Though it seemed that he also failed in that. "Listen Kane, I saw...what happened that night..." Dean confessed, figuring that it was about time that they spoke about this properly. It was better than simply watching Kane suffer. "I saw the two of you talking, and then saw...the kiss..." Dean had to swallow the lump in his throat as he tried his best to not imagine that image once more.

"You...saw?" Kane asked, his voice sounding as if he was horrified that Dean witnessed it. It was like all the color had drained from Kane's face as he realized just how much he messed up. How everything was quickly spiraling out of control and that there was no way he could fix all of it. Kane's heart was pounding against his chest, the fear rising that he messed up in more ways than he originally thought.

"Yeah..." Dean quickly nodded, only to clear his throat afterwards. "I'll be honest, I was numb after seeing it. I felt as if my ears were ringing and the world just felt hollow." It was hard to recount all the emotions that Dean was feeling, but he needed to let Kane know so that they could work it out. That they would be able to bounce back from this.

"Of course I did what I always seemed to do when things often go bad for me. I ran..." Not that Dean could really go anywhere, but he avoided Kane and Miles in the process. "I needed to understand what I was feeling." Dean paused, trying to collect his thoughts in an attempt to make Kane understand. "I mean, I was ready to head straight to Amelia's place so that I could finish the task on my own. I didn't know what else to do." Hearing that, it was clear that Kane was upset at the news. The way that Kane's mouth hung partially open as if to say something, but no words seemed able to leave past his lips.

"Of course that didn't happen." Dean remarked, a light shrug of his shoulders as a faint smile graced Dean's lips. "Miles was able to catch me beforehand." Dean continued with his story, not sure if it was a good or bad thing that the two men had a deep decision while Kane was suffering by himself. "Miles told me that he had something to talk to me about, so we went to his den to talk." Dean continued, moving to lean back a bit against the bed as Dean used his left hand to help support himself.

"Miles told me his dark backstory with everything that happened to his brother and his mother...." Dean continued before clearing his throat once more. "And by the end of it, he made a pretty good point that I shouldn't be angry at you or Miles because frankly, we're nothing more than friends." Dean had to swallow the harsh reality that he couldn't argue with that point, but it didn't help to wash away the bitterness that it lingered in Dean's mouth. "Then in the carriage, he made some random metaphor about boats and crews that made sense, but it still didn't take the pain away. Not at first anyways." After all, how could it? Dean never told Kane how he felt after all this time.

"What do you mean?" Kane asked, his brows knitting in confusion as he tried to follow Dean's logic with everything Dean was telling him, but it still wasn't clicking. But when Dean turned to look fully at Kane, the leader stopped all thoughts that were running through his mind. The look on Dean's face wasn't angry or disgusted, but rather peaceful, as if Dean was accepting himself for who he was for once.

"What I'm trying to say is that I like you Kane." The words weren't easy to say, but Dean had to express how he was feeling towards Kane that would allow the leader to know how Dean felt. "That, I have come to know myself a lot more because you were always by my side." Dean started off, a small flustered look crossing his face as he continued.

"When you're not beside me, I feel like a part of the person I've become vanishes, leaving this empty husk behind that just goes on auto-pilot." Dean didn't know if he was making sense at this point, but he wanted to get his feelings out one way or another. "I'm not really the best at saying how I feel, or even really knowing if what I am feeling is right..." Dean started to trail off, his nerves starting to get the best of him.

"Or if I even know what I'm feeling since I never got a chance to understand myself until I got here." Dean continued with a nervous chuckle towards the end. Reaching out to gently grab Kane's hand, Dean was starting to collect his nerves the longer that Kane was by his side. "But what I do know is that I care a lot about you. You've helped me to become a better person." Dean admitted, studying Kane's face the more Dean spoke about his feelings. "Before, I was full of bitterness and anger. But seeing this world and getting to know you, that anger and spite is gone." Dean admitted, giving Kane's hand a light squeeze.

"I'm still trying to figure out everything, and I don't know how to properly express my feelings. But if you give me a chance, I'd like to have a more proper relationship with you." Dean continued, his eyes focused on Kane's. "I want to experience the joys of living each day with you. To sail on a ship just for us. Whether we face stormy weather or calm seas. Have rough patches of ice to dig through, or tread through rocky streams. I want to do it all with you." Dean continued, moving his other hand to lightly cup Kane's cheek. With a small smile on his face, and a tilt of his head, Dean waited for Kane to answer.

Watching as some of the life came back into those silver eyes, a small smile seemed to creep on Kane's face. "You know Dean, as gay as I am, that was super gay." Kane teased, a bit of laughter escaping his lips as he saw the shocked expression on Dean's face. "Did you take that out of one of my romance books? Because that was super cheesy." Kane teased once more, moving to wrap his arms around Dean's shoulders, preventing Dean from getting off of the bed with a flustered look on his face.

"I'm trying to cheer you up and confess my feelings, and that's how you treat me?" Dean asked, his tone a bit huffy as he was quickly brought back down onto the bed. "If my dad said that to my mom, she would have probably swooned over him." Dean continued in a huffed tone. As the dark cloud that seemed to hang over Kane slowly disappeared, Dean was at least relieved that he could bring back the smile on Kane's face. It felt like ages since Dean was able to hear Kane laughing once again. Even longer seeing that smile on Kane's face.

After a few minutes, Dean cleared his throat once more as he figured he would be a bit more blunt with his question. "You never gave me an answer though, on whether or not you would want to be in a relationship with me. Where you would let me be your partner...." Dean trailed off, his heart beating against his chest as he looked up at Kane. Dean's face felt hot like he came out of the shower while his eyes studied Kane's movement in response to his question. The silence in the room felt like it was lasting an eternity.

With a small swing of his hips, Kane straddled Dean's waist as Kane braced himself to hover over Dean. "Well, let me think." Kane spoke, a coy smile lingering on his lips as he moved to be a few inches away from Dean's face. "Permission to come aboard?" Kane asked, his voice a little husked as he closed his eyes halfway. Seeing the embarrassed and flustered expression on Dean's face, Kane smiled as he tilted his head. "Yes, I would love for you to be my partner. That is, if you can handle me." With a small chuckle, Kane moved to rest his forehead on Dean's chest. Was it wrong to enjoy this banter? That this type of flirting was suiting? It didn't exactly matter what anyone else thought, if this was what made them happy, then so be it.

THE next morning had come quickly. Dean had changed into something a bit more fitting than the sweat covered clothes he was wearing the other day. With a pair of slightly faded dark blue jeans, Dean wore a buttoned up long sleeved white shirt with the sleeves rolled up to his elbows. Wearing a dark gray vest with black buttons, the hem of the vest neatly covered the shirt that was currently tucked into his pants. Around Dean's neck was a dark blue and silver pinstripe tie that was slightly loose as to keep Dean from feeling as if he was going to be hung by it. With his backpack over his shoulders Dean headed out of the inn while Kane rested from their intimate night together.

Walking along the streets as his boots splashed against some of the lingering puddles from yesterday, Dean headed towards the large clock tower that was visible from his location. It may not have been the tallest building around, but it was more intact than the buildings surrounding it. The interface of the clock was clear, acting like a large window that anyone could see inside and take note of the wooden interior. Some of the numbers had long since faded, yet the black hands of the clock still seemed to work.

Vines seemed to make their way up the sides of the building, offering light blue and purple flowers that were scattered among the green vibrant leaves. The outer rim of the clock glistened from the gold in the sunlight. On top of the clock tower rested a bell that was completely covered in moss, giving the impression that it hasn't been used in a long time. Watching as white birds scattered past the top of the clock tower, Dean couldn't even begin to tell what type of birds they were supposed to be from the distance they flew overhead.

Rounding the corner of a building that led to the clock tower, Dean was able to spot the large fountain that Miles had described the other day in front of it. It was exactly how Miles described it, but there was something more to it. With the scattered clouds hovering overhead, the true beauty of the global fountain seemed to become more evident when the sun started to peek out from behind the clouds.

Walking up to the large crystal fountain, the water seemed to make the planet that was made up of various scattered islands shine brightly. Just watching the fountain spin ever so slightly seemed to highlight just how beautiful this planet has become. Unlike the fountain on the Millennium, the one that seemingly screamed death and betrayal that shimmered in gold, this fountain gave Dean hope. Tracing the different crystals, Dean was able to get an understanding of how much the various leaders controlled. Looking down at a small plaque sign, Dean noticed a little inscription written in beautiful cursive: **Left To Be Divided, Came Together United.** It was rather short but beautifully described as to what Dean had seen.

Glancing up at the clock tower, Dean sighed as he knew the next part to come was facing Amelia on his own. He could have Kane come with him, but it would simply be best if Dean met with her alone. He was already able to get the approval of the others on his own, so maybe Amelia would be like the rest. Though remembering how she reacted at the banquet, maybe it would have been a better choice to Kane there. Mentally shaking his head, Dean knew that he had to face this final part alone.

Quickly crossing the street, Dean went up the brick steps towards the door resting just below the large clock. On the door was a strange logo that Dean never seen before. Taking a closer look at the logo, it almost resembled some type of family crest. In the middle was a bear that seemed to stretch its mouth open wide with its teeth visible. Inside of the mouth was the frame that had a ribbon design that waved in and out of the crests' badge. The top of the crest had a line of roses with thorns tracing along the edge of the bottom of the badge. It looked as if it was professionally done with details that one would almost expect from one of the members of the Elite. Remember what Keaton stated about Amelia's grandmother being originally from the Elite class, it seemed to match up with what Dean knew of the monsters in charge on the station.

Grasping onto the curved handle of the door, Dean pulled it open before heading inside. Glancing above him at the different gears seemingly turning to the seconds on the clock, Dean was surprised that it wasn't louder. In fact, it felt more like there was a small dull roar in the building with a constant ticking that could easily turn to white noise. As much as Dean would have loved to see more of the gears working with individual pieces to make the clock function after all this time, the ticking of the clock was just a regular reminder that he was starting to run out of time.

Spotting a singular woman sitting behind a desk, Dean started to head in her direction. Maybe she could point Dean in the right direction if he was in the right place. As he got closer, Dean noticed that the woman seemed to be absorbed into her book, failing to realize that Dean was standing in front of her desk. The woman's brunette hair was pulled back into a tight ponytail. By the looks of it her hair would be roughly shoulder length if it was down.

Small silver hooped earrings barely dangled from her earlobes. Besides the light blue faded jeans that clung to the woman's slender and petite frame, she wore a dark gray cardigan sweater with the smallest hint of a white shirt underneath. Upon her face rested a pair of thick glasses. Slender fingers pressed into the pages to keep it in place as steel gray eyes scanned the words that were printed on the pages. This girl seemed a bit on the meekly side, which was a nice change of pace from the rather loud company Dean had to deal with.

With a small clearing of his throat, Dean was able to catch the woman's attention. "Uh, hi." Dean started out, watching as the woman quickly slid the bookmark into the page and set the book aside. "I'm looking for the leader of the Greed clan, Amelia Park. Is this the right place to see her?" Dean asked, though he noticed that the woman was starting to frantically look for something amongst the small mounds of papers and books that decorated the woman's desk. It seems like Dean caught her a bit off guard as she seemed to look for something under the scattered documents.

"Sorry," The woman was quick to apologize as she found a clipboard that looked as if it had been rung through the ringer a few times. Pieces of the corner were broken or chipped away, appearing as if some of the pieces were being held together by tape. "If you could just, sign your name on the visitor sheet." The woman spoke, her voice a bit flustered as she grabbed a pen for Dean to use. "Sorry again, it's just, I was told we weren't expecting anyone for today." The woman quickly apologized before taking a deep breath in. "Unless, your name is Dean Torres, correct?" She asked, glancing up to see Dean's face as the male started to write his name on the sheet.

"Yeah. I'm here to talk to Amelia about some important matters." Dean didn't exactly want to go into details about what he was meeting the head of the other clans for. "Can I head up?" Dean asked once he was done and set the clipboard back down on the desk. Dean figured that the woman would be more comfortable with staying behind the desk to get back to her book more than anything else, though she did seem to be eager to guide Dean if he needed it.

"Oh yeah, just push the second to the top button to get to the floor where Amelia is on. The top button takes you to the roof and the doors won't budge open." The woman remarked, giving Dean the directions he needed in order to reach the right floor. As Dean turned to walk away, the woman noticed the skull that Dean had connected to his backpack. "Oh, before I forget." The woman called out, causing Dean to stop and look at her over his shoulder. "You'll want to make sure to wear the skull mask before you reach the top. It's an unspoken rule that those who go up have to wear theirs before being approved."

"Really?" Dean asked, raising one of his eyebrows in surprise. "Thanks for the heads up." Dean remarked with a small wave. Pressing the button to call the elevator down, Dean swung his backpack over to take the skull off. It was surprising that Dean didn't get a chance to wear the mask often even though he went through all that trouble to take down the large mountain goat.

As the elevator reached the floor, and Dean did as he was instructed, Dean felt as if time was slowing down the moment he got onto the elevator. Putting on the skull, Dean raised his head to watch the numbers go up one by one. The elevator creaked against each floor, causing a little concern to rise in Dean. What if the cable snapped or something? Dean couldn't let his story end this way. Taking a few deep breaths, Dean steadied his nerves, knowing that freaking out wouldn't help anything right now.

Stepping off of the elevator, Dean was greeted with the sound of a cello lightly playing off in the distance. The smell of wood shavings and coffee lingered in the air as Dean cautiously walked on the wooden floor that had a few small holes in it. Peering down the hole, Dean could see the top of the gears continuing to turn below. How could anyone be so calm working in a place that felt like one step could lead to a very painful death?

Trying to ignore those types of thoughts, Dean made his way towards the sound of the music playing. Though seeing how many books seemed to span throughout the tower's layout wasn't exactly reassuring that he would find Amelia. What if she was hiding behind them?

Watching where he stepped, and using his surroundings to find the right path that led him towards a more open area, Dean was able to spot Amelia right away. Towering over some of the books on a higher landing, Amelia was studying an emerald with what looked to be a miniature spy glass over her right eye. Dark red nails seemed to stand out against the green gem that Amelia was holding, causing Dean to wonder how someone who seemed to be disgusted with wearing anything that was deemed too feminine would still do her nails. It was only when Dean stepped on a creaky board that Amelia seemed to notice someone was close by over the soft cello music playing on an old record near to where Amelia sat.

"Crystal, sweetheart, I don't need any more coffee. If you want to come and grab a book, you can do without both-" Amelia started to speak, before her eyes adjusted to see Dean standing in front of her. "Oh..." Amelia trailed off as a small disgruntled tone and displeased facial expression swept over her face. Though taking note that Dean was wearing the skull of the mountain goat, and how it seemed to be custom made already, Amelia did raise an eyebrow which indicated that she was rather curious to see how far Dean had come since their last encounter at the banquet. "I see you've decided to become one of us." Amelia remarked, moving to tilt her chair back enough to put her feet up onto the desk.

Black laced boots kicked up onto the table, the studs that dug into the side of the boots appeared to be either chipped or missing. Tight black camouflage pants that had part bits of brown and green hidden in the black hugged Amelia's legs. There was a leather gun holster attached to Amelia's right leg, though no gun could be found. Whether it was hiding under some papers or didn't simply exist at all was still undetermined. The belt that Amelia wore had the left side of the belt lined with bullets that wrapped around the front part of her hip.

The hooded top she was wearing was black as it showed off her tanned shoulders as the holes of the top exposed the bony edges of her shoulders as it dipped down to her mid bicep. The hem of the top rested just shy of her belly button, exposing her torso as the zipper of the hood rested just shy above her cleavage. The hem of the sleeves rested just above her elbows. There was a small yet distinct sound of metal chains that rubbed against the wooden chair Amelia sat on. Amelia's brunette hair was braided along the side as her hair clung to her right shoulder. It seemed that her hair had gotten even longer as it rested against her right breast. Light silver eyes followed Dean's movements as he got closer.

"Well, I figured it would show you that I was serious about joining you." Dean remarked, a small shrug of his shoulders as Dean slid his hands into his pockets where he had the envelope that Miles gave him. "I'm sure you more than anyone would want to get their revenge on the Elite for what they have done to humanity." Of course Dean wasn't going to bring up the fact that Amelia's family was directly affected by the Elite from the impression that Keaton gave him.

"And why would you say that?" Amelia asked, reaching a hand out as if to demand for the envelope to be handed to her. "Let me guess, my stupid lover said something, didn't he? Perhaps spilling out a detail that he shouldn't have been sharing in the first place?" Amelia asked, watching as Dean fumbled with the envelope that got stuck in his pants. Seems like Amelia was sharp with her intuition after all.

"Yeah...but I wasn't going to ask." Dean remarked, handing the envelope over Amelia who proceeded to take the envelope without much incident. "But I am a bit curious as to how someone who was in the Elite could be banished from the station. I mean, I can see why they would do it for those who are in the Bronze section, or rarely with those of the Silver class. But to banish someone to their death that was an Elite member? What could someone in the Elite rank do that was so bad to warrant their death?" The only plausible excuse that Dean could come up with was that the person didn't fall in line with the rest of the Elites' views.

As Amelia opened the envelope while Dean was talking, it appeared that he hit a bit of a nerve with the questions. "It's simple." Amelia spoke, not even bothering to look at Dean as she folded the paper open. "It's because my grandmother went against them." Dean didn't know how he was supposed to internalize that type of response. There were a couple of ways that Amelia's grandmother could have gone against the Elite, the fact that she wasn't clarifying it left Dean to glance off to the side in thought. As Amelia glanced over to look at Dean, she sighed as she couldn't focus on the paperwork in front of her with someone who looked preoccupied.

"My grandmother didn't like the way that the Elite were treating the Bronze class." Amelia continued, though the annoyance in her tone was apparent. "She hooked up with a man from the bronze class because she didn't want to be another baby making machine to the Elitist ass-holes that surrounded her." Dean didn't know which he should have been surprised with. The fact that someone from the Elite class willingly hooked up with someone in the Bronze class, or the fact that women in the Elite class were nothing more than baby makers.

"Because my grandmother fucked a lower class servant, resulting in her getting pregnant, she had the same type of accident as you." Amelia continued, placing the paper down on top of her stomach. "However, she was being disowned by the people she called family, rather than having someone else kill her off that wasn't part of the Elite members." Amelia continued as she started to gently rock the chair on the last two legs while reading the form. "Upon crashing on the planet, she lost the baby she was carrying." Amelia spoke glancing towards Dean at the end of it.

"Wow. I didn't think that the Elite would go that far simply because she slept with someone who was lower class." Dean remarked, feeling a bit bad now for assuming something when he didn't know all the facts. Then again, Dean didn't know the rules that the Elite had to follow. It seems that knowledge was something that only Amelia would know about. "It's pretty bad crashing on a planet. Then to go as far as to lose a child, I couldn't imagine going through something like that.." Not that Dean had to worry about that sort of thing. But he could only imagine what could have been going through the woman's mind at the time.

"My grandmother was always a tough woman no matter what happened." Amelia commented, lowering herself back down on the chair. "She passed it off as a loose thread so that she didn't have to worry about it." Amelia remarked, bluntly. "As a coping method I guess." In a world where anything could happen, people had to find ways of dealing with their problems one way or another.

"Eventually she met my grandfather before having my father, who introduced her to Nero." Amelia continued to explain, not divulging the details as there was no need for Amelia to explain her grandmother's sob story. " The two of them came up with the system of several leaders to hold some type of accountability for their land, and to produce different types of crops that would benefit the growing population as we looked to reopen the shelters and bring people back. To make something great once more." The hostility seemed to waver from Amelia as she focused her attention on reading the paper to make sure she collected the information on said paper.

"Seems like you're grandmother knew what she was doing then. It's amazing just how much you guys were able to achieve on your own without alerting the Elite." Dean spoke, placing his hands against his waist. He could see Amelia's eyes move back and forth reading the page. Her eyes were a lot like Kane's, though Amelia's had a sharper glance to them.

"It was a lot of trial and error, but we eventually got a system working." Amelia spine nonchalantly about it. "Normally people who are in power want to pass it along to their families, but we decided that if anyone wanted to take over, we would start to show them the ropes." Amelia spoke up, grabbing the cup of coffee that lingered close by, only to bring it close to her lips as she continued to speak.

"But apparently it was too much work or hard for people to remember, so they would back off and allow us to lead them again." Amelia finished before closing her eyes to enjoy the coffee. "People started to realize that there wasn't much benefit in being a leader of the clan. therefore, they settle on allowing us children to make decisions that would benefit the clans as a whole. After all, they discovered their particular needs were a small drop in the bucket compared to everything else that was going on." Amelia finished before an audible sip could be heard from the cup. It seemed that Amelia did that when she was annoyed by something, and in this case, it was Dean.

The more that Dean listened to Amelia, it was clear that the leaders weren't being selfish at all. Sure there was some appeal of power that people thought was there, but remembering how large the Earth is and how much of the land was divided up into clans, there was a lot to consider in the way of goods that was produced in the clans, as well as making sure that the members were satisfied in how their issues were being addressed. For those who may not have been able to make time to see the leaders through the year, the banquet was a good way to make sure that those who could make it could have their issues addressed to the leaders personally. It was like a community coming together to make something amazing work.

"Now then," Amelia spoke as she set the cup down. "As you have visited the other clans, I'd like you to rate the clans from one to six in which you would be open to living in. After I say their name, give me a number and a reason why so I can write it down." Amelia instructed as she moved to lean back in her chair once more after fishing out a pen on her rather messy desk.

Dean was a bit nervous as Amelia seemed to tilt back, but it wasn't like he was able to say anything to her. "Ready?" Amelia asked, glancing over towards Dean who gave her a small nod of his head. Clearing her throat, Amelia placed the pen on the paper "Envy." The first one seemed like it would be in alphabetical order if Amelia was starting with that clan.

"I would say that would be a four." Dean commented, though he took note of the stern glance from Amelia as Dean didn't offer her a reason why. "Mostly because I'm not that very artistic. Even though I do enjoy the art and the concept of having some type of car is fascinating, I just can't find myself feeling like I would be beneficial there." Dean added, figuring that was a suitable answer for Amelia. The way that Amelia jotted the answer down as Dean spoke was rather impressive, but Dean knew to keep his mouth quiet as Amelia was wrapping up.

"Gluttony?" Amelia asked, raising an eyebrow as she figured that it would rank high on Dean's preference list. Not that she would have been wrong, but considering their new relationship, it felt like Dean was playing favorites.

"One." Dean quickly remarked before clearing his throat. "Mostly because I like growing food and it was something I picked up while living in the Silver class with my parents." Though it was a good excuse, Dean wasn't exactly sure if he should even comment on the fact that he was very much interested in continuing a relationship with the leader. Even if things don't play out in Dean's favor, he could still at least find something to do in the clan.

"You sure farming is the only thing you're interested in?" Amelia asked, moving her pen to gently tap it against a particular area on her neck. "Because it seems like you're more than interested in the farming aspect of it." Amelia remarked, causing a flustered look to grow on Dean's face. Not like he could deny it. There were a few marks that lingered from last night, but it wasn't any of Amelia's business.

Dean glanced away as he cleared his throat, indicating that he knew he was caught, but Amelia would just ignore it for now. "How would you rate my Greed clan? I know you haven't been here very long, but we do offer courses on how to grow a business." Amelia started with her selling points. "If you're looking more into being able to bring peace, we do have a type of police force that goes through a long training program that covers all kinds of situations to resolve issues peacefully. Or if those don't suit your needs, we also have a course which allows you to assist the leaders." Amelia seemed as if she was pushing for Dean to rate her clan a bit higher than she might expect him to rank it.

"I'd say a three." Dean remarked with a small smile on his face. "Not that I got to see much, but I think that if I were to want to learn a more useful skill, I wouldn't mind getting to know more about your clan and what you have to offer." Dean added, seeing a bit of tension in Amelia's face lessen. Was she expecting Dean to rate it lower? Seeing as how they weren't exactly starting out on the best of terms, it was unexpected to see Dean rate it so high.

"How about Lust?" Amelia asked, after jotting down the notes for the last two. It seemed that Amelia was easy to side track when she was trying to do some actual business that didn't seem to pertain to her own clan.

"A six. I'm not exactly the type of guy who likes to go about and party." Dean remarked, figuring that there wasn't much else to it. "Sure learning about how to give birth properly is a necessity, but I feel that I couldn't exactly handle the stress of so many people and the loud music playing all the time. Not to mention the dangerous crater close by with the toxic fumes." Just remembering how close he came into falling into the toxic area still gave Dean a bit of anxiety.

"Fair enough. Those who usually rate Lust high are the type who enjoy the thrill of the unknown." Amelia commented as she wrote down the explanation Dean gave her. "And how did you feel about the Pride clan?" Amelia asked, moving her pen towards the pride section, Amelia figured that Dean was ready to give it a two, considering that Dean was rather prideful when he first got there. At least, according to the reports given to her it seemed that way.

"A five." Dean remarked with a small shrug, but he could see the hint of surprise on Amelia as she had to adjust the placement of her pen. "Even though the idea of being able to build or craft spectacular devices is great, I just don't feel like I could offer much to Felicia." Dean remarked, watching as Amelia softly nodded her head at his explanation. "That place is like a well fined machine and I'm just not the right part for the job." Amelia seemed to be a bit speechless as she moved to put the five in Pride, leaving Sloth to be second.

"So you want Sloth as your second choice?" Amelia asked, raising an eyebrow. "That's honestly a first. Normally people rate Sloth as a one, three, or five." Amelia admitted as she wrote the number down. "So why would you rate Sloth as second?" Amelia asked, wondering if perhaps Miles was able to sweet talk Dean into giving him a higher mark.

"Well, it still deals with plants." Dean remarked as he watched Amelia scribble on the paper while tilting back a bit further. "But in a way, the aspect of being able to help make some medicine to help everyone is something that I know my dad would be into. After all, he was one of the few morticians on the station." If Dean was going to make sure that he could save people, why not use plants to do it? Besides, Dean never could deal with the stench of dead bodies, so he would have to use some of his medical knowledge he got from the books to be of some use.

"Hm," Amelia hummed as she quickly finished writing down the comment before pulling out a drawer from her desk. "I have to say, it's rather nice knowing that someone from the Silver and Bronze class wants to help us take back the control from the Elite." Amelia continued to speak before pausing. "But I have to ask," Amelia asked, pulling out a stamp and ink pad.

"Why do you want to kill the last remaining humans aboard the United Space Station Millennium?" Amelia started to ask her question, but didn't give Dean a chance to reply before she continued with her questions. "In doing so, you risk not only killing hundreds of thousands of innocent people if not more, but you risk collateral damage anywhere that the station lands on. Is it out of vengeance? Out of anger, or fear? Why put everyone on the planet they left for dead at risk if your plan doesn't work?"

Dean stood there in silence, trying to figure out the best way to answer Amelia since he wasn't exactly sure of his answers now. Beforehand he would have simply said that he wanted to get back at those who wronged him. To kill the people who killed his parents. He was full of anger and hatred, wanting to get back at those who tried to kill him. But being on Earth, traveling around to different places and seeing how much people were able to learn to adapt, Dean didn't know what he had going for him anymore. Taking a deep breath, Dean lowered his shoulders, relaxing his body as he studied Amelia's face. She was expecting some type of answer from him, so Dean might as well give her one.

"Because people here deserve a chance to be able to spread their wings again." Dean remarked, a gentle shrug of his shoulder since he knew that it might not be an acceptable answer, but it was something that he had noticed. "I want to see what great advancements humanity can still make." Dean remarked with a genuine smile on his face. "With everything being destroyed, and years of technological advances brought to a sudden stop, I want to see humanity excel once more." Dean continued, watching Amelia's expression to see if he was winning her over. "To live in a world that I know can be even better than where it was left off when the bombs dropped. That's what I want more than anything now." Dean was speaking from his heart. He didn't want to see the people who were left behind to continue to hide from the ever watching eye of the Elites.

Amelia listened to his Dean's words. Studying his face and body language to see if he was trying to give her some type of reason that was supposed to make her feel sympathetic to Dean. Keeping the stamp on top of the ink pad, Amelia planted the chair on the ground. Glancing from the papers in front of her to Dean, it seemed as if Amelia was debating on whether or not it would be beneficial to allow Dean into their community. Was he a threat or an ally?

Folding her hands in front of her face, Amelia lightly tapped her foot, listing off the pros and cons in her head before finally reaching a decision. Taking the stamp, Amelia pressed it into the ink pad once more before stamping the seal on Dean's papers. "You better not prove me wrong."Amelia muttered under breath as she stood up from her seat while allowing the ink to dry. "Congratulations Dean Torres. You're now officially one of us." Amelia spoke, though she sounded as if she was in a hurry. Collecting some papers from a small bin, Amelia started to make her way towards a seating area.

"Follow me." Amelia instructed, her boots pounding against the floor. Was she angry that Dean was accepted? It wasn't like Dean was able to read minds or anything, but the way that Amelia seemed to react to giving Dean the news indicated that she wasn't exactly thrilled at the idea of having him join the clans. Not like Dean could really blame her. With everything that had been going on, it was like letting some outsider that you didn't know much about coming in and acting like a spy for your enemy.

Following Amelia towards the sitting area, Dean pushed the skull up to rest on his head as it tilted backwards. The skull was starting to get heavy and Dean didn't understand how anyone could wear the skull around for hours if need be. The spot they went to seemed to be littered in books, giving Dean the impression that Amelia was a bookworm, but he kept his mouth silent about it. Watching Amelia take one of the chairs, Dean took one that was situated across from Amelia. The seat felt as if it had been worn down from constant use, but it wasn't as if Dean was going to sit there for hours on end, or at the very least he hoped not.

"So, guess it's time for you to hear about my awful truth now." Amelia huffed, seemingly hating herself for making the deal with the other leaders. "Considering that I made a little bet with Kane, I never go back on my word." Amelia remarked, moving to rub her hands against her legs as if she was trying to wash off blood from her hands. The way that Amelia's hands clenched and released indicated that her nerves were rattled. The normally cool, calm, and collective Amelia seemed to be struggling through an anxiety attack.

"Amelia, you don't have to-" Dean spoke up, only to cut his sentence off when Amelia raised a hand up. Dean blinked in surprise, not sure what he should do since it wasn't like he could exactly tell her to stop. A bet's a bet after all, and Amelia had lost.

"I have to Dean." Amelia spoke, her voice a bit shaky as she collected her thoughts. "You learned about some bits of and pieces of what happened five years ago. It's only fair you hear the last bit." Amelia stated, taking one last quick breath as if it would be enough to calm her nerves. Whether or not Dean wanted to hear what happened, he knew it would put everything into perspective. Why the leaders acted in certain ways. The fate of what happened to Ashley's mother, and everything else that followed afterwards. To learn about the dramatic change would be the final piece of the puzzle that Dean needed for the bigger picture.

CHAPTER TWENTY: *Sins Of The Past*

With Lily Greenlee in custody for the brutal murder of her husband with an attempted murder of her daughter Ashley Greenlee, the poor woman sat alone in a cage. The stone floor was cold and wet from the rain that seeped in from the street. A storm seemed to be blowing outside. With her hands bound to the wall, Lily could feel the iron shackles digging into her wrists. Her short blonde hair peeked out of the bandage wrap from the wound she received thanks to James' attempt to save Ashley. Large hand prints were imprinted onto her neck from when Michael tried to strangle her. Even while locked up she could still feel those hands trying to squeeze the life out of her, causing spouts of coughing fits and wheezing to echo in the semi-empty hall. The torn up black and white striped scrubs she wore were slightly baggy against Lily's thin and frail frame. The so called blanket rested underneath Lily was wet and cold, leaving her with hardly any warmth in that cell.

A man stood just outside of Lily's cell, gazing in on the Envy's leader in her sorry state. With medium length blond hair whose bangs broke evenly over his eyes, and piercing yellow eyes and sun-kissed skin the man had a concerned look about him as he reached out to grasp the cold bars. Wearing a dark robe that had white flowers spread along the bottom with blue butterflies scattered among the fabric, the man let out a small sigh as his fingers dug into the iron bars more.

"First Lucas, and now you." The man whispered to himself, his eyes glancing down to the puddle by Lily's feet. The man could see her hollowed gaze that seemed to linger in her eyes. "Just what the hell is going on? Why is everyone losing their mind?" The man asked himself out loud. It felt like everything was going crazy as the division among the survivors seemed to grow. Despite their best efforts to make everything change for the better, it always felt like the current leaders were facing an uphill battle.

"So this is where you've been Elijah." A man called out to Elijah, his voice echoing ever so slightly along the stone walls. The man was wearing a gray buttoned up shirt with white pinstripes that went down the man's body vertically. The first two buttons were undone as the shirt seemed to be tucked into some dark formal slacks. The man's feet were covered from getting wet by a pair of boots that peeked out from the hem of the pants. Unfortunately for Elijah, he was wearing some sandals with thin white socks that were getting wet from the ground. "How's Lily holding up? Is she talking yet?" The man asked, reaching Elijah's side to gaze at the woman.

"I didn't know you were here Ryan." Elijah spoke to the man, his eyes glancing towards his companion. Ryan Mayworth who was the leader of the Sloth clan while Elijah Flores was the leader of Gluttony. Like Celia, Ryan's hair was silver though it seemed that Ryan's hair was a shade darker than hers. Ryan's eyes were a piercing dark gray that Miles had gotten from him. With ivory white skin, the man seemed to glow even in darkness.

"Not good, if I'm being honest." Elijah started to speak, answering Ryan's question as the man reached the leader. "She seems to be cut off from reality at the moment. Almost like she doesn't even know where she is." Elijah remarked, moving the subject back towards Lily. "She looks as if she has completely checked out of this world. Much like Kane when I first arrived home..." Elijah closed his eyes, mentally shaking his head as he wanted to be free from that image. Even now it was a hard topic to think about.

"Can you really blame her though?" Ryan remarked, glancing towards Elijah with a concerned look on his face. "Her husband tried to kill her in a drunken state." It wasn't a good excuse, but with the evidence at hand, it was hard not to find some sort of sympathy for their friend. "If it wasn't for the kids..." Ryan trailed off, visibly shaking his head as he didn't even want to think about it. "She was desperate to survive. She wasn't in the right headspace." Ryan continued, as if trying to make some sort of sense about all of this.

"Makes me wonder what my son's head space was when.." Elijah spoke, though his words were soft and quiet as his mind went back to that night. The night in which he arrived home to see his home in nothing more than burned frames and Kane barely able to speak or look at him. It took everything in Elijah not to break down once he had seen the charcoaled remains of his family. Even now, when he was supposed to focus on deciding the fate of a dear friend, Elijah's mind always wondered towards the night that he was too late to save his family.

"That wasn't your fault Eli." Ryan quickly remarked, trying to snap Elijah back from that memory. "You don't know what happened." Ryan tried his best to reassure Elijah, but even Ryan knew that it was hard not to think about that night. "Miles has been trying his best to help Kane return back to normal. Though it's been especially tough on him dealing with his mother after the death of Parker." Ryan remarked, shoving his hands into the pockets of his pants. "It makes me wonder if life is just being cruel to us as a way to deter us from surviving in this world...." The way that everything has been going wrong lately, it made Ryan feel like nothing was ever good enough anymore.

"I know I had no control over what happened that night Ry." Elijah remarked, his eyes focused on the puddle closest to him. "But seeing Lily's face like that..." Elijah spoke, pointing a finger towards Lily. "It's exactly the same look Kane had after that night. You can't expect me to just back and let everyone condemn Lily when she looks that pitiful..." Elijah sighed, pressing his forehead against the cold iron bar. There was a lingering scent of rust from bits of the iron starting to rust from all the rain pouring in.

"It's the look of someone who has tunnel vision into a black hole." Elijah continued, taking a step forward to let his foot rest against the metal frame. "There's no light for her to head towards. Her mind will simply recall everything that happened in an attempt to try and figure out how things could have been different." Elijah continued, though he didn't know what was really going on in Lily's mind.

"I can only imagine the choices that she is reflecting on, trying to see if perhaps there could have been a better ending than this one. Where she could still be with her kids rather than sitting in an empty and lonely jail cell..." Elijah reflected on his own words, hoping that perhaps after this was all said and done, Kane would eventually open up to him once more. To tell him what exactly happened without the fear of being judged.

"Well, would you rather have Kane stare off into the void like Lily is right now or have Kane be an uncontrollable sobbing mess that can barely get up and function?" Ryan asked, moving to press his back against the iron bars. "You can't just expect Kane to get over something that traumatic overnight." Ryan remarked, resting his head against the cold bars. "You just have to give him time Eli." Ryan continued, trying his best to cheer the other man up.

"You don't want Kane shutting down completely like Lily, right?" Ryan asked, turning his head to look at Elijah with a straight face. "I know you. You would never want to see Kane sitting in the darkness while time passes by, barely eating anything or wanting nothing more than to make the suffering end." Ryan was speaking out of experience from witnessing his own wife recoil into herself like Lily was right now.

"After all, that's what I'm dealing with. Seeing how Rosa is handling Parker's death, it's hard on her. It's hard on even me, because I wasn't there to save my youngest boy..." Ryan commented, closing his eyes as he tried not to think about it. "When I'm home, I stay close to her, you know?" Ryan paused as he averted his gaze to look at the wall ahead of him. "I hold her close to me as she cries." Ryan paused, swallowing the lump in his throat.

"It pains me because there is nothing I can do when we're called out here away from our loved ones. It makes me feel like a failure as both a leader and a husband..." Ryan continued, the lump in his throat getting hotter the more he thought about it, but Elijah couldn't offer his friend support.

"Seems like we both know what it feels like to be helpless." Elijah finally spoke up, trying to break the tension. "This job isn't exactly easy on us, that I know all too well..." Elijah spoke, letting out a soft sigh as he twisted his hand on the metal bar once more. "We can't stay in the capital all the time. We have to make sure that our people get the supplies needed to make sure that the locust don't destroy the crops above ground once again." Elijah spoke, stepping back from the bars as he let go of them.

"But it seems that Nero is doing everything possible to anger Alan. Making it seem like he'll force Alan into agreeing that the best action to handle this swiftly, is to agree to killing Lily." Elijah didn't like the fact that only one of the seven leaders was asking for violence. "A life for a life doesn't seem like it is a fair decision if you ask me." Elijah muttered to himself as he turned away from Lily, facing the same wall that Ryan was gazing at. "That feels like all Nero wants to do is just kill off those who he thinks are not worthy or strong enough in his eyes. I don't understand why Davis even agreed to take Nero with him to finish up their mission." The man was clearly unstable since he left the shelter fifteen years ago.

"It's not exactly easy to forgive someone for taking a life, Eli." Ryan spoke, almost bitterly as he pushed himself off of the wall, bits of his clothing wet from the surface. "I regret every single day for letting that guy off for accidentally killing Parker. But it seemed like he was willing to repent for his actions and accepted being exiled rather than face death." Crossing his arms over his chest, it was clear that Ryan wasn't over it. But the damage was done, and it wasn't worth killing the poor hunter for it. "I'm sure Rosa hates me every single day for letting that man go without killing him, but it won't bring my son back."

Elijah softly nodded his head, knowing that there was no way to make this right without someone getting hurt. "Come on, let's head back up to the surface." Elijah spoke, pushing himself off the bars as he walked through some of the scattered puddles along the way. "I'm sure this dark and gloomy place isn't the best atmosphere to talk about these sorts of heavy subjects right now." Elijah remarked, glancing towards Lily one last time before walking past Ryan.

The sound of his feet shuffling against the floor echoed against the walls before being joined in by Ryan following him. It wasn't like Elijah didn't understand what was going on through Ryan's mind as they talked about forgiveness and death, but with the negative air in the holding cells seemed to amplify the negative mood, making them feel worse about this whole situation.

Upon reaching the top of the steps, the two men stopped to retrieve their skulls masks that they were to wear while in the town hall where the leaders often discussed important matters. Ryan was quick to pick his skull mask up. It was that of a cow skull that had rather small horns that were barely an inch in length. The nose of the skull had a metal ring around it while bits of green crystals decorated the eye sockets. Small black feathers dangled round the base of the small horns. Elijah's skull mask was that of a mountain lion with bits of red crystals seemingly filling the gaps of the skull as there was black paint streaked around the openings of the eyes and the nose.

"I still can't believe you were so lazy that you used the cow you raised and then slaughtered for the meat as the first animal you killed." Elijah remarked, watching as Ryan worked to make sure that it fit just right. "I know you're the leader of Sloth and all, but don't you think that didn't have much effort behind it?" The tone of Elijah's voice was that of teasing more than anything. After all, the two of them had been friends since they were practically children.

"Excuse me? I think you're just jealous that I was thinking smarter, not harder." Ryan remarked, moving to lightly knock on Elijah's skull decorative headpiece. "I still had to kill it after all. I loved my little Bessie." Ryan continued, shoving his hands into his pockets as the two men walked. "She would follow me anywhere I went. So, why not make her into my skull?" Ryan shrugged before reaching up to lightly pet the bridge of the skull's nose. "Besides, not like I have the brass balls that you have to go out and actually kill a frickin' mountain lion. Those things are deadly and you took it out like it was hardly anything." Whether it was praise or not, it was still a rather difficult task that the man pulled off.

"What can I say? I liked going after the thrill when I was younger." Elijah remarked with a small shrug of his shoulders. "How else do you think I was able to get Celia to agree to marry me? It wasn't for my good looks, that's for sure." Elijah spoke with a light smile on his face before it slowly faded. It hasn't quite set in that most of his family was gone. Hell, Elijah didn't even get to spend that time much with his new daughter Ava before he was called back to the capital. "Makes me wonder what I'll do now." Elijah spoke up, the frown still lingering on his face. "I only have Kane to keep me going at this point..." Elijah trailed off, wondering how he would be able to provide for his one and only son now.

"You're a good looking dude Eli. I wouldn't set yourself so low." Ryan spoke up, glancing over at the blond haired male. "After all, I remember seeing a lot of girls disappointed learning that you settled on marrying Celia instead of them." Ryan spoke, giving Elijah a small nudge, causing a faint smile to land on the males' face. "But you always said that she was your little piece of heaven. Glowing in the sunlight like a beautiful angel." Ryan paused, seeing Elijah avert his gaze at that comment.

"Never thought of you as the poetic type, but I guess I was proven wrong, huh?" Ryan added, trying his best to lighten his friends' mood to keep him from looking down in the dumps. Though in this day in age, it was getting harder to look on the right side of things. It seemed to have worked a bit as Elijah glanced back at Ryan with a sheepish smile on his face, appreciating what his friend was trying to do.

"What can I say? I guess my type is someone who tends to shine in this bleak world of ours." Elijah remarked, a small shrug of the shoulders as the two continued to walk down the hall. "In this world, it's the closest thing to being able to see an angelic figure without being the religious type." Elijah spoke as he glanced towards the ceiling that had broken in various places.

"To have someone so dear to us, that we have just the slightest bit of light in our lives, can make any darkness we face that much brighter." Elijah continued as they walked down the halls. "But now that is all gone." Elijah's tone dampened as he glanced down to the floor once more. "All I have left is Kane..." Elijah trailed off, feeling his heart sink as the two men walked. "He's a spitting image of her. Big heart, bright silver eyes that glisten when he's happy....though there isn't much in the way of a shimmer as it looks more like an empty pool of gravel now..." Elijah lowered his head, wondering just how he would even be able to make Kane happy once more. These past months have been a rollercoaster for the remaining members of the Flores family, making Elijah wonder if they could ever bounce back from this.

"You're not alone in trying to make him happy Eli." Ryan spoke up, earning a cautious gaze from Elijah. "You have us after all. My family is willing to help you in any way that we can." Ryan remarked, as they turned a corner. "You're like a brother to me. So I'll do anything I can to make sure that you and Kane are able to get back on your feet." It was a reassuring thought, but Elijah didn't exactly think it was right for him to intrude into Ryan's family like that. "Besides, maybe we could talk to Alan about finding ways that you could continue to do your leader work from a new location outside of your clan. That way you won't have to relive those horrible memories." Ryan suggested, figuring that it wouldn't hurt to try alternative means.

"Well, to be frank, I was thinking about stepping down as leader." Elijah spoke bluntly. The leader had spent that last couple of months trying to decide on how he should go about stepping down. Ever since his family's slaughter, it was unfair to Kane that Elijah still went about his business as a leader when his son was clearly still hurting. "Maybe we can try and find a replacement. It's clear that I need to focus on helping my family recover from all of this.." Elijah admitted, glancing towards Ryan and seeing the rather shocked expression on Ryan's normally calm demeanor.

"What? You can't do that!" Ryan snapped, grabbing hold of Elijah's shoulder to pull the other to look at him more directly. "You're a good leader. Your clan needs you!" Ryan practically shouted, shocking Elijah who was surprised to see this side of his friend. "Who else could easily replace you Eli?" Elijah stared up at Ryan's face, a bit surprised that he was so quick to be against the idea of Elijah leaving the leader position. Elijah tried to open his mouth to say something, but nothing seemed to come out at first.

"There will probably be someone more qualified than me Ry." Elijah finally spoke up, feeling Ryan's fingertips starting to dig into Elijah's arms a bit. It wasn't long before Elijah noticed that Ryan's hands were trembling the more that Elijah talked about stepping down. "I mean, it's not like I'm completely sure as to what I'm doing anyways." Elijah remarked with a small shrug of his shoulders.

"Besides, I need to focus on making sure that Kane is safe." At least, that's the lie that Elijah was trying to tell himself. "I want to be there for him. Traveling from there to here all the time, not being able to see my family even before everything went down, it's exhausting." Elijah lowered his head, not wanting to see the look on Ryan's face. Elijah already knew that Ryan would do or say anything to deter him from leaving. "Not like you can really stop me Ry. I've already made up my mind." Elijah continued, looking away from Ryan. Elijah didn't even have to look at Ryan to know the hurt expression on his face.

"You're really going to quit being the leader of the Gluttony clan?" Ryan spoke in a disbelieved tone, unsure if he was hearing his friend right or not. "Do you think that will bring your family back Eli?" Ryan asked, tilting his head a bit to the side as he took a step closer to Elijah, as if to try and talk him out of it. Despite wanting to convince Elijah to change his mind, it was the sound of familiar voices drawing close that caused Ryan to stop in his tracks. The two men glanced up to see two other leaders making their way towards them, seemingly discussing something that the two men couldn't hear from their current location.

One of the two males was a bit shorter than the other male. With a light blond hand that parted on the right side and flopped over towards his left eye, leaving a singular light silver eye exposed as the bangs curled towards his nose, small bits of freckles danced along the bridge of the man's nose. His skin was lightly tanned, giving him almost a sun-kissed color to him. Against the man's right exposed ear rested earrings that were scattered around the edge of his ear. Wearing torn up blue jeans, a flannel jacket that was green and white tied around his waist, a dark gray t-shirt rested against his slender frame. Around the man's neck were some old dog tags that lightly gleaned some of the sunlight pouring into the hallway. In the man's left hand was his skull mask as it seemed like he was explaining something to the taller man beside him.

"You wouldn't believe how long it took to get my old goggle lens inside of the skull." The man spoke as their voices seemed to get louder the closer the two men got to the other leaders, a small chuckle leaving his lips as the two men stopped in front of Ryan and Elijah. "Oh hey Ryan! Elijah." The man greeted the two men with a smile on his face. On the man's right cheek was a small black and blue mark that wasn't visible before he got up close to the two men.

"Simon, what the hell happened to your face?" Ryan asked, his eyes instantly noticing it. It wasn't that hard to notice it the closer that Simon got to the two men. It shined in the light against Simon's skin, almost looking as if it had been drawn on rather than being natural.

"Well, last night after you and Elijah left, this dude came up to me and slugged me in face." Simon remarked, moving to tap his cheek with his right hand. "He knocked my poor monkey skull off and chipped the right eye." Simon continued, almost boasting about the whole thing that went down. "Of course I couldn't let him get away with that and decked him right back." Simon continued with the story, bringing up his right fist that had some bruising on it. "It went on like that for a while before Matty here came to my rescue." Simon boasted as he gave Matt's chest a light slap with the back of his hand.

Matt was a bit taller than the three men, allowing him to stand out amongst the men. Matt was wearing the skull of a water buffalo with the horns seemingly being pulled back. The edge of the top jaw was slanted backwards, allowing for Matt's face to be more apparent. With peach colored skin against the medium long black hair that contrasted against his skin, bright yellow eyes glanced down at Simon. With bits of Matt's hair tucked behind his ears, it showed off the singular earrings that rested on each of Matt's earlobes.

The black leather jacket that Matt was wearing shifted a bit as he moved a hand to rest on Simon's shoulder. The white shirt was a bit tight against Matt's body, allowing for his well sculpted body to become visible in the sunlight. The black jeans were intact, unlike Simon's, with a belt that had a few studs on it. It was apparent that each of the men had their own style that they wore even to the meeting for the leaders.

"Well it's not like I could let someone hurt Simon." Matt remarked. Even if he lets his pride get the best of him." Matt remarked, moving his hand up to tussle some of Simon's blond locks. "Besides, it wasn't like he got completely hurt. Just a small shine on his cheek since the mask was able to protect him." Both Elijah and Ryan collectively sighed upon hearing what happened with the two other leaders.

"He probably would have gotten to me sooner if he wasn't trying to flirt with the ladies." Simon remarked, lightly elbowing Matt in the side. Elijah and Ryan had a skeptical look on their face as they looked Matt over. Seeing those bright yellow eyes caused the two leaders to avert their gaze.

"I was just sitting there, making sure you weren't going to get in trouble." Matt remarked, resting his arm over top of Simon's shoulder. "I know how you get when you drink. How easily it is to hurt your little pride." Matt continued with a small chuckle leaving his lips. "I was just surprised that you weren't the first one to swing this time." Matt continued, glancing down to study Elijah's and Ryan's face through the bit of interaction between Simon and himself.

"You guys need to be more careful." Elijah started to nag at the two leaders. "Just because you're the leaders of the Pride and Lust clan doesn't mean you can just go to any random pub and pick a fight." Elijah lightly scolded them as Ryan walked past the three. It seemed, for at least the time being, that their early discussion was going to be put on hold. Not that anyone could blame Elijah for not wanting to talk about it, but it didn't change the fact that Ryan didn't agree with the method of simply running away to solve his problems.

"Yeah....sorry about that Elijah." Simon apologized like he meant it. "Anyways, why were the two of you down this way anyways?" Simon asked, curious as to why the two leaders had headed off before the rest of the leaders went to see their prisoner. "Seeing Lily? How is she?" Simon asked, turning around to walk after Ryan as Matt and Elijah copied the blond.

"Yeah. We were trying to see if Lily could remember anything more from that night." Elijah remarked, knowing from the start that it was a bit of long shot to get answers from Lily. "But it seems like she doesn't want to talk with anyone. Not even her own daughter." Elijah explained, glancing towards the floor. Lily was pretty much acting the same way as Kane was. Closing herself off from people, refusing to eat or drink anything presented to her, and just looking as if her soul had already left her body with barely life left in her.

"Then again, Ashley seemed pretty reluctant to come and see her as it was. She only came because James begged her to come and talk things out with Lily." Elijah paused, moving to slip his hands into his robes as Elijah rested his arms against his chest. "As you can imagine, it didn't exactly go all that well." A sigh escaped Elijah's lips towards the end.

"Yeah?" Simon's interest seemed to perk up, curious as to how that whole interaction went down while Lily's daughter was visiting. "How did it go?" Simon asked, glancing over towards Elijah. Studying the male's face seemed to answer the question long before Elijah spoke about it. "Guessing from that facial expression, it didn't go down very well, huh?" Simon commented, seeing how Elijah's brows seemed to knit together and the blond averted his eyes from the other leader.

"Ashley kept demanding to know why Lily went after her that night." Elijah started off, knowing that he could hear the young girl screaming from the top of the stairs. "What purpose did it serve to try and kill her child? Only to spit on Lily's face before storming off." Elijah answered, giving them the rather short summary of everything that happened.

"I can understand why Ashley would be angry, but considering that we have to debate on what kind of punishment that Lily should get, do you honestly think that Ashley would be satisfied knowing that she would never give her mother a proper goodbye?" Elijah asked the other leaders briefly, watching as the men averted their gaze from him.

"All that hate is just going to sit inside of her until it eventually explodes into a huge ball of emotions." Elijah noted, feeling the same way on the night that his oldest killed each member of his family besides Kane. "I can only hope that Ashley will be alright when it finally blows up…" It made Elijah reflect a bit on the last argument he had with Celia the week before he came left for a pointless leader meeting. All the things he said out of anger because of how stressed he was, it seemed pointless now that she was gone.

"Well, not like there is anything we can do for her now." The comment from Ryan caught Elijah's attention as the male continued to speak. "Ashley will just have to live with the fact that she would rather have hate towards her mother in the end. Knowing that it will forever haunt her is something she decided." Ryan spoke up, giving his piece of mind on the whole situation. "Maybe in Lily's passing Ashley's heart will be free of that hate. But for now, she has to live by her actions and deal with the consequences of it all." The mood of the room seemed to shift from the rather heavy talk about the subject of regrets made in the past.

The look on the four men's face seemed to reflect the mood, causing Simon to try and swing the mood into a more positive spin. "Oh yeah!" Simon chimed up in a perky tone as he moved to walk backwards in front of the three men. "You guys didn't see my latest design for my mask, huh?" Simon remarked, holding up the monkey skull that had been resting in his left hand.

"Since it was fractured, I decided to use my old pair of goggles to put into the eye sockets of the skull. That way it would act as more protection to my eyes when we go into battle." Simon boasted proudly as he showed them the new and improved mask he made. "It wasn't easy, but it certainly was worth all the work." Simon's smile was widespread as he enjoyed showing off all of his inventions or creations. Seeing Simon's smile was almost infectious as Elijah and Ryan seemed to smile as well. Even if it was a lighthearted one.

In Simon's hand was the skull of a large monkey thanks to the years of radiation growing the once small prime ape to be bigger. The eye sockets were filled in with the goggles that had a small tint to them to block out the harsh lighting. Surrounding the goggles were white crystals to make the lens stick out more. The fangs that seemed to have been chipped or damaged were also replaced with white crystals given their more clear appearance than the actual teeth.

"You probably should put your mask back on. Don't want Nero or Alan to catch you without it on." Matt spoke up, knowing how strict either one of them were about that one particular rule. It was a rather silly rule where they all had to wear their skull masks when they were getting ready to perform meetings. It had to do with something about it being symbolic of the tribes coming together as one, but some of the leaders didn't exactly see why they should wear it. But it was one of the few rules that they had to follow.

"Oh yeah, you're right." Simon spoke, as if he had completely forgotten about what they were doing today. Sliding it over his face, Simon smirked as he glanced back up at Matt. "There we go, how handsome do I look now?" Simon asked, of course he was obviously joking, but it was to keep the mood light rather than have the rest focus on the negative thoughts that always seemed to creep back into his friends' minds.

"You look like an idiot." Elijah remarked, though he did have a small smile lingering on his face. It was appreciative to have someone in good spirits around them. "Frankly I just want to get this meeting done and over with. The less time I have to spend around that snake Nero, the better." It seemed like none of the other leaders like Nero. The man always seemed to give everyone the creeps and liked to push their buttons, making it rather difficult to get anything done in the meetings.

"That wasn't very nice to say Elijah." Simon lightly pouted as he shoved his hands into the pockets of his jeans. "Most of the animals on the islands are either some form of monkey, large felines, or birds." Simon listed off a few of the animals that he had, making it hard to find the right one to use for his skull mask that actually fit his head. "Not like I had much to choose from, unlike the rest of you." Simon continued with the pout on his face. Hearing the excuse caused some of the men to chuckle nervously.

"But you're right about that Nero guy." Simon continued, shifting the topic topic back to Nero. "He always makes up stuff about everyone. It's hard to tell what is true or not some-times." Simon remarked, tilting his head to the side as he continued. "I mean, the guy is a genius when it comes to being able to rig something up out of seemingly nowhere." Even Simon had to admit that Nero was basically a genius when it came to engineering the latest contraptions that were made out of old materials, but that was the only good thing that was associated with Nero.

"Being able to keep a low profile while coming up with alternative ways to get us power, with some restrictions to stay out of the cowards' radar, that's hard to accomplish with the limited resources and technology that we currently have." Simon remarked, almost awestruck like the first time he saw a rig that Nero came up on the fly. "I really hate working with that guy, but he does have a lot of talent. Really pisses me off..." Simon finished with a light sigh escaping his lips.

The other three leaders softly nodded in unison without uttering a single word. Working with Nero was like trying to work with someone who could easily switch on a dime. One had to be careful with what they said around the leader of the Wrath Clan. When a vast majority of the leaders tried to keep things civil between each other, and they had someone who, not only knew how to fight but could easily overwhelm someone if they were caught off guard by him, it was a rather scary situation that put everyone on edge.

As the four men walked silently in the hallway that led to the meeting room, a man walked out carrying a ring of keys. The man was a rather tanned man with long brunet hair that trickled down towards his shoulders. A permanent scowl seemed to land on the man's face as piercing silver eyes gazed at the group of men coming towards him. On top of his head was the skull of a ram that had horns that curled backwards and to the side where it seemed to hover over the man's shoulders. Wearing a dark red shirt with a jacket that seemed to end at his elbows, the man was wearing dark jeans with a matching belt that barely peeked out from under the red shirt.

A small silver beaded necklace clung to the man's neck as it was barely noticeable against the color of the shirt he was wearing. "Where have the four of you been?" The man asked. Exiting from the door close to the man was a young woman who followed behind him. "We were supposed to be meeting here five minutes ago." The man's voice was lightly scolding, but it seemed by his facial expression that he was used to this thing by now.

"Yeah, sorry about that Alan. Matthew and I were on our way to see Lily before everything would go down, and we ran into these two on the way." Simon explained as he jerked his thumb to point behind him towards Ryan and Elijah. "From what I could only guess, they must have been ahead of us to see Lily before our little private trial would begin." Simon continued, before taking notice of the girl behind Alan who seemed to be holding a pile of papers in her hands. "Whoa! Amelia! It's been so long!" Simon spoke excitedly as he walked up towards the two. "You've gotten so big. You look like a miniature version of your dad."

"Yes, it's been a while Mr. Manwell." A younger looking Amelia spoke up, looking up at Simon. "I trust that Felicia has been doing well since the accident?" Amelia asked in a curt tone but keeping in mind that she was speaking to the leaders. Her father Alan, who was in charge of all the leaders, was keeping an eye on her, making sure that she didn't say anything that would be deemed impolite.

"Well, the swelling has done down thanks to the medicine that Ryan has been able to give me." Simon spoke up, glancing over his shoulder at Ryan briefly before looking back down at Amelia. "Hopefully in a few months she'll be able to walk around easier with the makeshift leg I crafted for her. Then it'll be like she never lost her leg to that damn tiger..." Simon trailed off, recounting the events still even though it happened a few months ago. Even with a fake leg being attached, it would never stop the blood curdling screams that came from Felicia when she would have her nightmares.

"Let's not bring up that subject right now Simon." Alan remarked, giving a soft glare to Amelia, knowing full well she shouldn't have asked the question. "We have to get Lily ready for the trail soon." Alan shifted the topic while placing a hand on Amelia's head, giving it a few pats. "I'll be taking Amelia to the kitchen beforehand to get us some hot tea ready for when we need to take a break. This trial will be testing all of our nerves, so I want to time it out perfectly." Alan finished, trying to keep the subject matter from spiraling out of control. If any of the past meetings were an indication as to what could possibly go down with this trial, the leaders would certainly need something to help calm them once a judgment has been passed.

Amelia's hair was tucked mostly under the skull with the small tufts of her hair seemed to stick out from behind Amelia's ears. Wearing a black silk blouse, Amelia wore a black, red, and white flannel skirt with some fishnet stockings that tucked into small heeled shoes that had a small black ribbon on the top. "Is there anything else that I should prepare as well father?" Amelia asked, looking up at Alan. "Maybe some light cookies or some biscuits to enjoy the tea with?" Amelia asked, tilting her head a little to the side as she glanced towards Alan, waiting for his answer.

"I don't see the harm in it." Alan remarked, figuring that a little sweetness to take away the bitter that would soon follow from the meeting. It was never easy having to pass down a judgment on a friend. Especially with everything that was going on, how much disorder seemed to linger in the air, and the bad misfortunes already happening around them. It was like they were still being cursed by the Elite after all these years. "By the way," Alan continued as he glanced at the four men ahead of him.

"Nero will be arriving shortly." Seeing the light grimace on the men's faces, Alan knew that this was going to be like the other meetings that they had in the past. "I know that we don't exactly get along with him, but just for today, could we please just keep it civil?" Alan asked, his voice begging as his brows knitted together under the mask.

"If we can just do that, I'll try to figure out a way to see if we could do one of those group calls on the phone like they did before the bombs dropped." Alan still had to figure out how it worked, but seeing the relief wash over the men's faces at the compromise seemed to give Alan the answer right away. "It might take some work, but with your help Simon, I'm sure we could figure out a solution so we don't have to keep meeting in person." It was at least a compromise to get the men to behave, considering how all of them seemed to hate Nero, and it would make the situation run smoother, or at least that's what Alan hoped.

"No promises." Matt quickly remarked, crossing his arms over his chest. Alan sighed as he knew how much Matt loathed Nero. The two men often looked like they were ready to take swings at each other. Matt seemed to only hold back from decking Nero in the face because of the respect that he had for the other leaders. Not to mention he wasn't exactly a big fan of sitting in a cell for days at a time. Hearing that response caused Alan to sigh as his gaze moved towards Simon.

"I'll do my best to ignore him," Simon started to speak, knowing that it was the least that Alan could ask for. "But you know how he can be. He always knows what to bring up in order to get you riled up." Simon remarked, placing his hands on his hips. It's not like Simon was the type to get physical unless push comes to shove. "If anything, the worse I will do is verbally fight with him." Simon added, reaching a hand up to scratch his left temple. "As long as you don't get mad over that, then I'll behave." Not exactly ideal, but it was better than nothing, so Alan would simply have to accept that.

"Fine.." Alan exasperated as his eyes moved over towards Ryan and Elijah. At least Alan could count on the two of them to be somewhat decent. Granted Ryan was the mature one of the group, but if he were to ever lose his cool, it would only spell out disaster. Elijah on the other hand, he often held back his anger out of respect for Alan. But considering everything that happened in the leaders' life, Alan wasn't sure if Elijah would be able to hold back.

"I'm with Simon on this one." Elijah remarked, a bit out of character for this one. "Normally I'm not the type of guy to get into fists fights, and I keep my mouth shut for most things." Elijah paused giving a soft glare towards Alan. "But Nero will go for the weakness that we all have, the misfortune befalling on most of our kids." Elijah wasn't exactly wrong. The only ones who haven't been dealt with a heavy blow is Alan and Matt. "Felicia's leg being ripped off by a tiger, Parker's death, Ashley's trauma, and my son being barely able to function after the slaughter of the rest of my family. Do you honestly expect me to just keep my mouth shut while he taunts most of us where it hurts the most?" Elijah asked with a stern look on his face.

Alan's eyes glanced down to the ground. He couldn't exactly argue with that type of logic. After all, sometimes a family is all that a man has going for him. To attack them is like attacking a man's castle. "You're right..." Alan remarked, his voice softened as he glanced towards Amelia.

"After all, most of us only have our kids left." Alan spoke as he placed a hand on Amelia's head once more. "But just this once," Alan turned his attention to the four men in front of him. "I'm begging you to simply let it go." Alan continued, knowing he was asking a lot from the leaders. "Just this is the one time I'm pleading with you, as a fellow father and leader, to ignore Nero the best that you can and let me handle him."

The four men turned to look at each other, doubt rested on their facial expressions as they silently gazed at each other. It was only when Ryan stepped forward that Alan removed his hand from on top of Amelia's head, as if waiting for a verdict. "Fine..." Ryan spoke, though it seemed he wasn't exactly pleased with the idea. "But if he gets out of hand, we want you to be the one to handle him, within reason." Ryan continued with a stern look on his face. "You're the leader of us. You can't simply let him get away with this behavior anymore." Ryan spoke, his brows knitting together as his voice was stern.

What was Alan supposed to say? No? Letting out an annoyed sigh, Alan placed his hands on his hips. "Alright, fine." Alan relented, knowing that if he was going to get any peace at the end of it, he'll just have to take things into his own hands.

"It feels like you're asking me to kill him when you put it like that, you know." Alan half heartedly joked as a small smile landed on his face. "Anyways, go ahead and get settled in your seats. I'll be back with Lily so we can finish this before it gets too late into the evening." Alan remarked, moving towards Ryan before lightly patting the man's shoulder. Leaving the four behind, Alan knew that there was something heavy in the air as if something wasn't right, but he couldn't put his finger on it. If it wasn't the longest day of his life already, it certainly felt like it.

As the sun's glow was starting to turn a mixture of yellow and orange against the walls of the room in which the seven leaders sat, the room was filled with tension. Three tables rested around Lily, though she barely seemed to take notice as her gaze was focused down to the carpeted rug underneath her. On her left was Simon and Matt, to her left was Ryan and Elijah, leaving Alan and Nero to sit in front of her. Everyone but Nero had a sadden look on their face. Nero, who was wearing a red long sleeved shirt with dark gray pants with his red sash tied around his waist. A smirk seemed to rest on his face while his golden eyes studied Lily's depressed face with glee at the female leader's misfortune. It was evident that he was taking pleasure in seeing Lily reduced to nothing more than wetted scrubs that caused the leader to shiver in the warm room.

Nero had grown to be fairly tall over the years, his body becoming muscular yet lean. His tanned skin stuck out against his white blond hair. His lashes made it seem like he was wearing eyeliner, causing his golden eyes to stand out more. Unlike the others who wore either black or silver earrings, Nero wore gold. His lower ears were visibly pierced as the red head scarf that covered his forehead with the bits of hair both trapped and hanging over it covered the top of his ears. His normal golden bangles were done, which seemed to be unusual as the man never took them off. The snake skull that sat on top of Nero's head was encrusted with red crystals along the eye sockets, leaving only a sliver of black crystals to act like the snake' s pupils. The fangs almost went unnoticed as they seemed to blend in with Nero's locks.

The room felt heavy as Alan stood up with a piece of paper in his hand. "Lily Greenlee," Alan started to speak, pausing as he waited for Lily to look up at him, though she seemed to be rather slow to gaze at the one who addressed her. Even after all this time, Lily still didn't seem like she was really there, and that all of this was nothing more than a bad dream.

Alan knew that he couldn't give her pity considering the course of her actions, even if it was in self defense. "You've been charged with the murder of your spouse Michael Greenlee, and the attempted murder and child endangerment of your daughter Ashley Greenlee...." Alan trailed off, his nerves seeming to get the better of him. "How...do you plea?" Alan asked, his voice finding the confidence, despite the somber expression that was currently resting on his face.

".....Guilty...." Lily spoke, though her voice seemed to be low as if she was mumbling. The weakness was evident as she could barely say anything else. Lowering her head back down, it was like she had just given up all hope. All but one of the men seemed to share Lily's remorse, keeping silent in hopes that this could be done and over quickly. The sooner they get this done and over with, the quicker they would be able to treat this like a bad memory.

"Then let us....start debating her punishment." Alan continued, knowing full well that this part would be the hardest for all of them. They were about to decide the fate of one of their dear friends. It wasn't like Lily would fair off if she was simply exiled, she would starve herself or take her own life. Lily wasn't a bad person, her circumstances were simply put against her. So killing her right then and there was simply too cruel, but it seemed like it was what some people would want, but even that was too cruel. "Simon," Alan addressed the male who was to his right. "What is your proposition on how we shall go about with Lily's punishment?"

Simon seemed to be rather caught off guard by the question, but he knew that Alan was doing this to prevent Nero from speaking his mind about killing off Lily. "Well..." Simon started off before clearing his throat. "What if we remove her from being a leader?" Simon started off, thinking that maybe this could save his friend from certain death. "Maybe we will be able to rehabilitate Lily instead of killing her?" Simon asked, figuring that it would be a good alternative to exile or killing the poor woman. It seemed that most of the other leaders were pleasantly surprised by Simon's alternate plan, seeming to be on board with it.

"I'm sure if she were to be put into a hospital, she could very well make a better recovery and atone for what she did." Matt started to speak up, backing Simon's original idea. "Maybe have someone watch her in case she tries something? Matt spoke up, seemingly on board with the idea. "My son is currently on an expedition to see what he can learn about shelters that are more towards some of the surrounding cities. If I can get word to him, I'm sure he would be more than happy to see what he can collect out there as a means of helping people who mentally snapped from lack of nutrition..." Matt continued, realizing just how thin Lily was after learning of her husband's affair.

"I could start to see if maybe we could produce some kind of medicine to help her with the trauma as well." Ryan spoke up, knowing that the issues that Lily had gone through might have led up to her killing her husband. "If we can find some type of medical books from before the bombs dropped, it could very well become beneficial for future illnesses." Ryan remarked, crossing one leg over the other as he crossed his arms over his chest in thought.

"In the meantime, my clan is far enough away from the Envy clan that Lily can stay there." Elijah took this as his turn to speak up. "I'm sure we could find a way to treat her there. Maybe some fresh open air would help to clear the fog from her mind." If there was ever a place that had large clear lands with nothing but open skies, it was the Gluttony clan. "We always need painters to help restore some of the buildings. It could help her enjoy what she used to love doing before everything went down." Elijah finished, knowing how much Lily loved painting and restoring things that she often saw beauty in them.

"Are you all insane?" Nero quickly snapped when it was his turn. "Rehabilitation... Medical advances that we have no proof is even out there without being withered from the harsh weather over the years, and thinking that being stuck in the boonies would help her out?" Nero spat as he stood up from his seat. "Are you all saying this because she's your friend?" Nero asked almost bitterly at how the leaders were acting towards Lily. "Don't you think that is a bit hypocritical of you?" Nero scoffed. "Favoring one person above all the others that you were so quick to exile for similar things." Nero asked, glancing around the room at the other men.

"You honestly expect us to either kill or exile Lily?" Elijah was quick to snap back at Nero in a bitter tone. "If we exile her, we might as well be killing her. So we're trying to find alternative means to help her out." Elijah remarked, moving to stand up since he wasn't going to let Nero talk everyone out on helping Lily. "If we can find a way to help Lily out from her mental breakdown, we might be able to help others just like her." Elijah was quick to continue as he hoped that if they found something to help with trauma, then perhaps he would be able to help Kane.

"Is it because she reminds you of your son, Elijah?" Nero asked in a taunting tone, catching Elijah a bit off guard. "After all, look how pathetic she looks sitting there." Nero remarked, causing most of the leaders to glance at Lily's pitiful state before he continued. "Bet it reminds you a lot about your little boy right about now, huh?" Nero continued, causing Elijah's jaw to clench tightly.

"Knowing full well that he killed his older brother who had snapped and killed your beloved wife and daughter." Hearing that remark from Nero caused Elijah's fist to clench tightly, trying his best to keep his promise of being civil with Nero. "Then again, shouldn't we have your little boy Kane here on trail right now too? He is a murderer after all." Nero continued his taunt, watching as the rage seemed to build up inside of Elijah's eyes. Glancing down to watch Elijah's hands clench and tremble, watching the rage fill up inside of the leader of the Gluttony clan caused Nero to chuckle in delight as he got under the leaders' skin so easily.

"Nero, stop it." Alan growled, his eyes seemingly piercing daggers at Nero, but the Wrath leader simply brushed them off before moving towards Ryan. Slithering towards the other leaders like the snake that he was that seemed to crawl under all of the other leaders' skin.

"And what about you Ryan?" Nero continued down the line. "Do you really think that you could just sit by as the man who killed your precious baby boy walk out and get help?" Nero asked, his voice almost singsong like. After all, you wanted to kill the man with your own two hands, right?" Nero asked, watching as Ryan glanced away from him. This only seemed to cause a smirk to form on his face.

"What if that man who killed your son came back and raped your poor vulnerable wife?" Nero asked, raising an eyebrow. "After all, you did allow him to simply walk away the first time. Wouldn't it have been better if you simply killed him right where he stood?" Nero asked, studying the reaction from Ryan who looked like he wanted to punch Nero in the face.

"Don't you want to slash his throat and watch as the blood slowly drips down his neck as he gargles on his own blood?" Nero continued to ask, planting ideas in the Sloth leader's mind that Ryan could ever dream of doing. "Wouldn't you feel like the bastard got what he deserved then?" Nero asked, pressing Ryan's anger until he stood up quickly to say something, but stopped as Elijah gripped his arm to stop Ryan from speaking his mind. This only seemed to fuel Nero's ego as he was able to get under their skin.

Walking around Lily, Nero made his way towards Matt. Even if he didn't have anything bad on the leader, Nero knew he could get into the man's mind. "Speaking of expeditions, how crazy would it be if your son met with people who had a bunch of birth defects?" Nero asked, resulting in Matt glaring at him. "No amount of medicine can save mutated freaks like that. Maybe he would just do them all a favor and kill them off." Nero spoke before laughing as if he told a hilarious joke. But it seemed like Matt didn't feed into Nero's taunt. Watching as Matt simply leaned back in his chair a bit, Matt's jaw clenching tightly as he knew getting angry would only seem to fuel Nero. With a small shrug, Nero moved onto Simon.

"Given the fact that your daughter's leg was recently chewed off by a tiger, don't you think it's cruel to send our precious Lily out into the wild where such beasts can easily devour her thin figure?" Nero asked, raising an eyebrow at Simon who scowled towards the Wrath leader. "After all, she doesn't have a single muscle in her body any more. Maybe it would be better if we feed Lily to the dogs. I'm sure they would appreciate it better than-" Nero continued before Alan stood up from his seat.

"Nero! I said enough!" Alan shouted, slamming his hands on the table. "If we can find a new method to be beneficial to Lily, we can use it as a means of allowing people to recover from mentally snapping like she did." Alan was quick to point out.

"Granted it wouldn't be immediate justice for what she did, but given the circumstances that Michael tried to strangle Lily, it would be crueler to kill her off than allow Lily to actually make amends for what she did." Alan remarked, watching the smirk turn into a sour pout on Nero's face. "If we give Lily time to get the help she needs, then perhaps Ashley could come to understand the situation and they could become a family once more."

"Tch." Nero spat as he made his way over to Lily. It was easy to see that Nero had gotten under the leaders' skin, but now was his time to finish what he started. Kneeling down in front of Lily, Nero grabbed some of her blonde locks as he jerked her head back. Immediately all of the leaders stood up as they were ready to pounce if Nero tried anything on her.

"Step away from her Nero, this is your one and only chance." Alan ordered, the seething anger in his voice was evident in his tone. Hearing the anger in Alan's voice, Nero couldn't help but smirk once more as he glanced back at Alan with a glint to his golden eyes. Seeing the cold sweat drop against Alan's forehead was delightful to Nero. Seeing the head leader getting huffy was rather amusing to the sadistic leader of the Wrath clan.

"Relax. I'm just wanting to take a look at her neck." Nero remarked innocently, despite the venomous tone to it. "After all, you said that she was being strangled, right?" Nero spoke in a taunting tone as he moved his attention to Lily once more. His golden eyes locked with the dull blue of Lily's eyes, the smirk disappearing as he found the expression to become boring. There was no fight left with the leader that Nero once knew. She was nothing more than another weakling in front of him.

"N-Nero...." Lily softly called out as Nero brushed his fingers against Lily's neck. The tips of his fingers guided against her jugular that were stained with a purple hue from Michael's hands wrapping around her thin throat. When a coy smirk flashed across Nero's face, a gurgling noise soon spilled from Lily's mouth as a hidden dagger pierced into her neck.

"Now now Lily, you know the rules. If you kill someone, you should be killed as well. It's only fair, right?" Nero spoke, only to jerk his hand to gash Lily's neck wider. The blood spilled onto his red shirt, staining it a darker shade of red, making it almost turn black, as bits of blood spattered onto Nero's face and down his pants.

Letting go of Lily's hair, her body soon slumped over while Nero pulled up the hidden blade to admire the view of the silver blade being stained red. As Lily's body twitched and convulsed, Nero stood up with a relaxed sigh leaving his lips. Retracting the blade back into his sleeve, Nero looked around to see the horrified looks on the men's faces. "See? How hard was that?" Nero remarked, pulling out a red handkerchief to wipe the blood off of his face. "Guess I really have to do things myself." Nero muttered bitterly as the smile he wore faded.

"You...." Simon mumbled in disbelief, his eyes fixated on Lily's body as it went limp. "You just killed her... like that..." He trailed off, the shock overwhelming him as his body shook ever so slightly. "W-Why?! We could have saved her!" Simon yelled, jumping over the table and grabbing Nero's shirt. "We could have helped her! And you just decided to be her judge, jury, and executioner!!" Simon continued to shout, shaking Nero who didn't seem like he was at all affected by this.

Alan could barely hear anything over the ringing in his ears. It felt like Lily's dead eyes were now looking straight at him, watching as the life faded from her eyes. Alan didn't even watch as Elijah and Ryan grabbed Nero's arms as Matt tried to hold Simon's arm back to keep the leader from punching Nero. The ticking of the clock sounded louder in Alan's mind as the red sunlight from the setting sun seemed to illuminate the walls with a dark red. Turning his gaze towards the decorative swords that rested on the wall, Alan found himself moving towards them while the rest of the leaders were distracted.

"Stop it Simon! If we beat him to a pulp, we're no better off than he is!" Matt shouted, trying his best to get through to Simon who was fighting tooth and nail to beat Nero to an inch of his life. "The best thing we can do is let Alan decide what to do with him. Right Al?" Matt remarked, glancing at Alan to see his back turned to them. But it didn't seem that Alan heard the Lust leader's voice.

Seeing Alan holding the sword and gazing at it, Matt loosened his grip, allowing Simon a chance to punch Nero in the face. Hearing Nero's grunt snapped Matt's attention back to trying to hold back Simon whose knuckles were starting to turn a little red from the first swing. Alan on the other hand gazed at the blade as the ringing only seemed to intensify. Gripping the handle tight enough to turn his knuckles white, Alan proceeded to turn around and see the sight before him. His vision was as red as the color resting on the wall in front of him.

Carrying the sword in hand towards the group, Alan's eyes were fixated on Nero. With a bit of blood dripping from his nose, Alan's vision was tunnel with the desire to kill Nero where he was standing. But as Alan got closer, Matt let go of Simon once more to try and stop Alan from his blood lust. "Stop Alan!" Matt shouted, moving to get into Alan's way, only to feel the sharp edge of the knife pierce into his stomach. Looking down, Alan didn't even seem at all bothered by the fact that he just impaled Matt. Before he knew it, Alan kicked Matt backwards, causing Matt to groan as he fell onto the floor, pushing the table in the process.

As Simon started to beat on Nero in a blind rage, he only became distracted when he heard the sound of Matt falling down close by. Looking up to see the horrified look on both Ryan and Elijah's faces, Simon turned around to see Matt on the ground holding onto his stomach as blood pooled onto his white shirt. Glancing towards Alan with a blood soaked sword in his hand and some of Matt's blood splattered onto his shirt, Simon was equally horrified as the other two leaders who watched it happen.

"Alan, what the hell man?!" Simon shouted, turning his attention to Alan as Nero was left a bit bloody and panting from the beating he received while Ryan and Elijah still held Nero by his arms. "Are you crazy?! You just attacked Matt!" Simon continued to shout, but seeing that there was no getting through to Alan. It seemed that Alan was on a destructive path. Anyone who got in his way would just end up injured.

"Come on Alan, do you really want to go down like this as well?" Ryan asked as he finally found his voice after the horror he had just witnessed. "If you don't snap out of this, we'll have no choice but you put you down as well." Ryan called out, trying to reason with Alan, but it was no use. Alan was far gone. No words or actions could stop him now.

By the time that the lights had started to flicker on, Amelia was making her way towards the meeting room. In her hands was a tray with six cups stacked into three piles of two, a hot kettle with steam rising from the pot, and a plate of assorted cookies. The sounds of her heels almost sounded like a loud roar in the rather quiet hallway. Reaching the door of the room that was still shut from the trail, Amelia stopped in front of the dark wooden door.

Behind her the sun barely peeked out from behind the distant mountain top. Steadying the heavy plate to rest against her left arm and stomach, Amelia tapped three times before waiting. Surely they were done by now and they would just simply need time to pause their discussion for some refreshments. However, there was no answer on the other side of the door. Waiting for another few seconds, Amelia moved to knock three more times before waiting for an answer. When no was heard, Amelia grabbed the door handle to open it.

Pushing the door wide open, Amelia found that the room was dark. Surely they weren't having a meeting in the dark, right? Reaching over to turn on the light, Amelia dropped the tray she was holding at the sight in front of her, causing the cups to shatter on the marble ground below. The kettle containing green tea spilled onto the floor, mixing in with the blood that stained the ground. The assorted cookies spilled in every direction as the tray crashing to the floor echoed in the room. It was a complete blood bath in the room.

Cautiously stepping into the room Amelia looked at the dead bodies on the floor. Both Lily and Ryan had their necks slashed open. Taking a step closer, Amelia noticed Elijah was stabbed through his chest with slits along his backside. Simon's dead body rested on top of Matt's. It seemed that Simon's right eye had bits of shattered glass from his goggles being shattered with bits of the right side of his torso gashed open. Hearing heavy breathing coming from behind the desk, Amelia rushed towards the sound. She slipped on the blood ever so slightly, causing one of her heels to fly off.

Stumbling into the desk, Amelia saw her father holding onto his stomach, alive but barely breathing. The front of him was completely covered with blood as Nero was slumped onto his side. Blood pooled under Nero as he seemed to be just as covered in blood as her father. "Dad! What the hell happened?!" Amelia asked, causing Alan to look up at her with a mixture of shock and confusion.

"Amelia?" Alan called out weakly, "What are you doing here?" Alan asked, removing his hand with a wince as he looked down to see that he had small gashes in his stomach. "What.... Did I do?" Alan mumbled to himself, watching his bloody hand shake uncontrollably. "I.... I killed them...Oh god, I killed them!!" Alan shouted, realizing everything happened as it came back to him in a flash. Moving his legs to try and get up, Alan found that it was nearly impossible to move. Hot tears started to fall down his face as he started to choke up. "A-Amelia... what have I done?" Alan asked in a whimper, looking up at her with pleading eyes.

"Dad..." Amelia softly spoke before jumping over the desk to come to her father's side. "What happened?" Amelia asked once more, taking a survey of how bloodied her father was. It looked like he was cut deep by some kind of blade. "Can you recall what happened?" Amelia asked, trying her best to stay calm as she watched her father look around in a dazed state. She had to be strong enough to help her father realize what exactly happened.

"Lily... He.... killed her." Alan started out, his mind trying to put the pieces together, though some of it was still a bit hazy. "And then.... I blacked out ..." Alan paused, bringing a bloody shaky hand up to his forehead. "Matthew .... Simon .... Ryan .... Elijah .... Nero ...." Alan slowly listed their names as he tried to recount what happened.

"A-After I stabbed Matthew for getting in my way.... Simon and Ryan tried to talk me out of it." Alan kept recounting, before he looked up at Amelia with a bewildered look to his eyes. "Nero took that chance to try and escape." Alan continued in a panic, fearing that Nero might have escaped during that time. Despite being in complete shock of it all, Alan was able to remember all of what happened next, despite not wanting to remember it at all.

"He stabbed Ryan in the neck after breaking free in the confusion." Alan continued, moving a hand back down to his stomach as he slumped against the wall. "Elijah let go to try and help Ryan, allowing Nero to go after Simon." Alan took a shaky breath as he winced in pain when he tried to move. "He....stabbed Simon in the eye, causing Simon to turn towards me...." Alan continued, choking up as he softly shook his head, regretting what had happened to once of his friends.

"Then Nero started to stab Simon in the back as my sword pierced his right side as Simon fell on top of me." Alan paused to try and catch his breath, bringing up a bloody hand to wipe away some of the snort that started to seep out of his nose. "I pushed Simon off of me... and Nero took this chance to try and stab me with his hidden blade..." Alan continued, tears forming in his eyes as he remembered the next part clearly. "Elijah got between us....trying to break apart our fighting....only to have Nero push him into my sword and stabbed him as well." Alan explained through some of his sobs.

"And did you... kill Nero?" Amelia asked, glancing over towards Nero's body to see the thin piece of skin that attached Nero's skull to his neck. It was a pretty gory scene, but it seemed to establish that Alan was at the very least telling the truth. With a soft nod of his head, Alan looked back up at Amelia. His eyes were stained red as a defeated look rested on his face. Tilting his head back a bit, Alan rested it against the wooden panel behind him.

"He got a couple of jabs in.... but ultimately I slashed his neck open with pushing my strength behind the blade..." Alan nodded, grasping the sword in his hand as he brought it into view. He looked at the blood stained blade, barely able to see his own reflection on it. "Amelia...I have to ask you to do something that will haunt you for the rest of your life." Alan spoke, his hand holding the blade shaking ever so slightly as resigned himself to his idea.

"No dad.... don't make me do it...." Amelia spoke, already knowing where this was heading. "This isn't some cheesy movie you know, where there can only be one." Amelia pleaded a little, grasping onto her father's arm to put the sword away. "We can patch you up. Then you can continue to lead the Greed clan, like none of this ever happened." Amelia spoke through soft tears. The only ones who would know the truth of what happened to the other leaders would be Alan and Amelia, a sacrifice she was willing to make. "You did this in self defense dad... Nero was the one who killed them. Not you." Amelia spoke, softly sniffling as she gripped her father's hand tightly, her voice shaking as she felt like her throat was burning.

"That's what got us into this mess kiddo." Alan remarked, moving to try to sit up more, only to wince in pain. "You kids have to act as the leaders now. So it's only fitting that you judge me right here and now." Alan remarked, a soft smile on his face as he removed his hand from his stomach, only to gently place his blood stained on Amelia's cheek. "This will let everyone know that you are worthy enough to be the next leader of the clans." Alan spoke in a shaky voice, the tears rolling down his cheeks at the point. "Punish me with death....end my life as a way to repay for the lives I stole Amelia." Alan spoke softly, his vision was starting to give as he watched the tears fall down Amelia's face as he let go of the blade, forcing Amelia to take hold of it.

As Amelia caught the sword, she could feel the weight of it causing her hand to tilt. It wasn't like Amelia could say no to her father. He was the only one who remained in this bloody royal. If there was someone who had to give her father the justice he wished for, she would have to do the unthinkable.

Slowly standing up, Amelia sniffled once more as she stood up. Kicking off her other heel, Amelia stood on her bare feet with only fishnets to cover her bare feet. "Alan Park.... You lay there with the sins of assisting in the death of the leaders of the clans. How do you plead?" Amelia asked, her voice wavering as the tears continued to seep from her eyes. Amelia hated everything about this.

"Guilty..." Alan spoke softly, looking up at Amelia with a soft smile on his face. He knew above all else how hard it was on Amelia to have to take her father's life, but it needed to be done. Whether it was now or later, he would eventually have to face the music of what he did. Rather it was on purpose or an accident, he helped to kill the other leaders. If anyone was going to kill him, he was glad that it was his own daughter. Despite everything that Amelia had been through, she was truly a leader worthy of leading the Greed clan.

"Then I....sentence you to death..." Amelia spoke, grasping the sword tightly in her hand, bringing up and swiftly striking it into his chest. Closing her eyes tightly, Amelia clenched her teeth to keep from crying out. Despite the fact that she wanted to toss the sword to the side and plead with her father to find alternative means to punish him, there was a ruling for those who killed multiple people. There was no rehabilitation for them. It was an instant death as no amount of time served could atone for their victim's death.

"I love you, kiddo." Alan struggled to speak out. "You....made me the happiest dad in the world. I'm proud...of...you." Alan spoke through groans as he felt the sword pierce his heart and lung. Closing his eyes, Alan passed away with a smile on his face, knowing that Amelia was strong enough to take care of the clans. Despite knowing that this would forever haunt Amelia, it would only serve to toughen her skin.

Feeling Alan's body slump down, Amelia's eyes snapped open. Taking her hands off of the sword, she gazed down at her shaky bloody hands. Curling her hands into soft fists, Amelia slumped down onto the floor. Her soft weeps filled the room as she kept from screaming in despair. Her father was dead at her own hands. His blood, as well as all of the other leaders' blood, were on her hands.

THE next couple of days after the incident, Amelia felt hollow. Everything in that room was removed to be burned. The bodies of the leaders were cremated as it was tradition. The families came together and were presented with the urns that held the leaders' remains. Amelia knew that this was just as hard on them as it was for her, given the fact that she was the only one who had actually killed her father.

The surviving or oldest children were arranged to stay in the capital of the clans while they sorted everything out. They discussed plans in which they would disband those who were in the Wrath Clan and bring them towards re-entering the other clans. The land was divided evenly as it was surrounded by four of the six leaders.

The news of this didn't exactly settle well at first. Protests had started and people demanded that those who were involved in trying to act against the leaders be brought to justice. But Amelia was tired seeing pointless deaths and violence. Over the next five years, Amelia and the other leaders were able to make a more effective system that allowed for the leaders to meet once every crop rotation as a means to keep the clans more well in tune with everything that was happening. If there was an issue that needed immediate attention, they were able to use the phone system to reach out for official business.

With some of the plans that Nero had drawn out or put in place, Amelia was able to work with Felicia and Keaton to test out means of expanding the crystals and how much energy a household could use before it was endangering their chances of being found out. With Ashley, they were able to find ways of bringing back some of the arts through expeditions. Miles and Kane worked with Amelia to find new medicine that would help using the flora they had.

With the amount of research Amelia did with the books that were salvageable, the leaders were able to make a list of things that they could try out once they figured out a way to destroy the Elite. But that would mean that Amelia would have to sully her hands in blood once more, and she was not ready for that type of psychological punishment again. At least, not until Dean showed up. With him willing to sacrifice the innocent lives of those on the Millennium, they may very well stand a chance to further advance the human race that was left behind on the ruined planet known as Earth.

CHAPTER TWENTY ONE: *The Beaming Light In the Sky*

THE SMELL OF fresh damp mushrooms filled Dean's nose as he opened his eyes. The sun rested behind the hills as the wooden ceiling of the cabin Dean was staying in came into view. With the fall now approaching, Dean knew that he would have to get to work with finishing the last of the preparations for the device. After learning about the history of the leaders, and how everything seemed to fall on Amelia's shoulders to rebuild society, Dean had been working with Kane and Felicia to get the device finished before the deadline. The summer had passed rather quickly after Dean left with Kane to come back to the Gluttony clan.

Despite wanting to have a place of his own, Dean gave into Kane's suggestion of moving in with him. Kane even remarked with the fact that Dean didn't exactly have a place in which to move into, so he should move in with Kane. Regardless if Dean got a place of his own or not, Kane would have simply kept visiting and keep Dean company since there was no point in staying in a house Kane barely stayed at anyways. They did come to an agreement that if anything happened between them, Dean could move out at any time, if he so wished.

Pulling the sheets off of him, Dean let out a small groan as he sat on the edge of the bed. Bringing his two hands up, Dean started to rub his face, feeling the bristle of the facial hair growing on his face. His skin had a bit more color to it as he decided to work in the fields that Kane visited to lend them a hand. It might have been a rather short visit, but Dean was learning a lot about the various soils that the Gluttony clan had. Not only that, but he was able to learn about the various vegetation that the clan had to offer. Most of which happened to be more earthbound crops like potatoes and carrots. If one could even call them that.

Moving his hands to brush back the brunet locks that had started to creep over the top of his ears, Dean knew that it was time to get up. Looking over his shoulder, Dean noticed that Kane was still asleep. Seems that Kane had worn himself out the night prior when a storm had passed overhead. There were still times in which Kane would lock up when the lightning would hit close to the house, causing Dean to try anything he could to help remind Kane that he was in a safe place. Reaching over, Dean lightly brushed some of Kane's locks from his face, revealing more of a sleepy expression without waking him up. A small smile formed on Dean's face as he studied the rather peaceful expression on the leader's face.

It wasn't long before an orange glow started to seep past the white curtains. Turning to face the window in front of him, Dean retracted his hand before getting up off of the bed. The wooden floor beneath him creaked ever so slightly under Dean's weight as he grabbed some clothes that he threw over the chair the night prior to going to sleep. Draping the clothes over his left arm, Dean headed towards the staircase.

Resting his right hand on the metal railing, Dean walked down the spiral steps towards the landing beneath. The cabin that they lived in used to be part of the old barn that was on Kane's family property. Thanks to some of the villagers who came together to convince the former Leader Elijah, before his untimely death, that the old barn that was falling apart could be turned into their new family home.

The top of the cabin had a singular bed that was a queen size bed with a metal frame that had a few drawers on the bottom of the frame for extra storage. There was a singular win-

441

dow that was on the left hand side that faced the hills leading further into the clan's territory. Though Dean didn't get to see too much of the land past the few neighboring towns, there was still so much of the land that needed to be explored.

On the right hand side of the room was a large handmade wooden closet that was decoratively made that had two dragons facing off at the top. It was large enough to fit most of Kane's clothes, and nothing more. On either side of the bed had some night stands with matching crystal lamps that provided enough light for one of them to read without disturbing the other. In the corner on the left hand side was a full length mirror while a medium length horizontal dresser rested under the window.

On the main floor of the cabin rested a decent yet small sized living room that rested under the spiral staircase. There was a decorative rug that laid under a single couch and two chairs on either side. A dark wooden and glass coffee table was planted in the middle with some metal cups from the night before. The throw blanket that they shared was messily tossed on the side of the couch as a lingering glow of amber in the fireplace offered little warmth to the cool morning air.

The window to the left of Dean was partially opened to vent out some of the heat after the rain had stopped, allowing the cool air to enter. On either side of the fireplace rested bookshelves seemingly littered with books that Kane collected or traded from some of the merchants along his journey. There was a large double wide arch that led towards a kitchen that was directly under the bedroom, but where Dean needed to head towards was a bathroom that rested past the kitchen.

Moving towards the kitchen, Dean stopped at a small table that rested just shy in front of the bathroom by a few feet. Setting his clothes on the clean wooden table, Dean looked at the small mess of dishes that was left in the sink overnight. "I'll just do them after my shower and shave." Dean mumbled to himself as he headed back into the living room to collect the dishes that were left behind. With the collective of dishes resting on the wooden counter, Dean picked up his clothes to head into the bathroom. There wasn't exactly much room in the bathroom, but it was at least bigger than the closet of a bathroom Dean was used to on the station.

Entering into the bathroom, Dean set the clothes down on top of the toilet before pulling back the shower curtain. The steam was rather quick to rise after he turned on the water, warming Dean up in the process. After pulling off his pajama shorts, Dean stepped into the shower. It wouldn't be a long shower, but at the very least Dean would shave the facial hair that was plaguing his face once Dean was done. After all, today was a big day. They were about to blast the death ray beam at the Millennium! With careful calculations and tracking of the station from the ground, it seemed that the weather would permit the launch to happen without much issue. If luck was on their side, they could very well be witnessed to a spectacular light show tonight.

Once his shower and shave was complete, Dean collected the clothes to throw his outfit together. Sliding on a pair of black jeans over some white ankle high socks, Dean slid the dark brown belt through the loops before slipping it through the right hole to make it fit. He wanted it to be snug, but not too tight. Grabbing a light gray t-shirt, Dean was practically ready to head out at a moment's notice. The only thing would need is some boots and a jacket, both of which were both waiting by the door.

Opening the door to the bathroom, Dean was rather surprised to see Kane was not only up, but appeared to be just as ready as Dean was. With a pair of light brown pants that seemed to be cut off an inch above his ankles, Kane was wearing a white buttoned up long sleeve shirt with the sleeves rolled up to his elbows. A black muscular shirt could be seen underneath. Kane's hair had grown to be barely skimming along his decorative earlobes as Kane tucked bits of his hair behind his left ear. Kane's hands were deep in the water as the sound of dishes were being washed as they clinked and clanked under the bubbly surface.

"Ah, I didn't expect to see you already up and dressed." Dean remarked a bit surprised to see Kane up. Dean sighed as he felt bad that Kane had already started on the dishes since Dean wanted to surprise Kane. After the little scare from the other night, it was understandable that Dean wanted to make things easier for Kane. "You didn't have to do those." Dean started out as he tossed the towel into the hamper that rested outside of the bathroom. "I was going to get them after my shower." Dean continued, walking towards Kane before giving him an ever so soft kiss on his forehead. "Want me to make breakfast instead?" It was at least a fair trade off. "Maybe something light for your stomach?"

"I don't mind." Kane remarked, a small smile spreading on his face as Kane slid the freshly washed dish into the still water to clean off any suds that remained on the plate. "Besides, you helped me out last night when I was going through my panic attack." Kane reasoned before letting out a small sigh. "I just didn't expect the lightning to hit that close." Kane continued with a small shrug of his shoulders as Kane averted his eyes.

"Felicia is going to be picking us up in an hour or so." Kane started to speak up once more as he fished out to work on another dish. "Since we're going to be flying towards the location where she is going to build the device, I don't want to eat anything for now." That was Kane's way of politely declining Dean from making them some food. "Motion sickness and all, you know?" Kane finished, taking the last dish he was washing to slide it into the still water.

"Right. It's close by to a large field right? Away from any towns?" Dean asked, trying to remember what Felicia had said about their last encounter on their way back home from visiting Amelia. Not like Dean could really track all the terms that she was using to describe the process that went behind the new and improved death beam. It had some scientific terms that went above Dean's knowledge. It was a good thing that Felicia was on his side instead of the being on the station with the Elite.

"Yeah. It would be safer that way." Kane added, putting the last dish on the tray with a small click of the plates knocking together. "After all, we don't know exactly what to expect once the trigger has been pulled." Kane remarked as he pulled the plug from the soapy water. "We were also able to retrieve some special suits that people used to wear to protect from harmful radiation." Kane continued, glancing over his shoulder towards Dean.

"We're expecting that once it has been hit, the station might end up somewhere in the ocean." Depending on the location that they hit the station in, it was a safe bet that the Millennium would fall in the ocean close by to one of the clans. "We made sure to evacuate everyone from the islands closest to where it will land. The flooding from the tidal waves will be devastating to the coastlines nearby. Not to mention the amount of smoke from the station crashing and breaking up in the atmosphere..." Kane trailed off as his gaze went towards the water that was slowly spinning down the drain. It was clear that Kane was worried about the after effect of all of this going down.

"It's a big price to pay for everyone to be free from the monsters..." Dean remarked, placed a hand on Kane's back before softly rubbing it. "It's true that a lot of innocent people that I grew up around will be killed, but their blood will be on my hands. Not yours" Dean reassured Kane as he lightly pressed into Kane's side. "I was the one who decided to convince the others to be on my side. You are not doing anything wrong here. So put that out of your mind." As comforting as it sounded, Kane still had a worried expression on his face.

"But the monsters who left us to die had perished hundreds of years ago Dean." Kane started to speak up, glancing over to the other male. "We're just punishing their descendants now. Labeling them monsters simply because they came from the bloodline of those who did us wrong." Kane had a point, but Dean felt that this was their best course of action. Even if Kane didn't see it now, eventually they would be forced to deal with the Elites one way or another. "Aren't we just as bad for letting them die out in the ocean? Where they can't swim?" Kane asked, turning to face Dean more directly.

"Think about how much the Earth's gravity affected you Dean." Kane added, causing a worried expression to cross Dean's face. "How it took you weeks to just be able to move around. And then months afterwards to move around without much issue." Kane continued as his brows knitted together in worry. "Not only are we letting them sink to their death, but we're leaving them for the monsters of the ocean. Large apex creatures that show no mercy for intruding vessels that cross into their waters." The worry in Kane's voice showed that the leader had been thinking a lot about this. There wasn't much that Dean could even say that would lessen Kane's worry over this whole situation.

"You know that if we try to rescue them, we'll be putting a lot of our people in danger as well, right?" Dean remarked, placing his hands on Kane's shoulders. It didn't seem to relax Kane much, but at least it seemed that Kane was willing to listen. Even if the leader turned his head to avert looking at Dean. "Besides, the people who are in charge are still killing off the lower class as a means to control the population." Dean continued, recalling some of the rumors he had heard.

"You may not want to believe it, but the Elite are so messed up in the head that I heard some horrible rumors that made me wonder if they were true or not." Dean took a small deep breath in as he prepared himself to talk about the horrible rumor that unfortunately ended up being true. "Before they start to hurl people towards the Earth in their pods, the Elite used to force petty criminals into a chamber that would end up sucking them out into space." Dean continued, watching as Kane looked up at him with a concerned gaze. "The Elite sat in a room just above the chamber, watching the people suffocate in the cold harsh space. All the while they enjoyed smoking cigars from the freshly cut tobacco leaves they had gotten earlier that day. You really think that they shouldn't be punished for that?" Dean asked, studying Kane's eyes closely after finishing his story.

Kane glanced away from Dean as he knew that there was no way that this could end peacefully. "I know their behavior can't be excused Dean." Kane started to speak, averting his gaze once more. "But it just feels wrong to end people's lives just like that. Even if they deserve it."

Kane remarked with a pout on his face. "Just once we're done with this, can we leave all of this violence behind us?" Kane asked as he gently grasped Dean's shirt.

"I'm tired of watching the people I care about turn into killers as well. It's not fair to them to soil their hands with the blood of innocent people." Dean couldn't exactly blame Kane for feeling this way. It must have been hard seeing the person that Miles killed laying on the ground, blood seeping out of his neck while Miles seemed to lay on the ground unconscious. Or watching the blood pool up under his brother Lucas after stabbing him repeatedly. Kane had enough blood on his hands, and he didn't want to see how Dean would turn out after the station would crash to the ground.

"I promise you Kane. After all of this is said and done, the only time in which violence would ever occur would be if someone attacked us first." Dean spoke in a reassuring tone, giving a light smile to Kane to show he meant it. It wasn't as if there was much in the way of violence that would lead to Dean needing to get his hands dirty. For the most part, people tend to leave each other alone. It was a complete stark contrast to what Dean had gotten used to on the station. Where everyone needed to be in your business, never letting you have a moment's peace while in your own pod. The constant feeling of being watched always seemed to put people on edge.

"Alright." Kane started to speak, a gentle smile on his face. "I'm keeping you at your word then." Kane remarked, feeling a bit reassured, though the lingering thoughts about how this would affect their own people didn't seem to disappear. Would their community really blossom after they destroy the last bit of humanity from before the bombs drop? Maybe they would be able to figure out a way to memorialize those lost in the crash once this was all said and done. At least, that's what Kane was hoping for.

By the time the sun had peeked out from the hills, there was a knock on the door. Before either one of the two men could answer it, a woman walked in with a smile on her face. It was Felicia, and the outfit she was wearing was completely different than what Dean had seen her in. Her long platinum blonde hair was braided into a side french braid that hung over her left shoulder. Wearing a thinly strapped light gray tank top under a long white lab coat that reached down towards her ankles, Felicia wore black shorts that reached her mid thighs with a loose belt resting on her hips. A pair of dark stockings reached just above her knees, allowing for just a small bit of a metal rim to peek out of stocking. Dean's eyes seemed to be a bit fixated on the leg as it seemed what everyone had told him was true. Felicia really did have a prosthetic leg.

"Morning guys." Felicia called out, stepping onto the little greeting mat that had faded over the years with a pair of black boots that went up to her ankles. It wasn't long before Felicia took notice of where Dean's eyes had landed, causing her to become a bit self conscious. Tucking her hands into the pockets of her coat, she pushed the coat forward ever so slightly, causing the coat to drape over the leg as if to hide it. "Ready for the light show tonight?" Felicia asked, though there was a small waver in her voice, showing that she was rather embarrassed about Dean staring at her leg.

Dean realized the mistake he made once he noticed that Felicia was attempting to hide her leg, causing him to snap out of his gaze. "Oh, yeah!" Dean spoke up, clearing his throat a little before glancing to Kane to see if he would get scolded for staring at Felicia's leg. But to Dean's surprise, Kane kept his gaze forward, a soft smile lingering on his face.

"I'm taking it that everyone has been put into the shelters then? No worries about having our own casualties?" Kane asked, trying his best to help put Felicia at ease. It wasn't exactly Dean's fault for staring. Felicia always tends to keep it covered up with her outfits, so seeing her in something that wasn't exactly medieval looking or would completely cover up her right leg was something that Dean wasn't used to.

"Yup. I made sure that everyone was accounted for." Felicia chimed up happily, even though she was still hiding her leg with her coat. "They have enough supplies and room to last them a couple of months if things were to go sour." At least that much was reassuring the Kane that they didn't have to worry about running out of supplies soon. "But by my calculations, that shouldn't happen." Felicia remarked, sounding a bit more like her cheerful self as she kept her attention onto Kane. It was like she was doing everything she could to avoid looking at Dean at that moment. "So, the ship should be almost done refueling now. Shall we head towards the shore and get this train moving?" Felicia asked, though her voice seemed to waver again as she made a quick glance towards Dean.

"Yeah. Let me just get my jacket and shoes on." Kane remarked, moving towards the door to gather the last bit he needed to head out. Dean didn't exactly like the thought of Felicia feeling weird around him, but it wasn't like he didn't understand. It took a while for Kane to be comfortable not hiding his scar that lingered on over his right eye, but now Kane doesn't seem bothered by it anymore. Dean had to fix this while he still had a chance.

"Before we head out," Dean spoke up, catching Kane and Felicia off guard. "I just want you to know that I didn't mean to make you feel self conscious, Felicia. It's just," Dean trailed off, pondering how he was going to explain why Dean had the need to stare at her fake leg. "I've never seen a prosthetic leg before. Not even on the station." That wasn't a lie, but seeing how uncomfortable Felicia seemed to appear, Dean was going to correct this as soon as he could. "So, sorry if my staring may have come off as rude." Dean wasn't exactly the best at explaining himself, but the faint smile on Felicia's face revealed that she wasn't mad at him. There seemed to be a sense of relief coming from Felicia after Dean explained himself.

"It's alright Dean." Felicia spoke up with a soft nod of her head. "I guess I still get a bit self conscious about people staring at it. Especially when they don't know about it." She continued, bending down to brush her fingers gingerly against her prosthetic leg. "Miles told me that I should stop trying to hide it....but it's easy for his scars to be covered since they are on his back." Felicia continued, moving to stand up straight once more.

"Kane used to hide his scar with his long bangs as you noticed when you first arrived." Felicia continued, seeing a flustered look on Kane's face as he left to grab something before their journey. "It was actually nice to see him show more of his sweet face that I..." Felicia paused, briefly glancing towards Kane before her attention was brought back to Dean. "Decided to embrace my own scars." She continued with a soft angelic smile. "I want to accept myself for who I am completely." Dean was surprised to hear Felicia accept the fact that even she had a scar she couldn't hide for long. "If I can't even accept myself for all my flaws, then what good am I as a leader?"

Seeing the smile lingering on her face, Dean was rather surprised that Felicia was willing to reveal the very thing she had worked hard to keep hidden. It seems that everyone was starting to blossom since Dean had first met them. Beforehand the leaders had kept mostly to themselves, but now they seemed to have accepted Dean as if he was part of them. Not that Dean would ever want to be a leader, but the feeling that they accepted Dean as one of their own was something he never got to experience on the station. This made the decision to go through with the plan to blast the station out of the sky all that more crucial to restoring humanity and furthering the advancement needed to their survival.

After collecting their items, the three made their way towards the coastline where the airship had been anchored down to refuel. The pathway wasn't as long as the first trip had been when Dean first arrived on Earth. Walking about thirty or so minutes, the three came to the shoreline where their first encounter started. Unlike the last time however, there were barely enough people for a small fleet that seemed to linger around the docks. Even the oceanic waters felt still, as if setting the mood for what they were going to do.

Glancing up at the sky above, the thick clouds above barely allowed for Dean to gaze at the station passing overhead. A light scowl lingered on Dean's face as he waited for his turn to climb onto the airship. Gripping the metal railing, Dean boarded after Kane. Unlike the last time, Kane made his way over towards a small military cot that would allow for the leader to nestle down while they traveled. Taking a seat next to Kane, Dean would glance over to make sure that the leader was safely strapped in. This was the first time ever that Dean got a chance to see what happened in the cockpit of the airship during the flight from start to finish.

The interior was made out of a mixture of wood and metal pipes. There were panels all over the front of the ship that seemed to be used to monitor the condition of the airship. A team of two people sat down on swiveling chairs that made it easier to reach the necessary buttons if needed. In the middle towards the front of the cockpit that was lined with large glass panels was a seat that was turned to reveal a large wooden wheel with faint letters on each tip of the wheel. If Dean were to gamble on the wheel being from an old boat, he would be a winner. It seemed that the wheel was taken off and repurposed for the airship. There were a few small panels on either side of the chair that Dean could only guess belonged to Felicia. Though he wasn't sure as to what they did, Dean could only speculate their functions.

"Is everyone ready?" Felicia called out as she made her way towards the central chair. "I want to get everything set up by the time the sun goes down. Today will go down in history as the day the cowards in the sky get their just desserts." Felicia called out, grabbing a pair of black goggles with bright orange lenses with smaller similar lenses along the right side. Taking her rightful place, Felicia strapped herself in, the others in the room following suit, as the one remaining crew member closed and locked the door that they had previously climbed onto while boarding.

As the airship started to come to life, the cockpit started to shake ever so slightly. Much like the first time that Dean was on the ship, the sounds of pipes popping was similar to being on the station. As the ship began to rise from the ground, Dean glanced over to make sure that Kane was alright. Watching as Kane buried his face into the pillow, Dean knew that it would only be momentary. There was a feeling of pressure on Dean's stomach, but that soon faded as the airship got higher into the air. If it was this extreme up in the cockpit, Dean could only imagine how it must have felt underneath them in the cargo for anyone left down there. Now he understood why Felicia wouldn't allow for cattle to be transported on the air ships, their limbs may not support them, causing the poor animals to be in pain before they could even land.

Eventually the ship was able to break through the lower layer of clouds, allowing for the crew to move about if need be. Felicia was still at the helm, gazing out of the window as Dean glanced over towards Kane. "Hey, you alright?" Dean asked, unbuckling himself to stretch out his legs. "Need any ginger ale or crackers for your stomach?" Dean continued to ask, moving to kneel down as Kane softly gazed up towards him.

"No. I'll be fine so long as I don't eat anything." Kane mumbled, his hand moving to rest on his stomach. "It'll be a little while before we get there. Feel free to get yourself something to eat at least." Kane encouraged, though Dean didn't have much of an appetite at the moment. With the excitement of being able to see the station come down, Dean's appetite had been suppressed. "I'll have something when we land." Kane added, a soft groan leaving his lips. "Nothing too big. Just some buttered bread or crackers or something." Kane slowly shrugged, hating that they had to travel by airship in order to get towards the more isolated area that would let their plan go off without hardly any problems.

"Alright." Dean remarked, reaching over to brush some of Kane's hair out from his face. "If you need me, have one of the crew members come and fetch me." Dean knew that if he fussed over Kane, it might just make things worse. Considering that Kane was easily motion sickness on any type of transportation that rocked, it was hard to figure out a way to make it easier for the leader to not suffer.

As Dean moved to stand up so that he could look around, Felicia turned around in her chair after locking the helm in position. "Hey Dean, why don't you come over here and get a wonderful view that not many people get to see." Felicia called out over the sound of the dull engine roaring in the cabin. "It'll take your breath away." Felicia added, flashing a bright smile though the goggle she was wearing looked rather ridiculous.

Making his way over towards the helm, Dean braced himself by placing his hand on the back of Felicia's chair. Leaning forward, Dean was struck with awe at what was before him. Before Dean were massive clouds that ranged from large fluffy clouds that were darkened in color as it threatened to pour down rain it had collected onto the ground below, to small piles of clouds that looked like bits of smooth mashed potatoes. There were some clouds that seemed even tower above the rest, forming small arches connecting the two large masses of cloud. Passing through one of the large clouds, bits of rain drizzled onto the large panels of glass, making the sun that peeked out from the clouds to sparkle against the small water droplets.

As the ship continued to fly through the clouds, the ground slowly opened up in various patches, making it almost seem like the land below were elaborate puddles to another world beneath the clouds. From up high, Dean could see bits of farm land that had been cut back to a particular spot before the wilderness surrounded the lands' edges. Large homes with white panels were easily spotted even from high above. Dean had been both on the ground looking up, and floating above the Earth looking down, but this was the first time he was between those two worlds. It didn't even seem real to Dean. Like he was in a fantasy land.

"Whoa..." Dean trailed off, his eyes scanning everything to take it all in. It was almost as if he could simply step out of the plane and fly among the clouds, but sadly gravity wasn't his friend in that regard as he would simply fall back down to Earth. But being able to see this view from up high, it must have given Felicia an amazing show each time she would fly in the clouds. Despite the fact that Felicia's leg may have been gone, it didn't mean that her wings were clipped.

"Right?" Felicia chimed happily, a big smile on her face as she turned to see Dean's expression. "If it wasn't for the fact that it is dangerous to travel at night, I would be more than happy to fly all the time." Felicia continued, lightly gripping the helm in her hand. "In the morning or at dusk, when the sun hangs below the clouds, it's like I'm flying through a shimmering world of orange, red, and purple." Felicia spoke in a daydream tone, the smile never fading from her face. "I get to see a beauty unlike anything of this world and I wish I could share it with the rest of the world." Felicia continued, the smile slowly fading as her head lowered.

"You know, I heard stories from before the war..." Felicia trailed off before looking back up at Dean. "Stories of cities and towns shimmering like a river of golden diamonds." Felicia paused, moving to turn back to look out the window once more. "Lighting up the ground in vibrant colors that would make it hard to ever get lost. Shimmering brighter than any starry sky against the vast ocean..." Felicia trailed off, gripping the wheel in her hand once more, the smile slowly fading from her face as she wished to see it, but didn't dare to voice it.

"Yeah, I heard about that as well." Dean remarked, though he had never once seen a speck of light coming from the Earth. He wished that he could have seen those lights from his little pod on the Millennium. To be able to trace the continents by the lights shimmering like stars, revealing the life of those who were still alive. Despite wishing that for so long, he knew the reason why those who survived on Earth didn't make themselves known. They lived in constant fear that they would be wiped out once more. All because the Elite wanted to be the last true humans left in the universe. "You could tell how large a population was simply by how bright their lights glowed at night." Dean added, causing Felicia to glance back at him, the smile returning to her face once more.

"Exactly!" Felicia remarked, her voice showing how excited she was to know that someone felt the same way as she did. "I want to see those lights shimmering brightly once more. To be able to look down at a sea of lights while the stars continue to sparkle above me." Felicia remarked, turning in her chair to face Dean more directly. "It's always been a dream of mine to be able to find myself between two bodies of light. Where I could feel at peace with myself for once." What did that even mean? To find peace with yourself? Dean didn't know what Felicia meant by that, but it seemed like she was willing to explain it.

"Frankly the closest I've come to experience something like that was when Miles took me to a small island close by to my home." Felicia started to recall, a timid smile on her face as she brought her finger tips together in thought. "I had just gotten my prosthetic leg and was feeling down because of it." Dean was surprised to see how timid and innocent Felicia appeared right now with a small flustered look on her face.

"He told me to put on my sunflower sundress and meet him on the beach." Felicia continued, a soft hum leaving her lips towards the end. "That idiot…" Felicia softly muttered in a fond tone of voice before continuing her story. "We walked over the small sand bridge to an island that we use to grow some fruits." Felicia paused, a soft chuckle leaving her lips as she recounted the memory. "By the time we reached the shore, the tide was starting to come in." Felicia moved to cross her left leg over her right, a hand reaching up to tuck in some stray bits of hair from her right side to nestle behind her hair.

"Before I could come in further, Miles stopped me in my tracks. I could feel the warmth of the ocean pool up against my ankle as the warm tropical wind started to blow. The sound of water rushing under my feet felt like a dull roar." Felicia spoke in a fond tone as she remembered the whole thing as if it happened yesterday.

"I gaze upon him, only to have him lightly point upwards." Felicia continued to explain, her voice sounding almost dreamy. "Above us were the bright stars that twinkled so brightly between scattered clouds." Felicia paused, glancing up at the wooden ceiling through her goggles. "I've never seen so many stars in my lifetime, and the station wasn't hanging over my head at that particular time. So it felt like a type of freedom I never thought I would ever feel since the tiger took my leg." Felicia continued before shifting her gaze down towards the leg, only to idly reach down to caress her prosthetic leg.

"And then he told me to look down at the water that rested beneath my feet." Felicia added with a soft chuckle, closing her eyes halfway in thought before she continued her story. "I was surprised at how calm the water was back then, and how it reflected the stars above me. It made my heart feel so incredibly light that it brought me tears of joy that night." Felicia's eyes started to water a bit as she recalled that memory so vividly.

"Miles soon joined me, getting the hem of his robe wet in the process but he placed his hands on my shoulder. Leaning in close, he rested his forehead against mine." Felicia paused long enough to wipe away some of the tears that slowly trickled down her cheeks as it escaped the curves of her goggles. "And he said to me, though you may cry for the beauty that was lost, you will always be as beautiful as the night sky is right now. For beauty is nothing more than flesh to some, but to Miles, it's my soul that captured him." Felicia let out a soft sigh as if to let out the breath she held. "It's bright and beautiful, always shimmering even in the darkest of nights."

Felicia placed a hand on her chest, a sincere smile lingering on her face as bits of tears still clung to the sides of her face. "So I want to capture that feeling once more. Of being between two forms of stars and feeling the peace that Miles gave me that day." Felicia finished, looking up at Dean with a bright smile on her face. "So let's make sure we destroy the station so we can make the skies and land beautiful once again, okay?"

How was Dean supposed to say no to something like that? The way that the energy Felicia had changed as she told her story, it was oddly inspiring when she talked about how Miles helped to see the beauty within herself. "Yeah…" Dean trailed off, a soft nod of his head as he glanced out the window. "I would love to see the lights shimmer as well." Dean remarked, knowing that this was their one and only chance. If they messed this up, it would be all over. But Dean couldn't focus on that right now. He had to put faith that their plan would work. It just had to work. For all of their sake.

As the airship circled around a small island that looked as if it was nothing more than a large meadow with a few tents circling a rather large device, Felicia started to lower the airship. The people that rested underneath them seemed to rush towards the descending airship, ready to help anchor it to the ground. It took a bit of careful maneuvering, but eventually the airship was tied down to the ground. As the engine was turned off, Dean made his way over towards Kane who hadn't moved from his spot on the military cot.

"Hey, we're here." Dean spoke softly, placing a hand on Kane's shoulder, gently shaking the other away. Watching as Kane turned to look at Dean with a groggy expression and some of his silver hair messed up, Dean was quick to help tame the disheveled locks. "Need help walking around?" Dean asked, only to see Kane softly shake his head.

"No, I'll be fine." Kane grumbled, getting to his feet though Kane's right hand still lingered on stomach. Dean wasn't exactly going to argue with Kane, but at the very least he would keep an eye on the male. It wasn't like they had far to go, but knowing how Kane got when he was hit with motion sick, it didn't exactly help anything either.

Climbing out of the airship, Dean was greeted with grass that seemed to reach just below his knees. There was a clearing up ahead with the gigantic device standing proudly in the middle of it all. It was massive, much bigger than anything that Dean could ever think of. Surrounding the large cannon device was a bunch of rods with purple glowing orbs on top of them. A low hum could faintly be heard from each tower as they got closer, Dean was interested in knowing how all of this was being powered up. There were gauges along the length of the towers, some of which were fluctuating. Long wire tubes seemed to slither along the ground towards the canon, looking as if it was too heavy to be easily knocked over.

"Spectacular work guys. I'm impressed that you were able to set it up just right." Felicia remarked as she moved towards the cannon. Placing a hand on the metal, Felicia gently caressed the large device as if it was her own child. The cannon was seemingly attached to a wooden miniature deck to keep it from falling over. The top of the rim seemed to reach over seven feet tall. The barrel of the cannon looked as if it could fit five normal people inside of it with a bit of room to spare for them to move about. Even though Dean was curious as to how it looked inside of the cannon, he figured that it was lined with all kinds of wiring to make sure that it would actually work.

"Well we did follow your instructions." One of the men who was setting up the device remarked. "We had a storm last night, so we were able to get max energy stored up for today." The man continued as he walked over to the three. The man was wearing a pair of faded overalls with a dark gray shirt nestled underneath. The man was rather muscular as his arms looked to be the size of grapefruits. His black locks were pulled back into a tight man bun with the sides of his head shaved. Wearing a pair of protective goggles, it was hard to tell what color the man's eyes were, but if Dean were to guess, they probably would be a light green. As the man pulled off the goggles, it seemed that Dean's hunch was indeed right. "So," The man spoke as his eyes seemed to drift towards Dean. "Is this the outsider? The one who was crazy enough to convince you to follow through with your plan?"

"Mmhm." Felicia hummed in agreement. "This is Dean Torres. He's the one who fell from the station on a one way trip. " Felicia added, gently patting Dean on the back. "Surprised he is one of the few who actually made it in one piece." Felicia remarked, giving Dean a light smack on the back to push Dean towards the large man. "He got Amelia's approval and everything. So he's one of us now." Felicia finished, flashing a bright smile towards Dean.

"Nice to meet you Dean. " The man started to speak in a baritone voice. "I'm Adam Miller." The man introduced himself, holding out a hand for Dean to shake it. The man's hand was huge compared to Dean's. Even though the man looked like a complete beast who could probably rip Dean's arm off, his handshake was oddly gentle. Like he was nothing more than a big teddy bear.

"Nice to meet you as well Adam." Dean remarked, slowly retracting his hand once he was done shaking his hand. "So guessing this is the death ray then that Felicia was talking about?" Dean asked, looking up at the cannon with an impressed expression on his face. Who would have guessed that they had this sort of technology simply laying around? Even with all technology wiped out when the bombs dropped, to find something like this must have been a miracle.

"Yeah. She was working on it long before you came around." Adam remarked as he glanced back at the cannon, only to have Felicia lightly punch his arm. "What? It's the truth." Adam remarked with a small shrug of his shoulders. "You wanted to prove your father right after all." Adam added, smiling at Felicia. "That there is a way to take out the cowards once and for all. He would be proud of you. With everything that you accomplished on your own." Adam finished, a big smile on his face.

"Y-Yeah...but that doesn't mean that you should tell everyone about that." Felicia remarked with a small flustered look as she crossed her arms in a pouting manner. "Changing the subject back to the cannon," Felicia spoke, clearing her throat in the process. "Water didn't get inside the cannon or anything did it?" Felicia asked, glancing towards the cannon with a concerned look on her face. "I want to make sure that there is no possible way for this to get screwed up. This is our one and only chance to take them down." It seemed that one small thing could cause this whole operation to become nothing more than a bust, making Dean worry if they could pull it off or not.

"We made sure to keep it covered when the rain came." Adam spoke, pointing towards a tent that had people folding up a large blue tarp. Seems like they thought of everything. "We also made sure to get the other stuff you requested as well." Adam remarked, crossing his arms over his chest. "The barriers are made up of lead to protect from any type of radiation blast that may come from the cannon; specialize hazmat suits that people used to wear when dealing with radiation; and some food that we can cook over a little bonfire." Adam continued before glancing towards Kane who was leaning onto Dean while holding his stomach. "We even made sure to get some ginger ale prepped and chilled for a certain motion sick leader that we know." Adam finished, a soft burly chuckle leaving his lips as Kane looked towards him.

"Sorry... you know how my stomach gets when I am in some type of transportation vehicle." Kane apologized, knowing that it must have looked like some kind of inconvenience for people around the leader. "I'll go and get some now. Don't want to skip out on the delicious food you brought after all." Kane remarked, carefully making his way towards the tent that housed his relief.

"I'll run some checks on the towers and cannon myself. Make sure everything is in order before we relax. It'll be a few hours before the station is in alignment for the cannon to get a direct hit." Felicia spoke up as he glanced over towards Dean. "Go ahead and keep Kane company. You've done the hard work of convincing Amelia to allow this day to happen. So go ahead and relax with Kane." Felicia added, knowing that they were on the last bend of this journey that Dean was on.

"I'm sure he would be more than happy to have your company right now." Felicia remarked, glancing towards Kane in the tent who was settling down with a glass of ginger ale. "We got it from here." She added, giving Dean a light smack on the shoulder before turning her attention to tending to the towers. Not like Dean really had much of a choice in the manner. It was best to stay close to Kane, allowing Felicia and her crew to make sure everything was set up for the big night. Despite the calm and relaxed atmosphere, Dean's heart was pounding against his chest.

As the sun seeped into the oceanic horizon, those on the mission to destroy the United Space Station Millennium were sitting around a fire that was built closer to the shore as some of the equipment was flammable. One small bit of floating embers could very well result in their mission failing. With empty plates with bits of crumbs lingering on them from the meal they ate, Dean glanced up towards the darkening sky. For once there wasn't a single cloud hanging around to obscure their tracking of the Millennium. With his thumb and index finger resting on the rim of the plate, Dean was able to keep from having the wind that was blowing from the shore that could rip Dean's wooden plate off of his lap.

"Nervous?" Kane spoke up, catching Dean's attention as the male looked at Kane with a somber expression. "Or, are you realizing now that you're going to be killing off your own people in a goal to get back at the people who tried to kill you?" Kane asked, noting the change of expression on Dean's face from earlier.

"I'm not sure anymore." Dean spoke up, his gaze going back down to the plate in his lap. "It's not like we have much of a choice. Plus we've already come this far, so what's the point in backing out now." Dean remarked, a small shrug of his shoulders as the crackling of the fire started to sound like a dull roar in Dean's ears.

"It just feels like a heavy knot is in my stomach." Dean admitted, placing a hand on his stomach. "I don't know exactly how long I can handle this waiting though." Dean continued as his leg started to shake a bit, his nervousness showing. "It feels like we're about to go against an evil tyrant. To save the land, and free people from a threat that could kill them without a second thought. The very thought of it all is nerve wracking to say the least." Dean spoke as his fist clenched the shirt he was wearing.

"Trust me, I know that feeling all too well." Kane remarked, moving to lightly lean on Dean. "But we've come this far, like you said. We're staring at an unknown possibility and it's quite frightening." Kane continued, his gaze moving to look upwards at the purple sky with small traces of stars that were already visible. "If this works, we can finally advance our society to light up the darkness that we once used for cover to hide from the monster that floats above us." Kane continued, feeling the warmth of the fire close by. "The terrible all seeing eye that always felt like it casted judgment on us will finally be gone for good." Considering that the red light along the bottom of the pods always casted a red glow, it was easy to see how the Millennium looked like a giant eyeball in the sky. "But we're finally fighting back instead of hiding. We're taking our lives back, and it's all thanks to you." Kane spoke in a gentle voice as he moved his attention to Dean.

As Dean locked eyes with Kane, the leader softly smiled as he placed a hand on Dean's shoulder. Kane gave Dean a soft squeeze before moving to stand up. "Think about it this way, if those cowards did decide to fight back, we'll easily out fight them since we know this land like the back of our hand." Kane added, reaching to brush some of the sand off of himself.

"We'll capture them, and see if they're worthy of joining our rankings. That way we can avoid bloodshed." Kane continued, moving to toss the wooden plate into the fire. "Just like you were when they first arrived, they won't be able to walk in natural gravity. So capture is our second option. It's a peaceful way to resolve this whole issue. Wouldn't you agree?" Kane asked, giving Dean a reassuring smile at the end.

Thinking about it that way, Dean could see the logic behind it. After all, the first time that Dean tried to walk in the hospital, he nearly doubled over from the pressure his body felt. Everyone on the station was used to artificial gravity that they never experienced the real thing. "I guess you do have a point." Dean remarked, a coy smile on his face as he got up to toss his wooden plate into the fire as well. "Guess you guys already decided that as a second option in case we fail?" Dean asked, joining Kane's side as the male waited for Dean by the pathway that led back towards the cannon.

"I can neither confirm or deny." Kane teased as he started to walk ahead of Dean. "But let's just say that us leaders always make up backup plans in case the first option doesn't exactly pan out." Kane remarked, shoving his hands into the pockets of his pants. "If the station explodes right then and there, then we know our plan was a success. If not," Kane trailed off a bit before he glanced back at Dean. "Well, we would have no choice but to wait for them to make a move then." Not the best option, but it was an option nevertheless.

"If they want to surrender peacefully, that would be ideally." Kane added, though it was unsure if the members of the Elite would even surrender peacefully, or if they would put up a fight. "But knowing those cowards, it might get bloody. Not that we would want that to happen. But it's a sacrifice we're willing to make." Kane's voice expressed that he wasn't pleased with the idea of killing, but it was either kill or be killed.

"Hopefully it doesn't come down to that." Dean remarked, following behind Kane. Dean knew the heavy weight of worrying about the people that Kane had. Trying to be more tactful when it comes to the decisions that he made. Being an outsider made it a bit easier for Kane to come to Dean with his struggles as they talked about it before bed. Even if Dean didn't help much as he just simply listened to Kane's worries about certain subject matters dealing with his clan, it was still a way that Dean contributed to helping the clan he was a part of.

As they reached the top of the hill, Felicia walked over towards the pair with something in her hand. "Alright you two. Put these on and stand behind one of the barriers. It's getting closer to the time, so we're going to get things ready." Felicia remarked, wearing a pair of darkened goggles and some type of white suit over her current clothing. It almost looked like a type of jumper suit, but it was far too big on Felicia's slender frame. "You'll be given some noise canceling headphones, so don't expect to be able to hear what the person next to you is saying. Just sit back and enjoy the fireworks, okay?" Felicia chimed up happily, a bright smile landing on her face. Dean could already sense Felicia's excitement for her pet project to be put to the test.

"Already?" Kane asked, a bit surprised that they were already doing this. They must have taken longer than he originally thought. "Alright, we'll get set up. Let us know if there is anything we can do to help out." Kane remarked, though there wasn't much that he could help with. But it was at least worth the effort.

With the articles in hand, the two headed towards the barrier where some of the other members were already suited up and standing by. "By the way," Dean spoke up, setting the articles onto a table before putting the goggles off to the side. "Where are the other leaders? Why is it only you and Felicia here?" With all the talk about wanting to see the cowards being blown up in the sky, one would figure that a vast majority of the leaders would want to be there to witness history in the making.

"Well, they have to take care of their clans." Kane remarked as he started to get dressed. "Keeping everyone calm in the shelters isn't exactly easy." Knowing that the last time that they people had to head into the shelters meant that the Elite destroyed a vast majority of the population at the time. It was understandable that the people needed to have some type of figure head to reassure them that everything was going to be alright.

"Then how come you're here?" Dean asked soon after as he started to put the suit on. "Shouldn't you be in the shelter with your people as well then?" It was an honest question, though it seemed that Kane was hurt by it. Putting on the white jumper felt a bit awkward, but he would need it in case the unexpected happened and he would be part of the rescue team.

"Well, I wanted to be with you." Kane spoke bluntly as he pulled the sleeve over his arm. "I mean, we did see most of this through together. So, why not stay by your side through the greatest accomplishment of your life?" Kane added, moving a hand to zip up the front of the suit. "Besides, I could never stay down in the shelters for too long. I'm a bit claustrophobic after the incident with Miles and those of the Wrath clan." Kane finished, a small flustered expression crossing his face as Kane didn't like talking about his weaknesses.

"Way to make me feel like a dick." Dean remarked, zipping up his suit as well before putting on the goggles. "But if it helps any, I'm glad that you decided to stay with me then. To see this last bit with me means a lot." Dean spoke, moving to grab the headphones before making his way towards the group. It seemed like a lot of them had already put their headphones on, keeping to themselves as some looked up to see if they would be able to see the Millennium for themselves.

As if on cue, the Millennium could be seen in the distance. It slowly rolled through the skies, the large station looking intimating with the red lights slowly fading in and out amongst the stars. Felicia was quick to press a button that caused the purple glow from the towers to fade. The power lines that snaked through the wires on the ground started to glow purple as the power was being directed towards the cannon.

The wires looked like a bunch of slithered snakes as the power moved towards the cannon.

Before much longer the cannon started to glow a bright purple, indicating that it was ready to be fired as soon as it was in line with the Millennium. Those who didn't have their headphones on quickly scurried to put them on in fear of going deaf if they weren't fast enough as well as slip the goggles on to protect their eyes from the bright light emitting from the cannon.

Felicia rushed over towards another button that was behind its' own barricade. Her eyes were focused on the large red orb that was heading towards them, keeping track of the movement and the speed in which the Millennium was moving in their direction. The fact that Dean could barely hear a sound other than his heart beating was making him nervous. A million thoughts seemed to enter Dean's mind as he watched it get closer. Was Felicia going to press the button in time? Was it going to hit? Would the Millennium react in time as it was obvious that they couldn't hide the large purple glow coming from the cannon? All of the muscles in Dean's body clenched as a cold sweat started to form against his temples.

Just when it seemed like the Millennium might pass overhead, Felicia pressed the button that would send a bright purple wave towards the Millennium. It was blinding. The cannon lit up the area around them, shining bright like a star.

The sonic boom from the cannon could be felt through their bodies, almost knocking some of the people off of their feet. If it wasn't for the barrier, some of the people might have very well fallen down from the blast alone. The tent that held down their supplies barely stayed on the ground as it seemed that the stakes holding the tent in the ground stayed in place. The heat coming off of the cannon was hot, making it feel like it was high noon in the desert.

By the time that the last wave from the long stream of energy left the cannon, all anyone could do was watch in awe as the stream of light made its way towards the Millennium. Red meeting purple. Would it hit? Would it completely destroy the symbol of oppression? Would they finally be free?

Dean held his breath, his eyes staring towards the sky as he waited to see what would happen. Silence fell on the group as they all watched, wondering what would happen. Despite the loud roar of the cannon earlier, it was dead silent. No one dared to say a word. All they wanted to see was the eyesore in the sky of the Millennium exploding. To see the very symbol of their oppression fall from the looming skies. Time slowed down as the light disappeared. The long that everyone looked up, they soon realized that the light had faded. And there was nothing...

Nothing happened...

Not a single sign that the death ray did as it was supposed to do. Instead, the red lights of the Millennium continued on as if nothing happened. Dean and the rest were surprised that nothing seemed to come of this. As some of the people started to take off their goggles and headphones, Dean stood there in disbelief. How could they have failed? How did they miss? It wasn't like the Millennium had some kind of force field that would be able to stop it. So why? Why did it miss?

Slumping down to his knees, Dean felt his heart sink. All that hard work, and for what? For them to miss? To doom the planet once more? Hunching over on the ground, Dean dug his nails into the ground as he couldn't come to terms with it. His body shook with rage unlike anything Dean had ever felt before. "How did we miss? How did we fail?" Dean mumbled to himself, his voice sounded louder in his head with the headphones still on him. "It's not fair....

we planned it all out. And for what?!" Dean yelled, bringing his fist up to slam into the ground, only to be stopped by someone.

Dean quickly glanced up to see who had caught his wrist, only to see that it was Kane. There was no sorrow on Kane's face, nor was the other upset, but instead he had a genuine concerned look on his face for Dean. As Kane reached over to pull Dean's headphones off of him, the muscles that were tense from frustration slowly started to soften.

Moving to sit up on his knees, Dean pulled the goggles off of his face. The utter look of defeat rested on his face. "I'm sorry Kane....I let you all down..." Dean quickly apologized, his voice wavering as he still couldn't believe how the mission seemed to have failed. "I doomed you all with my ambitions to take down the Elite....I'm sorry....So...very sorry." Dean kept apologizing, though it wouldn't make anything better. How could it?

Seeing the pitiful state that Dean was in, Kane simply knelt down beside him. Not saying another word, Kane placed a hand on Dean's back. Softly rubbing his hand up and down on Dean's back, Kane let Dean wallow in his defeat. As the people around them mumbled inaudible words between each other, Kane did what he did best, comforting the person he cared for the best way that he knew how.

By simply staying by Dean's side, and letting the man get his frustrations out right then and there, that's all that Kane could do for the man. After all, what else could he do? Not like they could head up to the station to check on if there was any damage to it. All they could do now was simply sit and watch to see what would happen. If they were lucky, perhaps they could watch it crash and burn up in the atmosphere. But even that seemed like it was farfetched. After all, they did their best and still failed.

CHAPTER TWENTY TWO: *The Fall Of An Empire*

O N THE STATION a few hours prior, everything seemed to be working as it should. The Elite were busy with their own planning for the Hollow's Eve that was in just a few months. The Silver class were getting their crops ready for the autumn season, and the Bronze continued their normal tasks of serving underneath the two classes like the servants that they were seen as. A lone woman walked through the metal halls of the lower decks with a hand-made cup in her hand. Her legs were lengthy as the lower part of the uniform clung to her well fit body. Her torso was barren as part of the uniform code, showing off her fit stomach that had a few scars around her waist. The top of the uniform had a singular zipper down the middle that made it easier for her to get dressed in the morning. Her light tanned skin glowed under the lights that seeped out light from the metal ceiling. The woman's hair was a copper red with dark brunette roots that was pulled back into a loose ponytail. Hazel eyes scanned the area ahead of her before she reached a door that was for the main computer terminal.

As the doors parted, she walked in the room before covering her mouth to let out a long yawn. "Morning." She called out through the yawn to the man sitting in one of the two chairs. Different lights seemed to light up on the monitor in front of the man, outlining the different layers of the station that floated above the ruined planet below them. "Everything quiet on that blue pearl?" She asked, turning the chair around before sitting down at her station.

"Morning sunshine. See you had another late night." The man remarked, flashing her a side grin as he leaned back in his chair, a small creek from the metal chair could be heard over the dull roar of the ship. The man was rather well fit as well. His dark complex seemed to run all over from his hair to his skin, to even his eyes. Though could you call having a buzz cut with tufts of curled locks sticking out on top of his head hair?

The man seemed to wear a similar outfit to the woman, though the strips that were on the inside of his thighs and around the chest were black while the woman's strips were red. "As for the blue pearl," The man paused before looking at the Earth in front of them slowly spinning with large clouds covering most of the land. "She's just as big and pearly blue as ever." The man added, grabbing hold of his colding coffee before taking a sip.

"Then all is normal." The woman remarked before taking a sip out of her cup. "It's a shame that we can't go back down there, you know?" The woman continued, moving to rest her right elbow on the edge of the control panel that was lighting up with various colors like a Christmas tree. "We could easily rebuild a society down there and make things even better." She continued, almost in a day dream like state.

"Again with this Sofia?" The man exasperated, as if he had heard this a million times. "You know it's dangerous to go down there." Not that there was much evidence as no one sent down there has been able to come back from the planet. "It's a one way hell hole and you know it. There is nothing down there waiting for our return that isn't death." It was the same explanation that Sophia had gotten from the man every time they talked about it.

"Come on Ajay. You know that can't be true." Sophia started with her usual argument. "We've seen bits of light here and there on the planet. Like that giant opening that has beautiful bits of yellow and orange. Or the flying dots that we see every now and then." Sophia spoke up as she leaned back in her chair with the cup in hand. Ajay just seemed to shake his head, knowing that there was no point in listening to this go on.

"The light is probably from a malfunction in the old grid. And those lights you see in that exposed opening, it's a volcano Sofia." Ajay rebuttaled as his right hand pointed towards the Earth. "And that dot, is probably just some garbage being kicked up by some powerful winds." That was Ajay's usual rebuttal on the matter when it came to discussing the possibility of life on the destroyed planet. "I'm telling you, there is nothing going on down on the planet. There are no survivors. There are only mutated plants and animals that can kill us." The tone in Ajay's voice indicated that he was not wanting to talk about this again. They had hashed it out so many times before today, making Ajay ready to get up and leave whenever it was brought up.

"But...." Sophia trailed off, knowing that she had to be careful with her words, unless she wanted Ajay to get up and leave her all alone again. "What if there were people down there?" Sofia asked, hearing the click of Ajay's tongue as he leaned his head back and visibly shook it. "Just, humor me." Sofia remarked, a soft smile on her face as Ajay glanced over towards her. "Please? It'll make the day go by faster." Sofia pleaded once more with a soft weary smile on her face as she brought her cup up to her lips to take a sip.

"Fine...." Ajay remarked, showing that he gave up trying to fight Sophia on this. Letting out a small annoyed sigh, Ajay glanced towards the planet once more as he tried to think of something. "If we were to go down there, and we find out that the people there are not some type of mutated freaks but actual people who can understand us," Ajay spoke, trying to be specific with what he thinks would happen if they went back down to the planet. "I think we might be able to help them with building a proper society." Ajay finished, glancing back to Sophia.

"Well, that's a start." Sophia lightly teased as she looked at the planet before her. "If all of those conditions were met, what would you want to do in that society?" Sophia started to ask, clasping her fingertips against the mug that was handmade by Ajay. "Would you have any type of goal that you would like to have? Maybe start up a little farm with Omar?" Sophia asked teasingly as she could see the flustered look on Ajay's face in the corner of her eye.

"How did you know about that?" Ajay asked, a light scowl on his face. The look that Sophia gave him was like an all knowing Cheshire cat as her silence spoke volumes to him. It seemed like she wasn't going to give Ajay a hint as to how Sophia knew about the two men, so Ajay just simply continued to play along with the question. "But... having a sheep farm with him...wouldn't sound so bad." Ajay admitted reluctantly. "Maybe we would be able to breed our sheep with their sheep..... Make some interesting offspring that could help us learn how their sheep mutated or something." Ajay continued, his face burning bright red as he glanced away from Sophia.

"Awww." Sophia lightly teased Ajay with a big grin on her face. "But it's good that you two are seemingly doing well enough to talk about still wanting to be with him if we land on the planet. We may even help their society become a more practical one." Sophia added, an excited hum leaving her lips before taking a sip from her mug. "Not having to use a type of barter system and learn proper hygiene and all." Sophia paused, wondering for a second how anyone could stand to be around natural body order. "I could only imagine the smell of body odor they would have down there." Sophia remarked before she took another sip of her drink.

"Alright, your turn now." Ajay spoke up, moving to turn to face Sophia. "What would you do if we could establish contact with the people on the planet." Ajay asked, moving to lean his arm over the back of the chair. This should be interesting, considering that Sophia never really opened up about what she would want to do on the planet.

"Hm...good question." Sophia hummed before setting her cup down beside her. Crossing her leg over the other, as well as crossing her arms to rest under her chest, Sophia stared out the window towards the slowly circling planet. "I guess I would want to travel around the world to see how much everything has changed." Sophia spoke in an unusually serious tone. At least, it was a more serious tone than what Ajay was used to.

"I'd love to find a nice spot where I could rebuild a home that is in still good condition, and maybe learn how to hunt and grow my own crops." Being in the maintenance section of the station didn't allow for Sophia to grow her own little garden. "Or, I could live on a diet of fish if I find a place that is near a nice river in the woods." Sophia continued, a light smile on her face as she tilted her head to the side. "I know Issac would want to see the world with me. So I'll have to find a way to keep him close to me so he doesn't get hurt." Sophia finished, glancing over towards Ajay who had a sheepish grin on his face. "What?"

"Nothing." Ajay quickly remarked, twirling his chair to face the controls once more. "It's just nice to see you serious for once." The remark puzzled Sophia a little, but she figured it was best to keep quiet rather than argue about whether or not she was serious all the time. "Speaking of Issac," Ajay spoke up once more before he turned away from Sophia to pull something out of his side drawer.

"It's his birthday tomorrow, right?" Ajay continued before he twirled back around with a small bag in his hand. "You should hand this to him when you get home later on tonight." Ajay remarked as he handed her a light blue bag. "It has two pieces of strawberry short cake and a robot toy that Omar made out of some old recycled metal bits." Seeing the look of excitement and awe on Sophia's face made Ajay's day. "It took a while to paint it his favorite colors, but hopefully Issac loves it."

Sophia was a bit surprised when she heard what was inside of it. Opening the bag, Sophia pulled out the robot to inspect it. It was a light blue robot that had mismatched parts, but one couldn't exactly tell with the paint covering most of the pieces that would give it away. "Awww. It's adorable Ajay." Sophia remarked in astonishment. "I know Issac will love it." Sophia commented, putting the robot back into the bag. "It's hard to believe he'll be four tomorrow." The faint smile on Sophia's face slowly faded into a small frown as she lightly clenched onto the bag.

"You alright Sophia?" Ajay asked as he arched an eyebrow, his voice sounding genuinely worried for her. "You look down." Not that Ajya was a mind reader, but he knew Sophia well enough to know when something was weighing down on her thoughts. After all, these last four years haven't been easy on the poor woman.

"Yeah...just..." Sophia trailed off as she lightly caressed the edge of the bag with her right thumb. "Do you think that Issac is growing up feeling lonely?" She asked Ajay with a concerned look on her face. "I'm a single mom after all....I'm working awful hours and hardly get a break." Sophia paused, keeping her eye on the colorful bag in her hands.

"When he wakes up before me, he always is sitting on my bed with his toys out wanting to play….And I only ever get to see him on my break and when I go home." Sophia continued with a somber look on her face. "Even then it's not enough." Sophia trailed off, feeling the weight on her shoulders. "He always begs to come with me to work, and I hate seeing him cry when I tell him that I can't bring him." Sophia continued, reached a hand up to wipe away some of the tears from her eyes. "I just want to be able to spend what time I can with my son without being exhausted. Is that really so hard to ask for?"

Seeing Sophia in that state, Ajay lightly sighed through his nose as he glanced at the computer panels to his right. "You know...they were talking about transferring one of us to the night team." Sophia was surprised to hear of this news before Ajay continued to speak. "If you want, I could convince them to let you be on the night shift rather than me. That way, you can spend more time with your son during the day time."

It was a kind offer for Ajay to give Sophia the spot instead of him, but something told Sophia that it wasn't a good idea to take it. The look of sadness resting on her face seemed to give it away. "It won't be until the end of the month, so just give it some time. Think it over." Ajay reassured Sophia, bringing a faint smile on her face. Hearing that caused the soft smile to return to Sophia's face once more.

"I really appreciate the thought, Ajay." Sophia remarked, giving her shoulders a small shrug. "But Issac loves his babysitter. I can't exactly remove her from the picture you know." Sophia continued as she gently held the bag to her chest. "But...I'll think about it." It wasn't an exact answer on whether or not she would take it, but the seed had been planted at least.

"That's my girl." Ajay smirked, giving Sophia a light bump on her shoulder. "You know I care about you and Issac as if you were my own family." Ajay continued, hearing the soft chuckle coming from Sophia. "After all, when the news of me being in a romantic relationship with Omar comes to light, my family will probably disown me." The uncertainty in Ajay's voice was a bit worrisome. Unlike on the planet, there was still the bigotry of those who didn't fall into the social norm.

"Fuck them then if they can't accept you!" Sophia quickly snapped, her brows knitting together as she turned to face him. "If they disown you because you happen to swing for the same team, then I'll adopt you as my brother." Sophia quickly added. "I will go through the proper paper works in order to make sure you're part of my family." Sophia continued as she moved to place a hand on Ajay's leg. "You're family to me and Issac. No one can say any different." A gentle smile rested on Sophia's face as Ajay looked up at her with a slightly shocked expression.

"Really?" Ajay asked, only to get a small nod from Sophia as she reassured him that everything Sophia said came from her heart. "You know, having a friend who doesn't look at me as if I'm a freak, it really helps me to face each new day." Plenty of people would rather take their own life than let people know the truth about them. When the truth about someone's sexuality would come to light, people often feared the rejection associated with being different.

"Well, you know a lot of people are becoming more accepting since there are so many of us on the station." Sophia spoke up as she retracted her hand from the male. "It doesn't even matter what someone's sexuality is nowadays, if you think about." Sophia remarked as she gently set the bag down under the desk. "So, give it a bit more time before you come out to them. It's not like you have to rush anything. Let it come out naturally." That part was always easier said than done. Not everyone was willing to accept people who they really are.

As the hours passed, the two took their breaks, alternating between who was to leave first to keep from simply leaving the controls alone. As Sophia came back, she was greeted with Ajay looking rather bored as his eyes lazily glanced over the displays. "Guessing you're missing your lovely boyfriend already?" Sophia remarked as the doors closed behind her, causing Ajay to sit up straight before glancing over his shoulder petrified. Seeing that it was Sophia, Ajay was quick to relax.

"You can't just go and say that so openly Sophia." Ajay was quick to yelp out. "What if someone overhears?" Ajay remarked, slumping back in his seat, placing a hand over his heart. As Sophia walked over to her chair, Ajay was able to recover from his small panic attack "You know how it is here, Sopha." Ajay was quick to speak up once more, a somber expression crossing his face as his eyes glanced at the panel lights before him. "If the wrong people overheard you saying that, it's pretty much a death sentence for me." The way that Ajay looked so gloomy after stating that showed that he often feared the wrong people finding out about his relationship.

"There was no one around when I came in. So don't worry." Sophia remarked casually. "If it's any consolation, Issac simply adored that robot Omar made for him." Sophia beamed as she scooted closer to the controls, her fingers gently being placed on the keyboards to sign back in. "He was so excited to show it to his babysitter and was ready to get his other toys before I reminded him that there was cake." Sophia continued to smile as she pressed enter to log back into her work station. "Oh yeah, let Omar know that the cake was delicious." Sophia chimed happily, looking over to Ajay who looked more relieved now. "You could taste the love he put into making it."

"I'll make sure to tell him." Ajay remarked, the color coming back to his face as he moved to scoot up to the panel as well. "It seems that we're in for another boring day." Ajay casually remarked, leaning away from Sophia as he gazed at the panel with a bored expression on his face. "No explosions or much in the way of maintenance issues to report either." Ajay spoke as he brought up the display for the station on the large monitor in between the two of them. "There was a small blurb about an alarm going off, but thanks to your coding, I was able to reset it from here." Ajay remarked, pointing to the area where the incident had taken place.

"Well, I did make the coding for the system after all." Sophia boasted with a small cocky grin on her face. "With how dated the old one was, there were plenty of bugs that needed fixing." Sophia remarked, as she started to boot up the sequence to do a quick maintenance check to make sure that there weren't any other issues.

"It's amazing how easy the last one could be overwritten so easily." It was like child's play to Sophia. "But with this new coding, I'm the only one who can lock it if something were to come up." It was another bragging point that Sophia had under her belt, though not many people appreciated the hard work she put into making the station run smoother than before. "Whether it be an enemy attack, or some careless Elite trying to take over the controls like that one incident a couple of years ago." Sophia continued, feeling confident in her work as it made the job for the maintenance department to run smoother, making the crew less ragged over the years.

"Yeah yeah, we know you're a badass with a smart brain for coding and electronics. You super freak." Ajay lightly teased as the station started to make their way towards hovering over the cannon. "If it wasn't for you, we might not have been able to make it this far with minimal maintenance requests going out." The amount of workload that had decreased was slow at first, but with enough work and keeping the coding running, they were able to fix most issues straight from the monitors.

"Well, what can I say? I just..." Sophia started to speak before a bright light caught her attention. "What is that?" Sophia mumbled, squinting her eyes as she could barely see much of anything else as the light was getting closer. It was like there was a bright star shooting up at them from Earth, but it was supposed to be abandoned over five hundred years ago! It was approaching closer, making it hard to avoid being hit.

As Ajay and Sophia closed their eyes, the light seemed to hit the station, causing it to shake violently. It was a miracle that Sophia and Ajay weren't thrown from their seats by the impact alone. When it seemed that the light was fading, the control room was bright red with the alarm lights flashing and the sirens were blaring overhead. Quickly the two started to look at the monitor to see what happened. To their disbelief, one of the engines had been completely destroyed with some of the lower section of the station. Sections of the screens started to static over, some even going completely black in the process.

"What the hell is happening?!" Ajay shouted as it was hard to hear anything over the sirens that were blasting overhead. The monitor seemed to be freaking out as well, making it hard to get a proper assessment as to what was currently going on. Reaching forward to touch one of the screens, Ajay was shocked briefly, forcing his hand to retract from the damaged screen.

"I-I don't know!!" Sophia frantically shouted as she started to do what patch work she could in closing off the sections that were damaged from the strange light hitting them. "I'm going to redirect the fuel towards the other engines. In doing so, perhaps this could give us enough time to see if we could at least detach the busted engine so it doesn't-" Sophia tried to explain her train of thought before there was another explosion. A second engine was apparently damaged from the initial engine blowing up. "Fuck!" Sophia cursed as she quickly detached the two engines to keep from having any more of the engines explode.

"Sophia, what was that light? What is happening?" Ajay asked, trying his best to understand what was going on, working on his side to try and close off some of the other seals and try to assess the situation. This was something that they were unprepared for. This didn't make any sense, and the sound of the alarm blaring didn't exactly help with their thinking as it only seemed to get louder in their ears.

"I don't know! I don't know Ajay!!" Sophia panicked as her fingers started to override certain alarms going off. With a swift click of the buttons to turn off the alarms as the lights continued to flash in the room as well as outside. Sophia sighed in relief that she would be able to think without the alarms blaring overhead. The lights still flashed red and white, but it wasn't like it was as distracting as the alarm going off.

"I re-routed the fuel to the remaining engines, but it's going to take more fuel to stabilize us to keep from being pulled into the Earth's atmosphere." Sophia spoke, instructing Ajay to do the same. "If we don't, the Millennium will be sucked into the atmosphere and we'll all die from the impact alone if we're not careful with re-entry." Sophia spoke in a rather calm tone as she slumped back into the chair. Sweat started to pour from her forehead as it trickled down her face.

"We need to tell the Elites about this." Sophia remarked out loud, seeing that most of the screens had been fixed, allowing the two to properly see the assessment. "They have to know that we were just attacked by something on Earth." As much as Sophia would have liked to believe that there are good survivors on the planet, this just demonstrated that they would be at war with each other if the station fell. Who would win was still yet to be determined.

"But what was that? That blinding light?" Ajay asked yet again, figuring that he could get some answers now that they weren't rushing to fix the situation. "I've never seen something like that before in my life." Ajay spoke in awe with a hint of terror. "We can't just ignore that Sophia. What if they try it again?" The worry in Ajay's voice seemed to read the room. It wasn't like Sophia didn't know where Ajay was coming from, but she couldn't figure out how a blast like that could even reach them without there being some sort of intelligent life on the once dead Earth.

"I doubt that they would be able to do it again." Sophia spoke up, a serious expression landing on her face as Sophia's brows knitted together. "Considering that it was some sort of electrical beam as it traveled at the speed of light, there's no way they would be able to produce that much power again in a short time." Sophia added, crossing her arms under her chest in thought. "If we go by that logic, then this was their one and only shot." Sophia reasoned as she moved to sit up, correcting error codes that were still popping up on the screen. "The real question is, who should be the one to tell the Elite what just happened?" Sophia's gaze went from the screen to Ajay, who looked like he was freaking out in a cold sweat while staying silent. Lighting biting her bottom lip, Sophia turned in her chair to face Ajay.

"You know they will want an explanation, Ajay." Sophia paused as her brows knitted together with concern. "That blast shook the whole station. It took out two of our engines." Sophia continued before moving a hand to point towards the screens. "We can't fix it!" Not that Sophia needed to explain that much to Ajay.

"The places where they were able to blast a hole through, we can patch that. But there is no way to fix those old engines." Sophia continued to explain, only to let out a small sigh before bringing her hands up to rub her face. "Right now all I can do is patch up the damage...." Sophia trailed off with an exasperated sigh leaving her lips. "If you want, I'll try and talk to one of the members of the Elite." Sophia knew that she would have a better chance at talking to them than Ajay would, mostly because of a little secret she kept from everyone.

"You will do no such thing." A man's stern voice came from behind them, causing the two to turn. The man was rather old, wearing a white pristine outfit with a captain's hat that he bits of silver locks slicked back underneath it. A silver mustache enclosed around the man's upper lip as hazel brown eyes glared at the two people in front of him. His crow's feet were noticeable against the side of his eyes as bits of his cheeks sagged on his face.

"Captain!" Ajay and Sophia spoke in a shocked unison tone before they quickly stood up to salute him. The two were so caught up in trying to stabilize the station that they didn't notice that their captain had come in before Sophia's suggestion to see the Elite members. This could be bad for either one of them. That is, if the Captain sought fit to punish them for uttering this to the Elite members.

"I'm sorry to ask this sir, but why can we not tell any members of the Elite what happened?" Sophia asked, her brows knitting together in confusion as she tried to understand what reasoning there could be to not inform the higher ups as to what happened. "It would be negligence if we don't inform them right away." Sophia continued before hearing a low growl coming from the elderly man.

"Because they are in the middle of preparations for the biggest holiday of the year." The man spoke up, causing a soft disgruntled tsk to come from Sophia. "If word were to them that the station is in trouble, it will spell disaster for all of us." The captain remarked, looking sternly between the two of them. "I don't want a single word about what you had seen getting out to anyone on the station. Is that clear?" The captain barked out the order while glancing between Ajay's and Sophia's faces. It wasn't like either of them could go behind their captain's orders, but deep down Sophia felt like it was necessary for them to at least try to make an attempt to inform the Elite.

"But sir, what about the fact that the station shook from the impact?" Sophia started to ask her questions. "Or that we're down two engines?" Sophia knew that people were going to ask questions regarding what had hit the station. Considering the amount of damage that the station took, it wasn't something that they could easily brush under the rug. Then again, it wasn't like they could say how there was a large beam that came up from Earth that struck the station. It seems like it would be something out of a science fiction story.

"We'll just say that some space debris was able to temporarily knock out two of our engines." Hearing their captain say that caused both Sophia and Ajay to look at the man with a bewildered gaze. That's all the public needs to know." The captain finished, turning to face away from the two. "Is that clear?" The man asked, giving the two a side glance. Sophia didn't like the fact that they would have to lie to the public about what had happened, especially since they were put in charge of making sure that the station was running smoothly.

"Y-Yes sir..." Ajay softly remarked, glancing towards Sophia who didn't say anything. Giving her a small nudge, Sophia quickly spoke up as well.

"Yes sir..." Sophia agreed, though she didn't like it. Why were they trying so hard to make it seem like nothing was wrong? Why was the captain going out of his way to make it seem like nothing bad happened? This wasn't settling well with Sophia, but she kept her mouth shut for now.

"Good." The captain spoke up, a smug grin landing under his mustache. "I'll inform the night crew of the story." The captain spoke, sounding as if he was in good spirits now. "Sophia, you need to provide them with the codes to keep everything running smoothly." Even though Sophia didn't like the idea of sharing the codes, she had to do as her captain ordered.

"I'll dispatch some of the maintenance crew to go and fix the breach with double pay for the hazard they will face being close to the engines." The captain remarked, causing Ajay and

Sophia to glance towards each other with a concerned gaze. "Even if they die, their families will be well off." The captain mumbled to himself as he still faced away from the two as the door opened.

"Remember, if word of what has happened gets out, the guilty party will get the death sentence." The man warned the two, as if reminding them that his word was law. "It wouldn't be just you who has the death penalty, but your family as well." The captain spoke, glancing over his shoulder one last time before he left, leaving Sophia and Ajay standing there in shock at the threat their captain made. Did that just happen? Their captain ordered them to keep quiet at the cost of their lives, and their lives of their family members?

"He can't be serious...." Ajay mumbled in shock, stammering back to his seat. "Not only our lives, but our families? Is he that crazy?" Ajay asked out loud, meanwhile Sophia returned to her seat. Even though Sophia was just as concerned about the penalty as Ajay was, she had to work on fixing the codes to override the error messages, allowing for the flashing lights to turn back to normal. Ajay slowly turned to look at her, gazing at Sophia as if she was deaf or something. "Did you not....hear him Sophia?" Ajay asked in a rather concerned yet annoyed tone as Sophia seemed like she didn't witness the same thing he did.

"Of course I did Ajay...." Sophia trailed off, her voice monotone as she spoke. "But I have to get these codes in before it does more damage." Sophia lightly growled as her brows knitted together in concentration. With the lights returning to normal, and the display started to return to normal as well, Sophia sighed as she leaned back in the chair.

The tension in the room was thick enough to slice a knife though it was like melted butter. Pulling out a piece of paper, Sophia went to work writing out the procedure on how to override the codes in case some of the errors started to flare up while the other crew was on the scene. Not that Sophia enjoyed this, but it wasn't like she was given much of an option at this point.

After a few minutes passed since their captain left, and Sophia was done writing down the codes, she reached up to wipe the sweat off of her brow. "There... that should do it." Sophia muttered to herself, sliding the paper into a protective covering before glancing over towards Ajay. The look on the man's face showed his emotions as clear as glass. The guilt of knowing that the station was doomed, the fact that there were many people who would end up dying because the higher ups didn't want to let the public know, and being threatened with the death of not only you but the people in your family? It was a lot to unpack there. Sophia knew that there wasn't much she could say to ease Ajay's mind right now. So for now, she would simply stay silent.

As a couple of days passed, the station was starting to give way, causing some people to notice the shift as the Elite ordered for more trash to be burned. The reasoning behind it, or rather the cover up story behind it? To provide room for new resources to help expand into new ways of providing energy to the engine. Most on the ship failed to realize that with two engines gone, it put them at risk of drifting closer to the planet. Whenever the station would shake as the Earth tried to pull it closer, the engines would start to pick up speed to keep it from being pulled in. Eventually a week passed after the initial incident happened, and people were becoming uneasy. The tension in the room could be felt as Sophia and Ajay sat in the control room.

"It's.... getting closer each day, isn't it?" Ajay softly remarked upon hearing the door open. Turning in his seat, Ajay saw the tired expression that lingered on Sophia's face. "We're going to crash into the Earth.... and we're all going to die...." Ajay spoke in a strained tone as he appeared a bit thinner from the lack of eating. The bags under his eyes were evident that he hadn't gotten any sleep as well.

Sophia glanced away from him, moving to sit in her chair. It was true that they were getting closer to the Earth. That they couldn't exactly keep quiet about what was going on anymore. As Sophia sat down in her chair, she pressed her fingertips into the smooth surface below the controls. "Say... Ajay..." Sophia spoke up, her eyes focused on the lighted up controls in front of her. "You haven't introduced Omar to Issac yet, have you?" The sound of the chair turning let Sophia know that Ajay was turning to face her.

"Yeah...he's been busy with work." Ajay started to speak up, studying the side of Sophia's face as he was puzzled as to why Sophia would bring that up now. "Plus, I didn't think it would be a good idea to introduce Omar without your approval Sophia." Ajay spoke up, his voice cracking ever so slightly. "Do you honestly think now would even be a good time though? Considering the fate in which we're all doomed?" Ajay asked, his gaze drifting down to the metal floor resting underneath them.

Sophia was silent at first, her hands gently shaking as she closed her eyes. "Yeah. I think now is the perfect time to have them meet." Sophia remarked in a soft voice as she slowly turned to look at him. "After all, you are Issac's godfather." Sophia continued, though her stomach felt like it was in knots. "Why don't you use my lunch time with your lunch to visit Issac? I'm sure he would love a chance to spend time with his uncle Ajay." Sophia finished, holding in a small sniffle as her eyes started to burn.

"Are you sure Sophia? Don't you want-" Ajay started to ask before Sophia held up a hand to stop him from speaking more. Ajay's mouth hung open for only a few seconds before he closed his mouth, allowing for Sophia to speak her mind. It was clear that she wanted to get something off of her chest, and who was Ajay to stop her?

"I'm sure." Sophia softly but sternly spoke. "After all, we both know what needs to be done without them overhearing us." Sophia spoke, sparing a side glance towards the door. "Just, make sure you play with him a lot with his toys. And make sure that he gets tuckered out before you leave. It'll make things easier on him." Sophia spoke in a more cryptic tone as she turned to face the computer screens.

"Tell you what," Sophia continued before clearing her throat. "I'll even give you my card so you can buy him the mega robot toy he always wanted. Let him know that mommy never forgot his birthday gift. It was just coming late is all." Sophia finished as she reached up to wipe away the single tear that threatened to fall. "Let me just write down these new codes for the night crew before I forget." Sophia added, moving to grab a piece of paper before tearing off the lower part of the paper to write something down.

"Yeah, just give me your card around lunch time, okay?" Ajay spoke, knowing that this would be for the greater good after he caught on to what Sophia was insinuating. Even if one of them was to make the ultimate sacrifice in order to save people the rest of the station, Sophia figured that she might as well be the one to do it. "I'll make sure he gets the robot. I know he'll be more than happy to receive it." Ajay gave Sophia a reassuring smile as the weight had been lifted off of his chest. Though it was still a heavy burden on Sophia, at least Ajay wasn't the one to make the tough decision for either one of them.

TIME felt as if it was moving slowly. The passing of time as they drifted just out of the Earth's orbit was a constant reminder that they were on borrowed time. As the time for Ajay to go to his lunch break clicked on the digital clock, the male stood up with a somber look on his face. Sophia handed him her card with a small note attached to the side where the surveillance camera couldn't see it. Sophia didn't even utter a word as Ajay slipped it into his pocket as he headed out, only to stop at the door. Sophia made sure to keep her back towards him, making it appear like nothing was out of the ordinary.

"Hey," Ajay called out, glancing over his shoulder at Sophia who was still facing the monitors. "Try to join us when you can." Ajay quietly remarked before heading out, leaving Sophia by herself. A soft sigh escaped her lips as she frowned at the lights in front of her. This was harder for Sophia than she ever wanted to admit.

"I doubt that will happen...." Sophia muttered to herself as she could feel the weight of the world resting on her shoulders. She had to continue to remind herself that this was for the sake of everyone on the station. If she had to die in the process, then so be it. It was worth the price so long as Issac was able to live on without her.

After five minutes had passed, Sophia got up from her chair and left the control room as well. She had already made the camera in the control room have a repeating image of her working on the control panel so as to not raise suspicion. It wasn't like she had much time left. With her credit card out of her pocket, and the evidence that she gave to Ajay before he left, she couldn't be tracked.

Boarding the elevator that allowed her access to the Elite section, Sophia stood on the marble flooring in the elevator. The golden trimming always made her sick when she would make her way to see the Elite when they summoned her. Glancing at her reflection in the gold, though it was a bit distorted, Sophia could see the effects of the sleepless nights she had. The way that her eyes seemed to have dark circles around them, and how thin she was getting, it was hard to deny that it wasn't a good look on her. But now wasn't the time to be prideful, she was here on a mission.

As the elevator stopped at the floor, Sophia embarked off of the elevator. Glancing around, she felt sick with how much gold seemed to decorate the interior walls. Various sculptures of the founding leaders and some of their descendants lined the hallway with black and white checkered floors made out of marble paved the path towards the offices of the Elite members. There was a rather ominous choir singing that felt like it lingered above her on the ceiling. It gave Sophia the chills as the ego from the Elite thinking of themselves as gods was evident.

"If I can find Nicolas, then perhaps he might be able to help me. After all, he owes me." Sophia mumbled to herself as she glanced at the names on the panel, trying to find Nicolas' office. Even though Sophia hated to admit it, Nicolas was the father of Issac. They had an affair at one of the Hollow's eve dinners where Sophia had a bit too much to drink and made a horrible mistake. She hid it the best that she could from Nicolas until she started to show. They agreed to not make it known who Issac's real father was, simply saying that he was exploring space with the brave soldiers of a made up class. It was better than having Issac learn the hard truth of who his father really was.

Thinking back on that memory caused Sophia to pout, wishing that perhaps Issac wouldn't keep asking questions where his father was. It was hard keeping such a secret from him. As she seemed to be lost in her thoughts, Sophia bumped into a man who was coming out of his office. The man was rather tall, standing about 6'0 with a fair complexion. The man's light brown hair was slicked back ever so slightly as his green eyes casted a glance down to who had bumped into him. Wearing a dark blue pinstripe suit, the man wore a golden tie that seemed to stick out as much as his eyes did.

"Sophia? What are you doing up here?" The man asked, causing Sophia to step back to see who it was she absent mindedly walked into. To her surprise, the man that Sophia had been thinking of magically showed up, as if she summoned him. Even after all this time, it felt like Nicholas didn't age a single day since the night the two of them hooked up.

"Nicholas!" Sophia spoke up in a relieved tone. "Thank god I ran into you." She continued, grabbing his wrist in one of her hands. "I don't have much time to explain, but you've got to talk to your father and the others." The panic in Sophia's voice was evident as she gripped Nicolas' hand even tighter. "The station, it's-" Sophia started to speak in a more frantic tone before spotting an older version of Nicholas walking out of the room that Nicholas had just exited, causing Sophia to stop mid sentence.

"Nicholas..." The man trailed off, sounding rather displeased with Sophia hanging onto his son. "What is that woman doing here?" The man asked, sneering at Sophia with disdain that a lower class was being too familiar with his son. "Didn't I order you to take away her accessibility to get up here?" The man spoke in a rather deep tone compared to Nicholas. Upon hearing the remark, Sophia couldn't help but softly growl towards the man.

"Listen!" Sophia spoke loudly, causing her voice to echo in the hallway. "The station is going to fall to Earth!" Sophia continued to shout, her stern expression indicated that she was being serious. "If we don't start to release the pods with the people inside of it, they're going to die." Sophia explained, though it was mostly towards Nicholas as she heard a 'humph' coming from the older man.

"Who cares about the Bronze class." The man remarked, causing Sophia to glare at the man. The two always seemed to be at odds, making it rather difficult for Sophia to find any good in trying to make amends with Nicholas, so long as his father was around that is.

"I do!" Sophia quickly snapped, her brows knitted together as she always hated Nicholas' father Gregory. "Please Nicholas. Think about how many people you could be saving." Sophia started to plead towards Nichalos. "You know as much as I do that those people in the pods are the most important part of the station." Not that many members of the Elite would admit such a thing. "They risk their lives to help keep this station afloat. If it wasn't for them, we would have crashed into the Earth hundreds of years ago." Sophia continued, giving Nicholas' wrist a tight squeeze. "Your son is in one of those pods Nicholas.... you don't want him to die, do you?" Sophia asked in a more stern tone.

"You honestly think we would let your rat of a child sway our minds to save those pathetic wretches?" Gregory remarked in a boasting high and mighty tone of voice. "You honestly think you're the first woman on this station to get a big head and think she has the right to call the shots?" Gregory continued in almost a mocking tone as Gregory placed his hands onto his hips while raising a brow.

"Will you just shut up?!" Sophia snapped, tugging Nicholas close to her as she glared at Gregory. "For crying out loud! Do you realize that you'll be in the crash as well?" How could one person be so dense? "Everyone's lives are in danger here you moron!!" Sophia continued on with her rant.

"Of course you didn't realize that. You're only looking out for yourself right?" Now was the time for Sophia's sharp tongue to come into play. "Instead of being rational in realizing that humans can't stay up in space forever, you simply allowed for the station to run out of the resources needed to fuel the engines." Considering the fast thinking of burning up the trash to save their lives, the remaining humans would have crashed into the planet a long time ago.

"All that you have built, is being brought down. And you can't even bother to care about the safety of those on board?" Sophia asked with a scowl on her face. "You're a piece of shit and I hope when the station falls, you'll be crushed under your precious gold statues you ignoramus!" Sophia's face felt hot as her ears started to ring from the built up rage finally being released after all these years of abuse.

Both Gregory and Nicholas were taken back by Sophia's words, watching as she panted while still red in the face. "Forget it!" Sophia snapped, letting go of Nicholas' arm as she turned to storm off. "If you aren't going to save the station, then I will." It was a long shot, but at least Sophia tried. She tried her best to try and reason with some of the members of the Elite, but to no avail. She didn't want to have to resort to going with the worse case scenario, but it seemed like she had no choice.

On the way down on the elevator, Sophia crossed her arms to rest against her torso. Lowering her head she was trying to figure out how she would pull it off. She knew it would be risky, but what else was she supposed to do? Let every single person die without a chance to survive? To just let them be completely crushed under the weight of the Millennium? There was no way she could allow Issac to meet a fate like that. She would rather die than have let her son go through a horrific death like that.

As the doors opened, Sophia was greeted with two Enforcement officers standing in front of the doors. They looked as if they were expecting her. With a baton in each hand, the two officers stood there in a menacing stance, ready to beat Sophia into submission if she were to try and fight back.

Swallowing the lump in her throat, Sophia moved to press the 'close door' button, but one of the officers placed their hand on the elevator door to keep it from closing. The other officer took this chance to step on the elevator, closing the gap as to make sure that Sophia couldn't escape. With her heart beating against her chest, Sophia steadied herself against the wall, scanning to see if she could find an opening. There was a small gap that Sophia could slide through if she got her timing down just right.

Just as one of the officers moved closer to Sophia, reaching out as if to grab her, Sophia was able to duck down and use the strength of her legs to slip under the man's legs. In the process of her kicking off the side of the elevator as if she was kicking off of the side of a pool, the elevator shifted, causing the officer to lose his balance as his partner reached out to help stabilize him. Sophia slid on the floor through their legs before coming to a stop. This allowed Sophia to get back up on her feet, before she started to run towards the control room as fast as she could.

Running as fast as she can with the two officers behind her, Sophia ran as if her life literally depended on it. As one of the officers tried to jump to tackle Sophia to the ground, she was able to round the corner in time to hear the crash behind her. Not even looking back, Sophia made it to the control room just in time to shut it behind her.

Grabbing one of the computer towers, Sophia was able to pull it down to help block the door from opening. Rushing over to the computer, Sophia went to work putting in the codes that would set the pods to be ejected on a timer. To keep the officers from trying to take the controls over after they would bust through the door, Sophia worked on the control panels while listening to the officers trying to bust through the door. Before they were able to make much room with pushing the computer tower out of the way, Sophia turned off the artificial gravity as a means to give her more time to escape from the pursuit.

As she started to float over the control panel, Sophia pressed the 'okay' on the screen for the emergency evacuation order to be sent out on a timer. With one final code put in place, Sophia was able to lock the screen to keep from anyone trying to undo the emergency signal. Just as it seemed like the officers were ready to bust through the door, Sophia took this chance to push herself towards the large panel windows that showed the Earth creeping closer to the station. Sophia had two options before her. Either she could go up and hide in the wires and other electrical devices, or head down towards the computer towers and vents?

Without much time, Sophia headed upwards to hide among the electrical wiring that was there. To her luck, Sophia was able to spot the large pipe that she could rest on in case the gravity was to kick back on. As she found her landing, the officers had busted into the room.

"Where is she?!" One of the officers shouted as three officers followed behind him. The three men floated towards the control panel to see if they could find a way to stop the emergency signal that started to blare through the station. With each press of the buttons, it didn't seem that they were able to take back the controls.

"Maybe she is hiding underneath? She could always slip away in the vents." One of the other officers remarked, drifting over towards the edge. Seeing as how the officers were close, Sophia pressed herself as much as she could into the wires, feeling the electrical buzzing from the electrical current going through it, Sophia hoped that they didn't look up to see her reflection in the panel window.

"Let's go then. She couldn't have gotten too far." The previous man barked, sending all four of the officers down underneath the controls, unaware the Sophia was watching them in the reflection of the windows. Sophia didn't know if she should count her blessings just yet, but she was grateful that the officers thought so poorly of her.

As the officers moved further into the monitor towers that rested underneath, Sophia glanced out the door with the help of the window to make sure that the coast was clear. Leaping towards the wall opposite of her, Sophia slid down the wall a bit before pushing towards the controls. With a quick push of the button, she turned the gravity back on, trapping the officers down below. As the alarms started to sound off, Sophia hurried towards the stairs as the elevators would be chaotic from this point.

Entering into the staircase, Sophia could hear the panic of people shouting far above her. People were already trying to rush towards their pods as the evacuation order was being issued. **Thirty minutes until evacuation of all emergency pods are released. I repeat, thirty minutes until evacuation of all emergency pods are released unless the evacuation order is canceled.** The computer generated voice spoke, giving Sophia a timer to be able to reach her son, Ajay, and Omar. That is, if they haven't been taken in by the Enforcement officers. The very thought was coursing through Sophia's veins, driving her to reach them before the officers did.

"Third floor... gotta reach the third floor. Come on legs, we can do this!" Sophia grunted through her teeth as she ran up the stairs, through the vibration of the many people on the steps above her didn't make it easier.

As she reached the first floor, people from the maintenance level started to rush in, blocking her way. Glancing at the railings, Sophia knew that she could very well be crushed if she made her way into the crowd. People were willing to step all over each other if it meant that they could escape. Feeling the sweat pouring down her body, Sophia rushed over towards the railing and started to climb up them. She wasn't going to allow the officers a chance to trap her in the crowd, not when she had to go up only a few floors.

Using her hands and feet to climb the railings like a ladder, Sophia was able to reach the third floor without much issue. There were a few scary moments, like when someone tried to push her leg off of the railing, but other than that, she was able to make it above the rest of the crowd.

As she rushed into the third floor hallway, Sophia glanced around to make sure that no officers had either beaten her there, or were lying in wait. At this point Sophia's lungs were on fire, her breathing was getting ragged as she ran towards her pod. She had to make sure that Issac was alright. If she could protect him in the crash, it would all be worth it.

Rounding the last corner, Sophia saw her pod door open. Fearing the worst, Sophia stopped just shy of it. As the alarms rang through the hall, Sophia barely heard anything over the sound of her heart beating against her chest and in her ears. Slowly stepping towards the opening, Sophia peered around the corner to see Ajay's back as he sat at the table with three other people.

One was a tanned skin man with a brunet goatee, slightly long brunet hair that was tied back into a loose bun, and hazel eyes. The other adult was a female with soft red hair that was braided to the side. Her skin was paler than those in the room with bright blue eyes. On her lap was a little boy with a dark messy mop of hair on top of his head. Dark green eyes were focused on a robot toy that was almost as big as he was. The sight alone was enough to make Sophia want to weep in pure joy. Stepping into the pod, Sophia braced herself against the wall as she pressed the button to close the door to the pod. With another press of the button, she locked it to keep anyone else from coming inside.

"Mommy!!" Issac called out, spotting Sophia against the wall, causing the other three to look at her. "Guess what mommy? I flew with my robot today!" Issac spoke up, his voice sounding as energetic as he seemed to be. Sophia softly smiled as she walked towards them, ready to scoop up Issac in her arms.

"Sophia! What's going on?" The woman asked, setting Issac down as the boy rushed over to Sophia. "What's this about the pods being ejected? Ajay has refused to say anything to us." She continued, looking over to Omar who shared the same worried glance that the woman had. "Is everything alright?" She asked in a worried tone.

"I'm sorry Amy....i-it's just best if no one leaves right now." Sophia spoke through her pants as she was trying her best to catch her breath. Every muscle in Sophia's body was screaming out in pain, but picking up Issac was worth the pain. "The station is getting ready to crash into the planet." Sophia spoke bluntly as she held Issac in her arms. "There was an attack from Earth.... a beam of light. Messed up the controls...a-and we lost an engine." Sophia continued to explain, walking over towards the three. "I tried to warn people... but no one believed me" Sophia tried her best to explain it all, but the doubtful look on Amy and Omar's face showed that they didn't believe her.

"It's true..." Ajay collaborated, though he didn't exactly sound pleased about sharing the information. "I was there when it happened." Ajay added, causing Amy and Omar to glance at each other with a worried expression.

"There was some type of light beam that hit the station a week back." Ajay continued to back Sophia's story. "It caused two of our engines to stop working. Because of that, we're struggling to stay above the Earth's gravitational force." Ajay cleared his throat towards the end before turning to face Sophia. "You did good Sophia, but there is one thing you should know." Ajay continued to speak before glancing a spare shot towards the closed bathroom. "I just didn't expect *him* to show up before you started the emergency signal. Was that planned?" Sophia had a puzzled look on her face when Ajay spoke about someone showing up.

"Who?" Sophia asked, her brows knitting together as she had no idea who Ajay was going on about. It wouldn't be long before a familiar voice would pipe up, though Issac glanced over Sophia's shoulder to a man standing behind Sophia. Looking at a man looked similar to Issac, but not familiar to the young boy.

"Me." The voice of a man spoke up, causing Sophia to turn around to see someone emerging from the bathroom, Sophia was surprised to see that it was Nicholas. "I came down to see if it was true, and that if it was, I would talk to my father about it." Nicholas remarked as his eyes went towards Issac who moved seemed to be hiding against Sophia.

"But it seems that you and my father are too stubborn and set your ways for proper action to be taken." Nicolas added, moving his attention back to Sophia. "As a result, my father called the Enforcement officers on you, and you decided to take things into your own hands." The frustration was evident in his voice, but Nicholas kept a calm air about him. "Both of you have doomed this station, you know that right?" Nicholas added, a sigh escaping his lips. "Instead of trying to come up with a solution, you took matters into your own hands." Not that Nicholas was wrong, but was there any other way for this to end peacefully?

"I had no choice Nicholas." Sophia spoke as turned to face Nicholas, her legs feeling sore, barely allowing Sophia to keep her stance. "Your father wasn't going to listen to reason, Nichalos." Sophia knew the man well enough to know that Gregory was set in his ways. Like most Elite members. "The stupid captain tried to hide it because you and your kind were getting ready for your damn Satan worshiping holiday." Sophia spat, her anger rose in her voice.

"You did have a choice Sophia. All of us had a choice, and you chose to doom us all instead of looking for an answer." Nicholas spoke as he walked up to Sophia. "Do you honestly think that we can even survive down there? What if something were to happen to Issac?" Nicholas asked, his eyes studying Issac who looked almost like an identical version of Nicholas.

Fifteen minutes until emergency pods are ejected. I repeat, fifteen minutes until emergency pods are ejected, unless cancellation of emergency protocols is engaged. The computer generated voice spoke out over the speakers. It seemed people were rushing to find the pods that would secure their safety despite the officers warning about people abandoning their posts. Those who were smart enough would continue to stay in their pods, or allowed others into their pods if they didn't have time to make it to their own pod in time.

"How can you honestly stand there and say that you believe that there was a way for us to stay aboard the station as it crashes to Earth and survive it?" Ajay asked in disbelief. "Most of us would have ended up being burned up in the atmosphere if we stayed on the Millennium. Sophia saved us!" Ajay spoke up, not liking how this Elite bastard thought that he knew the answers to everything. "If Sophia didn't volunteer to do it, I would have been the one to try and evacuate everyone." Ajay added, his brows knitting together as he spoke. "I probably would still be in the control panel making sure that no one messed with it as the station would head down to Earth." Ajay spoke bitterly, causing a surprised look on Omar's face as he heard it for the first time.

"What? Why would you do something like that?" Omar asked, causing Ajay to glance back before realizing what he said. Not like Ajay would have wanted to be away from Omar, but if it meant that his lover would have been safe, then Ajay would do anything to protect him.

"Wait, what about my parents? They'll be worried about me if I don't go back to them!" Amy spoke up as she stood. "I can't let them think I'm dead." Amy started to walk towards the door, only to find that the lock wouldn't unlock. Sophia lightly shook her head as she knew that they were all locked in.

"The door is locked Amy. I can't unlock it now." Sophia spoke up, knowing that Amy would have to be brave and hope her parents can make it out alive. "Once the doors to the pods are shut with the emergency protocol activated, it's impossible to open it up." It was a fail safe from when the Millennium was first built hundreds of years ago. "If the pods are ejected from the station, they are programmed to head towards the nearest planet, which is Earth." Another fail safe plan from when the station was first being built. "Once they land, the computer will slowly release the pressure from the pod, allowing for people to get used to the atmosphere, and then allow them to exit." Sophia explained, finally getting enough energy to move or talk without being out of breath.

"So what am I supposed to do?" Amy asked, her voice wavering as she didn't like the thought of leaving her parents all alone. Not that she had much of a choice in the matter. She was locked in the pod with Issac, his mother, and three strange men. Wasn't the best company, but if she was going to die, at least she wasn't going to be alone. "Just sit here and wait for my death?"

"Or you could just at least try and survive." Sophia quickly snapped, showing that she wasn't in any mood to debate something that she had no control over. "If you're going to want to survive the crash landing, then help us." Sophia knew that it would be a rough landing, but if they were going to make it out of this together, they had to work together.

"We need to brace ourselves with the mattresses or anything soft. That way, when we crash land on the planet, it will minimize the damage we take from the fall." Sophia remarked as she knelt down to pick up the box with Issac's toys before lightly tossing them into the bathroom. "We have probably close to ten minutes left to get anything that could be potentially harmful to be in the bathroom." Sophia continued to explain, watching as Ajay was the only one to start helping her. "Then we get anything soft to help cushion our fall. It's going to be a bumpy ride, so let's do our best to keep from getting hurt." Sophia ordered, watching as the rest of the group glanced at each other.

"Come on! Let's go. Unless you all want to die in a horrific way." Sophia shouted. This seemed to make everyone move to do as she ordered. Sophia hated having to be bossy and order people around, but this was to make sure that they would all be able to live. Besides, she already did the hard work of timing everything out to let the pods eject one layer at a time to keep from having the pods collide in the air. If the other people in the pods were smart, they would try to find ways to protect them from getting injured on the way down.

After the preparations were done, the five huddled together as the first level pods were released, causing the station to shake. Anything that could be dangerous to the group was locked away in the bathroom. Sophia held onto Issac tightly. "Mom, what's going on?" Issac asked softly, holding onto Sophia tightly. "Are we going to die?" He asked, his voice sounding a bit strained.

"Not if I can help it sweetheart." Sophia spoke in a calm tone reaching up a hand to gently stroke Issac's hair. "Just close your eyes and hold onto me." Sophia softly instructed, knowing that she would be a fool if she lied to her son. It wasn't like they were going to end up dying, but Sophia was going to try her best to save everyone. "We're going to be free from this place and get to see that bright planet that we've been circling." Sophia remarked, trying to shift the subject from something as grime as death to something peaceful. "You'll get to feel real grass.... look up at a real sky, and feel the warm breeze for the first time." Sophia remarked, feeling the shake of the second floor pods releasing, indicating that they were going to be next.

Sophia tried to steady her breath, showing that she wasn't scared despite her body trembling. Amy was huddled between Omar and Nicholas, with Ajay huddling between Omar and Sophia. The five of them stayed close to each other before they felt the pod starting to disconnect from the station. The feeling of weightlessness was a lot like when the artificial gravity was turned off, but when the pull from Earth caught the pod, they could feel it starting to shake violently. Closing their eyes, everyone held onto each other as the pod pierced the atmosphere. Would they live? Or would they die? Sophia wasn't willing to risk opening her eyes to tell. For now, she simply put her faith that they would survive long enough to be able to see Earth from the ground.

CHAPTER TWENTY THREE: *The Shooting Stars In The Sky*

THE PASSING DAYS after the failed attempt, Dean couldn't do much but simply stare up at the sky. He couldn't find it in himself to eat or do much of anything. With the station still orbiting around the Earth, Dean felt like he put everyone in danger for even thinking that they could bring the station down. It's almost like he was trying to take down some mighty god while he was just a lowly mortal with a limited life span. The foolish nature of a naive child in the body of a man, it was a wakening experience to Dean, but what was he going to do now? Frankly there wasn't much that he could do. With a blanket resting underneath him while on the roof of the cabin, Dean gazed off at the distance. The smell of the autumn air and the cold chill of the onset night that was creeping in caused Dean to shiver a bit. It wasn't long before the sounds of someone coming up the ladder was heard, only to have Kane pop his head up over the ledge of the roof.

"So, how much longer are you going to sulk like this?" Kane asked, resting his arms over the edge of the roof as his feet were planted on the ladder underneath him. Dean didn't remark at the comment, not even sparing Kane a passing glance as Dean kept his gaze up to the sky with a soft frown and a scowl lingering on his face. "Another all nighter then?" Kane asked, moving up the ladder before stepping onto the roof that felt like a cat's tongue against his bare feet. "You know it might rain tonight. If you don't come in, you might end up sick." Kane continued to speak as he made his way over towards Dean who turned to face away from him. Seeing this stubborn and childish behavior coming from Dean caused Kane to audibly sigh.

"You can't keep sulking like this Dean." Kane remarked, moving to sit down next to Dean on the blanket that still had some Dean's warmth from the hours he laid on it. "I know you wanted results right away, but considering that we shot some type of ray up into the sky, we don't know if it would have hit or if it missed completely." Kane spoke up, watching Dean's back to see if he would have gotten some type of reaction out of the other. "It's been almost a week now since we launched the death beam into the sky. Maybe in a few more days we might actually start to see something." Kane remarked, moving to nestle behind Dean as Kane was trying his best to cheer the man up. Keeping his gaze against Dean's back, Kane waited patiently for Dean to finally speak about what was on his mind.

"And what happens if a week passes and nothing happens? How are we supposed to go on knowing that they still rule the sky over us?" Dean asked, moving to roll on his stomach. It wasn't as if Kane could say much to bring up Dean's hopes, but it didn't exactly help matters when Kane was being pushy enough to try and talk some sense into Dean. "With everyone in the shelters, they only have enough supplies for a month, remember? What if by the time they come out, that's when the station will fall? What if it lands in a populated area? What will we do then?" Dean asked, the thoughts that he tried so hard to hide from Kane seemingly slipping out without Dean meaning to.

"Then we'll deal with it the best that we can." Kane remarked with a small shrug of his shoulders. "If someone's property gets damaged from the station falling from the sky, then so be it. They can always rebuild. Not like we didn't plan for something like this you know.

You can't stop any of the devastation and destruction that follows with watching an empire fall Dean." Kane remarked, moving to lay on his back to gaze up towards the sky. "Besides, we told everyone in advance to pack up their valuables. They already know that the station is going to come down one way or another. Their safety is more important than material things." Kane reassured Dean, but whether Dean accepted it or not, it was clear that Dean was full of regret for the choices he made.

Hearing that, Dean couldn't help but sigh into the fabric of the blanket. It was a comforting thought that everyone was safe in the underground bunkers, but if the station was to crash now, they wouldn't exactly know where it would land. The thought that kept plaguing Dean's mind was how he would be responsible for the death of innocent people on both sides. If the station were to land on one of the shelters, it would trap the people inside, making it rather difficult to get them out. Could Dean handle the thought that he doomed innocent people from one of the clans to be trapped under a highly irradiated space station? Or deal with the fact that once it crashed, it could permanently change the landscape once more?

Turning to face Kane, Dean studied his face to see if perhaps Kane might have some lingering doubts that this was going to work out in their favor. However it seemed that Kane was rather confident that they would be able to handle any situation that came across them. That this was just another day where they have to figure out some minor problem that was brought to their attention rather than the major problem that was literally heading straight for them. "So I'm guessing this fall's crops are all going to be harvested in the shelters?" Dean asked, his voice a bit defeated as he knew that there was no point in trying to go about the subject that would just lead to the two going in circles as if it could change anything anyways.

"More than likely. Though it wouldn't be the first time." Kane remarked with a small shrug as he moved to sit up a bit more. "And it certainly won't be the last time either." Kane finished as he hugged his knees. Staring off towards the pathway that leads towards the ocean, Kane noticed a figure walking towards them. It wasn't someone that Kane recognized right off the bat. Usually only the other leaders took that path since it was easier than going through the normal route. Standing up, Kane squinted his eyes to see if he could get a better look at the individual, but to no luck. "Seems like we have a visitor." Kane mumbled, moving to stand up against the roof tiles.

Moving towards the edge of the roof, Kane jumped down, landing on his hands and his right knee like someone ready to start a marathon. Dean was surprised that Kane would jump off the roof so easily like some sort of madman. Dean slowly got up from laying on the roof before moving towards the edge of the roof to spot Kane running inside of the house. Sitting back down against the edge of the roof, allowing for Dean's feet to dangle over the edge, it wasn't long before Kane was coming back out of the cottage while wearing his skull decoration. Watching Kane walk with such grace was like that of an elegant deer spirit that was roaming through the woods. With his head held up high, Kane met with the mysterious man by the wooden fence that surrounded the cottage.

"Wonder what that's all about?" Dean mused to himself as his feet started to lightly swing back and forth in odd patterns. "Not like I would really get much in the way of answers by sitting up here." Dean remarked as he gazed up at the sky once more. He knew sitting up on the roof wouldn't exactly accomplish much, but it had grown to be rather comfortable to him. Perhaps Dean was spoiled by the nights that the two of them would sleep under the stars during their travels. Being able to change up the scenery everyday seems like a luxury now.

Eventually Dean got up from the blanket before folding it up. He had been sulking on the roof for a couple of days since they had gotten back from visiting Amelia, so he might as well at least see what was happening with Kane and the mysterious man. By the time that Dean got down however, the man was already starting to leave, though it seemed that they were at least talking for a couple of minutes before Dean reached the ground.

By the time that Dean came back down the ladder with the blanket in hand, Kane was making his way back with a letter. Whatever was written on the paper seemed to have Kane's full attention as the male barely looked up from it. Even Kane's feet were shuffling against the ground as those silver eyes were focused on the paper. By the time that Kane reached Dean, the male seemed to stop in place.

"So," Dean spoke up, catching Kane's attention from the paper. "What does it say?" By this point even Dean was a bit curious as to what it said. Trying to catch a quick glimpse as he peeked over Kane's shoulder but it seemed almost illegible to him as Dean could barely read the cursive writing that lingered on the piece of paper.

"Oh, sorry." Kane remarked, looking over the paper once more to make sure that he was able to collect the right information. "Apparently we were actually able to hit the Millennium." Kane spoke up with a small smile on his face while reading that bit from the report. "It might not have been the kind of damage we were hoping for, but we were able to take out at least one or two of their engines." Kane continued, looking up to see the shocked expression on Dean's face. "There was some debris that fell a few hours after we launched the death ray cannon. Most of the engine was destroyed in the reentry, but from the design of it, it was certainly an engine part." The news seemed to bring a small smile to Dean's lips after the initial shock wore off. The heavy weight that he had doomed his new home was lifted off of his chest. So they didn't completely fail after all?

"So, it was a success?" Dean asked, trying to hide the excitement in his voice, though the way that the corners of his lips tugging back gave it away. It might not have been an immediate destruction of the Millennium, but this was the best news that Dean had received in his life. "We were able to actually damage the station?" Dean asked, his turquoise eyes shimmered with delight as he moved closer to Kane to see if he could read the report better.

"Apparently so." Kane spoke softly, a faint smile on his face as he could see how excited Dean had gotten. "Not only that, but by Felicia's calculations, the station might land in the desert. Meaning that we won't have to worry too much about the casualties out there since that was where the Wrath clan originated. There aren't many people there, so it should be fine." Despite the fact that the Wrath clan was no longer much of an issue, it was still a place that didn't offer much in the way of resources for the rest of the clan to use. But with it being centralized around the other clans, it meant that if they were to rescue anyone, they would have a better chance than if it had landed in the ocean where the calculations first placed the station's descent.

"So when is it going to come down?" Dean asked, looking as excited as a child at Christmas with how wide he was smiling. "Will we be able to watch it come down?" Even though it sounded rather morbid, Dean felt that it was worth risking his own safety to watch his revenge come to the final conclusion. With everything being done in secret, including his parents death, Dean wanted the satisfaction of watching everything that the Elite built on the blood, sweat, and tears of the workers they used and abused to go up in a literal flame. To watch the mighty giant of the Elite come crashing down from their high throne in the sky.

"It'll be in two days. So if we leave on the airship within the hour, we could very well reach the Envy clan by nine tonight. Then we can watch it descend from the sky before we go into the shelter on the estate. Give it a couple of hours before we send out a scout party to see if anything happens, and then see if there is anyone we can rescue with the hazmat team." Kane explained as he looked at the paper. "So do you think-?" Kane started to ask before noticing that Dean was already making his way towards the cottage. "Hey!" Kane shouted, running after Dean with the paper in his hand.

"No time to waste. We gotta see this." Dean shouted back, only to make his way up the staircase to their bedroom. It wouldn't be much longer before Kane joined him to grab a small backpack to put in some spare clothes into it. It wasn't like they were going to be walking around the other clans this time. This would be a rather short trip. One that they would never be able to forget.

AFTER the long walk towards the cove, and boarding the plane with someone else that was piloting the airship, Dean was rather surprised to see that Felicia wasn't behind the wheel. Apparently the man piloting it was the same gentleman who had made his way towards the cottage. There wasn't much to describe about the man other than he was a tall older gentleman who barely spoke a word to Kane and Dean. It seemed he was someone who liked to keep things professional, unlike Felicia who would relish in talking to everyone to make the long flight feel shorter than it actually was.

The flight across the sea felt like it took an eternity, but eventually they were able to reach Ashley's clan just after the sun had set in the ocean. Unlike the last time, the streets were completely empty. No lights were visible around the houses that lined the street, except for the gas street lights that lit up the street. There was a small rain storm that hung in the air, causing small pellets of rain to greet those coming off of the airship. Dean glanced around to see if perhaps he could see some lights in the windows over shops that were closed, but there was no indication that there was much life left on the streets.

"We should head to the estate before the rain gets worse." Kane spoke up in a weakened voice. "I'm sure that Ashley will be wanting to give us an ear full." Kane remarked, grabbing a hold of Dean's hand. Despite being sick from the long trip, it seemed that the little pill that Kane took before getting on the ship seemed to help with the motion sickness. It was a bit of a relief considering that it was something that was discovered in an old airport a couple of years back, and Miles was able to collect the materials needed to make it into some form of edible pill. It seemed to do the trick to help lessen the effect of Kane's motion sickness.

Kane was wearing some black sacks with a light yellow buttoned up long sleeve shirt with some black suspenders draped along his outer thighs. Dean was wearing similar black slacks as Kane, however he wore a dark navy blue long sleeved buttoned up shirt with a visible bit of the black muscle shirt underneath. Taking a small black umbrella out of the side of Kane's backpack, Dean was able to open it up to cover the both of them since they were not wearing their skull decorations as the skulls lingered on their backpacks like when the first time the two traveled together.

"You really think she will give us an ear full?" Dean asked, walking beside Kane who looked a little pale, but not as sickly pale as he used to look like after flying. "I figure if there was anyone who would be excited to see the fall of the Elite, it would be her." Dean remarked, a small shrug of his shoulders as he must have guessed wrong.

"It's just a lot of work having to close everything and make sure that everyone is safe in the shelters is all. But I think at the end it, she'll be blown away by watching as the station would come down in a firing blaze." Kane spoke up as they walked through a puddle that had small pebbles resting on the bottom of it. "Who knows, maybe she might be inspired to paint a mural of it." Kane remarked, a soft chuckle towards the end as he couldn't figure out how an artist and their muse worked. It always seemed like a small fickle thing could become an inspiration to someone with a creative mindset.

"I wouldn't mind seeing something like that." Dean spoke up as he could only imagine it in his mind right now. "After all, she is a really amazing artist. At least from the bits I was able to see over her shoulder." Dean remarked, giving Ashley the benefit of the doubt. "Is there something that you're hoping to see for yourself when the station comes down?" Dean asked, glancing down towards Kane, who only seemed to be staring ahead of them.

"Not really." Kane replied with a small shrug of his shoulders. "I just want to be able to get this over with so we no longer have to live in fear." Kane started before letting out a small sigh towards the end. "Plus it would make the sky beautiful to gaze at when the stars peek out of the clouds." Kane continued softly with a light smile on his face. Not that Dean could really blame Kane for feeling that way. Often when they would gaze up at the sky, seeing the Millennium soaring over the sky was always a bit of an eye sore to Dean, and he was only seeing it for almost a year.

"Well, I'm sure we can find a way to celebrate the skies being liberated from the eye sore that is the Millennium." Dean suggested, giving Kane a small squeeze on his hand which only seemed to make Kane become a little flustered. The rest of the walk towards the estate was silent. The rain softly drizzled on the umbrella as they made their way around the corner to the estate. Surprisingly Ashley wasn't waiting for them like Dean figured she would.

Passing through the gates, Kane guided Dean towards a side path that Dean never paid much attention towards when he was there the first time almost a year ago. The path was barely visible as they made their way past some bushes that helped to cover the stone tablets that guided those who were heading towards the shelter. Eventually the path led towards some type of small hill with an entrance that was covered in thick vines. Closing the umbrella, Kane made his way past the vines until he came upon a metal door. Dean followed soon after him, just in time to hear Kane knocking three times. There was silence at first, but soon the sound of locks being unlocked could be heard echoing behind the door.

As the last lock clicked opened, Dean waited with baited breath before he heard the sound of one of the doors opening up to them with a loud creak. A small light that was similar to that of a lantern offered a bit of light to the two men. As the lantern came into view, a small hand was holding it up before a familiar scowl peeked out from behind the door. "Oh...it's you." Ashley remarked, sounding a bit displeased at who was standing before her. "Come on in." She called them in, waiting for the two men to enter into the shelter before closing it behind them. Dean took this chance to look around the shelter as this was his first time in one. It didn't seem like it was all that big. Besides having an art easel close to the door, there was only a ramp that rested in the middle of the room.

"The shelter is a bit further down." Ashley remarked, picking up the sketch book she was idly drawing in while waiting for two men to show up. "I have something ready for you two to heat up so you can enjoy some dinner. I'm sure you are starving making the long journey back here." Ashley continued to speak as they made their way down the ramp. Ashley was wearing her hair up into a single small ponytail as her hair grew a bit since the last time she cut it. Wearing a bathrobe with bits of her white long nightgown peeking out under it. Her feet were oddly bare.

As they reached the bottom of the ramp, laying in front of them was a singular mansion like one of the three that rested above them. The lights inside seemed to light up the whole area with the lingering smell of Chlorine from the fountain in the center of it. Dean couldn't help but look around in amazement before he noticed a tunnel that seemed to lead towards another section of the bunker. It was amazing at how well built this shelter was. Surely there was more to it than what he was seeing right now.

"So this is what you guys have been living in all this time?" Dean asked, his voice showing his shock and awe as he took a second or two to look around. If he was born on the Earth, what kind of shelter would he have been born in? Though considering that Kane spoke about how people were leaving the shelters close to fifty years ago, maybe Dean wouldn't have been born in a shelter. Either way, it was still remarkable with how well built this shelter was.

"Each shelter is completely different Dean." Kane started to explain before they were following Ashley towards the mansion. "You see, my family's shelter was more like a farm land than anything else while Ashley's family decided to use their riches before the bombs dropped to build a mansion so they could be comfortable while they waited out the radiation." Kane continued, only to see the small flustered Ashley, ready to snap at the remark that Kane made..

"It's not like I've spent any time down here. We had to do a lot of cleaning up the last few weeks while we waited for everyone to get their shelters ready as well." Ashley quickly snapped as they reached the gates. "I have plenty of canned goods in case the others run out. So even if we get locked down here for over a month, we should be good for a couple more months. Not to mention there are some farmers connected to this tunnel that would provide additional food to help us last for a couple more years." Seems like they really did think this through.

As they headed inside, Dean could feel his stomach start to growl. Placing his free hand over his stomach, Dean couldn't wait to head inside and get something to eat. Then it would be a nice quick hot shower, followed by getting ready for bed. They had a busy day ahead of them, the Millennium would be coming down for good, and at last Dean would get his revenge on the station that not only sent him to his death, but killed his parents and left Dean with nothing. With Kane by his side, Dean would revel at the sight of the Elite's demise. Or so he thought.

DESPITE his best efforts, Dean couldn't sleep that night. As the hours passed on by, Dean laid awake in a foreign bed while Kane slept peacefully beside him. Even at dinner Dean pecked at his food with the tip of his fork. His stomach just felt empty and anything he put in his mouth tasted like ash. The hot shower he had been looking forward to felt almost ice cold to him, even when he had set the temperature a little higher than normal. It just felt like he couldn't simply enjoy the fact that he was there to see the downfall of the station. Knowing that he was killing the last of his kind, it weighed even more heavily on Dean's mind than he originally thought. He was the last of the superior humans, or at least that's what the Elite would have him think.

Getting up from the bed, Dean quietly slipped on the clothes he wore when he first arrived. Taking his backpack with him, Dean glanced over his shoulder to make sure that Kane was still asleep before slipping out of the room. Making his way towards the front corridor of the mansion in the dark, Dean recalled his steps from when they first arrived to find his way to the front door. Picking up the shoes he took off, Dean exited the mansion before putting his shoes on. Though the area was dimly lit, he could still see where the entrance to the ramp was. All he had to do was make his way back up top before resting on the hill to get some fresh air. Maybe the cold morning air would help to clear his mind.

The walk felt like it was taking much longer than it did when they were walking down the ramp to get to the mansion, but once Dean reached the top he felt better as it wasn't locked up like when they first got there. Opening the doors, Dean could feel the cold fall air brush against his face as a small puddle from the rain started to seep inside of the bunker. Leaving one of the doors opened, Dean brushed past the vines hiding the entrance before gazing up at the sky. Though there were bits of dark clouds lingering in the sky from the downpour earlier, the late night sky still looked amazing as bits of purple sky shimmered above.

With a small deep inhale through his nose, Dean stretched his arms over his head before looking around. It was eerily quiet, making Dean's breath and heartbeat sound like a roar in his ears. Clearing his throat, Dean figured that he might as well find a place to sit down that would allow him a chance to sit and reflect on everything that has been going on. But first he needed to put the goat skull on as a way to symbolize that he was no longer Dean Torres, a member of the janitorial section of the Bronze class aboard the United Space Station Millennium, but a member of the Gluttony Clan.

With the skull resting on his head, Dean started to climb the small hill that was on top of the shelter, finding a tree stump that had been chopped down a long time ago. It was a rather large tree stump, allowing two to three people to sit on top of it. Pulling out a towel, Dean would use that for a makeshift cushion on the wet stump. Upon sitting on the fabric of the towel, Dean set his gaze up towards the sky once more. Leaning back to rest his hands on the wet cold surface of the stump, Dean reflected on the choices he made up until now. How every decision sent a ripple through the still water that the people around Dean had gotten used to their daily lives with nothing new and exciting, only to find themselves being swept up in the chaos of Dean's ripples, breaking their normal routines and possibly endangering them all for his own selfish gain. The one that seemed to be affected the most by Dean's decisions was Kane. Then again, Kane's life wasn't exactly a peaceful one, was it?

It felt like hours had passed before the first glimmer of orange seemed to pierce through the dark skies. Was it really morning already? Blinking a bit as if he was snapping out of a trance, Dean found himself leaning forward as the bags under his eyes felt heavier all of a sudden. It seems like Dean was more than ready to get some sleep, but would he really want to sleep through the Millennium falling down? He didn't exactly know when it would happen, but he couldn't risk being out in the open when it would come down. Reaching his hands up to rub his face with a groan, a familiar voice seemed to call out to Dean from the bottom of the hill.

"Couldn't sleep?" The voice asked, causing Dean to look down and see Kane standing there with a small smile lingering on his face. Wearing the deer skull with a light navy blue kimono on, Kane held onto some type of fabric that resembled a towel much like the one that Dean was currently sitting on. "And knowing you, you don't want to head back inside because you don't want to miss the station falling down, right?" Kane asked, making his way up the hill towards Dean who looked a bit amused.

"You seem to know me a bit better than I know myself." Dean half heartedly joked as he covered his mouth as a yawn seemed to escape him. "I just want to be here when the station comes down." Dean spoke as if he had to justify his reasoning for being out in the cold. "I want to be able to see those criminals pay for what they did." Dean spoke, his voice more serious now as his brows knitted together. "I know I can't watch the whole thing come crashing down in a ball of fire, but it would at least give me some satisfaction being able to see the beginning of it." Dean admitted as Kane put down the towel he brought up with him.

"Well then I guess it's' a good thing that I'm here then." Kane spoke, a soft mused chuckle leaving his lips as Kane moved to wrap an arm around Dean's arm. "If you want, you can take a small nap on my lap. I don't think the station will come crashing down right when the sun comes up, so you might be able to get a little bit of sleep. Like when we're at home and you want to take a nap on the couch, using my leg as your pillow." Dean seemed to be a little apprehensive about the idea, but it was better than nothing at this point. "Don't worry, I even brought a light read to keep me entertained for a few hours." Kane spoke as he pulled out a small thin book from his robe.

"You really do think far ahead, don't you?" Dean remarked in a small teasing tone. Not that he could exactly blame Kane for bringing something to read. If Dean was in the same position, he probably would have done the same. "Fine. But you better wake me up at the first sign that the station is coming down." Dean remarked as he stood up as he took off the skull mask and set it aside. He couldn't exactly sleep on the small folded up towel, so Dean had to adjust to laying out the towel so he could sleep without worrying about getting wet.

"How much longer do you think he'll be asleep?" Came a familiar voice of a female, causing Dean's eyes to slowly open up. He could feel the warmth of the sun basking overhead as the smell of lemon filled his senses with hints of green tea. As his eyes adjusted to the sun, Dean slowly sat up from his spot on the damp towel, Dean looked around groggily before seeing Ashley sitting on a type of picnic blanket that was spread on the stump. She was wearing her usual Lolita style dress that had the main part of the dress covered with white polka dots against a black background. The short sleeves of her dress were a solid black as she wore a skull choker while her trademark green skull hairpin rested above her left temple. In her white gloved hands was a cup of tea that she brought up in a thermos.

"Not long apparently." Kane remarked, as he glanced over towards Dean who seemed to still be a little bit out of it. "Morning sunshine." Kane greeted Dean before picking up one of the sandwiches that Ashley also brought up. "Did you have a pleasant nap?"

"Mm...yeah..." Dean grumbled, reaching up to wipe the crusts out of his eyes. Everything felt like it was still a dream to him, but perhaps if he were to eat or drink something, he could become a bit more awake. Taking a deep breath in, Dean stretched his hands up towards the sky as he stretched. A few joints popped into place before Dean opened his eyes as his head tilted back. To his surprise the Millennium was much closer than it had ever been, looking as if it was getting ready to crash towards the ground at any second. It was almost enough to make Dean fall backwards off of the stump. "Holy..." Dean spoke in awe as he stopped himself from finishing the sentence.

"Pretty massive, huh?" Kane remarked nonchalantly as he took a bite out of a sandwich that had a creamy peanut butter mixed with a red jam that one could only guess to be strawberry. "Wonder how much damage it will do once it falls." Kane asked himself out loud as soon as his mouth was free of food.

"Hard to say. But if it is going to hit the desert, then perhaps it won't be too devastating." Ashley spoke before taking another sip of her tea. "It kind of looks like a honey bee nest doesn't it? Or a wasp nest. Since you know, those bastards are nothing more than pests that don't really contribute to anything significant." Ashley remarked with a smirk on her face. Her hatred for those in the Millennium still apparent.

Dean could barely comprehend what they were saying as he stared at the station that was barely crossing the sky as it once had. It was only when Kane's hand gently slapped Dean's chest that he shifted his focus to the pair. "Uh...sorry..." Dean trailed off, lightly scratching the back of his head. "I just can't believe it's that big." Having only been on the inside of the station most of his life, Dean never fully grasped how big the station was in order to house so many humans. "I mean, I knew it was big in the first place, but just...not that big. It's almost like we're staring at another moon." Dean knew he shouldn't stare up at the station, but it was hard not to simply look away with how massive it hung in the sky.

"I'm just surprised it isn't already falling apart with how close it has gotten. But then again, they did have the best minds working on it to design a station that could hover easily around the gravitational pull of the Earth. I'm sure they had the hindsight to make the station strong enough to handle re-entry if something like this happened. Right?" Ashley remarked, glancing towards Kane who finished the last bit of his food, only to give her a nod in response, causing Ashley to let out a slightly annoyed sigh. "So don't worry so much about it Dean. Besides, isn't this what you wanted?"

"What I wanted, huh?" Dean thought to himself as he glanced down at the golden colored tea that Kane offered Dean before taking the hot cup into his freezing hands. "Yeah, guess it is what I wanted, huh?" Dean reaffirmed, mostly to himself as he brought the drink up to him. Drinking the hot lemon tea, the only thing it seemed to provide was a warm sensation going down his throat with a small ashy aftertaste. Setting the cup down, Dean picked up the ram skull mask before putting it on. Though he was there for the fireworks to begin, he couldn't exactly find the fun in watching his own people die anymore.

As the hour passed, the three sat on the edges of the stump before they watched the Millennium get closer towards them. The only one who seemed to express any joy in watching the space craft starting to be pulled closer to them was Ashley. As the station broke through the atmosphere, something unexpected happened. The pods circling the outside started to detach themselves, flinging the pods to be spread somewhere into the world. This took the three by surprise as they didn't expect anything like this to happen. All three seemed to stand up from the stump and watch in awe as it seemed that they were actually deciding to save people rather than allow all of those aboard the station to die in a fiery death.

"What's going on?" Kane asked, looking towards Dean to see if he knew what was going on. Kane didn't know that the red lights that caused the eerie glow of the eye could be easily detached like that.

"Those are the pods that people usually live in. They act like an emergency shuttle in case something like this were to ever happen, but I didn't think that they would actually allow people to escape." Dean spoke as he took a step away from the stump as it seemed the second wave of pods being ejected started to be released from the station as the bottom of the station started to become engulfed by fire as it started to descend towards the Earth.

"It's a good thing we had everyone evacuated then..." Kane trailed off before he noticed Ashley starting to pack up everything. "Alright Dean, time for us to head inside. We don't want to get caught up in the debris when the station finally crashes." Kane remarked, grabbing a hold of Dean's hand, but noticed that Dean wasn't moving. "Dean?" Kane asked, moving to wave a hand in front of the other, bring Dean back to his senses.

"Huh?" Dean spoke in a slight confused tone before looking down at Kane. Seeing the worried look on Kane's face, it clicked in Dean's mind that he had to move now. After all, what good would it do if Dean got crushed by either a pod or debris before knowing if there were survivors on the station or if they all died?

"We have to go." Kane remarked quietly but firmly, lightly tugging on the male's hand. Dean softly nodded his head before following behind the leader. Ashley was already making her way through the vines by the time that the two men reached her.

Heading inside of the shelter and locking the doors, the trio descended down the ramp with Ashley holding a little lantern in front of them to guide their way. "Do you think the others know about the pods ejecting?" Kane asked, figuring that he might as well break the silence, though his voice did echo through the tunnel.

"Amelia might have known thanks to her grandmother being one of the Elitists. Perhaps Miles as well since he is rather smart enough to think about how much the scattering debris is going to impact the land." Ashley spoke up as she carried her blanket and picnic basket in one hand while carrying the lamp in the other.

"But Keaton is probably busy with making sure that they have enough supplies while the rest of his citizens think that this is just a big night club rave or something." Ashley remarked, her voice seeming less caring about the other leaders currently. "I'll have to go and inform the recovery squad when we get down there. Kane you can head towards the radio tent and tell them to pass along the development to the other channels. Dean, you can..." Ashley trailed off, trying to think of something for the male to do. "Do whatever you want." Figures that she would settle on that since there wasn't exactly much that Dean could do at this point.

"You can go ahead and rest if you want. It'll be better than running around with us. You've done your part. So let us do our part now, okay?" Kane spoke up with a reassuring smile on his face, giving Dean's hand a squeeze before they reached the bottom of the ramp. Already there were people who seemed to be running around close to the other entrance that lead further down. It made Dean realize that he really didn't need to do much of anything. After all, what could he possibly provide now?

"Right. I guess I'll go inside and rest. Or at the very least get started with making some quick meals for everyone." Dean spoke in an uncertain tone, a soft gloomy look on his face. Watching as the two leaders walked off towards the group, Dean stood there. Simply watching at first as his mind raced with anything that he could think of to try and help out with the relief effort, besides making some food for everyone. He couldn't go out and help to retrieve bodies. He didn't know the codes or phrases to work the radios, he just felt completely useless, like he did on the station. Perhaps it was just simply best if he headed inside and occupied himself with a book once he was done. At least then he would be doing something then.

OUTSIDE of the shelter was a completely different story. As the pods crash landed to the ground, various structures were destroyed from the impact of the pods and ruined the already abandoned cities that were deemed too hazardous to live in. Some of the pods landed in the ocean or other various aquatic features like lakes or large rivers. Those that were fortunate not to land in places that would have been hard to retrieve them, landed in fields that were once used for grazing animals or growing crops. Though it would seem that there were some pods that were burned up on the descent down. The pod that carried Amy, Issac, Nicholas, Omar, Ajay, and Sophia was lucky enough to land in a shallow river bed with just enough water to cushion their blow of the impact towards Earth.

Inside of the pod was a mess. Some of the objects that were stored in the bathroom had spilled out, pelting some of the adults as they spun around in orbit. The inside of the pod was rather hot, but it was being cooled off thanks to the stream. Omar was the first one to try and stand from the fall, only to find his bones in pain from the gravity alone. "W-What the hell is going on? Why does it hurt to move?" He asked in a pained tone, his hands moving to touch his legs.

"We're not used to real gravity. So we have to take it slow." Sophia remarked, wincing as she tried to get up with Issac still clinging to her. "How is everyone? Is everyone alright?" Sophia asked, looking around to see the condition of the room. The toys were spread out everywhere, like a toy avalanche swept through the room. It would be hard to reach the door that had some bright light peering inside of it. The light seemed to be rather bright, despite them being further away from the sun than they were on the station.

"I feel heavy mom..." Issac softly complained, though that was to be expected. At least the little boy wasn't harmed from the crash landing. Gently placing a hand onto Issac's head, Sophia started to gently stroke Issac's hair as she spoke.

"I know pumpkin. But you'll get used to it. You gotta be patient, okay?" Sophia remarked, trying her best to comfort Issac who didn't understand the concept of how real gravity worked. "How is everyone else doing? Can you move?" Sophia asked, watching everyone seemingly get their bearings.

"I'm alright, considering that I had that giant toy robot hit my head." Ajay remarked, reaching up to rub the back of his head. The toy in question was currently laying on the floor, it's light flashing as it was saying some kind of garbled message.

"I'm fine." Nicholas remarked as he glanced over towards Sophia. "If that's any consolation." Sophia simply rolled her eyes before she looked at Amy who seemed to be holding her wrist. Though Sophia couldn't exactly see what was going on, she could faintly hear Amy sobbing.

"Amy, are you okay?" Sophia asked, gazing at Amy with a concerned look on her face. Slowly Amy held up her hand, resulting in showing everyone a bent right index finger that seemed to broken in three sections. It seemed to be swollen bright red with splattering of black and blue along the skin. "Oh my god..." Sophia whispered before holding Issac's head close to her chest. "How did that happen?"

Amy couldn't exactly answer, but she pointed to a broken toy that was the toy that Ajay and Omar had made for Issac a week prior when the attack happened. Tears seemed to be streaming down Amy's face as she gripped the injured hand with her other hand. Amy was trying her best to keep it all together, but the pain she must have been going through was immense.

"Here, hold Issac." Sophia ordered, passing the little boy over to Ajay. It wasn't like Sophia could sit back and let someone suffer. Not when she had the tools to help them out at least.

"What are you doing Sophia?" Ajay asked, watching as Sophia struggled to get onto her hands and knees. Trying his best to hold onto Issac, the extra weight felt like it was pinning Ajay in place.

"I'm going to get the first aid from the bathroom. What else do you think I'm doing?" Sophia grunted, pushing the toys out of her way as she fought against the pain of the gravity pushing against her body. It felt like an unseen force pressing against her body that made it hard to move, but she was determined to get a hold of the first aid kit that was located under the bathroom sink. One of the perks of being a maintenance personnel was receiving better medicine kits that had a powerful pain medicine that was for emergency situations like this. Considering that this was an emergency, Sophia was glad that they escaped in the pod rather than accepting certain death on the Millennium.

Making her way into the bathroom on her hands and knees, Sophia glanced around to see that the bathroom was in an even bigger mess than the rest of the pod. There were a bunch of exposed wires that dangled from the ceiling. Water was spilling out from the shower, making Sophia a bit nervous if one of the wires fell down. Sure there wasn't anything to continue the current, but it was still a bit nerve wracking nonetheless. With a quick inhale, Sophia used her legs to help push off of the door to reach the sink. The doors of the cabinet were barely hanging on, say for maybe one screw holding it to the wooden frame. Reaching inside, Sophia pulled out the medical kit. Opening it up, she was happy to see that the syringe and clear medicine were intact. Pressing it against her chest, Sophia let out a small sigh of relief before closing it up. Sticking the handle of the kit into her mouth, Sophia rolled onto her stomach so that she could crawl back out, allowing her to miss the wires dangling overhead.

By the time that Sophia crawled out of the bathroom, a large explosion could be heard from outside of the pod. Unsure as to what was happening, Sophia's only concern right now was getting the medicine to Amy. But as soon as she started to make her way towards the crew, the blast from the Millennium crashing down sent powerful shock waves that started to rock the pod that they were currently in. The way that the pod rocked back and forth in the water had knocked Sophia towards the group, causing Sophia to crash into Omar and Nicholas with a loud thud.

"Ugh! Get off of me!" Omar spat, trying to push Sophia off of him. "You're crushing me!" Trying his best to push Sophia off of him. Hearing that remark, Sophia glared at him before spitting the handle out of her mouth.

"Like I want to be on top of you." Sophia snapped before crawling over him towards Amy. "Geeze, thinking you're the only one in pain right now. How pathetic can you get." Sophia muttered under her breath as she reached Amy. "Alright Amy. I'm gonna give you a small injection to numb the pain. Then, we're gonna bandage it up to see if maybe your fingers will heal on their own. I won't use too much, but I'll give you more of the medicine if or when the pain gets to be too much, okay?" Sophia spoke in a more calm tone as she started to get the syringe ready with the medicine.

Amy didn't say anything to her, but simply nodded with the tears still rolling down her cheeks. Bringing up the needle, Sophia pushed the air bubbles out of the tip of the needle before gently taking Amy's hand. "You might feel a burning or stinging sensation at first, but afterwards the pain will go away." Sophia gently coaxed Amy as she pressed the needle under the skin. Carefully watching Amy's reaction, Sophia waited for the medicine to kick in before she went to work splinting Amy's finger with the two medicine sticks and gauze.

"So what are we going to do now?" Nicholas asked, watching Sophia bandage up Amy. "We're stuck on the planet that our people set out to destroy. It's not like they are going to give us a warm welcome." Granted Nicholas had a fair point, but it seemed like they would have no choice but to at least try and work with those who survived after all these years.

"You mean your people tried to destroy it." Ajay quickly remarked, his brows knitted together in anger as he held Issac close to him while balancing holding onto Issac. "We didn't start this mess. You did. You and your damn family who wanted to rule the rest of humanity and keep the survivors under their thumb." It was clear that Ajay was bitter towards the Elite, though with good reason. "Killing off anyone who got in your way, no matter who it was. Oppressing your own people and making them live in small pods like this one. Like it was some sort of jail cell!" Ajay continued, the anger seeming to rise up in his voice.

"Ajay!" Sophia snapped, tying off the splint. "Nicholas isn't like his father, okay?" Sophia spoke up, though she wasn't exactly trying to defend the man, but she knew that it was wrong to single out a person simply for what their parents' choices were. Or rather in this case, the choice of one's ancestors that lead to the fall of humanity. "After all, if you want to talk about his family, then you would be directing that anger towards my son you're holding." Sophia never told Ajay who Issac's father really was, so the surprise on his face wasn't too shocking for Sophia.

"So Issac's dad is..." Ajay trailed off, looking between Issac and Nicholas, the dots starting to connect. The same shade of hair and the coloring of their eyes were a dead give away that the two were related. Ajay let out a small annoyed sigh towards the end, not like he could find it in himself to hate on Issac. The little boy was like a nephew to him, even if they weren't related by blood.

"Yes. It's Nicholas." Sophia finished the sentence before moving to crawl over to Ajay. "Now that the cat is out of the bag, we should probably find a way to get out of here and look for any survivors." Sophia remarked as she took Issac from Ajay's grasp. "The sooner we can find survivors, the closer we can see if we can get them some kind of medical attention." Sophia continued, grabbing onto one of the chairs to help her stand up. It was hard at first, but she managed to finally stand up. Swinging Issc over to the left side, Sophia struggled to walk towards the only exit that they had.

"And how would we get her medical help Sophia? Those people tried to kill us?" Ajay spoke, crawling after Sophia before reaching the chair. It took him a bit of time to get up on his two legs, but when he got up, it took everything in Ajay's power to stay standing up. "You honestly think that they would offer us aid? That they have the tools and equipment to deal with her broken fingers?" The concern about getting them medical help was apparent, but there was more to worry about outside than being able to find someone who would be able to assist them with the medical needs they needed to treat Amy's injuries.

"Yes!" Sophia snapped, adjusting Issac to rest on her hip as the boy was starting to slip. "Look, these people have every right to be angry at what our ancestors did. Blowing up the world for their own gain. Leaving trillions of people to die while we hovered in space, looming above them." Sophia continued, moving to the counter to hold herself up. "But if we try to make amends, then it's one step closer to being a functional society once more. Can't you see that this is punishment for what happened?" Sophia didn't want to believe that everything for the last five hundred years was for nothing.

There had to be some good behind people, even if it was faintly. "Omar, Nicholas," Sophia spoke, looking at the two. "Help Amy to her feet. We can't waste time just sitting here." Sophia ordered before looking over at Ajay. "I'll need your help Ajay. You know I can't do this alone." Sophia continued, studied Ajay's face to see if he was willing to comply with her. "We'll scout ahead to make sure it is safe. If we find anyone else's ship, we'll do what we can in order to help them. The more people we have on our side, the greater the chance that we can all make it through this." Despite looking like a newly born calf with how weak her legs were, Sophia was moving on pure adrenaline at this point.

"Hold on!" Omar shouted, doing his best to stand up without the use of anything to support his weight, but his own willpower to keep him from falling down. "Who died and made you the boss of us?" Omar remarked in a disgruntled tone as he used the mattress to keep himself from falling back onto Amy or Nicholas.

"Are you kidding me Omar?" Sophia scoffed as she looked at him. "If it wasn't for my quick thinking, we would be just as dead as everyone else." Sophia snapped, the gull that Omar had seemed to bewilder Sophia. Why was this guy trying to fight her at every turn? "I gave people plenty of time to get to the emergency pods even if they were rushing to get to those said pods. I made sure that the pods would eject one layer at a time to prevent them from colliding in the air. And you have the nerve to ask me why I am putting myself in charge? When I am willing to risk my neck for someone so ungrateful as you?" Sophia asked, glaring at Omar as she took a step forward, only to have Ajay stepped between them.

"Now isn't the time for fighting, right Sophia?" Ajay spoke up, trying to keep her level headed. Sophia bit her lower lip to keep from saying something that she might very well regret, instead turning to face away from the group. As Sophia walked towards the door, Ajay sighed before turning to look back at Omar. "Really? You gotta push her buttons now?" Ajay asked, though he didn't exactly sound pleased with the man. "Just, be civil until we can figure out what is going on. Can you at least do that for me?" Ajay pleaded with Omar, trying to find a way for them to keep things peaceful.

Omar was silent at first, but seeing Ajay's eyes begging him to work with Sophia, he couldn't exactly say no to the man. "Fine.... but if this comes back to screw us, it'll be on both of your heads. Afterall, we don't know what to expect out there. What if they try and kill us? These savages aren't willing to work with us." Omar remarked, causing Ajay to let out a sigh since he could see where Omar was coming from.

"If it bites us in the ass, you can complain all you want then. But for now, we should at the very least regroup with everyone." Ajay remarked as he looked over at Nicholas who was still on the ground. With a disgruntled sigh, Ajay walked over towards Nichalos before extending a hand out to help the man up.. "Now come on Mr. Elite. Time for you to start making it up to the planet that your kind tried to destroy. It's the least you can do after putting us through hell over the years." Even though Nicholas was a bit weary at first, he figured that it was better than struggling to get up. With a small grunt and using what he could as leverage to get up, the two men were able to stand before helping the injured Amy up to her feet.

Sophia on the other hand put in the code that was the number above the door to allow them to get out of the pod. Smoke seemed to fill the air from where the station fell in the distance. Feeling the wind brushing against her body, Sophia shivered before a smile landed on her face. She was finally on Earth, the place that she could only admire from the station. The sound of the river rushing underneath them was like the rivers on the silver section of the station. The sound of the trees rustling from the wind blowing was unlike anything that Sophia heard. Being used to the sound of the station with the metal pipes and the roar of the engines, it was something else to behold. Carefully jumping out of the pod with Issac holding onto her, Sophia gently fell back onto the pod. The water was freezing against her legs as she held onto Issac who kept slipping from her grasp.

Gazing up at the bright blue sky, Sophia smiled brightly before pointing up to the sky. "Look Issac. We're on that beautiful blue pearl you gaze at every night. You can tell by the blue reflecting up against the sky." Sophia chimed happily, looking at Issac who seemed to be in just as much awe as she was. Retracting her hand, Sophia lightly rested her head on top of Issac's. "This is our home now. What do you think of it?" Sophia asked in bliss, only to spot a weird hybrid being running towards her. The smile quickly faded as the rest of the individuals came out from the pod to find themselves falling into the river as they didn't brace themselves against the pod.

"Wait, are those people? Are there actual humans still living here?" Ajay asked, looking a bit concerned when he noticed the animal skulls on top of people's heads while others were wearing some type of hazmat suit that one would have seen on the station. As they got closer, Sophia wasn't able to comment on what they were seeing as they were soon surrounded by these tribal men. Some of the people had weapons in their hand while others seemed to be ready with medical supplies. Gazing towards the center of the people, one figure seemed to stand out the most. It was Amelia, who was wearing a hazmat suit though without the helmet to protect her. Instead she had what looked like a bear skull resting on her head. "What's going on?" Ajay asked as the group of people. The water felt freezing against Ajay's hands, but he couldn't stand up on his own thanks to not being used to gravity.

"Seems that you people at least still speak our language, so that's good." Amelia spoke as she glanced over the people. Amy was draped over Nicholas and Omar's shoulders, her body was covered in sweat. Spotting the bandaged finger, Amelia glanced over towards the personnel that was used for their medic. "Grab her and take her to the medical tent." Amelia ordered, before her eyes went back to Sophia. "It looks like her fingers are injured. So be careful when handling her."

"Hold on! What do you think you're doing?" Sophia demanded, watching as the man moved towards the rest of the group. Ajay started to get back up, moving to try and stop the man from taking one of their injured members but to no avail. The medical personnel didn't have much patience as he quickly kneed Ajay in the stomach, causing Ajay to double over back into the cold water. "Hey! What the hell do you think you're do-?!" Sophia shouted before she was met with a spear close to her face, forcing Sophia to quickly halt what she was going to say. If she wasn't careful, Sophia might say something that would make things worse for them.

"We're getting her medical attention. Clearly she is injured." Amelia spoke, placing her hands on her hips. "For now all of you are being captured. If you resist, we won't hesitate to kill you. Is that clear?" Amelia asked, raising an eyebrow as she looked around at the group's faces, trying to see if one of them was going to fight back. "I'll take your silence as an understanding." Amelia continued, tucking her hair behind her ear. "After we evaluate you all individually, we will determine where you are to be placed. If you wish to join our society and follow our rules, you'll be able to make a living for yourselves. If you don't want to join us and rather try your luck outside of our society, you are free to do so, but it will be much harder on you than it would be on us." Amelia spoke as if she had recited it a million times, only to have Omar interrupt her.

"Society?" Omar seemed to scoff. "What kind of society do you even have if you wear dead animal skulls on your head? You're nothing more than a bunch of-" Omar started to rant before Ajay lightly punched his leg. "Ow! What the hell Ajay?" Omar asked, a scowl on his face as he looked down to Ajay who was struggling to stand up once more.

"Omar I love you, but just shut your mouth on this one." Ajay growled under his breath as he finally was able to stand up. Even an idiot would know that it was best to simply follow the captores directions and not try to fight back. If they did, they may end up as just another skeleton for the Earth to take back.

"As I was saying." Amelia spoke, a displeased look lingering on her face. "If you wish to join our society, you will have your choice of six clans to join based on your skills. In order to be a part of the society, you will need to kill an animal that you will wear as both your battle helmet and a decorative headpiece for special events. You will go around to each clan and see which one is right for you. Take our classes to help you with childbirth without the use of medicine. If you do this, and follow our rules, you'll no longer be part of the cowards, but rather one of us instead." Amelia continued, before sighing as she was getting tired of sounding like a robot.

"It doesn't matter what your status was before you came down here, but if you wish to live your own life and experience true freedom for once, you're free to join us. If you don't, then good luck in the wild because this planet is a death trap waiting to kill you if you aren't prepared." Amelia spoke, reaching her hand out to them. "So, with that being said, would you like to join us, or try and fight us?" It wasn't like Amelia was giving them much of a choice, despite the fact that she made it seem like they had a choice.

Sophia glanced back towards the three men. Seeing as how Amy was being guided away from them to get her injuries looked at, the men looked at Sophia as if it was her call. Glancing down to look at Issac who was focused on the spear pointed towards them, Sophia sighed before she reached out to take Amelia's hand. "Well, if we're going to have a choice, I'd rather go with the one that lets me make my choice." Sophia remarked, knowing that it was better than simply wondering around the planet aimlessly. At least this would give Issac a chance to experience a world outside of the metal cage he was born into.

With the handshake, the spears were pulled back and the people wearing the hazmat suits moved in to help the others walk to the relief tents. It seemed to be a bit hectic, and the smoke seemed to continue rising to the sky in the distance. They were at least a hundred miles away, and it was evident that the Millennium was going up in smoke. Their home and everything that they knew was simply gone. The sky above them was clear for the first time in years.

The stars that the remaining survivors once floated among seemed to fall from the sky. Lines of stars darted in a spectacular show, almost as if they were celebrating the fall of the station. It gave them an odd sense of comfort knowing that they were free to do as they wished. To never be controlled by a group of people who could easily destroy everything they worked for. It was an oddly liberating feeling that broke the chains of oppression. Their lives would now be their own, all thanks to humanity coming together to witness the downfall of the Elite.

Epilogue

FIVE YEARS AFTER the fall of the Millennium had passed. Society has been able to stabilize after the fall, giving way to better technological advances that was once thought lost. The land was slowly being reclaimed and production of new food supplies was able to be distributed among the clans. Over the years the coast line had started to light up, allowing for more traveling across the scattered land. During that time, a lot has changed even for the leaders as well.

Felicia and Miles had gotten married and had a child who was currently two. Amelia and Keaton had one child as well, though the child was only a few months old. Kane and Dean had made it official and were wed before any one of the other leaders once everything had settled down. Even Ashley was able to meet someone who seemed like a bit of a pushover, but was a decent man who was loyal to her. After going through the tragedy with her mother, some worried that Ashley would never be able to find someone, but she proved them wrong.

In the cottage close to the sea, Dean sat on the patio chair that looked over the coast line. With his hair lingering down to the middle of his ear, Dean was wearing a dark gray robe with small silver lined clouds that swept along the bottom towards the hem. Turquoise green eyes scanned the horizon to see the airships drifting through the clouds. On his left ring finger rested a silver wedding ring that glinted in the sun. On the table to his right was a nearly empty glass of water with beads of water from condensation dripping down it. A small boxed radio rested close by, though the music was rather faint, almost hard to hear. A familiar figure walked towards Dean with a drink in his hand.

"So, anything new going on?" A man asked, his silver locks pulled back into a loose bun with the silver rings decorating his ears. "I know we're going to have to go to the memorial next month, but I still hate traveling." The man remarked, sitting down in a light orange robe that had red autumn leaves seemingly swirling along the hem of his robe. "Even after all this time, I can never get used to it." The man lightly whined, placing left hand onto his stomach, gently stroking it with a silver wedding band resting on his left ring finger.

"Yeah, it's hard seeing the lingering metal frame of the Millennium still embedded into the Earth." Dean remarked, looking over at Kane who moved to settle down on the other side of the small table, taking a drink from his cup. "But considering that it landed in the desert, we were lucky that when it exploded that it didn't destroy the neighboring clans." The only real damage was to the abandoned towns. They would still have to wait a bit on building there, thanks to the radiation from space. Eventually they would be able to build there, but that would be a couple of hundreds of years from now. "Speaking of which, I heard that Sophia woman is going to speak at it, right?" Dean asked, looking over at Kane who softly nodded.

"Yeah. It was thanks to her that many of the people survived the crash." Kane remarked as he set the cup down before leaning back in his chair. "We've been able to recover a lot of data that was once lost thanks to her skills. It's only fair that she gets a chance to address everyone." Kane spoke as he pulled out a book. "To think, a brilliant mind like hers could have been lost to the ages if we blew up the station right then and there." Kane lightly chuckled as he turned to the page he left off on.

"I also heard that Felicia was considering backing her to be the new leader of the Pride clan." Dean remarked as he moved to place his hands behind his head as he relaxed in the chair. "Amelia and Keaton also finished setting up their place between their clans, making it easier for the both of them to continue on with their duties as leaders." Dean remarked as he gazed up at the sky, watching the clouds slowly drift by in the sky.

"Yeah. It's hard to believe that so much has happened in the last five years." Kane softly chuckled before sliding a bookmark into his page since he wasn't in the mood to read while they were talking about current events. "To think, this would have never been possible if you didn't arrive, Dean." Kane spoke, a soft smile lingering on his lips. "We would have still been trying to keep out of the eyes of the Elite. Never being able to grow and spread out our wings. And now that there is no lingering threat, just look at where we are. Able to restore old cities to their prime and unlock lost technology that can help us understand what life was like before the bombs were dropped." Kane continued, moving to get up from his seat as a song had started to play on the little radio.

"It's all thanks to our chance meeting that we were able to get this far." Kane continued moving to grab Dean's hand to pull him up from the chair. A playful smile seemed to grow on Kane's face as he pulled Dean closer to him. "Now we're married, and we are able to continue to grow and reclaim the world properly. No more wars over what land belongs to who. No division between where people come from, and most certainly no war over resources. We share everything and we've been thriving. Kind of like a storybook ending, huh?" It was rather hard to believe that they could accomplish so much after integrating the survivors of the crash after they agreed to join the clans.

"Well, to be fair, you were already doing that way before I got here. The thriving part, not the war part." Dean remarked with a small smirk on his face as placed his hands on Kane's waist. Dean leaned in close to rest his forehead against Kane's, moving to lightly sway with Kane to the music that started to play on the radio. "But, I will admit it seems that things have become calmer since the Millennium fell. Everyone can breathe a sigh of relief as they work hard to make this world even better. Everyone has helped to really make the dream possible." Dean spoke, knowing that if they didn't rescue everyone, there was no way for humanity could spread as far as it has. With all the technological advances they made, and how they were able to recover some old medical information to help to treat the new members of the clan, the information would help society advance by hundreds of years rather than waiting thousands to recover old information.

"Speaking of being able to breathe easier," Dean spoke up as he gazed down at Kane who looked rather puzzled at the statement. "Seems like you're slowly getting over your motion sickness. That must make you feel better when we fly, right?" Dean remarked, remembering how crippling it was for Kane when they would travel. But with the recent medicine being developed, it has helped Kane more than anything Dean could do to help the other out.

"Well, it was thanks to Miles that I was able to get over the motion sickness with that chalk based pill he gave me. Making it easier for me to move about on the airship. But I still wished there was a better way to travel through the sky than the airship." Kane remarked, placing his hands on top of Dean's shoulders. "The only downside to the medicine is the fact that I can't read as much as I used to while traveling." Kane remarked as he tilted his head to the side. "But that just means I get to spend it with you." Kane remarked with a soft chuckle. "I'm surprised you're not exactly sick of me yet."

"Maybe I'll just take some chalk medicine if I start getting sick of you. But then again, I have a hardened stomach." Dean remarked before feeling a light smack on his shoulder. "What? Take it as a compliment." Dean spoke with a smile still lingering on his face.

"Don't be a smart ass." Kane lightly scolded as he reached up to pinch one of Dean's cheeks. "But I do have to admit. Being able to do things a bit more remotely is far more satisfying than having to run around everywhere." As long as it saved Kane from the long drawn out trips that he used to take every season, Kane was more than willing to stay put and allow Miles to come to him for once to get the crop rotations. "This way I can use the time I would be heading all over the place to stay here and look after my people." Kane spoke, moving to rest his head on Dean's shoulder.

"Oh yeah, we're getting some new people right to join the clan soon, right?" Dean asked, at the mention of the clan. "A fair amount of the survivors wanted a decent chance to either help raise farm animals or grow crops. Seems like you'll be fairly busy the next couple of days." Dean remarked, as Kane seemed to lightly cling to Dean as they rocked back and forth to the music.

"Don't remind me." Kane groaned as he buried his face into Dean's shoulder. "I gotta help to figure out farming space for some of these people. Convert old houses with plenty of land around them. And make sure that they get the hydroponic system built in to help people grow crops in a greenhouse to see how they fare in the coming winter months." It seemed like a lot more work than Kane was used to, not allowing for much free time in the up and coming days ahead of them.

"Why not have a sort of community garden in some buildings? That way people can help each other out?" Dean suggested, causing Kane to lift his head as if a light bulb went off in his head. It was always rather amusing to see the look of astonishment on Kane's face with something Dean suggested that could make everything easier for them.

"Why didn't I think of that?" Kane mumbled to himself, only to give Dean a soft smile. "That would save me so much time and people can still live in the city without much issue." Even though a lot of the land was open for people to start their own farm, there were plenty of places that were still too dangerous for people to live. "We'll have to try different ways of growing the food on the roof tops though. Make sure that it doesn't get too cold or that the building can handle it." Kane continued before smiling up at Dean. "You're a genius Dean."

Hearing the compliment, Dean couldn't help but lightly chuckle as he glanced to the side. "It's not a big deal really." Dean remarked as he could try to pass it off as a simple suggestion. "I had tried something like that when I was on the station. It was working for a bit, but the Elites didn't seem to like it." Dean continued, glad that his old ideas could at least be of value here. Unlike the night that the station had fallen, Dean had felt rather useless. He was still recovering from that empty feeling, but with Kane listening to his suggestions, that empty feeling was going away.

"Oh yeah, I heard that Maiti took over Keaton's lectures and it's been a huge success."

Kane piped up as he pulled back from leaning against Dean's shoulder. Ever since the baby was born, Keaton had devoted himself to be a full time father rather than being a leader. "She has a far more gentler touch and not as demeaning about other people's sexuality as Keaton was." Kane knew that Keaton meant well, but he didn't have the right approach to it.

"Good." Dean was quick to remark. Even though the two never really saw eye to eye, Dean knew that Keaton's heart was in the right place. "Frankly it felt like Keaton was talking out of his ass for most of it." Dean remarked, a bit miffed about the encounter at the Fox Den five years ago. "She has that one lady helping her out, Amy something? I never got her last name." Dean asked, shrugging off the last part since it didn't exactly matter. She was just another member of the survivors of the crash, not like Dean paid much attention to her besides knowing that she had some missing fingers.

"Yeah. I can't recall her last name either." Kane remarked as he tried to recall it, but it simply kept escaping the tip of his tongue. "And the new assistant that Amelia got has been doing a decent job helping her get through those documents. Nicholas was his name if I can recall correctly." Kane remarked, though the last name of Nicholas seemed to escape him as well. Kane was always bad with last names. "Apparently his father was related to Amelia's grandmother. So I guess that would make them cousins. Who would have guessed?" Kane remarked, a small chuckle leaving his lips as he thought how crazy it was that they were related. Though considering that Nicholas was a former member of the Elite, it wasn't too surprising to Dean. However Dean didn't like the idea of an Elite working with one of the leaders after everything that they were put through. Not like he could really say something about it.

"Seems like everyone is finally able to live out their lives in relative comfort and peace now, huh?" Dean remarked as they parted once the music had died down. Walking back over towards the patio chair, the wind started to pick up, causing Dean to glanced up towards the sky. There was a feeling of bliss that swelled in Dean's chest, making him feel as if he was finally free from the hatred that once bound him to seeking revenge. "I won't lie Kane," Dean started to speak while gazing up towards the sky. "I feel really good about the future from here on out." Dean glanced towards Kane with a smile on his face.

"Who knows, maybe in a couple of years we'll be able to get some television stations back up and in working order. After all, we got radios to work again. So televisions will probably be coming sooner than we think." Dean suggested as the excitement was starting to build up inside of him. "Just imagine being able to watch some fresh new shows at night while eating dinner, or to have it on for background noise like how we have our music playing as background noise." Dean continued as he grabbed a hold of Kane's hand. "Or we can start launching satellites up into space to get that thing called the internet back up. Then we can send out information all over the world at the speed of light." Dean finished, intertwining his fingers with Kane.

"Well I heard that Sophia was already coming up with a way to be able to restore that net. With the Pride clan's help, I'm sure we'll be able to get that running in no time." Kane remarked as the two started to head back to the chair to relax. Sitting down, Kane leaned back in the chair with a soft sigh escaping his lips. "Who knows, maybe we'll be able to find out a lot about the past and learn from the mistakes." Kane suggested, knowing that history was an important part of being able to grow. "That way, we never have to go through this ever again." If they could avoid using total nuclear war, the better. "There was a lot of information that was lost to that day, but we're slowly getting it back. And that's what I'm looking forward to the most." Kane remarked, seeming hopeful as he took his glass into his free hand before taking a sip of his drink.

"I couldn't have said it better myself." Dean softly chuckled as he glanced over to Kane. "Even if the future of the world may not be completely certain, I'm just glad that I get to spend every day of my life with you by my side." Despite it being a cheesy yet romantic remark, Dean felt happy to be able to say something like that to the person he cherished in this world. Just to spend each and every single day with the person who made him feel blissful after entering this world spiteful and set on revenge, it made each and every single day worth it. After all, this journey was a rather long one, but Dean wouldn't want to spend it with anyone else other than Kane.

Special Thanks:

Anya Radulovic

Kaycee Morgan

Edward Garrett, my loving husband

The Daily Family (Jon and Caitlin)

My family members

Ricco Fajardo and the community

Crystal and James Goff

Stephimus Prime

And the lovely readers who took time to read my very first novel.

About the Author

Laura Garrett was born and raised in the countryside of Western New York in a small village. Traveling stateside with her husband, she was able to see a lot of the country while pursuing a degree in Business Administration from an online college from Ashford University. However, after suffering from a work related injury, Laura took to writing as a way to cope with the injury. As a means of being able to make something of herself, Laura dedicated her time to writing her first novel while trying to broaden her skills despite her injury.

Taking her love of Japanese animation and instrumental music, Laura was able to weave ideas into her story. After making some friends online, Laura was able to find strength in the fandom community that drove her to finish her novel and pushed her further into writing about vast and wondrous stories that have yet to see the public eye.

At home Laura continues to get inspiration from various sources of media. When she isn't writing, Laura spends time with her husband and her beloved cats. Despite the injury, Laura hasn't given up on her writing as that fulfills her passion and creativity.